A Cold,
Bleak Hill

RON CARTER

BOOKCRAFT
SALT LAKE CITY

PRELUDE TO GLORY

Volume 1: Our Sacred Honor
Volume 2: The Times That Try Men's Souls
Volume 3: To Decide Our Destiny
Volume 4: The Hand of Providence
Volume 5: A Cold, Bleak Hill

Library of Congress Cataloging-in-Publication Data

Carter, Ron, 1932–
  A cold, bleak hill / Ron Carter.
    p.   cm. — (Prelude to glory ; v. 5)
  ISBN 1-57345-956-9 (Hardbound : alk. paper)
    1. Pennsylvania—History—Revolution, 1775–1783—Fiction.   2. Howe, William Howe, Viscount, 1729–1814—Poetry.   3. Washington, George, 1732–1799—Fiction.
4. Brandywine, Battle of, 1777—Fiction.   5. Germantown, Battle of, 1777—Fiction.
6. Soldiers—Fiction.   I. Title.

PS3553.A7833 C65 2001
813' .54—dc21

                                                                    2001003368

Printed in the United States of America   72876-6809
10   9   8   7   6   5   4   3   2   1

This series is dedicated to the common people
of long ago who paid the price.

This volume is dedicated to my grandchildren,
the twenty-three who have already arrived
and the many more to follow.

A Cold, Bleak Hill

December 22, 1777

To The Hnble Henry Laurens, President,
Congress of The United States:

Sir:

It is with infinite pain and concern that I must again dwell on the state of the Commissary's department. I do not know from what cause this alarming deficiency or rather total failure of supplies arises, but unless more vigorous exertions and better regulations take place, and immediately, this Army must dissolve.

Regarding the Pennsylvania Supreme Executive Council and their declared wish that this army should attack the enemy, I can assure those Gentlemen that it is a much easier and less distressing thing to draw remonstrances in a comfortable room by a good fireside than to occupy a cold, bleak hill and sleep under frost and snow without clothes or blankets. However, although the Council seems to have little feeling for the naked and distressed soldiers, I feel superabundantly for them, and from my soul pity those miseries they are now suffering, which it is in my power neither to relieve nor prevent.

George Washington

PREFACE

★ ★ ★

The reader will be greatly assisted in following the *Prelude to Glory* series if the author's overall approach is understood.

The volumes do not present the critical events of the Revolutionary War in chronological, month-by-month, year-by-year order. The reason is simple. At all times during the eight years of the conflict, the tremendous events that shaped the war and decided the final result were happening simultaneously in two, and sometimes three, different geographical areas. This being true, it became obvious that moving back and forth from one battlefront to another would be extremely confusing.

Thus, the decision was made to follow each major event through to its conclusion, as seen through the eyes of selected characters, and then go back and pick up the thread of other great events that were happening at the same time in other places, as seen through the eyes of characters caught up in those events.

The reader will recall that volume 1, *Our Sacred Honor*, follows the fictional family of John Phelps Dunson from the beginning of hostilities between the British and the Americans in April 1775, through the Lexington and Concord battles, and then moves into the experiences of Matthew Dunson, John's eldest son, who was a navigator in the sea battles that occurred later in the war. In volume 2, *The Times That Try Men's Souls*, Billy Weems, Matthew's dearest friend, survives the terrible defeats suffered by the Americans around New York and the disastrous American retreat to the wintry banks of the Delaware River. In volume 3, *To Decide Our Destiny*, Billy and his friend Eli Stroud follow General Washington back across the Delaware on Christmas night 1776, to storm and miraculously take the town of Trenton and then Princeton. Volume 4, *The Hand of Providence*, addresses the tremendous, inspiring events of the campaign for possession of the Lake Champlain–Hudson River corridor, wherein British General John Burgoyne, with an army of eight thousand, was sent by King George III to take Fort Ticonderoga, proceed to Albany, and in conjunction with the forces of General William Howe and Colonel Barry St. Leger, cut the New England states off from the southern states and defeat them one at a time. To oppose Burgoyne, the United States sent General Arthur St. Clair, with less than half the army commanded by General Burgoyne. The heroics of men on both sides, the battles, the unbelievable tricks, the startling performance of General Benedict Arnold, all seen through the eyes of Billy and Eli, are probably among the most gripping stories of the entire Revolution. Historians have long since included the events of the summer of 1777 in the single term *Saratoga*, and it is clear that this battle changed the history of the world.

Volume 5, *A Cold, Bleak Hill*, addresses the events of the summer of 1777, following General George Washington as he seeks a way to stop General William Howe on the eastern seaboard. Caleb Dunson, age sixteen, the rebellious runaway son of John Dunson, has already joined Washington's army and is rapidly learning the brutalities of camp life and war. Mary Flint, the beautiful, plucky widow of wealthy Marcus Flint, now destitute and seeking a new life, finds Eli and Billy, the only two persons she can look to for help and understanding, and love blossoms between Mary and Eli. The battles of Brandywine Creek and Germantown, both defeats for the Americans, followed by the "Paoli Massacre" and the political efforts of ambitious American officers Horatio Gates and Thomas Conway to undermine General Washington present trials unheralded. The bitter, heartbreaking story of Valley Forge, the darkest hours of the entire Revolution, is presented, with the ultimate rising of the Americans above all the terrible hardships, to march out of Valley Forge in June 1778, a new, inspired army, to continue their work of winning freedom and liberty for America.

And, reader, again, be patient. Matthew and Kathleen are going to be reunited, and the wait will make it all the sweeter. Billy has given his heart to Brigitte; however, she sees him only as a dear friend of the family. These wonderful young people are going through that painful but exciting time of finding each other and experiencing the blossoming of young love into mature love. It's all yet to come.

CHRONOLOGY OF IMPORTANT EVENTS RELATED TO THIS VOLUME

★ ★ ★

1775

April 19. The first shot is fired at Lexington, Massachusetts, and the Revolutionary War begins. (See volume I)

June 15. The Continental Congress appoints George Washington of Virginia to be commander in chief of the Continental Army.

June 17. The Battle of Bunker Hill and Breed's Hill is fought, which the British win at great cost, suffering numerous casualties before the colonial forces abandon the hills due to lack of ammunition. (See volume I)

September. King George III of England and his cabinet agree upon a strategy for putting down the rebellion in the American colonies, as well as the British officers who shall command and the armed forces that will be necessary.

1776

February–March. Commodore Esek Hopkins leads eight small colonial ships to the Bahamas to obtain munitions from two British forts, Nassau and Montague. (See volume I)

March 17. General Sir William Howe evacuates his British command from Boston. (See volume I)

July 9. On orders from General Washington, the Declaration of Independence (adopted by the Continental Congress on July fourth) is read publicly to the entire American command in the New York area, as well as the citizens. (See volume 2)

Late August–Early December. The British and American armies clash in a series of battles at Long Island, Kip's Bay, Harlem Heights, White Plains, and Fort Washington. Though the Americans make occasional gains in the battles, the British effectively decimate the Continental Army to the point that Washington has no choice but to begin a retreat across the length of New Jersey. He crosses the Delaware River into Pennsylvania and establishes a camp at McKonkey's Ferry, nine miles north of Trenton. (See volume 2)

September 21. An accidental fire burns about one-fourth of the city of New York.

October 11. General Benedict Arnold leads a tiny fleet of fifteen hastily constructed ships to stall the British fleet of twenty-five ships on Lake Champlain. The hope is that Arnold's forces can at least delay the movement of thirteen thousand British troops south until the spring of 1777 and thus save George Washington's Continental Army. (See volume I)

December 10. Benjamin Franklin travels to France to persuade the French government to support America in the Revolution.

December 14. General William Howe closes the winter campaign, and the British troops retire into winter quarters. Howe stations General James Grant at Princeton with a small force of British soldiers. Colonel Carl Emil Kurt von Donop is given command of three thousand Hessians along the Delaware River opposite the American camp, and he quarters fourteen hundred of his men in Trenton under the command of Colonel Johann Gottlieb Rall.

December 22. John Honeyman, an American spy posing as a British loyalist, is under orders from General Washington and makes a reconnaissance journey to Trenton, is later "captured" by the Americans, and reports his findings to Washington directly.

December 25. Washington's three-point attack of Trenton begins as he and his army cross the Delaware River at McKonkey's Ferry at night and during a raging blizzard. General James Ewing attempts a crossing at the Trenton Ferry, and General John Cadwalader moves into position at Dunk's Ferry.

December 26. The Battle of Trenton is fought to a dramatic conclusion.

December 29. Benjamin Franklin meets with Comte de Vergennes to discuss French aid for the Americans.

December 31. Enlistments for the majority of soldiers in the Continental Army are due to expire at midnight.

1777

January 2. General Charles Cornwallis leads a British force of 8,000 men out of Princeton with orders to destroy what is left of Washington's army. Colonel Edward Hand and a small force of 600 Pennsylvanian riflemen are dispatched to stop the British before they can reach Trenton.

January 3. Washington and his army of over four thousand men endure a midnight march out of Trenton and into Princeton, where they surprise British colonel Charles Mawhood's command shortly after sunrise. The Battle of Princeton is fought with surprising results.

January 7. The Continental Army establishes winter quarters in Morristown, New Jersey.

February 25. As the political relationships between England, France, and America tighten, Comte de Vergennes receives news regarding the outcome of the battles of Trenton and Princeton and plans a course of action for France.

April 2. General William Howe advises Lord Germain, British Secretary of State for America, that he intends to abandon New Jersey in favor of taking Philadelphia, which is seen by the British as the capital city of the

United States. Lord Germain agrees and instructs General Howe to assist General John Burgoyne in his mission to come south down the Hudson River.

May 6. British General John Burgoyne arrives in Canada to begin his campaign down the Champlain–Hudson region.

Late May. General Washington marches the Continental Army from winter quarters at Morristown south to Middlebrook, in the Watchung Mountains.

June 12. General Arthur St. Clair arrives at Fort Ticonderoga to take command of the American forces.

July 4. The British scale Mt. Defiance to mount cannon that are within range of Fort Ticonderoga.

July 5. The Americans discover the presence of the cannon and recognize that the British are now capable of destroying the fort at will, together with the men therein.

July 5–6. General St. Clair abandons Fort Ticonderoga to the British and retreats with his men, part of them moving south in boats to Skenesborough, the balance marching toward Hubbardton, intending to join the boats at Skenesborough.

July 6. The British fleet sinks every American boat at Skenesborough and scatters the Americans.

July 7. The Battle of Hubbardton is fought, in which the Americans make a good accounting until British reinforcements arrive, driving them from the field.

July 9. Preparing to move his army to Philadelphia, General Howe loads his soldiers and equipment onto 260 ships in New York Harbor, where the fleet remains while waiting for favorable winds.

July 16. General Howe receives an exuberant letter from General

Burgoyne, who has taken Fort Ticonderoga on the Hudson. Howe decides it is not necessary to go north to assist Burgoyne and instead makes preparations to march on Philadelphia via the Delaware River.

July 23. Favorable winds come in from the north, and General Howe sets sail from New York for Delaware Bay. General Washington is unable to determine if Howe intends to move north to assist Burgoyne or south to take Philadelphia.

August 16. General John Stark leads his American New Hampshire militia against German Colonel Friedrich Baum in the Battle of Bennington and soundly defeats the German column and their reinforcements.

August 19. General Horatio Gates arrives at Stillwater to replace generals Philip Schuyler and Arthur St. Clair as American commander of the Northern Army. Congress has ordered Schuyler and St. Clair to explain their actions in abandoning Fort Ticonderoga, and they are to report to General Washington, ostensibly to face courts-martial.

August 25. After a series of baffling maneuvers, the intent of which has confounded historians ever since, the British fleet and army sails south past the Maryland Capes and Sinepuxent Inlet into Chesapeake Bay, landing finally at Head of Elk, on the northern tip of the Bay. The forty-seven days aboard ships in the summer heat of July and August leaves Howe's men, horses, food, and supplies in terrible condition. He starts toward Philadelphia, and General Washington marches to meet him.

September 11. The two armies collide at Brandywine Creek, where the Americans make a strong showing but are defeated. The Paoli Massacre immediately follows.

September 18. The American Congress, convened at Philadelphia, anticipates the arrival of the British and flees to York, eighty miles to the west.

September 19. The American and British forces clash at Bemis Heights, and the Battle of Freeman's Farm is fought. Neither side claims victory.

September 26. General Howe sends General Cornwallis to Philadelphia, and the British are able to occupy the city without firing a shot. A British feint had left Washington marching to protect American supplies at Reading, which he believed the British intended to seize.

October 3. The American army attacks the British forces entrenched at Germantown. Through a series of American tactical errors and the presence of a thick fog that confounds his battle plan, Washington is again defeated and prepares to march to winter quarters in Valley Forge.

October 7. The Battle of Barber's Wheat Field is fought near Bemis Heights. General Benedict Arnold, against orders from General Horatio Gates and with spectacular leadership on the battlefield, leads the Americans to victory.

October 17. General John Burgoyne surrenders his army to General Horatio Gates.

October 22. General William Howe sends a letter to Lord Germain, resigning his office as commander in chief of the British forces in America.

December 2. King George III is informed of the surrender of Burgoyne's army, and Horace Walpole reports that "the king fell into agonies."

December 12. Benjamin Franklin, American ambassador to France, meets with Comte de Vergennes, French foreign minister, to persuade him, and eventually King Louis XVI, to enter the war on the side of the Americans.

December 19. Starving, freezing, and destitute, the Continental Army arrives at Valley Forge.

December 20. General Washington issues orders to begin building the small huts for which Valley Forge will become famous.

December 22. General Washington writes a letter to President Henry Laurens of the United State Congress, describing the terrible plight of his men and including the statement about their existing on "a cold, bleak hill."

1778

February 23. German General Frederich von Steuben arrives at Valley Forge to take charge of training and disciplining the American troops, a feat which he accomplishes beyond all expectations.

April 4. In an exchange of prisoners, American general Charles Lee, held prisoner by the British since before the battle of Trenton, is released. He arrives at Valley Forge on April 6.

May 4. The United States Congress ratifies the treaty with France, bringing France and its invaluable assistance into the Revolutionary War on the side of the Americans.

May 25. His resignation having been accepted by Lord Germain and the British Parliament, General William Howe sails for England. Command of the British forces in America is given to General Sir Henry Clinton.

June 17–18. In a nighttime maneuver, General Clinton evacuates Philadelphia and marches his troops toward New York.

June 28. General Washington's forces attack General Clinton's British column at Monmouth Courthouse, New Jersey. General Charles Lee is in command of a large American division assigned to lead the attack. When Lee retreats, General Washington intercepts him and reprimands him severely, then turns the division around and resumes the attack. Following a fierce engagement, the British flee during the night and the Americans claim victory.

1779

September 23. Commodore John Paul Jones, aboard the *Bonhomme Richard*, engages the larger British man-of-war Serapis off the east coast of England in the much-celebrated night battle in which Jones utters the now-famous cry, "I have not yet begun to fight!" (See volume I)

PART ONE

CHAPTER I

★ ★ ★

*H*ave someone walk this horse until she's cooled out, then rub her down and grain her. Gather all the officers you can find for a council."

General George Washington dismounted his tall gray mare and for a moment stood stiff-legged on the frozen ground, in the manner of horsemen who have been in the saddle too long. He handed the reins to Captain Tench Tilghman, a member of his staff, and tipped his head to squint at the sun, calculating the time. It was not yet ten o'clock in bright, frigid sunlight.

Fitzgerald nodded. "Yes, sir."

Steam rose from the hot hide of the bone-weary horse, crusted with sweat and lather that had built up around the bridle and saddle blanket. Fitzgerald handed the reins to the nearest sergeant, gave orders, then swung back onto his own smoking, jaded bay gelding and raised it to a trot. He stood tall in the stirrups to search through the press of Continental Army soldiers for the ones wearing the gold braid of officers on their black tricorned hats.

For a time Washington stood in the patches of light snow, vapor rising from his face. His eyes were narrowed, chin set like granite as he studied the smoldering remains of the campus of the College of New Jersey at Princeton. His heart swelled as he watched the men of his

3

command working their way through the scattered buildings and the nearby homes, searching for British stores or ammunition—anything they could find that might ease their desperate need for food, clothing, gunpowder, blankets, medicine. They carried wooden packing crates from homes and warehouses and rolled barrels of flour and salt meat out into the streets to be picked up by their wagons.

Half naked—most without shoes—sick—starved—scarecrows—falling asleep on their feet—Trenton eight days ago—now here at Princeton—victorious in both engagements—been marching and in battle for two days and two nights—outgunned, outmanned—how did they win?—how?—only heaven knows—and only the Almighty knows what sustains them.

He turned slightly to look at Nassau Hall, the largest structure in the thirteen American states. The stained glass windows on the first floor were smashed out. The tall, double, heavy oak doors hung at odd angles on their great wrought-iron hinges, blackened and splintered by American cannon wheeled into place by Alexander Hamilton and Joseph Moulder when British soldiers barricaded themselves inside and refused to surrender. Wisps of smoke still rose from the wreckage. One cannonball had ripped through the doors, passed the length of the great assembly hall, and struck a huge painting of King George II, removing his head as neatly as if done by a sword.

The soldiers slowed as they passed Washington, nodding, mumbling "Gen'l" to pay their respects. None remembered they should salute, nor did Washington remind them. In their minds they were seeing him once again as he wheeled his big gray horse away from General Sullivan's command south of Princeton and kicked her to a stampede gait across open ground for more than a mile, cape flying, before he brought her to a lathered, sliding halt in front of the terrified Pennsylvania militia. Alone, he lead them into the battle that routed the line of British redcoats commanded by Colonel Francis Mawhood. At battle's end, there were bullet holes in his cape, but not one musketball had touched him.

No, sir, the musketball or cannonball can't be made that'll git him—not him—not Gen'l Washington—right out there where it's thickest—nary a sign of concern—just sits that big gray horse like he was borned there—leadin' right into them British redcoats

*and their bayonets with bullets whistlin' everywhere like angry hornets an' not one touchin'
him—no, sir, not Gen'l Washington.*

They could never speak their innermost thoughts to his face. All
they could do was nod their heads as they passed and mumble, "Gen'l."

He turned at the sound of a horse cantering in behind, and
Tilghman spoke as he reined in his gelding.

"The officers are on their way, sir—the ones I could find."

They came on tired horses: Sullivan, Hitchcock, Greene, St. Clair,
Cadwalader, Knox, Wilkinson. Washington stood tall to peer over the
college campus searching for others, then turned to Tilghman in
question.

"That's all I could find, sir."

Washington led them into Nassau Hall, to a classroom with shattered window glass littering the floor and a table and chairs thrown about
at random by the terrified British. He set the table upright while the men
gathered the chairs and sat down. They saw the fear in him as he spoke.

"Has anyone seen General Mercer?" he asked.

General Hugh Mercer, Washington's oldest and dearest friend, was
missing from the gathering of officers.

General Cadwalader could not meet Washington's eyes as he
answered quietly: "General Mercer's aide, Major Armstrong, gave me a
message. He found General Mercer near a barn on the Clark farm. His
skull is broken. He has more than fifteen bayonet wounds. Major
Armstrong and Dr. Rush are there with him in the Clark home, but
there's little hope, sir. He's dying."

"Haslet?"

General Nathanael Greene answered. "A bullet through his head. He
felt nothing."

For just a moment the men saw the searing pain in Washington
before he cleared his throat and continued, giving general instructions in
rapid order.

Get all the British stores you can find—especially gunpowder—burn
what we can't take. General Knox, find the Morven estate where General
Cornwallis had his headquarters—search it for every record you can find.

Get a casualty count—the British have a large store of supplies and munitions at Brunswick, along with seventy thousand pounds sterling—a very tempting prize. We could arrive in Brunswick before morning—I want your opinion—Can this army march all night tonight and fight in the morning?

The answers were unanimous. Doubtful—utterly fatigued—it would be tragic to lose all we've won so far.

Washington heaved a great sigh. "I concur. I have considered where we should go for winter quarters. It appears to me that Morristown would be our best choice. The town is small, located on a plateau at the foot of the Thimble Mountains. Nearby, on the east, is another ridge, the Watchung Mountains. They run from the Raritan River on the south to the northern borders of New Jersey. From outside those mountains, the only access to Morristown is through narrow passes that we can easily defend should the British attempt an attack. We will be just thirty miles from New York City, where we can keep a constant watch on General Howe and his movements. I recommend that we winter there to allow our men to regain their strength, and to refit the army for spring. Are there other suggestions?"

There were none.

★　★　★　★　★

Morristown, New Jersey
Early May 1777

"Sir, the officers are assembled. The council can begin at your convenience."

Washington raised his head, pushed his chair back from the small corner table, and stood. "Thank you, Major. I'll come at once." He folded the large map he had been studying as Tilghman nodded and backed out of the private study. Washington heard the steady cadence of his boot heels fade as the major walked down the narrow hallway toward the library.

The faint, sweet scent of mountain laurels hung light in the warmth of the late spring air as Washington followed, stepped into the library, closed the door, and set the dead bolt. Chairs scraped as the officers seated around the long, plain table stood, came to full attention, and waited.

"Be seated, gentlemen." He laid the folded map on the table as they settled back onto their chairs. He glanced quickly up and down the table. Knox, St. Clair, Sullivan, Cadwalader, Hitchcock, Wilkinson, and Hamilton.

He came directly to it.

"I have lately received information that will likely affect all plans for the coming summer campaign." He saw in their eyes that they had already heard.

He continued: "Lord Germain of his Majesty's government has sent General John Burgoyne together with an army to arrive momentarily in Quebec. Roughly half British regulars, half German Hessians."

He waited while brief comments dwindled and died. British regulars were bad enough; Hessians, with their long mustaches and pigtails, were feared, hated.

Washington went on. "General Burgoyne's orders are to proceed south on Lake Champlain, then the Hudson River, take Fort Ticonderoga and continue south to Albany, then east to New York. With the cooperation of General Howe from New York, and Colonel St. Leger from Fort Stanwix, it is apparently the British plan to cut the thirteen states into two sections. Divide the northern states from the southern, then reduce them to British control one at a time."

He paused for a moment, waiting for comments, but there were none. The great convoy of British ships bringing Burgoyne and his command across the Atlantic, with the largest number of cannon ever recorded in British history to support such an expedition, had been too well observed in international waters by too many ships of all flags. When the British ships flying the Union Jack turned west into the mouth of the St. Lawrence River, there was no doubt who they were or where they were bound. The sightings were reported in New York and Boston harbors, and within days, the news of the armada had spread throughout New England.

Eyes downcast, Washington continued: "I see you already knew. The problem this gives us is critical." He raised his eyes. "I'm asking for your counsel. Do we remain here to try to stop General Howe if he moves north up the Hudson to meet and join General Burgoyne? Or do we go north to stop General Burgoyne, and leave New York and the seacoast to General Howe? If we remain here to engage General Howe, can the northern militia stop Burgoyne from coming on down the Hudson, behind us? This army cannot survive if we're required to fight both Burgoyne and Howe at the same time, one behind us, the other in front."

Washington paused. He could not hide the deep fatigue that crept into his eyes and the deepening lines in his face. The officers saw it, and they averted their eyes to stare down at their hands on the table in front of them. In the dead silence they could hear the birds outside arguing over territorial rights and the buzz of the new crop of spring insects. No one spoke.

The commander in chief took a deep breath and exhaled slowly. "May I state my own convictions? I am certain that General Howe intends taking Philadelphia during this summer campaign, one way or another. If that is true, then the questions are, when and how? Before General Burgoyne comes down the Hudson? After? And if General Howe does go after Philadelphia, will it be by land or by sea? Common sense suggests an overland march from New York to Philadelphia. Ninety miles. But General Howe's brother, Lord Admiral Richard Howe, has more than four hundred British transports and warships at anchor in New York Harbor. If General Howe is concerned about exposing his army to us in a ninety-mile overland march, he could load most of his men onto the ships and sail up the Delaware to within sixteen miles of Philadelphia."

He stopped speaking to rub at his eyes with a thumb and forefinger. "That raises the question, is Philadelphia strategically important to us? I'm well aware of the rules. If you capture the capital city of your enemy, you've won the war. But, gentlemen, we're fighting a new kind of war. We're making new rules as we go, and this old rule must be discarded if we are to survive. Congress is keenly aware that if Philadelphia falls, the

British will crow like roosters, and our people will feel a loss all out of proportion to its actual value in the war. Congress will be very reluctant to let Philadelphia fall, but fortunately for them they are not the ones who will be doing the fighting. We will. They can be gone from Philadelphia in half an hour should the need arise and continue their work in any one of half a dozen other cities. Losing Philadelphia would not be good, but its loss certainly won't be fatal."

Again he paused, and every officer moved in his chair as the weight of what was descending on their army, and on the United States, settled in. Washington continued:

"One heavy question is, what can our army do to stop General Howe, no matter what he does? We are outnumbered about four to one. We have far too few cannon. Half the men are still barefoot. True, some French arms and munitions are trickling in, but some of our soldiers are still without muskets. And we are low on gunpowder, food, blankets, and medicine."

He dropped his hands to his sides. "It's obvious that we cannot commit ourselves to a battle on open level ground. Nor can we commit to a battle on their terms. We can only harass them and wait for a time and place that will favor us." Again he paused, searching for words. The officers seated around the table leaned forward, sensing that his silence and the obvious care in selecting his next statement signaled that all he had said was but prologue. The live-or-die issue was coming.

Washington spoke slowly. "Should Burgoyne be successful in joining Howe in New York, I fear for our entire revolution."

There it was! The chairs creaked as each officer leaned back, mouth pursed, eyes narrowed in deep concentration. Every man in the room knew that if Burgoyne and Howe were to succeed in joining forces, the days of the Continental Army would be numbered.

"Questions? Comments?" General Washington was standing straight, silently waiting.

General Enos Hitchcock cleared his throat. "Did I hear that St. Leger has Joseph Brant gathering a force of Mohawk Indians to take Fort

Stanwix? And then come east, on down the Mohawk River to join Burgoyne?"

Washington nodded. "You did. It's true."

Murmuring broke out as Hitchcock continued. "Joseph Brant and a thousand Mohawk up there in those woods could inflict more damage on us than five thousand British or Hessians. Any way to stop him?"

Washington slowly shook his head. "I don't know. We'll try to get help from the Iroquois, but no one knows if we'll succeed. The Iroquois have a confederation, a written constitution, that binds them together, and they've taken an oath to remain neutral. They won't fight for either side. Last Monday, May fifth, I sent two men north to do what they can."

Hitchcock was incredulous. "Two men? To stop Brant?"

Washington nodded. "One is a white man who was raised Iroquois for seventeen years—speaks all Iroquois dialects, including Mohawk, as well as French, fluently. A remarkable fighting man. I've used him before. He works with another man. Do you recall our cannon blowing open the doors of Nassau Hall at Princeton to clear out the British barricaded inside? The first two men through the smashed doors are the ones I've sent north."

Each officer fell silent, searching his memory to identify the two men. Suddenly Knox, the corpulent twenty-six-year-old former bookseller turned soldier, and now general in command of artillery for the Continental Army, straightened in his chair. "I was there with those cannon, sir. Did one of those men have a tomahawk?"

A rare, faint smile crossed Washington's face. "Yes."

Knox leaned back, grinning at the remembrance of the tall man following the husky one, sprinting through the shattered, smoking doors, swinging his black tomahawk over his head, and the high, shrill Iroquois war cry echoing inside the cavernous assembly hall.

Hitchcock continued. "Did he say how he intends stopping Brant? Or the Mohawk? Is he planning an assassination? Murder Brant, and the whole Mohawk nation could rise against us."

"No, no assassination. He knows Brant, and Brant knows him. It's possible this man can do something. In my judgment, it would have been a mistake not to send him."

"The names of those two?"

"Private Eli Stroud and Corporal Billy Weems. Both from the Massachusetts Regiment."

Hitchcock settled back in his chair and said quietly, "Two men? To stop Brant and his Mohawk?" He shrugged and softly blew air through rounded lips as he shook his head in disbelief.

Washington leaned forward, arms stiff, palms flat on the table. "Coming back to the issue before us, I need your advice. What can be done to prevent Generals Burgoyne and Howe from joining forces and dividing the States?"

Open talk broke out between the officers, and Washington let it go on for a time before he raised a hand.

"Are there any clear-cut proposals?"

There were none.

"Then I suggest the following: First, General Burgoyne made his reputation as a light cavalry officer at the battles of Valencia de Alcantara and later at Villa Velha in the British war with Spain. Since then he has made his regiment the finest light cavalry in the British army. I am convinced he believes he can now lead his light cavalry as he always has—all mounted on horses, swords in hand, straight ahead at the gallop."

He paused, then changed direction with his thoughts. "I think he will move his entire army south in boats on Lake Champlain probably to within striking distance of Fort Ticonderoga. Remember, most of the cannon at Fort Ti are set to cover the lakes—both Lake Champlain and Lake George. That means that in order to take Fort Ti with the fewest casualties, he'll have to come at it from the land side. So he'll have to put most of his army ashore north of Fort Ti."

A light went on in the heads of most of the officers.

"If he takes Fort Ti, he'll have two choices in moving on south. Move his army overland, or move it by boat on Lake George and the Hudson River. To take the Hudson River route he'll have to portage his entire army and all its artillery across the Chute—the spillway that empties Lake George into Lake Champlain—and then twelve miles to the Hudson River. I do not think he can portage all his boats that distance because some of them are too large. The result is, he'll have to find boats when he gets to the Hudson. If he does, and moves south on the river, his entire army will be exposed on the open water for thirty miles. American cannon hidden on shore can reach him the whole distance, and there is no way he can shoot back."

Half the officers were leaning forward as their minds leaped ahead. Washington stopped for a moment to further arrange his thoughts.

"Considering the unacceptable risk of moving in boats on the Hudson River, I conclude that if he succeeds in taking Fort Ticonderoga, he'll move his entire army south by traveling over land."

He stopped, waiting for the officers to settle in their minds. "Now let me put it all together. I believe General Burgoyne does not understand that he cannot move his army through those northern forests the way he has done in Europe. It's true he's had limited service here in America, but I do not think he understands that his worst enemy here will not be our forces, but the terrain. The notion of mounted light cavalry charging through those woods is utter nonsense. There are places they'll be fortunate to make one mile in one day. There are swamps where they'll have to build causeways very close to a mile long. There will be no forage for their horses and cattle. Wagons and cannon will be virtually impossible to move. His supply line will stretch over two hundred miles, clear back to Quebec. It can be cut off at will."

He straightened. "In short, I think General Burgoyne's army will be vulnerable. It is my judgment that with the right leadership, and with the natural barriers the British will face in the New England forests and woods, our northern militia can stop them."

He looked around the table. "Do you have advice?"

Talk rose, slowly at first, then more excitedly as the officers spoke, giving and taking, gesturing, sorting through the flood of reactions. Washington listened with silent intensity until Cadwalader raised a hand and the room quieted.

"Who will be sent up to take command?"

Washington's answer was firm. "That will be for Congress to decide."

Hamilton thrust his tiny, thin hand into the air. "Permission to speak freely, sir?"

At Washington's nod, he continued.

"Congress could put the northern campaign under command of a politician—or perhaps some French dilettante. That notable warrior General Roche de Fermoy leaves much to be desired. That any commander would get drunk and abandon his command in the face of the enemy is unacceptable. We have Heaven to thank for Colonel Hand and the success of the action at Princeton the following day, or we would all be prisoners. Or hanged. I know the importance of respecting Congress's authority, sir, but we must concede that they have not always exercised it with wisdom or judgment."

Washington turned understanding eyes on small, slender, young Alexander Hamilton, who had been in command of a cannon battery at the battle of Trenton and then at Princeton. Hamilton had performed heroically and was a promising officer, with but one considerable flaw: he never questioned but that his opinion on anything was ultimate and final.

Washington spoke with quiet emphasis. "So long as I am in command, the military will be subject to the will of Congress. Congress will select the commander of the northern forces."

He reached for the map. "Assuming Congress agrees with what I have explained and sends a general to the northern militia to stop General Burgoyne, we will undertake to hold General Howe in check here."

He unfolded and spread the map before them. "If General Howe intends taking Philadelphia, I have concluded the following location will be the best to watch his movements, and hold him." He raised his face to them. "I repeat, we cannot engage him on open, flat ground. He knows that, and will try to draw us out for a battle we cannot win. We'll have to be watchful and prudent and pick the time and place for any engagements."

He tapped a long forefinger on the map. "We are here, at Morristown. Right now General Howe's army is here, at New York, about thirty miles east of us." He shifted his finger further down the map. "Here is Philadelphia, south and a little west of us about eighty miles, on the Delaware River." He began moving his finger slowly. "If General Howe marches his army from New York to Philadelphia, the most logical route will be from Amboy, here, to New Brunswick, here, southwest through Princeton, across the Delaware at Trenton, and on down the river past Germantown to Philadelphia."

He moved his finger back up the map to Morristown. "If he follows that route, it is my judgment that the best place for us to watch his every move, and to harass him effectively, would be here, at the village of Middlebrook, about thirty miles nearly due south of where we are now. We'll have to cross the Raritan River, but once across, we will have several advantages."

Again that long finger tapped the map. "The village is small—just a few homes at a crossroads. It is located at the foot of the Watchung Mountains, near the stream that bears its name—Middlebrook. The stream runs here, past the town, on past a copper mine here, past the smelting furnaces here, and on north to the Raritan River." He shifted his finger back. "Here, on this hill just outside the village, is a huge rock, four hundred feet above the valley floor. From that rock, one can see all roads, nearly to Amboy, New Brunswick, and on down to Philadelphia. We can camp here"—he tapped the map—"near the mountains, and build redoubts and cannon emplacements, here and here, to defend our camp. Should General Howe choose to force a major battle, we can disappear into the Watchung Mountains within minutes. I believe that is where we should move our forces immediately. We will leave the sick and wounded here at the Morristown hospital until they can travel. Then they can join us."

He raised a hand to thoughtfully touch his chin. "Have I forgotten anything?" He dropped his hand. "Yes. I think you all know I have sent General Putnam with his command to Princeton. General Nathanael Greene is at Basking Ridge. General William Heath is at Peekskill, and

General Anthony Wayne is at Ticonderoga. So long as we hold those positions, we can constantly watch the British and move to prevent them from severing the northern states from those in the south."

Satisfied, he straightened and directed his gaze up one side of the table and down the other. "Do you have questions? Is there a better plan?"

The silence held.

Washington nodded. "Thank you, all. I'll have written orders for each of you by evening."

★　★　★　★　★

The road from Morristown to Middlebrook
Late May 1777

They came striding along the dirt wagon road that wound crookedly from Morristown, south across the Raritan River. They were more than six thousand, and they came loud, boisterous, confident, carrying their rifle or musket in one hand, or across their shoulders with their arms hooked over them, dangling. The column was strung out for three miles in groups and clumps that bore no resemblance to a marching army. They called bawdy stories to each other, or humorous insults, or openly berated their officers in the ancient tradition of enlisted men.

They walked laughing, jostling, nearly jubilant, spirits soaring, buoyed by the incomparable, pristine beauty of another New England spring. Oak and maple trees, standing so thick one could hardly see the blue heavens, had burst their buds and turned the world into an ocean of green. Dogwood and mountain laurel blossoms spangled the forests with splotches of white and pink, and emerald skunk cabbage lined the banks of the unnumbered brooks and streams carrying the roiling spring runoff from the mountains to the great rivers, and on eastward to the sea. Birds of every size and hue flitted in the scrub oak and maples and pines, filling the air with their warbles and chirps as they established rights. Red squirrels and striped chipmunks, still shedding their long winter hair, darted about, pausing only long enough to study the strange procession in disgust, then disappearing in an instant. A mother raccoon interrupted her washing of a crayfish in a stream to cuff her two new-borns into silent obedience, then study the boisterous procession as it passed. A porcupine waddled into the road and hunkered down for a moment to stare, then moved on. A fresh new world, burgeoning with life and the promise of rich harvests surely to come, had dimmed the men's memory of the harshness of their winter encampment on the outskirts of Morristown.

They wore the tattered homespun that had survived the New England winter. Most were naked from the knees down, swinging along barefoot on the hard-packed New Jersey dirt. They gleefully ignored the orders of their officers, who had long since abandoned any hope of enforcing any military discipline or maintaining any order in their line of march. After all, the captains and lieutenants had not been selected on merit, nor commissioned by any recognized military authority. To the contrary, this army had reversed the entire process. Lieutenants and captains were elected by the popular vote of those they were to command, and such elections were held as often as a captain or a lieutenant forgot who was in fact running the army.

They knew who they were. They were the Continental Army of the thirteen United States of America. Shopkeepers and farmers, backwoodsmen and city folk, literates and illiterates, artisans and laborers, sinners and saints, whites, blacks, reds, and yellows, from north and south, practical, hardheaded, independent. No uniforms. Dressed in homespun. Bearded. Long-haired, mostly bareheaded. Burned from the suns of summer and the snows of winter. Officers wore jackets made from blankets, epaulets sewed on their shoulders. A few had battered hats. Horses with their heads down labored to pull wagons that grumbled along, overloaded with camp kettles and bedrolls, cooking tripods, ammunition, gunpowder, and too few barrels of salt meat and flour.

Behind the military came the women and a few children—the wives and families of soldiers—and with them a ragtag band of camp followers. They made do with what they had and shared the fortunes and misfortunes of this marching army. They earned their keep by washing the ragged remains of clothing and by cooking and by tending the sick and wounded. They plodded along behind, the mothers watching, scolding the children as they cavorted and darted about the road or into the woods to chase the squirrels or to pluck wildflowers.

The men knew they more closely resembled an undisciplined horde than a marching army, but wore the fact like a badge of honor. No matter their appearance, they held their heads high, spirits soaring in the glories of spring. After all, weren't they the ones who had crossed the Delaware River, west to east, in a blizzard on the night of December 25, five months before, and caught the Hessians at Trenton by surprise at eight o'clock the morning of the 26th? Finished the battle before noon? Killed or captured the entire garrison, with only four Americans wounded, none lost? And when the furious British general Howe sent his best field general, Lord General Charles Cornwallis and eight thousand of his best troops to trap and destroy Washington and this upstart Continental Army, weren't they the ones who wrapped the wheels of their cannon with blankets to muffle them, and overnight marched around Cornwallis to take Princeton the morning of January 3, then carried on to Morristown in the Thimble Mountains, where the British dared not try to reach them? The news of their impossible victories had magically raced through New England overnight, then leaped the Atlantic to strike King George III and his Majesty's government like a thunderbolt out of a clear blue sky.

Weren't they the ones who had performed the magic? The impossible? Weren't they the ones doing the work of the Almighty? Their catastrophic defeats of 1776 at Long Island, White Plains, Fort Washington on Manhattan Island, then Fort Lee, and their panic-driven, headlong retreat across New Jersey to escape total annihilation were but dim memories as they swung along, nearly cocky in their confidence that they could now whip the British any time, any place. Just so long as ammunition held and they knew General Washington was out there in front, leading, as he had in both the Trenton and Princeton battles. He was the one officer they openly revered. They cursed and jabbed at all the others, each in turn, but not Washington. Not their Gen'l Washington.

Gen'l Washington? Can't be kilt. The way he sat his big gray horse there in Trenton in the twilight, on the south end of the Assunpink Bridge. Musketballs thick like mosquitoes and the cannonballs blasting all around. And the way he come charging back the morning we took Princeton. Over a mile he ran that big horse, right out in front of the Pennsylvania militia when they was hiding scared in them trees. Him all alone, in plain sight of the British. Talked the militia out of the woods, into the open, and led them across that open field, right up to thirty yards from where that British officer, Mawhood, had his troops all in a line ready to fire their opening volley. Only Gen'l Washington shouted "Fire!" first. The mustketballs was buzzin' both directions like mad hornets. Knocked holes in his coat and his hat, but nary a one touched him. No, sir. Not Gen'l Washington. He can't be kilt. He's favored by the Almighty, he is!

News of their movement south from Morristown spread outward to excite and fire the imagination of boys and restless young men who dreamed of adventure and glory, drawing them from their homes, as marching armies have from the dawn of time. They trickled into camp in ones and twos, or in small companies, to swell the ranks of the Continental Army with each passing day.

★　★　★　★　★

It was of little note when a rather tall boy with a decidedly Boston accent walked into the camp of Third Company, New York Regiment, in early July, as they were setting up their kettles for evening mess. No one paid him any attention until he stopped the nearest soldier.

"Can you tell me where to find an officer?"

"What for?"

"I've come to join the army."

The man snorted, "Where's your musket? Bayonet?"

"I don't have one. I thought—"

"You thought the army had one for you. Well, it don't, at least not right now." He pointed indifferently. "That man with the beard is a captain. Talk with him."

The boy did. He was sent to Sergeant O'Malley.

"What's your name?"

"Caleb Dunson."

"Ever cut meat?"

"Yes."

For half an hour Caleb Dunson stood shoulder to shoulder with the supper detail of Third Company and diced fresh venison for their evening mess, then piled the bones onto a torn, bloody tarp to drag them away to a fly-infested pit. He shared a steaming stew and watched as a big, bull-necked, thick shouldered Irishman named Conlin Murphy beat a man named Jamie senseless. Caleb made the innocent mistake of standing up at the wrong time and quietly asking the man next to him a question. In less than two minutes Murphy had beaten him to a bloody, half-conscious pulp. From nowhere, an aging stranger appeared, with an odd tenderness in his touch. By nightfall, the bone-deep cut on Caleb's cheek was stitched closed, and a cold, wet compress had been pressed to his swollen cheek and eye.

The boy smoldered and swore one thing: It was not over with Conlin Murphy.

★ ★ ★ ★ ★

The Continental Army camp, early July 1777

The jumbled tangle of anger festering deep in his soul found its way to his hands as sixteen-year-old Caleb stood hunched forward, elbows tucked in, while he hammered the huge double-burlap sack filled with one hundred eighty pounds of river sand and New Jersey dirt. He shifted his weight from foot to foot to drive his canvas-wrapped fists into the bag, catching it solid as it dangled on its short tether looped over the branch of an oak tree. Caleb's teeth were set, jaw clenched, as he swung each hand with every pound he had, and he grunted as each ripped into the dirty, worn burlap. Stripped to the waist, sweat glistened on his upper body and dripped from his nose and chin. His eyes shone, and his face was a mask of dark, animal release as he pounded away, oblivious to time, concentrating fiercely on but one thing. Learn. Learn to hit quick and hard with either fist. Learn to move, to protect the head, the ribs, to make the other man miss, to slip a punch, to set the feet quickly, strike, then move, always moving. Shuffling on the balls of his feet, it became a rhythm—set, strike, move, set, strike, move.

The sun slipped below the western rim, and still he pounded while the gray of evening settled over the sprawling, chaotic camp, scattered near an unnamed stream on the road to Philadelphia. He had taken evening mess, cut his assigned share of firewood to heat the big black cast-iron kettles of wash water that dangled on chains from the apex of the great, smoke-blackened iron-legged tripods, then gone to the bank of the stream with a shovel and Charles Dorman to fill the burlap bag with sand and earth. They worked in silence, the aging, gray-haired Dorman holding the bag open while Caleb pitched it full. Together they dragged it to the oak nearest Caleb's bedroll, cast the rope over the lowest heavy branch, raised the bag six feet, and tied it off, swaying slowly in the golden glow of a setting sun.

Patiently Dorman had wrapped Caleb's hands with canvas strips, then stepped back to watch in critical silence as Caleb squared with the bag and began his evening ritual. Dorman's eyes narrowed in intense concentration as he saw the rage, the consuming hate welling up in Caleb, driving him to swing with all his strength, grunting as his fists slammed in.

Too much anger—more to this than Murphy beating him—deeper—dangerous—headed for trouble—ruin—too young—what could it be?—what?

With the experience and finely honed instincts of one who had spent much of his life in the harsh, brutal world of two gladiators facing each other in a squared ring with the all-consuming purpose of beating the other man senseless, Dorman missed nothing as he studied Caleb. The boy stood nearly six feet tall, one hundred sixty pounds, with brown hair, blue eyes, and a smooth, unmarked face that could only be called handsome. He had reached his full frame, but not his full weight. His knees and elbows were a little too prominent, his feet slightly too large. His movements lacked full coordination, but with each passing day they were a heartbeat faster, more accurate, more confident, smoother.

Dorman's eyes narrowed as he watched—slowly, steadily framing a mental picture of the boy before him.

He has heart—intelligence—balance—he'll gain speed—but what's driving him?—too much for a boy his age—the wrong reasons will bring trouble.

As he dropped his eyes to study the movement of Caleb's feet, he found his thoughts reaching back into the gray mists of his own childhood, filled with heartrending pain and soul-destroying ugliness. He felt once again the seething rage at the evil into which he had been born and the hot lust it had shaped in his breast to strike out against all authority. For twenty years he had disciplined himself to push away from the terrible torture of those memories, but now, watching a boy with an unknown inner torment that could ruin him, he let the memories come as they would.

Dorman's fifteen-year-old unwed mother had died giving him birth in the filth of a waterfront alley in the great seaport of Liverpool, England. His father, a Dutch sailor, never knew he had left an unborn child behind when his ship sailed from Liverpool for Minorca seven months before the sweating, terrified girl delivered her child alone in the squalor of the narrow alley. She lived only long enough to wrap the infant boy in her bloody skirt and crawl to the street. A grizzled old sail maker heard the cries of the newborn and took the shivering, wrinkled infant to an orphanage not fifty feet from the stench and unending sound of water lapping at the heavy oak pilings that supported the wharves.

The newborn infant was accepted with a cold disgust by the tall, wiry beadle and his wife, who saw nothing more in the boy than another one pound sixpence each month from the coffers of a stingy, reluctant public charity that paid to keep the shame of Liverpool's fatherless children hidden. They entered him on their pay vouchers as Jonathan Smith.

For fifteen years Dorman endured the Spartan poverty of the Liverpool orphanage before he exploded in a fit of rage. The beadle had once again ordered him to the front of the crude dining hall for a caning with an oak stick, the consequence of Dorman having dipped his spoon into the greasy supper gruel before the pronouncement of "Grace." Dorman dutifully walked to the beadle, obediently bent over and seized his ankles, and tightened every muscle in his body to take the first blow when something inside him, primal beyond anything he had ever known, came surging in wild rebellion. The hickory struck, Dorman jerked erect and tore into the tall, wiry beadle with both fists flailing wildly, tears streaming, screaming like one demented. He struck again and again as the startled man stumbled backwards and went down. Dorman was on him like an animal, fists pounding at the eyes, nose, mouth, while he screamed his rage. He leaped up and shrieked at the man to get up, get up, but the man lay curled on his side, arms thrown over his head. Dorman kicked him in the stomach, then the throat, then wherever he could while the other horrified orphans turned the dining hall into bedlam. He seized his wooden bowl and hurled the container of thin, steaming soup at the man's head, then turned and ran to the great doors, threw them open, and disappeared into the dark of the rain-slick cobblestone streets of the Liverpool docks.

The following day, with the authorities combing the waterfront for a runaway orphan worth one pound sixpence each month to the beadle of the orphanage, he gave himself a new name and a new position in life. Thus it was that Charles Dorman became cabin boy on the *Pelican*, a ship whose captain, Abijah Morton, cared more for profits than his crew. Dark stories spoken quietly in dingy taverns told of Abijah Morton selling part of his own crew to slave traders on the African coast.

At age eighteen Dorman had brawled his way through every major seaport in Europe, Africa, the Orient, and the Mediterranean. He had learned to use his hands and feet to break bones and disable men with deadly efficiency. Twice he had taken knife wounds that had nearly killed him. Once he was certain he had broken a man's neck and killed him, but with the police pounding on the door, he had fled before he was certain. At nineteen he jumped ship at midnight as she lay anchored in the Thames River a mile below London town, waiting to have her cargo of China silk unloaded. Two days later he was a seaman in the Royal British Navy.

Within three months his explosive temper and deadly fists had his shipmates silently avoiding him, while his superior officers gleefully entered his name in the Royal Navy boxing register to compete for the title of fleet boxing champion. The best trainer in the British navy saw the talent that lay beneath the wild flailings of this tavern brawler. He arranged to meet the angry young man and began the yearlong training that slowly gave direction to the volcano that seethed within. At age twenty Dorman was fleet champion. At twenty-one he was champion of the southern half of England. Five feet nine inches tall, one hundred seventy-three pounds, dark wavy hair, his relentless training and many fights had made him thick-necked, heavy in the shoulders and arms. There was very little bridge left to his nose, and his bushy eyebrows showed deep scars, as did his lower lip and both cheekbones. He had not been beaten, nor had he ever learned to completely control his hot rebellion against authority.

In 1757, at age thirty, Dorman the British sailor found himself in a vast, strong, primeval land, at war with the hated French for possession of the thirteen American colonies and Canada. Within days he realized two things: he was drawn to the power and strength of the pristine wilderness called America, as to no other place on earth, and there was a sense, a spirit, of unfettered freedom among the colonial people like none he had ever felt. With the surrender of the French forces in 1763, Dorman let his enlistment with the British navy expire, then remained in America as a soldier in the New Jersey militia. He chaffed against the authority of the British Stamp Act, and when King George III and Parliament passed the Boston Port Act that blockaded Boston Harbor, Dorman became an open rebel against his native England. He joined the headlong retreat of the American Continental Army across New Jersey after its catastrophic defeat at Long Island and crossed the Delaware River into Pennsylvania to try to save anything they could of the shattered, beaten, freezing, starving Continentals. He was with General Washington when they recrossed the Delaware River in a blizzard on the night of December 25, 1776, to strike and take Trenton at eight o'clock the next morning, then moved on to Princeton. He wintered with the army at Morristown, knowing in his heart he had found a home and a people and a cause to which he could pledge his life. America. Liberty.

At age fifty his hair had grayed. He had never lost the inner fires of anger and rebellion, but with age had learned to bank and control them.

With the onset of the spring greening of 1777, and the eruption of color as the flowers flooded the Morristown mountains and valleys, Dorman rolled his few belongings in his blanket, took up his musket, and followed the march of most of the Continental Army from Morristown south to Middlebrook, probing to find General Sir William Howe and the British army.

It was in the early evening of an eventless day that a panting, wide-eyed private came running, shouting for Dorman. The young soldier was one of the few in camp who had previously seen the single occasion in which Dorman had quietly stepped between a big, raw-boned North Carolina braggart holding a tomahawk in his right hand, and a smaller, white-faced youth with a rock clutched in his fist. "You best put down the tomahawk," Dorman had quietly said, looking up eight inches into the big man's face. The man had laughed and reached to wrap Dorman inside his arms to break his back. Dorman stepped within the encircling arms and swung once. It had taken a North Carolina sergeant more than an hour to get the unconscious man to open his eyes, and the regimental surgeon four hours to set and tie his broken jaw.

Dorman stopped unrolling his blanket and stood with narrowed eyes as the sweating soldier gasped, "Murphy's beating on a boy down by the river. Might kill him. You better come."

Conlin Murphy! Dorman knew well the proclivity of the Irish to settle things with their fists, sometimes for fun, sometimes to break the monotony, sometimes in anger. But not Murphy. Murphy took a depraved delight in picking fights with his inferiors and pounding them bloody. Despite his fifty years, Dorman had never risen above his over-powering hatred for a bully. The pain and remembrance of endless beatings with a hickory stick until he bled still burned bright in his memory.

Dorman nodded, the private pivoted, and Dorman followed him at a trot, working his way toward the river, through the disorganized clutter of ragged tents and ragged soldiers and evening fires. A knot of men opened a corridor for him, and he strode to the center of the circle, where a boy lay on his side, trying to rise. His face and shirt were smeared with blood. With a bone-deep cut on his left cheek streaming blood, he was shaking his head, sending blood and gore flying from his nose and mouth. His eyes were glazed, the left one purple, swollen nearly closed. Two men held him while he feebly fought to rise, shouting, sobbing, "It's not over. Bring him back! It's not over!"

Dorman spoke. "I'll take care of him." The two men turned to see who had spoken, and Dorman repeated. "I'll tend to him."

"Are you the regimental surgeon?"

"No, but I understand these things."

Both men rose and backed away while Dorman knelt beside Caleb, who was still struggling to rise. Dorman placed a hand on the boy's shoulder and pushed him down, and Caleb slowly settled. Dorman tenderly pressed the angry swelling of the left cheekbone. He shifted his thumb and finger to the bridge of the swollen nose, closed his eyes, and carefully pressed first to the right, then the left. He studied the cut on the left cheek, then forced the left eye open to study the pupil. Moving his fingers gently, he worked his hand down Caleb's left rib cage, collarbone to belt.

"Son, can you hear me?"

Caleb nodded.

"You're lucky. No bones broken. The bridge of your nose is cracked. I think it will heal without showing. I don't know about your left ear. We'll find out if it's been hurt in the next couple of days. I think you got two cracked ribs, but none broken. I'm going to get some of my things, and I'll be right back. Don't move."

Blinking to make the world come back into focus, Caleb waited until the man returned with an old, small, dented metal box; a canteen; and some clean sheeting. Dorman stripped Caleb to his trousers, washed him from the waist up, then soaked the cut on the cheek with alcohol, threaded a needle, and spoke.

"This will sting."

"Go ahead."

Caleb jerked when the man took one stitch to close the cut, then smeared a strong, thick, foul-smelling salve on it.

"Still taste blood?"

"Yes."

He uncorked a small bottle, poured a thick, dark liquid into a tiny cup, and said, "Wash your mouth with this. Don't swallow it. Spit it out."

Caleb drained the cup and for a moment thought his head was on fire. He held the foul mix as long as he could, then spat it onto the ground. "What is it?" he choked.

"Carbolic salve and alcohol. It'll help heal the cuts in your mouth. Where's your bedroll?"

They both turned as a corpulent, officious man with gold epaulets on the shoulders of his homespun coat came puffing up behind them. "I'm Major Waldron, the regimental surgeon. Is this the injured boy?"

For five minutes Waldron examined Caleb, then rose, eyebrows raised in surprise. "Seems it's all taken care of. If you need me, send word." He rose and was gone as quickly as he had arrived.

Dorman looked at Caleb. "Where's your bedroll?" he asked again.

Caleb pointed.

"What's your name, son?"

Caleb lisped through bruised, swollen lips, "Caleb Dunson."

"Come on."

With Caleb's arm over his shoulder and his box and canteen under his arm, Dorman walked Caleb to his bedroll and sat him down.

"Who are you?" Caleb asked.

"Name's Charles Dorman. Company Five, just north of here."

"Why are you doing this?"

"I got my reasons."

"Like what?"

"We'll talk about that later. For now, we get some water from the creek and keep a cold compress on that cheek and eye. I don't think there's any permanent damage, but you'll want to get that swelling down." He turned on his heel and walked toward the river.

With the sun now below the western horizon, the world was cast in dwindling shades of bronze when the man returned. He wrung water from a rag and positioned it over the closed eye and swollen cheek. "Hold that," he said, and Caleb reached with his hand.

The following morning the reveille drum echoed through a silent camp, and Dorman quietly watched Caleb grit his teeth against the torments of the worst aches he had ever known. His face was puffy, the left eye swollen, purple, and yellow. It took the boy ten minutes to put on his shoes and roll up his blanket. Dorman turned his head to listen as Lieutenant McCormack sang out the work assignments for Third Company, then stopped to speak to Caleb.

"I heard about it. Murphy's on report. You're off duty for today."

Dorman's ragged eyebrows raised when Caleb shook his head. "No, I'm not. Give me my orders."

McCormack's mouth fell open. "What?"

Caleb glared through swollen eyes. "Give me my orders."

McCormack shrugged. "All right. Fire detail. Haul wood for the cooks. Where's your musket?"

"Don't have one."

"Then you carry a spear. Make one."

Caleb bobbed his head. Dorman watched with deep interest as Caleb, hunched over to favor cracked ribs, winced as he used his left hand to load wood on his right arm, dumped it by the great black kettles, and went for a second load. Finished, Caleb picked up an ax from the woodpile, cut a nine-foot pine sapling, trimmed it clean, then with nearby soldiers glancing at him as they worked, held it against a log with one foot while he swung the ax one-handed to sharpen the end. With his pine sapling spear in hand, he shouldered his bedroll and marched out with Third Company, eyes straight ahead, chin set against the pain of cracked ribs.

Evening mess was finished when Captain Venables came striding, calling for Caleb. Men crowded around as the captain spoke.

"We're going to have a hearing. What charges do you want to bring against Private Murphy?"

"None."

Venables started. "What? After what he did to you?"

"It was a misunderstanding."

"A misunderstanding of what? Have you seen your face?"

"No charges."

Venables turned and called, "McCormack, come over here."

McCormack approached, and Venables pointed. "McCormack, this man says he does not want to bring charges against Murphy, and I want a witness." He turned back to Caleb. "Do I understand you do not want to hold a hearing? You refuse to bring charges against Murphy for what he did to you?"

Caleb looked from Venables to McCormack, then glanced at the faces of the other men in the circle. "That's right. No charges."

Venables tossed his hands upward. "Well, I can't force you. If you bring no charges there won't be a hearing because we have no bill of particulars to bring against Murphy. You understand that?"

"I do."

"I'll write it up just that way in the regimental orderly book. All you men, go on about your business."

Caleb had settled onto his blanket, hunched over his aching ribs, when a sound came from behind. He tried to turn his head but could not because of the pain.

"It's me, Dorman." The man settled cross-legged, facing Caleb as Caleb spoke.

"I want to thank you for all you've done."

The man nodded and Caleb went on.

"You said we would talk. Why did you take the trouble with me?"

The man's eyes dropped. "I can't stand a bully. And I thought there must be something about you, the way you swung back at that man, and tried to get up when you knew you didn't have a chance, and then wanted them to bring him back because you didn't want it to be over. And I've noticed you today. Hauling wood. Making that spear."

Caleb asked, "You saw it yesterday?"

"No. It was over when I got there. Others told me."

Caleb remained silent and Dorman went on. "I know something about fighting. I did it for a living for a time. I was champion in the southern half of England a long time ago."

Caleb's eyes widened in stunned surprise.

"I can teach you a little about it. At least enough to take care of the bullies of the world, like Conlin Murphy. If you're interested."

"I'm interested."

"It won't be easy."

"I'm interested."

"When you're able, we'll start."

"I'm ready now."

Dorman's eyes widened. "You can hardly raise your arms."

"Start now."

For a time Dorman studied Caleb's face, especially his eyes, then rose to his feet. "All right. Stand up."

Caleb winced as he stood.

"We'll start at the beginning." Dorman raised one hand. "Watch. This is how you make a fist." He clenched his hand, knuckles forming an even bridge, his thumb tucked tightly against his fingertips. "Keep your thumb tucked in. You can dislocate it if it is sticking out, in the way. Do it."

Caleb raised his right hand, folded his fingers in, and tightened his thumb over the fingertips, then looked at Dorman, waiting.

It had begun.

The following evening Dorman had brought burlap, a sailmaker's needle, and heavy cord. Within an hour they had cut and sewed a double-burlap bag, filled it with sand and dirt, and hung it from the branch of a heavy oak tree. Five minutes later, with Dorman hovering over him, Caleb felt for the first time the solid jolt up his arms and across his shoulders as he slammed his clenched fists into the swaying bag.

Over the next nine days, after evening mess was cleared, Dorman patiently dissected the fundamentals while Caleb soaked up every word, every move, quietly repeating to himself over and over again each sentence Dorman spoke, miming Dorman's every motion, slowly at first, then more quickly as he struggled to perfect it.

"You don't hit a man just with your fist, you hit him with your entire body—every pound—got to set your feet right to do it—footwork's the trick—watch—like this—now you try it—no, don't step, slide your

feet—you get a foot off the ground you're vulnerable—try it again—
better—again—better—a good blow doesn't have to travel more than
eighteen inches if your arm is only an extension of your body—watch—
try it—no, keep your elbows tucked in, not out—try again—better—
again—better—watch your feet—keep your toes slightly in—you're
right-handed, so lead with your left foot and left hand—keep your hand
up level with your chin for protection—elbows in—tuck your chin inside
your left shoulder—three fundamental blows—the jab, the hook, the
power blow—the jab just keeps your opponent off balance—the hook
comes in from either side and can hurt him—the power blow can knock
him out if you hit him right—the point of the chin—the temple—the
forehead—watch the jab—you try it—flick it out and back fast, like a
snake strikes—try it—no, no, no, out, back, quick—try again—better—
again—better—try the hook, like this—watch, you've got to raise your
elbow outward and keep your arm bent but set and bring it in hard—
aim for the temple—come in over your opponent's arm—like this—try
it—no, no, keep your arm bent at the elbow—try again—better—now
the power blow—straight out with your right hand—elbow locked, arm
stiff, just an extension of your body—hit with your right foot planted,
slide forward with your left foot—lean into it with all your weight—aim
for the point of the chin or the forehead or the temple, whichever gives
you the clearest target—there are nerves where the jaw joins the skull—
hit the point of the chin and you stun those nerves and the man will go
down—like this—you try—fair—be sure your arm's stiff—hit off that
right foot—keep your toes slightly in—slip that left foot forward—don't
step it, slide it—try again—better—there! that's it!—good!

"While you're trying to do all this to your opponent, he's trying to do
it to you. Trick is, learn how to avoid it—make him miss you altogether
if you can—if you can't, at least avoid letting him hit you hard—that's
called slipping a blow—let him hit you, but not solid—can't hurt you that
way—keep your elbows in to protect your ribs and belly—a man can
knock you out with a power blow over your heart—can stop you in pain
with a blow over your kidneys—got to learn to slip his punches—keep

your head moving slightly—keep your hands up in front of you, elbows in—try it—that's it—good!

"Time we start with combinations of blows. Watch it slow. Jab—hook—power—one, two, three—fast—left hand jab, left hand hook, right hand straight in—watch—try it slow—good—again slow—again a little faster.

"Questions?"

"I thought men stood toe-to-toe and just hit until one was beaten."

"King's Rules—wrong—if you want to win you do what I'm showing you—the Conlin Murphys of the world don't know the King's Rules—and what I'm teaching you will beat the bullies or a professional in the ring—look at my face—every scar you see taught me something, and I'm trying to pass it on to you—spare you looking like me—so you listen and you learn, understand?"

"Yes, sir."

And now, on the ninth day, in the light of the evening campfires, Dorman paused, eyes lowered, staring blankly at the ground, and Caleb recognized he was struggling with his thoughts and searching for words. Caleb waited. Seconds stretched to half a minute before Dorman raised his head, and Caleb started at the strange mix of emotions on the battered face. For the first time Caleb saw traces of doubt, mixed with a feeling of suppressed anger, but most of all he saw a tenderness, a compassion that reached deep. Dorman spoke slowly.

"That second night, I warned against being a bully. Remember? Tomorrow we talk about the single most important thing."

The sound in Dorman's voice froze Caleb. "What is it?"

"Why you're doing this."

For long moments Caleb locked eyes with Dorman, and it seemed that those aging, steely blue points of light beneath the gray, shaggy brows sliced to his very center and laid bare his every thought and secret. Caleb dropped his eyes and swallowed, and in that instant Dorman sensed the wall the boy had built within, thick and high, to shield something dark and foreboding that was consuming him.

Caleb tried to speak. His voice cracked, and he tried again. "Why is that important?"

"Because what I'm teaching you can become something good or something bad. That's up to you. You think on that. We'll talk tomorrow." Dorman fell silent and for a moment dropped his eyes to the ground while he pondered whether he had said enough. Then he turned and walked away with Caleb staring at his back as it disappeared in the shadows.

Caleb sat staring into the fire for a long time before he went to his blankets. The fires dwindled to coals and ashes before the regimental drum sounded tattoo and the camp quieted. The boy lay on his back, hands behind his head, staring unseeing through oak and maple branches into the starry heavens. Unwanted thoughts and images came flitting into his mind, beyond his control, without logic or reason. He threw an arm over his eyes to shut them out, but still they came, bright and scalding. He rolled onto his side and curled up, eyes clenched, unaware of the small moaning sounds coming from his throat as the inner pain grew.

Father—in his bed dying—was it a Wednesday?—No, Thursday—the Concord battle was on Wednesday, April nineteenth—Tom Sievers brought him home from the battle the night of the nineteenth—shot in the back—a British musketball in his right lung—bleeding inside—Mother wiping blood from his mouth—Doctor Soderquist shaking his head—nothing to be done—Tom Sievers, the town derelict, who loved Father, silently weeping—all of us there helpless—me—Mother—Matthew—Brigitte—the twins, Adam and Prissy—it was the morning of Thursday the twentieth he died—he asked us all to leave while he talked to mother alone—he died in her arms—she called us all in—he bled to death in his lung—face white, sagging—dead—dead—dead.

Caleb clenched his eyes shut but could not close out the image of his dead father, an image that was burned into his memory forever. He balled his fists in the blackness as new scenes came.

Mother alone—heartbroken—how she loved him!—struggling to take care of us— no time to mourn him—taking in laundry—anything to get food—working dawn to dark—Matthew—home from the university—stepped into Father's place—the letter from General Washington—needed Matthew as a navigator on a ship—Matthew gone to sea—Mother trying to be both father and mother to us—me and Brigitte taking work

*after school to help—Matthew and Kathleen—loved each other since childhood—
separated by the war—never see each other again—Billy Weems—like a brother—shot
and bayoneted in the battle at Concord—should have died but didn't—gone to the
army—his mother, Dorothy, alone with Trudy—making candles, taking in ironing—
anything to stay alive.*

*All gone—the life we all had—no more—dreams gone—hope gone—everyone
saying this war is the work of the Almighty—America destined to be free—they're
wrong—if we're doing the work of the Almighty, then why is Father dead?—Matthew
gone?—Kathleen gone?—Billy gone?—Dorothy and Trudy alone?—Mother killing
herself for us?—everything we lived for gone forever? —if that's the work of the Almighty,
then he's someone I don't want to know.*

Suddenly he sat up, and in the black of a moonless night pounded
his fist on the ground, muttering, "They'll pay! I'll make them pay!"

He did not know when he drifted into a sleep filled with tortured
dreams nor did he know when he cried out in the night, the sound echoing strangely through the woods. He was awake at dawn when the drummer hammered out reveille. He cut his share of wood for the breakfast
fires, then hung his blankets on a clump of scrub oak to dry from the
morning dew. While he and the other men were finishing their fried
mush and burned sowbelly, Captain Venables came striding.

"We march out at nine o'clock. Due west, right down that dirt road.
Be ready."

With eyes squinted nearly closed against the morning sun, a dour
sergeant wiped greasy fingers in his beard and asked, "Cap'n, we been
marching up and down for ten days—east, west, east, west. Anybody
know 'zactly where we're goin', or why?"

Venables shrugged. "Orders are we march west. We'll know why
when we get there."

The entire command—now more than six thousand soldiers—
marched sweating eight miles west on the narrow dirt wagon trail winding through the thick New Jersey woods. They forded three streams—
two shallow, one chest high and running hard with the muddy brown
runoff from the Appalachian Mountains. The wagon mules balked at
stream's edge, and the men had to blindfold them and jump them,

bucking and kicking, into the swirling water. In the late afternoon they set up camp, their tents and bedrolls scattered along the banks of a clear-running brook. Caleb took his place with the crew assigned to set up the tripods and hang the smoke-blackened kettles from their chains. They set fires under them to boil up an evening mess of bitter, shriveled turnips and fatty chunks of meat from a sow they had butchered three days before.

After eating, Caleb was assigned to a detail that hauled fresh water to heat for cleanup, scrubbed out the kettles with sand, rinsed them, and tipped them against a log to dry. Then, with the evening campfires burning, Caleb went to his bedroll, shook out the burlap punching bag, and waited, tentative, unsure, undecided about what he would tell Dorman if he pried into the past.

Dorman came with shovel in hand, and they walked to the brook to fill the bag with sand and some leaves and dirt. Five minutes later it was swaying from its tether as Caleb began the established routine. Fists up, left foot and left hand forward, chin tucked in, elbows over the ribs, move, slide the feet—don't step—jab, hook, power, jab, hook, power.

With eyes that had survived battles, in and out of the ring, reaching back thirty-five years, half of them long since forgotten, Dorman studied Caleb's every move. He saw the intense concentration, and he felt a rise of excitement at the skill that was slowly emerging. *Knees and elbows and feet still slightly too large for the rest of him—but the reflexes are a little more refined— He's an instant quicker with his fists each day, a fraction smoother on his feet, hitting the bag more solidly with most of his weight. Only a matter of time—let him grow into his frame, keep him working, and one day soon he will be deadly.*

Dorman narrowed his eyes to study Caleb and reflect on what he knew of him.

Good breeding, educated, intelligent, Puritan Boston.

He considered the rage in the boy's eyes, the ugly hate that contorted his face, driving him past his limits as he poured an inner wrath out through his fists. Dorman saw it, and he remembered the white-hot hatred that had consumed him, driven him from the orphanage, out into the harsh world of the sea. And he remembered the wicked joy of release as he learned to pound out his anger with his fists.

Caleb was stripped to the waist and sweating when Dorman called, "That's enough for now." Caleb threw a final, vicious punch at the bag, then walked to the brook, where he splashed cold water on his face and torso. He dried himself on his shirt as he walked back to Dorman, who had lowered the bag and dumped its contents out. Dorman motioned, and they sat on the ground, facing each other across the fire.

Caleb held his silence. *It's coming.*

Dorman picked a sprig of green oak from the ground and began peeling the new, tender bark with his thumbnail. "You have family in Boston?"

Caleb answered warily, and Dorman caught the telltale hesitation.

"Yes. How did you know I'm from Boston?"

"The way you talk. Mother and father? Brothers? Sisters?"

"Mother. Two brothers. Two sisters."

"Father?"

"Passed on."

Dorman's eyes dropped for a moment. "I am truly sorry to know that."

Caleb saw pain come onto Dorman's face and fade, and suddenly he wanted to know more about the aging fighter.

Dorman continued. "How long ago? Your father?"

"Two years."

Dorman stopped picking at the oak twig while he made time calculations, and suddenly he knew. "How did he die?"

"The battle at Concord. Shot. In the back."

Dorman could see the barely controlled flare of anger in the boy and fell silent for a moment while he let the developing picture settle.

"Your brothers. Older or younger than you?"

"One older, one younger."

"Where's the older one?"

"At sea. Navigator on a ship. Graduated from Harvard."

"Warship?"

Caleb nodded.

"If your father was gone, why did he leave?"

"Got a letter from General Washington. They needed navigators to go down to the West Indies and get cannon and gunpowder. Matthew is one of the best navigators on the coast."

Dorman saw the pride, coupled with the rising sense of rebellion as the boy spoke. Dorman went on. "Is Matthew married? Still alive?"

Caleb wiped at his mouth before he answered. "Matthew was going to marry when he got the letter. Now he's gone, and the war has changed that forever. He was alive when we got his last letter." Caleb shrugged. "I hope he still is."

"Your sisters. Older or younger than you?"

"One older, one younger. My younger brother and sister are twins."

"The older sister—still at home?"

"Yes."

"Church?"

"Do you mean did I go to church?"

"Yes. Your family."

"Congregationalist. Every Sunday. All of us."

"The Bible?"

"Father and Mother read it to us, and we read it ourselves. We prayed every day."

"You attend school?"

"Yes. Preparing to go to Harvard, like Matthew."

"What was your father's work?"

"Clockmaker. Gunsmith. Made the best clocks and muskets in Massachusetts." Again, deep pride sounded in Caleb's words and shone in his face, and then was lost in defiance and pain. Dorman paused for a time as he pondered the dichotomy of the two boys sitting before him: one raised in a genteel, Puritan Boston home to become a true gentleman and leader, the other consumed by an inner rage.

"You were the oldest man remaining in the house, and you left?"

"Yes."

"Your mother agreed?"

"She knew I was going."

"I didn't ask that. Did she agree?"

"She didn't try to stop me."

"That's not the same as agreeing. Now she's alone with your older sister and the twins?"

"They'll be all right."

Dorman rounded his mouth and softly blew air while he let the implications of the answer settle in. He raised his eyes to look squarely at Caleb's face.

"Why did you join the army?"

The prologue was finished. The waiting was ended. Caleb's breathing slowed. He did not change expression as he made his answer.

"To fight the British."

With insight born of being a nameless, fatherless orphan, a child of poverty and pain and anger at the ugliness of the only world he knew, Dorman reached past Caleb's words to the brutal truth. Silence lay thick between the two men while he decided it was time to lay it bare before Caleb.

"You mean revenge. Make the British pay for what they did to your father. Your brother. Your mother. Your family."

It had come too quick, too harsh, and Caleb recoiled slightly. "I mean, fight the British."

Dorman leaned forward, elbows on knees. His words were spoken softly, but they cut deep. "Some things you need to know about me. No one ever knew who my father was. My mother died when I was born in a Liverpool alley. Some old sailor took me to an orphanage. For fifteen years I watched as people came to adopt children, but no one ever looked at me. We were taught to read and write, and that's all the school we ever had. We worked eleven hours a day making brooms and rag rugs. Make a mistake, and the beadle would beat us with a hickory stick. I still have the scars. At fifteen, I beat him and left. I signed onto a ship, and I knew only one thing: the world was my enemy. I was so filled with hate and anger that scarce a day went by I didn't fight someone, and it made no difference who or where. I think I killed a man—broke his neck in a drunken tavern fight. When I was seventeen I joined the Royal Navy. Someone there saw me in a fight and trained me. I became fleet champion at age twenty, then champion of southern England at twenty-one."

Caleb was scarcely breathing, not daring to move.

"I was thirty years old before I got enough of the hate worked out that I could see things more clear. By then I was in America, a British sailor, fighting the French. There was something about this country . . . I don't yet know exactly what . . . a spirit, or a feeling . . . like I had finally found someplace I could belong . . . it got inside me. I stayed on here after my British navy enlistment ended—joined the New Jersey militia. I came with General Washington when he made his run from New York across New Jersey and then the Delaware to Pennsylvania last year, and I been with him since. Trenton, Princeton, then on to Morristown for the winter, and now here. I never married because when I was young enough all I knew was how to hate. I have no home, no children. I'm an old man with nothing to show from a wasted life."

Suddenly something spontaneous and powerful was happening between the two. Caleb straightened, staring intently at the man seated across the fire from him. Never had an older man thrown his life open to him as Dorman had. Dorman sat motionless, unable to speak. It was as though a door in his heart that had been sealed had suddenly opened far enough to reveal emotions he had never admitted to anyone. He yearned to reach out to Caleb, touch him, plead with him, *Stop the hate— it will only bring bad,* but he could not because he did not know how.

After a time, Dorman spoke again. "You're divided inside. Part of you still loves your home and family, and part of you hates the British so bad you left it all to get revenge. Hate. Revenge. They've been my study in life." He lowered his face and for a time worked bark from the twig with his thumbnail while a look of deep, wistful regret clouded his eyes. He drew and released a great sigh, then raised his head once more.

"Until you've settled which way you're going, you won't be worth much to yourself or anyone else."

Caleb could not move, nor speak. He felt Dorman had seen completely through him, stripped his life so completely that he felt defenseless, unable to hide his feelings, as if he were standing exposed in the hot light of truth.

Dorman rubbed weary eyes, then concluded. "If I teach you boxing, how will you use it? For good or bad? I won't teach a bully."

The momentous revelations and the surging emotions of the past few minutes washed over Caleb like a wave, leaving him confounded, confused, unable to answer. He opened his mouth to speak, but could not, and he licked at dry lips and dropped his eyes.

Dorman rose to his feet. "I'll come by in the morning."

Dawn found Dorman approaching Caleb, seated cross-legged by the ashes of a dying fire, a blanket wrapped about his shoulders. The boy turned weary eyes upward to the aging fighter, and it was obvious he had had little sleep. Dorman dropped to his haunches and waited.

Caleb looked him squarely in the eyes. "I'm no bully. I will not do wrong things with what you teach me." The boy's gaze was steady.

Dorman nodded. "I'll see you after evening mess."

★ ★ ★ ★ ★

General Washington's command headquarters, Middlebrook
July 1777

"Sir, that French gentleman is here to keep his appointment. The one Benjamin Franklin and John Adams wrote about. He has three in his party."

General Washington raised his head from studying the map on his worktable and reached for two letters near his right hand. "You mean the Marquis de Lafayette?"

Hamilton could not suppress a smile. "I'm sure that was somewhere in the names he recited."

"Have them wait just a few moments while I review the letters, then I'll have you show him in."

"Yes, sir." Major Hamilton backed out the door of the small library and closed it, smiling again as he walked back down the hall to the tiny reception room. *The Marquis de Lafayette. I'll bet he had six other names before he got to that one.*

Seated in the small, austere library of a home he had rented from a citizen on the outskirts of Middlebrook, Washington quickly reread the letter signed by Benjamin Franklin. Lafayette, nineteen years old—born into privilege and nobility—one of the wealthiest men in France—well connected in all French courts—has immediate access to King Louis XVI and his prime minister, Vergennes—unusually gifted in spite of his youth—fully committed to the success of the American cause—I judge him to be a natural leader—most of all he can be of immeasurable help in bringing the French into the revolution in support of America—critically important he be given due consideration—recommend him to become a major general earliest—keep him close to you.

Washington leaned back in his chair, reflecting on the content of the letter. *Benjamin Franklin—shrewd—unusual judge of human nature—sees this young Lafayette as critical to his efforts to gain French support.*

He laid the Franklin letter aside and reread the brief note from John Adams. The Marquis de Lafayette a tremendous surprise—dresses like a peacock—Doctor Franklin highly impressed—the American Congress recommended Lafayette return to France, but he responded in writing, saying, and I quote, "After the sacrifices I have made in this cause, I have the right to ask two favors at your hands: the one, is to serve without pay, at my own expense, and the other, that I be allowed to serve at first as a volunteer in the ranks"—Absolutely unprecedented—recommend you give Lafayette every consideration. Please forward your decision earliest.

Washington turned the two letters face down and thoughtfully rose. *Congressman John Adams—the man who nominated me to become commander in chief—unusual for him to give such a recommendation for a Frenchman. If Franklin and Adams agree on this, there must be something worth looking at. We shall see. We shall see.*

He opened the library door and spoke to Major Hamilton, waiting just outside. "Bring Mr. Lafayette in." Washington returned to his seat at the worktable to wait. The sound of approaching boot heels echoed in the hallway before Hamilton rapped on the door.

"Enter." Washington rose to his full height as the door swung open. Flanked by a young man, Hamilton strode three steps into the room, stopped at full attention, and announced, "General Washington, may I present the Marquis de Lafayette." He turned on his heel and closed the door as he left.

Washington took in the man at a glance. Just over six feet—tall for a Frenchman—reddish brown hair, very close to the color of Washington's, a chin that thrust ever so slightly forward, long triangular nose, forehead that sloped back to a receding hairline. His face could not be called handsome but was intriguing. His hair, like Washington's, was unpowdered, and he had on his face an expression that was at once respectful and confident. His uniform was resplendent, flawlessly tailored of blue fabric, trimmed in gold.

Washington did not move from behind the worktable. Instead, he bowed slightly from the waist. "Sir, it is my honor."

Lafayette's heels snapped together as he stiffly returned the bow, betraying a slight aura of awkwardness in his movements. He found himself in the unusual position of looking upward at a man taller than himself. "Sir, I am your humble servant." His English was colored by a French accent.

Washington gestured to a chair. "Would you be seated?"

Lafayette sat across the table, his posture erect, facing Washington and waiting in silence.

"I am embarrassed that I do not know your full name, sir."

"I am Marie Joseph Paul Yves Roch Gilbert du Morier de Lafayette. My father was the Marquis Gilbert de Lafayette, my mother, Julie de La Rivere. My father lost his life at the battle of Minden in 1759."

"I am sorry to hear it. May I inquire your age?"

"Certainly. I am nineteen years of age. I was born September 6, 1757. I will be twenty years of age in less than two months."

"I trust your sea voyage was pleasant."

"Acceptable. We were fifty-nine days on the water. I became a bit melancholy as time wore on. I found it necessary to busy myself with exercise, writing letters, and the study of military tactics."

"You arrived in Boston?"

"We anchored near Charleston, in the state of South Carolina on June fifteenth. From there we traveled overland to Philadelphia, where it was my honor to present myself to the American Congress. I bore papers from the Honorable Benjamin Franklin. Congress was reluctant. I was told the American Minister Silas Deane had exceeded his authority in offering me rank and position. I volunteered whatever services I might tender, at no compensation. They accepted and recommended this visit with yourself."

"Has your ship returned to France?"

"No. The French government was insistent that I remain in France. The governor of Bordeaux sought to arrest me as a means of holding me there. I disguised myself, returned to Los Pasajes, bought a ship—the *La Victoire*—and set sail with my companions. They remain with me."

Washington leaned forward. *Bought a ship!* "Do I understand, then, that you have volunteered your services in the American cause at no compensation?"

"It is true. I have no need for money."

"You have resources in France?"

"Yes. Inherited from the families of both my mother and father. My great-grandfather, the elder Comte de La Rivere, was appointed my legal guardian when my mother passed on. I was eleven years old at the time. He is most capable in matters of investments and money. I have no idea the size of my fortune, only that it is immense."

Washington's expression remained formal, cordial. "May I ask, sir, do you have a wife? Family?"

"It was my honor to marry Adrienne d'Ayen, the daughter of Marshal Duc d'Ayen, on April 11, 1774. We have one child. My wife and child remained in France."

"You have had military training?"

A light came into the eyes of the young Frenchman, and he leaned forward. His voice rose, and his words came tumbling, reckless, filled with a fire that startled Washington, settled him back in his chair.

"It has been my lifelong dream to serve the cause of justice for all humanity—both the privileged and the peasants. I know in my heart that Nature and the Almighty meant for all men—all races—to be free. Nothing has moved me so powerfully as the revolution now in progress in this country. I am committed to give all I possess—my life, my fortune—to it, if it will free the common people."

For long moments the two men sat in silence, eyes locked as each stared into the core of the other—the most powerful man in the Continental Army, five months past his forty-fifth birthday, and the Frenchman, just ten months beyond his nineteenth birthday and the wealthiest fugitive from a French arrest warrant in the world. One a colonial American, the other a European aristocrat. The older man never having had children, the younger never having known his father. In that silent, electric moment, age and circumstance became meaningless as each man recognized in the other an all-consuming passion for freedom. Neither knew, nor cared, how long they remained in silence, not moving, while a powerful, unspoken bond formed between them.

Washington broke the silence. "You hardly knew your father, and I've never been blessed with a son. Has nature wrought something here?" He continued, "You received military training?"

"I apologize for failing to answer your question. My early education was from the Ignasius Loyola Jesuits. They were banished by the Papacy, and my later education was at the feet of Abbe Fayon. It was he who taught me mathematics, spelling, literature, and English. I read much of Voltaire. My mother later took me to Paris where I was enrolled in the College du Plessis and enlisted in the king's Musketeers. I learned fencing, firearms, riding, military history, and science. From there it was my honor to be accepted into the king's Black Musketeers. I discovered I was not skilled at politics—could not control my passion for freedom and justice for all men. I spoke too freely of my feelings and was transferred. Then I learned of the revolution in this country and was captivated by it. I purchased my ship, and I am here."

For two full seconds Washington did not move while his thoughts settled. *The Black Musketeers! The king's select! The best of the best!*

"You have companions with you?"

"Yes. Among them, Baron Jean de Kalb, a trained officer. He shares my feelings in being here."

Washington leaned forward, carefully selected his next words, and came to the pivotal question. "Do you have a preference where you serve or the rank you will bear?"

The answer was instant. "Those considerations are of no consequence. Use us according to your need. I and Baron de Kalb stand ready to obey your orders without compensation."

Washington settled back in his chair and carefully covered his astonishment. He could not remember one officer among the multitude who came from Europe seeking to join the American revolutionary forces who had not demanded high rank and high salary.

"Is there anything else you wish to discuss?"

Lafayette considered for a moment. "I think not, sir."

Both men rose. "I will have Major Hamilton settle you and your companions in suitable quarters. You will be notified of the outcome of all this as soon as possible. In the meantime, you have immediate access to this office at any time. Should you need or desire anything, notify my aides. Thank you for your appearance here."

Lafayette bowed from the waist. "Sir, it has been my honor." He turned on his heel, and Washington followed him to the door, where he gave orders to the waiting Major Hamilton. Washington watched the two men march down the hallway to the ante room before he stepped back into the small library and closed the door.

Remarkable! Wealth, position, education—every reason to become a wastrel—and he turned his back on it all! He's a rebel in the finest sense of the word! A born rebel!

The chair creaked as Washington sat down at the worktable. For a time he remained in reflective silence.

Franklin and Adams—I understand now—and I agree. Adams wants my recommendations at once, and he shall have them. Must be careful of the politics Congress has to deal with—can't thrust young Lafayette to the top in one stroke—must take this one short step at a time—recommend him to become a major general, but only honorary for now until he proves himself—de Kalb with him on the same terms—no salary for either until they've earned it.

He reached for quill and paper, thought for a moment, then began his usual careful, artistic drafting of a letter.

"Congressman John Adams . . ."

Notes

This chapter is intended to be a foundation for what is to come, and therefore includes some information that has appeared in prior volumes.

The events depicted at Princeton are taken from volume 3, *To Decide Our Destiny*, chapter XVI.

The war council at Morristown in early May 1777 is taken from volume 4, *The Hand of Providence*, chapter III.

General Sir William Howe was ordered to take Philadelphia, since taking the capital city of the enemy was deemed tantamount to winning a war. Higginbotham, *The War of American Independence*, pp. 180–83.

Sending the fictional characters Billy Weems and Eli Stroud north to deal with Joseph Bryant, great leader of the Iroquois and Mohawk who had joined the British, is described in volume 3, *To Decide Our Destiny*, chapter XIX.

British General John Burgoyne rose to fame by leading his cavalry to victories at Valencia de Alcantara and at Villa Velha, in the British war with Spain. Leckie, *George Washington's War*, pp. 366–76.

The French built Fort Ticonderoga to resist the British approaching from the south; hence the cannon faced south, covering Lake Champlain and Lake George. To take the fort, Burgoyne was expected to come from the north. See volume 4, *The Hand of Providence*, chapter VII.

George Washington refused to commit his inferior army to any battle in which the British could destroy it altogether. Ketchum, *Saratoga*, p. 48.

From Fort Ticonderoga, there were two possible routes for Burgoyne to take his army south to Albany and on to New York. Either the Hudson River, which would expose his boats to American cannon nearly the entire distance, or marching his army overland. See Mackesy, *The War for America, 1775–1783*, p. 132.

From Morristown, where General Washington wintered his army in 1776–1777, he marched to Middlebrook, at the foot of the Watchung Mountains. The area and the strong attitude of the American army with the coming of spring is described. See Ketchum, *Saratoga*, p. 46; Leckie, *George Washington's War*, p. 344.

The events described concerning the fictional character Caleb Dunson were presented in volume 4, *The Hand of Providence*, chapter XX. Charles Dorman is also a fictional character.

Spears, sometimes called spontoons, were a weapon regularly used by soldiers in the Revolutionary War. See Wilbur, *The Revolutionary Soldier 1775–1783*, pp. 12, 35, 49, 52.

The reflections of Caleb Dunson regarding his father, Tom Sievers, and others, as well as his family descriptions, are based on events depicted in volume I, *Our Sacred Honor,* chapters I and X–XV.

The information regarding the French General Lafayette is found in Leckie, *George Washington's War,* pp. 336–44.

CHAPTER II

★ ★ ★

*G*eneral Sir William Howe was not a politician. As a member
of the British Parliament his blunt, sparing use of words quickly convinced those in London's high political whirl that his talents were immea-
surably more useful on the battlefield than in the halls of government.
To stand in the hallowed chambers of Whitehall to argue before British
parliamentarians required wit, lucidity, and a fluid command of thought
and language, as well as a measure of dramatic flair. To stand tall at the
head of a regiment of charging redcoated British regulars required a few
well chosen words, courage, and the nerves to face a hail of enemy musketballs and cannonshot. Howe's spectacular rise to success as a combat
officer was equaled only by his failure to rise as a parliamentarian. When
he had something to say, he said it with as few words as possible and usually with an abruptness that was at least unsettling. Decidedly, he was a
warrior, not a politician.

Tall and laconic, the commander of all British forces in the United
States had been born in 1729, the son of the second Viscount Howe of
Ireland and Mary Sophia, daughter of Baroness Kielmansegge, known in
the court of King George I. The family was blessed with two other sons,
and the three were named William, George Augustus, and Richard. True
to their Hanovarian heritage, all three brothers early committed their lives
to the military—William and George to the army, Richard to the navy.

At age seventeen William purchased a cornet's commission in the light dragoons under the command of the Duke of Cumberland. Less than a year later he was a lieutenant leading a headlong charge of regulars against the French Marshal Saxe, at Flanders. Following the War of the Austrian Succession, he served in the British Twentieth Foot, under the watchful and approving eye of the legendary General James Wolfe. With the outbreak of the Seven Years' War between the French and the English for sole claim to America, William and George came to the great, sprawling North American wilderness—William under command of General James Wolfe, George under General James Abercrombie.

At the critical second siege of Louisbourg on Cape Breton Island, just off the northern coast of Nova Scotia, William was ordered to command a regiment in an amphibious landing. With drawn sword, he led his men ashore, then stormed into the muskets and bayonets of Frenchmen crouched in trenches and behind breastworks. In fierce hand-to-hand fighting the British forces overran the French, and with his sword high over his head, William swung his command in behind the center of the French army to flank them, engage them, and pound them into surrender.

General Wolfe was effusive in his praise of young William, whose stock had risen like a meteor in the British military. It was amidst laurels and with honors ringing in his ears that William learned of the heartbreaking battle for Fort Ticonderoga. General Ambercrombie, who had no cannon, had attempted to storm the sixteen-foot-thick walls of the five-sided fort using nothing but his infantry. With the need for the missing cannon so painfully obvious, he had thrown his regulars against the north and west walls again and again, while the French slaughtered them with grapeshot and musketball. Three decades later occupants of the fort would use the unburied skulls of Abercrombie's decimated regulars for drinking cups and their shinbones for tent pegs.

Tragically, among the fallen was Viscount George Augustus Howe, respected and beloved by his troops and by the Americans as well. For a time William deeply mourned the death of his brother, one of the brightest and finest in the British military. Those nearest to William often wondered if he ever fully recovered from the loss.

Wars do not wait on those who mourn. The following year it was Colonel William Howe who led his regiment into battle, fighting its way up the steep path to take the high ground at the battle of Quebec. In a spectacular attack he pounced on the flank of General Montcalm, turned it, and fought on to victory in the decisive battle of the Seven Years' War. In 1760, as a brigadier general famous on both continents, he once again led his troops in the taking of Montreal. Two years later, as adjutant general, he was with the army that wrested Havana from Spain.

Thoughtfully he considered a phenomenon he had observed among the Americans, and the Indians, in the vast, sprawling forests. With only their weapons and a small pouch of cheese and bread, they could move eighty miles through impenetrable forests in one day, strike with deadly efficiency the next, and return the next. There was not a single military command in all Europe that could match it. Thus it was that in 1762 he introduced to the British army the startling new innovation of elite troops trained to travel light and fast, strike hard, and disappear. Within months such military units sprang up wherever the British army was found.

With the surrender of the French in 1763, the now famous Brigadier General William Howe was rewarded with the nominal title of governor of the Island of Wight, located just off the English coast, southwest of London. The title was honorary, his responsibilities almost nonexistent, and he let neither interfere with his weakness for a cup, a deck of cards, and a woman on his arm. His elegant coach was constantly on the winding road to London, where he indulged himself in his chosen pleasures. The rather good-natured, tall, dark-complexioned brigadier with the prominent nose and large, black, brooding eyes, who spoke little, soon became prominent in London's high social circles.

He had never lost his fascination with and admiration of colonial America and the Americans. Never had he known the raw power he felt in the forests and mountains and rivers of that vast, primeval land. He sensed in her people a passion for freedom that moved him profoundly, and he saw in them a backbone of steel, a hardheaded practicality, and a rough wit and humor that carried them through the worst of times. He felt a bond, a kinship, with these Americans, and they reciprocated his friendship. When General Howe's brother George Augustus fell at the battle of Fort Ticonderoga, the Americans mourned the loss. The grieving Massachusetts Assembly caused a monument honoring the beloved Viscount George Augustus to be erected in Westminster Abby in London. Neither William nor his illustrious brother, Richard, who had risen to the office of viscount and admiral in the Royal British Navy, ever forgot the honor the sympathetic Americans had bestowed on George Augustus.

In troubled silence Howe watched the storm gathering over the American colonies. He chaffed at the imposition of the tax stamp act, by which the British intended to bring the colonials to heel, but held his silence as a member of the British House of Commons, where he represented the Nottingham District. It was no surprise to the general when the Americans burned the tax stamps and hung the British tax collectors in effigy. Nor was it a surprise when on December 16, 1773, the colonials disguised themselves as Mohawk Indians, boarded the British cargo ships *Dartmouth, Beaver,* and *Eleanor* as they lay at anchor in Boston Harbor, and dumped three hundred forty-two chests of British Ceylon tea into the sea rather than pay the tea tax imposed by His Majesty's government. General Howe murmured, but held his peace. It was only when King George issued orders to close down Boston Harbor until the hotbed of rebels was brought into obedience that General Howe broke his silence. He was no politician, but with his understanding of the Americans, and America, and the battle-experienced eye of one of the finest brigadiers in Europe, he saw what the politicians did not.

The colonies would fight for their declared rights if pushed to it.

General William Howe took his stand. In the winter of 1774 he openly informed his constituents in the Nottingham District that if war erupted, he would not accept a command against the Americans, if the King should offer it.

If King George knew of Howe's sympathy for the Americans, it was not apparent in his decision on how to crush the rebellion that was taking shape in the colonies. In naming three generals to send as advisers to

Governor Thomas Gage in his efforts to subdue the rebellious patriots in Boston, the King selected William Howe, John Burgoyne, and Henry Clinton. Howe, the taciturn warrior; Burgoyne, the bon vivant dandy; and Clinton, the obstinate planner. Gage was to remain in command but rely heavily on their advice. In the King's reckoning, Howe's seniority and prior experience in the colonies during the Seven Years' War made him the premier and obvious choice to lead this mismatched triumvirate of British military authority.

Howe startled his Nottingham constituents, who held strong sympathies with the struggling colonies, when he suddenly reversed his prior declarations by stating, "A man's private feelings ought to give way to the service at all times." Having inexplicably reversed himself, Howe, with Burgoyne and Clinton, boarded the *Cerberus*, and on May 25, 1775, thirty-six days after the Americans had stunned the world with their catastrophic defeat of the British at Concord, walked down the gangplank onto the docks of Boston Harbor.

The orders King George III had given General Howe all rested on one fundamental: destroy the American army.

The American militiamen dug in on Breed's Hill, Bunker Hill, and Dorchester Heights, at Charlestown, just across the bay from peninsular Boston. Gage fretted, then ordered Howe to kill or capture them all. After British ships in the harbor had pounded the American positions with cannon, Howe set his teeth and led 2,500 of Britain's best up Breed's Hill. From behind their breastworks, American marksmen cut them down in rows. Howe licked dry lips and led his men up the hill a second time. They never reached the breastworks. With dead and dying regulars scattered all over the hill, Howe took a deep breath and led what was left of his men up the hill a third time. This time, with ammunition and gunpowder running out, the Americans backed off the hill and gave it to the British. Howe shook his head in disbelief. Nearly half his command lay behind him, dead or dying.

Never had he paid such a price for one hill.

Gage blockaded Boston Harbor to starve out the rebels. The rebels blockaded the same harbor to starve out the British. In March 1776 the

King, Gage, and Howe had had enough. Gage was relieved of command and ordered to return to London. Howe was given full authority over all British troops in the colonies. He immediately ordered them to prepare to evacuate Boston, and on March 17, 1776, led them out as they marched to the critically important colonial seaport of New York to prepare for the battle that was sure to come.

General Washington, newly appointed commander in chief of the fledgling Continental Army, followed. On the morning of August 27, 1776, General Howe trapped the unwary Americans on Long Island and crushed them. Within days Washington's army had been defeated again at White Plains, Fort Washington, and Fort Lee and was in panic-driven flight across New Jersey to save anything they could of their decimated force. In December, beaten, huddled, and starving on the Pennsylvania side of the Delaware River, Washington led the remains of his army in one last desperate attempt for redemption. On the night of December 25, 1776, he crossed the Delaware in a blizzard and stormed the town of Trenton on the morning of December 26. The entire Hessian garrison of nearly 1,400 men was killed or captured. Infuriated, Howe ordered General Charles Cornwallis to take 8,000 men to Trenton with but one objective: get rid of Washington and what was left of his army. January 3, 1777, overnight, Washington marched around Cornwallis, then continued twelve miles north to take Princeton, then moved on to winter quarters in Morristown, New Jersey, a geographic enclave protected by the Thimble Mountains.

Cornwallis was apoplectic. Howe was in a towering rage. He paced, grinding his teeth, knowing he dared not launch a winter attack on Washington in his mountain stronghold. He could only remain in his command headquarters in New York City, lay his plan, and wait.

He cooled. No matter. Washington would be nearby when the greening of spring provided enough forage in the hills and valleys for Howe's 3,000 horses. In the meantime he would enjoy his cup, his gaming table and, with the beautiful, blue-eyed Mrs. Betsy Loring on his arm, becoming the darling of the New York social swirl. Employed as the very well-paid British commissary of prisoners, Betsy's husband, Joshua Loring, was content to travel about, take care of business, and look the other way while Howe and Betsy blatantly flaunted their affair.

★ ★ ★ ★ ★

Those who had lived on the New York islands knew what was coming. Briefly stirring the early morning July heat, an onshore breeze had blown in from the Atlantic, moved west the length of Long Island, then across the East River and New York Harbor to Staten and Manhattan Islands, on past the mighty North, or Hudson, River, and over the sheer, towering Palisades—the three-hundred-foot-high granite cliffs on the New Jersey side. By ten o'clock the air had turned sultry, muggy. By noon all movement of air had stopped, and New York was locked in a dead, stifling vacuum. A breathless hush settled over the lush forests and woods, the farms, and the villages and hamlets.

For a hundred miles in all directions, people cast nervous eyes southwest, searching for the first signs of a gray-purple line to come creeping over the horizon, listening for the deep rumble of distant thunder and watching for lightning flashing in the bowels of billowing storm clouds. Nervous farmers herded their sheep and cows out of the fields and into barns or pens, confident that Ben Franklin's lightning rod would reach into the heavens and magically draw lightning away from their buildings and livestock.

On Manhattan Island people glanced nervously south toward the waterfront, where unnumbered commercial ships were tied to the wharves and piers. Beyond the docks, out in the harbor, a forest of masts marked more than four hundred British warships and transports lying dead at anchor under the command of Lord Admiral Richard Howe. Eight thousand anxious British seamen scrambled in the ropes in the rigging high above the decks, checking the lashings that bound the gathered sails to the yards, adding to them where howling wind might find loose canvas and shred a sail.

On the southern end of the island, where the great fire of September 21, 1776, had turned half the buildings on the waterfront into blackened skeletons as far north as the Trinity Church, thieves and beggars and castoff human flotsam crawled sweating from their makeshift hovels into the vacant streets. These were the dregs of society, and they had infiltrated the waterfront wreckage while it was yet smoldering, to turn scorched planks and rotting canvas into a camp now called Canvastown. They emerged from the squalor of their dark world to test the dead air and shade their eyes as they squinted into the heavens, judging how long before the storm would come thundering. A New York summer lightning and thunderstorm could rip a ship from its anchor or moorings and drive it smashing into the wharves. Frantic shipowners and salvage crews would then come swarming. Behind them would come insurance agents to reckon the insurance claims. And behind them would come constables. The prospects made the inhabitants of the squalid camp nervous. Far too many of those living in the filth of Canvastown were wanted for crimes ranging from assault to murder. They studied the southwest horizon and peered at the glassy harbor surface, then disappeared back into the charred blackness of the gutted buildings.

Across New York Bay, on Staten Island, two British sentries stood at rigid attention on either side of the huge doorway leading into the mansion that General William Howe had appropriated to serve as his command headquarters. In the strange quiet, they held their Brown Bess muskets at their sides, sweltering in their heavy red coats and long white stockings and casting furtive eyes toward a clear, blue sky—waiting, wondering.

Inside the mansion, General William Howe closed the French doors into the huge library and walked to a great, ornately carved and upholstered chair at one end of a black, two-ton, imported ironwood table. He laid a rolled map down before he glanced around at his staff of officers, who were standing at attention. To his right was his brother, Lord Admiral Richard Howe, face passive, nearly apathetic. General Sir Henry Clinton stood beside him, short, thin-lipped, corpulent, combative. Lord General Charles Cornwallis, with his round, fleshy face, peered past Clinton, watching General Howe. Beyond Cornwallis was Colonel Charles Stuart, known for his accuracy in grasping harsh realities. Across the polished expanse of the table, General Philip de Heister stood at attention. Next to him the Earl of Percy waited patiently, and beyond him stood Lieutenant Colonel Joseph Vaughn. The last man was General James Grant, who had his mouth set in disgust. It was Grant who had made it contemptuously clear that if he had command of five thousand British regulars he could march from one end of the United States to the other and bring every adult male to heel. Four engraved silver trays were spaced down the center of the table, each bearing a decanter of red wine and an array of crystal goblets.

The wall behind Howe was a huge stone fireplace with a thick, twelve-foot-wide oak mantel. Murals and paintings from the finest European artists of the day graced the other three walls. Above the table a two-hundred candle, cut-crystal chandelier caught the light and turned it into a thousand tiny prisms. The carpet was thick, plush, with an intricate hand-design from a master carpet weaver in Bombay, India. The windows were all partially open for circulation, but an hour earlier the dead calm outside had turned the room into a sweltering oven.

General Howe gave a hand gesture. "Be seated."

He pursed his mouth and waited while each man pulled his upholstered chair back from the table and sat. Howe's forehead was furrowed as he struggled in his straightforward mind to force the nonstraightforward pieces of a gigantic, jumbled puzzle to come together. He reached to unbutton the top three buttons of his tunic.

"Loosen your tunics or take them off, if you like."

Half the officers loosened the top buttons while the others slipped theirs off and hung them on the backs of their chairs. Each drew a white handkerchief from his pocket and wiped at the perspiration that had formed on his forehead and had begun to trickle down his cheeks and nose.

Richard Howe raised his eyes to his brother. *He'd rather be leading a charge with a broken back than conducting this staff meeting.* He began inspecting his hands, working with his fingernails.

"I think a little history is in order," General Howe began.

The men settled back in their chairs and wiped again at the sweat on their faces.

"The King's orders were to bring the rebels into submission. To do that Lord Germain sent the biggest armada in history. Over four hundred forty ships and thirty thousand troops. We hurt General Washington's army here in New York last year, and at White Plains, and they retreated clear to Pennsylvania. They came back across the Delaware and surprised the Hessians at Trenton and then took Princeton."

Cornwallis's face reddened at the word *Princeton*.

Howe continued. "Then they went into winter quarters at Morristown, where we couldn't make a winter attack."

He paused to order his thoughts and pick his words. The men continued wiping at their faces while they attempted to keep their minds focused. Not one word of what Howe had said thus far had given them anything they did not already know.

Howe wiped at his own face, then unrolled the map and anchored the four corners with small leather pouches filled with sand. "Last month General Washington brought his army out of the Thimble Mountains and camped them here." He dropped a long, slender finger on a place marked "Middlebrook," just south of the Raritan River. "That camp is surrounded by the Watchung Mountains, and it gives him a strong advantage if we should try to attack him there. The price would be too high, and he has too many places to retreat."

His finger traced the roads. "From that camp he can watch all roads west of here. He has regiments at every critical point, from Middlebrook down to Princeton. We can't move without him knowing it."

He raised his eyes. "I tried to draw him out onto level ground for a decisive battle last month. It was June nineteenth, if you recall. He took the bait, but the moment we moved to cut him off on June twenty-sixth, he fell back into those mountains in time to avoid the trap. We engaged one of his divisions briefly but did no real damage."

Howe cleared his throat, then said, "I don't think we'll be able to draw General Washington into a decisive battle on open ground. And I am not going to try to engage him in those mountains. It gives him too much the advantage."

Cornwallis reached to wipe sweat, then dropped his hand as the thought struck his brain. *Philadelphia.*

Howe reached to rub a thumb and forefinger into weary eyes before he changed directions. "You're all aware that Lord Germain sent General Burgoyne up to Quebec to take command of eight thousand troops. He met with General Carleton up there and is on his way down now. His orders are to take Fort Ticonderoga and come on south to Albany, then east to New York. The plan is to divide the northern states from the southern and then subdue them at will. You may also know that we are to give him support."

Clinton's eyes narrowed. *Support? Idiocy! The orders were for us to meet him in Albany! He's at risk if we fail!*

Howe continued. "As far back as April I suspected this might happen, and I so informed Lord Germain in a written message. I told him it was my opinion that the only way to end the rebellion is to eliminate General Washington and the Continental Army. To do that I would have to have reinforcements, and soon."

Again he paused to choose words and thoughts and again change direction. "We know that France is at this moment shipping arms and supplies to the Americans. Lord Germain is concerned that if those shipments continue, it could bring France into the war against us. If France goes with the Americans, Spain will likely follow, either directly or indirectly. There is unrest at Minorca and Gibraltar in the Mediterranean and in our colonies in India. Catherine in Russia has lately been less receptive to us—won't consider letting us hire Russian mercenaries. In short, gentlemen, with half a dozen crises in our worldwide empire making demands on our men and resources, we are rapidly being stretched to our limits. The result is that while we have received a limited number of reinforcements, we will get no more. We must proceed with what we have."

Howe paused. Richard stopped working with his fingernails, wiped at sweat, and glanced at the officers surrounding the table. Clinton was visibly agitated. Grant's face was a contortion of impatience and disgust—*Just give me five thousand men, and I'll settle this whole matter in time to be back in England by September.* Cornwallis was lost in thoughtful reflection. Stuart was pensive, calculating. Richard reached for a decanter of wine and a goblet and poured. All the others followed. Howe waited for a moment, then reached for the nearest decanter and goblet, and there was an unexpected, silent pause while they all drank.

A breath of breeze moved the French lace curtains at the windows, and each man turned for a moment to look.

Howe wiped at his mouth, then continued. "Over the winter I sent four different proposals to Lord Germain as to how to destroy Washington and the Continental Army. Each one addressed the problems we faced at that time, both here and in Europe. The latest proposal is the one Lord Germain has approved for the circumstances we are facing today."

Cornwallis straightened and slowly leaned forward, head turned to Howe, watching intently. Richard glanced at Cornwallis, then leaned back in his chair and worked with his wine goblet in his hands. Stuart's face was a puzzle of disbelief.

Howe hesitated while he considered how to proceed. "I used the entire month of June trying to draw Washington into a decisive battle in New Jersey. He wouldn't fight. I ordered all our forces back here to New York and Staten Island because holding New Jersey means nothing if he hangs off our flank, in those mountains where we can't attack him, and refuses to come out. We are now in July. I can waste no more of the summer campaign."

Howe turned his eyes on each man in rapid succession as he spoke in slow, measured words. "So long as Washington and his army survive, this accursed revolution will continue. To do what the King has ordered, we must first destroy them both."

Stuart's mouth was dry as he wiped his perspiring face.

Howe cleared his throat. "So Lord Germain agrees that we should not return to New Jersey. That we should abandon it."

Audible gasps erupted, then open murmuring. Clinton turned to Howe. "Do I understand we are simply going to give New Jersey back to the rebels? After all the cost, all His Majesty's loyal subjects over there did for us? In the name of heaven, two thousand men sacrificed—millions of pounds in money—simply forgotten? Abandoned?"

Howe shook his head. "No. Not forgotten, nor abandoned. Useless. We had to learn, and we did. This war is like none other we have ever fought—the forests, the rivers, the distances. But mostly the people." He shook his head. "They're a whole new breed." Howe leaned forward on stiff arms, palms flat on the table, black eyes points of light. "Make no mistake. They do not think like us. They have no concept of soldiering, but on their own ground, fighting for what they believe to be their rights, their freedom, they rise above themselves. Mark my words! The only chance we have of putting down this ridiculous revolution is to destroy their leader, and their army."

For three long seconds no one moved or spoke. Never had the officers surrounding the table seen their commander so intense, or heard him speak with such feeling. In those moments the bright July sunshine that had filled the room dimmed, and again the curtains stirred, then fluttered in a fresh, cooling breeze. They felt more than heard a deep rumble coming from a great distance, and their breathing slowed for a moment while they listened and then turned back to Howe.

Cornwallis raised his hand. "Sir, if we abandon New Jersey, precisely where are we to go?"

For a moment Howe pursed his mouth. "As you know, Philadelphia is the capital of the thirteen American states."

Cornwallis set his goblet down hard, and at the same moment Stuart dropped his right hand flat, slapping the table. For a split second all eyes flitted to Cornwallis, then to Stuart, then back to Howe. Howe looked at each of them, waiting for either to speak, but both remained silent. He continued.

"And as you also know, the so-called American Congress is there."

Stuart shook his head. "I didn't know the rebels had a capital. I don't think I've ever heard anyone declare Philadelphia to be such."

Howe nodded. "No one has said as much, but it is an acknowledged fact. They met there to form their first congress, and their second. It was there they drew up that document—their Declaration of Independence—

to sever themselves from the mother country. I am convinced—nay, certain—that General Washington will fight to keep us from taking Philadelphia. I do not believe the American people, nor their congress, will allow him to do otherwise."

Grant cracked a smile. Stuart snorted. Cornwallis appeared smug. Clinton cast his eyes toward heaven. Richard reached for the nearest wine decanter. Howe dropped his finger onto the map and slowly traced a road as he started to speak.

Without warning the room darkened. The sound of heavy wind arose outside, blowing the curtains inward, snapping. The gloom was suddenly pierced by fierce light, and a moment later thunder boomed less than one mile to the southwest. De Heister and Richard quickly strode to the windows to drive them slamming down. The curtains settled, and the two men returned to their chairs. Howe continued, finger still on the map.

"It is about ninety miles from here to Philadelphia, overland. If we make the march, it will take at least ten days, and we will be exposed to attack the entire distance. There are at least four places where we would be vulnerable to ambush, and you can be certain that General Washington knows each of them." He paused to shake his head. "I will not expose my men to that. There's a better way."

Every man leaned forward, eyes turned to Howe, waiting in hushed silence.

"I have proposed, and Lord Germain agrees, that the best way to take Philadelphia is by sea."

Outside, the wind came howling around the house and murmuring in the chimney. Every man at the table paused for a moment, humbled in the face of the terrible power of nature. Then talk erupted. Stuart spoke directly to Howe. "And what of Burgoyne? If we go after Philadelphia by sea, we will essentially abandon Burgoyne. He'll be coming down through the most troublesome and populous state of all and in country he doesn't understand. I thought Germain's orders were for us to join him and St. Leger up on the Hudson River. And what if

Washington doesn't choose to fight for Philadelphia? What if he marches north to engage Burgoyne instead? What then?"

Howe was adamant. "My orders are to support Burgoyne. Not necessarily meet him. And I've thought about how we can support him and take Philadelphia at the same time." He moved his finger on the map. "We'll go up the Delaware River. We can disembark from the ships within sixteen miles of Philadelphia, and from that position we can march north to help Burgoyne on a moment's notice. If Washington marches north to attack Burgoyne, we'll have him out in the open, and with Burgoyne north of him and us south of him, we'll have him trapped."

Stuart set his bulldog chin. "Have you considered the number of rebel militia that will rise all along Lake Champlain and the Hudson? With the right leadership, they could outnumber both Burgoyne's forces and ours, and with their knowledge of those accursed forests, we could be the ones who are trapped."

"Burgoyne will have eight thousand of the finest British regulars and Hessians. My command will be at least fourteen thousand. I have no fear for the outcome should the rebels choose to fight."

Suddenly Clinton straightened. "Fourteen thousand? We have in excess of thirty-two thousand troops available. Where will the balance of them be?"

Howe turned directly to him. "The plan is to leave a force here in New York under orders to protect the Highlands and to go to Burgoyne's aid if necessary."

"And who will command those forces?"

"You."

It had come too quickly. Clinton's eyes widened as he slowly leaned back in his chair. He started to speak, stopped, and held his silence, humiliated that he was the one to be left behind—excluded from the campaign to take Philadelphia or destroy Washington or both. Ever since armies had been organized, most major officers dreamed of leading men into the vortex of the great battle that would bring victory and eternal glory. To be robbed of his dream by a single word stunned Clinton speechless.

Howe stood in thought for a moment. "What questions do any of you have?"

For five minutes questions flowed, and Howe impatiently answered in terse, clipped sentences.

Then Stuart raised a hand, and talk ceased. "When do we begin loading the ships?"

Howe turned to Richard, who answered. "The ships will be ready by next Wednesday, July ninth."

Howe picked it up. "Each of you prepare your commands. Baggage, laundry, munitions, cannon, food, horses—everything. We'll be in the field until we succeed."

The room fell silent as the enormity of the undertaking sank into each man.

Howe gave a small hand gesture. "I'll have written orders delivered to each of you soon. In the meantime, begin making your preparations now, today. You are dismissed."

Blinding light flashed through the windows at the same instant as a deafening thunderclap shook the entire house. Costly chinaware rattled in the hutches against the west wall. Wisps of soot settled from the chimney into the fireplace. The wine in the decanters sloshed, then settled.

For five seconds not one man moved nor spoke; then Grant muttered, "Did it hit the house?"

Richard spoke up. "I don't think so. But close."

Howe pointed. "It might be better to move out of this room, away from these windows. Go out the back way. There's a covered walkway to the stables."

With their aides following, the men filed out of the room, down to the reception room to get their hats, then walked rapidly to the rear entrance of the great, two-storied house. In single file they trotted down the covered breezeway to the stables, where enlisted men were soothing the nervous horses.

Richard remained behind with William. With the wind howling

amid lightning and deafening thunderclaps, he reached for the wine decanter, poured, and sipped before he looked at William.

"They're divided. Most don't like this business of going after Philadelphia in ships."

William's eyebrows arched in surprise. "Which ones?"

The first huge drops of rain came splattering against the windows, and in an instant the incessant din of a cloudburst filled the room.

Richard could hardly be heard above the storm. He raised his voice. "I think Grant and Cornwallis are the only ones who take your side of it. The others?" He shrugged. "They disagree."

"Why?"

"Clinton doesn't want to miss taking Washington down. Stuart thinks you're leaving Burgoyne to the wolves. The others? Who knows?"

His face flushed in anger as William slammed his hand down on the table. "We'll be close enough if Burgoyne needs help. Clinton was raised right here on Long Island. His father was governor of New York! Who better to take command here?"

Richard's answer was calm, unruffled. "No one. He's the obvious choice." He raised his goblet of wine to inspect the cherry-red spot of light in the center, while the wind screamed and the storm thundered. "Ambition does have its price."

William settled. "How many ships will this take?"

"About two hundred sixty."

"Will you have them ready?"

"By midnight on Tuesday, July eighth, Commander. But there's one thing you have to know."

William asked the silent question, and Richard answered it.

"The prevailing winds are from the south and west, which is exactly the direction the ships will have to take to get out of this bay. That means we'll have to wait until the winds shift to the north. We can begin to load on the ninth, and probably be finished by the twelfth. But until we get favorable winds, we can't sail."

William pursed his mouth in thought. "Are you suggesting we put off loading until the winds change?"

"Not at all. If we wait for better wind before we load, it could change before we finish. We load on the ninth, and we wait."

They heard the pounding of running boots in the hallway and then a hammering on the door. William jerked at the handle, and a white-faced aide blurted, "Sir, the two pickets at the door—both injured—the lightning!"

Whatever their weaknesses, whatever their faults, both William and Richard Howe had shaped their military lives around one polar star. *Care for your men!* In the years since command had been given to them, their men came to know that either one, Richard or William, would walk where their men walked, fight when they fought, starve when they starved, and share their losses and victories. No British commanders were more respected by those they led.

Immediately both men sprinted down the hallway and through the ante room, threw open the front doors, and burst onto the great porch. The two pickets lay sprawled on the stones with the wind driving sheets of rain past the twelve marble columns that supported the high portico. One lay still, white, unmoving, while the other was pawing with one hand to reach past the knee of his right leg. In moments both William and Richard were drenched. Without hesitation, each seized one of the fallen sentries and half carried, half dragged him back into the ante room, where they lay them on the carpet while the aide slammed the doors.

Richard knelt beside the still one, ripped open his tunic, and pressed his ear to the man's chest. He closed his eyes, concentrating, listening for a heartbeat. William cradled the other man on his arm, staring into the glazed eyes as the man clumsily tried to reach his right leg.

"What's wrong?" William demanded. "What happened?"

The man tried to focus his eyes but could not. He tried to speak, but no words would come. He tried again and slowly stammered, "Don't know. Something . . . pain . . . leg . . ."

William quickly reached below the right knee and felt for broken bones. There were none, but instantly he felt the calf muscle drawn up in a knot the size of his fist. He laid the man back onto the carpet, seized the leg with both hands, and began to work it with all his strength, kneading the calf muscle, pounding, trying to make the cramp relax and subside. Slowly the knot softened, and then it was gone. The man's reaching hand dropped, and his eyes closed in relief.

William looked at Richard, and Richard raised his head from the man's chest. He slowly shook his head and said quietly, "This one's gone."

William turned back to the man before him, and once again raised his head on his arm. "Can you hear me?"

The eyes opened, still glazed, still disoriented. "Yes."

"Do you know who I am?"

The man tried to focus his eyes. "Not sure—an officer—maybe the general."

"Can you tell me what happened out there?" Howe asked.

Again the man shook his head, then mumbled, "Wind—rain—a big light—sound—my feet—legs—something bad—never felt anything like it."

"Lightning? Were you hit by lightning?"

"Don't know—something."

William turned to his aide. "Get this man to my quarters and wrap him in blankets. Then get the surgeon general." He turned back to Richard. "Help me with the other one, down to the sewing room."

With the dead man covered in the sewing room and the surgeon general upstairs in Howe's quarters giving the injured man sips of brandy, William and Richard went to the front door, both soaked to the skin. Their wigs were a sopping, bedraggled tangle of artificial hair as they opened the door and walked out and across the porch into the teeth of the storm. Shoulders hunched, they ventured seventy feet out onto the spongy grass and turned to look at the house, searching for a blackened hole or for telltale smoke from a still-smoldering fire on, or inside, the roof. There was nothing.

Suddenly Richard raised his arm and pointed. "There!"

William pivoted, searching in the blinding rain for several seconds before he saw it. Twenty-five yards to the west, the five-foot-tall iron uprights that had supported the sixty-foot flagpole on all four sides were peeled outward, nearly touching the cement block in which they were anchored. One-half-inch thick, they were warped, twisted, nearly unrecognizable. Awestruck, the two brothers started across the grass, heads ducked against the rain, when they slowed, staring. Furrows, like small trenches, had been ripped a foot deep in the earth, to run in ragged, zig-zag patterns in all directions from the base of the flagpole. Several ran toward the house. The deepest one reached the porch, and they could see it had raised stones and broken the mortar.

The men cautiously approached the cement base and stopped. They could hear the hissing as rain pelted the four mangled strips of iron. Richard reached to touch one and jerked his hand back from the heat. They peered at the ground, searching for the flagpole but saw only tiny shards of scorched wood scattered in all directions. William pointed, and they walked to a large, blackened, distorted lump of smoking copper, still hissing in the rain.

"That was the ball on top of the flagpole," William murmured. It had once been round, sixteen inches in diameter. It was now blackened, unrecognizable.

Richard spoke. "Where's the flag?"

The two moved through the grass, searching, and William stooped to pick up a strip of charred cloth two feet long. On each end was a blackened brass eye, with an iron snap still in place. The remaining two feet and the third brass eye were missing. Without a word William handed it to Richard, and he recognized it as all that was left of the heavy strip of canvas with three brass eyes through which snaps were placed to hang the flag. There was no other trace of the Union Jack.

For a time the two brothers stood still with the rain driving against their backs. These two had command of more men, more firepower, than any other two men on the earth, save kings and cabinets. Thousands of cannon, tens of thousands of men, hundreds of thousands of muskets, but they stood cowed in the growing awareness of their own insignificance, their own smallness. They looked around at the trees that were split and uprooted and thrown about and at the debris that was scattered everywhere by the fury of the storm, and they felt a creeping consciousness of how helpless they were in the face of the incomparable power of Nature and He who controls it.

The wind slackened, and the deep purple clouds and the lightning and thunder passed as the storm moved toward the narrow neck of water separating Staten Island from the New Jersey coast, where the Raritan River empties into the sea. With rain dripping from their noses and chins and fingertips, Richard looked at William.

"It appears Doctor Franklin was right about his lightning rod. We'll have to remember that."

William faced his brother squarely. "Doctor Franklin thinks he can bring France in against us. Could he be right about that, too?"

For a time the two men faced each other in silence, neither caring to answer the question. Then Richard turned back toward the house, and William followed.

"Will you have damage among your ships?"

Richard nodded. "Probably, but we'll be ready by the ninth."

By four o'clock in the afternoon, Staten Island and all of New York were bathed once again in hot, muggy July sunlight. By five o'clock, eighty wagons heaped high with huge canvas bags filled with laundry, each marked by regiment and company, rumbled eastward from the massive British camp, the six-foot-tall wheels mired halfway to the axles on dirt roads that had been turned into quagmires. Draft horses strained to pull the loads, slogging through puddles of rainwater and mud that reached to their knees and splattered their bellies. By six o'clock sixty more wagons settled into the ruts while the horses dug in and labored. The drivers cursed and gigged their horses and plowed on, mumbling under their breath in the ancient rite of all enlisted men.

Don't mean nothin' to them officers—they just give the orders and it's the rest of us got to do the work—gather the laundry, they said—no reason—never is—just do this, or do that an' don't ask why—just do it.

East of the vast British camp, the thousands of wives and families of enlisted men and the traditional camp followers stood with hands shading their eyes as they studied the incoming wagons. These were the women who for a pittance washed and ironed the clothing of an army, cooked to feed them, and nursed the sick and wounded. Bound by family, or by choice, to the lives of soldiers, they had long since accepted the hard, unsparing lives of nomads, uprooting themselves with the army, moving, settling again, ready for the next move. In the deadly heat of battle some of them moved among the men, comforting the wounded, carrying water, sometimes stepping up to load or fire a cannon for one who had fallen. They were the unsung heroines who do the mundane, necessary things that hold armies together.

Short, stocky, gray, and aging, Milly Stringer squinted at the incoming wagons, counting. She spoke between teeth that were brown, decaying.

"More'n seventy of 'em, and there's bound to be more comin'. Laundry. We better get out the kettles and scrub boards and start the fires. How they expect us to git clothes clean in this mud?" She shook her head. "There'll be little sleep tonight."

Beside her Sookey finished her count and nodded. Tall, slender, round-shouldered, Sookey's black face and black eyes showed a weariness that seemed to hover over her continually. She had never known her real name, or if she had one. She had been called Sookey all her life, first on the Virginia plantation where she was born in the slave quarters, then in Massachusetts, where she had stopped when she ran away as a girl of thirteen. She coughed her hacking cough and answered Milly.

"Looks such. Land, would you lookit them wagons. Looks like cotton harvest all over again the way they's loaded. Never seen so much laundry in one pile."

By nine o'clock, in the glow after sunset, more than a thousand fires burned beneath black cast-iron kettles, and the women had settled into the mind-dulling sequence of washing. Carry steaming water to the brass wash and rinse tubs—cut brown soap and stir to a froth—in with the shirts—the pants would come later, then the socks—start the back-breaking work of rubbing the hot, wet laundry on the corrugated scrub boards—fold it and wring it until your fingers cramped—into the hot rinse water—poke it down with a stick—repeat it—wring it out—put it on a clean board for those who would hang it on long, strung lines—dump the dirty water—fetch fresh—start again. Don't think—don't question—don't dream—don't mind your hands are smarting in the heavy lye soap—skin cracking—don't think about being soaked from your shoulders to your ankles—disconnect your mind from all around you—scrub—rinse—dip—fetch—repeat it—repeat it.

At midnight Sookey put her hands on her hips and struggled to straighten her back. "Goin' to fetch a drink and set down a minute," she said and coughed as she made her way stiff-legged to her tent. She paused at the entrance to drink long from the wooden canteen hung on the ridge pole, then sat down on her cot. For a time she sat with her elbows on her knees, hands buried in her face. Then she lowered her arms and sat in silence, watching the shadows of those passing between her tent and the campfires and listening for anyone approaching. Satisfied, she reached beneath her cot into the small canvas bag where she kept the few things she needed, or valued, in life, and drew out a small pad of brown parchment paper and a piece of lead that served as a pencil.

Without a light she held her face close while she made crude marks on the parchment, then silently mouthed what she had written. Satisfied, she folded it twice, replaced the pad and pencil in her bag, and slipped it back beneath her cot. Again she waited for a time, then stood and bent forward to walk out through the tent flap into the heat of the fires and boiling water and a muggy July night. She walked a different route on her way back to the kettles, and on the way she dropped the folded parchment beside a twelve-year-old girl, who covered it with her foot until Sookey disappeared. Quickly the girl bent to sweep it up, then stuffed it into her apron pocket. Five minutes later she was at the edge of the clearing, where she paused, looked about for a moment, then thrust the paper beneath a rock near a scrub oak tree and walked casually on. Within minutes a seventeen-year-old boy plucked the paper from beneath the rock and disappeared in the darkness. At two o'clock in the morning, with the oarlocks wrapped in burlap to silence the oars, a rowboat silently pushed off from Staten Island, moving west toward the New Jersey coast on a moonless night. At eight o'clock in the morning a picket at the Middlebrook camp of the Continental Army raised his musket as he watched a rider come in at a gallop. Ten minutes later

General George Washington unfolded the small brown piece of parchment, laid it on the worktable in his quarters, and examined every mark.

"7–3. Two hundred wagons laundry—more coming. S."

He read it once more, then a third time, mouthing the words to be certain there was nothing hidden, nothing he had missed.

In thoughtful silence he leaned back in his chair. *General Howe is preparing to make his move. Will it be by land or by sea?*

He drew a small brass saucer from the drawer of his workdesk, raised the chimney on his table lamp, touched the parchment to the flame, laid it on the saucer, and watched it burn to a small ash.

Notes

British General William Howe, his origins, military history, experience in America, attitudes toward Americans, and his personality characteristics are described. See Higginbotham, *The War for American Independence*, p. 68; Mackesy, *The War for America, 1775–1783*, pp. 74–78; Leckie, *George Washington's War*, pp. 145–48.

The battle of Princeton was described in volume 3, *To Decide Our Destiny*, chapters XVI and XVII.

The tremendous British armada sent by King George III to subdue the rebellious colonies is described. See Mackesy, *The War for America, 1775–1783*, p. 82; Leckie, *George Washington's War*, p. 258.

The Americans spent the winter of 1776–1777 at Morristown, New Jersey, as described in volume 3, *To Decide Our Destiny*, chapter XIX.

British General William Howe realized he could not draw General Washington into battle on open ground and that he dared not attack the Americans in the mountains. See Leckie, *George Washington's War*, pp. 344–45.

Lord Germain, British secretary of state for the American Colonies, sent General John Burgoyne to Quebec, Canada, with eight thousand troops under orders to proceed south down the Hudson River to New York to cut the northern colonies, now states, from the southern colonies. See Mackesy, *The War for America, 1775–1783*, pp. 131–32; see also volume 4, *The Hand of Providence*, chapter III.

The British knew the French were shipping arms and supplies to the Americans in 1777. See Mackesy, *The War for America, 1775–1783*, p. 127.

The British also knew that if France entered the war on the side of the Americans, Spain would likely follow, and, further, they knew that Catherine the Great of Russia would not help the British. See Higginbotham, *The War of American Independence*, pp. 130, 226–38.

Over the winter of 1776–1777, General William Howe sent four different proposals to Lord Germain in London, each addressing the problems of subduing the Americans. Howe knew the only British solution to the American rebellion was to eliminate both General Washington and the Continental Army and, further, that General Washington also knew it and therefore would not be drawn into a battle that might bring those results. Howe concluded the British should abandon New Jersey and go directly after General Washington and destroy him and his army. Included in the plan was the taking of Philadelphia, which the British saw as the American capital city and therefore critical to the conquest of America. Howe proposed taking it by sea to avoid marching across New Jersey and exposing his army to American attack, and Lord Germain agreed. See Higginbotham, *The War of American Independence*, pp. 177–83; Leckie, *George Washington's War*, pp. 344–45.

British Generals Stuart and Clinton violently disagreed with General Howe and openly said so. See Mackesy, *The War for America*, p. 123; Higginbotham, *The War of American Independence*, pp. 181–83.

General William Howe's brother Admiral Lord Richard Howe was commander of the British fleet sent to America, and the brothers agreed to load the army onto two hundred sixty ships on July 9, 1777, and sail for the Delaware River with the first favorable winds. See Mackesy, *The War for America*, p. 125; Higginbotham, *The War of American Independence*, p. 183.

One of General Washington's greatest spy networks was among washerwomen for the British army. Sookey is a fictional person; however, she is used to represent hundreds of such washerwomen who rendered invaluable espionage services to the Americans. See Flexner, *Washington, The Indispensable Man*, p. 119.

CHAPTER III

★ ★ ★

*C*aleb thrust the last small piece of dark brown bread into his mouth, followed by a soft, crumbling piece of white goat cheese and reached for his wooden canteen. He drank the tepid water, smacked the corncob stopper back into the spout, and leaned back against the trunk of the maple tree that was shading him and half a dozen other soldiers of Company Three, the Irish company of New York's Ninth Regiment. He tipped his head to squint through the leaves that made a lacy network of the blue sky and the overhead ball of fire that pounded down on them. *About one o'clock. Five more hours.*

Sweat plastered his hair to his forehead and ran in small rivulets down his face. His shirt was stuck to his back where he had carried his bedroll. Huge mosquitoes and summer insects buzzed and clicked, swarming. He covered his face with his arms for protection and closed his eyes to let every muscle in his body go limp while he tried to think of nothing. He did not move nor open his eyes when the raspy, decidedly Irish growl of stocky, red-headed, red-bearded Sergeant Randolph O'Malley passed nearby.

"Awright, finish your eats. Five minutes. We march in five minutes. Stragglers get double picket duty. Five minutes!"

For one full minute Caleb did not stir. Then, with other silent, sweated men he walked the ten feet to a running brook and sank his canteen, swatting at the clouds of mosquitoes and flies that rose from the thick summer grasses and flowers and the water. He watched the bubbles cascade upward, then stop, and he jammed the stopper home before he splashed chill water on his head and face. Back at the base of the tree, he slung his bedroll on his back once more, hung his canteen about his neck, picked up his crude spear, and made his way back to the two faint wagon wheel ruts winding through the New Jersey wilderness.

He stood tall, searching for Sergeant O'Malley and the place where Company Three would take its place in the two-mile-long column. Caleb was the only soldier in the company who was armed with a handmade pine spear, and he carried it at his side. The spear marked him for what he had been two short weeks ago—a young innocent-come-lately filled with dreams of glorious soldiering. He had carried the spear proudly over his shoulder for one week before he understood that it drew silent, sarcastic smiles. He had begun carrying it low.

He picked out Sergeant O'Malley thirty yards north and worked his way forward, pushing through silent men who were focusing themselves on but one thing—survival through another five hours of marching in the worst sweltering heat of the summer. The morning march was vivid in every man's mind. By ten o'clock all talk had ceased. By noon canteens had been drained to replace sweat that ran dripping. More than a hundred men had dropped from heat exhaustion, seven of them from the Ninth Regiment. One had died. Others plodded on with glazed eyes, muttering, out of their heads, held between the wagon tracks by those around them. The officers rode nervous, sweat-streaked, lathered horses that threw their heads constantly against the insects that swarmed about their eyes.

They had called a halt at noon and ordered every man into the shade to move as little as possible while they ate the hard, brown bread and cheese that had been rationed out at the morning mess. The officers dismounted, unsaddled their horses, rubbed away the sweat and caked lather with burlap, and led them to the nearest stream to let them drink, slowly at first, then their fill.

As Caleb pushed through the milling soldiers toward O'Malley, he was startled by a voice to his left.

"Are you needin' help with that spear?"

In the moment of hearing he recognized the heavy Irish brogue of Conlin Murphy. He did not stop. He turned his head only enough to see the sneer on the broad, bearded face and the smiles of the men who had heard it, then walked on with rage swelling in his chest. He reached to touch the pink line of tender skin that had knitted on his left cheek. It would leave a scar. He silently repeated what he had said to himself a hundred times since Murphy pounded him senseless two weeks before. *It isn't over, Murphy. It isn't over.*

He took his place in Third Company and waited while O'Malley walked up and down the line of march, waving and shouting his men into a semblance of rank and file. As he passed Caleb he paused for one moment to quietly ask, "Murphy givin' you trouble?"

Caleb shook his head. "Murphy's fine."

"In a pig's eye," O'Malley muttered and moved on while Caleb waited for him to bawl out the order, "Foorrrrd, harch!"

At two o'clock the sun was at its zenith, hammering heat down like something tangible, and a halt was called. The men stumbled to a nearby stream to drink and refill their canteens before dropping to the ground to lie in the shade for half an hour, their precious rest plagued by the relentless hum and buzz of the ever-present cloud of insects. Then they were on their feet again to endure another mind-numbing march of four hours. Finally, at six o'clock the order came rolling down the column.

"Halt for evening camp."

By eight o'clock, with mess finished, bone-weary men sat on their blankets, where the inevitable camp talk started in the gathering twilight, sparse at first, then more.

"Been marchin' for three days—where we goin'?"

"North to the Hudson—didn't you hear?—Burgoyne's comin' down from Canada an' Howe's loaded about half the British army into them ships over in New York Harbor. Gen'l Washington figgers the whole lot of 'em is goin' north to meet Burgoyne. If Howe joins up with Burgoyne, they can cut the states in two, and this here revolution's finished—so we're goin' up there to stop one or the other of 'em. Gen'l Washington already sent Sullivan and his command up there in the Ramapo Mountains, just west of the Hudson, waitin' and watchin' for them ships comin' north right on up the river. Sent two divisions 'cross the river to Peekskill and told 'em to guard the highland passes. Stop Howe from goin' north."

"Yer wrong—I heard Gen'l Washington got news that them ships is loaded with enough supplies for a month, so he figgered they was goin' to Charleston."

"Well, if that's true, how come we're headin' north while Charleston's a long ways south?"

"Don't know—Gen'l Washington's usually right. I reckon we just keep marchin' where we're told."

"Yer all wrong—I heard Howe figgers to take Philadelphia—thinks that's the capital and if he gets it we'll just naturally quit."

"No, sir. If that's true, why aren't we gatherin' everybody around Philadelphia, 'stead of marchin' up this road?"

"Well, I don't know exactly. Only that's what I heard."

"Maybe you're all right, partly. Maybe Washington sent Sullivan up into the Ramapos to set cannon along the Hudson and stop them ships and figgers to confuse Howe by marchin' us north for a while and then turnin' around and goin' back to protect Philadelphia."

"Has them ships actually sailed from New York yet? Which way'd they go?"

"No, they're just sittin' there —about fifteen thousand soldiers and three thousand horses—for upwards of ten days—doin' nothin'—just waitin'."

"If they're just sittin' there, then how does anybody know which way they're goin' when they leave?"

"Well, I don't rightly guess anybody knows for sure—just have to wait and see."

"Sounds to me like this whole revolution has come down to a guessin' game. Howe's got ships loaded and is guessin' where he best take 'em, and Gen'l Washington's got an army marchin' tryin' to guess which direction he oughter go. That's not exactly encouragin' when we're the ones that's got to do the marchin'."

"Well, it can't be much better for those redcoats sittin' in them ships. With this heat, half those horses'll be dead by now, an' a fair share of those regulars'll be wishin' they was dead right along with 'em."

"Heard about that Frenchman that come over? Joined up with us? Fancy dresser. Some sort of a high official in France. Name's Lafayette. I heard he's just nineteen years old, and he's a general."

"I heard Gen'l Washington wrote Congress about him. That's how he got to be a general."

With the first hint of a cooling breeze, Caleb pulled the burlap sack from his blankets and filled it with sand and dirt, then hung it from a low-hanging branch of a maple tree. He pulled off his shirt, wrapped his hands, then began his evening ritual. Set the feet—move—jab—hook—punch—hit off the correct foot—elbows in—fists high enough to protect the head and face—move—jab—hook—punch.

Those nearby watched him for a time, then drifted back to their idle talk around low campfires. The mosquitoes settled for the night while thousands of fireflies left their signatures in the gathering gloom. In the distance, unnumbered bullfrogs began their raucous nightly belching. Nightbirds darted, taking night insects. Eyes appeared in the woods to stare at the unwanted intruders for a moment, then disappear. The evening star rose prominent in the east, and tiny points of light appeared overhead as the last vestige of sunset died.

Drenched in sweat, Caleb finally unwrapped his hands, lowered and dumped the bag, and walked back to his blankets. He was wiping his face with his shirt when the sound of excited, raised voices came through the trees. The men around him listened for a moment, then rose and trotted toward the cluster of men that was gathering around a large fire. One breathless, sweating man wearing a tricorn was talking loudly as he pointed north.

". . . and they're up there now, all scattered out, running for their lives. Maybe they're headed for Skenesboro. Gen'l St. Clair's with 'em, but no one knows where, or where they're headed."

"Wait! Who's up there scattered and headed for Skenesboro?"

A hush fell as it broke in the minds of the soldiers of the Ninth Regiment. This man was pointing north. He was talking about someone on the Hudson River, and there were but two forces up there: the British under Burgoyne, and the Americans at Fort Ticonderoga under St. Clair. They held their breath waiting for the answer.

"St. Clair and his whole command. Every man. Burgoyne got cannon up on top of Mount Defiance, and St. Clair found out. Those cannon could wreck Fort Ticonderoga in one day right along with the men inside, so St. Clair saw nothing to do but abandon it! So he did! More'n ten days ago. Overnight. Just gave Fort Ti to Burgoyne without a shot! What's left of his army is scattered out running southeast, probably trying for Skenesboro."

For five seconds the Ninth Regiment stood wide-eyed, stunned in disbelief. Fort Ti? The Gibraltar of the North American continent? The gateway to the thirteen United States? Given to Burgoyne without a fight? Not one single shot? In their wildest imaginings, not one man among them could ever have dreamed it.

Buzzing broke out, then open excited talk, then anger. Caleb listened for a time, then turned to slowly walk back to his own blankets while excited men gathered around fires, arguing, gesturing heatedly.

"If Burgoyne holds Fort Ti, then that's where Howe's headed with all those ships and men, right up the Hudson to join him. And if those two get together, there's hardly a way we can stop 'em from coming right on down the Hudson and cutting the north from the south."

"Don't ya see? That's why we're marching north. Gen'l Washington knew about Fort Ti, and he's headed up there to stop Burgoyne."

"Then what happens when we get halfway there and Howe shows up behind us with more troops and cannon than we got, and Burgoyne's in front of us with his army? We can't fight both front and back at the same time. This war might be over in the next two weeks if that happens."

The arguments raged on, and concern ripened into fear as the men realized the magnitude of what was happening both behind and in front of them. The drummer rattled out tattoo at ten o'clock, and the men went to their blankets, but the talk did not stop. At ten-thirty O'Malley came striding through Company Three.

"You men trying to start a panic? Stop the talk. Get to sleep. Reveille's five o'clock like always, and you got another long day tomorrow. Gen'l Washington knows what he's doing. So stop talking."

With quiet, fearful talk still going on among the men, Caleb dropped into a dreamless sleep. It seemed only minutes had passed when a rough hand shook him awake. An overcast had drifted in through the night, and the first light of dawn was turning the underbelly of the eastern clouds a deep rose color. Slowly Caleb focused on where he was, then looked up into the square, bearded face of Sergeant O'Malley.

"You awake?"

"Yes."

"You know Cap'n Venables?"

"Yes. The tall one."

"That's him. Git on up to the head of this regiment right now and find him. Two wagons of French muskets got here in the night, and they're goin' to whoever don't have one and gets there first. Take that spear to show 'em what you been carryin' and get one of them new muskets. And be sure to get a bayonet and some cartridges and flints."

Caleb jerked on his pants, then his shoes, shrugged into his shirt, scooped up the nine-foot spear, and jammed his shirttail into his trousers as he sprinted around and between men still asleep in their blankets. In the gray light preceding sunrise, he stopped where men were clustered around two wagons. Captain Charles Venables stood in the box of the one leading, with a book of records and a pencil in his hands. Two lieutenants were using bayonets to pry the tops off wooden crates with French wording stenciled on the sides.

Venables spoke, sharp, curt. "These muskets are for the Ninth Regiment only. Other regiments got their fair share. If you don't belong to regiment nine, you don't belong here." He pointed. "So form a line. We're going to do this orderly. When I ask, tell me your name and your company, and you better know the name of your sergeant and the color of his hair, because if you don't, you don't get a musket."

Caleb was eleventh in line. Without looking down, Venables barked, "Name?"

"Caleb Dunson, sir."

"Company?"

"Three."

"Your sergeant?"

"O'Malley. Red hair, red beard."

Venables signaled one lieutenant to hand down a musket, the other, a bayonet in a scabbard, and a canvas pouch with one hundred cartridges and six flints.

Caleb spoke. "You want this spear?"

Venables raised amused eyes and for a moment flashed one of his rare smiles. "Do I remember you?"

"I remember you, sir. Want the spear?"

"No, you . . . on second thought, put it in the wagon. One never knows."

Caleb tossed the spear to the nearest lieutenant, who dropped it clattering into the wagon bed, then handed down the new French musket. The other lieutenant handed him a bayonet, scabbard, and a canvas pouch with French markings. Caleb nodded, turned, and walked away, hefting the new musket, inspecting it. The reveille drum banged as he went hastily back to his blankets. O'Malley was waiting.

"You got it."

Caleb nodded.

"Know how to load it? Shoot it?"

"My father was a master gunsmith. I've made muskets with him."

O'Malley's chin dropped. "You *what?*"

"I've made muskets. This is a pretty good one, maybe two pounds lighter than the British Brown Bess, and a little better tooled. The frizzen fits tighter, and the trigger pull is smoother. It's a sixty caliber, like the ones my father made. Not as heavy as the seventy-five caliber ones the redcoats carry." He raised defensive eyes. "Not as good as father made, but better than the British. It will do."

O'Malley covered his surprise. "Well, you take care of it, and it'll take care of you."

"I'll remember that."

O'Malley turned to go when Caleb stopped him. "Sergeant, I appreciate it, you looking out for me this way."

O'Malley's eyes dropped, and he fumbled for a moment. "I was lookin' after Third Company. One man without a musket can make a difference. You be careful with that thing." He turned and was gone.

The overcast held throughout the day, blocking some of the oppressive heat from the sun but adding to the humidity. In the evening a north breeze moved the leaves in the trees, and a light rain came softly while Caleb was pounding the bag. The shower continued until midnight. At noon the following day the first rays of sun broke through the gray clouds, sending shafts of light onto the forests of New Jersey to illuminate a gigantic patchwork of gold and emerald green as the column marched on. At two o'clock they crossed the Pompton River, and by three o'clock were two miles into the Ramapo Mountains, following the Ramapo River toward Stony Point on the west bank of the Hudson River, across from Peekskill, New York.

They made camp on both sides of a stream in late afternoon, and a little after eight o'clock Caleb once again filled his canvas bag and hung it from the lower branch of a great oak. He was wrapping his hands when he became aware of someone approaching from behind, and he turned to face Charles Dorman. Caleb nodded, remained silent, and continued working with the frayed strips of canvas.

For a moment Dorman studied the wrapping, then quietly said, "Close your fist between wraps. It'll all fit better when you finish."

Caleb closed his fist, opened it, wound the canvas around his knuckles, closed his fist again, and continued as Dorman spoke.

"When you finish those wraps, we'll start the next step."

Caleb paused to look at him, questioning.

"Working with a man, not a bag."

Quickly Caleb finished, tied off the ends of the strips, and rose, facing Dorman. For a moment he felt awkward, hesitant, not knowing what to do, what to expect.

Dorman began. "I'm going to raise my hands flat, and you're going to hit at them. First thing you learn is don't look directly at my hands. Pick out a spot in the middle of my chest and look there, but see all of me. Feet, hands, head, eyes. Learn to see all of me at the same time. Do you understand?"

"Yes."

Dorman raised his hands shoulder high, palms outward. "Now do what you've been practicing—feet, elbows, move, jab, hook, punch. Don't think how you look, just do it. Start now."

He waited. A few men turned to watch as Caleb raised his fists, elbows in, left foot slightly forward, chin tucked in, and he jabbed, then hooked and punched while Dorman continued his instructions.

Good—good—don't look at your feet—don't look at either of my hands—look at my chest and see all of me—jab—hook—punch—good—circle me—hit off the correct foot—good—keep circling—good—good.

The onlookers smiled and drifted away. For half an hour Caleb circled under the watchful, critical eye of Dorman, who maintained his unending stream of comments, instructions. A pattern developed in Caleb's footwork and in the rhythm of his fists. He concentrated on a spot on Dorman's chest but saw the whole man, including his eyes. He began to strike with more authority, more accuracy, one heartbeat quicker.

Sweat was dripping from Caleb when Dorman finally dropped his hands. "That's enough for now. Think on what you learned. I'll be back tomorrow. Let's get that bag down."

Amidst the fireflies and the croaking of frogs from the Ramapo River and the marshes, Caleb sat on his blankets for a time, then as the night cooled, lay down. He clasped his hands behind his head, peering through the leafy canopy to study the myriad stars in the black velvet above. He reached to touch the French musket, then tucked his hand behind his head once more. From far away to the north the regimental drummer pounded out tattoo, echoing strangely loud in the forest. The camp quieted, the fires burned low, and Caleb found his thoughts wandering.

Through with the spear—the French musket—Father made them better—made most things better—tried to make Boston better—said he was right—had to go fight for the right—what's right and what's wrong?—Father said one thing, the king another—can a thing be right in one place and wrong in another? Right in England and wrong here? If Father was right, what did it get him? It got him dead—dead and gone—it got Matthew gone to sea—Billy gone north—the women home alone—doing laundry to buy food—that's what the right and wrong question got us.

He turned on his side, arm under his head.

Right or wrong doesn't matter on the battlefield—only who's got the most men and muskets and cannon—that's the truth of it—I don't care who's right or wrong—I only care about giving back to the British what they gave Father—bring the scales back to level—they took Father's life, they owe us a life—they caused pain to Mother and the family; we owe them some pain and suffering. That's the way of it.

He didn't know when he drifted into restless sleep. He only knew that he was at his father's familiar workbench, stroking a trigger assembly with emery cloth to make the pull smooth. He paused to watch his father tighten the three large, consecutive vises that locked a musket barrel blank in place, then carefully set the drill and begin the precision turning that would cut the bore. He had seen it countless times, done it himself with his father's hands guiding, knew the procedures, the moves. He raised his eyes to his father, but his father refused to look. He spoke and reached for his father's arm, but there was no response, nothing. With panic rising, he called his father's name, then shouted it. He was still shouting when he awoke, crouched on his blanket, the echo ringing in the stillness of the black forest.

From the darkness came voices, curt, angry.

"Stop the hollerin'!"

"Hard enough to sleep without someone yellin'!"

"Wake up or go to sleep, but quit callin' out."

For long moments Caleb stared in the darkness while he came from his father's workbench in Boston, back to the camp of the Continental

Army on the Ramapo River in northern New Jersey. He sat upright for a long time, afraid to fall asleep for fear of unwanted dreams. The morning reveille drum found him still sitting, head tipped forward, chin on his chest as he slept.

He swallowed at the sour taste in his mouth, then walked to the stream to splash cool water on his face, rinse out his mouth, and return to begin rolling his blankets. O'Malley barked orders, and Caleb walked into the forest with the other three men assigned to gather firewood. With morning mess completed, and a ration of one hard biscuit and one piece of crisped sowbelly for their midday meal in their pouches, the Ninth New York Regiment assembled on the road that wound north through the mountains.

An odd quietness hung over the column. The men repeatedly peered north as though they were expecting to hear cannon, either American cannon bombarding the two hundred sixty British ships they believed were moving up the Hudson toward Burgoyne, or British cannon shelling the American shore batteries, or both. They knew the Hudson was nearly forty miles away, but still they looked and listened.

Captain Charles Venables stood tall in the stirrups, hand high to give the signal. Sergeant O'Malley bawled out, "Forraard harch!" and the column began moving on the winding road like a great, creeping reptile. They had gone less than one hundred yards when O'Malley suddenly shouted, "Third Companyyyyy, halt!"

Some men stopped and some didn't, and in an instant the regiment was a mass of startled, confused soldiers. They craned their necks to see what had happened ahead that could stop the entire column but could see no cause. Confusion turned to fear.

"We been ambushed up there?"

"Has a sniper kilt Gen'l Washington?"

"Look sharp in the trees—maybe we're surrounded."

O'Malley came striding. "We just got orders from Gen'l Washington. We're to stay right here 'til he says move."

"Why? What's happened?"

"Didn't say. Only that we're to stay right here for now. So git off the road into the shade and wait."

Disgruntled, mystified, nervous, the men divided, half moving into the woods on either side of the road, seeking shade and water, brushing away mosquitoes that rose in clouds. Caleb dropped his bedroll beneath a white pine and sat on it, musket across his knees, fighting the insects. One hour became two, then three. Canteens were running low. Some men began to gnaw at their piece of crisped sowbelly.

O'Malley sounded a warning. "Better be careful with your rations. Don't know how long we'll be here. Won't be moving until orders come."

Half an hour before noon, four men wearing colonel epaulets on their shoulders came loping sweating horses south, back down the road they had just gone up. Ten minutes later Captain Venables hauled his horse to a stop in the road and gathered the Ninth Regiment around.

"Listen close. I only want to say this once. This morning, five minutes after we started to march, a messenger from New York got to Gen'l Washington. He rode all night. Wore out two horses. He said Howe got a letter from Burgoyne about a week ago. You already heard Burgoyne's got Fort Ti. He's coming right on down to Albany, and the letter said he didn't need help."

The horse tossed its head at the mosquitoes, and Venables took the slack out of the reins as he continued. "When Howe got Burgoyne's letter, the winds in New York Harbor were from the southwest, and the ships couldn't make it over the big bar by Long Island. They had to wait for better winds and tides. Well, yesterday the winds shifted, coming in from the north. Howe sailed, but not up the Hudson, because Burgoyne doesn't need him. Howe's two hundred sixty ships sailed east, past Sandy Hook, out into the Atlantic, and haven't been seen since. Gen'l Washington's sure Howe's headed down past the New Jersey Capes to the Delaware River, then up the river to Philadelphia. The minute the messenger told the Gen'l, he called a halt, and then a war council. They all agreed. We got to get back down to defend Philadelphia."

Once again he paused to gather his thoughts. "We got the women and all the wagons at the south end of the column, so Gen'l Washington sent four officers back there to get 'em off the road so we can march past 'em. Then they'll have to unhook all the horses and turn the wagons by hand, because the road's too narrow to turn 'em otherwise. While all this is happening, you men stay right here and be ready to march the minute the order comes down."

He turned to O'Malley. "You know what to do?"

"Yes, sir. How did the messenger know Howe got a letter from Burgoyne?"

"Spies," was all Venables said before he reined his horse around and spurred it back up the road.

A torrent of talk erupted.

"All this marchin' north for nothin'?"

"How come we didn't wait 'til we knew what Howe was goin' to do?"

"This here whole thing's a great big plot by Burgoyne and Howe, and it worked!"

"How do we know those ships are headed for Philadelphia? Why not Charleston?"

O'Malley raised a hand and the talk died. "Get back in the shade. It'll take just as many days goin' back as it took gettin' here, so save your strength. Don't eat your rations until I say."

Days and nights became a blur of the grinding routine of setting up camp in the evening, tattoo, reveille, striking camp in the morning, cursing mosquitoes, insects, the relentless sun or summer rainstorms that turned the dirt road to a river of mud, endless gathering of firewood, marching in sweat-soaked clothing, going to blankets in damp clothing, getting up in damp clothing, eating food that all tasted like boiled sawdust.

In the late afternoon of the fourth day, west of the Passaic River, Caleb picked up an ax and with three other men from Third Company walked past the fringes of camp into the forest in the unending quest for firewood. Two of the men were bearded, dressed in buckskin leggings and hunting shirts. The third wore a soiled linen shirt, homespun trousers, dirty knee-length white stockings, and battered, square-toed shoes. Ten yards into the trees Caleb stopped before a tangle of brittle, wind-felled pines that had been toppled by a great storm in a time long forgotten. Without a word he began swinging the ax, scattering the branches while the others gathered them.

The buzz came without warning. From the corner of his eye Caleb caught the flash of movement near the ground, next to the gnarled roots of the fallen tree, then the ringing yell as the man in the linen shirt dropped his load and jerked erect, right hand clamped on his left wrist.

"It got me, it got me," he shouted as he staggered backward in white-faced panic.

The other two dropped their loads and were on him in an instant, while Caleb searched the ground, trying to understand what had happened. It wasn't until the buzz came again that he could distinguish the coiled rattler from the leaves and spots of sunlight, and he drew backward violently at the sight of the ugly, triangle shaped head and wide=set, serpent eyes. Shaking, he stepped forward and swung the ax with all his strength, once, twice, three times, and the buzzing slowed and died. When he was sure, he turned toward the three men behind.

The two in buckskin had the third one sitting on the ground, battling to hold him as he fought, shrieking, "Help me, help me, I'm going to die, I'm going to die!"

In one fluid motion, the man on his right drew his belt knife, grasped the struck arm, slit the sleeve past the elbow, and rammed the knife point deep into one of the purple marks left by the fangs of the dead snake. Clean red blood gushed. With the other man straining to hold the writhing victim still, he jerked the knife out and thrust it into the other fang mark, then dropped the knife to the ground as he lowered his mouth to the dripping cuts and sucked. He turned and spat the blood onto the soft, spongy forest floor, then sucked again and again and again. The other man tore the linen shirtsleeve from the right arm, wrapped it above the elbow of the left arm, knotted it, jammed a stick through it, and twisted the stick hard.

Wiping the blood from his mouth and chin, the nearest man turned to Caleb. "Get the surgeon!" he barked.

Caleb dropped the ax, spun, dodged through the trees back to the campsite, and sprinted south. O'Malley appeared to his right, and Caleb slowed long enough to gasp, "Where's the surgeon?"

O'Malley pointed. "What's happened?"

Caleb hooked a thumb over his shoulder. "Back there in the woods. Snakebite. What's the surgeon's name?"

"Waldron," O'Malley exclaimed as he broke into a sprint toward the woods, while Caleb continued his headlong run, dodging around startled men. He recognized Fifth Company as he sprinted through and slowed to call to the nearest officer, "Waldron. Surgeon. Where is he?"

"Up front. Who's hurt?"

Caleb ran on without answering, watching for men with gold epaulets on their shoulders. Two minutes later he slowed near an evening cook fire with five officers gathered nearby. Sweat running, he stopped, fighting to control his panting enough to speak.

"Regimental surgeon. Waldron. Is he here?"

Corpulent, balding, lipless, a major narrowed his eyes at Caleb.

"I'm Major Waldron."

Caleb pointed. "Back there. Third Company. Snakebite."

Waldron turned on his heel, ran to his tent, snatched up his satchel, and came puffing back. Without a word Caleb pivoted and led out at a run, Waldron grunting to keep up. He was wheezing when Caleb approached the cook fire of Company Three and slowed. Most of the men were gathered in a circle that opened, and Caleb led Waldron into the center. O'Malley and the two men in frontier buckskin were kneeling in front of the stricken man, who was seated on a log.

Without a word Waldron pushed his way to the man while O'Malley and the others drew back to let him kneel. Breathing hard from his run, he stared into the man's eyes for a moment before he spoke.

"Can you understand me?"

"Yes."

He grasped the arm above the tourniquet. "Can you feel this?"

"Yes."

Waldron raised the forearm to study the cuts, still open, with the black blood caked and clotted and a trickle of bright red still dripping. He turned back to Caleb.

"When did this happen?"

"Maybe ten or twelve minutes ago."

"Who did the cutting?"

Caleb pointed, and Waldron turned to the two men. "When?"

"Right after it happened."

"The tourniquet?"

"Same time as the cut."

Waldron jerked open his satchel, drew out a bottle, pulled the cork, soaked a rag, and washed away the blood. Carefully he looked above the cuts, past the elbow, then above the tourniquet, searching for gray or blue lines creeping upward. There were none. He reached into the armpit, found the nodule he was looking for, and pressed.

"That hurt?"

"A little. Not much."

He put two fingers in the man's left hand. "Squeeze as hard as you can."

The man's hand closed and he bore down.

Waldron nodded and the man released his fingers.

"Feel light-headed? Like you're going to pass out?"

"No."

"Well," Waldron said, "I'm afraid you're going to live. We keep up this marching up and down through these woods, you might wish you hadn't, but that's between you and the Almighty. I'll stay around for a while to be sure, and then we'll put a stitch or two in those cuts to close 'em."

He turned to the two bearded frontiersmen. "For whatever it means to you, I think you saved his life."

Embarrassed, the men let their eyes drop for a moment and said nothing.

As an afterthought Waldron asked, "Where's the snake?"

Caleb spoke up. "Dead."

"They usually don't strike like that unless you corner them, sometimes accidentally. How'd it happen?"

"Gathering wood. The snake was under a tree we were working on."

"Figures. Watch next time." He stopped and for a moment studied Caleb. "Do I remember you? That scar on your cheek?"

"You looked at it three weeks ago."

"A fight—something about a fight?"

Caleb shook his head. "No fight to speak of."

"Didn't someone else stitch that cut?"

"Yes."

Waldron reached to pinch his lower lip for a moment in thought. "Well, son, you stay away from snakes and fights. They're no good."

Half an hour later Waldron washed the arm again, gave the man a long pull from a bottle of brandy, set a sixty caliber musketball between his teeth, and put two stitches in each of the cuts. He smeared thick carbolic salve over it all, wrapped it in clean sheeting, and looked the man in the eye.

"You start feeling faint or funny, send for me. That young man knows where to find me. Get to your bedroll, and stay there 'til I get back in the morning to change the bandage." He closed his satchel and stood, muttering, "I'm getting too old and fat to be running around like this." He turned on his heel and started back north when the man called after him.

"Thank you."

Waldron waved a hand without turning and was gone.

O'Malley led the wounded man to his bedroll and sat him down. "I'll send supper. Where's your canteen?"

He walked back to the cooking kettle and called to Caleb, "Where's the ax?"

Caleb thought for a moment. "In the woods. I dropped it."

"We still got to have wood. Go get the ax, and fill this while you're out there." He handed him the canteen, then gave hand signals to the two bearded men in buckskin.

"Finish gettin' in the firewood."

The three of them walked back into the woods, the two frontiersmen striding out, Caleb walking gingerly behind, hearing every sound, eyes cast to the ground for everything that moved. A grasshopper took flight clicking, and Caleb jumped. Twigs crunched underfoot, and he flinched. He was seeing coiled rattlesnakes near every tree, under every bush, beside every rock, and hearing the deadly buzz of the rattles in every sound of the forest. The frontiersmen smiled in understanding and waited while he found the ax, then once again began knocking the dead branches from the tangle of wind-felled trees.

Half an hour later firewood was stacked by the evening cook fire, and Caleb tracked down Sergeant O'Malley.

"Know where I can get some paper and a pencil?"

"For what?"

"Write the snake story while it's still fresh."

"You a writer?"

"Worked for a printer. Once in a while wrote articles for his newspaper."

"In Boston?"

"Yes."

"You another Ben Franklin?"

Caleb grinned. "No, there's only one of him."

"Go find Cap'n Venables. He keeps the records. Maybe he can spare some paper and a pencil."

With evening mess behind them, Caleb wrapped his hands and waited for Dorman, who spoke.

"I heard about the snake. Were you there?"

"Yes."

"That could have been bad."

"It was."

Dorman glanced at Caleb's wrapped hands. "Let's get started."

Dusk had settled before Dorman lowered his hands. Caleb was sweating, breathing hard, wiping with his shirt.

"It's coming. Soon we take the next step."

"What's that?"

"You try to hit me. Head, chest, anywhere."

Caleb stopped wiping the sweat. "Hit? Your head?"

Dorman smiled in the deepening gloom. "Don't worry about it." He turned to go when Caleb called to him.

"Wait. I'll walk with you. I got to find Captain Venables."

Dorman's eyebrows peaked. "Venables? What for?"

"To ask for some paper and a pencil."

"A letter home?"

"No. I want to write the snake story while it's all in my head."

Dorman exclaimed, "You a writer?"

"Worked for a printer. I wrote a few things once in a while. Might send the story back to him."

Dorman shrugged. "I got some paper and a pencil in my things."

In full darkness the sound of tattoo came echoing. In the silence of a tired camp, Caleb sat near the banked coals of the supper fire, a pad of paper on his knee and a piece of lead that would serve as a pencil in his hand. He closed his eyes to capture the sick terror of stumbling into the snake, then searched for the right words. Thoughtfully he began to write.

"The buzz and the strike and the shriek of the terrified man came in the same fleck of time, and sick fear came flooding inside of me. It wasn't until the buzz came the second time that I saw the coils and the dead eyes of the rattler ready to strike again. I don't remember swinging the ax. I only remember the snake dead, cut in three pieces, and the two men behind me frantically working . . ."

It was close to midnight before O'Malley came, gruff, demanding. "What are you doing?"

"Just finishing some writing."

"The snake story?"

"Yes."

"You get onto your blankets. We don't need tired men. Things go wrong when men are too tired. You get to sleep. Move!"

Notes

The messenger who came with news concerning the loss of Fort Ticonderoga and the defeat and scattering of the American forces in the ensuing battle was described earlier. See volume 4, *The Hand of Providence*, chapters XVIII and XXI.

For a visual description of the route of the American army as described herein, see the map in Mackesy, *The War for America*, p. 91.

Having loaded his army onto the two hundred sixty British ships on July 9, 1777, General Howe was obliged to wait for favorable winds until July 23, at which time he sailed out into the Atlantic. Thus began one of the strangest and most confusing odysseys between two armies in the history of warfare, with General Washington utterly baffled by the unbelievable route General Howe followed, as we shall see. Mackesy, *The War for America*, p. 126; Leckie, *George Washington's War*, pp. 346–47; Higginbotham, *The War of American Independence*, pp. 181–83.

Caleb Dunson, a fictional character, worked for a printer in Boston. See volume I, *Our Sacred Honor*, chapter XXV.

The Delaware River, New Jersey

July 29, 1777

CHAPTER IV

★ ★ ★

*M*ounted on his dappled gray mare, General Washington stood full height in the stirrups and shaded his eyes to peer south from the high crest of one of the lush, rolling hills of southern New Jersey. "There," he said, pointing. "We'll camp there tonight."

Beside him his aides raised their hands to block out the stifling July sun, studying the silvery thin line that meandered in the distance, west to east. They said nothing as they spurred their horses to follow their leader down toward the great Delaware River and Pennsylvania on the far side. Each man struggled with the one concern that had ridden him heavy since Washington had ordered the entire column around for a forced march from the Ramapo Mountains and the Hudson River, far to the north. It had dogged the men day and night, made them edgy, surly.

The stand-or-fall, do-or-die question was: could the two hundred sixty British ships carrying more than fifteen thousand troops with horses, food, and munitions, move out of New York Harbor, south along the New Jersey capes, west into the Delaware River, then back north to Philadelphia, in less time than General Washington could march his column from just south of Stony Point on the Hudson River to the same place?

A half mile behind Washington and his officers, plodding on a winding dirt road, came the core of the Continental Army—in a long column that stretched north out of sight in the rolling New Jersey hills. They had labored fourteen hours a day since reversing their line of march, crossing the Pompton, Whippany, and Raritan Rivers and countless streams and brooks in their headlong plunge toward the Delaware, where they hoped to intercept Howe. If Philadelphia was Howe's objective, the Continentals meant to make a fight of it.

Washington put his horse down the south slope of the hill, raised her to a lope across a quarter mile of lowlands, splashed through a small stream, then slowed to a walk as they began the next climb. His back was straight, man and animal moving as one through the undulating hills. Finally, with the sun directly overhead, he called a stop near a brook.

"Loosen your saddle girths and water your mounts. We'll continue in twenty minutes."

At two in the afternoon the dank smell of the river reached them, and half an hour later they reined in their sweating horses on the New Jersey bank of the broad, rolling, green-brown waters of the Delaware. For a time they remained mounted while they studied the river and searched the distant Pennsylvania shore for anything that would tell them if Howe had been there.

Square barges and the familiar Durham freight boats, filled to the gunwales with iron ore and riding deep in the water, were being poled upriver by sweating crews, toward the smelters above McConkie's Ferry. Other traffic was moving downriver, boats and barges filled with pig iron, wheat, sheep, cattle, and fresh vegetables for the Philadelphia market. Rowboats moved in all directions as farmers, merchants, bearded frontiersmen, itinerant preachers, and countless others with untold business moved on the great water-highway that served three states. Among all the vessels, there was not a military ship to be seen, nor a sign of the red, white, and blue of the British Union Jack, nor a single red-coated British regular.

Washington broke the silence. "They might be above us or below us." He turned to General Nathanael Greene. "We have about six hours of daylight. Take three officers and go south." To General John Cadwalader, he said, "Take three men and go north. I'll go back to bring the column in. Report back when you've found the British, but not later than midnight."

Both officers saluted, nodded to those who were to accompany them, wheeled their horses, and cantered away in opposite directions. Washington and his two aides turned their horses and walked them east, searching for a clearing in the woods that would provide enough open land, firewood, and fresh water for the oncoming column to make camp for the night.

★ ★ ★ ★ ★

They came sweat-soaked, footsore, standing in respectful, expectant silence as General Washington reined his horse to a stop and spoke to the leading regiment.

"The Delaware is two miles ahead. There are no British ships or soldiers in sight."

A hushed murmur arose and quieted. Washington continued.

"We have patrols moving up and down the river. Until we know the location of the British, we will camp and wait. There's open ground just over a mile ahead with two streams running through. We'll camp there until further notice."

He turned to Lieutenant Colonel John Laurens, the nearest of his two aides, pointing. "The two of you ride on and give the message to those behind. I'll lead back to the campsite."

Murmuring in the marching ranks began before the aides had covered a quarter of a mile. By the time they had gone half a mile, there was open talk.

"From Morristown south to Middlebrook, then back north halfway through the Ramapos, and turn right around south clean back here to the Delaware, and what did it get us? Nothin' but wore out!"

"Marchin' in circles! That's what we're doin'! Won't even know when the war's over 'cause we'll still be out somewhere marchin' in circles!"

Reaching the meadow, Washington reined his mount around and faced the leaders of the column. Wordlessly he pointed to each succeeding regiment as it entered the campground, directing each to its position. It was after six o'clock before the wagons arrived. Overloaded with the sick and the precious little equipment, munitions, food, and medicines the Continentals had to meet the unending demands of a marching army, the wagons came creaking and rattling into the clearing.

The women and children rode in the wagons when they could, or walked silently beside when they couldn't, waiting to see the place that would be their new home. They would remain until the next day, or two days, or until an advance or a retreat or a battle won or lost would force them to once again quickly pack their meager possessions, load them into a wagon bed, and march on to a new meadow or a field or a hill or a valley they had never seen before. They had learned not to attach themselves to a place, or to things, but only to each other. All else was fleeting, transient.

By dusk, a haze of smoke from the cook fires hung in the sultry dead air above the camp, dimming the stars and blurring the treetops. Tents for the officers and women and children were scattered about. Blankets and bedrolls littered the ground wherever the soldiers had dropped them for the night. With evening mess finished, camp talk flourished in the deepening shadows. New York's Ninth Regiment, Third Company, bedded on the south side of the sprawling camp, finished scrubbing the supper cook pots with clean sand from a brook, and the weary men sought the comfort and reverie of an evening campfire. They sat cross-legged on the ground, in clothes damp from sweat, elbows on knees, fingers interlaced before them, studying the shifting, dwindling flames.

"We should've had scouts out before we come all this way, so's we'd know if we was goin' to finally catch Howe."

"Gettin' ready to fight's bad enough. Gettin' ready and havin' nobody there to fight is worse."

"We oughta go on down to the river and shoot at *somethin'*. That'd be better'n comin' all this way to do *nothin'*."

Caleb Dunson sat among the men, listening for a time, then went to his bedroll for the worn canvas strips to wrap his hands. He was finishing when the familiar voice of Dorman came from behind.

"Too tired tonight?"

Caleb shook his head and stood. "I'm ready."

Dorman hesitated for a second. "We start the next step. You try to hit me any place you can above the waist."

Caleb started. "Hit? How hard?"

"As hard as you can."

Caleb stammered. "I . . . that doesn't . . . don't you—"

Dorman cut him off. "Don't worry. Go ahead. Remember your feet. Start."

Caleb took his stance—left foot slightly forward, hands up to protect his face, chin tucked into the hollow of his left shoulder, elbows close to his ribs. He centered his gaze on Dorman's chest but took in the whole man, then began moving to his left, slowly circling Dorman. His left hand flicked out, aimed at Dorman's forehead, but Dorman tipped his head to the side, and the blow missed its mark. Caleb flicked his left hand out again, but to no effect—Dorman turned his head just far enough that the blow brushed harmlessly by. Surprised at how easily Dorman avoided being hit, Caleb jerked his fist back, cocked his arm, and brought a left hook aimed at Dorman's right temple. Dorman's right hand moved up and out to deflect the punch while it was yet six inches from his head, and Caleb's fist harmlessly grazed Dorman's rounded shoulder.

In the grain of time between Dorman's hand coming up and Caleb pulling back from his missed punch, Dorman was inside Caleb's left arm. In that instant it flashed in Caleb's mind—*He's inside my guard—could hurt me bad—break my ribs.*

Dorman said nothing nor did he change the dead expression on his face. Only his eyes were alive, focused on Caleb, closely watching every movement, every expression as it flitted over Caleb's face.

The dance went on. Again the boy jabbed and hooked, and once more Dorman slipped or picked off Caleb's punches. Frustrated, Caleb threw all his weight into a power punch aimed between Dorman's elbows, at his chest. Instinctively, Dorman brought his forearms together in front of his chest and twisted slightly to one side, deflecting the blow while

Caleb tried to recover. In that fleck of time Caleb knew. *He could hook my ribs or my head, hard.*

Men seated around nearby campfires turned to watch the two spar—the gray-haired man and the smooth-cheeked boy—warily circling each other, the boy swinging, the man blocking. They watched for a few moments, then smiled and shook their heads and turned back to cursing the British, their officers, the weather, and the fact they had come prepared for a battle that was not to be.

In full darkness, with only the shadowy light of the campfires showing their perspiration, Dorman finally backed away and dropped his hands.

"That's enough for now. Questions?"

"How do you know when I'm going to swing?"

"Your eyes. Your expression. How you position yourself."

Caleb's eyes widened. "My eyes?"

"A split second before your hands move, your eyes narrow just a little. Concentrate on not changing your expression. No matter what happens, try to keep the same expression. You hit him, he hits you, he gets hurt, you get hurt, it's all the same. Don't change your expression. And learn to set your feet a little closer to the time you swing. If there's too big a gap between the two, you've told the other man what you're doing. It has to be quick."

Caleb stood still for several seconds, memorizing the words he had just heard, putting them in place in his mind. Then he began to unwrap his hands.

Dorman turned to go, and Caleb called, "Tomorrow night?"

"Unless we're marching." Dorman reflected for a moment. "You're learning. Doing well. A few times tonight you came close. Could have hurt me."

Caleb started. "I don't want—"

Dorman raised a hand, smiling. "I know. Let me worry about that. A little more work, and I'll start hitting back."

Caleb's mouth dropped open. "You'll fight back?"

"Let's say you'll learn to slip and block, or you'll have a bruise here and there."

A thrill surged through Caleb as Dorman turned and was gone.

In the moment Caleb dropped his eyes to finish unwrapping his hands, a shadowy movement in the trees forty feet away caught his eye, and he jerked his head up, peering into the darkness. The shape of a blocky, bearded man stepped back out of the glow of the fire and disappeared while Caleb stared, uncertain of who it was or what the man had been watching.

Was it Murphy? Conlin Murphy? Watching? He shrugged. *Let him watch.*

He rolled the hand wraps and was putting them back into his bedroll when Sergeant Randolph O'Malley came striding, red hair and beard shining in the firelight. He slowed, and his gravelly voice came rasping.

"You got that writing you did about the snake?"

Caleb stood silent for a moment, caught by surprise. "In my bedroll. Why?"

"Cap'n Venables is looking for someone who can write, to help keep the regimental orderly book. Wants to read it."

Caleb's head fell forward in shock, then he asked, "What's the regimental orderly book?"

"Nothin' much. Just a book that tells what the regiment done each day."

"Venables wants *me* to keep it? How did he know?"

O'Malley cleared his throat, and for a moment his eyes dropped as though he were about to confess having done something wrong. "He asked me if I knew anyone. I told him."

Caleb started forward, unaware he was moving. "O'Malley, I won't do it!"

O'Malley waved a hand to brush aside Caleb's refusal. "Cap'n Venables will decide, and if he orders you, I don't reckon you have a choice. Now where's the snake story?"

"I wrote that to send back to Boston to the print shop."

"You'll get it back."

"When?"

"Likely tomorrow mornin'."

Caleb rounded his lips to blow air for a moment while he accepted what O'Malley was forcing on him. Then he turned, dug into his bedroll, and brought out the sheaf of papers. He folded the first two sheets and handed them to O'Malley.

O'Malley bobbed his head once, turned, and walked away into the darkness.

At ten o'clock tattoo sounded. Men banked the glowing coals of their campfires for the morning cooking fires and broke away from their small groups to seek their blankets. From a long distance to the north came the mournful sound of wolves baying at the thin crescent moon as it cleared the eastern skyline, and for a long time the soldiers stared north in the blackness, not moving as they listened, unconsciously counting the voices of the pack.

For a few minutes the baying quieted, and then came the sounds of the pack in full voice, first one, then another, and another as they took their rotation in running something to ground. A moose? Elk? Deer? In the darkness, each man created his own scene of half a dozen of the tireless, long-legged, gray and black wolves, yellow eyes glowing in the night as they relentlessly, patiently, worked their prey, maintaining a chase that was divided among the six of them, driving their terror-stricken prey to exhaustion. When the victim could run no more, it would find a rock or a wind-fallen tree, whirl, and back up to it with lowered head, antlers poised, ready for the death struggle that was coming. It would end as quickly as two wolves were able to attack the throat long enough for two others to seize and rip the big tendons in the hind legs. With the hindquarters down and the animal unable to rise, it would be over in less than two minutes. Quick, efficient, the end known from the beginning.

None of the men were conscious that they were lying motionless, staring into the blackness. Nor did any of them ponder the reason the entire Continental Army camp on the Delaware was hushed, quiet, listening to the progress of the chase. Who knows what the primal sound of wolves in full voice touches in the deep recesses of mankind? Is it the ultimate fascination of knowing the eternal cycle of hunter and hunted, of life and death, is playing itself out somewhere in the night? That something will die that another might live? Is it the subtle, unspoken sureness that the seeds of hunting and being hunted, of killing or be killed, lurk within the human heart, tenuously restrained by the rules of civilization? In their minds, are men seeing themselves when they hear wolves in the night? Hear the rush and snarling and snapping as they rip at throat and tendon? Are they seeing men of one uniform facing those of another, each with cannon and musket to kill? Listening to the wolves, are they seeing themselves?

Who knows? The only thing the men and women of the sprawling Continental Army camp knew was that they listened until the voices stopped because they were unable to do otherwise.

In the quiet that followed, Caleb turned on his side, away from the north, and closed his eyes. He let his muscles go slack while his mind reached for a warm, dark, quiet place. He was brought back from the comfort by a whisper from behind.

"It's me, O'Malley. Cap'n Venables says you can get your paper back in the morning. Might want to see you."

Caleb rolled toward the sergeant. "You hear the wolves?" the boy asked.

"Yes."

"Makes you think."

"Wolves always do."

Caleb drew a deep breath before he continued. "A lot of the men were surly today when there were no British. Why?"

O'Malley arranged his thoughts before he answered. "The Almighty put it in a man to want to live. In the end, maybe that's the strongest thing men feel. Maybe that's what makes men want children. So something of them can live after they're gone. I don't know. But I do know that it's hard for a man to get ready to kill another man, and it's worse to get ready to die. When a man's gone through that misery and then finds out there won't be a battle, he'll complain. It's normal. Don't worry about it as long as they're complainin'. The time to start worryin' is when they quit and just get quiet. That usually means they're plannin' to run."

Caleb remained silent in the darkness.

O'Malley finished. "I'll bring that paper in the mornin'."

Caleb watched the dark shape disappear in the darkness before he turned on his side and curled his arm under his head. He did not remember drifting to sleep.

Sometime in the night a faint vibration of the ground reached him through his blanket, and his sleep-fogged brain identified the sounds of saddle leather creaking and shod horse hooves hitting the ground somewhere to the west, closer to the Delaware. That small, quiet, vigilant voice that never sleeps whispered to his mind, *It is all right—you need not awaken.* He sighed, shifted set muscles, and slept on.

Half a mile to the west, General Nathanael Greene swung down from his weary mount. For a moment he stood on stiff legs, hands on his hips, seeking to ease muscles cramped from fifteen hours in the saddle. The three officers with him also dismounted and handed the reins of their spent horses to waiting soldiers, then walked the ten feet to the pickets standing on either side of the entrance to General Washington's tent. The pickets drew the tent flaps aside and held them.

"The general's waiting."

In the pale yellow lantern light that cast huge, misshapen shadows, Washington seemed to tower larger than life, standing behind his desk, his tired face showing the crushing weight of ultimate command.

Greene and those with him came to full attention and saluted. Washington returned it as he spoke.

"Report."

"We went as far as the outskirts of Philadelphia. I personally talked to some of the officers in the Pennsylvania militia." He shook his head in bewilderment. "No one has seen the fleet, or any sign of Howe, or his command. Nothing."

Washington started. "Nothing? Have they heard anything reliable?"

Again Greene shook his head. "Only what we already knew. Howe sailed out of New York into the Atlantic and hasn't been seen since. They thought he was on his way to Philadelphia, just as we did, and did what they could to get ready. But so far, not a word of his coming."

The air went out of Washington, and his shoulders sagged for a moment. "Is it possible he put his troops ashore at the mouth of the river and is marching them to Philadelphia?"

"No. I asked about that. It would be impossible to put fifteen thousand troops with three thousand horses and cannon ashore and march them up the banks of the Delaware without half the populace knowing it. No one has seen such a thing. Howe is simply not on the Delaware, nor anywhere near it, or Philadelphia."

"Then where?" Washington demanded.

Greene tossed a hand in the air. "Who knows? Maybe on the way down to Charleston. Maybe his sailing into the Atlantic was only a feint. Maybe he intended to draw us back here so he could turn around and sail back to New York and up the Hudson to meet Burgoyne."

Washington dropped a large hand on the tabletop. "I was afraid of that." He straightened, squared his shoulders, and continued. "Return to your commands and get some food and rest. Make a written report. I'll wait for General Cadwalader. He should be—"

He stopped at the sound of incoming horses and waited as they halted just outside his tent. The pickets spoke and drew back the tent flaps to let General John Cadwalader enter, followed by his three officers. They nodded to General Greene, straightened, saluted General Washington, and waited.

"Report."

"We moved north nearly to Coryell's Ferry. There was no sign of Howe or his ships or his army. We talked to militia officers up there. They knew Howe had sailed out of New York into the Atlantic and had thought he was coming to Philadelphia. But no one has seen or heard a thing."

Bewilderment showed plainly in Washington's face. "General Greene proposes that going into the Atlantic might have been a feint to draw us down here while he goes north to meet Burgoyne. Was there any indication that might be true?"

Cadwalader lowered his face for a moment in thought. "Maybe. But I doubt it. If he did that he'd have to get past General Sullivan up in the highland passes above New York, and I think Sullivan would have sent a message before now. I don't think Howe intends going up the Hudson."

Washington shook his head. "Then what does he have in mind? Those men and animals have been aboard the ships in this heat since July ninth. Twenty days today. It's been six days since they disappeared into the Atlantic. Common sense says he should have done something by now that would show his objective. Burgoyne, or Philadelphia, or some other place. Do any of you have an answer to this?"

Agonizing bewilderment showed in the face of every man. For several seconds they talked among themselves, then shrugged and turned back to Washington, unable to offer any plausible answer.

Washington lowered his eyes for a moment before he spoke. "All right. Return to your commands. I will send for you tomorrow morning for a war council. That's all for now. You are dismissed."

Washington remained standing to watch the officers file out and listened to the creak of saddles as they mounted. The sound of the horses' hooves in the night had faded before he sat down at the small worktable in the center of the tent. In the stillness with the light of the single lamp before him, he placed his palms flat on the table and stared unseeing at the backs of his hands. By force of iron will he drove the fatigue from his mind and once again sought to explain the puzzling, erratic movements of General Howe and his colossal armada.

He must have a plan. He would never prepare as he has, unless he has a major objective. More than fifteen thousand regulars—food—munitions—horses—enough to mount a major assault—onboard ships for three weeks. He could have been up the Hudson to Burgoyne, or the Delaware to Philadelphia, ten days ago if that was what he intended. But the lot of them disappeared into the Atlantic six days ago and haven't been seen since. He's wasting men and food and horses every day. Where's the sense to it? How do I meet him if he can't be found? What do I tell the war council in the morning?

It was nearing two o'clock in the black of night before the general drew and released a great breath of frustration. The lamplight etched deep furrows in his forehead as he cupped his hand around the chimney to blow out the light. He hung his tunic over the back of his chair, unbuckled his spurs, worked to pull his boots off, and lay down on the cot in the corner of his tent in his stocking feet. It was half an hour before his mind would let go of the enigmatic question that had to be answered before he could take decisive action.

He was back on his feet before the drummer banged out reveille and the jumbled camp of the Continental Army began to stir. He bent over the porcelain basin on the washstand in the corner of his tent to wash himself and shave, changed his shirt, and sat down to his breakfast of hot chocolate, fried ham and eggs, and brown bread. Finished, he rose and called for his aide.

"Colonel Laurens, notify Generals Greene and Cadwalader and their officers to be here for a council at eight o'clock. They're expecting it. And arrange chairs for eight at the table."

Twenty minutes later he raised his head to the sound of incoming horses, and the morning picket pulled aside the tent flap. "Sir, Generals Greene and Cadwalader and their staffs are here."

Washington stood. "Show them in."

They entered without a word, eyes not leaving Washington as they searched for any indication of his thoughts.

"Be seated." He gestured, and they took their places in the crowded tent, waiting.

His face was set, his eyes noncommittal. "No news has arrived since our discussion last night. I do not know where General Howe has gone with his army, nor do I know his eventual objective, be it the Hudson, Philadelphia, or some other place."

The officers shook their heads, and for a moment there was talk between them. It stilled when Washington continued.

"This is July thirtieth. We are deep into the summer campaign. I am unable to understand why General Howe has wasted so much time when it is obvious he must engage us and try to destroy our army. The only thing I have concluded is that it would be a mistake to take up our march again without some reasonable expectation of intercepting him. At present we lack not only a reasonable expectation, but any expectation at all. Consequently, I believe it would be best to remain where we are, encamped here on the New Jersey side of the Delaware. Should Howe appear on the Hudson going north, we will be able to march immediately without crossing the Delaware. Should he come up the Delaware toward Philadelphia, we will have enough warning to cross the river and move down to meet him. Is there any discussion?"

Open talk went on for two minutes before Washington raised a hand, and it stopped. "Do you have any proposals to make?"

There were none.

Washington nodded. "Then we remain here until further notice. Keep your patrols out. Report anything that might suggest where the British are. Dismissed."

With the sound of their horses fading, he sat down at the table, eyes narrowed, forehead creased in deepening bewilderment. He unrolled a map of the New England coast, anchored the corners with leather bags of sand, and traced the Atlantic shoreline with a long finger.

Here in New York Harbor three weeks ago—then seven days ago into the Atlantic—and disappeared.

He shook his head. *At sea with fifteen thousand men and three thousand horses, in this heat? Is he insane? He could have made Albany ten days ago, or Philadelphia. Where is he? What's his plan? With a force that size he has no reason to hide from us. To the contrary, it is I who must play the game of hide and wait for the right time and place. Then why is he hesitating? Why?*

He dug a thumb and forefinger into weary eyes, then looked once again at the map before he raised his head and looked to the southeast, as though he could see through the canvas wall of his tent, down the Delaware to Philadelphia, and beyond, to the place where the river broadens to empty into the great Delaware Bay, and on to the mighty Atlantic Ocean.

Is he down there? Or New York and the Hudson? Or moving down the Virginia Capes toward Charleston? Or some other place? Where? Where?

★　★　★　★　★

Far to the southeast, riding the Atlantic sea swells rolling toward Delaware Bay, Captain Sir Andrew Snape Hamond, commander of a small British squadron of patrol ships stationed nearby, and captain of the *Roebuck*, stood grasping the starboard railing in tense silence while he identified all the water traffic on the broad expanse of the bay. Seagoing ships, pilot boats, barges, freighters, ferries—all that moved—fell under his eye. Again and again he brought his gaze back to the place where the bay meets the great Atlantic Ocean, searching for a forest of masts cutting the line where the blue sky and the green-black ocean meet. His square-rigged, blunt-nosed ship had all canvas unfurled, bulging in the wind, and it left a long, foaming wake as it plowed on southeast, dividing the bay in halves.

Hamond involuntarily started at the excited call from the crow's nest, seventy feet up the mainmast. "Ships to starboard! At anchor just inside the south bay shore!"

Hamond fumbled for his telescope as he shouted back, "How many?"

"More than two hundred, sir."

"What flag?"

"Ours, sir."

Hamond extended his telescope and leaned forward, silently glassing the distant shore of the bay, searching for the great gathering of ships lying at anchor, loaded heavy and riding deep, all sails furled, masts and arms undulating in the swells. Suddenly he pointed and exclaimed, "There they are! That's what we've been waiting for—Admiral Howe's armada. They came in the night, or somehow got into the bay unnoticed." He jammed the telescope closed and drew his watch from his tunic pocket. Twenty minutes past nine o'clock. He raised his arm to point and barked orders to his first mate.

"Set a course for those ships. Admiral Howe's flagship is the *Eagle*. As soon as you identify it, bring us alongside. I'm going aboard."

The first mate cupped his hands to shout the orders to the helmsman, and the *Roebuck* slowly turned south, plowing a furrow in the waters of Delaware Bay as it came quartering south across the southwest wind. Twenty minutes passed before the first mate jerked his arm up, pointing excitedly. "There! The *Eagle*." He turned to the helmsman, still pointing. "Put us on the starboard side of that ship. Captain wants to go aboard her. And be careful. Admiral Lord Richard Howe is aboard and is commander of the entire armada. And likely his brother General William Howe is also quartered there."

The helmsman swallowed hard, spun the great spoked wheel, and the *Roebuck* corrected course to come in on the leeward side of the *Eagle*, away from the wind. Every sailor on the *Roebuck* was on deck, staring in fascination at the greatest gathering of warships they had ever seen.

The first mate turned to the bosun. "Get men into the rigging to spill the wind on command. We're going to drop anchor on the leeward side of the *Eagle*, close enough for the captain to go aboard."

"Yes, sir."

The bosun barked orders, and sailors scrambled up the ropes and onto the arms, where they grasped the lines that would have to be released the moment the order was given, spilling the wind from the sails. They waited and watched as the helmsman skillfully made the last of the small needed corrections. The ship straightened and approached parallel to and twenty feet from the hull of the larger ship. From habit, every sailor counted the closed cannon ports on the two decks of the gunship. Eighteen on the top deck, fifteen on the second deck. Thirty-three heavy cannon on the starboard side; sixty-six guns on the *Eagle*. Members of the *Roebuck* crew glanced at each other for a moment, awed by the firepower. The *Roebuck* had only thirteen guns on each side, twenty-six lighter cannon in all.

Captain Hamond cupped his hands to shout, "Hallo, the *Eagle!* Captain Andrew Hamond requesting permission to come aboard."

The call came back, "What is your authority and for what purpose do you request permission to come aboard?"

"I am commander of the Delaware Bay Squadron and captain of the *Roebuck*. The purpose of my request is to inform General William Howe of critical information regarding Delaware Bay and the river."

There was a long pause. "Permission granted. Come alongside. You and one officer of your choice will board the *Eagle*."

The bosun shouted orders up to his crew in the rigging. Instantly they jerked knots loose, and the sails were released to spill their wind and flap free while the sailors on the arms worked frantically to pull in and fold the canvas, then lash it to the arms. The ship slowed and stopped, dead in the water, parallel to the *Eagle*, top deck eight feet lower than that of the larger ship. The helmsman rounded his mouth to blow air, and his shoulders settled in relief.

Half a mile northwest a small pilot boat flying American colors was cutting a wake southeast when suddenly she dumped her mainsail and slowed in the water. On deck her captain walked to the starboard rail, raised his telescope, and for a long time studied the stern of the *Roebuck* as it moved away from him, then raised the telescope to glass the south shore of the bay. His eyes widened and his breathing quickened as he was able to distinguish the masts of the British fleet from the trees and shoreline beyond, and then the flags fluttering in the morning wind. Slowly he lowered the telescope to stare, then once again raised it to count. He counted fifty, estimated the balance, turned, and gave orders. The helmsman swung the wheel to bring the bow of the small craft on a bearing of nearly due south.

Once again the captain studied the ships on the shoreline and watched the *Roebuck* align with the *Eagle*, spill her sails, and stop dead in the water twenty feet from the larger man-o-war, starboard to starboard. He pondered a moment, then once again gave orders. The helmsman spun the wheel to bring the craft full around, moving slowly back to the northwest on the zig-zag course as she tacked into the wind, moving in the direction from which she had just come.

On the *Eagle*, twenty sailors lined the rail, armed with muskets at the ready, remaining silent as they watched every move on the *Roebuck*. The bosun gave orders, and his crew hurled ropes across the twenty feet of water. The crew of the *Eagle* caught them and secured them on either side of the section of rail that was cut and hinged for boarding the ship. Captain Hamond took his place in the wooden bosun's chair, the first mate closed the buckles on the tie-down straps, and two men on the *Eagle* began the rhythmic, steady pulling of the rope that drew the chair across the gap on the lines and pulleys, while two men on the *Roebuck* held a slight tension on their rope to maintain control as the chair moved to the opening in the rail. The empty chair was returned, and the first mate followed Captain Hamond to the deck of the *Eagle*.

An officer came to attention and saluted. "I am First Mate Samuel Whitcomb of the *Eagle*."

Hamond returned the salute. "I am Captain Andrew Hamond of the *Roebuck*. This is my first mate, Derwin Kiley."

Whitcomb bowed. "I am ordered to request you wait. General Howe will see you shortly."

Hamond started. "Is he indisposed? I can return at a more convenient time."

Whitcomb dropped his eyes for a moment while he fumbled for a reply. "The general is well, sir. He was . . . uh . . . not expecting such a visit."

The facade was transparent, the message clear. Captain Hamond had caught General William Howe in bed at ten o'clock in the morning, while the entire armada and fifteen thousand soldiers waited in the sweltering heat of July thirtieth! In red-faced mortification, Hamond opened his mouth to speak, searched for words that would not come, and finally blurted, "I shall return to my ship until a more opportune moment."

Whitcomb shook his head. "That will not be necessary. I have orders to invite you to my quarters while we wait."

Hamond stammered, "I would rather remain on deck."

"As you wish, sir."

Hamond clasped his hands behind his back, glanced at the blank faces of the embarrassed sailors and officers of the *Eagle*, and turned to peer back at the crew of his own ship, riding the swells twenty feet away. His men stood stock-still, foreheads wrinkled in puzzlement as to why their captain had not been escorted to the quarters of General Howe. With no way to tell them the unbelievable truth, Hamond could only stare back at them while the color rose ever deeper in his face.

Within minutes that seemed hours Whitcomb cleared his throat. "The general will see you now, sir."

Hamond drew a handkerchief from his pocket and wiped at nervous sweat as he followed Whitcomb toward the stern of the ship. Whitcomb opened the ornamented door and held it while Hamond, followed by his first mate, entered the richly appointed cabin. The only source of light was a bank of paned windows at the far end of the small room, and Hamond blinked for a moment while his eyes began to adjust from the glare of the bright July sun. General William Howe rose from behind a worktable while Hamond and Kiley both came to attention and saluted. Whitcomb stood to one side, out of the way, silently watching and listening.

"Captain Andrew Hamond of the *Roebuck*, sir. May I present my first mate, Derwin Kiley."

With an expression that was casual, nearly bored, Howe returned a spiritless salute and gestured. "Be seated."

Hamond and Kiley sat opposite Howe, and Hamond sought to quell the shock he experienced as his eyes adjusted to the detail inside the cramped quarters. General William Howe, commander of all British forces in the thirteen United States, had not washed, nor shaved. His shirt was open at the throat, and his tunic was tossed carelessly on the foot of his bed. One could not miss the sour stench of liquor, nor fail to see the evidence of last night's drinking in the face and the bloodshot, bleary eyes of Howe.

Hamond straightened, thrust out his chin, brushed aside his shock at the breach of military deportment that hung in the room like a pall, and launched into his message.

"Sir, may I presume your intention is to proceed up the Delaware River?"

Howe bobbed his head once, then reached for a cut-crystal decanter of wine sitting on a silver tray. He poured, then pushed the tray toward Hamond and Kiley. Hamond ignored it while Howe drained his goblet.

Hamond cleared his throat and continued. "Then it is part of my assigned duties to report to you that to do so with the ships in this armada would be extremely dangerous, perhaps impossible."

Howe's eyes narrowed, and he tossed a hand in the air, silently bidding Hamond to continue.

"The channels for deep-sea ships are intricate. It will require a seasoned pilot to navigate each of these ships through, and it can be done only when the tides are favorable. If it can be done at all, it will take weeks."

Howe leaned forward on his elbows and spoke to Whitcomb. "Get Admiral Howe."

"Yes, sir."

Whitcomb reappeared in three minutes followed by Admiral Lord Richard Howe. Tall, clearly the brother of William Howe, Richard entered the small room, looked at William for an explanation that did not come, and turned to face Hamond and Kiley, who were standing at attention.

William spoke. "Admiral, this is Captain Hamond and his first mate, Mr. Kiley."

The two lesser officers saluted, Richard returned it and turned back to William, waiting.

"Captain Hamond's squadron patrols the bay. He is here to make a report you should hear." William turned back to Hamond and gestured for him to continue.

"Admiral, the river channels deep enough for these heavy ships are intricate. It would be catastrophic to attempt sailing upriver without a pilot to guide each ship. If it can be done at all, it will have to be when the tides are exactly right; otherwise the ships will run aground."

Richard reached to tug at his chin thoughtfully. "Go on."

"The closest place to Philadelphia where troops and cannon and horses can be unloaded is between Reedy Island and Chester, fifteen miles below the city. At that place it will take four miles of anchorage for this armada."

Hamond paused and leaned slightly forward to emphasize his next statement.

"And the ships will be within range of American shore cannon the entire four miles."

Concern was growing in Richard's face. "Anything else?"

"Yes. The place you will have to unload is laced with marshes and creeks. Getting horses and cannon ashore will be difficult at best."

Hamond stopped. Richard pursed his mouth for a moment, then gestured. "Is there more?"

"The American fleet is much lighter and can maneuver freely any place on the river. In short, the Americans can position themselves to bombard this armada without fear of return fire. And there are obstructions sunk in the river, and chains, that will hull these heavier ships should they run onto them."

"How many gunboats do the Americans have available here?"

Hamond shook his head. "Many, and more coming in daily."

"Why haven't our lookouts seen them?"

"They hide in the creeks and marshes, sir. Unless you know where to look, they're hardly visible from the bay."

For a few seconds Richard stared hard at Hamond, then turned to William. A silent communication passed between the two brothers before William spoke to Hamond.

"Is there anything else, Captain?"

Hamond reflected for a moment. "No, sir. I felt it my duty to make this report." Hamond's chin was high, spine straight. His face bore the expression of one who had done his duty and was now waiting for his reward.

Howe nodded and spoke in a mechanical monotone. "Thank you. You are dismissed."

The abruptness startled Hamond. The usual courtesies that protocol required between officers in His Majesty's Royal Navy were brutally lacking. No suggestion of a written commendation for his work? No invitation to stay and dine with the famous Howe brothers? Not even the expected query, "Is there anything you need that is within our power to give?"

None of it! Only a hollow "Thank you! You are dismissed!"

Numbed by the abrupt end to his only meeting with the Howe brothers, Hamond could find nothing more to say. He glanced at Kiley, stood, did an about face, and marched out the door into the sweltering, humid heat. Within five minutes he was back on the deck of the *Roebuck*. Ten minutes later her sails billowed full, and she drew away from the *Eagle*, turned to port, and made her way through the northern fringes of the armada, back into the open waters of Delaware Bay.

Aboard the *Eagle*, alone in the quarters of General William Howe, the brothers faced each other. Richard dropped onto an upholstered chair facing his brother and spoke quietly.

"Do you believe him?"

William tossed a frustrated hand upward and let it drop. "He's a British commander. Captain of a ship. He knows Delaware Bay and the river. I see no reason he shouldn't be trusted."

Richard leaned forward, elbows on his knees, and began to rub his palms together as though it helped him think. "Neither do I." Seconds passed while he formed his thoughts and words. "Even if only half of what he said is true, it's enough to turn a foray up the Delaware into a disaster. One ship run aground in a narrow channel, or with a hull ripped open on a sunken chain or logs could stop the entire armada for days. If our anchorage would be four miles long, Yankee cannon on both sides of the river could cut us to pieces, and we would have nearly no way to stop it because we would be unable to move, while they could."

After pausing for a moment, he continued. "If we tried to put our men ashore, their boats would be raked by both solid shot and grapeshot. Horses and artillery the same. I don't know how many would make it all the way, but we have to presume the worst. We could lose half our force on the water, before they set foot on land."

He stood suddenly, decisively, voice firm, loud. "The ships are mine, the army yours. We're here to deliver you. If you decide it's worth it to go on up the Delaware, we can be under way within three hours. If not, we can carry you farther south to the Chesapeake and back up to the place where the Elk River empties into the bay—Head of Elk. We can put you ashore there. It'll take about ten more days but will likely save thousands of men. From there it's about fifty-seven miles overland to Philadelphia. The decision is yours."

The two brothers stared into each other's eyes in a room charged with a terrible intensity. Richard waited in silence. William did not move a muscle for a full fifteen seconds as he reckoned his choices. In his mind he was seeing General Abercrombie years ago, shouting orders to his infantry to take Fort Ticonderoga, knowing all too well the fatal imbalance: the fort was bristling with French cannon, while the British had none. Thousands of good British regulars rose from their trenches with their muskets and without cannon marched toward the thick, towering stone walls, and there they died, row upon row, bodies on top of bodies. He was seeing his own command at Breeds Hill and Bunker Hill just fourteen months earlier, when General Thomas Gage gave him the order to teach the rebels a lesson. Three times Howe marched his men up the hill while Yankee gunners at the top continued to stack up the bodies with grapeshot and those terrible Pennsylvania long rifles. He took the hill, but only because the Americans had run out of ammunition. When he stopped at the top to look back at the thousands of crimson coats of his men lying face down on the slope in the June grass, he had sworn he would never again pay such a price for a hill. Whatever his weaknesses, whatever his shortcomings, William Howe held his men in supreme regard. There was no city nor state, no glory nor honor, that would justify ordering them into needless slaughter.

He spoke abruptly. "We go up the Chesapeake to Head of Elk."

A light came into Richard's eyes, and he stepped out the door onto the deck of the *Eagle*, calling for his second in command. He paid no attention to the track of white water churned by the *Roebuck* as it moved north, away from the *Eagle* and from the great fleet of British ships.

Captain Andrew Snape Hamond stood for a long time on the quarterdeck at the stern of his ship, staring back at the armada growing smaller in the wake, struggling with emotions that alternated between confusion, anger, elation, and amazement over the meeting just ended with the Howe brothers. He had expected something glorious. What he had gotten was something vulgar.

He clasped his hands behind his back, shook his head at the remembrance, and continued staring. He did not see the small pilot boat under the American flag off the port bow of the *Roebuck*, tacking into the wind, moving into the northbound channels of Delaware Bay without a seagoing ship following. A pilot boat piloting nothing. A suspicious thing in this time of war, with two hundred sixty British military ships riding at anchor in the bay.

The little boat continued her course, tacking zig-zag against the current as she worked her way slowly up the Delaware. In the late afternoon the wind shifted to the south, the sails caught full, and the bow of the boat cut a four-foot curl as she sped northerly. In the early evening the captain glassed Newcastle on the west side of the river, and an hour later, Wilmington, in the distance, where the Brandywine Creek emptied into the Delaware. In the glow of sunset the small vessel passed Chester on the port side, then the Red Bank Redoubt with her cannon on the starboard, just past the place where the Schuylkill River joined the Delaware. In full darkness the captain stood at the port rail to watch the lights of Philadelphia slip past on the port side, with Germantown out of sight not many miles to the west. He positioned himself at the bow of his small boat to call orders to his helmsman as he moved beyond Philadelphia, to where the river narrowed and navigation became a matter of knowing the sandbars and the snags and the tricky channels. At four o'clock in the morning he sighted the few lights of the village of Trenton off the starboard and called orders.

The boat took a heading toward the New Jersey shore, to drop anchor and run a small blue flag up the mainmast. With the first colors of dawn showing purple and rose in the east, the captain retired to his tiny quarters, where he labored for ten minutes over a brief written message, read it, reread it, then folded and sealed it with wax. He had a rowboat lowered into the water and, with a crewman at the oars, made for shore. They beached the boat and waited in the light of a sun not yet risen, watching for movement in the forest that lined the shore. Two minutes passed before a man in dark clothing came trotting. He stopped at the boat only long enough to take the sealed note, then grasp the bow of the rowboat, throw his weight against it, and drive it back into the water. He watched the oars dig in, the boat turn and move toward the pilot boat. Then he splashed back to shore and disappeared into the trees. On board the pilot boat, the crew lowered the blue flag that fluttered in the morning breeze and threw lines to the rowboat bringing their captain.

Two hours later, farther north, up the river, the soldiers of the Continental Army camp who were cleaning their pots and pans after morning mess raised their heads at the sound of a running horse and watched a mounted rider gallop a lathered gelding to the tent of General Washington, rein it to a sliding stop, and hit the ground at a trot. The pickets at the tent flap challenged, and he handed the nearest one the sealed writing, then went back to loosen the saddle girth on his winded horse while he waited. He straightened in surprise when the picket pushed aside the tent flap and emerged, followed by Lieutenant Colonel John Laurens, Washington's aide. Laurens walked directly to him.

"The general has read and understands the message. He has no reply. He has authorized you to grain and care for your horse with the officers' mounts and take breakfast at the officers' mess. You can rest in the officers' quarters if you wish. If you'll come with me, I'll show you."

Laurens led the way east two hundred yards to the rope enclosure that held the officers' mounts. A dozen soldiers milled about, working the horses with large, stiff-bristled curry brushes, checking feet and ankles, rationing oats from a large wheelbarrow. Laurens spoke to the lieutenant in charge.

"Give this man whatever he needs for his horse. When he finishes, show him to the officers' mess and quarters for food and rest if he wishes."

"Yes, sir."

Laurens turned back to the man. "Should you need anything else, send word."

"Tell the general I will give his message to the pilot. I thank him for his courtesies." The messenger followed the lieutenant to the north, toward the tent that housed the horse fodder and four tons of oats in barrels. Laurens watched him, a tired man leading a tired mount, knowing he would care for his horse before allowing himself to eat and sleep.

Laurens turned to the sergeant in charge of tack. "Have my horse saddled at once."

Minutes later Laurens swung onto his own sorrel mare, tapped spur, and loped off to the north to rein in at the tent of General Nathanael Greene. Inside he delivered his message in one sentence.

"General Washington requests you be in his tent immediately."

Greene's eyes widened. "I'll be there."

Laurens reined in once more at the tent of General John Cadwalader and delivered the same terse message.

Ten minutes later both generals were standing at attention, facing Washington across his worktable. The light in his eyes and the animation in his face held them in expectant silence, aware something significant had happened. Washington wasted no time.

"I have just received information from a river pilot who lives in a small Delaware town named Lewes. He shall remain nameless. Yesterday morning at ten o'clock he personally observed about two hundred fifty or sixty British ships with sails furled, loaded heavily, and lying at anchor on the south shore of Delaware Bay. A Captain Hamond commands a small squadron of British ships that patrols the bay, and his ship named the *Roebuck* visited the *Eagle*, which is the flagship of the British armada."

Both Greene and Cadwalader slowly exhaled as the news sank in.

Howe!

Washington leaned forward, his eyes points of light. "We've found them." He straightened. "The message states there is no question General Howe intends coming up the Delaware to take Philadelphia. Congress believes it is imperative that we stop him if we can. So I believe we have no choice but to cross the river and proceed down to engage him. Do you have any suggestions?"

Greene felt the rise of excitement in his chest as he glanced at Cadwalader, then back at Washington. "Did he see them unloading?"

"The message did not say."

"Do we have defenses in place? Cannon on the riverbanks? Obstructions in the water?"

"Very few cannon and no obstructions in the water. Not enough of either to even slow them down." Washington paused for a moment while he weighed the advisability of revealing what had, until that moment, been held secret. He made his decision and continued. "I have had people in key places quietly spreading the rumor that we have hidden cannon all the way up both banks of the Delaware and have underwater chains and logs in the channels. If those rumors have reached General Howe, he has apparently disregarded them, or has intelligence that they are only rumors. Either way, it now appears certain he is coming up the river. If he has some other destination in mind I do not think he would be foolish enough to waste more time simply anchored in Delaware Bay."

Cadwalader's mind leaped ahead. "It'll take two days to move our men and supplies across the river. Then six or seven more to march them down and take up defensive positions around Philadelphia and throw up breastworks. It will be a close thing as to whether we can do it before Howe arrives."

"I plan to give orders immediately to begin the crossing. Do you concur?"

"Yes."

"Prepare your men. I'll have written orders delivered to all the officers within the hour. We start crossing by noon."

Far to the south, in bright morning sunlight, the small pilot craft sped steadily back down the Delaware, sails full and masts creaking as she ran with the wind and the current. The small craft skimmed past Philadelphia, then Chester, and on toward Wilmington and Newcastle. The captain spoke to his first mate, then the helmsman, then descended the narrow passage into his tiny quarters. Bone weary from twenty-eight intense hours on deck, he pulled off his shoes and lay down fully dressed on the small cot against one wall. Within minutes he was breathing slowly in deep, dreamless, exhausted sleep.

The excited voice and the rough hand shaking his shoulder brought his slumbering mind back to the world, and he opened his eyes, trying to remember where he was. He stared up into the face of his first mate, who was shaking his shoulder with one hand, pointing south with the other as he exclaimed, "Captain, they're gone! The whole British fleet! Gone!"

The captain swung his legs off the cot and sat up, groping to understand. What British fleet? Gone where? His brain was still fogged with sleep when it struck. He lunged from his cot, swept his telescope from the table, leaped up the four stairs and out onto the starboard deck, head thrust forward as his eyes swept the south shore of Delaware Bay.

There was not a mast nor a British flag in sight. Staggered, he jerked his telescope to full length and held it to his eye to quickly scan the south shoreline from the Atlantic to a point ten miles inland. The usual small vessels of river freight and traffic moved about, but the tremendous armada had vanished, as though plucked from the earth by some mighty hand from the heavens. He pivoted to glass north, but there was no sign of the British warships.

Reeling in disbelief, he stared at his first mate. "Where? Did we pass them coming downriver?"

"No, sir. We did not pass a single British warship going either direction between here and Trenton. They've gone back to sea! They're in the Atlantic somewhere!"

The blood drained from the captain's face as he realized the horrendous tactical blunder he had innocently set in motion at the Continental Army camp on the banks of the Delaware north of Trenton. For a moment he stood in shocked silence, then blurted, "General Washington! The Continentals! They're crossing the Delaware to meet Howe at Philadelphia." Instantly he ran to the stern shouting to his helmsman, "Turn her about! Turn her about! Back to Trenton!"

The startled helmsman spun the wheel, and the pilot boat leaned to starboard as she turned hard to port, slowing as she came around and straightened. The first mate barked orders, and the small crew began the tricky task of handling the sails as the helmsman began the slow, zig-zag course of tacking into the crosswind and against the current.

Time lost meaning for the captain as the boat crept up the river. He walked the deck with telescope in hand, searching every cove, every inlet, for any sign of heavy British ships, but there was none. In the late afternoon, clouds covered the sun, and a warm, heavy summer rain fell until midnight. The crew took four-hour shifts, eating and sleeping, then taking their rotation on the sails and lookout. At two o'clock in the morning the captain went to his cramped quarters to sleep until five o'clock, when once again he was on deck, pacing, still searching in dawn's first light for any sign of the British armada. They labored past the Red Bank Redoubt, the Schuylkill River, then Philadelphia, through the normal bustle of river traffic that was unimpeded by any sign of British men-o-war.

Twenty-four miles above Philadelphia the lookout on top of the cabin sang out, "There, sir, port side, American soldiers on shore!" Instantly the captain was at the bow railing, telescope extended, holding his breath as he glassed the northwest bank of the river. They were gathered there, under the stars and stripes, men, cannon, horses, and wagons, preparing to march southwest toward Philadelphia.

The captain called to the helmsman, "Hard to port," then turned to the first mate. "Bring her to within one hundred yards of shore and drop anchor. Launch the lifeboat and wait." He trotted to the deck door down to his quarters and disappeared. Ten minutes later he burst back through the door onto the deck just as the lifeboat touched into the brown waters of the Delaware. The first mate straightened as the captain thrust a paper to him, sealed with wax.

"I am not to be seen contacting any American military, so you'll have to take that to General Washington. In his hands only. Do you understand?"

"Yes, sir!"

"Take one man to row the boat and get ashore as fast as you can. Insist that you deliver that to General Washington yourself. Then return and report."

One hour later Lieutenant Colonel John Laurens was observing the confusion of an army that had spent nearly two days crossing the Delaware River and was now trying to assemble itself into a marching column. He cast a puzzled glance on a knot of agitated men who were making their way in the massive jumble of men and equipment. He reined in his horse and waited as they approached and stopped.

An American wearing the epaulets of a captain on his shoulders looked up apologetically at Laurens.

"Sir, this civilian insists he has a message for Gen'l Washington personally. No one else."

For a moment Laurens studied the first mate. "Who are you?"

"First mate on a pilot boat."

"What boat?"

"I can't give her name, sir."

"Who's the captain?"

"I can't give that name, either, sir."

"Show me the message."

The man raised his hand defensively. "I can't, sir. Only General Washington."

"I'm Colonel John Laurens, a personal aide to General Washington. I'll deliver it to him."

"Sorry, sir. My orders is firm. I'm to deliver it myself."

It flashed in Lauren's mind—the sealed message of two days ago—and now one that appeared identical.

"Very well. Follow me."

Laurens reined his horse around and held it to a walk as the first mate hurried along behind on foot. They threaded their way through the bustle of men two hundred yards, then Laurens stood tall in the stirrups to search. He reined the horse to his right and pulled it to a stop, watching as three mounted riders approached at a lope. The first mate stopped beside him, eyes narrowed as he studied the incoming riders, and suddenly his mouth dropped open.

The man in the lead was tall, square-shouldered, riding a blooded gray mare. His uniform showed the wrinkles and stains of having been worn constantly for the past thirty-six hours, but he wore it with an aura of dignity. He sat his tall horse easily, his back ramrod straight, his boots in the stirrups, slightly ahead of the saddle girth, toes up and pointed a little outward. He rode the rise and fall of the loping horse as though the two were one and was without question the finest horseman the first mate had ever seen. As the lead rider approached Laurens, his eyes dropped to the first mate, and he came back gently on the reins, bringing the horse to an easy stop. The first mate clacked his mouth shut as he looked for the first time in his life into the face of General George Washington.

A black tricorn sat squarely on the general's head. The prominent nose and firm chin did not flex nor move as the general made an instant appraisal of the man, his pale blue eyes seeming to reach into and through the sweating messenger. Then he turned to look at Laurens, waiting.

"Sir, this man has a written message that he insists he must deliver to you personally."

The voice was soft, but it reached deep. "May I see it?"

Without a word the first mate extended his hand and Washington took the folded, sealed paper. Instantly he recognized what it was, broke the seal, and scanned the handwriting. Without a change in his expression he refolded it and worked it inside his tunic, then spoke.

"Do you need anything? Food? Rest?" There was a strange tenderness in those pale blue eyes.

"No, sir. I'm under orders to report back to my captain as fast as I can."

"I understand. Give him my regards."

"Yes, sir. I'll do that, sir."

The man stood as though rooted to the ground, still staring up at Washington.

The hint of a smile crossed Washington's face. "You are dismissed."

The first mate blinked as though coming from some far place in his mind. "Uh . . . oh . . . yes, sir. Thank you, sir." He turned and left at a trot, stopping only once to look back at the sight of Washington giving orders to Laurens.

"Colonel, get Generals Greene and Cadwalader as fast as you can. I'll meet them at my tent."

Twenty minutes later a picket pushed back the tent flap. "Sir, Colonel Laurens is here with Generals Greene and Cadwalader."

A minute later the four men were facing each other, three of them waiting for what they knew had to be catastrophic news. Washington wasted no time.

"I have a written message from the same river pilot who reported the British fleet to be anchored in Delaware bay, coming this way. That was two days ago, July thirty-first. This message now informs me . . . let me read it."

He drew the document from his tunic, unfolded it, and read steadily.

"Returned to Delaware Bay July 31 to find all British warships and transports vanished. They are not to be found in Delaware Bay nor any other place on the Delaware River. The fleet has disappeared to the east, out into the Atlantic; whether they are bound for New York or Virginia is not in my power to tell."

Washington's eyes were a mask of disciplined control. Greene, Cadwalader, and Laurens all expelled air as they shook their heads in puzzlement. Greene recovered first.

"Gone? Simply vanished? Two hundred sixty men-o-war? Ridiculous!" he exclaimed. "In the name of heaven, what does General Howe think he's doing?"

Washington shook his head. "I do not know, nor can I conjecture what it means. He has had an entire army with supplies and horses on those boats since July ninth. This is August second. Twenty-four days in the hottest part of the summer. Some of those horses have to be dead and others dying. The men should be near mutiny. If any of you can make sense of it, I'd be most grateful."

Cadwalader asked, "Does the message suggest where he's going? Charleston? Back to the Hudson?"

"Not a word. It's possible that this adventure into Delaware Bay might have been a deep feint to draw us to Philadelphia, so he can reverse himself and go back to New York and up the Hudson in support of Burgoyne. Or, he could be going south to Charleston, although that makes absolutely no sense because Burgoyne, or Philadelphia, are far greater military objectives than Charleston, at least at this time. What he's doing is a profound mystery to me."

Laurens spoke. "Sir, this army is about to march. Do we delay it while we gather further information? Determine the proper direction?"

Washington looked at the two generals. "Any proposals?"

Greene spoke up. "Wait right here until he shows his hand. Without some definite intelligence about the whereabouts of the British fleet and army, we're simply wandering about the country like a band of Arabs. We're wasting what little supplies we have on nothing, and maybe that's exactly what General Howe wants us to do."

Washington looked at Cadwalader, waiting.

"I agree. I say we wait until we know what we're doing. Or more accurately, what he's doing."

Washington pursed his mouth for a moment before answering. "I was about to order a march back to the Hudson because it makes sense that if General Howe isn't going on up the Delaware to take Philadelphia, he is going back to the Hudson to help General Burgoyne." He shook his head. "But the more I think on it, the more convinced I am we should remain right here until we get word that the British have arrived at Sandy Hook. Once we know they're inside New York Harbor, it will be clear that their objective is the Hudson River and reaching General Burgoyne."

He stood for several seconds, head bowed, as he weighed the thing out in his mind. Then he spoke.

"We camp here until further notice."

Notes

On July 29, 1777, General Washington's army arrived at the Delaware River, only to find that the British were nowhere in sight. The gigantic game of cat and mouse between the British and American armies was now in full swing. See Leckie, *George Washington's War*, p. 347.

Caleb becomes involved in making entries in what is called an "orderly book." An example of such a book is *Valley Forge Orderly Book*, see the bibliography.

Captain Sir Andrew Snape Hamond, commander of a small British squadron of ships patrolling the Delaware Bay and River and captain of the ship *Roebuck*, was a real person, and his activities related to discovering General Howe's fleet inside Delaware Bay and the mortal embarrassment of finding General Howe still in bed at ten o'clock A.M. are historically accurate. The information given by Hamond to General Howe regarding the dangers of sailing the British fleet up the Delaware was in great part incorrect and resulted in General Howe putting back out to sea. See Higginbotham, *The War of American Independence*, p. 183.

An American pilot boat stationed in Lewes on the Delaware River observed the British fleet and sailed up the Delaware to warn General Washington, only to return and find the entire British fleet vanished; the same boat immediately reversed course and sailed back up the river to tell Washington. See Leckie, *George Washington's War*, p. 346.

Generals Washington and Greene were utterly baffled at the erratic, non-sensical sailings of the British fleet. Greene commented that the Americans were wandering about like Arabs, trying to find them. Washington decided to stay where he was until he knew where the British intended to land. See Higginbotham, *The War of American Independence*, p. 184; Leckie, *George Washington's War*, p. 347.

Morristown, New Jersey

Early August 1777

CHAPTER V

★ ★ ★

Seated in a battered rocking chair, Mary Flint started, jerked awake, and sat in the darkness, still seeing in her mind a huge gravestone with the name "RUFUS BROADHEAD" carefully carved into the polished marble. She wondered what had awakened her in the half-hour before dawn. She peered into the darkness and listened while the squeak of the rocking chair echoed in the emptiness of the great room of the squat, square log building that had served as the Morristown hospital for the Continental Army.

Seven months before, the sick and the wounded from the battle of Princeton had been brought there. Then, with the greening of spring and General Howe on the move in New Jersey, General Washington had moved the army south to Middlebrook. Command of the hospital was given to Major Leonard Folsom, the only competent medical doctor and surgeon General Washington could spare. Washington's orders were brief: Return as many wounded as possible to active duty and discharge the remainder to return to their homes. The orders were ominously silent regarding those whose wounds prevented either.

For seven months Mary and the doctor, with half a dozen untrained volunteers from the small village of Morristown, had slept in tiny quarters within the hospital, exhausting themselves in mind and body as they met the needs and demands of those in the hospital. Some had healed and were sent to find the marching Continental Army. Some had died, their bodies carried to a great stand of oak and pine south of the hospital to be buried. Others who could never again bear arms were sent back to their homes, where they would learn to live without a foot or a leg or a hand or an arm. They had walked out of the hospital on crude crutches or with a tattered coat sleeve pinned up—penniless, pale, hollow-cheeked, grimly pondering how wives or children or sweethearts would accept a crippled man and wondering how they would survive in a world that finally came to rest on the bone and muscle and sinew of its men and women.

By the last week in July there were only seven men remaining in the hospital, and it was clear none of them would leave alive. Their wounds had gone progressively putrid. Six times since mid-July, Mary had strapped them on a wooden table where the short, corpulent, balding doctor forced whisky into them. He thrust a piece of leather belt between their teeth and while she held them down, screaming, he cut away the dead flesh. For the five who had lost arms or legs, he sawed off infected bone and closed the gaping wounds with needle and silk thread. They could do no more, and in silence they watched the seven men daily drift deeper into a world of pain and hopelessness in which their last thought would be the blessed relief that death would bring.

Then, only a few days before, Doctor Folsom had quietly ordered Mary and his untutored staff to box the surgical equipment and medical supplies, ready to be loaded into the few wagons that had been left for them to use when there were no wounded to hold them longer in Morristown. He ordered that seven graves be dug among the fifty-three already in the grove and that seven simple headboards be provided, bearing only a name and a date of birth. The date of death was left open, waiting.

By the first day of August, five of the seven open graves had been filled and closed. Only two wounded men remained in the hospital, tossing, turning, delirious from fever. Then, within minutes of midnight, five hours before, one of them had stopped mumbling and grown still. In the hush of night Mary and the doctor prepared the body and lowered it into its final resting place, and with only a half-moon and numberless stars as their witnesses, read a passage from the Bible, closed the black grave, filled in the date of death, and set the simple headboard to show the passing of another rebel soldier.

The last of the wounded was a slender boy of seventeen, whose foot had been smashed by a British Brown Bess musketball on January third, as his Pennsylvania regiment followed General George Washington storming from the woods into the face of the redcoats under the command of Colonel Charles Mawhood, south of Princeton. The young soldier's name was Joseph Selman. A surgeon had cut off the mangled foot but could not stop the creeping gangrene that smelled of death. They had cut again, just below the knee, and fifteen days later, above the knee, then at the hip. They did not tell the boy there was no hope of saving him.

It was his mumbling that had wakened her. It came again, then stopped, and Mary settled, waiting, sensing what was coming. In the dark silence she felt the dull ache in her back and her legs and shoulders and the coolness of her dress on her back. It was still damp from the perspiration of twenty hours spent moving everything from the building into the wagons in the wilting heat and humidity of yesterday and the exertion of the haunting, lonely midnight burial a short five hours ago. She yearned for a time and place to sit in cool water while the stiffness left her muscles and her weary mind drained itself of every thought and she could once more feel the luxury of fresh, dry clothing.

"Mother!"

She flinched at the unexpected call, and in an instant was on her knees beside the low cot. The gray of dawn filtered through the four small windows on the east side of the room, and she could see the shape of the boy's pale face. His eyes were open, too wide, and he licked at lips parched from fever.

"Mother?" He raised his head to see her more clearly in the gloom.

"Yes, I'm here, Joseph. I'm here." She slipped an arm behind his shoulders to lift him, cradle his head against her. She felt the raging fever and heard the quick, shallow breathing. She could see his eyes, too wide, too bright. He clutched at Mary, and his voice came too excited, too loud, too high, his words too fast, incoherent, spilling over each other as he stared up at her.

"Mother, my foot was hurt, but it is all right now. The doctor said it is all right—I could come home—so I came—it hurts but you can fix the bandages, and it will be better—it got hurt—a bullet broke the ankle, but the doctor fixed it, and it's all right, and I could come home— where's Father and Jenny? It hurts but you can fix it, Mother—I can hardly see you, Mother. Where are you? There you are—will you fix the bandage so it will quit hurting?"

He stopped speaking, and Mary's heart ached with the sure knowledge of what was now only moments away. She spoke calmly. "I know, son. It will be all right. I'll change the bandage in a few moments, and it will be all right."

He closed his eyes and ran his dry tongue again over fevered lips. "I'll help with the milking when you're through—is Jenny all right? Where's Jenny? Sweet Jenny, she must be thirteen now—thirteen the twelfth of June—will she come talk to me while I do the milking, will she?"

"She's outside now, son, bringing in the cow."

"Matilda? Did she have her calf? She was going to have a calf."

"Yes. A strong little heifer. Just like Matilda."

Joseph smiled weakly. "A heifer calf—more milk later—so good to have milk." Suddenly he sobered. "I can't see Father. Where's Father? Is he out in the grain—is the grain ripe? It's too early for it to ripen—where's Father?"

"In the barn with the calf."

Joseph's clutching hands relaxed, then fell away, and Mary felt the wasted body slump in her arms. His face was turned up to hers, eyes wide. His words slowed, and he spoke with great effort.

"Mother, I can hardly see you. Are you leaving? Mother, don't leave me."

"No, Joseph. I'm here. I'll not leave . . ."

The boy drew a great breath, and his shoulders settled as it left him. A smile crept across his face. Then his head fell back, and Mary felt his spirit leave. She stayed on her knees beside his cot for a time, holding the body to her, tears trickling as she felt the wrenching pain that awaited a mother and a father and a sister named Jenny, when they received the letter that would break their hearts.

The soft tread of stocking feet behind brought her around, and she turned in the gray light to look up into the round, jowled face of Dr. Folsom. His hair was disheveled, and he was lifting his suspenders over his shoulders. His face softened as he saw her tears.

"He's gone?"

"Yes. Just a few minutes ago."

The first rays of a rising sun suddenly slanted through the windows, and for a few moments the aging doctor stood looking down at Mary as she cradled the body of a smooth-faced boy, who had given all he possessed on this earth for an idea with which he was scarcely acquainted and the depth of which in his seventeen years he had little grasp.

Liberty.

From the dawn of time, how many men had placed greater value on the indomitable, inborn need for liberty than on their lives? How many had left wives, children, hearth and home, all they held dear, in their unquenchable thirst for freedom? How many knew that without it, the sweetness of all else in life was lacking.

In the silence of the empty hospital, looking down at the tear-stained face of Mary Flint as she held the body of Joseph Selman, the question struck Dr. Leonard Folsom as never before. Was it worth it? The pain, the suffering, the death, the heartbreak— was it worth it?

Standing there in the room that had been filled with the maimed and the dying, staring down, a thought jolted Folsom to his very foundations.

I am here! Just a country physician—nothing in my life that sets me apart—just one common, aging man among many. Still, I left all to come here to do what I could! Why? I don't recall thinking about liberty. Yet, I'm here. Is the need for freedom so strong that men will have it without conscious thought? Is it? Is it?

A feeling arose in his breast, faint at first, then stronger, then overpowering. *It is!* He could not doubt the source, nor dared he challenge the transcendent power of the conviction. It startled him, cowed him, humbled him, stripped him of all pretense, all defenses.

When he could, he choked down the lump in his throat and tenderly went to one knee beside Mary.

"Let me take him."

He laid the boy back and covered him with the blanket, then stood. "I'll get help for the burial, and then we've got to leave."

"I'll help bury him."

Folsom looked into her dark eyes and at the beautiful face that was drawn and lined and shook his head. He raised a hand to gently touch her cheek.

"No, Mary. You still have traces of pneumonia in both lungs. I don't know how you've survived this past month. Eighteen hours a day— surgeries, deaths, burials—you're drained, body and soul. I'll take care of it. You get your things ready, and then you ride in my wagon. I've made a bed from blankets. You're going to rest. That's an order."

At ten minutes past nine o'clock—the tearful good-byes having been said between doctor Folsom's little command and the townspeople who had labored at their side—the doctor helped Mary climb the wagon wheel to the wagon seat. He followed her and settled her in the wagon box on blankets stacked two feet deep. He took his place on the seat, gathered up the reins to the four horses, threaded them between his fingers, and nodded to the six mounted, armed men riding escort. They turned their horses south, and Folsom slapped the reins on the rumps of his team and talked them into a walk. Behind him, eight more loaded wagons rumbled into motion, taking their place in the line.

He turned to look at Mary. Shaded from the sun by the canvas wagon top, lying on blankets that smoothed the rutted road, she was already lost in deep, dreamless sleep.

At noon they stopped on the banks of a stream to water the horses and unhook them from the singletrees to graze while the men and women sought the shade of nearby maples to take their midday meal of brown bread, cheese, cold mutton, and dried apple slices. At half past one, they were once again moving steadily south, under an August sun that bore down unmercifully.

An evening breeze came down from the Watchung Mountains, cool on their faces, and they made their camp in a stand of oak trees near a stream that flowed south toward Bound Brook. They watered and hobbled the horses in grasses that reached their bellies, then kindled small cook fires for their simple supper. With the evening star winking in the west, they sat near the low flames—quiet, thoughtful, reflecting on the chapter in their lives they had just closed as they left Morristown, and the one they were now opening as they moved south to find and join the army as it prepared to engage General Howe and his British regulars in mortal combat.

Doctor Folsom found Mary seated on an aging wind-felled log, lost in reveries as she gazed into the glowing embers of a dwindling fire. He picked up a long stick, then sat beside her, and for a time they remained still, each with his or her own thoughts—a round, aging, balding, homely little man and a beautiful young woman with dark eyes and dark hair. They had known each other for only one month, yet as they sat beside each other, bone-weary, leading a tiny column of nine wagons searching for an army that was committed to the wrenching horror of cannon and musket, the walls people normally build around themselves for protection from the unwanted intrusions of strangers and society had vanished. Age, upbringing, social status, appearance—none of it mattered. A rare, unexpected feeling came stealing over them. Instinctively they understood that they both desperately needed to freely speak their thoughts and their hurts and fears, as they really were.

Folsom poked at the fire with his stick. "Today, in the wagon, you spoke a name in your sleep. I think it was Rufus."

"My father. Rufus Broadhead. He died not long ago. The last of my family. He's buried at the family plot in New York."

Folsom nodded, and for a time the quiet held. "Then you're married to a man named Flint?"

"I was. Captain Marcus Flint. He was killed unloading cannon from a ship at the Catherine Street docks in New York."

Folsom turned far enough to see Mary's face in the firelight. "Accident?"

"No. Murder. A British agent."

Folsom slowly shook his head. "I'm so sorry. So sorry. No children?"

"Our first child was stillborn within days of the time Marcus was killed. I have no children."

Folsom felt the pain, and his head bowed for a moment. Mary continued.

"You? You must have a wife and family somewhere."

"White Plains. On the mainland near New York."

Mary nodded. "I know about White Plains. You were a doctor there?"

"Yes." A wistful smile crossed his face. "A country doctor."

"Family?"

A light came into his eyes. "My wife, Emily. Our three children are grown and married and gone. The ones who lived. We lost two. A long time ago. Smallpox."

"Your wife is well?"

"Yes. After Concord and Bunker Hill I said I had to go. She agreed. Almost insisted. She's there now, sewing clothes for the soldiers. Most of the women are." He bowed his head for a moment before continuing. "Your husband's family?"

"All gone."

"You have no one left on either side?"

"No one."

"I know you come from high breeding. Did either family leave you assets?"

"My father had an estate in New York. The Flint family was wealthy. The British took my father's mansion for their command headquarters. They took the Flint mansion for a hospital. They seized everything. I was left with the clothes I was wearing and what I could carry in one valise. I was forced to serve for a time as a nurse in the Flint mansion hospital. A British doctor named Otis Purcell taught me. One night the mansion burned. I was on the third floor, asleep. Dr. Purcell saved me. I was very close to dead from the smoke. That's where I contracted pneumonia. I was thirteen weeks recovering."

Folsom reached with the stick to stir the coals and waited.

"Dr. Purcell was a widower—had no family. The day after the fire he was dying of a stroke, and he wrote a will leaving me thirty-two thousand pounds, British Sterling. I put the money in a New York bank managed by a man named Charles Partridge. Later I was told a British court had entered an order to hold it all. A man in England named Alfonso Eddington had brought a lawsuit. He claimed to be a distant blood cousin of Dr. Purcell and contended that my claims were a fraud, that the will was a forgery. The money is still in the bank, but I cannot get it."

"Have you tried? Hired a barrister?"

"I have no money to hire one. But I gave the documents to my father's barrister, a man named Lawrence Weatherby. He said he would see what could be done." She shook her head, and Folsom saw the sad hopelessness in her eyes. "He also told me the lawsuit is filed in Liverpool. I'm afraid there is no hope that a British court in Liverpool is going to deliver thirty-two thousand pounds in British Sterling to an American rebel accused of claiming it on a forged document."

She paused for a time, then added, "The truth is, Dr. Purcell died while I was unconscious in the hospital after the fire. His body was found by a British general named Jarom Hollins, along with the will. I didn't learn of what had happened until thirteen weeks later."

Folsom stared at the dying flames while he let the story settle in. "How did you get from New York to Morristown?"

"Spent the last money I had, then drove a freight wagon for my keep."

He turned to her in surprise. "You drove a freight wagon? How far?"

"From the Raritan River to Morristown."

He broke off staring at her and said quietly, "Amazing. Amazing." Again they sat with the night breeze moving cool on their faces, stirring the leaves of the oak trees.

"Why did you leave New York? All your friends?" Folsom asked.

"The British came. I was working for the patriots, and the Tories turned on us. I was with General Washington's army when it crossed from New York to Long Island. Stayed with them. That's where I met two men. One from Boston, the other a white man who was raised as an Iroquois Indian. They seemed to understand."

Folsom could not miss the softness that had come into her voice and her face.

"Their names?"

"Billy Weems is from Boston. Eli Stroud was orphaned and raised by the Indians."

"Where are they now?"

She shrugged. "The last I heard, somewhere up north. Eli thinks he can do something to stop the Indians Burgoyne has gathered to fight our army." A brightness came into her eyes. "Maybe he can. I hope he can."

Folsom sensed it. "You have a . . . a special feeling for these men?"

She turned earnest eyes to him. "They were kind. They understood."

He stirred the fire, and a shower of sparks spiraled upward, then winked out as they settled.

"Is that the reason you came to Morristown? To find them?"

She sat without moving for so long he thought she was not going to answer.

"Yes."

"Eli?"

"Yes."

His words were so soft they could scarcely be heard. "I hope you find him."

"I hope Emily is safe and well when you return."

For a moment his chin trembled, and he reached to wipe at his mouth without saying a word. After a time he started to rise, and Mary reached for his arm. He settled back down, waiting.

Her voice was low, steady. "Is life just a matter of endings? All things ending? Mother, father, husband, child, home, health—all gone?— ended?"

Folsom didn't immediately answer. Never had he talked of such things with a person he had known for such a short time, yet, sitting on a log in the wilderness, before a dying fire, it seemed natural, even needed.

After a time, he said, "All things change. Good, bad—all things. Maybe it's less an ending and more of a change. Emily and I lost two of our five children. For a time I thought she would never smile again. But she did. She changed. Now she takes her greatest joy in our eleven grandchildren. Two lives ended. More lives began. An ending? Maybe. But maybe more of a change."

There was torment and pain in her voice as she spoke. "Everything I knew, everything I loved, is gone. Not just changed. Gone forever. There seems to be no end to it."

The doctor leaned forward, knees on elbows, looking at his hands as he slowly rubbed his palms together. "Life can be hard. But the thing is, it moves. Good times pass, but so do bad ones. It seems like the Almighty meant for us to taste it all, one way or another. Maybe more good or bad for some of us, but in time we share it all. Rich, poor, high, low—it makes no difference. Maybe that's what life's all about—finding out if we can take it all, and learn, and keep going. And it seems like somehow it's all linked back to freedom. Is that why we're fighting the British? We have to be free to find out what we are?"

"I hadn't thought of it that way."

"I have, more lately than before. I sometimes mourn to be home with Emily, but lately it seems like I have to see this thing through with the British. There's something about liberty—freedom—it just sits there like a stone. Won't go away."

"I know. I've felt it."

The call of a distant owl came floating from the north, and they quieted for a moment, staring into the darkness of the forest. The strange mood had been interrupted. They were both aware it was receding, and oddly, it seemed right to let it go—that clinging to it, or speaking of it, would somehow diminish it. They did not move for a long time, storing the rare feeling in their hearts so they could draw it out in quiet times and feel once again the gift of having touched souls for a moment in the vast, uncharted ocean of life.

Finally Dr. Folsom stood with the dwindling light of the glowing coals casting shadows on his round, homely face. He had returned to the thorny world of duty, obligation, trouble, decisions, and safe distances between humans.

"You sleep in the wagon tonight, on those blankets. Keep one over you to protect your lungs. The pneumonia has not yet gone. I'll be nearby."

"Thank you. I will."

She watched him disappear in the darkness, then turned back to the fire. The soft call of the owl came again, and she looked north for a few moments.

Eli's up there somewhere. Is he alive? Safe? He has to be. He has to be. He and Billy. The Almighty has taken everything else from me. Surely He will not take Eli. He would not do that.

Notes

Mary Flint and Dr. Folsom are both fictional characters. The feeling between Mary and Eli Stroud is somewhat explored in volume 2, *The Times That Try Men's Souls*, chapter IX.

Neshaminy Creek, thirty miles north of Philadelphia, Pennsylvania

August 10, 1777

CHAPTER VI

★ ★ ★

"*What?*"

General George Washington thrust his head forward as he sat his gray horse, facing the sweating messenger who was fighting to hold his winded, lathered horse still in the wilting, midday August heat. Two hundred yards to the east, through a narrow strip of thick forest, Neshaminy Creek ran south toward the mother river, the mighty Delaware, thirty miles behind them. General Washington's two aides, Colonel John Laurens and young, slender, diminutive Colonel Alexander Hamilton, flanked him on either side, stunned wide-eyed as they waited for the answer to the blurted question.

The messenger's horse threw its head impatiently as the man raised an arm to point south. "Like I said, Sinepuxent Inlet, sir. Thirty-two miles below the Delaware Capes, in Maryland. The whole lot of them. We counted the flags. Two hundred sixty, all British, sailing south. I come as hard as I could to tell you. Wore out three horses."

Shaken, Washington struggled to regain his composure. "Are you certain? Did you see it yourself? Make the count?"

"Me and four militia officers, sir. We was all there. We all had telescopes. We all counted. The whole British fleet is headed south. We don't know where to, but south."

Washington turned in the saddle and spoke to Hamilton. "See that this man gets food and rest for himself and his horse." He shifted to

Laurens. "Stop the column here, and put the war council on notice. I will likely need to assemble them before day's end. Do not repeat what you've heard to anyone. Both of you report back to me as soon as possible."

Hamilton turned his horse and led the messenger away at a lope, moving south to find the wagons loaded with oats for the horses, while Laurens spurred his horse north at a gallop to catch General Nathanael Greene, leading the two-mile-long column. Washington reined his mount into a small break among the oak trees and swung down, pacing, head bowed as his mind raced to make sense of the incomprehensible intelligence he had just received.

South! South to where? General Burgoyne's to the north, up the Hudson! Philadelphia's up the Delaware! And General Howe is taking that armada with fifteen thousand troops south? Ridiculous! His army's been on those ships in this heat for over a month! Reports are he's thrown more than a thousand dead horses overboard! This is August—he's wasted half the summer campaign on those ships going everywhere except to join Burgoyne or to take Philadelphia. And now he's sailing south?

He shook his head in bewilderment, then forced his racing, fragmented thoughts into some semblance of order.

Charleston? Maybe. But if he wanted Charleston, he'd have been there weeks ago. I can't take this army down there to oppose him, and he knows it. That leaves only two logical objectives: Philadelphia, or the Hudson and Burgoyne. He sees Philadelphia as the capital city and thinks taking it will hurt us and elevate him in the eyes of Parliament and King George. We can give him Philadelphia and survive quite well. But we can't give him the Hudson River corridor and survive. So it has to be the Hudson, and a rendezvous with Burgoyne. If that's true, then sailing his ships to the south is nothing more than a deep feint to draw this army down there, so he can turn around and sail back north, up the Hudson, without opposition.

He stopped pacing to silently repeat it all to himself, testing whether it had the ring of sound judgment, common sense. It felt right. He gathered the reins to his mount and raised his left foot to the on-side stirrup before he caught himself. He lowered his foot back to the forest floor while holding the reins with his left hand, his right hand resting on the neck of the horse.

Maybe Charleston really is his objective. Conquer the south and use it as a base to move north. Maybe. Maybe. Always a maybe. Maybe he intends leading us all over the coast. A matter of attrition—which of us runs out of food and men first. He can move faster on the water than we can on land. Is that the answer? Simply grind us down?

Again he paused to look the thought straight in the face, to test the sound of it, the feel of it. It would not pass the test of good sense. If Howe had wanted Charleston, he could have been there, almost unopposed, weeks earlier. And the notion that fifteen thousand men on ships, limited in both food and water, could outlast an army on land with an endless supply of food and water and replacements was sheer nonsense. There was no plausible explanation.

He turned at the sound of horses cantering in and waited while Hamilton and Laurens dismounted and stood, waiting for his orders. Both men saw the anguish on his face as he spoke. "Report."

Hamilton spoke first. "The man and his mount are taken care of. Food and rest. He'll sleep for a while, then be available for further orders."

"When he's rested have him return to his command. There is no return message." He shifted to Laurens, waiting.

"The column is stopped until further orders. The war council will convene on your notice. They know nothing of what the messenger said, so far as I know."

"Good. I need time. Have my tent erected. I'll be along shortly. Don't go far. I'll want both of you at the council."

Startled, Hamilton stiffened. "Sir, are we to leave you alone out here in the woods?"

For a moment Washington considered. "I'll be all right. I won't be long."

Both men mounted their horses, and Washington watched their backs as they rode the fifty yards to the column of agitated men, milling about in a loud, confused muddle, their attitude nearly mutinous. From the grove of trees where he held his horse, Washington watched and listened to the frustrated men.

Stop? We've done nothing but march every which direction, and now we just stop here in the forest? For what? Are we trying to find the red-coats, or trying to *not* find 'em?

Washington turned back to his mount and loosened the saddle girth. For a time he stood beside the horse, one hand holding the reins, the other unconsciously patting the horse on the neck while he stared at the ground, working to force some conclusion to the pieces that would not come together. Half an hour passed before he tightened the saddle girth and mounted, then reined his horse around and tapped spur.

His tent was ready, and he entered. Both Laurens and Hamilton were waiting.

"Gather the war council." He removed his tricorn and settled onto his chair facing the long table while he waited, then rose at the sound of a horse coming in at a gallop. General Nathanael Greene pulled his mount to a stop, and a moment later the picket pulled the tent flap aside to give him entrance. His eyes searched Washington's face as he came to attention.

"Take a chair. The others will be along shortly."

"May I inquire, sir. Have the British been located?"

"They have."

"May I know where, sir?"

Seconds passed before Washington answered. "Sinepuxent Inlet, Maryland."

Greene gaped. "*Where?* Did I hear you correctly, sir? Sinepuxent Inlet? Maryland? Clear down past the Delaware Capes?"

Washington's expression remained fixed. "Correct."

Greene was foundered, astonished. "South? To where? What's to the south?"

Washington exhaled a weary breath. "Charleston, perhaps. But if he wanted Charleston, he could have been there five weeks ago, and there is very little we could have done about it."

At the sound of horses they both fell silent, waiting. The officers of the war council came in from different directions: Stirling, Lafayette, Cadwalader, Stephen, Wayne, all with the same blank expression on their faces. They filed into the tent and waited for direction. Washington remained standing to speak.

"Take your places." Chairs squeaked, and Washington waited until they were settled. "I have just received reliable information that General Howe and the British fleet were seen and counted yesterday south of the Delaware Capes, at Sinepuxent Inlet in Maryland."

Instantly the air was filled with exclamations, loud, raucous. Washington gave them a moment to vent their disbelief, then raised a hand, and the talk ceased.

"You will recall that when the fleet was sighted in Delaware Bay, and then disappeared, I had decided to wait at the Delaware River for him to show his hand. Then it seemed he must certainly be headed back north, up the Hudson to join Burgoyne, and I ordered this march north to meet them. Now he's down off the coast of Maryland, moving farther south."

The only sounds were the creaking of saddles outside as their horses moved, breathing hard, mingled with the buzzing of summer insects and the chortling of birds in the trees.

"I cannot recall such contradictory maneuvers in all the military history with which I am familiar. It should not be difficult to find an army of fifteen thousand men with horses and cannon and supply wagons, but we have now spent two months and two weeks trying to do so, and all we have to show for it is a footsore army that has rightly concluded that we do not know what we are doing. I'm sick to death of it. If any of you has a rational explanation, I would be most grateful to hear it."

General Anthony Wayne spoke first. Average size, blazing eyes, he had earned the title "Mad Anthony" from the headlong, devil-take-the-hindmost way he led his men into battle. He knew only one way to fight—straight on, shouting at the top of his lungs, sabre swinging wildly at anything resembling the enemy.

"Send out patrols in both directions. North and south. He's bound to be one place or the other—Philadelphia or the Hudson. I have men in my division who could handle it."

Washington nodded as Greene broke in.

"He can hurt us worse if he joins with Burgoyne. Together they could cut the states in two. It could end the war."

Washington's expression did not change. "I agree."

Cadwalader interrupted. It was General John Cadwalader who had been assigned to cross the Delaware River at Bordentown the night of December 25, 1776, to seal off the escape route for the Hessians following the battle of Trenton. He had made the crossing in a raging blizzard, only to discover it was impossible to bring his cannon across the ice-choked river. He had recrossed back to his men and waited. Washington had commended his judgment and his action.

Cadwalader spoke up. "It's possible he's after Charleston, but if he is, there is nothing we can do about it because of the distance. The most sensible thing would be to do what General Greene suggests—pick the spot where he could do the most damage, and go there. That would be the Hudson."

Stirling nodded in agreement but said nothing. William Alexander Lord Stirling was the only American in the Continental Army with a British title, which, however, had never been confirmed by the crown in England. It was Stirling who had made the heroic stand to cover an American retreat south of the Gowanus Swamp on August 27, 1776, during the catastrophic defeat of the Americans at the battle of Long Island.

Washington turned to Stephen, who met his gaze but said nothing. He turned to Lafayette, standing to his right, and waited. The nineteen-year-old, untried French major general spoke, his French accent prominent.

"I am not here to advise, but to learn. However, it seems to me that if General Howe is as far south as Maryland, his true objective must be Charleston. That defies all military reason, and further, if it is true, there is nothing this army can do to defend that city because of the distance. It would seem better judgment to move north to meet Burgoyne to prevent finding ourselves between the two armies as time goes on."

Washington stood still for a moment: tall, face a study in perplexity bordering on anger. He wished the fiery Benedict Arnold and tough backwoods fighter Daniel Morgan were in the group, instead of up north somewhere trying to rescue St. Clair's battered army from Burgoyne and Fraser and Phillips and Riedesel.

But he had sent them, and they were gone, and Washington had long since learned that in the end, he who bears the weight of final command must deal with what he has—nothing more. He must make the soul-wrenching decisions, guided only by the hard facts, instinct, and whatever inspiration the Almighty chooses to impart at that moment. "If only" and "I wish" were useless luxuries.

He raised his face. "I'm tired of playing the part of the fool. The single course that appears to be reliable is to go north to stop Burgoyne. Unless there is some better suggestion, that is what we will do."

His eyes went around the circle, but the silence held.

"Prepare your men to march in the morning. You are dismissed."

The officers looked at him for a moment while they accepted the order. Each nodded his agreement and then stood, each with his mind leaping ahead, making the never-ending small calculations and decisions that hold an army together. With Hamilton and Laurens at his side, Washington watched the other officers file out the tent flap, mount their horses, and wheel them about to work their way back through the sprawled camp of distraught soldiers. He watched until he heard the captains and lieutenants bawling out orders to prepare the camp for their overnight stay, then get ready to march north in the morning.

Minutes passed before he turned to his two aides.

"Colonel Hamilton, would you have my horse saddled? Both of you should accompany me."

Hamilton's eyes opened wide in surprise. "Yes, sir. May I inquire where we are going?"

"To move among the men. Listen. Watch. Be seen."

"Yes, sir." Hamilton left the tent at a trot to reappear minutes later with the horses saddled and waiting.

Washington mounted his mare and reined her out into the open with Hamilton on his left, Laurens on his right. He sat erect, straight, chin up, as he walked the tall horse north, intently watching the faces of the soldiers, listening to their voices, sensing their mood while he let them see him, stoic, calm, unperturbed. He returned the salute of officers as he passed them and acknowledged the slight bow of the head of the enlisted as they showed their respects. He reached the head of the column and returned southward, walking the horse among the men as they turned east toward the creek and began the work of unloading the great black iron tripods and cook kettles, then the bedrolls and the few tents they had, to set up their camp.

He passed the New York Regiment, and tall, hawkish Captain Venables saluted. Washington returned it as his horse walked on. Sergeant O'Malley was facing the creek, his back to the approaching Washington. He saw his men slow, then stop in their work while a sense of awe came into their faces, and he turned, looking for the cause. He instantly came to attention and saluted as Washington passed a scant twenty feet away. Washington looked him in the eye, touched the brim of his hat, and moved on. It seemed that time stood still as they watched him disappear into the trees and the bustle of men and equipment.

As he departed, murmuring broke out among O'Malley's men.

"Why're we stoppin' again? We was already goin' north up towards the Hudson, and now we're stopped, with orders to make camp and then get up in the mornin' and keep marchin' north again. Seems like this is the contrariest army since creation."

"He musta had a reason. Don't do nothin' without a reason."

"Well, it would be just dandy if he'd tell us what it is. Stoppin' just to stop?"

"He'll say when we need to know."

O'Malley let it run for a minute before he called out, "All right, you heard Cap'n Venables's orders. Get your bedrolls on your backs and your muskets in your hands. We're settin' up camp over by the creek. Move!"

In the oppressive midday heat of the dead August air, the men shouldered their equipment and moved east through the swarms of mosquitoes and flies and brulies and the tangled undergrowth and oak trees to drop their bedrolls where they chose. Sweating and swatting at the flies, they sat where they could to wait for the wagons to rumble in with the heavy cooking equipment and the tents for the officers.

With sunset approaching they set the fires beneath the smoke-blackened cook kettles, carried water from the creek, waited for it to boil, and dropped diced beef brisket, turnips, and onions into it, followed by moldy flour for thickening, and salt. They cut, trimmed, and peeled tree limbs and thrust them in to stir until the stew was all thick, with great clumps of floating fat. O'Malley called Third Company, and the men came with their wooden bowls and spoons to get their ration of beef brisket stew and a chunk of heavy, hard, brown bread.

Caleb carried his bowl to his bedroll beneath an oak tree and sat down to stir the smoking mix while he blew on it. He sucked air as he touched his tongue to the first wooden spoonful and jerked it back, singed. He grimaced as he broke his bread into the bowl, stirred until it was softened, and forced down the salty, greasy gruel. After eating he walked to the creek to fill his canteen, scrubbed the bowl and spoon with water and sand, then returned to his bedroll to sit for a time, watching the familiar muddle of untrained citizen-soldiers trying to set up a camp and settle in for the night.

Half an hour passed before he opened his bedroll to dig out his burlap bag and fill it with dirt and sand, then hang it from a tree branch. He wrapped his hands with the dirty, frayed canvas strips and dropped easily into the stance of a boxer and began his nightly ritual—left jab, left hook, right hand in hard. He had raised a sweat before he saw Dorman working through the men and bedrolls.

For a time Dorman watched in silence with a critical eye, making mental notes of the things Caleb did that were right, and wrong, with his feet, his elbows, his shoulders. *It's coming. One day soon. Sooner than I thought.*

After a time, Caleb dropped his hands and turned to face his mentor, waiting.

Dorman's face was almost expressionless as he said, "Now we take the next step. I hit back. Not hard, just enough."

A smile flickered on Caleb's face. "Enough to what?"

"Teach you."

Caleb shrugged and raised his hands. Dorman did the same, watching as Caleb began the circling. The boy's left hand flicked out to jab. Dorman's right hand came up just enough to deflect the punch, then drop back, and the circling continued. Caleb jabbed again. The next sequence of movements were a blur as Dorman again blocked it with his right hand while his left hand came ripping through Caleb's spread arms to thump his chest over his heart. The blow was harmless, but in that instant Caleb knew Dorman could have knocked him down backwards, maybe unconscious, if he had not pulled the punch at the last instant. Shocked at the ease with which Dorman had penetrated his defense, Caleb dropped both hands for a moment, and in that split second Dorman jabbed with his left hand and punched with his right. All Caleb saw was both hands start to move and in the next instant felt the fingertips of both touch, left on his chin, right on his forehead, scarcely hard enough to be felt.

He gaped at Dorman, unable to believe the speed with which the gray-haired, round-shouldered old man had struck and withdrawn. He started to speak, and once again Dorman's hands flicked out with the blinding speed of a striking snake, and once again Caleb felt the tap on his left temple, then his chin. Dorman began to circle him, his face a mask of concentration, eyes locked onto Caleb's chest while he took in the whole boy—feet, hands, head, eyes, his every move.

Caleb raised his hands again, eased his left foot forward, tucked his chin into the hollow of his left shoulder, and began circling clockwise with Dorman, eyes on his chest, vision decentralized to take in the whole man. The men who were lounging nearby turned to watch, fascinated to see the two of them, an old man with finely honed skills, and a young one learning, warily stalking each other, one swinging hard, the other carefully. Minutes passed to a quarter of an hour, and Dorman backed away to drop his hands.

"Enough for now?" he asked Caleb.

"Tired?"

Dorman shook his head.

"Then let's go again."

Twice Caleb's hands got through Dorman's defenses and landed hard, once in the chest, once on the forehead. For two seconds Dorman saw the familiar white and yellow spots dancing before his eyes but gave no sign and kept moving. A quarter of an hour later he backed away once again.

"We're through for tonight."

Caleb used his fingers and teeth on the knots of his hand wraps. "Did I hurt you? Those two times? I didn't mean to."

Dorman shook his head. "I felt it. No harm."

"I'll try to be careful."

"No, don't. The whole idea is for you to learn to hit hard while you're moving. The only way you'll learn that is to do it. I've been hit hard before. I'll tell you when it's enough."

Billowing white thunderheads piling high in the western sky were alive with spectacular reds and yellows as Caleb jerked the knots holding the bag to the tree branch, and it dropped. While he was loosening the rope and dumping the sand and dirt, Dorman spoke once more.

"You're coming along. See you again tomorrow." He had turned to walk away when Caleb called after him.

"Can you talk for a minute?"

Puzzled, Dorman turned back, waiting. Caleb folded the bag and tossed it onto his bedroll, then spoke haltingly. "You've . . . uh . . . been in battle before?"

Dorman looked intently into Caleb's eyes. "Several. Sea and land."

Caleb sat down on his bedroll. "What's it like? The shooting, I mean. Men hurt. Killed."

Caught by surprise, Dorman reached to touch his chin, sorting out his thoughts, searching for words. "Worried?"

Too quickly, too nonchalantly, Caleb shook his head. "Worried? Oh, no, not . . ." He caught himself. "Yes, a little. I just wanted to know."

Dorman sat down on the ground, feet crossed, elbows on his knees, and he spoke with slow deliberation. "I doubt one man can tell another how it is. I can tell you about the shooting and the bayonets and the cannon. The screaming. I can tell you about men being wounded. Dying. I can say all the words, but you won't know how it is until you've been through it. It's a little different for each man."

"Is it . . . bad?"

Slowly Dorman locked eyes with Caleb. "I think it will be for you, at least at first. It's different from man to man. It seems like some find they were made for battle. Born for it—love it. Others find out they're cowards. Still others—maybe most of us—find out it's a terrible thing, but we learn to live with it."

"Any way to . . . uh . . . know . . . what you'll do?"

"You afraid of what you'll do?"

"Not afraid, exactly. Just . . . wondering."

The older man didn't answer immediately. Then he said, "I think you'll do fine."

Caleb sat without speaking for a time, staring at his hands, and he did not raise his head as he asked, "Did you ever . . ." The words trailed off, and he did not finish.

"Run? You worried you'll run?"

The answer came too quickly, too decisively. "No. Not worried. I just . . . yes. Worried."

"Don't be. I never ran, but sometimes I was so scared I wanted to. Sometimes I was so full of anger I charged when I shouldn't have—should have been killed half a dozen times. Twice they declared me a hero, but I wasn't. I was just so filled with hatred and anger I wasn't responsible for what I did. It was foolish."

"What did you do?"

"It doesn't matter."

"Yes it does."

Dorman shrugged. "Once I refused to retreat. Stood off a British attack with a bayonet and a sword. Another time I cleaned out a British redoubt alone."

"You? One man?"

"Don't make it something it wasn't. The cannon in that redoubt killed seven men in my company. I saw it—my companions blown apart.

I got inside the redoubt and to the cannon before the British could reload. It was all over quick."

"Did you feel . . . fear?"

Dorman shook his head. "No. Not that time. Even after things quieted and I realized what I had done, I felt only anger. I had to punish those redcoats. A terrible feeling. A terrible thing."

"How many?"

"Six. The cannon crew."

"You had your musket? Bayonet?"

"No. I used the sword I took away from their officer. A captain, I think."

Caleb slowly leaned back. "You charged six men, empty-handed?"

"Don't make more of it than it was. It was a bad thing."

"You weren't wounded? Hurt?"

"That night I found a bayonet hole in my right side. Went clear through. I don't remember it happening."

"You *what?*"

"A bayonet. I didn't know it."

"How bad? How long were you in a hospital?"

"I didn't go to a hospital. I didn't report it. I bound it up with some jimsonweed and carbolic salve. It healed."

Caleb wiped at his mouth and tried to speak but had no words.

Dorman rocked up onto his feet. "Don't worry about battle. Worry can bring on mistakes. Keep a clear head. Handle it when it comes." He waited until Caleb raised his face and looked directly into his eyes. "You'll do well. Hear?"

Caleb nodded, and Dorman bobbed his head before he turned on his heel and walked away through the dusk and the evening fires and the thick undergrowth and oak trees, toward his own company.

Caleb sat on his bedroll for a time, struggling with the startling things Dorman had confided to him, going over again and again the advice he had been given. Keep a clear head—don't worry—worry makes mistakes—you'll do well.

The evening star winked on, huge in the purple of the western skies, and then others came twinkling until the dark sky was a sea of lights. Caleb raised his eyes, and the thought struck him—*Is Mother looking up at these stars right now?—Prissy and Adam?—Billy and Eli?—Matthew? Where's Matthew?*

And then without warning the thought froze him: *And Father? Is he up there somewhere?*

It had come too fast, and he could not stop the warm tears that trickled down his face, onto his shirt, and he didn't care. Slowly a hard caste formed on his face. *No, Father is dead. Just dead. And dead is nowhere.*

He felt the wrong of it inside, but more than that he felt the hot, bitter anger rise to drive out all other thoughts, all other feelings. *The British killed him. They shot him in the back, and Matthew had to go and Billy and Kathleen, and Mother was left alone to provide for us, and I'm going to make the British pay. They'll pay.*

A high voice rich with Irish came calling, and he started, then quickly wiped at his eyes with his shirtsleeve.

"Dunson! You here somewhere? Caleb Dunson?"

Caleb stood and answered. "Here."

Barrel-chested, bearded Sergeant O'Malley came striding, followed by tall, lanky, Captain Venables.

"Here he is, sir." O'Malley said, stepping aside.

Venables spoke. "You did the writing about that snake story?"

Caleb's eyes narrowed in question. "Yes, sir."

Venables cut to the heart of it. "Once in a while we need someone to keep up the regimental orderly book. We give you the facts, you write 'em. Never know when someone's going to ask to read them, someone like Gen'l Washington, or maybe Congress. The way we're going through courts-martial, that'd keep Congress busy for about eight years, just tryin' to catch up."

Caleb's mouth dropped open, then clacked shut. "Courts-martial?"

Captain Venables flashed a wry grin. "Three or four every day."

"For what?"

"Just about everything you can think of. Stealing food, assault, disobeying direct orders, fighting, desertion, sleeping on picket duty—it goes on and on." Venables caught himself and concluded, "Anyway, once in a while we need someone to do the writing. Any reason you can't do it when that happens?"

"Well, no, except I've only been here just over a month. I don't know—"

"You don't need to know nothin' but how to write, and you do that good. So you're it. Next time we need you, I'll tell O'Malley. Understand?"

"Yes, sir."

"Good." Venables shook his head. "Be just my luck for you to stop the first British musketball that comes whistlin'." He thrust a bony finger under Caleb's nose. "You stay out of the way of those redcoat musketballs, hear?"

"Yes, sir."

"All right." He turned to O'Malley. "I'll send for him when we need him."

"Yes, sir."

Venables turned to go, and Caleb called to him, "Sir, could I get back that writing about the snake? I'd like to have it back."

"Oh, yeah. I meant to bring it. O'Malley, remind me tomorrow."

"Yes, sir."

Venables quickly became a black shadow in the campfires, then disappeared, and O'Malley turned to Caleb.

"I'll get that writing back." He pointed to the folded bag on Caleb's bedroll. "You still trying to learn fighting?"

Caleb shrugged but said nothing.

"You intend getting Murphy?"

"Maybe."

"Let it go. Nothing good can come of it."

"That depends on Murphy."

"Well, you stay away from him."

O'Malley waited, but Caleb remained silent. O'Malley bobbed his head in emphasis, turned, and walked back the way he had come. Caleb watched him disappear, then continued to stare for a time, in heavy thought. *He's wrong. Murphy can't go on beating people. Someone has to stop him. Just like the British. They can't go on like they are. Someone has to stop them.*

The drummer hammered out tattoo, and the camp quieted. For a long time Caleb lay on his back, hands clasped behind his head, staring into the infinity of stars overhead. *If the Almighty is up there, where? Which star? So many. Too many. What makes us think He cares about us—even knows we're here? If He cares, where is He now when we're getting ready for battle? If killing is wrong, why doesn't He stop it? If He hears prayers, why didn't He hear Mother's when she asked for Father to live? Why?*

He felt a dark cloud creep into his mind, coloring his thoughts with doubt and hopelessness that turned to frustration and anger. He turned on his side, his face drawn in cynicism. *It always ends this way when you try to understand. Better to let it go. Let the Almighty take care of the Almighty. I'll take care of me.*

He drifted into troubled sleep filled with incoherent snatches of scenes, both real and imagined. One moment he saw his mother hanging fresh wash in the backyard behind their house in bright Boston sunshine, ignoring him when he called to her. The next moment there was an old man with long hair and decayed teeth and a thin face, pointing at him, laughing insanely. In an instant the man faded, and he saw Adam and Prissy crying.

Tossing, turning, he jerked awake sweating and heard his own voice echoing in the woods. Angry calls came from the darkness, and he lay back down, fighting to stay awake.

The line of light separating earth and sky was faint in the east before he once again slept, and less than half an hour later the drummer came walking through camp banging out reveille. Caleb rose from his blankets with the jumbled, disjointed, bizarre visions of the night flicking through his mind. He swallowed at the sour taste in his mouth as he tied his shoes, then walked to the woodpile and picked up the ax to wait for the rest of the morning wood crew. They came hitching suspenders over their shoulders, and Caleb led them away from Neshaminy Creek, into the oaks, watching the ground for snakes.

They had carried their first load back to dump it at the cook fires and were turning when the sound of a running horse brought them up short. A rider came in from the south on a lathered horse while men scrambled to get out of his way, then raised their fists at his back as he plowed on. O'Malley shook his head in disgust.

"That fool's going to kill someone, he keeps that up."

They watched the horse out of sight, then went on about the dull, mindless duty of preparing morning mess.

The rider found the tent of General Washington, with its rounded ends and flagpole, and brought his horse to a skidding stop, throwing a shower of soft, decayed flora from the forest floor. He hit the ground at a run and pulled up before the two pickets, breathing hard while the horse stood spraddle-legged, fighting for wind.

"Message for Gen'l Washington," he exclaimed. He patted his chest where the message was wrapped in oilskin inside his shirt.

"I'll take it."

The man shook his head violently. "My orders is to deliver it to the gen'l personal. I got to do it myself."

"Wait here."

The picket disappeared through the tent flap and thirty seconds later pulled it aside. "The general will see you."

Inside, the rider came to rigid attention, heels together, chin sucked in, and saluted with one hand while he dug out the oilskin packet with the other. He didn't wait for Washington to return the salute. Standing to Washington's right was Alexander Hamilton.

"Gen'l, sir, I was sent special with this here message yesterday evenin'." He thrust it forward. "Cap'n Iverson said it had to be here this mornin'. Took all night and two horses, but it's here."

General Washington laid the message on the table to unfold the oil-skin, then the message, and read it. The only change in his expression was a slight widening of his eyes. He read it once again, then raised his face to the messenger.

"Do you know what is written here?"

"Well, sir, I don't because, well, I can't read, but I got a good idee."

"What?"

"I was there, sir. I seen 'em. Right there where the Elk River hits the Chesapeake, sir. Head of Elk. The whole bloody bay was filled with them sails and British flags."

"You're certain?"

"Certain. Counted as many as I could see. Way over two hunnerd of 'em, sir. I expect they was close to two thousand cannon snouts stickin' out the cannon ports on them ships. Maybe fifteen, twenty thousand redcoats on board. They was gettin' ready to come on ashore. Dumpin' dead horses all over the bay. I seen it. I reckon that's what Cap'n Ingersol wrote, sir. Told me to get it here like the devil hisself was nippin' at my hocks, so I come a-foggin' it, sir."

Washington pursed his mouth and turned to Hamilton. "Take this man and his mount for food and rest and then return as quickly as possible. Neither of you is to say a word about this to anyone until further orders. Send Colonel Laurens the minute you find him."

"Yes, sir."

With his usual quick movements, the slightly built Hamilton led the larger man out into the bright August morning sun, in a straight line toward the fodder wagons.

Inside his tent, Washington grabbed a map, quickly unrolled it, and weighted down the four corners. He shifted it once to lay true to the compass, and instantly began locating places with his finger.

Three minutes later the picket ushered Colonel John Laurens through the tent flap to stand facing Washington. Laurens had been inside his tent shaving when Hamilton burst in. He had swept the lather from half his face and come at a run.

"Sir, are you all right?"

"Yes. We'll wait for—"

The sound of running horses interrupted, and moments later the tent flap was once again thrown aside as Generals Greene and Cadwalader pushed inside. They saw Laurens half-shaved and Washington standing motionless, as though he had been chiseled from granite, and they stood in silence, waiting. Thirty seconds later a winded

Hamilton threw aside the tent flap and quickly stepped inside, followed moments later by Generals Stephen, Stirling, Lafayette, and Wayne.

With his war council assembled, Washington took a deep breath. "I have just received a message from a Captain Bosley Ingersol of the Maryland Militia. The British fleet is at Head of Elk, at the top of Chesapeake Bay."

For a split second a stunned silence held, and then the tent exploded with wild exclamations of shocked disbelief. Half the generals lunged to their feet, gesturing.

"*What?* Head of Elk?"

"Insane!"

"In the name of heaven, what is Howe doing? Has he lost his mind?"

Washington let it run for a full minute before he called them to order. "I make no attempt to explain it because I find that impossible. I only know that I am reliably informed they arrived there yesterday. The messenger saw it himself and also carried the written message from his captain."

Again raucous exclamations resounded, then quieted.

"Let me show you." Washington spent one moment orienting himself to the map spread before him, then tapped it with a long index finger.

"This is Amboy, on the New Jersey coast, just opposite Staten Island. This is where General Howe had his army assembled last June. The distance overland from Amboy, here,"—his finger traced a line—"to Philadelphia, here, is just about sixty miles, north to south."

He straightened. "I believe General Howe feared we could hurt him badly if he marched his troops through New Jersey to Philadelphia, so he decided to avoid it by taking them on ships. He probably meant to go up the Delaware River and land them at Chester or Red Bank Redoubt, some fifteen or sixteen miles from Philadelphia, and march them overland from there."

He once again tapped the map. "But he didn't do that. He stopped in Delaware Bay and for some reason known only to him and the Almighty sailed right back out, down the coast past the Virginia Capes, then Maryland, and turned west, then right back up the Chesapeake Bay to drop anchor, here, at the very top of the Chesapeake, at Head of Elk, where the Elk River empties into the bay."

He paused to shake his head in profound bewilderment. "I believe he intends marching his army overland from Head of Elk to Philadelphia." He raised his face. "The distance is about fifty-seven miles, south to north."

All the officers in the tent leaned back in their chairs, their faces dead blank in wonderment.

"He loaded his army on those ships on July ninth. He will probably have them unloaded by about August twenty-fifth. I am not able to invent an explanation as to why he would have his entire army on those ships in the worst heat of the summer for forty-seven days, and at the conclusion be just as far from Philadelphia as he was when he started."

Every man on the war council stared at the map, re-creating the movements of General Howe and his fleet, trying to understand. It was impossible.

Washington called them back to attention. "Why it happened no longer matters. What does matter is that it is now on us to march our army back to Philadelphia as quickly as possible. We have a mandate from Congress to defend the city and keep it from British hands if we can."

Every man at the table sobered.

"When you leave, go immediately to your commands and give orders that we march for Philadelphia the moment we're ready."

Greene rounded his lips and blew air for a moment. "We're going to have some rather confused troops. They think we're marching north in the morning. We've changed directions so many times the past few days, they're starting to think we're trying to avoid the British, not find them."

"I know. There's nothing to be done about it, except to let them know we've acted on the best information we've had. Make it abundantly clear that if this message is correct, and I'm certain it is, we finally know where the British are and where they are going. This army will engage them at or near Philadelphia in the next few days. Tell them. They're good men. If they know we are finally going to have our battle, it will quiet them and settle them. Tell them."

Notes

In the forepart of August 1777, a messenger informed General Washington that the British fleet had been sighted off Sinepuxent Inlet, off the Maryland coast. The news utterly confounded Washington. Then, about August twentieth, another messenger arrived informing Washington the fleet had been sighted at the northern tip of Chesapeake Bay, at a small place called Head of Elk. General Howe unloaded his army on August twenty-eighth, after having them on board the ships for forty-seven days. See Leckie, *George Washington's War*, pp. 349–50.

General Anthony Wayne earned the title "Mad Anthony" by his habit of riding headlong into battle. Ketchum, *Saratoga*, p. 43.

General Lafayette was ever dedicated to learning about America. Leckie, *George Washington's War*, p. 343.

CHAPTER VII

★ ★ ★

*T*he lightning bolt leaped thirty miles through the belly of the purple storm clouds that sealed the heavens and for three seconds turned the gloom of the rain-swept world whiter than midday. The officers seated around the council table inside General William Howe's command tent gritted their teeth, ducked their heads, and rounded their shoulders against the thunderclap. Two seconds later the tent bucked, and the ground shook as if hit by the sound of a hundred thousand cannon. For half a minute their ears rang while the wind howled, tearing at the tent as they sat in silence, cowed by the awful powers of nature.

General William Howe glanced at his brother, Admiral Lord Richard Howe, seated at his right. "That might have hit one of the ships."

Richard shrugged. "If it did, it did. The fleet's weathered storms before."

William turned back to the war council of officers seated around the long table, wrapped in capes that were soaked from the ride they had made from their various quarters in the great British camp. They had slogged through the Chesapeake cloudburst to the command tent, with their horses splashing through mud that reached well past their fetlocks and splattered their mounts' chests and bellies with each stride. The officers now sat in uniforms that were soaked, in boots covered with dark Maryland mud. The close, musty odor of wet wool and soggy felt hats was thick inside the canvas tent.

Howe raised his voice to be heard above the incessant drumming of the wind-driven rain on the tent roof and walls. His manner was one of complete detachment as he looked at his pocket watch, then placed it on the table beside stacked documents.

"It's ten o'clock. We have a lot to do. The first order of business is to carry out the sentences on the prisoners convicted at their courts-martial."

He picked up several documents and droned on. "The charges were plundering, and molesting females of the local citizenry, all prohibited by specific orders, which stated the penalties for offenders." He watched his officers lower their faces to stare at their hands or at the tabletop, hiding the thin veil of defiance that crept into their eyes and faces as he continued. "The sentences are specific. Two men are to be hanged, and five are to be flogged. If any among you have reason for delay, state it."

He waited. Every eye in the tent was now on him, and in them he saw the accusations leveled against him, which had spread through the ranks—whispered sparingly at first, then spoken openly, and finally running rampant. He knew them all too well.

For forty-seven days, July ninth to August twenty-fifth, he had held his entire army onboard the fleet of ships, during the worst heat of the New England summer. Uniforms had moldered in the humidity. Sunstroke and heat exhaustion had felled men by the hundreds. Burials at sea were conducted nearly every day. Stale drinking water and decaying food had been rationed. There was no space for exercise. Sickness became epidemic. Horse fodder ran out the fourth week, and two thousand seven hundred dead and dying horses had been thrown overboard. Insignificant trifles between comrades had blossomed into deadly confrontations, sometimes with drawn bayonets. The world-renowned discipline of the vaunted British Army had degenerated to a state of near mutiny.

When Howe finally gave the order to go ashore, the three hundred emaciated horses that remained alive plunged into the nearest cornfield to gorge; within hours all were standing spraddle legged, heads down, shaking with colic. Many died. Two days of whistling wind and pounding rain, with lightning that streaked from horizon to horizon and thunder that jolted the trees had turned the Maryland countryside into a quagmire. Wagons and cannon sank to their axles. Lacking horses, men lashed ropes to the cannon trails and sank to their knees in the ooze as they strained to move them. Creeks became rivers and overflowed their banks to flood the rows of tents. The soldiers, filled with smoldering outrage at the suffering they had endured aboard those accursed ships and now in their muddy tent city, turned on the countryside to vent their fury. Homes, barns, livestock, granaries, orchards, fields were ransacked, plundered, burned. Men were attacked, women molested.

Too late Howe had issued orders against the offenders, specifying harsh penalties on the written document that forbade depredations of the civilian population. Those who disobeyed would be made to answer before a court-martial. Today the leaders among the guilty were to pay the price. All too many soldiers, both enlisted and officers, laid the whole of it at the feet of General William Howe.

He stared back at his officers, aware of the silent condemnation they held in check and of the single burning question they needed to have answered. With his high reputation for care of his men, why had he sub-jected his entire command to the sufferings that had very nearly destroyed them all?

Howe cleared his throat and took a moment to order his thoughts. His legendary lack of political skill was never more evident as he spoke in a low, flat, emotionless voice, in terms that were short, blunt—approaching brutal.

"I'm aware of what's being said. Maybe even by some of you. I mean to be clear on two points: First, the orders I received from the king and the conditions I found here in the colonies both required that we remain on board the ships until we reached this place." He paused to judge whether he had said enough. In his cryptic view, he had. "Second, by its very purpose and nature, the life of a soldier is often unpleasant. It rests on the foundation of obedience to orders. Those who take exception are in the wrong profession." Again he stopped and pursed his mouth, this time pondering if he should expand on the sometimes cruel military axiom "orders are orders." In the split second of considering it, he perceived a danger. Someone at the table might see it as an oblique attempt at an apology or a sign of weakness or regret. He shook his head, closed his mind on the subject, and moved on.

"If no one has reasons to the contrary, the sentences will be carried out today at one o'clock before the entire army. Have your men assembled."

Lightning flashed as he looked down at his notes, and he waited for the thunder to boom and recede before he went on. He still held the documents on which the minutes of the courts-martial were recorded.

"We march for Philadelphia tomorrow morning."

The chairs squeaked as the officers moved. For a moment there was brief talking muffled by the steady sound of wind and rain on the tent.

Howe squared a map with the compass and weighted down the corners before he dropped a slender index finger at the top of Chesapeake Bay. "We're here, at Head of Elk. The line of march will be east to the Delaware"—his finger moved as he spoke—"to Newcastle, then north past Wilmington, up this side—the west side—of the river. We'll pass Brandywine Creek, here, on past Chester, and to Philadelphia, here." He raised his finger. "Fifty-seven miles."

Every man leaned forward to study the map, memorizing the winding course of the Delaware and the succession of towns and hamlets and landmarks—Newcastle, Wilmington, Chester, Red Bank Redoubt, the Schuylkill River, and Philadelphia, with White Marsh, Germantown, and Valley Forge away from the river, not far to the northwest. Howe gave them time to satisfy themselves before he continued.

"To make the march, we will divide into two divisions. The first division will be under the command of General Lord Cornwallis."

Startled, the rotund, fleshy Charles Cornwallis jerked erect so abruptly his jowls jiggled. He started to speak, thought better of it, and eased back in his chair.

"The second division will be under the command of General Wilhelm von Knyphausen."

True to the rigid discipline drilled into the very bones of every German-born and trained army officer, the general neither moved nor changed expression. Orders were orders. It was a matter of total indifference to him what they were.

Howe dropped the court-martial documents onto the table and leaned his long frame forward, once again orienting himself to the map.

"Latest reports place Washington and his army somewhere near here." He tapped a finger on the area above Philadelphia. "Apparently he's spent weeks marching around the countryside, first one direction and then the other." A wry smile formed for a moment. "He likely had reports of sightings of our fleet and tried to guess our objective. Apparently he thought it might be north to join General Burgoyne, but he wasn't sure." He sobered. "Whatever he thought, he has lately crossed the Delaware and is marching south. Obviously he now knows we're here and has correctly guessed we intend taking Philadelphia."

For a few seconds the only sound was the storm passing outside.

"Our best agents tell us he has about fourteen thousand soldiers. About three thousand of them are sick or otherwise disabled from battle. That leaves eleven thousand effectives. Of those, many are militia, which means they will be the first to run at the sight of a bayonet charge."

Howe paused to run a thumb down his jawline. "He has sent Benedict Arnold and Daniel Morgan with a few of his riflemen up north to help Horatio Gates. I judge General Burgoyne will have little trouble with the lot of them. If we succeed in taking Philadelphia soon, I will send a force to Albany to meet General Burgoyne. In the meantime I'm sure he can fend for himself."

Half the officers moved in their chairs, unwilling to look Howe in the eye. Too many of them knew the temper and the fighting capability of the New Englanders in the forests. They had heard the stories of British officers who led their commands into the New England woods, never to be heard of again. Leave Burgoyne to fight the New Englanders and their forests alone? They feared for him.

Howe shifted his weight from one foot to the other and wiped at his mouth. "At this moment we have fifteen thousand regulars, battle ready. That gives us a slight numerical superiority, but more than that, our forces are both trained and experienced. In short, should we engage the rebel army, the odds favor us."

Lightning flashed in the distance, and he waited for the grumble of thunder to reach them. There was an urgency in his voice as he continued.

"I want each of you to understand what I am going to say." An edge came into his voice. "We are not here *just* to engage the rebels. We are not here *just* to take Philadelphia. That city is little more than the bait to draw Washington out in the open." He leaned forward, eyes narrowed. "We are here to destroy the Continental Army. Utterly destroy it. There is no other way to end this rebellion. So long as Washington and any part of his army survives, he can gather more men, and we will have accomplished nothing. Nothing! If he loses a thousand men, he can get a thousand more. If we lose a thousand men, we cannot replace them. It's that simple. Either we crush the entire army, and Washington with it, or we have lost."

Howe did not realize that in his ardor he had raised his clenched fist. Nor could he remember ever making such a lengthy speech to his officers. He lowered his hand and took a moment to recover his composure and his thoughts.

"Are there any questions?"

Cornwallis raised a hand. "Do we have intelligence on the number of cannon Washington is bringing?"

"Not current. Twelve days ago, there were not many. He may have picked up some on the way."

"Has it been decided where we will meet him?"

"No. Until we know his plan and marching speed, we won't know. He may stop in Philadelphia, or he may come on through. We'll have to wait."

Knyphausen spoke up. "Would it be prudent to wait until the mud has firmed? Wagons and cannon will be hard to move."

"If the storms the past two days reached Washington, he'll have the same trouble. We move on. More questions?"

"We have only one regiment of cavalry. The Sixteenth Dragoons. Is that enough for the battle?"

Howe shook his head. "Questionable. We didn't have enough space on the ships for all the cavalry, so I left one regiment behind in reserve. There isn't time to get them here. We'll move without them."

"Do we have enough horses left to mount the Sixteenth?"

"It will be close."

The officers shared glances and remained silent while Howe concluded.

"We march out at eight o'clock in the morning. I'll lead with General Cornwallis. Following will be the wagons and cannon. General Knyphausen will bring up the rear. I'll have written orders for all of you when we assemble at one o'clock. You are dismissed."

The heart of the storm had moved north. The lightning was now but dull flashes in the black, bulging clouds, with the thunder a low, distant rumble, more felt than heard. The wind had slowed, and the rain fell steadily. The officers draped and latched their wet capes over their shoulders and settled their soggy hats onto their heads. As they filed out of the command tent, with its pennants hanging rain-soaked and limp, each was irresistibly drawn to pause in the mud and the rain to stare northward.

There, near the center of the camp, rising stark and sharp against the leaden sky, a gallows had been constructed. Ten steps led to the raised platform over which two ropes dangled, each with the thirteen wraps and the knot that locked the hangman's noose. None of the officers pondered the reason that no man was able pass a gallows without stopping to stare, white-faced, wide-eyed. Was it because the conscience of most men condemns them to their own gallows in their hearts?

Every officer in General Howe's command had seen hangings before. Some had ordered them. Each knew the procedure. The reading of the charges. The sentence. The question, "Is there anything you wish to say?" The nod to the hangman. The pulling of the long handle. The loud clicking as the trap sprung. The downward swinging of the door. The sudden dropping of the bodies. The muffled snapping of the bones. The creaking of the overhead beam as the body swung, twisting.

They had seen hangings, but they could not force themselves to mount their horses and move on to their commands before they had stopped with the rain tapping on their hats and shoulders while they stared at the gallows.

Then, shoulders hunched against the pelting rain, they scattered, each spurring his horse through the muck back to his command. As their mounts picked their way through the brown puddles, each of them turned in the saddle to look once more to the north, beyond the gallows. In their minds they were seeing George Washington, tall on that dappled gray horse, while their thoughts ran.

He's up there. With that gathering of rabble he calls an army. How far? Coming which direction? Will he stop at Philadelphia? Come on past? Where will we meet him? Where will the battle take place? How many cannon are we facing? He's hard to bring to a stand. Survives. Win or lose, somehow he always survives to gather up more rabble and fight again. Will we be able to crush him this time? End this ridiculous rebellion? Will we?

★   ★   ★   ★   ★

Fifty-nine miles to the north, two miles beyond Philadelphia, General George Washington sat at his table in the command tent of the Continental Army, head bowed, eyes closed to concentrate. The deep rumble came again, faintly, and he rose to walk to the tent flap and push it aside to peer south. Thick, purple storm clouds lay low on the horizon, creeping steadily up the Delaware River in the afternoon sun. As he watched, the first gentle ground-breeze passed, to stir the flag and move the canvas tent walls.

Another one coming.

A look of concern crossed his face as he glanced about the camp. Steam rose from the mud and the puddles left by the storm that had passed through the day before and that had dwindled and died in the night. Wet firewood for the morning and noon meals had left a hazy canopy of gray smoke hovering above the camp. The soldiers slogged through the sticky morass that sucked at their shoes and moccasins, leaving them mud-caked to their knees as they went for water to finish the cleanup and to fill the kettles for the supper meal. Humidity hung like a dead weight, stifling, sweating the men.

Another storm—it will be hard to move the cannon and wagons. But harder for General Howe, if my reports are right.

He was turning to go back to his chair when the sound of horses stopped him. Laurens and Hamilton came cantering in, mud-splattered mounts throwing dirty water high as their hooves sank out of sight. They slowed to a walk as they approached Washington and dismounted. He held the flap for them to enter his tent.

"Report."

"The officers are on their way."

They came two or three at a time, wearing mud-speckled uniforms and dirty boots, riding dirty horses. Washington waited until all had hung their hats and were seated at the council table.

"You know that General Howe has landed his army at Head of Elk. Latest reports say he is preparing to march, probably east, then north up the Delaware. There is now no doubt he is after us, and Philadelphia, probably in that order."

Cadwalader interrupted. "When? Any reports on when to expect him?"

"None." He stopped, then added, "There are some matters we have to settle."

He spread a map on the table, weighted the corners, and tapped an index finger. "We're here, two miles north of Philadelphia." He shifted his finger down to the northern tip of the mighty Chesapeake Bay. "General Howe is here, fifty-nine miles south of us. The storm yesterday, and the one coming up the river right now, are going to slow both him and us."

He shifted his finger back to Philadelphia. "Both armies are on the west side of the Delaware. Our line of march is going to be down the river, generally southerly. I expect Howe to be coming north, up the river. With the new storm coming, there is no way to say how rapidly the

British can move through the mud, which means we have no way of knowing where we'll meet them. We will have to wait and see."

He tapped the map once more. "Tomorrow we are going to march through Philadelphia on parade. The citizens are expecting us to defend the city. We have to give them cause to hope. Do everything you can to present your commands in their best dress. They must march in rank and file, muskets cleaned, on their right shoulders, bedrolls tied and slung on their backs."

Knox raised his hand "This mud is going to make it hard to have them presentable."

"Do the best you can." Washington pursed his mouth for a moment. "My reports state that the British have lost virtually all their horses. I have no idea how they intend moving their cannon and all their supply wagons. Fortunately, we have enough horses."

He turned to General Henry Knox, the round little man who had been a librarian before he led the historic 1775 expedition to Fort Ticonderoga to bring back most of the cannon for the successful siege of Boston. His fierce love for cannon had compelled him to read everything he could find about them. In time he became a leading authority, although he had never fired a cannon, and Washington had promoted him to the rank of general and charged him with the responsibility of being commander of all cannon in the Continental Army.

"Be certain the cannon are prominent as we pass through."

There was a hint of pride in Knox's response. "Yes, sir."

Again Washington paused for a moment. "General Howe brought only one regiment of cavalry. The Sixteenth Dragoons. And my information is he likely does not have enough horses to mount them properly. I mention this because in the event we do engage in an all-out battle, knowing he lacks effective cavalry could be critical to us making the correct decisions in the field. Lack of effective cavalry means he has no highly mobile force to reinforce his infantry, should they be in need."

He moved on. "They have a slight numerical superiority—about fifteen thousand to our eleven thousand effectives. But, there are some things in our favor that we have not had before. First, we will not have a river at our back. Only open country. We can maneuver much more freely, even retreat quickly should that be required. Second, we have in our ranks several companies that are familiar with the Delaware River basin and the country surrounding."

Lafayette raised a hand. "Will we acquire more cannon from the militia in Philadelphia?"

"Yes. How many, I cannot tell. But there will be some. That brings us to the question of military supplies."

Washington straightened and for a moment compressed his lips in a straight line. "I have sent written orders to the militia in Philadelphia. They are to clear the city of everything that could be used by the British to support their army—food, gunpowder, shot, cannon, muskets, blankets, medicines—anything. Get it out of the city, into the country where it can be scattered in all directions should the British get past us and succeed in taking Philadelphia."

He paused to take a new direction. "I have also notified Congress that we are expecting a battle and that the delegates should be prepared to vacate Philadelphia on one hour's notice, should the need arise. They are prepared."

He took a deep breath and slowly exhaled. "I want to impress on you the foundation on which this army will proceed until further notice. We will meet the British, and we will defend Philadelphia because Congress and the citizenry expect it of us. But we will not defend it to the death."

For a moment all movement, all comment, ceased. He paused to allow the statement to settle in, then continued. "General Howe has spent his entire summer campaign trying to maneuver us into a position where he can destroy this entire army, including this war council. He knows that only then can he stop our fight for freedom."

An unusual intensity crept into his voice. "I will not let that happen. Should the battle go against us, we must save the core of this army to fight on. As long as we have the heart of the army intact, we can acquire replacement troops and supplies. General Howe cannot, and he knows that. He has to crush us totally and quickly. So, I repeat. I will not let that happen. I trust you will all abide that simple fundamental."

For long seconds silence held in the tent before Washington moved and spoke.

"Any questions?"

General Thomas Conway, the French-Irish officer who had notably trained his command to the highest state of readiness in the army, spoke up.

"Will the men be issued shot and gunpowder for the parade?"

"No. There is no chance we'll meet the British in Philadelphia. I see no need to run the risk of mistakes or accidents. Further questions?"

"Is it possible Burgoyne will get past Gates and come down on our flank?"

Washington rounded his mouth and slowly blew air for a moment. "You know General St. Clair gave him Fort Ticonderoga without a fight. You probably know our forces have been in a steady retreat since. General Arnold is up there now, with Daniel Morgan and some of his riflemen, to support General Gates. I learned this morning that on August sixteenth there was a decisive battle at Bennington, a few miles east of the Hudson. General John Stark of the New Hampshire Militia and Colonel Seth Warner with his Green Mountain Boys took down nearly the entire commands of Generals Baum and Breymann and their Hessians. Roughly one thousand of them. General Burgoyne is hurt, and in my opinion is finding out that the wilderness is his greatest enemy. I repeat to you what I have recently put in a letter. 'Now, let all New England turn out and crush Burgoyne.' I have no fear that without General Howe's forces to support him, General Burgoyne will fail."

Washington paused, then concluded. "We'll march out at eight o'clock in the morning. We'll pass through Philadelphia sometime around noon. It is possible some Tories and British sympathizers will attempt to interrupt us. I doubt it, but it's possible. Order your men that should that happen, they remain in rank and file and keep moving." A rare smile came and was gone. "I expect it will be a memorable thing, marching past Independence Hall, where Congress is convened, and past the print shop where Benjamin Franklin had his beginnings. Tell your men to step smartly. I'll have written orders delivered to you in the morning. You are dismissed."

The officers filed out, and although their boots were already mud-caked, they stepped judiciously over and around the worst of the mire as they walked to their horses.

General Henry Knox grunted as he lifted his left foot high to the stirrup and hauled his short, heavy frame into the saddle. He paused to peer south at the menacing storm clouds moving steadily toward them. Concern was evident in his voice as he spoke of his beloved cannon.

"Seems like all we've had the last while is storms. Rain and mud, mud and rain. Hard on cannon."

Cadwalader studied the rising purple billows. "That storm's not good for a marching army, but that's not the concern. The concern is the storm that's coming behind it."

He turned to Knox, and Knox nodded but said nothing as the two of them reined their horses around, splashing in the mud.

Notes

New England experienced frequent and violent summer storms in August 1777. General Howe had held his men on the ships for forty-seven days through the worst of the summer heat of July and August. Twenty-seven hundred horses died on board and were thrown into the bay; the three hundred that survived were unloaded and went into a nearby cornfield to gorge on green corn and became sick with colic. Men became sick and died. Heat prostration was rampant. Fresh water became stale, the food rancid. The rains turned the Maryland countryside into a quagmire, the rivers and streams overflowing. The men became surly, nearly mutinous, and in anger plundered the countryside. Howe issued orders to cease; the men refused, and Howe held court. Two men were sentenced to hang, five to be flogged, and their sentences were carried out.

General Howe divided his army into two divisions, one under General Cornwallis, the other under German General Knyphausen, and began his march for Philadelphia. See Mackesy, *The War for America*, p. 126; Leckie, *George Washington's War*, pp. 349–50.

For a visual presentation of the route and the towns, see the map found in Freeman, *Washington,* p. 321.

Howe's orders were to destroy the Continental Army and General Washington. To do so he had brought but one regiment of cavalry. See Mackesy, *The War for America, 1775–1783,* p. 128.

On his way to meet General Howe, General Washington paraded his troops through Philadelphia. See Flexner, *Washington, The Indispensable Man,* p. 103.

Corpulent, short General Henry Knox was a librarian and bookseller before joining the Continental Army. Higginbotham, *The War of American Independence,* p. 105.

Washington gave orders to remove everything from Philadelphia that might help the British, and it was done. See Mackesy, *The War for America, 1775–1783,* p. 129.

The battle of Bennington is described, with the fact that Daniel Morgan and Benedict Arnold were both in the north to assist in the fight against General Burgoyne. See Ketchum, *Saratoga,* pp. 306–38.

General Washington repeats his fundamental principle herein, of not engaging in any battle that could result in loss of the core of the Continental Army. Ketchum, *Saratoga,* p. 48.

CHAPTER VIII

★ ★ ★

*I*n the lantern light of his cramped hospital tent, Dr. Leonard Folsom sighed and drew the sheet up to cover the sightless eyes of an old soldier. He turned to the table in the corner, glanced at the clock, dipped his quill in the inkwell, and scratched the time, date, and cause of death in his medical ledger: ten minutes past two o'clock A.M., Sunday, September 7, 1777, fever. He dropped the quill on the ledger and turned to Mary with a weary sadness.

"Name's Welles. Casper Welles. Said he was from Company Three, Ninth New York Regiment. Find an officer from that regiment and have him tell the sergeant to burn everything the man had—everything. Wrap the body in something for burial—don't take time to build a coffin. Don't mention fever—don't want to start a panic—and don't let anyone get near. Can't let it infect others. Dr. Waldron and I will examine the people who've been near this man lately. This army doesn't need an epidemic. Stay until he's buried; then report back to me."

Captain Charles Venables of the Ninth New York Regiment held a lantern high to lead Mary through the darkness of the silent, slumbering Continental Army camp, four miles east of the Brandywine Creek in southern Pennsylvania. He stopped at the place where Third Company was bedded. In the humid air the grasses were drenched with dew, and Mary's shoes and the bottom of her skirt were both soaked. Mary waited as Venables shook the shoulder of a stocky, red-bearded sergeant who grunted awake. Venables hunkered low to speak softly in the lantern glow.

"O'Malley, remember Casper Welles felt poorly at evening mess? Went to that new doctor who came in from Morristown a couple days ago?"

"Yes, sir."

"Welles died a few minutes ago. Doctor says he has to be buried right now. Burn everything he had. No time for a coffin—wrap him in something, maybe a blanket. Get someone to help. Do it now, before the camp wakes up. Doctor's orders. Understand?"

"Buried now? In the middle of the night?"

"Doctor said."

"Why?"

"Don't know. Maybe it's something bad. Like smallpox or plague."

Mary heard a sharp intake of air, then a perfunctory, "Yes, sir."

Venables jabbed a thumb over his shoulder. "Doctor sent this nurse to see it done. She has to report back to him. Pick a man and follow me."

"Have the girl turn her back."

O'Malley pulled on his breeches, then his socks and shoes and signed to Venables and Mary to wait. He faded into the darkness to return in less than a minute with a sleepy-eyed young soldier following, struggling to clear his sleep-fogged brain. O'Malley's Irish brogue sounded as he spoke low to Venables. "Private Dunson. The one who writes."

The two followed Venables and Mary back through the night, stopping but once at a regimental supply wagon to silently collect a pick, a shovel, and a lantern, then continue on to the small hospital tent, glowing dully from the lamp inside.

Venables raised a hand. "Don't forget to burn his things."

"Yes, sir."

Venables left silently while O'Malley dropped the pick and shovel, held the tent flap for Mary and Caleb, then followed them inside.

The three crowded into the small space, then stood staring at the eerie scene before them. The lamp on the corner table was turned low, and the faint yellow light cast great, grotesque shadows on the canvas walls and ceiling. Draped with a white sheet, the small, wiry body of Casper Welles lay full length on a rough pine surgical table in the center of the small space. Caleb gaped at the scene and held his breath against the stench of death. He shuddered, shrinking from the haunting impression that a departed spirit was among them, lingering in the night. For a time he and the others stood rooted, caught up in an uninvited, weird sensation that raised the hair on the backs of their necks.

O'Malley was the first to move. He set the unlighted lantern down on the floor and spoke. "We'll need something to wrap him in."

Mary pointed, and O'Malley turned to the corner nearest the tent flap, where discarded bedding was folded and stacked. On top of the pile was a ragged quilt, hand-stitched in a forgotten time and place by women seated around a quilting frame in a frontier cabin. He handed the quilt to Caleb, then tucked the white sheet under the body from both sides. As he lifted the remains of Casper Welles, Mary and Caleb slipped the quilt beneath the body, then waited while O'Malley lowered the thin corpse. They wrapped the remains and for a moment stood in the grip of the shadowy silence before Caleb spoke to O'Malley.

"I'll carry him. You lead with the lantern."

O'Malley picked the lantern from the floor, and while Caleb folded the small body over his shoulder, O'Malley raised the chimney on the lamp in the corner and used the flame to light the second lantern. He held the tent flap open and followed Caleb and Mary out into the night with the lantern held high. Mary stooped to lift the pick and shovel from the ground.

O'Malley held out his hand. "Let me carry those."

The few soldiers who stirred from their slumbers to peer at them as they passed in the darkness made no movement or sound as they watched a lantern float past, casting a circle of yellow light on a man with a pick and shovel in his hands, followed by a second man carrying a wrapped corpse over his shoulder, and a third shadowy figure that appeared to be a woman. Those who witnessed the silent procession settled back into their blankets while their sleep-drugged memories reached back to early childhood. Once again they were wide-eyed children sitting cross-legged before glowing embers in the great stone fireplace of their homes, terrorized by hushed stories of grave robbers and ghouls. When they finally found the courage to make their trembling way to their beds, they pulled the quilts over their heads and waited to be snatched up by warlocks and witches.

With the camp more than one hundred yards behind them, O'Malley halted. Caleb stooped to lay the frail, wrapped body in the wet grass and then reached for the pick. For more than an hour Mary watched the two sweating men dig in the rocky soil, alternating in their use of the pick and shovel, working steadily to pitch the dirt and rocks out of the hole onto a growing mound. Mary raised her eyes to the quarter-moon, hanging low in the west, then to the numberless points of light in the black heavens, and her thoughts ran.

All His. So huge. Vast. Endless. How small we are. Yet—He knows when the sparrow falls. He knows we are here now to give the remains of this man back to mother earth. One of His children.

She lowered her eyes and peered at the black hole, dim in the moonlight.

How many of His children have I seen crippled in this war? Dead? Five hundred? One thousand? Two thousand? How many times have I stood beside graves? Too many. An involuntary shudder surged. *So much suffering. Pain. All needless. Love one another. So simple. So simple.*

The first gray of dawn was separating the earth from the black velvet dome when the men climbed out of the hole. It was but four feet deep and scarcely long enough and wide enough for the wrapped corpse, but the unrelenting pressures of time and war would allow no more. The two men knelt at either end of the grave, seized the quilt, and bent low to settle the remains of Casper Welles into its final resting place. They stood and wiped sweat with their sleeves as they stared down.

O'Malley cleared his throat. "I . . . uh . . . someone ought to say a little something. I'm not good at it."

Mary stepped forward, and the two men bowed their heads. With the morning star fading in the east, she spoke softly. "We commit the remains of this child of the Almighty to its final resting place. May he find the peace of our Lord and Savior. From dust are we created, and to dust shall we return."

"That was fine," O'Malley murmured. They stood quietly for a few seconds, each with his or her own thoughts before O'Malley reached for the shovel.

After filling in the grave, they turned their backs on the unmarked mound and strode back toward the camp. With the eastern sky glowing rose-red, it seemed the work of the night was but a strange dream. They did not look back. They returned the pick and shovel and the lantern to the supply wagon and continued on to the hospital tent.

"I'll burn his things," O'Malley volunteered. "Tell the doctor and Captain Venables."

"I will. Thank you both."

The high wisp of clouds was shot through with the golden rays of a sun not yet risen when Caleb paused for the first time to look into Mary's face—the dark eyes, dark hair, striking features. She met his gaze, and he quickly lowered his eyes to stare at the ground, then at O'Malley. He felt the color rise in his face, and he moved his feet, awkward, unsure, wishing he were somewhere else.

"Ma'am," O'Malley said, "I don't know your name. Private Dunson here sometimes keeps the regimental register. We might need your name."

"Mary Flint. I'm a nurse with Dr. Folsom. From Morristown."

"Thank you, ma'am. We should get back to our company."

The men nodded their respects to her and were turning to leave when the banging rattle of the reveille drum came echoing through the trees. At the same instant the vibrations and sounds of a galloping horse coming hard from the south reached them, and both men stopped. A horse pounding through camp at stampede gait at this time of morning meant but one thing. Something catastrophic—good or bad—had happened. They stood still, straining to see movement through the trees.

The tall bay gelding was lathered, sweated, as it flashed past them in the heavy, dead morning air with forelegs reaching, hind legs driving. The rider was low over the neck, giving the horse loose rein, kicking the mount with every stride. Caleb and O'Malley watched him disappear into the trees and listened until the sound was lost in the clamor of an army camp waking up.

O'Malley reached to run his sleeve across his mouth, eyes narrowed, mind racing. "Something's happened. We better get Third Company ready."

The rider reined the horse past the morning fires and around startled men until he came to the command tent of General Washington, with its flagpole and pickets at the flap. He reared back in his saddle and hauled the reins to his chest. The horse threw its head high against the pressure, stiff front legs skidding in the soft earth, hind quarters nearly on the ground as it came to a stop, blowing, dancing sideways, as the rider swung down, hanging onto the reins, fighting the winded gelding. Panting, the man called to the pickets, words coming too fast.

"Gen'l Washington here? I got a message. Important."

"I'll take that rifle."

The messenger puzzled for a moment, then reluctantly surrendered his long, beautifully tooled Pennsylvania rifle.

The picket continued. "A message from who?"

"Colonel Pollard. Pennsylvania militia."

"About what?"

The man's arm shot up to point south. "We seen the British!"

The picket started, then spun to disappear into the tent. Five seconds later he emerged and blurted, "General Washington will see you now."

The messenger, average height, wiry, quick, dressed in fringed buckskins and moccasins, dodged through the entrance and came to an abrupt halt facing the imposing figure of General Washington seated behind the council table. The flustered man started to speak before he remembered he should salute, and then he could not remember if he should remove his wide-brimmed, low-crowned felt hat first. He swept his hat from his head with his left hand, saluted with his right, and plowed on, excited, breathless. His four-day beard moved as he spoke.

"Gen'l, sir, we seen the British. Thousands of 'em. And their cannon." He pointed south, through the tent wall. "Right down south, not far from—"

Washington raised a hand, and the man stopped, confused.

"What is your name?"

"Uh . . . Abram Dearborn."

"What regiment are you from?"

A look of pained frustration crossed the man's face. "Don't rightly remember, sir. Don't recall anyone ever tellin' me. All I done, I joined the militia lately and didn't ask no questions."

"Who is your commanding officer?"

The man brightened. "Colonel Marvin Pollard. Pennsylvania Militia."

"What's the message?"

"The British are down the river, comin' this way." Again he caught himself and quickly added, "Sir."

"Did you see them?"

"It was me seen 'em first. Spent well nigh onto a whole day movin' quiet in the trees, countin'."

"How many troops?"

"Well, sir, I have a little trouble countin' above a thousand, so I counted 'em in thousands."

"How many?"

"Fifteen. Fifteen thousand of 'em, or close thereabouts."

"What color were their uniforms?"

"Three colors. Red, blue, and green."

Washington pursed his mouth for a moment, making calculations. "Cannon?"

"Hundreds."

"How were they moving them?"

"Mostly by men with ropes. A few horses in poor flesh. Some oxen they stolt from farmers."

"How was the column arranged? In sections?"

"No, sir, they was just one long column. Redcoats up front, wagons, cannon, blue coats, green coats, and a few redcoats in the rear."

"Did you see the officers?"

"Some. Most."

"Do you know who they are?"

"Only one. Howe. He's tall enough you can't miss him. Like you." The man caught himself and dropped his eyes for a second. "Beg pardon, sir."

"Did Colonel Pollard tell you to deliver this message verbally?"

The man licked lips that were suddenly dry. "Verbally? I don't know what—"

"Did he tell you what to say, or did he write it out? Did you bring a written message?"

The man's eyes rolled upward in pain. "Ohhh, sir, I don't remember ever bein' so dumb. He wrote it." The man jerked a wrinkled, sealed paper from his leather shirt and thrust it to Washington. It was damp from perspiration. Washington carefully unfolded it and for a full minute read it, read it again, then raised his eyes to the man.

"This says the British are somewhere near Newcastle. That's in Delaware, on the Delaware River. Do you know exactly where they are?"

"Yes, sir, I do. They was moving north."

"When did you last see them?"

"When I mounted my horse to make the run here."

"How many hours?"

"Maybe four, a little more."

"In the night?"

"Yes, sir. The colonel says you had to know quick. Picked me because of my horse. He's a good one."

The sound of an incoming rider stopped both men, and Dearborn turned his head to look. Three seconds later the tent flap was thrown aside and the slight form of Alexander Hamilton burst in. He came to an abrupt halt and saluted.

"Sir, forgive the intrusion. I heard this messenger had arrived. I took the chance you might need me."

Washington nodded. "He has just informed me that we have located what appears to be the entire force under command of General Howe."

Hamilton formed his mouth into a silent, startled "Ooo." "How far, sir?"

"Not far from Newcastle." He turned back to Dearborn. "Could you show me on a map where they are?"

"Easy, if you got one."

Washington anchored the corners of a map and waited. Dearborn laid a finger on it, traced the Delaware, then stopped, finger tapping.

"Right here. Just north of Newcastle. A swampy place. On their way up the river. They was movin' slow because they didn't have horses. I figger they'll likely be at Wilmington in the next two days, right about here, where the Brandywine meets the Delaware."

Washington leaned over the table for a time, intently studying the meandering of the Brandywine Creek. He straightened and turned to Hamilton.

"Help this man with food and drink for him and his horse. Then get Colonel Laurens and assemble the war council here in one hour." He looked at Dearborn. "Well done. Dismissed."

For a moment Dearborn stared into the pale blue eyes, where he saw the iron-willed discipline and the resolve. He shrugged. "Weren't much. Horse done all the work." He was turning to leave before he remembered. "Sir."

Hamilton was grinning when he led him out of the tent.

Washington took a great breath and exhaled slowly, then leaned over the map, palms flat on the table, arms stiff, as he stared intently at the crooked course of the Delaware River, then at Philadelphia, then Newcastle.

He's coming. If we know where he is, I must assume he knows where we are. And if that's true, the question is, does he want Philadelphia more than he wants to crush this army? I do not think so. I think he knows by now the only way he can conclude this war is to eliminate the Continental Army. So the question is, where best to meet him? We will need open country behind us and something in front of us.

Thoughtfully, slowly, he traced the river, pausing at every village, every tributary. His finger stopped where the Brandywine Creek flows into the Delaware.

There. Brandywine.

Twenty minutes later an aide brought his breakfast, and without a word Washington pointed to the small table in the corner. The breakfast was only half eaten and forgotten when the first of the war council arrived thirty-five minutes later, with the others following. Washington waited until all were seated, all eyes on him, intense, waiting.

"I received a written message one hour ago. General Howe and his entire force are just north of Newcastle, on this side of the Delaware."

There was a sharp intake of breath, but no one spoke.

"I do not think he is interested in taking Philadelphia. Before he does that, I believe he means to destroy this army completely."

Open talk erupted, then quieted.

"Does anyone disagree?"

The silence held for several seconds while Washington arranged his words.

"Then I propose we give him his chance."

No one moved. It was over. The weeks and months of frustration, marching, endlessly marching nowhere, were finished. At last, at long last, they were going to meet the British head-on in pitched battle. A mixed sense of relief and apprehension came over them as the full realization of what was to come reached inside.

Washington referred to the map. "Remember, we are outnumbered. And we have fewer cannon than they. With that in mind I've examined the country between where we are and where he is, looking for a place that gives us some advantages. I believe we need open country behind us to maneuver or retreat, if necessary, and we need something in front of us to slow him down."

Murmurs of approval arose and faded.

"I think I have found such a place." He tapped the map. "Here. At Brandywine Creek. It is wide enough and deep enough and straight enough to be a major obstacle to an advancing army. There are some shallow fords, and they can be patrolled by our forces. Should he try to cross at the fords, we can concentrate both men and cannon on them."

He straightened and cleared his throat.

"The only remaining question is, have I judged him correctly? Will he come up the Brandywine to meet us?"

CHAPTER IX

★ ★ ★

*T*here was nothing remarkable about the Brandywine. It was a small, beautiful stream like a hundred others traversing the lush, rolling hills of New England. The two forks, east and west, converge about four miles or so above Chad's Ford to run south. Its length, measured from the headwaters of either fork to the Delaware River, is about thirty-four miles as the crow flies; perhaps thirty-seven miles if one follows the meander line. It runs year-round. Heavy and brown and roiling in the spring with the snowmelt, lighter in the summer and fall, frozen in the winter. Too shallow and narrow for heavy watercraft, the stream was used by farmers as a highway for travel in rowboats, and to water stock and grow crops, which they moved up and down the stream to market in small boats. Philadelphia, Germantown, Whitemarsh, Valley Forge, Chester, Red Bank Redoubt, Wilmington, Newcastle, and Lancaster all lay within thirty miles of the stream, one direction or another.

That this tranquil place would be forever remembered as a pivotal battleground in the war that changed the history of the world is an anomaly made understandable only because many of the events that change history occur in anomalous places. Jeanne d'Arc was born in the quiet country village of Domremy in the beautiful Meuse Valley in France. At age thirteen that simple farm girl heard the voices of angels. At age nineteen she was burned at the stake for obeying them. Mary birthed a son in the obscure little village of Bethlehem. At age twelve he

confounded the priests in the temple. At age thirty-three he was cruci-
fied for it. An unknown shepherd boy walked out into an unremarkable
mountain valley called Elah and struck down a giant with his sling. In a
forgotten field of crops that he himself had planted and nurtured, Cain
slew his brother.

Consistent with the ever unpredictable, often puzzling patterns of
life that become fully discernible only in retrospect, two opposing armies
found themselves facing each other on opposite banks of the
Brandywine, east and west, preparing for battle. The disparity between
the two powers was ludicrous, nearly profane.

The British army, with fifteen thousand of the finest soldiers in the
history of the world were drawing up their battle plans and lines on
the west side, each highly trained man sworn to defend England from all
who would wound her.

The American force, with eleven thousand common citizen-soldiers,
resembling little more than a mob, were entrenching on the east side, each
man in the ragtag army driven by an idea that would not let him do
otherwise. Freedom.

Thus the issue was framed: could the mightiest military power on
earth destroy an idea?

★   ★   ★   ★   ★

The only sound inside the huge, elaborate British command tent was
the buzzing of the late summer flies.

Outside, the still, sultry air weighed heavy in the hot mid-morning
sun. Sweating red-coated soldiers cursed their heavy woolen uniforms as
they worked through the endless daily rituals of a disciplined military
camp. Reveille. Wash. Shave. Straighten bunks, tents, grounds. Gather firewood. Morning mess. Inspection. Inventory food, munitions. Compile
sick and disabled reports—always reports, unending reports. Clean horse
droppings. Feed the stock. Stand for inspection. Drill. Repairs—wagons,
cannon, caissons, muskets, bayonets, picks, shovels, uniforms.

An unsettled feeling crept into the soldiers as they remembered the
two messengers who had ridden in on sweated horses during morning

mess. The two men had spent close to half an hour with General Howe before they emerged from the great tent. They walked their jaded mounts to a water trough to let them drink, then on to the horse pens for a ration of oats before the men went to the enlisted men's mess, where they shared burned sowbelly and fried mush. Finished, they tightened the saddle cinches on their mounts, swung up, and loped out of camp. Through it all, they had refused to answer any questions.

Thirty minutes later the generals began arriving at the command tent, sober, faces set, paying little heed to the bustle of the camp around them. The nearby soldiers studied the twelve saddled horses at the tent entrance and looked again at the aides holding their reins. All officers. Then they turned their eyes to peer east, and their foreheads furrowed as the pieces of the puzzle came together.

The signs were all there. The Americans were just across the Brandywine. Messengers had arrived. Every general in the entire command was inside the command tent.

The enlisted men wiped at sweat as the questions came in a rush. Were the rebels coming? Going? Who would cross the river to attack? The British? The Americans? When would the cannon start? The not knowing and the waiting escalated the uneasiness to a nervous tension. Talk spread.

"If we're headed into a battle, let's cross the bloody creek and get on with it."

"You haven't heard? The rebels won't fight! Those two messengers carried terms of surrender! That's why all the generals are with Howe right now—to hear the terms."

"Surrender? In a pig's eye! The whole lot of 'em don't have the brains to know when they're whipped. Heard about Bennington? Up near the Hudson? Not three weeks ago. One thousand of Burgoyne's Germans gone in one afternoon. No, sir, those lumberin' fools don't know when they're whipped."

Inside the tent, Major General Sir William Howe gave a head nod and an aide dropped the tent flap into place. He turned back to the council table, surrounded by red coats, crossed white belts, golden epaulets, and powdered wigs. Not one man moved. All eyes were wide, all faces masks of concentration.

True to his nature, Howe did not waste a minute or a word.

"Washington has set up his defenses. Two messengers delivered drawings less than an hour ago. He's inviting us to come across the Brandywine and get him."

There was the brief sound of released breath, and the rustle of uniforms as the men moved, then settled. Howe's eyes were glowing. His body and his movements had a feral grace, like a panther gathered, crouched, waiting for the right grain of time to strike an unsuspecting doe at a spring hidden in the forest. In the hallowed halls of Parliament he was awkward, unsure. Here, facing a battle that could decide the war, he was without peer. He was doing what he had been born for. Every officer at the table felt the animal instinct reaching out to touch him, subjecting him to Howe's will, and none resisted.

Howe's long frame leaned slightly forward as he spoke. His words came deliberate, measured.

"We have spent the entire summer campaign waiting for this. We can end this war tomorrow, if we strike hard enough and quick enough. Get every word of this."

On the table before him was a large, detailed map of the Delaware River, from the Atlantic Ocean to McConkie's Ferry, nine miles north of Trenton. Close to the center was the village of Wilmington, near the confluence of Brandywine Creek and the Delaware. The Brandywine angled north from Wilmington, to the place it divided into the east and west branches, above Chad's Ford. He dropped an index finger on the stiff parchment, at a spot a little distance from the west bank of the Brandywine.

"This is the Kennett Meeting House where we arrived several days ago." His finger moved east and stopped near the bank of the creek. "This is where we are now." He moved his finger to the Brandywine. "The creek runs shallow in some places, deep in others, narrow some places, wide in others. There are fords all up and down." He shifted his finger down, reading from the map. "Here is Pyle's Ford. To the north is

Chad's Ford, Brinton's, Painter's, Jones's, Wistar's, Buffington's, Trimble's, Jeffrie's, and up here, Taylor's Ford."

He straightened, and his eyes swept the faces of the officers. The only sound was the quiet buzz of insects in the stifling heat of the tent.

"I'm going to go over this once, working south to north, so get it right. This is how the rebels are positioned." He returned his finger to Pyle's Ford.

"This is the southern end of the rebel positions. Washington's extreme left. John Armstrong has a brigade of Pennsylvania Militia there, nothing more."

He waited until he was satisfied everyone was ready to move on, then moved his finger north, up the creek.

"This is Chad's Ford. Nathanael Greene is entrenched here with two brigades. Washington is with him. I believe Washington intends holding Greene and his command in reserve to reinforce any breakthrough in his lines farther north. I'll come to that."

Again he waited before he moved on.

"North of Chad's Ford, less than two miles, is the center of the rebel line. John Sullivan is entrenched there with two regiments. There's a ford in front of him, but I don't know the name. It makes no difference."

Again he paused, waited, and went on.

"Just north of Sullivan, between Painter's and Brinton's Fords, Adam Stephen has a brigade, here, and just to his right and a little behind him, William Alexander Stirling—Lord Stirling—has a brigade. Stephen and Stirling anchor the right of Washington's positions."

Contemptuous smiles flashed and were gone at the mention of Lord Stirling, the British officer who had claimed the title "Lord" before abandoning England to join the Americans.

"There are small patrols up and down the river, none of them large enough to be of consequence."

He straightened, cleared his throat, and waited until no one was moving.

"Now I want to point out some landmarks you must not forget." Once again his finger tapped the map. "Here, seven miles above Chad's

Ford, is Trimble's Ford. Take a hard look." He waited. "Nearly due east of Trimble's Ford, here, is Osborne's Hill. Both Trimble's Ford and Osborne's Hill are about two miles north of Stirling and Stephen." Again his finger moved. "Between Osborne's Hill and the Americans, here, is a road called Street Road. It runs east and west. Behind Stirling and Stephen, here, not far from Street Road, is the Birmingham Meeting House. Now, study this map until you have all those places well in mind."

He straightened and waited for three minutes while each officer committed the landmarks to memory.

"Let's move on. You will remember the battle of Long Island. Our forces moved up the Jamaica Road to come in behind the rebels, and we caught them by total surprise. The same at White Plains. We circled behind them again, and they broke."

Instantly the plan that was coming clarified in the minds of most of the officers, and they stiffened, then leaned back, waiting.

Howe's finger tapped Trimble's Ford. "The rebels have no one here. It is not patrolled. Either Washington or Sullivan—most likely Sullivan—has simply ignored it, exactly as he did the Jamaica Pass on Long Island. We're going to take a major force of men to that ford, cross the Brandywine, move on around Osborne's Hill, turn south toward Street Road, past Birmingham Meeting House, and come in directly behind Stirling, Stephen, and Sullivan. They're the center of the entire rebel army. If we can catch them by surprise, we can destroy the center, and from there it will be a simple matter to crush Greene and Washington and then Armstrong. The heart of the Continental Army."

Excited talk broke out as the officers caught the vision of it. Simple. Practical. Workable. Howe raised a hand and went on.

"To do it, we shall divide into two divisions. General Cornwallis and I will take ten thousand troops north to Trimble's Ford, cross it, and come in behind the American center."

Cornwallis nodded his understanding.

"General Knyphausen will take the remainder of our forces—about five thousand men and most of the cannon—and move east. He will stop just short of the Brandywine Creek bank and make a strong show out where the Americans can see, of getting prepared for battle. He will then commence a general cannonade of Sullivan's positions to hold them where they are. He must make Sullivan think we intend crossing the Brandywine in a frontal attack."

He turned to look at Knyphausen. The German general's lower lip was thrust forward, face passive. He neither looked at Howe, nor spoke. Orders were orders.

"General Knyphausen, you will maintain the cannonade until you hear shooting from the rear of the rebel positions. That will be General Cornwallis and myself. The sound of our artillery will mean we're in position behind them, and that will be your signal. When you hear it, you cross the Brandywine and commence a direct frontal assault on Sullivan. With us behind him and you in front, the center and the right wing of the rebel positions will be ours almost immediately. From there, we go south immediately to take Greene and Washington. Do you understand?"

The German bobbed his head once. "Ja. I understand."

Howe reached with a white handkerchief to wipe at the sweat on his forehead. With the flap closed, the temperature inside the tent was becoming unbearable.

"Timing will be critical. General Cornwallis and I will march out at precisely four o'clock tomorrow morning. That means everything has to be in readiness tonight before tattoo. Tell your men only two things: Be ready, and that we march at four o'clock. Nothing more is to be said until we are at Trimble's Ford."

He stopped and partially closed his eyes while he searched for anything he had missed. He could think of nothing.

"Questions?"

"What about the cavalry? With whom does it go?"

"What little we have will be with General Cornwallis and myself. We will likely need the riders to strike at the first place the rebel lines show weakness. Anything else?"

No one spoke.

"I will have written orders delivered to you this afternoon."

He stopped, waited for silence, then leaned forward, palms flat on the table, arms straightened. His eyes met each of theirs as he spoke.

"I told you before, and I repeat it now. To end this revolution, we must first destroy the rebel army and Washington himself. We cannot let him escape with any remnant of his army. If he does, he will gather more of his rabble and fight on, and we will have failed. Tomorrow we take them down. When the sun sets, Washington and the rebels must be ours."

Notes

The description of Brandywine Creek and the surrounding towns, villages, and fords is accurate. The battleground, the location of the opposing armies, the general battle plan of General Howe and the British, the commanders of the two great British divisions, Generals Cornwallis and Knyphausen, and the progress of the two armies as the battle approached were as described. See Leckie, *George Washington's War*, pp. 350–52; Freeman, *Washington*, pp. 349–50. In particular, see map opposite page 321, Freeman, *Washington*, and map opposite page 352, Leckie, *George Washington's War*.

CHAPTER X

★ ★ ★

*T*homas Cheyney, husky, bearded, square-faced, burned brown by winter snows and summer suns, softly closed the plank door to his kitchen, hitched his suspenders over his shoulders, and walked ten steps out into the hard-packed dirt of his dooryard. He stopped and slowly turned completely around, eyes turned upward as he studied the cloudless heavens, gray in the approaching sunrise. The early morning Delaware River breeze coming up the Brandywine, a quarter mile east of the house, was soft and cool on his face. He glanced at the rutted wagon road that ran past the barn to Trimble's Ford, half a mile north.

He scuffed his shoe in the dirt beneath his feet and studied it for a moment. The earth was still damp from the torrential storms that had swept through ten days earlier, and the three summer rains that had fallen since, but the sun had dried it in the last three days enough to support horses and a loaded wagon. He felt a rise of satisfaction as he strode on toward his low, unpainted, slab-sided barn.

He had won. This year he had won. Most of the fourteen acres of wheat he and the children had planted in the spring and nurtured throughout the summer had survived the first storms of fall. The heavy heads were full and golden in the dawn, the stalks swaying gently, like waves on the ocean in the morning breeze. They would have wheat through the winter for their pigs, and the cow and steer, and the chickens. And there would be enough for Mother to bake her twelve loaves of

bread each Tuesday and cakes and pies for the German Christmas celebration and birthdays and once in a while on Saturday, for a Sunday
afternoon feast after church. The dawn-to-dark, rough, unending work
had been rewarded this year.

Last year? He had lost. Two nights before the harvest, nature had
rebelled. A violent storm had struck and held through the day. Howling
winds had stripped trees and lifted shakes from the roof of the barn.
Rain had fallen so thick that from the small south window in the
kitchen, the barn was only a gray blur. Twice that morning he had
slogged through mud a foot deep to reach the wheat field. By the second
visit, not one stalk was left standing. The wind had laid the entire field
down and stripped the stalks to leave the full heads of wheat soaked,
swollen, useless in the mud. He trudged back to the house to sit down
at the table for a long time in silence, shoulders sagging, while he slowly
worked his hard, callused hands before him.

His wife knew. With silent gestures she warned the fourteen-year-
old twins, Edith and Esther—sturdy, heart-faced copies of their
mother—to quietly do their chores and twelve-year-old Samuel to go to
his place in the loft at the north end of the house. Careful not to dis-
turb her husband, she and eight-year-old Sarah continued working
silently in the kitchen. The baby, eight-month-old Damon, was asleep in
his crib.

It was half an hour before Thomas rose from his chair, squared his
shoulders, and brought his book of accounts from its place behind a
stone in the fireplace to the table. He began making adjustments and
fresh entries. He could trade the heifer calf and six of the weaner pigs
for wheat. Maybe work for Heinrich Steinman up the road for some
more. Steinman had more than three hundred acres of crops. He kept
two hired hands, year-round. He had gotten half of his fifty-five acres
of wheat harvested before the storms hit. He likely had thirty, maybe
thirty-five tons in his bins. Steinman was a hard, frugal man, but he was
fair. Thomas had worked for him twice before, once for a calf, once for a
colt, and though Steinman's severe, humorless expression never changed,
Thomas was sure Steinman approved of his work. Maybe Steinman

would part with some of his wheat for work. Maybe his barn needed a new roof or his pens needed new rails or his fences new posts. Maybe. Thomas worked on his ledger in silence for an hour before he turned defensive eyes to his wife.

"Polly, the wheat's gone."

He used her name only in unusual times. She stopped and nodded, waiting.

"I'll try to trade the new heifer calf for some wheat, and maybe some of the piglets at Birmingham or at Kennett Square. Maybe Steinman will trade wheat for work."

She nodded and went on with her unending work. Once again her world was safe, secure. Thomas would be all right. They would survive the loss of their year's wheat, and they would go on with the unending cycle of planting, nurturing, harvesting, and enduring through the winters. That night in the quiet of their bed she would reach for him and would hold him, giving her strength to him, her assurance that she knew he could find his way through.

Next year? Come spring, they would plow and plant again and nurture and pray and watch the weather. And now next year had come, and the heavens had smiled on them. The Cheyney barn and sheds and root cellar would be full.

Those who do not till the soil to sustain life will never know the primal satisfaction that comes to those who plant and nurture in faith and trust the Almighty to reward them according to His will.

There was strength in Thomas's stride as he marched to the barn and opened the door to the pen where their Guernsey cow waited, bag full and dripping. Four years before Samuel had named the cow Chronicles. He didn't know why. He only knew he had heard their minister, tall and rigid in the pulpit, read from a place in the Bible he called Chronicles, and Samuel thought it was a fine name for a tan and white Guernsey cow with short horns that curled inward.

Thomas held the door open while the patient animal entered the barn and walked to her milking stanchion. He dropped the lock bar into place and forked dried grass into the manger before her, then settled onto the one-legged milking stool. He leaned his forehead into the cavity of her flank and began the rhythmic pumping that would drain her udder. The fresh milk came warm and frothy, hissing into the wooden bucket, to be taken to the cool of the root cellar. What remained of yesterday's milk was there in jars, and today Eva would begin the process of separating it—butter to trade and sell across the Brandywine at Birmingham or west at Kennett Square—cheese for the winter, whey for the sow and her annual litter of ten piglets.

Finished, he tossed the locking block on the stanchion upward to release Chronicles. She would remain until she had finished the dried grass hay, then return to her pen to be turned out to pasture later in the morning. Thomas dropped the milking stool into the corner and walked out of the barn with the rope handle of the wooden milk bucket in his left hand.

He cast his eyes east, across the creek, as he remembered the day just over a week before when the Continental Army had marched past on the far road. He had gathered the entire family into the wagon and driven the team to Trimble's Ford to watch them as they marched, muddy to the knees, muskets over their shoulders, loud, shouting at their horses as the jaded animals struggled to pull first the cannon and then the wagons in the rutted road. Fourteen thousand of them, with General George Washington, tall and erect near the front, leading them south to meet the British.

Shy, with diverted eyes, Edith and Esther, just on the cusp of sensing the power women exercise over men, had watched the soldiers pass and felt the delicious color rise in their faces when some of the marching men tipped their hats and smiled or called to them. Samuel had stood spellbound and pointed wide-eyed at the cannon as the horses dragged them past, mud-splattered, jolting between the five-foot-tall wheels that sank in the muddy road halfway to the axles. The campfires of the army had glowed in the southern sky that night, and then they were gone.

Thomas lifted the door into the root cellar and descended the five steps to the cool, damp earthen floor. While he carefully poured the morning milk into great jars, his thoughts were still with the Continental Army.

The soldiers are somewhere down there now, across the creek, looking for the British. Will they find them? I wonder if they'll find them. If they do, will there be a battle? He finished pouring the milk and climbed from the cellar back out into the bright sunlight and the quiet beauty of the late summer September morning. As he strode to the house with the milk bucket to be washed, his mind came back to practical, hardheaded New England conclusions. *Well, they'll find them or they won't find them. There will be a battle or there won't be a battle. Either way, it won't get the wheat harvested and into the bin.*

He set the bucket by the kitchen door and walked inside, blinking as his eyes adjusted. He poured water from a pitcher into a pewter basin on the washstand in the corner and washed his hands and face, then reached for a towel.

"Places," he called, and two minutes later he was seated at the head of the table, Polly facing him at the far end, with the children on both sides. He bowed his head, uttered a perfunctory grace over clasped hands, and waited. Polly circled the table, a large bowl of steaming oatmeal porridge on her hip, working with a great wooden spoon to portion generous helpings into the bowls before each of them. A little molasses, a little milk, a thick slice of Polly's bread piled heavy with butter, and the chatter quieted while breakfast was finished.

Thomas pushed his empty pewter bowl away, and the children settled, knowing the signs, waiting for his orders.

"Wheat's ready," he said. "Samuel and I will hitch up the team. Edith, you drive. Samuel, you're in the wagon stacking. I'll cut, and Esther and I will shock for a while, then Edith and Esther will trade. This is Thursday. We've got to have it all in the bin Saturday night, before the Sabbath."

Without a word they all rose and quietly went about preparing for their assignments. The foundation of their existence, the place their thinking began and ended, rested on the hard fact that they ate or starved, prospered or suffered, lived or died by the crops that were in the bin and the barn and the root cellar.

The girls, dressed in worn, plain cotton, ankle-length work dresses covered their hair with white bandannas. Thomas and Samuel wore loose cotton shirts and trousers that reached below their knees but left their lower legs bare. They all wore heavy, hard-leather work shoes.

Thomas backed his team of two big, heavy-boned Percheron draft horses on either side of the wagon tongue, swung the heavy leather harnesses over their backs, shoved the big U-shaped horse collars upward ahead of the horses' shoulders, and snapped them into place while Samuel connected the tugs to the singletrees. Thomas threaded the reins through the rings, back to the driver's box, and wrapped them around the brake pole while the three children climbed a wheel and sat down inside the two-foot-deep walls of the wagon. Inside with them was a three-tined wooden pitchfork and the big scythe with its peculiar S-shaped handle and three-foot-long blade. Samuel glanced at the cutting edge, shiny where Thomas had worked on it with the long whetstone he carried in his back pocket when he cut wheat or oats or barley or weeds. He would use the stone half a dozen times during the morning, stroking the cutting edge quickly, refining it. A sharp scythe cut clean, and a clean cut did not shake the ripe wheat heads from the stock into the dirt. To lose wheat heads during cutting was waste, and waste was a sin. They all knew the rules.

Thomas mounted the wagon box, gathered the reins, slapped them down on the big rumps of the two brown horses, and clucked the team into motion. The empty wagon rattled as it rocked and bounced over the rutted dirt road to the wheat field, where Thomas came back on the reins and crooned "hooo" to the horses. He climbed to the ground and waited while Samuel handed him the scythe. Edith took her place in the driver's box while Esther climbed down to stand beside Thomas.

The children watched their father lay the top of the seven-foot-long scythe handle over his right shoulder, seize the hand-grip, and begin swinging the blade in a great semi-circle, right to left. They listened to the familiar pinging sound as the cutting edge sliced through the stalks, and they watched the wheat topple to the right, the direction from which the blade had come. Two minutes later Esther was on the ground, ten feet behind her father. She bent forward at the waist, gathered her left arm full of wheat stalks, deftly wrapped half a dozen stalks around the bundle and knotted them once before she carefully laid the shock on the ground away from the wagon. She moved on, gathering the next armload, setting a steady rhythm.

When Thomas was sixty feet ahead of the horses, he stopped, returned to the wagon, set his scythe in the driver's box beside Edith, and took his place beside Esther, working to tie the loose wheat into shocks. Twenty minutes later Samuel handed him the wooden pitchfork, and Thomas began forking the shocks up to the boy, who carefully laid them in the wagon box, full heads toward the outside, then two rows of shocks down the center. He laid the bundles close, careful not to shake the wheat heads loose. At day's end they would sweep all the loose wheat from the wagon to save it.

At the end of the field, Edith turned the wagon left, stopped the horses, and changed places with Esther while Thomas paused fifteen seconds to run the whetstone scraping down the scythe blade, twice on the top, twice on the bottom, before he once again returned to the twisting, circular cutting motion.

By nine o'clock dark spots of sweat were showing between their shoulder blades. By ten o'clock Samuel was on his knees atop the stacked wheat, nine feet from the ground, when Thomas forked up one more shock and nodded to Edith. Esther climbed into the wagon box next to Edith, who turned the wagon back toward the barn, with Thomas following on foot as the heavy load jolted and swayed out of the field.

Polly brought cold well water, and they drank, then spread great sheets of canvas on the hard-packed earth next to the barn. Thomas brought the jointed flails from the barn while the children threw the shocks down onto the canvas, and five minutes later they were swinging the flails, thrashing the shocks, knocking the wheat heads free on the canvas. The stripped shocks were cast aside to be used for animal bedding, and they began the winnowing. They used small shovels to throw the kernels high in the morning breeze, where the heavier heads fell first, and the chaff drifted away. The precious winnowed wheat was shoveled into baskets and carried into the barn to be dumped into the bin. They drank cold water once again, then took their places to go back to the field for the next load.

The wagon was half full when Samuel suddenly straightened on his knees and his arm shot up, pointing south. "Look!" he shouted.

Instantly Edith hauled the wagon to a stop while all heads jerked around to peer at Samuel, then swivel south, following his point. For five seconds they stared before they saw the flashes of red, green, and blue moving through the heavy growth of trees lining the banks of the stream.

For a moment Thomas's blood froze in his veins. "British," he blurted. "They're coming to cross at the ford."

The girls gasped and turned to him in white-faced terror. Samuel stared down from the loaded wagon, eyes on his father, lower lip trembling, on the brink of tears of outrage and fear. "They can't have our wheat! They *can't!*"

They had heard the stories at the church and at the tiny trading post at Birmingham and at Kennett Square. They knew. In New Jersey, before they marched out to New York, what the British and the Germans wanted, they took at bayonet point, and what they couldn't use they burned to keep from the hands of the Continental Army. On their fifty-seven-mile march from Head of Elk, despite the orders of General Howe to the contrary and hangings and floggings for the offenders, the soldiers had vented their wrath at being in the purgatory of the ships for seven unbearable weeks. They had pillaged the countryside—crops in the field, the winter's food stored in root cellars, cattle, sheep, horses, munitions— anything—and the smoke from the fires they set to destroy the surplus was a dark smudge that could be seen for miles, rising in the blue skies. The stories of what the rampaging soldiers had done to girls and women were spoken in hushed tones wherever adults met.

In one fluid motion Thomas tossed the fork up to Samuel, then vaulted into the wagon box, crowding the girls to one side. He seized the reins and swung the wagon around hard, then slapped the leathers down on the horses and shouted them to a run. With the wagon bouncing crazily behind, the heavy horses galloped to the house, where Thomas brought the startled horses to a sliding stop in the yard. The commotion brought Polly running from the kitchen, white-faced, horrified to think that someone was hurt or dead. Thomas hit the ground running to meet her.

"British! Coming up the creek road."

Polly clapped both hands over her mouth to stand wide-eyed, mind numb. She saw the panic in his face and stood stock-still, waiting for him to speak. He put his hand to his forehead, and she watched him bring his stampeding thoughts and his fear under control. His voice was loud, firm, as he spoke.

"They haven't come for us. They've come for the Continental Army, south of us on the other side of the creek. I don't know what's happened down there, but I believe the British mean to cross the creek and come in behind the American lines. That could be bad."

He paused for a moment. "Someone's got to warn them."

Polly gasped at his meaning. "Thomas—" She bit down on the rest of her sentence and left it unuttered. She would have to take charge of the farm and the children, and she could not let them see her waver.

A faint, low rumble reached them from far to the south, and Thomas cocked his head to listen. It came again, stopped for two seconds, then picked up again like distant, ragged, ongoing thunder. Polly squinted, looking for deep purple clouds looming on the southern skyline, and there were none. She turned to Thomas, her face drawn in question.

"Cannon," he said softly.

Her breath caught in her throat, and he cut her off.

"We're a quarter mile from the road. I don't know if they'll come this far to steal, but we can't take a chance. Polly, you and Edith get sticks and drive the sow and her pigs down to the slough. Leave them. They'll root in the mud and stay there. Go right now and come back as fast as you can."

Eyes alive, flashing, he turned to Esther. "Lead Chronicles out into the woods and tie her to a tree where there's some grass and get back here."

Taking his son by the arm, he said, "Samuel, you're going to have to be the man of the house. Come with me." He led the boy running into the house. "You stay here with Sarah and Damon. I'll be back in a few minutes."

He strode to the fireplace and seized a stick of firewood, to plunge it into the glowing coals Polly had banked from the morning meal. Fifteen seconds later he drew it out, blackened, with flames licking. He shielded it with his hand as he trotted out the door and turned toward the chopping block, where wood chips lay thick on the ground. Ten seconds later he had a small pile of the chips smoking, thirty five feet from the house where two cords of firewood and kindling were stacked. A minute later flames were rising from a dozen sticks of kindling. As fast as he could move, he grabbed rungs of firewood from the stack and piled them onto the flames. He didn't stop until one full cord was heaped on the fire and the first wisps of smoke were seeping upward through the stack, drifting with the breeze into the blue heavens.

He ran back to the house, into the kitchen, where Samuel was holding Sarah to his chest, trying to stop her crying. Thomas went to one knee beside the child and tenderly turned her to him and wrapped her in his arms. Slowly her sobbing stopped. He held her away from him, still within his arms.

"It's all right. Don't be afraid. Mother will be back in a few minutes, and then you'll all go over to the woods. You can take some bread and maybe some butter and jam and a jar of milk and have a picnic for a while. Samuel will be there. And the twins. It will be all right."

As she gazed at him, the trust in her blue eyes tore at his heart.

He turned back to Samuel. "Go to the root cellar and get a jar of fresh milk and a block of wrapped butter and some of the blueberry jam."

Samuel bobbed his head and disappeared into the bright September sunlight, to return in three minutes, breathing hard. Thomas got the woven reed shopping basket and placed the milk and butter and jam inside, then raised his head, listening. A moment later a breathless Esther burst into the kitchen.

"Chronicles is tied. Mother and Edith are coming. What's the fire?"

Thomas raised a hand to silence her as he listened to the running steps, and then the two women were in the kitchen, both wide-eyed. "The sow and pigs are at the slough. There's a fire!"

Thomas bobbed his head. "I set it. If they mean to come here to steal, they'll see the smoke from the road and maybe they'll think someone has already been here and set fire to the place."

Polly raised an alarmed hand. "But the wood—"

"I can cut more wood. Now, Esther, get a loaf of bread and some cups for the shopping basket and take it out to the wagon. You're going to have a picnic in the woods. Edith, take Sarah outside with her. Samuel, you go along to help. Polly, wrap Damon. I'll bring his crib."

With the children outside waiting and Polly wrapping Damon in a blanket, Thomas reached to the pegs above the door and lowered his long Pennsylvania rifle, then the powder horn and leather shot pouch. He turned to Polly, who froze at the sight of the rifle. The unspoken question was plain on her face. *You're going to join the war?*

He spoke quickly. "Edith will drive the wagon with the load on it. Esther can ride on top to watch Samuel and Sarah. You ride beside Esther, with Damon. Go west into the woods and hide. I'll leave the rifle with you. If they come into the yard, don't show yourself. Let them do what they will with the house and barn. Stay hidden with the children and the horses."

He stopped, and she saw the awful fear in his eyes. "Polly, if they find you, and they come for you and the girls, use the rifle. Pick the officer in charge and tell them if they come close you'll kill him. If they don't stop, shoot him dead. Do you understand?"

She was beyond words. She nodded.

"Can you do it?"

Tears brimmed in her eyes, and she nodded again.

Thomas swallowed hard. "Polly . . ." He couldn't finish. For one brief moment he wrapped her and the baby within his arms and held them close before he led them out into the yard and helped them all to their places on the wagon. He quickly ran back to the kitchen to return with Damon's crib and toss it up to Samuel.

Edith called, "Won't you need one of the horses to ride?"

"No. I'll swim the creek and get one from the neighbors. Now go."

He watched the wagon move out of the yard and swing left, away from the Brandywine, toward the woods, a quarter of a mile distant. Samuel raised a hand to wave, and Thomas waved back to the boy. Then he turned and ran to the road, which paralleled the creek, and stopped for a moment, fighting to hold his breath while he listened. The faint rumble of the approaching army reached him, and then he heard the unmistakable rattle of drums from far off. Ten seconds later he heard the tramp of thirty thousand marching feet, and heavy wheels moving closer each minute.

He crossed the road and was ten feet from the Brandywine when the first musketball came whistling high above his head, followed instantly by the unmistakable cracking report of a British Brown Bess musket fired from more than two hundred yards to the south, too far for accuracy.

It flashed in his mind—*Patrol. I didn't think of a patrol*—and then came a shouted command.

"'ere, you blasted rebel! Stop! Or we'll shoot you dead!"

He plunged into the stand of willows at the stream's edge and hit the water running, splashing on until it reached above his waist, and then he was swimming strong. He heard three more musket shots and saw water leap high ahead of him as one of the heavy, .75-caliber musketballs tore into the stream. He sucked his lungs full of air and dove, swimming blindly toward the far shore, feeling the current move him downstream, toward the oncoming British. He came up for air once and then he was in the willows on the east bank, legs churning, driving as he plowed through them. Two more shots cracked out before he made the tree line east of the creek and dodged through the oak and maple to the road beyond. He heard angry shouts from the patrol in the trees on the opposite bank as he sprinted to the far side of the road and turned south, running, dodging through the low trees and foliage. He held the pace for more than half a mile, glancing west across the creek to see flashes of the red, green, and blue uniforms marching north. With sweat dripping, he bolted into the dooryard of the Tredwell place and, breathing hard, pounded on the kitchen door. Lucy Tredwell opened the door a crack, wide enough only to peer out with one eye.

"I heard shooting," she exclaimed. "Who's shooting?"

Gasping for air, Thomas panted, "Mrs. Tredwell, the British are marching north on the far side of the creek. They intend crossing at Trimble's and coming right past your farm. Tell your husband. I need a horse to go on south and tell General Washington."

Lucy's face blanched white, and her words came high, hysterical. "The British! We'll all be killed! Killed, I tell you."

"Where's Henry?"

"In the wheat with Phillip. Oh, may the Almighty have mercy!"

"I'm taking your horse. I'll tell Henry. You get ready to leave the house."

Three minutes later Thomas led Henry Tredwell's saddled sorrel mare out of the barn, swung up, and kicked her to a gallop. He reined in three hundred yards south of the house to shout across the fence at Henry and his son in the wheat field, "The British are coming past your farm within half an hour. Clear out. I need your horse to go tell General Washington."

For three full seconds Henry stood transfixed, then waved Thomas on as he frantically barked orders to Phillip and leaped to the wagon box. Thomas reined the prancing horse around and once again raised her to a run, bent low over her neck, holding her back to save enough for the long ride.

Notes

Thomas Cheyney was a resident of the Brandywine Creek area, whose activities in riding to warn General Washington of approaching British troops on September 11, 1777, are accurately described. See Freeman, *Washington*, p. 51; Leckie, *George Washington's War*, p. 351.

The British looted and burned many farms on their march from Head of Elk westward. See Leckie, *George Washington's War*, p. 349.

CHAPTER XI

★ ★ ★

*S*ergeant Randolph O'Malley, New York Ninth Regiment, Third Company, raised his head above the earthen and timber breastworks and for a long time studied the shadowy movements deep in the emerald green of the oak and maple trees eight hundred yards to the west, across the Brandywine Creek. He wiped a dirty, rough sleeve across his sweated eyes and concentrated, squinting against the bright sunlight of a rare Pennsylvania September morning. The breeze came warm from the south, up the creek, moving the leaves beneath a cloudless sky, touching the tense, perspiring faces of the eleven thousand soldiers of the Continental Army as they crouched in the trenches.

The southern end of the American lines was anchored by the commands of Generals Armstrong and Greene at Chad's Ford, with General Washington among them, waiting, impatient. To the north, upstream two miles, the commands of Generals Sullivan and Stephen held the center of the line, and a little behind and north of them, Lord Stirling's command was entrenched well over a mile from the winding Brandywine. Altogether the Continentals were spread five miles, north to south.

Howe had spent the entire summer campaign playing a deadly game of cat and mouse, watching, waiting for Washington to make the mistake that would allow the British general to crush the Americans. And now the Continentals were dug in across the creek, out in the open, in plain sight, army to army, face to face. Clearly they were inviting him and his redcoated regulars, and the blue- and green-coated Hessians to come across, rank upon rank, drums pounding, brass band blaring, their big Brown Bess muskets thrust forward with the sun glinting off their long, polished bayonets—to come across the creek and get them. If they could.

For the American soldiers, the hated waiting was over. The bragging, the bravado, the campfire heroics were forgotten, stripped away by the stark reality of the killing and being killed that was coming. In the face of such a struggle, ordinary things seemed strange, detached, unreal. Men with frayed nerves started, flinched at the voices and the sounds of every-day camp life, as though somehow they were hearing them for the first time. Raw recruits, untrained and untried, avoided the eyes of others, paralyzed by fears that ate at their minds, their hearts, driving them to the fringes of abstraction.

Can I kill a man? Can I pull the trigger? Can I run a bayonet through a man so close I can smell him? What if they come at me with a bayonet? Will I break? Run? Will I? Will I? If I'm wounded what will Mother say?—an arm gone—a leg—what will Mother say? If I'm killed? What will they tell Mother?

O'Malley looked up and down the line at Third Company, dug in close to the middle of General John Sullivan's command in the center of the American lines, hunched forward behind the breastworks, heads raised just far enough to peer west. The nine o'clock morning sun was hot on their backs as they studied the ground sloping gently down to the creek, then rising slightly on the far side to the thick woods. The American cannon were entrenched, half with muzzles elevated to reach the woods across the creek with solid shot, half loaded with canister and grapeshot, muzzles level to cover Brinton's Ford and Chad's Ford, where the British would have to cross.

"Look sharp, lads," O'Malley called. "What colors do you see in those trees?"

Half a minute passed before one answered, then another. "Blue and green."

"How much red?"

"Almost none."

O'Malley settled back, forehead furrowed in puzzlement. *Last night, mostly red—this morning, almost no red—no redcoats—blue and green—German Hessians. Where are the British? There was noise in the night—someone was moving over there. Did the British leave? If they did, where are they?*

He rose again to point. "Can you see their hats? What shape are their hats?"

Seconds later the answer came. "Tall. Shiny."

"Any tricorns?"

"None I can see."

Hessians—where are the British?—something's wrong. O'Malley was turning to trot up the line to find Captain Venables when the first showing of white smoke blossomed in the distant trees, and he came to a sudden halt.

"*DOWN!*" he shouted, and crouched, face down, hands clapped over his ears. One second later the ground thirty yards in front of the breastworks erupted with a roar all up and down the American center as sixty eighteen-pound cannonballs ripped into the earth and exploded to blast black Pennsylvania dirt fifty feet in the air. Falling clods and stones rained down, pelting the Americans as the thunder of the British cannon rolled over them.

More than half the Americans had remained standing, their heads exposed, brains locked and fumbling at the shouted command. Two of them were dead with iron fragments in their heads. Half a dozen had dropped their muskets to throw their hands over their faces, moaning, cut by hot, flying metal. One man scrambled from the trench, staggering, arms flailing as he screamed incoherently.

O'Malley leaped from the trench and raced to the man. He seized his shirt front and half-carried, half-dragged him back to the breastworks, where they tumbled into the soldiers in the trench with the man swinging his arms, voice raised like one demented. With strength beyond anything human, the dying man swept O'Malley aside, reaching, grasping blindly as he staggered to his feet and turned, still in the trench, blood streaming from his scalp and mutilated face, stumbling among the soldiers. O'Malley seized him from the back and lifted him off his feet, to throw him down again. Like a wild animal the man twisted, groping, screaming, as the two grappled among the scrambling men of Third Company.

Suddenly the flailing arms slowed and fell slack. The insane screaming dwindled and died. The mortally wounded soldier turned his head as though trying to see through eyes that were missing, then mumbled something as his head slowly nodded forward and he died. O'Malley released his hold, and there was deep pain in his face as he lifted the body from among the tangle of soldiers and laid him in the trench. He straightened the dead man's legs, then turned to a white-faced man who had been caught in the melee. His shirtfront was soaked with the dead man's blood.

"Dunson, are you hurt?"

Wide-eyed and shaking, Caleb's eyes never left the dead man. Horrified, he stared at the head. The upper part of the face was gone—leaving nothing but a mass of blood and gore.

O'Malley seized his shoulder. "Dunson, were you hit?"

Caleb shook his head as though coming from a trance and looked at O'Malley. He tried to speak but could not make a sound. He shook his head and finally forced out a single word, "No."

At that instant the second barrage of British cannonballs came whistling to rip into the breastworks. Shards of timber and clods of dirt leaped high and came raining down. Caleb doubled into a ball and threw his hands over his head while the booming wave rolled past. Then he straightened, unable to tear his eyes from the faceless soldier lying dead next to him. O'Malley leaped from the trench to shout, "Keep your heads down! Heads down! They're getting the range. Heads down!"

The next second the ground trembled as the heavy American cannon blasted a reply. A dense cloud of white smoke rose from the center of the American lines to drift lazily northward, and two seconds later geysers of dirt erupted in front of the oak and maples across the creek. Some cannonballs tore into the trees, shredding them, knocking leaves and branches loose to fall to the ground. For thirty seconds silence held in the beautiful Brandywine Creek basin, and then once again the British cannon boomed, and the cannonballs came whistling. Twenty seconds later the American guns answered.

The gun crews on both sides of the stream settled into the loading and firing of the cannon. Dip the huge swab into the barrel of water and run it hissing down the hot barrel to kill all lingering sparks; one live spark could ignite the incoming gunpowder and blow the arm off the soldier delivering it. Scoop one measure of gunpowder from the budge barrel and carefully push the ladle down the cannon muzzle, then twist the long handle to dump it. Jam the dried grass or the large cloth patch into the muzzle and use the ram to drive it home to lock in the gunpowder. Drop the next cannonball into the muzzle and use the ram once more to seat it against the patch. Smack the smoking linstock onto the touch hole and wait until the powder caught, then step back from the cannon's blast and recoil. Soak the swab and start again.

O'Malley turned to Caleb. "Get the man's blanket."

Caleb turned and grasped the dead man's bedroll and with trembling fingers untied the knots in the two cords. One minute later the body was wrapped, lying at their feet in the trench.

O'Malley asked, "Know his name?"

Caleb licked dry lips, and his voice cracked as he spoke. "I think it was Evans. Hosea Evans."

"Remember it. For the regimental record."

The pounding of the cannon and the exploding of cannonballs became an incessant roar. Minutes seemed unending, and time became meaningless. The sun continued its arc and came hot on their shoulders as the morning wore on. O'Malley timed the rhythm of the incoming volleys, and in the thirty seconds it took the British to reload, he was out of the trench, walking among his men, calming them, watching for the first signs of panic. Well he knew the harsh realities of what a sustained artillery attack could do to the nerves and the resolve of soldiers crouched in trenches behind breastworks, knowing the next cannonball could blind them, cripple them, kill them and that they were helpless to do other than crouch and pray to their God to be spared. One terrified soldier breaking from ranks to run could take five with him, and five could take ten more. He watched and waited.

It was shortly after ten o'clock that O'Malley slowed and stopped, then raised his head above the breastworks far enough to study the ford where the British or the Germans would have to cross. There was no one in sight. A look of wonder crossed his face as the next cloud of white smoke erupted from the distant trees and he dropped into the trench while the cannonballs came whistling, some into the breastworks, some overhead to plow into the earth fifty yards behind the trenches and explode.

They're not coming—two hours of cannon and they're not coming—should have started across an hour ago—something's wrong—something's wrong.

The inescapable conclusion struck him, and he stiffened. *They're not going to cross here—crossing somewhere else—north or south—can't be south because the cannon are firing down at Chad's Ford just like here—if they were attacking at Chad's, we'd hear muskets, not cannon. They're going to cross somewhere to the north—maybe Brinton's Ford, where Stephen and Stirling are.*

He raised his head once more, squinting north, but could not see the shallows at Brinton's Ford. He was settling back into the trench when movement to the east caught his eye, and he turned, startled. An American officer was kicking a hot, blue roan horse in the ribs, holding a steady lope south through a harvested oat field two hundred yards behind the lines.

Messenger! Who? From where? What message? A look of increasing concern passed over O'Malley's face as he settled down. *Something's wrong. Time will tell. We wait.*

Twenty minutes later the winded rider reined in a spent horse behind the breastworks at Chad's Ford, shouting above the din of the cannon, "Where's General Washington?"

An officer pointed, and the rider raced past to pull his horse to a stop ten yards from a group of huddled officers. Two walked out to meet him, hands on their swords.

"Identify yourself."

"Major Lewis Morris. Aide de camp to General Sullivan. Carrying a message to be delivered to General Washington personally."

Diminutive Colonel Alexander Hamilton stepped forward. "I'll take it." He turned on his heel and strode back to the group of officers to hand the written message to General Washington, who stood six inches taller than any other man. They all flinched as the next barrage of cannonballs came whistling and exploded; then Washington opened the written message. His breathing slowed, and he carefully read it again.

There was hardly a change in his expression as he spoke, cool, clear, aggressive. "We were wondering why the British haven't attempted to cross the ford and attack. We have the answer. Colonel Moses Hazen up at Jones's Ford wrote this message to General Sullivan less than an hour ago. He personally observed a large British column marching north. He thinks they're going to the forks of the Brandywine with the intent of crossing and coming down on General Sullivan's flank."

He paused for a moment, mind racing as he adjusted his thoughts and his battle plan to the startling new information.

"If that's true, then the British positions opposite us are considerably weaker than we thought."

They all flinched as the American cannon roared. Washington waited three seconds and continued.

"I think—"

The sound of a second incoming rider interrupted, and they all turned to peer east at a young lieutenant reining a bay gelding to a halt. He hit the ground running and stopped as he approached the knot of officers.

"I've got a dispatch from Lieutenant Colonel James Ross of the Eighth Pennsylvania. Up north near Osborne's Hill." He thrust the sealed document forward, and Hamilton took it to Washington. Again Washington paused, and his head came up, eyes bright as he read aloud from the paper. "From every account five thousand with sixteen or eighteen field pieces marched along this road just now."

For a split second he hesitated, then exclaimed, "With five thousand of them marching north, the force across Chad's Ford is half what we thought. Now is the time to cross and crush them." He turned to Laurens and Hamilton. "Write orders for my signature. Tell Generals Stephen, Stirling, and Sullivan to cross the Brandywine immediately and attack. Tell Generals Armstrong and Greene to prepare their commands to cross Chad's Ford and attack. The moment those orders are ready, get them to me, and find the best horsemen you can to deliver them. Understand?"

The cannon fire slowly slackened, and for a time it stopped. The soldiers in the trenches looked at each other, oddly disquieted at the sound of silence. A little before two o'clock in the afternoon, Washington sat tall on his gray mare and looked up and down his battle lines. His men were ready. Greene and his command, and Armstrong with his, far to his left, were crouched behind the breastworks. All eyes were on the officers, waiting for the order to rise and charge. For one moment Washington paused to reflect. *By now General Sullivan should be prepared to cross. We'll hear the muskets when he starts. We can wait no longer.*

Washington was reaching for his sword when the sound of a running horse coming in from behind turned the heads of the nearest officers. The rider held a paper high above his head as he brought his horse in, sweated, winded.

"From General Sullivan, sir. Urgent, he said."

Quickly Washington broke the seal and read.

"Since I sent you the message by Major Morris, I saw some of the militia who came in this morning from a tavern called Martins on the forks of the Brandywine. The one who told me said he had come from thence to Welches Tavern and heard nothing of the enemy above the forks of the Brandywine and is confident that they are not in that quarter. So that Colonel Hazen's information must be wrong. I have sent to that quarter to know whether there is any foundation for the report and shall be glad to give your Ex'y the earliest information." Washington read the signature. It was unmistakably that of General John Sullivan on information delivered to him by Major Spear, Pennsylvania Militia.

Washington's mouth became a thin, straight line as his mind leaped. *Hazen and Ross both wrong? Who is this Major Spear? Martin's Tavern? Welches*

Tavern? Where are these taverns he's talking about? Who told Major Spear? Reliable? Unreliable?

The eyes of fifty officers were on him, waiting, poised, sweating in the hot afternoon sun. Thousands of men were crouched behind breastworks, prepared to surge over the top, down the slope, shouting, shooting, directly into the grapeshot and musketfire and bayonets of whoever remained in the trees and trenches across the Brandywine. If those trenches were filled to full strength, too many Americans would be slaughtered before they reached the far side of the creek.

Go? Wait?

For long seconds Washington weighed it in his mind with the loneliness of ultimate command riding heavy. He shook his head. *I can't go forward until I know.*

He spoke to his officers and gave his orders. "I have information that prior reports of British movements to the north are mistaken. I refuse to risk this army until I know the facts." He stopped, and every officer within earshot stared, mesmerized, knowing what was coming. "Colonel Hamilton, there is no time for writing orders. Send a messenger at once. Tell General Sullivan to remain where he is. He is not to cross the Brandywine until further orders. Send another messenger to Generals Greene and Armstrong with the same orders. All other officers present, order your men to stand down."

Hamilton wheeled his horse and was off at a gallop. The other officers stared for several moments in disbelief, then quickly returned to their commands to give the orders that would bewilder the soldiers, tear at their resolve. Preparing to charge into grapeshot and musketballs and bayonets made strong men quiver. To be crouched in a trench, sweating, shaking, ready to make the desperate run over the top of dirt breastworks, down a slope, and wade a creek knowing half of the first ranks would never reach the far shore took all the courage a man had to give. To be steeled for the order and then be told to stand down, left soldiers limp, cursing, hating war, their officers, themselves.

For half an hour the cannons continued to blast, first on one side, then the other, while Washington held an iron check on his impatience, his rising need to know what was happening to the north. He paced, turning his head every few minutes to listen, waiting for the sound of the distant cannon to dwindle and for the unmistakable rattle of muskets to begin in the north.

He flinched at the sudden outburst from Laurens. "There, sir!"

He spun and raised a hand to shade his eyes from the afternoon sun while he peered to the east. A man was coming in from behind them. He was clearly a farmer, bare-legged, riding a horse that was running stumble-footed, near collapse. With Hamilton and Laurens beside him, Washington waited while other officers came running.

The farmer was dripping sweat as he reined in his spent horse. He leaped to the ground and came running toward Washington, panting, long hair plastered to his forehead and face. There was no pretense of military decorum as he pointed north, shouting, "The British are on this side of the Brandywine marching south. Thousands of them. They'll overrun the breastworks up at Brinton's Ford."

Washington stared at the man. "Who are you?"

"Thomas Cheyney."

"Where do you live."

"Across the creek, near Trimble's Ford."

"Who sent you?"

Cheyney's voice rose. "No one. I was at home. The British came. I swam the creek. They shot at me. Chased me. Thousands of them. Cannon. Don't you understand? They're coming in behind you!" He stood there, stunned that neither Washington nor any of his officers could grasp the fact that their entire army was caught in a trap.

Washington turned to Laurens and Hamilton. "What do you make of this?"

Laurens shook his head. "I don't know, sir. Could be a trap. This man could be a Tory sent to trick us."

Cheyney could take no more. He fairly shouted, "I'd have you know I have this day's work as much at heart as e'er a blood of ye!" He dropped to his knees in the dirt and quickly made marks, then raised angry eyes to Washington, pointing as he spoke, "There's a map of it, sir. I live there. The British came marching past this morning. I swam the Brandywine there. They shot at me, chased me. Henry Tredwell's farm is there. I stopped to warn him, and I took his horse—that sorrel mare you see behind me—and I've likely killed her to get here. That's the truth of it!"

Washington stood silent, torn, indecisive, then shook his head.

Cheyney sprang back to his feet. "You're mistaken, general. My life for it, you're mistaken. By heaven, it's so! Put me under guard till you find out it's so!"

Washington fixed him with cold blue-gray eyes, probing to the very core of Cheyney, searching for assurance the man was genuine. Cheyney stood solid, barely hanging onto his anger, eyes locked with Washington's while he waited.

From the east came another rider, horse covered with lather, eyes rolling from exhaustion. Hamilton shook his head. How many messengers in half a day?—five, six? He could not recall a battle with so many messengers, each with information they swore was the truth, yet in direct conflict with information already received.

The man dismounted, threw down the reins, and came directly to Washington. "From General Sullivan, sir. Urgent."

Once again Washington broke the seal and read. "Colonel Bland has this moment sent me word that the enemy is in the rear of my right about two miles coming down. There are, he says, about two brigades of them. At two o'clock P.M. he also saw a dust rise back in the country for above an hour."

For three seconds Washington was torn by self-condemnation. *We didn't scout the terrain—didn't know all the fords—didn't have enough patrols out—Sullivan didn't investigate the conflicted messages—I thought Howe would cross at Chad's Ford—wrong—wrong—wrong. No time for recriminations—must act.*

He spoke to Cheyney. "Your information is correct."

He turned to Hamilton and pointed to the messenger just arrived. "Get this man a fresh horse." He turned back to the messenger. "There's no time for written orders. Ride back to General Sullivan. Tell him to take the entire right wing—all three divisions—and march instantly to meet

Howe. He and Generals Stirling and Stephen are to seize the high ground around Birmingham Meeting House and hold it. Do you understand?"

"Yes, sir."

Hamilton handed him the reins to a tall, strong black gelding. The man swung up, spun the horse, and was gone.

Washington spoke to Laurens. "Find General Wayne. Tell him to remain at Chad's Ford with two brigades and his artillery to hold General Knyphausen across the Brandywine."

"Yes, sir." Laurens vaulted into the saddle and kicked his horse to a gallop to the south.

Washington turned back to Hamilton. "Locate General Greene. Tell him he's to be ready on an instant's notice to move either north or south—down to support Wayne or up to support Sullivan. We won't know which until the battle takes shape. Move!"

Washington glanced at the sun arcing toward the western horizon. He drew his pocket watch and studied the hands thoughtfully. *Four o'clock. Maybe it will be too late in the day when Howe reaches the Birmingham Meeting House. Maybe night will prevent a battle. Maybe we can build breastworks in the night. Maybe. Maybe. We can't live on maybe.*

The terrible tension was building with each minute. Washington paced as he held his impatience under control, waiting, waiting, turning his head to listen for the battle that would erupt three miles to the north when Howe collided with Sullivan.

At the stroke of four-thirty, the blasting roar of cannon came rolling down the Brandywine.

Across the creek, shielded by the oak and maple trees, General Knyphausen sat his horse and listened for two full minutes. There was no break in the rolling thunder, and then the staccato rattle of muskets and the sharp crack of rifles joined in. Knyphausen drew his sword and spurred his horse the length of his lines, shouting orders to his men. "That is our signal. Commence firing! Commence firing! In ten minutes the infantry will cross the ford." Five seconds later the ground shook as the German cannoneers touched off their first barrage and began to quickly reload.

It took Washington ten seconds to grasp the British strategy. Howe was going to crush Sullivan while Knyphausen engaged and held Greene and Armstrong out of the fight. Instantly Washington turned and spoke to Generals Anthony Wayne and Nathanael Greene, standing within five feet of him, waiting.

"General Wayne, you must hold this position with your two brigades. I will take General Greene and his command north to support General Sullivan and hold the road open to Philadelphia. We have to do all possible to keep the British from closing that road."

"Yes, sir!" Wayne mounted his horse and galloped south toward his command while General Greene trotted to his horse, then turned, waiting for Washington. Only then did Washington realize he knew the direction he had to go but not the route. He had no reports, no information on what roads to follow, what open fields to cross to get to Sullivan quickly. He cast his eyes about, looking for someone who might know. Scattered behind him were half a dozen of the local citizens, drawn to the battle like moths to a flame. Washington strode to an elderly man dressed in the garb of a local farmer.

"What is your name?"

"Joseph Brown."

"Do you know this terrain?"

"Lived here forty years."

"Will you guide us to Birmingham Meeting House?"

The old head shook emphatically. "No, sir, I will not. Too old for such. I come to watch."

Alexander Hamilton set his teeth, drew his sword, and strode to face the old man, sword tip a scant six inches from the grizzled old throat. "You will lead us, sir, or I will run you through where you stand."

The watery old eyes opened wide for a moment, and Hamilton gave a hand signal to two soldiers. Without a word they seized the old fellow and hoisted him into the saddle of the nearest horse. The gnarled old hands grasped the reins, and in a moment the horse was galloping north with General Washington right behind, shouting, "Push on, old man!" while Hamilton, Laurens, and half a dozen others of his staff followed, leaping fences and streams, cutting cross-country for the three-mile run to Birmingham Meeting House.

General Nathanael Greene spun on his heel and vaulted into his saddle. "Follow me, men," he shouted and turned his horse north, holding it to a trot as his entire command broke into a run, streaming out behind him as he followed the fast-disappearing back of General Washington.

Three miles ahead, the three divisions under command of General Sullivan pounded north and east, toward the slopes of Battle Hill and the crossroads near the Birmingham Meeting House. But in the wild, chaotic melee of exploding British cannonballs, the division led by Sullivan became separated from that of Stirling in the middle and Stephen to the far right as they swept on to seize and hold the high ground just west of the meetinghouse. Sullivan suddenly realized he was ahead of the two divisions to his right and half a mile away. He slowed his command until the three divisions were aligned, and then kicked his horse to a gallop through the shot and smoke to reach Stirling and Stephen.

"Can you hold?" he shouted.

Stirling shook his head violently. "They mean to come around our right and flank us and then come in behind you!"

Stephen pointed. "You need to be over here to present a solid front to take their attack."

Sullivan did not hesitate. "Hold here! We're coming!"

With cannon shot ripping the ground around him, Sullivan galloped back to his men, eight hundred yards to the west, and hauled the horse to a skidding stop before them, sword drawn, pointing to Stirling's command as he shouted his orders.

"To the right! To the right! Join Stirling! Follow me!"

Captain Charles Venables turned to the New York Ninth Regiment and shouted, "To the right! Close with Stirling's men! Move!"

Sergeant O'Malley gave his orders to Third Company. "Close the gap!" he bellowed. "To the right!"

Caught by surprise the bewildered division turned right and began to move, slowly at first, then faster as the officers rode among them, slapping laggards with the flat of their swords, shouting, demanding they move.

Clutching his French musket before him, Caleb Dunson fell in behind Sergeant O'Malley, trotting, moving with the sea of sweating men. It seemed they were no longer individuals, rather, they had become a tide, flowing down one grassy incline, then up another that rose to the top of Battle Hill. The smoke and the sound of the guns became a blur.

Get to the top—the top—join Stirling at the top.

It was the single thought that rose above all else to bind them together as they started up the incline toward the summit of Battle Hill. From the top, looking east, one could see the white spire among the trees that marked the settlement of Birmingham. To the north, Battle Hill faced Osborne's Hill, with the country lane named Street Road winding its way through the gentle valley between.

We can hold them if we get to the top.

The Continentals had climbed less than two hundred yards when the cannon suddenly ceased, and movement and a strange new sound across the small valley brought their heads around to the north to stop them in their tracks, staring in utter disbelief.

Caleb gaped, and his breath caught in his throat. In perfect alignment, the British forces crested Osborne's Hill and started down the incline toward Street Road. Their cannon and muskets were silent, and neither an officer nor a soldier uttered a sound. The oncoming ranks seemed to reach out of sight. Never had he seen so many bright red coats with crossed white belts. He looked to the east, where the green- and blue-coated German Hessians and Anspach jaegers marched in their twenty-pound stiff, black leather boots that reached above their knees. Every soldier carried his musket with muzzle thrust forward, with its long, slender bayonet mounted. The light of the late afternoon sun turned their uniforms into a kaleidoscope of blinding bright colors, and it touched the hated steel bayonets to turn them into glistening instruments of death. They came ten thousand strong, rank upon rank, marching down the slope like one monstrous, silent, disciplined, terrible, flowing organism.

Faintly at first, then with strength, the sounds of their band reached across to the Americans, flaunting the inexorable power of the British Empire, insulting the Americans, intimidating them with the strains of "The British Grenadiers."

Then, from the far right came the harsh battle cries of the Germans as they surged forward, still in perfect alignment. Across Street Road, then up the slope of Battle Hill they came, shouting as they ripped into the far right of Stephen's command, bayonets flashing in the sun, thrusting. General Stephen watched in helpless agony as the three regiments of Marylanders under his command, led by General Prudhomme de Borre, took the charge. In less than two minutes they were in wild retreat, terrified of the naked steel and the overpowering onslaught of the Germans. As by magic General Stephen found himself with his right wing shorn away and his flank wide open to attack. He rode shouting among his men, slapping them with the flat of his sword, ordering them to stop, to stand their ground and fight, but his command had become a panic-stricken horde, unstoppable in their headlong retreat from those dreaded bayonets.

Sullivan realized that with Stephen's command gone, Stirling's right flank was defenseless, and with the British coming head-on and the Germans coming in from his right, Stirling was trapped. In desperation Sullivan turned and screamed an order to his men, "Forward! Join Stirling! Join Stirling!"—before he jammed spurs to his horse and sprinted ahead to reach the American cannon clustered on the hilltop, while his mind raced ahead, *The guns—must be loaded with grape and the muzzles depressed to shoot downhill—must get there—must get there.*

At that moment, the red-coated regulars surged up Battle Hill in full-throated battle cry. They came running, rank upon straight rank, like a flowing carpet of crimson, with the sun sparkling off the tips of their bayonets. Those in Sullivan's command were running with all their strength to reach Stirling, directly across the face of that first rank of red-coated regulars, when they realized that their leader—General

Sullivan—was no longer with them. And then the awful sight of the oncoming crimson line with their bayonets lowered struck into them. The Americans slowed. One turned to the right, threw down his musket, and ran. Half a dozen more broke away and turned to follow, racing away, down the slope of Battle Hill. In twos and threes and then in companies they broke.

Six hundred yards to the east, at the cannon at the crest of Battle Hill, Sullivan looked back at his men, and for a moment his breath caught. Too late he realized his fatal mistake. He was not there to lead them, rally them. It flashed in his mind—*too late, too late*—and he kicked his horse to stampede gait back to his disintegrating command. He plowed into them as they retreated, shouting at them, pounding them on their backs with the flat of his sword. They dodged and swarmed past him, hearing nothing, feeling nothing but terror, possessed by but one thought. *Run! Run!*

Caught in the chaotic panic, Caleb was swept one hundred yards down the back side of Battle Mountain before his numbed mind caught and began to function. All around him white-faced men were throwing down their muskets, running. He raised his head, searching for Sergeant O'Malley, and he was nowhere before him. He slowed and twisted, peering back up the hill, and there found O'Malley's red hair and beard. The sergeant was fifty yards above him, cursing, shouting, swinging his musket at his own men, knocking them sideways as he tried to stop Third Company's retreat, turn them back to meet the British.

Caleb turned into the oncoming rush of men, dodging, shoving, pushing, making his way back one yard at a time. He reached O'Malley, and with only half a dozen men from Third Company following, they climbed back to the crest of the hill. There, alone, was Stirling's command, grim, bracing for the bayonet charge they knew was coming. Three thousand Americans facing six thousand of the flower of the greatest military force in the world. O'Malley, with Caleb beside him, broke through to the front of the American lines and settled to one knee, staring down the hill at the oncoming tide, ready.

From behind came shouts, and the Americans turned to look. Tall on his unmistakable gray horse, knocking the retreating Americans left and right, rode General George Washington, sword in hand, racing for the crest of the hill. Stirling's command opened passage for him, and he brought his blowing mare to a stop at the crest, instantly taking in the length and breadth of the oncoming British, less than one hundred yards down the slope of the hill.

"Form ranks! form ranks!" he shouted. "Prepare to fire!" From his right the remnants of Stephen's command came running, and from his left, what was left of Sullivan's men. Generals Sullivan, Stirling, and Stephen, and the proud French-Irish General Thomas Conway came in from either side, shouting, "Stand fast! Stand fast!"

Kneeling beside O'Malley, Caleb raised the frizzen of his musket to check the powder in the pan, locked it back in place, then tapped it to be certain it was ready for the hammer and flint to fall. Then he looked down the hill. At one hundred yards the first ranks of the British were faceless forms, laboring up the incline, muskets thrust forward, bayonets gleaming. Not one of them had fired a shot. Clearly, they intended to take the hill with their hated bayonets.

Washington held his sword high, gauging time and distance—eighty yards, seventy, sixty, fifty.

At fifty yards the faceless men suddenly had faces. Young, old, smooth, bearded, frightened, disciplined, short, tall—they took shape and form, individuality—each became a living person, like people in the streets of Boston or New York or in the shops of Morristown or Amboy or Middlebrook or from the farms of Pennsylvania or New Jersey.

Caleb drew back the heavy hammer of his musket and lowered the muzzle to bury the thin sight at barrel's end just below the place the white belts crossed on the chest of the redcoat coming directly at him. He took up the slack in the trigger and waited for the order to fire.

Then, for the first time in his life, the stark reality of what he was doing rose to paralyze him. *I'm going to kill that man! Kill him! Forbidden of God! Forbidden!*

General Washington whipped his sword downward as he shouted, "*FIRE!*"

The first American volley hit the leading ranks of the British, and men all up and down the line stumbled and went down. Those behind stepped over them, filled the empty places, and came on, steady in those terrifying red coats and crossed belts while their band arrogantly blared out "The British Grenadiers."

Caleb suddenly stood, musket still at his shoulder, and then he raised the muzzle. As though in a dream he looked dumbly at the hammer. It was still cocked. The frizzen was still upright, waiting for the flint to knock the pan open and strike the spark. He had not fired!

O'Malley grasped his arm, jerked him down to his knees. "Get down! Shoot! Shoot or be killed!" he shouted.

Without a thought and without aiming, Caleb thrust the muzzle forward and pulled the trigger. The frizzen leaped, the pan flared, the musket bucked, and the white smoke belched from the muzzle. Caleb saw the hit on the young man's chest and heard the grunt, and he saw the man's brown eyes glaze in shock and pain as he pitched forward. He tried once to rise, then relaxed, and died.

Caleb stared, unable to move, to think. In his heart and mind was but one thought that filled his soul with terror. *Forbidden! Forbidden!* He was not aware that he was crying, tears running.

O'Malley's hand came down hard on his shoulder as he bellowed, "Reload! Reload!"

Tears mingled with sweat and gun smoke to streak his face as Caleb jerked a fresh paper cartridge from the box on his hip, ripped the sewn end open with his teeth, tapped powder into the pan, smacked the cover closed, jammed the remainder of the paper cartridge with the powder and ball into the muzzle, yanked the ramrod from its housing beneath the barrel, slammed it down the muzzle once, replaced the ramrod, cocked the hammer, and took aim. He closed both eyes to fire but could not block out the image of another man groaning as he stumbled and fell forward to die.

From behind came a clamor, and the officers turned to look as the Americans opened a path. Charging through came the young Marquis de Lafayette, galloping into the center of the battle, pant leg soaked with blood from a musket ball that had ripped through his foot. He reined his foam-flecked horse in beside General Washington with sword drawn, waiting for orders.

Outnumbered two to one, the Americans stubbornly defended the crest of Battle Hill until they could no longer hold the relentless British. Slowly they backed off the hilltop, and then they stiffened. With General Washington leading and the other officers rallying, they stopped, and in full battle cry they doggedly fought their way back up the hill to drive the British before them, to the top, then down the far side.

Five times the British took the top of the hill, and five times the Americans regrouped and stubbornly fought their way back up to reclaim it. Bodies of the dead and wounded littered the slopes. A pall of white gun smoke settled to shroud the battle, and still they fought on, both sides exhausted from the forced marches of the preceding night and morning—sweated, loading and firing mechanically. Despite their bulldog tenacity, their determination, their willingness to fight as long as General Washington commanded, the numbers were against the Americans. Once more they backed off the hill and gave it to the British. Quickly the redcoats rolled four cannon to the crest, depressed the muzzles, and fired. As General Washington watched, twenty pounds of grapeshot tore into the retreating Americans.

We will fight but not to the death. We must save the core of the army, or the revolution is finished.

"Fall back! Fall back!" he shouted. "Fire and fall back, reload, fire and fall back."

Then suddenly a tumultuous shout rolled from the throats of the Americans. Behind them came the fresh division of General Nathanael Greene. Some of them had done the impossible by running four miles in forty-five minutes, knowing from the sound of the raging battle that the Americans were in desperate need. The exhausted ranks opened to allow General Greene, followed by Colonel Peter Muhlenberg and General George Weedon, to come through at a run, straight into the British, firing as they came, surprising the red-coated soldiers, stopping them in their tracks, giving the retreating Americans time to rally, regroup.

Greene's men formed into ranks and stormed into the British lines. What had been a musket and bayonet battle became hand-to-hand, face-to-face with musket-butts, rocks, fists, bayonets—anything they could grasp to stop a man. Colonel Peter Muhlenberg, commanding a brigade, led his men in a furious charge. German born and raised, he had been trained in the arts of war in his homeland, among his fellow Germans. Some of his old comrades in arms were now in the ranks of the Hessians, and they recognized him. He heard them shout, *"Hier kommt Tuefel Piet!"* "Here comes Devil Pete," and for one split second Muhlenberg hesitated in surprise, then plunged on, sword swinging as he led his men into the blue-coated Hessians.

Obedient to the orders of General Washington, Greene's men began a masterful retreat, covering the backs of the exhausted men who had met the best the British had to offer and, outnumbered two to one, had fought them to a standstill five times. With the sun below the western rim, they backed away from Battle Hill and into the open fields and onto the dirt roads behind. In deep dusk they reached the Chester Creek Bridge, and while the exhausted Americans poured across, Lafayette pulled his horse to a stop and turned, calculating.

The British must cross that bridge if they mean to follow us.

He raised his hand and shouted the order to his men, "Halt! Form ranks and reload!"

While the remainder of the Continental Army clattered across the bridge to scatter in all directions into the night, Lafayette sat his tired horse, positioning his men, first rank kneeling, second rank standing, muskets loaded and cocked at the ready. The wound in his foot ached. His boot was filled with blood, and his wound was still bleeding as he sat waiting in the first shades of night, waiting until he could see the white belts crossed on the chests of the pursuing British as they reached the middle of the bridge.

Only then did he shout, "Fire!"

Muzzle flashes leaped three feet from the American muskets, and those in the leading ranks of the British went down. The red-coated regulars had been marching since four o'clock that morning. They had stopped but once to eat hard rations, drink from a stream, and collapse in the grass for twenty minutes before they marched on. The heat of the late summer day, the eighteen-mile march in full battle gear, the agonizing draining of their strength in the battle, it all caught up with them as they faced Lafayette in the deep gloom.

Again Lafayette shouted, "Fire!" and again the American muskets blasted orange flame in the darkness, and the second rank of pursuing British went down.

They had had enough. Lafayette heard the shouted command, "Fall back! Fall back!" and then the sounds of men searching in the darkness to take the bodies of their dead and wounded with them as they retreated, boots thumping hollow on the wooden bridge. Lafayette held his position until he could no longer hear the British retreating, and then he too turned to lead his men away into the night.

South of Battle Hill and the Birmingham Meeting House, General Anthony Wayne pulled his jaded horse to a halt in the stubble of a harvested wheat field two miles east of the breastworks that his weary, beaten regiment had abandoned three hours earlier at Brandywine Creek. He twisted in his saddle, peering back in the dark, trying to see how many of his men had survived the wild fight on the banks of the stream and the chaotic, fragmented retreat that had scattered them in all directions. He could see the dark forms of those nearest and hear the rustle of feet in the wheat stubble behind them, but he did not know the count of those who had followed him.

He raised his hand and hissed, "Halt. Sit down and listen. They might still be following." The whispered order was passed on as the survivors sank down in the wheat straw and dirt, ears straining for any sound that could be the blue- and green-coated Hessians coming upon them in the black of night. Minutes passed, and the only sounds were the creak of the saddle as Wayne's tired horse breathed, bullfrogs in the creek that they had crossed to get into the field, and crickets. Far away the bark of a farm dog came furious, then quieted. There were no sounds of pursuit.

From his right came the voice of one of his captains. "Sir, are we going to find the others tonight? General Washington?"

"No. First we've got to find a place to tend our wounded, and then we've got to send out patrols to find the rest of our regiment and regroup."

Quiet held for a moment before the captain spoke again. "What happened back at the breastworks?"

Wayne dismounted. "You mean where did those British regulars come from?"

"Yes. We could have held the Germans right across the creek, even after some of them crossed Pyle's Ford to the south of us and came up on our left flank. But where did those redcoats come from that charged in on our right?"

Wayne shook his head in the dark. In his mind he was again feeling the bewildering shock of hearing the shouts of his men from behind, "The redcoats, the redcoats," and turning to see a horde of British regulars already into the rear of his command, muskets blasting, bayonets thrusting as they drove into them.

He drew and released a great, frustrated breath. "I don't know where they came from. I doubt Howe or Cornwallis sent them from the big battle up at Birmingham Meeting House. I think they got lost somehow and walked into our fight by mistake."

There was a pause, then, "We didn't have a chance. Not fighting in three directions at once. Surrounded."

Wayne spoke wistfully. "Battles come on their own terms. One never knows. General Washington's orders were to fight but not to the death. We've got to save enough to keep an army."

"Save any of the cannon?"

There was pain in Wayne's voice. "Not one. No time. They got them all."

"That's bad."

"Maybe we'll have to go get some of theirs. Maybe we can get some from the French. We'll need cannon for what's coming."

"Something big coming?"

"Philadelphia. Congress wants us to keep the British out. Could be heavy."

Silence held for a time, with both men lost in their own thoughts. Then Wayne turned to his horse and loosened the girth on the saddle as he spoke.

"Sounds like we lost them. Work back among the men. Find out who's here and who's not. Get a count if you can. I'll send out a patrol to find a farmhouse where we can take the wounded. Tell them."

"Yes, sir."

Wayne watched the dark shape rise and listened as the captain quietly made his way back through the decimated regiment.

★ ★ ★ ★ ★

Nine miles west and north, across the Brandywine, Thomas Cheyney cautiously dismounted Henry Tredwell's trembling horse and led it forward in the darkness through the trees lining the path from the road to his home and barn. Lamplight shone dully from the inside on the drawn window curtains. A great mound of ashes glowed where he had set fire to the cord of wood. He stopped and listened, but there were no sounds other than the crickets. He walked into the open yard, watching in the dark, listening. There was nothing, no one.

He dropped the reins to the horse and sprinted to the kitchen door, jerked the latch-string and burst in. Polly was seated at the table, head leaned forward on her arms, asleep. Across the table before her was the long Pennsylvania rifle. At the sound of the door opening she jerked erect in her chair and grabbed for the rifle, trying to focus her eyes, when she recognized Thomas in the yellow light. She came to her feet running and threw herself into his arms, shoulders shaking silently as she clung to him.

The battle of Brandywine Creek was over.

Notes

The battle of Brandywine Creek, from beginning to end, is accurate as described herein, including the officers of each opposing army, their assignments, their efforts in carrying them out, their strengths, and their mistakes and weaknesses. The heroics of Generals Lafayette and Greene were critical to saving the American army. Thomas Cheyney's participation is accurate, including his drawing a map in the dirt. His conversation with General Washington is nearly verbatim from recorded history. See Higginbotham, *The War of American Independence*, pp. 185–86; Mackesy, *The War of American Independence, 1775–1778*, pp. 128–29; Freeman, *Washington*, pp. 349–52; Leckie, *George Washington's War*, pp. 352–56.

CHAPTER XII

★ ★ ★

*G*iants wearing crimson coats and black tricorns and crossed white belts came in perfect ranks that extended into infinity, marching over the rolling hills, each man identical to the next, each with dead eyes in a dead face, each with a gigantic Brown Bess musket, muzzle lowered, with a steel bayonet five feet long shining, the tip pointed directly ahead. A band marched in the first ranks, drummers hammering, brass section blowing, but there was no sound.

Caleb fired his musket at the giant directly in front of him, and in the instant the ball hit, the huge creature was transformed into a man smaller than Caleb, with brown hair and pleading brown eyes. There was anguish in his face as he fell forward, eyes locked on Caleb, and he died, except for his eyes. They remained open, unblinking, staring at Caleb, accusing him.

Scalding pain leaped searing in Caleb's breast, and he threw down his musket and clapped both hands over his eyes to shut out the accusing brown eyes, but he could not. They were still there before him, unblinking, staring vacantly. A strangled sound came surging from his throat, and he fell to his knees, hands still over his eyes, trying to shut out the oncoming giants with their monstrous bayonets, and the silent blasting of the muskets, and the dead men that were everywhere, all staring with unblinking eyes.

Then one of the giants seized his shoulders, and the world became an impossible tangle of writhing motion and confused thoughts. The huge hands lifted him up, shaking him, and Caleb screamed at the giant, and the jumbled scene faded into blackness. He heard the echo of a human voice, and then there were stars above and a dim quarter-moon shining on the dark stands of oak and maple and pine trees nearby, and there was a face before him with a red beard and a pair of rough gnarled hands clamped on his shoulders as Caleb recognized the fading echo of his own voice.

O'Malley's voice hissed, "Wake up! Yer scarin' half the company!"

Sweat was running as Caleb blinked, wide-eyed, struggling to find his way from the battle with the giants back to the blackness of the Continental Army camp on the outskirts of Germantown at three o'clock in the morning. His voice croaked as he spoke.

"I . . . there were . . . giants."

"You were nightmarin' again. Are you waked up enough to let it go?"

"I'm awake. I'm all right."

"You're still sufferin' from your first battle. Get back to sleep. Reveille's in two hours. We march in three."

Caleb nodded. O'Malley released his grip, rose, and disappeared into the night while disgruntled voices mumbled at Caleb in the dark, then quieted. For a time Caleb sat still, listening to the sounds of the night while his heart slowed from its pounding and the grotesque images slowly faded. At four o'clock the chill of an early fall had settled over the camp, and he gathered his blanket around his shoulders as he sat cross-legged with his troubled thoughts running.

War—battle—like a dream—another world—so many dead—dead men everywhere—pain—suffering—evil—all evil—why doesn't God stop it?—if He's there and He's so good why does he let it go on?—is it because He's not there?—only another dream?—the killing was no dream—the men I killed are dead—God didn't stop me—and He didn't stop them when they tried to kill me—didn't stop them when they came with their bayonets—didn't stop them when our men cried out and died—got to stop thinking about it—got to stop.

The soft call of an owl came from far, and nearer was a sharp squeal and then silence as something large caught something small in the night.

Killing—everywhere killing—no end to it—got to stop thinking about it—think about Mother—home.

Without warning a lump rose in his throat to choke him. His eyes brimmed with tears, but he did not cry.

She'll hear about the battle at Brandywine, and she'll worry—must write a letter— tell her I'm fine—tell her I think of her—the twins—Brigitte—Matthew—and Father—Father, who is dead—gone—in a battle—killed.

He caught himself and by force of will drove thoughts of war and killing from his mind.

We march in the morning—where?—why?—men been coming in for four days— scattered everywhere in the battle—whole companies—half of Third Company gone— lost, dead, wounded, deserted—who knows?—haven't seen Dorman—him or Fifth Company—what happened to Fifth Company?—Captain Venables missing—General Wayne's command lost somewhere for two days—half our cannon gone— ammunition—gunpowder—blankets—winter coming—how do we replace it all?— where do . . . Slowly his head slumped, and his eyes closed, and he drifted into a fitful sleep, still sitting with the blanket about his shoulders.

He jerked awake at the rattle of the reveille drums and for several seconds struggled before he remembered where they were camped, nine miles north of Philadelphia. The lights of the farms surrounding the small village of Germantown in the lush rolling hills of Pennsylvania were winking on in the gray of dawn. Caleb winced at the sour taste in his mouth and stood, stretching to relieve stiff muscles. He turned at the sound of O'Malley's voice.

"On your feet. We march at six o'clock."

A grizzled old veteran called, "We just got here. Which way this time?"

"South. Across the Schuylkill."

"We goin' to Philadelphia?"

"Don't know. We'll find out when we get across the river. Breakfast crews, get at it."

The wood detail dumped firewood beside the iron tripods while the cooks filled the black iron kettles with creek water and stirred in milled oats and a handful of salt. Others poured poached ground wheat into pots of boiling water to make a strong, bitter drink. Third Company gathered around the smoking kettles, each man waiting for the cooks to ladle steaming oatmeal porridge into his wooden bowl and dip the seething brown drink into his cup, to be followed by a measured spoonful of molasses.

While they ate, men drifted from the trees into camp, gaunt, starving, weary, some wounded. They stared at the hot oatmeal and wiped at their mouths before they asked the nearest officers if anyone from their regiments or companies had made it back from the chaos of the nighttime retreat following the battle of Brandywine Creek. Officers pointed, and the men moved on.

With the sun cresting the eastern mountains, the captains gave orders, and the sergeants bawled their companies into ranks. Five minutes later the remnant of the Continental Army was marching south on the winding dirt road from Germantown, toward the river. At ten o'clock the column stopped, and the men sought the shade of the woods on either side as they drank long from their wooden canteens. Caleb wiped his mouth, smacked the corncob stopper back into his canteen, dropped his bedroll, and sat down with his back against the rough bark of a pine tree, listening to the soldier talk.

"We gave the hill to 'em, back there at Brandywine, but we held 'em five times. Outnumbered two to one we was, but we held 'em. The best they had."

"If we'd of had the numbers they had, we'd of beat 'em. Drove 'em clean back to New York."

"Scared 'em good. They got the hill, but every man-jack among 'em knows we only had half what they had, and we fought 'em to a standstill five times. They knew if it had been an even matched fight, we'd of won. Scared 'em."

"We get some rest and reg'lar food, and a little ammunition, and next time they'll see who gives up the hill."

Caleb listened, and thought, and remained silent.

They reached the Schuylkill River in the early afternoon, and by five o'clock had crossed it to continue their march south.

Throughout the afternoon stragglers came from the woods and the fields looking for their regiments. They brought stories of hiding in woods and caves and under bridges during the day while roving patrols of Hessians and British prowled the countryside searching for them. They moved at night, eating what they could find in the fields or in barns, silent, refusing to be seen by the farmers, to save them from the wrath of the British and Hessians who burned barns and crops and slaughtered animals of any who had harbored or helped the Americans or even knew of their passing.

They made evening camp in a small meadow near a stream, and as Caleb finished wiping his bowl with the crust of his hard brown bread, a familiar voice interrupted.

"You came through all right?"

He turned to watch Charles Dorman stride by the evening cook fire to stand before him. Caleb did not expect the swell of emotion that welled up into his throat to choke him for a moment as he looked up into the lined face and at the gray wavy hair that was growing long.

"I'm all right. You?"

Dorman grinned one of his rare grins. "Hard to kill." He sat down in the grass beside Caleb.

"Lose many from Third Company?"

"Some. Quite a few. Can't find Captain Venables."

Dorman was sitting with his elbows on his drawn-up knees, and for a moment he studied his clasped hands.

Caleb continued. "Fifth Company?"

"We were right in the middle of it. Lost some. Too many. Lost three officers." They fell silent for a time before Dorman went on. "Were you there at the end? When Greene came up?"

Caleb turned to look at him. "You mean, did I run?"

Dorman looked back at him in silence, waiting.

"I was there."

The slightest look of relief crossed Dorman's face and was gone. "We stood 'em straight up five times," he said. "They had twice the numbers, and we stood 'em straight up. It was a proud thing."

Dorman saw the flat, dead look creep over Caleb's face and waited a moment before he spoke again. "There are many reasons to take a life. Some good, some bad. Seems like we all have to make up our mind about which is which. I think freedom is a good reason."

Caleb's eyes dropped, and he would not raise them. Dorman continued, "I don't think revenge is. It grows bitter with time."

Caleb stared into the fire and would not look into Dorman's face. The older man finally stood. "You need to do normal things. Come on."

Caleb glanced at him. "Normal? Like what?"

"Get your hand wraps."

Ten minutes later, fifty yards from the campfires, with the last arc of the sun sitting on the western horizon, Dorman raised his hands while Caleb started the slow circling, hands raised, chin tucked into the hollow of his left shoulder, eyes trained on Dorman's chest, unfocused, to take in the entire man. His left hand flicked out, and Dorman slipped it, then caught Caleb's right hand on his shoulder as his own right hand blurred, coming across to slap Caleb on his left cheek. Caleb settled and continued. Five minutes later Dorman stepped back. "Enough."

"No. Let's go."

Dorman shrugged, raised his hands, and once again Caleb came circling, watching. Again his left hand flicked out; then he started his right hand across, and again Dorman raised his arm and shoulder to absorb it, and again Dorman started his right hand across. At precisely the right instant, Caleb checked his own right hand and cocked and swung his left in a perfect hook. Startled, Dorman saw it coming and had begun to check his own right hand to raise it but knew he was too late. Caleb's left hook came in over his right arm and caught him on the temple, solid, hard. Instantly the familiar spots came dancing, jumping before Dorman's eyes, and though he could see everything before him, he knew he was in that strange world of being conscious but unable to raise his hands to defend himself. He tried to step back, but his feet would not move. He saw Caleb cock his right hand, and he saw the fist start across the twenty inches that separated his jaw from the wrapped hand, and he knew he would not be able to stop it. And then he saw Caleb pull the punch and step back, concern springing into his eyes, his face.

"You all right? Dorman?"

For three seconds Dorman stood still, waiting for the spots to clear, waiting until his hands and feet would obey his commands.

"I'm all right."

"I didn't mean . . ."

"It's all right. It was good. Where did you learn that?"

"Learn what?"

"To start a power right and check it while you deliver a left hook? Not many can do it."

"I didn't learn it. It just came."

In that instant, for the first time, Dorman knew. The boy had those peculiar, inborn instincts that cannot be taught or learned. They were there, or they weren't there, and Caleb had them.

Dorman raised his hands. "Let's go again."

"Sure?"

"Sure. Go."

"I'll be careful."

"Don't. I'm going to hit back a little. Time you learned how it feels. Keep your mouth shut tight, so your teeth don't get chipped."

Once again they faced each other, and the wary circling commenced. Within three minutes both men were sweating. Within five, Caleb's eyes were narrowed with intensity. Within eight minutes the war, the Brandywine battle, the dead, the wounded, were forgotten as he bore in, testing Dorman, dancing, moving, giving, taking. At fifteen minutes, Dorman had a swelling over his right temple where Caleb's hook had landed. Caleb had a purple bruise on his left cheekbone, and it was swelling. Dorman backed away.

"That's enough for now."

Caleb dropped his hands, chest heaving, shirt soaked and clinging. "You hurt?"

Dorman shook his head. "You?"

"No. Feels good. Feels fine." He used his teeth to work at the knots in his hand wraps. Only then did he notice that soldiers had gathered in clusters, three here, four there, half a dozen another place, silently watching. They turned and walked away, talking among themselves with Caleb peering after them, searching. Conlin Murphy was not among them.

Caleb folded the long strips of canvas once and draped them over his shoulder. "Again tomorrow?"

"Depends on where we are. What we're doing." Dorman had recovered his breathing. "You having any nightmares?"

Caleb stared for a moment. "How did you know?"

Dorman shook his head. "After my first battle I had 'em for a year or more. Still do, sometimes."

Caleb's eyes widened. "You do?"

Dorman bobbed his head. "Better have a good reason for killing a man, even in a war. Better be right. It's bad enough at best, and the only relief is knowing you did right." He said nothing, waiting for Caleb's reaction.

Caleb dropped his eyes and studied the ground for a few seconds, weighing, pondering. He looked back at Dorman but didn't speak.

Dorman broke the silence. "Better get back to camp. Tomorrow could be a hard day."

They separated in the purple shades of twilight, Dorman back to Fifth Company, Caleb back to his bedroll. The boy stuffed his hand wraps among his things and drew out an oilskin and unwrapped a badly frayed pad of paper and the stub of a lead pencil. He thought for a time, then in the fading light began to write.

September 15, 1777

My Dear Mother:

I know you will hear of the battle at Brandywine Creek and will worry that I was there and that things did not go well for me. I was there, and I remained until General Washington ordered us to fall back. I am fine. I was not harmed. You will hear that we were defeated at Battle Hill; however, we held the hill through five heavy assaults, although we were outnumbered two to one.

General Washington ordered the retreat, but our army takes pride in the fact we held them through most of the day. Had our army been as large as theirs we would have driven them off. In the retreat, our army was scattered, but we are mostly back together, and General Washington has ordered us to cross the Schuylkill River. We were not told why, but most of us believe he intends trying to stop the British from capturing Philadelphia.

I would like to know if you have heard from Matthew. I trust Brigitte and the twins are safe, as well as yourself. I have thought of you many times and send my best wishes to you all. You are not to worry about me. We have a good sergeant and good officers who look after us.

I do not know where I will be after tonight. I will write you again as soon as I can, and when possible I will give you an address where I can receive your mail. I miss you all.

Your son,
Caleb.

Holding the pages to the flickering firelight, he read what he had written, then laid the pencil down and for a time sat motionless in the deep gloom of the darkness that had gathered. *Mother will look for a mention of the Almighty—thanking Him, somehow acknowledging Him—but I can't do it. I can't! Where was He when the cannonballs were blowing off arms and legs? The bayonets were working? If this is His war for freedom, why are we outnumbered two to one?*

He folded the letter and carefully wrapped it inside the oilskin with his pad and pencil and put it with his things.

In full darkness, tattoo came echoing through the trees, and the camp quieted. The waxing quarter-moon rose in the east and had made half of its nocturnal journey toward the west when clouds came drifting to blur the stars. By morning the heavens were a dull gray overcast, and sunrise was but a brightening of the clouds in the east. By seven o'clock the army was once again marching southwest on the rutted dirt road that wound through the Pennsylvania hills.

The midmorning halt had just been ordered when a rider carrying a musket and with a tricorn pulled low came galloping past Third Company on a grunting, winded mare, heading for the front of the column. Twenty minutes later an excited Colonel John Laurens came pounding up on his bay gelding, and the officers of the Ninth New York Regiment gathered around as he pointed and exclaimed, while Third Company listened in rapt silence.

"There's a column of British marching east on the road from Lancaster to Philadelphia—about eight miles from here. They're strung out for two miles, the worst position possible to defend themselves, and they don't know we're here! General Washington is certain we can hit them hard if we move fast. He's picked out a place called Warren Tavern for the attack. We're going to have to march double time. Get your men back into ranks immediately and have them load their muskets. When we move, it will be at a trot. Understood?"

"How do you know all this?"

"You saw that rider come in? A militiaman from over there. He was sent with a message to General Washington. Get ready!"

Laurens rammed his blunted spurs into his horse and galloped on to the next regiment.

Half an hour later the entire column was moving south at double time, muskets loaded, men silent as they worked to prepare themselves for another battle. At noon the first breeze came stirring the leaves in the trees. At one o'clock the breeze was a high wind. At half past one, it was a howling gale from the northeast, ripping leaves and limbs from the trees, and twenty minutes later torrential rains came whipping down on the hunched backs of the soldiers. Within minutes the dirt road was a quagmire.

Every man in the Continental Army had learned to shrug off the seasonal nor'easters that came roaring in from the Atlantic, and none of them faltered as they hurried on through the thick mud, but suddenly the officers realized the threat was not to their men—it was to their ammunition. A halt was called as they shouted orders above the screeching wind.

"Check your gunpowder! Check your cartridges!"

Half an hour later the reports began coming in from the companies and the regiments, to divisional officers and finally to Colonel Laurens, who turned his horse back to the southwest and rode through the cloudburst, splashing mud in all directions, to deliver the message to General Washington.

"Sir, some cartridge boxes turned the rain, but most of them did not. Poorly made. Tens of thousands of paper cartridges are soaked. Worthless. Tons of gunpowder are soaked. At this moment we are an army that cannot fight!"

General Washington stared in disbelief. He could not recall an experience in his life when an entire army was stopped in its tracks because of poorly constructed cartridge boxes that would not turn the rain.

Laurens continued. "Sir, there's more. We have more than one thousand men barefooted. No shoes. No tents. No shelter. Our food is nearly gone. If this storm holds, I suggest we would have no chance in a fight with the British." .

Reluctantly Washington gave the only order he could. "We camp here until the storm breaks. Get patrols out."

"If the British discover us?"

"I expect they will, and we'll have to handle that when it happens. In the meantime, tell the men to make whatever shelters they can from the trees hereabouts and search for dry firewood. Try to dry the cartridges and gunpowder through the night."

There was no dry firewood. They ate cold rations for their meager suppers and built crude lean-tos as a partial shield against the rain and wind that held through the night. The men slept sitting up, shivering, with soaked blankets wrapped around their shoulders. Morning broke gray with the wind still driving the slanting rain. Camp was a mass of sodden men in sodden blankets, slogging through mud to get a ration of cold pork and one soggy biscuit per man to appease their gnawing hunger, while they listened to their officers call out the orders of the day.

"Remain here. Improve your lean-tos. Dry your cartridges if you can."

The soldiers shook their heads wearily as they made their way back to their dripping blankets and set about cutting branches to heap onto their lean-tos. In the afternoon the wind died, and with evening coming on the rain was falling straight down. All eyes followed a rider as he passed, loping a mud-splattered horse toward the front of the column, throwing dirty water twenty feet at every step. The man reined in the steaming gelding ten feet from the entrance to General Washington's tent.

"Message for General Washington. Urgent."

"From whom?"

"General Pittston. Pennsylvania militia."

Inside, the messenger stood at attention while General Washington unfolded and read the hastily scrawled lines, then spoke.

"Do you know the contents of this message?"

"I know what it's about."

"What is that?"

"The British have scouted this column. They know you're here, and they're coming to get you. I'm the one who saw them. They split their command. Looks like they mean to hit you on both flanks at the same time as soon as the weather breaks. Maybe before. I told General Pittston, and he sent me here with that message."

"Are we in danger tonight?"

"No, sir. Not a chance. Their cannon are mired down to the axles. They can't march fast enough to get here before tomorrow noon, earliest."

"Go back to General Pittston and tell him we'll take evasive action. Thank him."

"Yes, sir."

General Washington watched the man disappear through the tent flap, then stood with his head bowed while his mind raced. He forced his thoughts to a conclusion and strode outside to the pickets. "Get Colonels Laurens and Hamilton here at once."

Minutes later his two aides were standing before him, soaked to the skin, dripping tricorns in their hands.

"We're discovered. The British are coming in on both our flanks, probably midday tomorrow. We're going to move the army back across the Schuylkill River at daybreak. We'll cross at Parker's Ford. We will leave General Smallwood and his brigade on this side of the river, with General Wayne and his division. Their orders will be to find the British and harass them. Delay or stop them if they can. Try to get their baggage train."

He gestured to Laurens. "Pass those orders verbally at once." He turned to Hamilton. "Prepare them in writing for delivery as soon as possible."

Making cook fires or campfires was impossible. The soldiers ate cold sowbelly and gnawed on hardtack, then huddled under makeshift lean-tos, which did little to shelter them from the incessant downpour. With soggy blankets wrapped about their shoulders, they shivered through the night. At midnight Caleb stood his two-hour picket shift on the edge of camp, then returned to his lean-to. At four o'clock the clouds thinned. By four-thirty the rain stopped, and the moon and stars were visible. Sunrise was a spectacular light and shadow show. At six-thirty the heavens were a cloudless blue.

The soldiers of Third Company were finishing the remains of a breakfast of one chunk of cold mutton and a crumbling, wet biscuit when O'Malley returned from receiving the marching orders of the day.

"We march at seven o'clock. They're leaving Smallwood and Wayne on this side of the river to cover our crossing and harass the British. Wayne's division is short of men. He needs more, bad. They're asking for volunteers to stay with him. Anybody want to stay with Wayne? He'll catch up to us later."

Caleb watched two men step forward, and then for reasons he himself did not understand, he walked forward to stand with them. Three more men followed.

O'Malley turned puzzled eyes on Caleb, then spoke to the six of them. "You sure?"

They all nodded, and O'Malley turned, pointing. "Down there, maybe three hundred yards. Ask an officer for Wayne's division. General

Anthony Wayne. When he comes across the river and joins us, all you report back here to Third Company."

By eight o'clock the army had begun their crossing of the Schuylkill River at Parker's Ford: a long, serpentine line of men in wet clothes, with wet bedrolls strapped to their backs, carrying wet muskets and wet cartridges that would not fire. Half of them were bare-legged and barefoot. Some paused at the crossing to look back for a moment at the place they had left Generals Smallwood and Wayne with what remained of their commands.

Caleb watched the New York Ninth Regiment, with his Third Company, march away and out of sight around a bend in the road that wound its way through the woods to the river. Only then did the realization seize him that he was in unfamiliar country, alone among strangers, under orders to find and fight the dreaded British and Germans. A moment of overwhelming loneliness washed over him as he stared at the disappearing column. Suddenly it was important that he explain to himself why he had volunteered to remain behind with Wayne's command, and there was no answer—nothing. For an instant, hot panic seized him. He battled the need to cry out, to run, to catch the column and the safety of Third Company and O'Malley and those he knew. He flinched at the voice that came booming from behind and turned to face a major he had never seen before.

"You new men fall into ranks here with First Company."

There was only time to trot forward to First Company and fill in six of the vacant places left by missing men in the last two ranks before the orders came loud and strong, "Fordddd, harch!"

They moved away from the river, traveling nearly due west, following two muddy ruts made by wagon wheels that followed an unnamed stream through the wooded hills. They passed places where trees, long dead, were stacked on the wayside, along with the stumps that had been dug out of the ground and dragged aside by oxen and chains to clear the ground. They rested at noon in a small meadow, and at one o'clock they were back in ranks, moving steadily west beneath blue skies and bright, warm sunshine. As they marched, they kept the covers to their ammunition pouches open, and by midafternoon the paper cartridges and the precious powder inside were drying.

The sun was setting when they made a hasty camp in the stubble of a small harvested wheat field surrounded by trees. They were within sight of a tavern with a small cluster of homes about and half a dozen farms nearby. They built their evening cook fires and had their first warm meal in four days—salty gravy with chunks of diced mutton on boiled rice, and hard brown bread. Half an hour later every company had fires burning, with their blankets hung on lines tied between nearby trees. The dank smell of wet wool hung heavy in the air. They boiled water to make their strong drink from parched, milled wheat, and sat around the fires with their wooden cups, quietly talking, watching the flames dance. They saw the windows in the distant tavern and the homes begin to glow in the dusk, and they drifted into silent reveries of wives and children and hearths left behind.

Caleb took a place at one of the fires of First Company, listening, letting the warmth creep in. A young soldier came to sit beside him and for a time silently nursed his smoking wooden cup with the others. After a time he turned to Caleb.

"You a volunteer?"

"Yes."

"From New York?"

"A New York company. I'm from Boston."

The young soldier, shorter than Caleb, barefooted, dressed in worn homespun, brightened. "I'm from Whitemarsh. Not far from here—east, across the river. Always wanted to see a city. Boston or New York or maybe Philadelphia."

Caleb sipped at his drink. "Philadelphia isn't far, is it?"

"Oh, maybe twenty miles from Whitemarsh. Never had time to go there. After the war's over I'm going, though. I got to see a city."

"What's this place?"

"It's called Paoli. Not much." He pointed. "A tavern over there and a few homes. Some farms."

"How far from Philadelphia?"

"I'd guess maybe fifteen miles."

They both stopped talking as an older man, slight, hunch-shouldered, strode into the circle of firelight.

"Picket duty is two hours. Four men each, according to your place in the ranks. Lead rank first, rear rank last. First four men are on duty now. Next four at ten o'clock. We cover them trees right over there. Keep a sharp eye."

He walked on and four men rose, collected their muskets, and disappeared into the darkness.

At ten o'clock tattoo sounded, and the camp quieted. The pickets came in, and fresh ones went out. Men gathered their blankets from the lines and for the first time in four days lay down in dry clothing, on dry blankets, with warm food and drink in their gaunt midsections.

Caleb lay on his blanket, calculating his picket shift. He had marched in the last rank. He would not be on duty until tomorrow night, earliest. Maybe the next night, if they were still on this side of the river. He stared into the black, boundless heavens with the unnumbered pinpoints of light and the moon and pondered what had caused him to volunteer to leave his New York company to join General Wayne's command. He could still see and feel and hear the horror of the cannon and muskets and the bayonets at the fight for Battle Hill—the men on both sides, dead, maimed, screaming—the endless screaming that wakened him sweating in the night. How long ago? Eight days? Nine? Ten? He could not remember. How could he have volunteered, knowing the risk of another such battle? Pride? Vanity? Revenge? He drifted into a dreamless sleep, still searching for the answer.

In the trees three hundred yards due west of the American camp in the wheat field, Major General Charles Grey, His Majesty's Royal Grenadiers, dropped to one knee and strained to see in the dim light of the quarter-moon. The gold epaulets on his shoulders and the gold braid on his tricorn hat were barely visible, as were the white belts that crossed on his crimson tunic.

"They're settled for the night," he whispered to his aide.

"I agree, sir."

Grey tapped him on the shoulder and quietly faded back to where his regiment waited. Quickly he gathered his officers.

"Have all the men remove the flints from their muskets. We cannot chance an accidental discharge." He turned to Colonel Henry Maguire. "Take the Second Regiment and circle wide to the east side of their camp and come up on them without a sound. Surprise is essential. Locate the pickets and silence them first by stealth. We are going to take that camp with bayonets. Do you understand?"

"Yes, sir."

"Check your watch. Mine says it is exactly twenty minutes past midnight."

"Mine is but twenty seconds ahead of yours, sir."

"At exactly two o'clock by my watch, I will lead my men into them. At that same time you come in from the east. Not a sound. No shooting. Bayonets only."

By one o'clock more than fifty of the small campfires were still glowing in the wheat field, making dark silhouettes of the slumbering soldiers. Their muskets were laid in the wheat stubble, ten feet from their blankets. The officers' horses were tied to picket ropes strung between nearby trees.

At three minutes before two o'clock, one of the horses suddenly pricked its ears and raised its head to stare into the night, eyes wine-red in the firelight. Another one blew, then whickered, and then they were all moving their feet, nervous, unsettled.

Two American officers came to their feet and went to the horses, sensing something was wrong, peering into the trees, searching for the yellow eyes of a panther or wolves.

At two o'clock they seized the halter ropes of two of the horses and were talking low to them, settling them. They did not see the British soldiers slipping silently through the trees. At the last moment they heard them, and the horses snorted and shied, and then reared. The officers were still clutching the halter ropes and had opened their mouths to shout a warning when the bayonets struck.

In the next twenty seconds the American camp became a purgatory of screaming men with sleep-fogged minds trying to rise from their blankets, stunned, bewildered, scrambling for their muskets while British regulars drove into them from both sides, their red coats and white belts vivid in the firelight while they relentlessly thrust their bayonets home again and again and again.

In the instant of the first scream, Caleb jerked erect, trying to focus his eyes in the dim light. Then the night was filled with the sounds of men in mortal agony, and Caleb's brain cleared. He threw his blanket aside, mind racing.

The light—got to get out of the light—into the trees—into the trees.

In one fluid move he rolled to his feet, legs driving away from the camp. Then a British soldier was in front of him, bayonet lowered, thrusting, and Caleb swatted it aside with his left hand and stepped in close and swung his right with every pound he had. His fist caught the man squarely on the point of the chin and the soldier went over backward, unconscious, jaw broken, his musket cartwheeling to the ground.

Caleb swept the weapon from the wheat stubble as two more red-coated regulars closed on him, bayonets gleaming in the firelight. He swung the Brown Bess to knock the first bayonet upward, then threw the heavy rifle, its stock smashing butt-first into the face of the second man, then swung around to face the first man as he recovered and came with his bayonet lowered once again.

Balanced, feet spread, hands forward, moving, circling, Caleb waited for the split second the man made his thrust. He twisted to his left and dropped his right arm to knock the bayonet far enough that the tip ripped his shirt and drew a trickle of blood as it grazed his side but did not penetrate. He cocked his left hand, and it flashed over the soldier's right shoulder in a perfect hook to his right temple, dropping the man like a stone.

Caleb leaped over both men and sprinted into the night, running low, dodging through the wheat stubble to avoid the scatter of oncoming redcoats. With their ten-pound Brown Bess muskets in their hands and their backpacks slowing them, they could not catch him as he sprinted, weaving through the gaps in their ranks. Then they thinned, and he was beyond them, running free in the darkness, when it flashed in his mind. *They didn't shoot—why didn't they shoot?*

He plunged into the trees, chest heaving, running hard. After a time, he stopped to look back and listen. Just over one hundred yards away, the dying campfires made a jumbled confusion of dim silhouettes of outnumbered Americans trying to fend off the deadly bayonets with their bare hands. The heartrending cries of the wounded and dying filled the night and rang echoing through the trees. A few scattered Americans broke through the wall of redcoats to run into the night in any direction that offered escape. Caleb did not know how long he crouched in the trees, horrified beyond thought, his gorge rising to choke him, unable to tear his eyes from the brutal carnage.

Then, almost as quickly as it had begun, the British slowed, the sounds of dying men stopped, and it was over. Some Americans were on their knees, hands thrust high in surrender, encircled by British. Other red-coated regulars walked among what remained of the campfires, pausing only to drive their bayonets downward, and move on. He heard orders shouted, and the regulars worked their way out of the camp with a small cluster of captured Americans, into the wheat field, where they all stopped, and while he watched, began working on their muskets, faces down, hands busy. Minutes passed before it suddenly broke clear in his mind. *Flints! They're putting flints in the hammers! They didn't fire a shot because they couldn't!*

He moved quickly farther back into the trees and then slowed for a moment. *North to the river, then east. We traveled west all day—Washington has to be east.*

The moon had reached its apex and was settling toward the west when the dank odor of the river reached him. Ten minutes later he pushed through the willows out into the current of the Schuylkill and stroked for the far shore. He pushed through the green foliage on the far bank and walked dripping, shivering, fifty yards north before he came to a trail running east and west. He turned to his right and set out at a trot on the rough, uneven path used to drive sheep and cattle up or down the river.

He startled a small herd of deer, which bounded away, and he dodged from the trail into the woods, heart in his mouth, until the sounds of their flight faded and died. He flinched at the inquiry of an owl, "*whooooo,*" in the trees ten feet from his right shoulder. The incessant belching of the bullfrogs came from the river, with the rhythmic chirping of crickets. He trotted on.

The eastern skyline was showing the separation of earth and heaven when he slowed to a walk, chest heaving. *Will the British have patrols out? Will they cross the river to follow? Where was Washington taking the army?*

He had no choice. He picked up his pace once more, moving steadily eastward. The gray before dawn had defined the branches on the trees that bordered the trail when he heard it faintly, from a far distance to his left. North. The unmistakable rattle of snare drums banging out reveille, and he stopped.

British? American? American! It has to be American. He took his bearings on the place the sun would rise in half an hour, and struck out cross-country, working through the thick underbrush and groves of trees, moving along the fringes of the pastures and open farm fields. Lights appeared in windows of farmhouses, and he trotted on past them. He stopped once to drink from a stream, then splashed through and trotted on, wet to the knees.

He heard them before he saw them—the sounds of axes ringing, cutting morning firewood, and the clanging of cast-iron tripods and kettles being set up to cook the breakfast meal. He crested a rise and saw through the trees the cook fires and the disorganized sprawl of bedding and tents of an army that had not yet learned the need for military order in setting up a camp. He trotted on, holding a steady pace. The tip of the sun was showing above the horizon when a voice boomed from his left.

"Who comes there? Stand and declare yourself!"

He stopped, hands raised to shoulder level while he peered into the trees, searching for the picket. He did not see him until the man moved and walked into the open. His Pennsylvania rifle was aimed directly at Caleb's breastbone.

Caleb called, "Private Caleb Dunson. Looking for the New York Ninth Regiment."

"You lost?"

"Yes. I was with Wayne. General Wayne."

"Deserted?"

"No. We were ambushed."

The man lowered his rifle and came at a trot. "When? Where?"

"Last night. A place called Paoli. Across the Schuylkill."

"You alone?"

"Yes."

"The others?"

Caleb shook his head. "Mostly dead. Some captured. A few got away."

The man rounded his mouth and blew air. "You better come with me."

Ten minutes later they stopped before the command tent, and the soldier spoke to the picket on duty at the entrance. "Private Owen McKinney. Massachusetts Sixth. Urgent business for General Washington."

The picket took McKinney's rifle and disappeared into the tent, then emerged immediately with a short, slight officer. Colonel Alexander Hamilton's eyes narrowed as he studied the two men before him, one clearly a backwoodsman, the other a boy who appeared to have been badly handled.

"What is your business with the general?"

The picket gestured. "This man just come in from Gen'l Wayne's command on the other side of the Schuylkill. Says they was ambushed."

Hamilton peered at Caleb. "Your name?"

"Private Caleb Dunson. New York Ninth."

Hamilton turned on his heel and entered Washington's tent, to emerge a moment later. "The general will see Private Dunson."

Inside the tent Caleb came to attention, looking up four inches into the face of General Washington. In those blue-gray eyes he saw every human emotion, but most of all he saw a will of tempered steel. He felt as though the general was looking through him, had seen everything inside. With Colonel Hamilton standing to one side watching, listening, Caleb saluted, and Washington returned it, then spoke.

"Your name and unit?"

"Private Caleb Dunson, sir. New York Ninth Regiment, Third Company."

"Your commanding officer?"

"That was Captain Venables, sir."

"Was?"

"We haven't seen him since Brandywine."

"Your Sergeant?"

"O'Malley, sir."

"You were with General Wayne?"

"Yes, sir."

"He does not command the New York Ninth."

"General Wayne was short of men after the Brandywine battle. They asked for volunteers, sir."

Washington nodded. "Colonel Hamilton said something happened last night?"

"Yes, sir. About two o'clock in the morning the British attacked our camp with bayonets. Killed a large part of the division. Captured some others. Some escaped. I got away."

"We heard no shooting."

"There was none, sir. They took the flints out of their musket hammers. It happened too fast. One second there was no one, and the next second they were on top of us with bayonets. Our men never got to their weapons. There wasn't a shot fired by either side."

"You saw all this?"

"I fought my way out and stopped to look back. I saw it."

Washington saw the awful revulsion in Caleb's face. "Where are the others who escaped?"

"I don't know. They scattered in the night. I swam the Schuylkill and came here."

"You're a soldier without a musket?" There was a trace of suspicion in Washington's eyes.

"Yes, sir. No time to get it when they came charging."

"Did the British follow you? Are we to expect them to attack us here?"

"I doubt it, sir. No one followed me, so far as I know."

"Was General Wayne killed?" Washington's breathing slowed as he waited.

"I don't know, sir. We had a lot of fires burning to dry our ammunition and blankets. All I could see were silhouettes. I don't know how many officers were killed."

"You're hurt? Your shirt is torn. There are traces of blood."

Caleb glanced at his side. "A bayonet. From the fight while I was escaping. It's nothing."

Washington turned to Hamilton. "Take two pickets and escort this man to the New York Ninth Regiment. Find a Sergeant O'Malley and have him verify that this man is from his company. If he is, leave him, then return and report. If he is not, put him in irons and bring him back."

"Yes, sir."

Twenty minutes later Hamilton reentered the command tent. "There's no question Private Dunson is from the New York Ninth. O'Malley says that if Dunson tells us General Wayne was ambushed and his command decimated, then it was attacked and decimated."

For a moment Washington's shoulders sagged, then he sat down at his table and for a time did not move as he concentrated. Hamilton shifted his weight from one foot to the other, and Washington gestured to him to be seated.

"We gave General Howe the field at Brandywine. It will be recorded as a defeat for us. But the men performed well. With courage. Bravery. Outnumbered two to one, but they gave as good as they got five times with the best England has to offer before we had to withdraw." He paused, and Hamilton could see he was putting pieces of the puzzle together in his mind, voicing them to judge how they sounded.

"I believe our soldiers took pride in their performance at Brandywine. I have information that General Alexander McDougall is on his way from Peekskill with nine hundred Continentals. General William Smallwood is coming with eleven hundred of the Maryland Militia. David Forman is sending six hundred irregulars from New Jersey. All that bespeaks the fact that we have strong support, despite the loss at Brandywine."

Washington stopped, waiting for a reaction from Hamilton, and Hamilton nodded his agreement.

Washington continued. "Now we are told that General Wayne's command was ambushed and largely destroyed. Another untoward event. Will the support continue?"

Silence held for a moment while Hamilton weighed the matter. "I believe it will."

"Have you heard any comments to the contrary?"

"None, sir."

"Good. There is one other matter. You know that we removed everything that could be used by the British out of Philadelphia. A large supply of food and clothing and ammunition is in a magazine in Reading, more than forty miles up the Schuylkill River."

"I'm aware of that, sir."

"Information received this morning indicates General Howe has been informed of the value of those stores and has marched out this morning up the river in that direction. I believe he intends capturing those stores."

Hamilton's mind jumped ahead, and with held breath he waited for Washington to conclude.

"I am ordering a march to intercept him. We cannot lose those supplies."

Hamilton reached to scratch beneath his chin. "And Philadelphia? What of Philadelphia?"

Washington heaved a great sigh. "If General Howe is marching to Reading, he cannot be a threat to Philadelphia."

For a long moment the two stared at each other before Washington broke it off and gave his orders.

"See to it our entire right proceeds up the Schuylkill to counter General Howe. We must not lose those supplies at Reading."

"Yes, sir."

Notes

The description of the soaked munitions in this chapter is historical. See Freeman, *Washington*, pp. 353–54.

The description of the Paoli massacre is historical. See Freeman, *Washington*, p. 354; Leckie, *George Washington's War*, p. 356.

Washington was in fact informed that General Howe and a column were marching toward Reading, Pennsylvania, to take valuable munitions and supplies stored there by the Americans, and Washington marched his column away from Philadelphia, toward Reading to save the supplies. See Freeman, *Washington*, p. 355.

CHAPTER XIII

★ ★ ★

*T*here is a transcendent power in the New England earth and air that is evident when the suns and rains of summer have done their work to draw abundance from the rolling hills, and the fields and orchards are ripe with the time of harvest. The benevolence of the Creator is evident in the richness of the produce of forests, stream, and field, and the human soul is stirred by the annual fulfillment of the eternal law of the harvest and the realization that man's labor is once again rewarded. For those who have eyes that see and hearts that feel, there is a quiet sense of rightness that settles over the land, affirming that life is good, living satisfying.

In the warmth of the late afternoon September sun, General William Howe reined his horse away from the head of the two-mile-long column of marching British regulars and stopped, caught in an unexpected moment of awe and wonder as he peered at the patchwork of emerald forests and white wheat fields and meadows and rows of green corn, all delineated by zig-zag rows of split-rail fences and meandering streams. Sheep grazed in pastures with cattle, their muzzles buried in the deep grasses.

He sat still in the saddle, caught up in the sweeping immensity and overpowering beauty of the land, sensing its profound, raw power and the vigor of the people it produced. In his heart of hearts the unspoken question that had haunted him while he was yet in the hallowed halls of the British Parliament rose once again. *Can they be beaten? Can men and women nurtured by this vast land be subdued?* The question remained unanswered, either because he could not answer it or dared not answer it, neither dared he try.

The sound of two running horses brought him abruptly back to the reality of his army marching westward near the Schuylkill River. He turned and took the slack out of the reins of his mount as General Earl Charles Cornwallis, with an aide-de-camp beside him, reined in their horses and stopped, their crimson tunics and gold epaulets sparkling in the westering sun. Howe waited, and General Cornwallis spoke.

"Sir, I just received a message from one of our patrols." Cornwallis leaned from his saddle, and Howe reached to take it. He opened it, studied the hastily scrawled words, and a sudden intensity came into his face. He read it again to be certain, then raised his eyes to Cornwallis.

"It appears Washington has taken the bait."

"So it does." Cornwallis pointed across the river. "At this moment he is across the river, two miles ahead of us, with most of his army, marching for Reading. There is no indication that he intends to stop before he reaches the town and the magazines with his stores. It is apparent he means to protect them. I presume that is according to plan and that your orders have not changed."

"My orders remain as they were. We make camp immediately. Your four divisions are to take food and rest at once. At midnight you will march them back to the east in a forced march, cross the Schuylkill, and take Philadelphia. If this report is correct, there won't be a single rebel soldier to defend the city. You should be able to occupy it without firing a shot. Capture the rabble that call themselves their Congress if you can."

He paused to arrange his words. "I shall continue the march west for one more day to be certain Washington's patrols think we are still marching for Reading, and then I will turn back for a forced night march to cover your flank, should Washington discover he has been tricked and try to catch you to attack."

Cornwallis nodded his affirmation as Howe went on.

"Then I will take about half our forces to camp out near

Germantown, six miles north of Philadelphia, and hope the defeat at Brandywine and the taking of Philadelphia will have angered Washington to the point that he will take the bait one more time and attack us there."

A look of intense calculation came into his eyes. "He escaped from Brandywine before we could destroy his army, and since that time his ranks have expanded with fresh troops from Peekskill and Maryland. Our losses were half his, but our ranks remain depleted because we can't replace them. It is now manifestly clear that the undoing of this rebellion rests on whether or not we can provoke him into a battle from which he cannot escape. Until the rebel army is destroyed, and him with it, it makes no difference how many battles we win. The result will always be the same: his ranks will swell, while ours diminish. Either we eliminate him and his army, or we lose."

He brought his eyes to Cornwallis. "Are there any questions?"

"No, sir."

"We make camp now. You march out at midnight. No lights, no sounds."

"Yes, sir."

Under cover of darkness, and the watchful eye of General Howe, General Cornwallis mounted his horse at the stroke of midnight, pumped his arm, and started east with four divisions of regulars, moving silently on the road over which they had just traveled marching west.

In the six o'clock sunrise General Howe listened to the drummers in camp bang out reveille. At seven o'clock he sat his horse at the head of his command and called out his marching orders. One minute later the band struck up its marching music, and the column marched out westward. They nooned near the river, reassembled, and marched on, to make their evening camp at six o'clock with the river to their right and wooded country to their left. They went to their blankets at dusk, tattoo sounded at ten o'clock, and at midnight they silently fell back into ranks. With General Howe leading, they marched east, over the tracks they had made just six hours earlier.

At dawn a rider caught up with General Howe. "Sir, our patrols have seen no pursuit by the rebels. It appears they are not yet aware we are marching back to Philadelphia."

At noon the weary British column sought the shade of the forest for two hours, with General Howe watching their back trail like a hawk, waiting for his patrols to report. The force was reassembling for the afternoon march when a red-coated officer rode in.

"No pursuit yet, sir. The rebels are still marching west on the far side of the river."

Howe shook his head in near disbelief that someone faithful to the rebellion—farmer, militia, or soldier—had not discovered the unbelievable ploy that had drawn Washington and the Continental Army away from Philadelphia and laid the city wide open to being taken at will. Howe's force marched on, gaining steadily on the four divisions led by General Cornwallis. At six o'clock they stopped to make camp for the night. By eight o'clock they could see the glow of the cook fires of General Cornwallis's command, four miles ahead, and far beyond the camp, two miles past the Schuylkill River, the flecks of light that marked Philadelphia.

In the deep shadows of late dusk, General Howe walked from a cook fire to his command tent, set a cup of steaming tea on his worktable, and checked his calendar. Then he spread a map, weighted the corners, and leaned over it to study the roads leading into the city.

General Cornwallis will come in from the west and be inside the city by ten o'clock in the morning. September twenty-sixth. Will there be shooting? And will he catch their so-called Congress?

At nine-forty in the morning, under a bright, warm sun that turned the Schuylkill into a winding golden ribbon and the woods and fields into a great patchwork of beauty, General Cornwallis, surrounded by his staff, rode his horse through the outskirts of the largest city in the United States, into its narrow, winding cobblestone streets. Tories and loyalists were everywhere, voices raised in a tumultuous, hero's greeting. The men in the first regiment behind Cornwallis marched with their muskets unslung, loaded, watching every window, every rooftop, eyes sweeping the crowd.

There was not a patriot or a soldier or a militiaman in sight.

Cornwallis rode on to the square, brick building where the American Congress had been convened, where he stopped and dismounted. The Tory sympathizers pressed in on all sides, reaching to touch him, shouting their praises for their liberating heroes. Cornwallis raised a hand, and the crowd silenced, waiting.

"I declare this city to be a possession of our Sovereign, King George III of England."

A roar went up, then subsided when Cornwallis again raised a hand.

"I further declare the rebel Congress to be a body without authority and guilty of sedition against the Crown. I demand to know their whereabouts this instant."

A portly man wearing the badly ink-stained apron of a printer answered. "They left eight days ago. The whole lot of them. Packed up and snuck away in the night, they did!"

Cornwallis turned to the man. "Where did they go?"

"York. Over eighty miles west, past the Schuylkill, across the Susquehanna River."

Disappointment crossed Cornwallis's face as he continued. "Where are the rebel stores? Ammunition? Cannon?"

The printer spoke up once more. "Gone. All gone. They took everything. This city is an empty shell."

Cornwallis set his jaw. "So be it. We shall quarter our soldiers within the city so far as possible. You will cooperate. General William Howe shall arrive later, and you shall accommodate him and his troops as well."

Midafternoon, the Tories and loyalists filled the streets once again, to once more shout their hero's welcome, this time to General William Howe as he entered the city on his horse, sitting tall and straight, leading his foot-weary men. He was met by General Cornwallis's aides and taken directly to the mansion Cornwallis had commandeered as his headquarters. Howe dismounted, walked across the spacious porch with its white columns and two-storied portico, into the ante room. One wall was a mural of the Adirondack Mountains. A great stone fireplace filled another. On the third wall was an original oil painting of King George II, eight feet by ten feet, with another like it of his son, King George III.

Cornwallis came quickly from the library.

"Sir, the city is ours. Congress fled eight days ago to York, eighty miles west. The rebels stripped everything of value before they vacated."

Howe shrugged it off. "I'll bivouac my troops at the edge of town tonight. Tomorrow we march for Germantown. I'll take the master suite here for the night."

"Yes, sir."

Howe turned to his nearest aide. "Prepare a message for my signature immediately. It will be delivered earliest to Joshua Loring in New York. You'll remember he's the commissary of prisoners. I order him to come to Germantown at once, and he shall bring his wife, Elizabeth."

"Yes, sir." The guard strained to maintain decorum. *He's simply got to have that blue-eyed, blonde-haired vixen at his side.*

Howe walked back out into the crowded street and mounted his horse. For a moment he paused, eyes cast west, mind running.

We took Philadelphia without firing a shot. I wonder what Washington will do when the news reaches him. And I wonder what he'll do when he finds I'm six miles west in Germantown, with only half my forces. Will he come? Will he?

Notes

General Howe's trick succeeded. While Washington was marching to Reading to protect his precious supplies, Howe reversed his march and sent General Cornwallis ahead to take and occupy the city of Philadelphia without firing a shot. The United States Congress had fled Philadelphia eight days earlier, to reconvene at the small town of York, eighty miles west, beyond the Susquehanna River. Howe realized he had won the battle of Brandywine, but though the Americans had lost more men than the British, the Americans could replace their losses, while the British could not. Upon arriving in Philadelphia, General Howe immediately sent for Joshua Loring, Howe's commissioner of prisoners, and his wife, Elizabeth, known as Betsy, to join him. See Freeman, *Washington*, p. 355; Higginbotham, *The War of American Independence*, pp. 186, 356; Leckie, *George Washington's War*, p. 356.

CHAPTER XIV

★ ★ ★

*T*here was frost on the blankets of the sleeping soldiers of the Continental Army when the sound of the reveille drum came rattling through the trees. The men stirred, then rose shivering against the sharp bite of early fall in the crisp air. Overhead the leaves of the maples and oaks and sycamores caught the first rays of the rising sun, and the forest became a blaze of incomparable reds and yellows and greens.

In the command tent at the south end of the camp, General George Washington cupped his hand about the top of the chimney to the lamp on his worktable and blew out the flame. With the tent roof glowing gold in the sun, he leaned forward, forearms on the table, and stared unseeing at his long, interlaced fingers. He was fully dressed in the wrinkled, wilted uniform he had worn for the previous twenty-four hours, and he had not shaved nor cleaned himself for the day.

He had paced in his tent until after three o'clock in the morning, until exhaustion drove him to sit at his worktable. At four o'clock his head tipped forward, and he slept for forty minutes with his head on folded arms before he jerked awake. His face lined, drawn under the relentless weight of command, he checked his watch and once again began pacing in the yellow lamplight, head down, hands clasped behind his back, laboring with conflicted thoughts.

Brandywine—defeated—Congress blamed Sullivan for not scouting the terrain—

not all his fault—partly mine—his failure understandable under the conditions he faced—I told Congress—they relented—the miracle is the soldiers don't see it as a defeat—outnumbered, they still held the British regulars five times—took great pride in it—marvelous men—but still, we were driven off—defeated.

He reached to wipe at his dry mouth.

Paoli—Wayne's command—the massacre—tragic—avoidable—nothing to be done about it now.

He stopped his pacing for a moment, reflecting. *Philadelphia—General Howe outmaneuvered me completely—I was twenty miles away protecting the stores at Reading from an attack that never happened while he reversed the march of his entire command and took Philadelphia without firing a shot—not one shot—made me look like a bungling fool.*

A look of pain crossed his face. *And then John Adams—Congress— publicly shouting: "O, Heaven, grant us one great soul!"—aimed directly at me.*

The scalding humiliation rose once again, and he forced his mind to move on.

The Country rallied after all of it—McDougall came with his New York Brigade—one thousand fresh militia from Virginia—more from New Jersey—Heath's Massachusetts' line—some of Morgan's riflemen—our strength is slightly higher than before the Brandywine battle. Despite all the blunders—the mistakes—the losses—the errors—the Country still supports us.

Once again he ceased pacing, caught up in the vortex of the dark thoughts that would not let go.

But Congress?—and my own officers? He drew and exhaled a great, weary breath as the stark reality came rushing once more.

General Gates—decisive victory against Burgoyne at Nielsen's farm up on the Hudson—deliberately sent his report of his victory directly to Congress and not to me although I am his commander in chief—openly talking against me—consumed by ambition—he wants my position. General Thomas Conway—driven by blind ambition just like Gates—Adjutant General Timothy Pickering—General Jean de Kalb— and even Nathanael Greene—all murmuring against me.

For the first time, anger surged hot. He set his chin and battled with the compelling need to strike out against all those who perceived themselves to be his superiors without ever having tasted the grinding, soul-destroying demands of feeding an army of untrained citizens when there was no food, clothing them when there were no clothes, leading them into battle when they were little more than a mob, shaping them into a unified command when they came from states with nothing in common to bind them together.

He softened at the thought of his men. Half of them barefoot, all of them hungry—no uniforms, short of ammunition, beaten—and still they remained. His thoughts ran on.

Redemption—there must be a way to achieve redemption—something that can be done to regain what has been lost. . . .

The sound of the tent flap being drawn brought him up short, and he turned to see diminutive Alexander Hamilton step inside the tent. Hamilton stopped at the sight of Washington, uniform wrinkled, unshaven, and then spoke with a quiet intensity.

"Sir, our patrols have intercepted two British letters. They could be important." He thrust them forward, and Washington quickly broke the seals and read them, then read them again, carefully. When he raised his eyes back to Hamilton all appearances of fatigue and frustration were gone, and there was an eager ring in his voice.

"Gather the war council here at nine o'clock!"

A trace of a smile crossed Hamilton's face. "Yes, sir."

At nine o'clock, washed, shaven, in a crisp, fresh uniform, Washington stood at the head of the council table as his officers entered and took their seats. Sullivan, Greene, Conway, Armstrong, Wayne, Moylan, Maxwell, Nash, and Stephen. His two aides, Hamilton and Laurens, were seated at his side. On the table before him were two large scrolls.

He wasted no time or words. "I have received a letter from General Lafayette. You will recall he was grievously wounded in the foot at the battle at Brandywine. A woman by the name of Liesel Beckel of Bethlehem—a Moravian sister—took him into her home and has nursed him back to health. He will be returning soon. I shall see to it she is rewarded. I thought you would like to know."

Each officer at the table exclaimed his relief at learning of Lafayette's imminent return to duty. Battle-wise, every man knew that all too many soldiers had made their way home lacking an arm or a leg, simply because battlefield wounds were too often untreatable and battlefield surgery was rudimentary, brutal. That one of their own would be spared such agony was deeply gratifying.

Washington waited, then raised a hand, and his officers sensed something compelling. They waited in quiet expectation.

"We have intercepted two British messages. First, General Howe has sent a rather large force north, up the Hudson River. It is his intent to open the south end of the Hudson River by eliminating all the obstructions our forces have put in the channel and by taking whichever of our forts necessary to allow free passage on the river. That might include Fort Montgomery, Fort Constitution, Fort Clinton, and any others he chooses. I know he is aware that General Burgoyne was badly defeated by General Gates's forces at a place called Nielsen's farm near Saratoga on September nineteenth. I do not know if he intends moving troops on up the Hudson to relieve Burgoyne, but I doubt it."

Open talk broke out, then subsided as he continued.

"The second message is that General Cornwallis remains in Philadelphia with enough men to control that city, while General Howe has moved the balance of his force to Germantown, where they are camped at this moment."

Every man at the table spoke at once, loud, excited. Washington waited until they settled.

"He's split his command. With part going to the Hudson and part in Philadelphia, he has only about nine thousand troops in Germantown. Our good fortune is we have received substantial replacements. Numerically our forces exceed his by about three or four thousand. In short, we have the advantage of General Howe at Germantown."

The entire council perceived what was coming, and Washington did not hesitate. He put the question to them: "I am of the opinion that conditions are right to attack General Howe at Germantown. Can you support such a decision?"

The answer was instantaneous and unanimous. "Attack!"

Washington nodded. "It is agreed." He unrolled one of the two large scrolls and anchored the four corners with small leather sandbags, then turned the map slightly to square with the compass.

"This is a map of the area." He dropped a long index finger onto the parchment. "This is Germantown. The countryside round about is largely in farms with split-rail fences dividing them."

He moved his finger north. "The general British camp is here, north of town. Here, about one mile north of their general camp, they have breastworks and trenches on both sides of Skippack Road, under command of Generals Grey and Grant. Their defenses face north and are clearly intended to hold the road."

Vociferous murmuring broke out, and Washington waited until it died. His generals had not forgotten it was British General "No Flint" Grey who had ambushed Wayne's command at two o'clock A.M. with bayonets at Paoli, in what had instantly become known as the "Paoli Massacre." And it was General James Grant who had contemptuously declared that with five thousand British regulars he could march from one end of the United States to the other, destroying any part of, or all of, the Continental Army should it oppose him.

He moved his finger as he continued. "We are here in Worcester Township, about twelve miles north and west of the British." He stopped until every eye was on his hand as it moved. "From where we are, there are three main roads that run north and south. The center one is the Skippack Road, which I identified a moment ago. You can see it runs past the British breastworks, on past the British camp, and continues south to become the main street running through Germantown."

He retraced Skippack Road. "Here, about three miles north of the British camp, is the second north-south road. It runs generally parallel to and east of the Skippack Road to this point, called Chestnut Hill, where it joins the Skippack."

Again his finger moved. "The third north-south road is here, about one mile west of the Skippack Road and less than three hundred yards from the Schuylkill River. It is called the Ridge Pike Road, and it runs past Van Deering's Mill, here."

He straightened for a moment, then continued. "Now we examine the roads running from east to west. We begin at the Van Deering Mill, where this road runs east for about a mile to cross the Skippack Road. The British breastworks are here, on the south side of this road, facing north, on both sides of the junction."

He paused to satisfy himself everyone was tracking, then continued. "Moving on south, the next east-west road is called the Lime Kiln Road. It comes in from the east, past Luken's Mill, here, to join the Skippack Road, here, where there is a large stone house called the Chew House because it is owned by Chief Justice Benjamin Chew."

His finger moved on. "Farther south is this road, called the Old York Road. It comes in at an angle to join the Skippack Road, here."

He stopped to tap the spot. "The British have a second camp here, in the angle made by the junction of Skippack Road and Old York Road. They have forces there in reserve to support the breastworks if they get into trouble."

He straightened for a moment, and his eyes went around the room, pausing for a moment on each man.

"This is the plan of attack. General Sullivan will move down Skippack Road with Generals Stirling, Conway, Wayne, Nash, and Maxwell. To the east, General Greene will lead a force that includes Generals Stephen and Smallwood in a sweeping curve that will bring them in south of the Lime Kiln Road. They will take Luken's Mill and continue west to come in south of the Chew House. From there they can protect the left flank of Sullivan's attack as they move south to the British breastworks and the support camp on Old York Road."

General Greene concentrated, then nodded his understanding, and Washington went on.

"Here, to the west, General Armstrong will bring a force down Ridge Pike Road and will turn east on the road at Van Deering's Mill, then leave the road to come in behind the breastworks and trenches of the British, here."

Washington straightened. "Make yourselves acquainted with the detail of the map and the part you play in the general plan of attack."

For three minutes he remained standing while the generals stood, hunched forward, tracing the roads with their fingers as they memorized them and began making the decisions that would guide them through the battle.

Washington waited until they were all seated once again, then spoke.

"Let me bring this to its simplest terms. Generals Sullivan, Conway, Wayne, Maxwell, Nash, and Stirling come down the Skippack Road. Generals Greene, Stephen, and Smallwood come in from the east. General Armstrong comes in from the west. Thus the breastworks and the main British camp are caught front, left, and right. With superior numbers, we will at least be able to hurt the British badly. With good fortune, we could take down the entire British force in Germantown."

The members of the war council looked at each other, caught up in the possibilities, calculating, judging. *It's possible! Take down General William Howe! "No Flint" Grey. James Grant. It's possible.*

Washington interrupted their thoughts. "General Greene will need about four hours more marching time because his command has the greater distance to cover, and some of it is cross-country. I have arranged for a guide who is familiar with the area. His command will leave first, then General Armstrong, then General Sullivan and his forces."

He paused and leaned slightly forward for emphasis. "We will march in the evening hours tomorrow, October third. The attack will begin at five A.M. the next morning, October fourth, and it will be done with bayonets." His eyes narrowed with intensity. "It is critically important that the first assault be a total surprise. That means we must silence their pickets before they can raise an alarm. To do that we must know where their picket stations are located. I will leave it to each of you to pick a few men who can leave camp tonight, move ahead in the dark, locate those British picket posts, and return undetected before morning to make their report. Tomorrow night those same men will move ahead of each command to the British pickets and silence them any way necessary. Is that understood?"

"Yes, sir."

Washington straightened. "Good. Issue ammunition and rations. Have your men rested. Tomorrow will be a long night followed by a heavy battle. Dismissed."

Two hundred yards south of the command tent, New York Third Company was laboring through midmorning drill when the war council officers ducked out through the tent flap and walked to their tethered horses. The reflection of the sun off the glittering gold on their epaulets caught the eye of Sergeant O'Malley, and he glanced at them, then turned back to his men. "Halt," he bawled, and the ranks came to a ragged, uneven halt while O'Malley studied the officers as they mounted their horses.

"Nine of 'em," he muttered, and for a moment he pursed his mouth. "Somethin's happenin'." He glanced at the officers once more. "Guess we'll hear about it soon enough."

It was during the noon meal that a young, thin officer with a trimmed Van Dyke beard came riding a high-headed, high-blooded bay gelding through the trees to the cook fire. His clothing was homespun, save for his tunic, which was new, with the gold epaulets of a captain prominent on each shoulder. O'Malley stood and came to attention while others nearby raised their heads from their wooden bowls to watch. Caleb walked within hearing distance to listen. The captain stopped but remained mounted while he eyed the men critically, then spoke in a high voice.

"I'm looking for Sergeant O'Malley."

O'Malley saluted. "I'm O'Malley, sir."

The man frowned. "I don't see your chevrons."

"No one ever gave them to me."

The man shrugged it off and tossed a hand indifferently. "I have orders to discuss with you in private. Follow me." A sense of superiority flowed from the man as he turned his horse away, expecting O'Malley to follow.

"Sir," O'Malley called, "who are you?"

The man turned in the saddle, eyes flashing. "Do you see these epaulets? Does it matter who I am?"

"It does to me, sir."

The man reined the horse around to face O'Malley. He pulled himself to his full height and thrust out his chest. "I am Captain Gerald Allen Furniss, lately placed in command of the New York Ninth Regiment. I am your commanding officer." He stared at O'Malley.

O'Malley showed no emotion. "What happened to Captain Venables?"

"His death at the battle of Brandywine was confirmed two days ago."

O'Malley looked at the ground while he accepted the shock. Most of the men of Third Company came to their feet to stand quietly, seized by their own thoughts about the death of their captain. Caleb walked to within six feet of O'Malley and stopped, still watching in silence.

O'Malley spoke. "I'm sorry about Captain Venables. He was a good officer. A good officer."

"I did not know the man. Follow me, Sergeant."

The noon mess was finished, and the men of Third Company were at the Skippack Creek washing out their bowls and utensils with clear, cold creek water and sand when O'Malley returned. They gathered around him, waiting, Caleb among them.

O'Malley's face was a mask of disgusted restraint as he spoke. "That's our new captain. The whole army's under orders to get ready for an attack. Tonight Third Company's got to send eight men down to the British camp and find their pickets. They go in pairs. The British can't know they been scouted. Tomorrow night the whole army goes down there, and we got to silence those pickets before they raise an alarm."

An old, bearded soldier asked, "What was all this business of takin' you somewhere, like this is all secret? Why didn't he just tell us all at once?"

O'Malley shook his head. "I don't know. That youngster acted like this was the biggest secret since Noah's Ark." He heaved a sigh. "Don't matter anyway. An attack's an attack."

He cleared his throat. "About their pickets. I figger the fairest way is volunteers. Some of you men from the woods who's trained in Indian fighting—you want to volunteer?"

A tall man with long hair tied back spoke. "Don't kill 'em? Just find 'em and come back?"

"Yes. They can't know you was there."

"Do we take our rifles?"

"I'd say no, but that's up to you. Just don't fire them."

An older man dressed in ancient fringed buckskins and moccasins grinned. "I kin smell one of them redcoats for about half a mile, rain or shine, day or night. I'll go if someone'll watch after my rifle 'til I get back."

Three more stepped forward, then one more, then two more.

O'Malley looked around the circle for a moment. "One short." He glanced at Caleb. "How about you, Dunson? You move good, with all that boxin' you been studyin'."

Caleb started, wide-eyed. "Me? I've never been out at night looking for pickets. I don't know the woods."

"Seems like you did fine in the dark when the British hit Wayne's camp at Paoli. You'll have a partner. Maybe someone who knows the forest."

The old man in the fringed buckskins raised his chin to scratch at his scraggly beard. "I'll take him. If he got outta that Paoli mess with a whole hide, he knows enough."

O'Malley bobbed his head. "Dunson, you just volunteered, and that makes eight. You men team up, and tonight after mess I'll meet you at the cook fire. By then I'm supposed to have a map tellin' what part of the British lines we're responsible to scout, and we'll work out which pair goes where. After tattoo, you slip out of camp. Tell our pickets when you leave, so they'll know you when you get back. You got to get there and be on your way back before daybreak. And remember, the British can't know you was there. This afternoon we're supposed to make sure our weapons are clean and workin' and then go get forty rounds of ammunition each. Let's get at it."

The old man walked over to Caleb and eyed him, top to bottom. "What's yer name, sonny?"

"Dunson. Caleb Dunson."

The old eyes widened in surprise. "Caleb, you say?"

"Caleb Dunson."

A wry grin slid across the whiskered old face. "Now that oughta get someone a little confused. My name's Caleb, too."

Caleb's eyebrows arched. "Caleb? Your last name?"

The old man dropped his eyes for a moment. "I been called Caleb so long I near forgot the last half. Pryor. Caleb Pryor."

"You've spent time in the woods hereabouts?"

"Since I was younger'n you. Family was taken by smallpox. I been in the woods ever since. I know what the momma panther says to her cubs. Tonight I'll get you there and back. Where you from?"

"Boston."

"Boston? Boston City?"

"Yes, sir."

"How'd you get mixed up in a New York regiment?"

"That's a long story."

"Meet me at the cook fire after evening mess, and we'll get our assignment. Then we'll get back together at the fire after tattoo and leave from there. Don't bring your musket or canteen. An' wear somethin' dark. That shirt'll show up in the moonlight."

In full darkness, Caleb hunkered down by the dying coals of the evening cook fire and listened to the sounds of the tattoo drum fade in the trees. The camp quieted as he waited, peering into the night for Pryor while his thoughts ran rampant.

In the dark—in strange country—with a man I don't know—searching for British pickets! Insane!—O'Malley's insane—Pryor's insane—I'm insane—this whole war's insane.

The voice came from six feet directly behind him. "You ready?"

In one fluid move of pure instinct, Caleb dodged to his right and spun, crouched, balanced, prepared.

Pryor stopped and raised both palms defensively. "Easy there, son. I'm on your side, remember?"

Caleb straightened, and there was a shade of anger in his voice. "Coming in from behind like that, in the dark . . ."

Pryor raised a pointing finger. "Better learn to expect anything from any direction, day or night." He dropped his hand and knelt by the remains of the fire to pick out a charred stick. He blackened his hand with the ash, then rubbed it onto his face and into his beard

He gestured. "Get a stick and black your face."

Caleb did not move.

"Do it. That dark coat hides your shirt, but there's going to be a three-quarter moon tonight, and what we don't need is the light coming off a white face. Black it!"

Three minutes later he inspected Caleb's blackened face, nodded approval, and asked, "You bring any weapon?"

"No. You said not to."

"A belt knife?"

"No. I don't own one."

Pryor shook his head. "City folk," he mumbled. "Let's go. You follow behind me. Step where I step."

"You been in these hills before?"

"I been on the Schuylkill River and the Skippack Creek many a time, and I know these hills, if that's what you're askin'. We'll follow the Skippack on south right to them British breastworks, where we're assigned. There's a road runs east and west right there, an' my guess is the pickets will be on the north side of that road. We work our way west lookin' for 'em, and about a quarter mile before we reach Van Deering's mill, we turn back north. The Wissahickon Creek's right there, and we can follow it back north a ways, and then on over to the Skippack Road an' back to our camp. Understand?"

Caleb paused long enough to form a mental picture of Pryor's instructions, then nodded.

Pryor rose. "Let's go."

Silently they moved south in the dark, Pryor guided by the stars, the skyline, experience, and the instincts of a child of the wilderness. Twice he stopped to raise a hand and listen, and twice something ahead moved, then bounded off through the woods.

"Elk or deer," he whispered, and they moved on, the Skippack Creek thirty yards east, to their left. The moon rose to cast pale silvery light that sifted through the trees to turn the forest floor into a patchwork of lacy light and shadow. Pryor moved steadily, in near total silence, with Caleb behind, watching his feet, stepping where Pryor had stepped. One hour became two, and Pryor raised a hand to signal a stop. He huddled with Caleb and spoke in a whisper.

"Not long now. You thirsty? Tired?"

"I'm all right."

"We'll stop a minute to listen. The forest says things at night."

They sat cross-legged in the chill of the October night, breathing silently, listening intently. An owl spoke from the west. From the east came the sound of something rustling in the thick forest foliage, close to Skippack Creek. The sounds of night continued to come softly from both east and west, but nothing from north or south.

Caleb leaned close to Pryor to whisper. "No sounds from north or south?"

Pryor nodded his head. "We come in from the north. The British are just ahead to the south. In the woods things go quiet where men are."

They went on. The taint of campfire smoke in the crisp fall air reached them, and Pryor dropped to his haunches to point and whisper. "Road's one mile ahead. The pickets ought to be about fifty yards this side of it. It's cold enough they might have a small fire goin', but I doubt it."

He rose and continued south. The forest became silent, and then they heard the faint sound of water moving over stones in the Skippack Creek as it angled in from their left. The odor of campfire smoke became stronger as they moved, and twenty minutes later Pryor halted and dropped to his haunches.

He made hand signs to Caleb. They were close to the road that fronted the British breastworks. They would turn right and make their way west, searching for the pickets.

Overhead, the moon had reached its zenith and was slipping toward the southwestern horizon. Moving slowly, silently, picking the places he stepped, Pryor moved on, Caleb following. They had gone less than two hundred yards when Pryor dropped out of sight, and Caleb went soundlessly to one knee, waiting, listening. The sounds came faintly, ahead and from their left, and Caleb's eyes widened when he recognized human voices followed by a rustling and then silence.

Pickets! They just changed pickets!—one coming, one going!

Pryor angled slightly to their right, then back due west, and continued. They did not see the picket as they passed him, but they heard him shuffling his feet against the chill of the night and the beginning of the gather of frost. Time became meaningless as they picked their way forward, caught up in the intensity of moving silently in a dark and hostile forest. They had covered three hundred yards when Pryor froze, then raised his head, obviously testing the air. Caleb breathed gently but could smell only the dank, musty scent of the forest floor, mixed with the smoke from the British campfires that had died six hours earlier but still tainted the air.

Then he smelled it. Tobacco smoke! A picket was smoking his pipe!

They passed the tobacco smell and silently continued west. Five minutes became ten, and still there was no sound, nothing.

The voice came loud in the silence, twenty yards to their left, close to the road. "Who comes there?"

Instantly Pryor uttered a small bark, and for a split second Caleb, a scant six feet behind, believed it to be the authentic voice of a fox. He marveled as Pryor rustled the ferns with his right hand, and then both men froze in utter silence, Pryor with his hand on the handle of his belt knife. They heard mutterings from the picket, but he did not challenge again, nor did he venture into the woods looking. They waited for what seemed to Caleb an eternity before Pryor once again slipped quietly into the night, nearly invisible in his buckskins, with his face blackened.

They had covered three hundred yards when Pryor stopped and

raised his arm to point southwest. There, in the center of a small clearing, the moonlight reflected off the white belts that crossed on the chest of a British regular. Beneath the belts, the white stockings showed faintly. Pryor paused only long enough to mark the place in his mind, then turned nearly due north to cut a circle around the clearing. Fifteen minutes later he paused once again, searching in the night, and again raised his arm. Four hundred yards to the west was a large building silhouetted in the moonlight. Van Deering's Mill.

Pryor turned right and moved north through the woods, cautiously at first, then more rapidly. They had covered three hundred yards when they waded soundlessly through a stream running west, then moved east for forty yards onto the bank of a creek that flowed due south. Twenty minutes later Pryor stopped at a bridge that spanned the creek and a road that led east and west. For a moment he studied the eastern sky, now showing the first light of dawn. The morning star was fading. For the first time in hours he spoke, and it sounded strangely loud in the night.

"We're clear of the British. Four pickets." He gestured. "We been followin' the Wissahickon Creek. The road we're on runs east, right back to Skippack Road. We can be back in camp just after sunrise if we don't waste time."

They dipped their hands into the icy, crystal clear water of the creek and drank, then started east at a trot while they wiped their mouths. Frost was forming on the roadside as they turned north onto Skippack Road, and the sun, still below the eastern rim, was painting the light drift of eastern clouds rose and yellow and the billions of leaves in the forest red and gold. As they crested the last swell, the two men heard the rattle of reveille in the Continental Army camp and saw the smoke from the morning cook fires rising straight into the azure sky. They sought their own pickets, identified themselves, and moved on into the camp where they found O'Malley waiting for them beside the black tripod and steaming cook kettle of Third Company.

"Trouble?"

Pryor shook his head. "None. Got that map?"

O'Malley spread it on the ground, and Pryor knelt, studied it for a moment, then pointed with his finger. "Four pickets. Here, here, here, and here."

"They know you were there?"

"No."

"Can you find 'em again tomorrow night?"

"Yes, if they're in the same place."

O'Malley bobbed his head and spoke with a sour, wry look. "Good. Fetch your gear. Get some of this real good, hot, moldy mush and some of that sowbelly fried so crisp you got to bust it with a rock. And be sure to get a chunk of that bread over there. Only eight days old. You got a choice with it. You can load 'er into a cannon like grapeshot and stop about forty British redcoats with it, or you can soak it in that real good, hot moldy mush for about an hour and try to eat it. If you survive breakfast, get some sleep. We march outta here tonight, and it looks like we got a battle tomorrow."

Pryor grinned as O'Malley looked at Caleb.

"You all right?"

"Yes."

"Learn somethin'?"

"A lot."

Pryor broke in. "He did good. Got a natural knack for the woods."

O'Malley continued. "You got a new musket after you lost that one at Paoli?"

"Yes."

"Get some breakfast and then some sleep."

The sun was casting shadows eastward when O'Malley shook Caleb's shoulder and Caleb raised onto one elbow, brain sleep-fogged.

"Captain wants to see you. Something about writing."

Caleb fumbled for a moment. "Furniss. Was that his name? Furniss?"

"That's the last part, and you better remember it all. He's Captain Gerald Allen Furniss, and I think there's nothin' he loves more'n hearin' all of it."

Caleb paused at the creek long enough to splash icy water on his face to wash off what remained of the blackening and run his hands through his hair to hold it back, then walked through the camp to the tent with two pickets by the entrance.

"I'm Caleb Dunson. Sergeant O'Malley, Third Company, said I'm to report to Captain Gerald Allen Furniss."

Three minutes later Caleb was inside the tent facing the shorter man with the thin, hatchet face.

"So you're Dunson?"

Not Private Dunson. Not Mr. Dunson. Just Dunson. For a moment Caleb studied the man.

"Yes, sir."

"I am told you write."

"Some."

"We're going into battle tomorrow. It appears my orderly is stricken with an illness. Dysentery. Matter of fact, four members of my staff are stricken with it. You will take paper and pencil and keep notes of the important events as they occur. At battle's end you will write a full report."

"I'm to go in advance of the main body to silence the British pickets."

Furniss bristled. "I'm to go in advance of the main body to silence the British pickets—*what?*"

It took Caleb a full three seconds to understand. "To silence the British pickets, *sir!*"

"Remember that." Furniss suddenly stood and locked his hands behind his back and paced for a moment. "I do not see why you cannot go in advance and still take notes and make the report. Am I understood?"

"Yes, sir."

"Good. I will expect the report within twelve hours of the battle's end."

"I'll need pencil and paper."

"I was told you had them."

"I lost them at Paoli. I lost everything at Paoli except what I was wearing."

"Very well. I'll have them delivered to you by evening mess. You are dismissed."

"Yes, sir."

Caleb turned on his heel and walked out the tent entrance into the cool air of late afternoon. He rounded his lips and blew air as he walked away. He had gone only ten feet when a booming voice stopped him, and he turned. A large, fleshy man was marching up behind him, spectacles low on his substantial nose. He was followed by a young woman.

"You just come out of Captain Furniss's tent?"

Caleb looked for epaulets, but there were none. "Yes."

"You part of his staff?"

"No. I'm from Third Company, back there." He pointed a thumb over his shoulder. "I don't believe I know who you are."

"I'm Dr. Ubecht. A major, but I don't like fooling with those epaulets. I was told Furniss's staff has a bad case of dysentery. What we don't need is another outbreak. You wait here 'til I come out of his tent."

"Yes, sir."

Ubecht strode past the pickets without a word and disappeared into the tent. The young woman remained behind, and for the first time Caleb had a moment to look at her.

She was five inches shorter than he, comely built, with a white kerchief tied to hold back her auburn hair. Her eyes were large and green, face beautifully shaped. There was a sense of weariness about her as she stood in shy silence, smiling.

A full minute passed, and the silence between them became awkward.

Caleb cleared his throat. "You with the doctor?" *Of course she's with the doctor. You think she's a soldier?*

Her voice was low. "Yes."

"A nurse?" *No, you idiot, she's a blacksmith!*

"I'm helping at the hospital. Whatever they need. I'm learning to be a nurse."

"Uh, my, uh, name's Caleb Dunson."

"I'm Nancy Fremont."

"Nice to meet you, ma'am. You . . . uh . . . from around here?" *Nancy.*

Fremont. Beautiful names. She can't be more than eighteen. Seventeen. She's seventeen. I know she's seventeen.

"Philadelphia." She raised her eyes to him. "May I ask your reason for visiting the captain?"

Caleb assumed an air of nonchalance. "Yes. The captain requested that I write the official regimental report on the battle tomorrow." *Requested? Furniss? Ordered, you mean!*

Her eyebrows peaked in sudden interest, and Caleb could not miss how striking she was. "You're the one they put in charge of the orderly book?"

"Uh, yes, the orderly book. Yes." *Is that what it's called? The orderly book?*

She went on eagerly. "Then you must be one of the captain's aides. An officer?"

"Well, uh, no, I'm in Third Company." *You're a private in Third Company. Tell her you're a private, not an officer. Tell her! . . . No, I won't!*

"How is it you were selected to keep the record?"

"I've done some writing before. I didn't ask for the job."

"Well." She smiled up at him, and there was an innocence in her face and her eyes beyond anything Caleb had ever seen before.

At that moment Ubecht strode out of the tent, pointed at Caleb, and spoke as he walked by. "You can go on your way. Nancy, follow me."

As she fell in step with the doctor she turned back and said, "Good fortune to you, Caleb Dunson. Perhaps we'll meet again."

Caleb's brain became a perfect blank. "Uh . . . yes. Maybe we will." *She wants to see me again—invited me!—I heard it.*

Her stride was firm, her shoulders square. Rooted to the spot, unable to move or think, Caleb watched her until she was out of sight. Finally he shook his head and came back to the Continental Army camp and the evening cook fires boiling the evening meal. He looked once more in the direction she had disappeared, then walked back to Third Company and took his place in line for evening mess. He tasted nothing as he ate his boiled mutton and turnips, and he saw only auburn hair and large, green eyes and a lovely mouth that was always smiling.

The men of Third Company were washing their cook kettles when the sounds of marching men and rolling cannon brought all their heads around toward the east. The men all stopped work to silently watch the men under command of General Nathanael Greene with the gold of sunset on their backs as they marched out of camp and disappeared into the woods.

It had begun.

At nine o'clock General Armstrong mounted his horse, raised his arm, and led his command west into the gathering shades of deep dusk.

At nine-thirty, O'Malley called Caleb and Pryor and the other three teams of Third Company's advance scouts together near the glowing coals of the dying cook fire. As they gathered, Caleb noticed for the first time, an iron-headed, black-handled tomahawk in Pryor's weapon belt, and a chill rose up his backbone.

O'Malley wasted no time. "You got to get those British pickets silenced before the main body gets to the British breastworks south of that road. When you've finished with the pickets, wait right there until we catch up, then take your places in Third Company. Remember, Gen'l Washington means to start the attack at five o'clock in the morning, so you got to be finished and waiting by then. Any questions?"

There were none.

"All right." He thrust a small packet wrapped in oilcloth to Caleb. "Cap'n Furniss says there's paper and pencil in there. You know what to do with it?"

"Yes."

"Good. All of you, leave now."

The eight men paired. Pryor stopped at the dying fire long enough to blacken his face and watch Caleb smear the ash onto his own. As they walked south toward the dark of the forest, Pryor handed Caleb a bone-handled belt knife in a leather sheath, fringed and beaded.

"Put that on your belt. Never know when you'll need it."

Caleb hesitated. "I can't pay you for it. I don't know how to use a knife."

"Never mind pay. You'll learn to use it quick enough if some red-coat comes at you with one of those long British swords. Remember one thing. If you have to use it, keep it low, in front of you, with the cutting edge up. A stroke upward has a better chance at a man's vitals than one coming down. Understand?"

"Yes."

"Get it on your belt. Left side if you're right-handed."

There was the tang of fall in the air as they moved south. By midnight the moon was well up to turn a skiff of high clouds silver and cast shadows in the woods. They followed the same trail as the previous night, and Caleb recognized most of the landmarks as they moved on. The streams, the high, denuded hill to the right, a gigantic, burned-out tree stump that had been struck by lightning in a century long gone, the split-rail fences that divided the farms. At one o'clock a cold north breeze stirred the air against their backs, and Caleb shivered as they worked their way on south.

It was approaching two o'clock when Pryor dropped to his haunches and they stopped while he whispered, "Two hundred yards. The first picket. They should be changing about now. We wait."

On bended knee they waited and watched until Caleb felt the muscles in his legs begin to cramp. Silently he shifted, stretched his legs, and settled once again. Minutes passed before the sounds of a man tramping through the forest came clear. They listened to two voices, then the sounds of a man leaving before Pryor picked a stone from the forest floor, gave a hand sign and moved forward silently. They were less than twenty feet from the picket before they saw the black form suddenly jerk alert and bring up a musket.

In that instant Pryor lofted the stone over the man's head to land forty feet beyond him, bounding through the forest foliage. The picket spun, and they heard the flat sound of his musket hammer being drawn to full cock as Pryor dropped his rifle and sprinted. The man was turning when the tomahawk struck. Pryor caught the picket as he fell and laid him silently on the ground. He detached the bayonet from the picket's Brown Bess musket and threw it into the forest, then threw the musket the other direction. He shoved the tomahawk handle back through his belt, and Caleb waited while he retraced his steps to retrieve his rifle from the brush. One minute later they were once again moving west, searching for the next picket.

There was no tobacco smoke. There was nothing. They nearly over-ran the man before his voice came booming from the shadows less than fifteen feet away. "Halt! Who comes there? Answer or I shoot!"

They saw the raised musket as Pryor spoke loudly, his voice echoing in the forest. "Loyalist scout. I'm coming in. My hands are raised." He gave Caleb hand signs and for a moment Caleb could not believe it. Pryor shoved him to his feet and pushed him forward. Caleb walked slowly toward the man, his heart in his throat, hands high, clasping his musket, feet rustling in the fall leaves on the forest floor. Pryor silently disappeared to his left. When Caleb had closed to within six feet of the picket, the man opened his mouth to speak as the tomahawk struck from behind, and he dropped like a stone.

Pryor threw the man's musket and his bayonet in different directions, and they continued on west, picking their way through the trees. They had gone nearly three hundred yards when Pryor stopped. For ten seconds he stood straight up, testing the frosty air, listening for anything that would betray the third picket. It came quietly in a hoarse whisper.

"Henry, is that you? I heard talking over there." The voice was soft, young, strained, frightened. Pryor pointed to a stand of pine trees and gave Caleb a hand sign to walk, while he again disappeared into the night, crouched low, reaching for his tomahawk.

They left the third man in the trees where he fell. Pryor paused only long enough to slip his tomahawk back into his belt and peer eastward at the heavens, judging the time until sunrise. The morning star was still strong in the velvet black of the heavens. He turned to Caleb long enough to hold up one finger. Only one picket left to find and silence.

Twenty minutes later Pryor stopped and dropped to his haunches with Caleb right behind. Pryor waited until their breathing slowed before he closed his eyes, bowed his head, and listened intently to the sounds of the night. From their right, at a distance, came the soft gurgle of the Wissahickon Creek flowing over rocks. For a moment something small stirred the brittle fall leaves on the forest floor and was gone. Then, silence. All summer insects were gone. The toads were buried in the mud for the winter. Overhead a night bird glided on silent, silken wings.

Pryor was rising when the brush less than eight feet to their left erupted, shattering the quiet. He had only time to partially turn toward the black shape of a man hurtling at them and raise his rifle at the bayonet that came flashing in the moonlight. From behind Pryor, Caleb heard the gasp as Pryor went down backwards, and Caleb saw the British picket jerk his musket back and poise it for a second thrust. In that grain of time Caleb's right hand reached for the bone-handled knife on his left hip, and he dived. He struck the picket from the side, and they went down in a tangled heap. Caleb rolled free and came to his feet with the knife drawn, low in front of him, cutting edge up as the picket came to his knees. He was rising when Caleb reached him with his right hand swinging forward in an upward arc. Caleb felt the knife strike the softness of the man's belly, just below the place the white belts crossed on the man's chest, and he heard the grunt as the man sagged away from him, clawing at the wound. Caleb jerked the knife free and struck again, and a third time. A strange, unearthly whine came from the man's throat as he sat down backwards, then toppled onto his side and became still.

For a moment Caleb stood over him, waiting, and when the man did not move again he spun and in two strides was beside Pryor. The old man had risen to one knee.

"How bad?" Caleb demanded, and Pryor could hear the fear in his voice.

"Nothin'. I think that frog-sticker got a little piece of my arm." He pulled the left sleeve of his leather shirt toward his elbow and raised his forearm to look. "Yep. Got just a little of it. Nearly missed. No real damage. We'll let 'er bleed a little to clean 'er out and then we'll bind it with somethin'. Can I borrow a chunk of your shirttail?"

Caleb opened his coat and pulled out his shirttail, cut a long strip with the knife and handed it to Pryor. Pryor flexed his hand while he spoke.

"Used the knife?"

It had happened too fast. Caleb raised his right hand, still clutching the knife, and he stared as his mind caught up with the fact that he had killed a man with it, face to face. He felt a sudden surge of weakness come over him and for a moment was not sure his knees would support his body. Knowing that he had again taken a human life rose to choke him. He licked dry lips in the cold October night air and stared back at Pryor.

"Yes. The knife."

Pryor could hear the flat, dead sound in Caleb's voice and for a moment his thoughts reached far back. Forgotten images rose in an instant, and he saw himself at age fifteen standing over an Indian writhing on the ground with a knife embedded deep in his chest. He remembered the leap of fear as his heart told him he had offended God and nature by killing another human, and it did not matter that the man was an Indian who had tried to kill him.

He looked at Caleb in the shadowy moonlight. "It's a hard thing. Hard."

Caleb heard the anguish and the hope in the voice, and Dorman's words came back to him—*It's a hard thing.*

"Might help to remember you likely saved my life."

It did not help.

Pryor handed him the strip of shirttail and gestured, and Caleb wiped the knife blade before he pushed it back into its sheath. Half a minute later Pryor quietly said, "It's bled enough," and Caleb carefully wrapped the cloth around the wounded arm and tied it. While he worked his shirtsleeve over the bandage, Pryor looked to the east. The black velvet of night had changed almost imperceptibly to a deep purple.

"Sunrise in less than an hour," he said. "We're just about in the middle between Skippack Road to the east and Van Deering's Mill's on Ridge Pike Road to the west, which is where we should be. If Gen'l Washington's on time for the five o'clock attack, we should be hearin' from him soon. If it gets too far past sunrise the British are goin' to start wonderin' where their last shift of night pickets are, and things could get testy. We wait."

They sat on an ancient wind-fallen log, nearly hidden by overgrowth as the minutes stretched on, until suddenly Pryor raised a warning hand at the same insant Caleb heard it. From the Skippack Road half a mile to the east, came the sound of coordinated feet moving at a trot.

"That's a patrol, and they're movin' fast," Pryor said softly. "Question is, ours or theirs?" They listened intently for a full minute before Pryor spoke again. "They're movin' south. It's got to be theirs."

Caleb heard the instant concern in Pryor's voice and felt the rising tension as they both peered into the darkness as though in the staring they could see the distant road.

On the Skippack, a panting British lieutenant kept his ten-man night patrol moving at double time down the center of the dirt road, breathing hard and sweating, despite the cold bite in the air. They crossed the road leading west to Van Deering's Mill, and five minutes later swung toward the east end of the breastworks, barely visible in the darkness. The young officer answered the camp pickets and led his patrol to the tent of General James Grant, British commander of the eastern breastworks.

Three minutes later he stood at rigid attention in the dim light of a lantern before a disheveled General Grant, who was wearing his night-shirt and pants, with one suspender looped over his shoulder.

"Sir, Lieutenant Robert Cartwright reporting. Sorry to awaken you, but I thought you would want to know. There is a massive movement of rebels coming south on the Skippack Road."

Grant's mouth dropped open, and he clacked it shut. "How many? How far?"

"Thousands. We saw them up at Chester Hill just after three o'clock A.M."

"Show me." Grant scrambled to lay a map flat on his worktable.

"Right there, sir." The lieutenant tapped with a finger.

Ten minutes later a gasping British captain pulled a winded horse to a sliding stop before the command tent of General William Howe, pitched where the Old York Road intersects Skippack, just over one mile south of Grant's tent.

"Sorry to interrupt, sir, but General Grant sends this message and ordered me to wait for a written answer."

A scowling William Howe, clad in a nightshirt and robe, broke the seal and read the few lines.

Ten minutes later the laboring horse was standing with its head down, fighting for wind while the captain once again stood before General Grant in his tent at the breastworks. "General Howe sends his respects and this message, sir."

Grant read the message and a smile formed. "Get my officers here as quick as you can, and send word to General Grey to get his officers over here, too."

Half an hour later Grant stood at the head of his council table. The eastern sky was bright with a sun just ten minutes from rising, and a heavy mist was beginning to rise along the creek beds and in the forest.

Grant spoke loudly. "The rebels are coming down the Skippack Road in force from the north. General Howe has issued written orders. Put all your men under arms immediately. Issue ammunition and rations for two days. General Howe's doing the same at the camp to the south of us. We do not go out to meet them. We wait here and let them show their hand first."

General Grey interrupted. "Are we certain this isn't just a scouting party? A small force to probe our defenses?"

Grant shook his head. "A Lieutenant Cartwright brought his night patrol in at double time for four miles to tell me he personally saw them. Thousands of them. This is no small force. Get your commands under arms and wait."

Grant watched the officers file rapidly out of the tent, then stood for a moment in deep contemplation. *So Washington's bringing his rabble down to engage us.* He slowly shook his head in wonderment. *Did he think he'd catch us by surprise? Another Trenton? The only surprise is that he's able to attack us so soon after the beating he took at Brandywine. I wonder where he is right at this moment.*

To the north, Washington drew his watch from his vest pocket. *Nearly five o'clock—late—too many fences—too many wooded hills.* He glanced to his right at General Sullivan, prodding his men along, then to the east, where the sky was already bright. The rising ground mist was beginning to obscure trees and split-rail fences. *Nearly sunrise—perhaps the mist will hide us for a while—General Greene should be nearing Lime Kiln Road soon—he'll be moving in to protect our left flank and hit the British on their right—is he on time?—he has to be—has to be. Armstrong will be coming in from the west.*

Four miles to the northeast a frantic General Greene sat his horse, walking it beside his guide, a man who had spent his entire life within thirty miles of Germantown. The ground mist swirled about them, blurring, obscuring known landmarks.

"Where are we?" Greene demanded. "We should have crossed the road just south of Chester Hill an hour ago. We've got to be at the Lime Kiln Road marching on Luken's Mill and the British breastworks at five o'clock. Where's the road? Where are we?"

The man peered back up at Greene. "I followed the marching orders you gave me, but they were wrong. I can't see in this mist. Too many fences, too many woods. Lime Kiln should be right here."

"Speak plainly, man! Are you lost?" Greene was barely holding himself under control.

The man shrugged. "It's hard when you can't see. We got to be close. Keep pushing south."

Greene bit down on his anger and his rising sense of desperation. He turned in the saddle once to peer to his right in the mounting fog. *Where's Washington?—no sound of battle to the west—is he waiting for us?—got to find him.*

More than three miles to the west, Washington held his place at the rear of the column and helplessly watched the sun rise, a dull orange ball barely discernible in the heavy mist. He sat erect in the saddle, watching, listening, every nerve alive. Ahead of him was the division commanded by Maxwell. In front of Maxwell were the divisions of Stirling, then Wayne, and leading, Conway.

Sun's up—it's past five o'clock—we're late—where's Greene?—if he gets to the Lime Kiln Road junction before we do, what will he do?—he won't know if he's ahead of us or behind us—what will he do?—what?—and what's happening at the head of our column?—what's Conway doing?

Nearly two miles ahead of Washington, hunkered down in dense cover, Pryor and Caleb heard the hushed sounds of British voices giving orders south of them and then the rustle of men pushing through the forest foliage in the thick mist. In two minutes the sounds were all around them, and they saw the shapes hunched forward, muskets and bayonets at the ready, as the red-clad troops moved north. Instantly Pryor clamped a hand onto Caleb's shoulder and shoved him down behind the log and whispered softly, "Something's gone wrong—too many British going north—don't move!"

Minutes passed while the two men lay behind the decaying log, barely breathing, as the British soldiers flowed silently past them, quietly moving through the fog toward the oncoming Continental Army.

More than a mile dead ahead, Captain Allen McLane, commanding the Delaware Light Cavalry that was leading General Conway's division, leaned forward in his saddle, squinting, trying to make out the dim, shadowy figures moving in the swirling ground-mist forty yards ahead. As he walked his horse forward, the figures took form and shape, and suddenly they were British regulars with the white belts crossed on their crimson tunics. In that instant McLane knew they were an advance patrol and had seen him. The trap was sprung. There would be no surprise bayonet charge. There was but one command he could give.

"Charge!"

He jerked his sword from its scabbard and jammed his blunted spurs into the shoulders of his horse. In three jumps he was at a gallop with his full cavalry command thundering right behind. The British patrol stood stock-still for the split second it took to realize the Americans meant to overrun them, and then they fired one volley before they turned and ran before the swinging swords. They came pounding back past Caleb and Pryor with McLane's cavalry crashing through the brush right behind them. Pryor shouted, "That cavalry's ours! Follow them!" In an instant both men were surging forward with the Americans as they chased the running British.

At the rear of the column Washington heard the British muskets, and he tensed as he stood tall in his stirrups to peer into the impenetrable mist. *Too soon!—too soon—the British are warned—who's firing?—what have we* run into?—*I should be there, not here!* He reined his horse out of the column and dug his spurs home.

At the front of the column, as by magic, the red-coated regulars of the British Second Light Infantry came marching out of the fog in a line, bayonets lowered, straight into McLane's oncoming American cavalry. In five seconds the opposing armies were locked in a wild melee, swords swinging, the hated bayonets thrusting, muskets blasting orange flame and .75-caliber lead balls in the thick mist that was now mingling with a fog that came rolling, and gun smoke. Within minutes the fog and smoke were so thick no one could discern what was happening thirty yards away.

McLane's cavalry slowed, confused, unsure of what they had run into and which direction they should attack. Then, out of the mists, Colonel Thomas Musgrave led his British Fortieth Light Infantry into the bedlam to support the Second Light Infantry, a battle cry surging as they came. They plowed into the fight in a bayonet charge, and McLane began to fall back onto his own infantry coming in from behind. The fog, mingled with the gun smoke, cut vision to less than twenty-five yards, and the din of the battle was strange, distorted in the blinding mist. No one—enlisted man or officer—knew what was happening up and down the battle line—who was winning, losing, advancing, retreating.

When McLane's cavalry stalled and began to fall back, the infantry behind them stopped, then began backing up in the dense fog. Only then did Conway realize his leading regiments were in full retreat. *I've got to stop them—turn them—before we're thrown back on Wayne and Stirling and Maxwell— can't let them start a panic—must prevent a full-scale rout!*

He drew his sword and spurred his horse forward into his own men, shouting, "Stop! Form a line! Make a stand!" His officers picked up his voice in the fog and echoed his command, and the entire division surged forward to meet the charging British, slow them, stop their advance, but in the fog it was impossible to know the tide of the battle, and the entire front ground to a standstill.

Behind, Sullivan paused long enough, listening in the fog, to understand that the line of battle was not moving and shouted his first command to his own division.

"To the west! To the west!"

His command went charging to the sound of the guns, headlong into the British Fortieth Light Infantry, muskets and rifles blasting, bullets whistling as the redcoats stubbornly met them with bayonets, and once again the two armies stalled.

In desperation Sullivan turned and shouted, "General Wayne!—Forward!—to the west. Charge!"

"Mad Anthony" Wayne's division did not hesitate. The men remembered Paoli—seeing the British come out of the night with their bayonets to massacre the American command, giving no quarter or mercy, running men through while they were trying to surrender. They came charging out of the fog like an avenging horde, bayonets flashing as they shouted, "Remember the Paoli Massacre—have at the bloodhounds!"

They swept the British before them like an avalanche, asking no quarter, giving no quarter, using their bayonets like demented men, showing no fear. The redcoats faltered, then began to fall back, and panic seized them as the wild-eyed Americans came on. Twice the routed British dug in their heels to make a stand, and twice Wayne's men ripped into them like men possessed, and twice the British broke, falling back.

And then, floating over the battlefield, came the sound of British bugles sounding retreat. Never had an American army heard music so inspiring, so sweet! They smelled victory, and like a tidal wave they swept on.

Racing his horse toward the front, General Washington turned his head to listen to the British bugles, and his heart leaped with elation. *They're in full retreat! We've routed them!*

Ahead of him, Wayne's command led the charge, with Sullivan's and Conway's divisions right behind, as they drove Musgrove and the British back, one field, one split-rail fence at a time, half a mile, then a mile, before General William Howe himself came in from the south, spurring his horse to the battle line. Furious, he pulled his mount to a prancing stop before his men, livid with anger, cursing, shouting at them.

"Shame! You've never retreated before! They're just a scouting party! Form! Form!"

By coincidence, or accident, or providence—no one ever knew—at that precise moment an American cannon blasted in the fog, and the canister of grapeshot exploded directly over Howe's head. Howe ducked, and his horse shied violently as the one-inch lead balls kicked dirt for thirty yards in all directions, and though none of them struck him or his horse, half a dozen red-coated regulars buckled and went down all around him. The screaming Americans burst through the mist and the smoke, and the British withered before them as Howe's command broke into full retreat, hurling themselves through the trees and brush with the howling Americans following less than ten yards behind.

Fighting his panic-stricken horse, pounding his own men on their backs with the flat of his sword, British Colonel Thomas Musgrave suddenly found himself on a dirt road, and moments later there was a split-rail fence less than ten feet to his left, and beyond that the great, gray shape of a building dim in the fog. For a moment he stared, unable to grasp where he was, and then it burst in his mind.

We're on Skippack Road—Lime Kiln Road is just south of us! That's the home of Judge Benjamin Chew! The walls are stone—nearly two feet thick!—a natural fort.

Instantly he shouted orders. "Companies one through six—over the fence and into the building! Take the second floor and fire from the windows!"

The one hundred twenty men from the first six companies, who were still able, bounded over the split-rail fence and tore open the two doors into the spacious, elaborately decorated home. They slammed and locked the shutters to every window on the main floor, barricaded every door, and bounded up the stairs to throw open every window on the second floor. Thirty seconds later they had one hundred twenty muskets leveled against all comers, waiting for the shouting Yankees to materialize in the fog.

The Americans came surging over the fence north of the home and were but twenty-five yards from the thick stone walls when they made out the shape of the huge structure looming in the fog. They could vaguely see the dark shapes of the windows as they came on, never suspecting the second floor was crammed with British regulars. They were a scant thirty feet from the back wall when the orange flame leaped from every north-facing window, and the blast of the first British volley tore into them. Shocked, confused, the rebel Americans stopped in their tracks for one split second before they understood what had happened, and then they scattered. The momentum of their attack, and of the British retreat faltered and slowed.

At that moment Washington jumped his laboring horse over the north fence and reined it to a sweating halt in the Chew House yard, shouting in the fog, "Why have you stopped? Move on! Move on!"

The second volley boomed out from the second-story windows, and again the musketballs came whistling. Washington held firm as the Americans scattered, and then he reined to his right, back toward the Skippack Road. He turned to his aide Colonel John Laurens. "Get the generals here as fast as possible."

Precious minutes passed with Washington tenuously controlling his need to drive on, maintain the attack, not give the British time to rally. Then the officers came on tired, sweaty horses, uniforms damp in the fog. They remained mounted while they waited for their commander to speak.

Washington pointed. "The British have a force in the second story of the Chew House. We have the British in full-blown retreat! I say we leave a company behind to surround the house and wait them out. What is your advice?"

Wayne nearly yelled, "Leave them! Move on! We've got half the British army on the run!"

Conway joined in. "We can drive Howe clear back to Philadelphia! In the name of heaven, leave the Chew House behind!"

Knox shook his head violently as he raised his voice. "A maxim of war! Never, never leave an occupied castle in your rear!"

Sullivan cut him off. "That's not a castle! That's a house, and there couldn't be many inside. We've got Howe himself running! Move on!"

For three seconds Washington weighed it in his mind. "Get an officer from one of your commands and have him go in under a white flag to offer surrender terms!"

Sullivan turned, shouted orders, and a young captain came cantering in, eyes wide in question. Sullivan handed him a large, white handkerchief. "Put that on your sword and walk your horse to that house. Offer the British inside safe passage and humane treatment if they surrender."

The young captain made it to within ten feet of the rear door before a musket cracked and he tumbled from his saddle dead.

Washington gritted his teeth. "Bring up the cannon."

For ten minutes, six-pound cannon blasted at point-blank range. The cannonballs splintered the ground-level doors off their hinges but did nothing more than knock chips and mortar from the thick stone walls.

"Storm the place!" Washington called.

Wayne shouted orders, and two companies from his command came charging. The muskets from the second-story windows knocked the first two ranks backward, and those behind stopped, then retreated.

"Let me go," Colonel John Laurens said, and Washington looked at his aide.

"To do what?"

"Burn them out. I'll need a volunteer to help." Chevalier du Mauduit du Plessis, a French officer, spurred his horse forward. "I will go."

Laurens sprinted to the Chew House stables and came out with a great load of fresh wheat straw in his arms as Mauduit ran dodging to the house, broke open the shutters to a window, smashed out the glass, and swung himself over the windowsill into the house. A British officer with a raised sword burst into the room.

"What are you doing?" he demanded.

Mauduit shrugged his shoulders. "I am only taking a walk."

For a moment the British officer struggled at the nonchalance, the sheer insanity of Mauduit's reply, then strode forward, sword leveled. "Surrender, sir."

A British regular burst into the room behind the British officer, saw both men, instantly raised his musket, and fired at Mauduit as the officer closed with him. The musketball struck the British officer in the back. As the officer fell forward onto his face, Mauduit leaped back to the ground outside the window, Laurens threw down the straw, and both men sprinted back toward their horses. They were yet three steps from their rearing mounts when a musketball took Laurens in the shoulder, and he went down to one knee, recovered, made it to his horse, and the two men returned to the gathered American officers.

Washington sat his horse, weighing what to do. Leave the Chew House filled with British regulars behind, with the possibility they could strike his advancing army from the rear? He stood tall in the stirrups, probing, listening for the approach of Greene and his large command. He jerked out his watch and felt the grab in the pit of his stomach. Past nine o'clock. *Where's Greene? Where is Greene?*

Half a mile due east, General Nathanael Greene paused in the fog and turned an ear to listen intently. The unmistakable sound of cannon came through the fog from the west, and Greene tensed. *Whose cannon?*

He spun around to an aide. "Where's General Stephen? Have you seen him lately?"

"Sir, there's something you should know. I think he's been drinking. He might be drunk."

"*What?*" blurted Greene. "Where is he?"

"I believe he has just ordered his division west, toward the sound of the cannon."

Greene gaped. "Without orders? He left without my orders to do so?"

"He led his division away, sir, including his cannon."

Greene bit down on the rage that sprang in his chest. "So be it." He twisted in his saddle and shouted, "Follow me! We must take Luken's Mill and then hit the British breastworks."

Five minutes later the American brigades of Muhlenberg, McDougall, and Scott were running forward, following Greene in a full-out charge against the red-coated regulars at Luken's Mill. The fog covered both sides until they were sixty feet apart, and then the roar of the muskets and the orange tongues of flame leaped from both sides as they closed in mortal combat. For long minutes the fighting was hand-to-hand, face-to-face, and then the British line began to sag. The shouting Americans sensed the weakness and charged again, and the British began to fall back.

"To the right," the British officers shouted, and the line shifted as the British tried to flank Greene's charge.

"To the left," Greene shouted to his men, and they veered to their left to meet the British counterattack head-on.

American General "The Devil" Pete Muhlenberg had had enough. He stood in his stirrups, sword raised, and shouted to his men, "Follow me, boys. CHARGE!"

He ripped into the British lines with a renewed fury, scattering the redcoats, tearing great holes in their leading companies. His brigade shattered the British formation, and suddenly Muhlenberg realized he had plunged completely through the battle lines. He was inside the British camp!

"Surrender or die," he shouted, and hundreds of the startled British regulars threw down their arms and raised their hands.

Behind Wayne's charging division, Stephen's division swept in toward the Chew House, wheeled their cannon about, and began firing at the walls. Washington squinted in the fog to recognize who they were and instantly sent word. "Return to assist Greene! We are in control here!"

Stephen struggled with his alcohol-fogged brain for several minutes before he understood, and he swung his division around to return to support Greene.

Wayne heard Stephen's cannon battering the Chew House, and then the firing stopped. For a moment Wayne pondered, face drawn in puzzlement. *Who's up there with cannon? Sullivan? Is Sullivan in trouble? It has to be Sullivan. If Sullivan's lines collapse, my command will be trapped between two major British forces!*

Instantly he barked orders. "Back! Find and support Sullivan!"

When Wayne gave the order, he had no idea Stephen's division was behind him, running the wrong way to support Greene. The plan clearly called for Stephen to be far to the east. In the fog and the confusion and the incessant roar of cannon and musketfire from guns and men that could not be seen, Wayne's division suddenly found itself within forty yards of the shapes of men running through the fog and gun smoke.

There was no way for him to know he had struck Stephen's misguided division broadside.

It flashed in Wayne's mind, *It has to be the British!* "Open fire!" he shouted, and all up and down the line American muskets blasted orange flame and musketballs into Stephen's men. Caught by total surprise, shocked, they staggered back, then knelt and delivered a full volley back into Wayne's men in the fog. Neither side knew who the other was. As fast as they could reload, the two lines fired, then each began to fall back, and finally both disintegrated into a full-blown retreat.

At that moment, to the east, Major General James Agnew led his fresh division of British regulars, joined by the divisions of General Grey from the west and General Grant from the east, headlong into the command of Nathanael Greene. The Americans had marched all night and had fought in a maddening fog all morning. They were exhausted, confused, disoriented, and burning with thirst. Greene knew they could not hold, and he took control.

"Fall back! Fall back! Fire from behind walls or fences or trees. Do not run. Bring the cannon. Bring the cannon. Do not run. Fire as you retreat!"

Behind Greene, Sullivan's aides hauled their horses to a stop, pointing as they reported to Sullivan. "Sir, the men are running out of ammunition. Maybe three, four cartridges per man is all they have left."

At that moment a cavalryman from the light brigade came storming up in panic. "We're surrounded, we're surrounded," he shouted and galloped off northward into the fog. Sullivan's men, who had carried the center of the attack on their shoulders, looked at each other, then at the empty cartridge boxes on their hips, and they began to fall back, slowly at first, then in a full retreat. They came streaming past Washington, cartridge boxes held high to show him they were empty, and Washington groaned inwardly. *We had them! We had taken the field, and now we are losing it!*

He kicked his horse to a gallop, headlong into the fog, riding to the sound of the hottest fight, where Muhlenberg was trying to break through to support Greene's well-organized retreat. Again and again Washington rode within yards of the British, trying to rally his men back to the attack. Musketballs whined and whistled all around him, but none struck him. Within minutes it was clear the Americans were in a panicked retreat, and there was no stopping it. Washington followed his men, covering their retreat, back to the north from whence they had come.

He did not know that General Cornwallis had just arrived from Philadelphia with three fresh divisions, nor did he know that Howe had ordered them to pursue Washington and the Continentals until they were far from the battlefield.

For eight miles Cornwallis followed the retreating Continentals, trading cannon shots, before he turned back. General Washington continued with his army for another eight miles to Pennypacker's Mill before he called a halt. His men fell asleep where they dropped. General Muhlenberg nodded off in his saddle.

Washington sat his horse with his head down, heartbroken, knowing he had been on the brink of a victory that could have ended the war, but his blunders and those of his men and the morning fog had allowed it to slip from them. Once again they were a beaten army.

I misjudged at the Chew House—should never have stopped the momentum— Greene arrived too late—Stephen left Greene without orders—Wayne blundered into Stephen—we had them beaten—in full retreat—and we gave it all away—lost it all. What will Congress say? What will our people say? Can we rise above another defeat? Is this the end of the revolution? Have we lost all we held so dear?

Once again the iron in his backbone straightened him. *The men fought magnificently. We survived. We still have an army. Howe won the field but lost what he had to have—he did not destroy us. We will fight another day.*

He reined his weary horse about to look at his men, then gave orders to his officers. "Move on to Whitemarsh. We'll rally and resupply there."

To the south, General Howe dismounted his horse and for a time listened to the exchange of cannon fire far to the north. The deep boom of the big guns stopped, and he waited for the return of Cornwallis with his thoughts running.

It was a near thing—we knew he was coming, and we prepared but still he very nearly succeeded—but for their blunders and the fog, who knows?

Impatiently he waited for the return of Cornwallis, then gathered his war council.

"We will return to camp to tend our wounded, and then I want a company of men to proceed north to locate the rebels. It is still possible to destroy them before the summer campaign closes."

Two days later, at Whitemarsh, near the Wissahickon Creek, Caleb sat down near the evening fire, huddled against the cold, and unwrapped the oilcloth packet. He drew out the pencil and paper, reflected for a time, then began to write.

"The Battle of Germantown began on the night of October 2, 1777, when American scouts located the British pickets north of their breastworks near the Skippack Road . . ."

He stopped writing for a moment to stare into the flames. He was seeing auburn hair and green eyes, and he was silently repeating to himself, *Nancy—Nancy—Nancy.*

He drove her from his mind and once again put pencil to paper.

★   ★   ★   ★   ★

Days passed while British companies prowled through the hills and draws surrounding Whitemarsh, reporting back to Howe regularly on the fortifications Washington had set up around his camp and the numbers of men still gathered in the rebel army. Patiently Howe waited for the opening through which he could send his army to smash the Continentals beyond recovery, but none came. He ordered his men to engage the Continentals in any way they could to try to draw them out into a full battle, but all efforts failed. As the days grew shorter and the nights colder, Howe shook his head. *Too late—the summer campaign is over—must return to Philadelphia for the winter.*

Then he paused to ponder deeply.

Twice in the past three months we engaged them to destroy them—twice they fought and lost—but still they are there and still the rebellion goes on—their losses were greater than ours in both engagements, but at this moment they have replacements for every man they lost, and we do not. I do not believe we will be able to destroy their army.

Brooding, his mind filled with dark foreboding, Howe drew himself up to his worktable and reached for paper and quill.

"October 22, 1777.

It is with utmost regret that I herewith tender my resignation as commander of His Majesty's forces in North America . . ."

He studied the words, scratched out some of them, added others, continuing to write the rough draft of his letter of resignation.

To the north, at Whitemarsh, General Washington sat at his worktable in his command tent near trees whose branches were stark and bare. Outside the brittle leaves of winter lay on the ground. On one side of his table were half a dozen written reports from scouting parties that had combed the countryside for twenty miles in all directions, searching for a place to build their winter camp.

Washington's face was lined with fatigue. His thoughts were running, and he let them go unchecked.

Gates defeated Burgoyne at Saratoga—took his entire army—Congress and the people are hailing Gates as a savior—the British forces on the Hudson have taken Forts Clinton and Montgomery—are in control of the river passage to the north—Congress is making official inquiries into my defeat at Germantown—Conway openly criticizing me—Gates has joined him—other officers support them—winter is coming—no food—no clothing—no shelter—sickness—no end to it.

A great sigh escaped him as he reached for the scouting reports. *And now we must find a place to establish winter camp.*

For a time he shuffled through the documents, then laid them down.

"Here," he said quietly to himself. "We shall make winter camp here."

He stared for a long time, then murmured, "Valley Forge."

Notes

The loss at Brandywine followed by the Paoli Massacre and the occupation of Philadelphia by the British resulted in a rising outcry from many Americans and their leaders. Congressman John Adams publicly declared, "O, Heaven, grant us one great soul!" which General Washington correctly believed was directed at him. See Leckie, *George Washington's War,* p. 357.

Nonetheless, the country did rally by sending more troops from Virginia, New Jersey, Massachusetts, and many of Daniel Morgan's riflemen. However, the initial success of General Gates against General Burgoyne on the Hudson River resulted in Gates sending his official report directly to Congress, and not to Washington, his commander in chief, which was a serious breach of military protocol. Then General Thomas Conway wrote Congress, highly critical of Washington. See Leckie, *George Washington's War,* pp. 357–59; Higginbotham, *The War of American Independence,* p. 187.

Lafayette had received a serious wound to his leg or foot at the battle of Brandywine and was nursed back to health by a Moravian sister named Liesel Beckel at Bethlehem, Pennsylvania. See Claghorn, *Women Patriots of the American Revolution,* pp. 22–23.

Two British messages were intercepted. One stated Howe had sent a force to Billingsport in New Jersey to open the south end of the river. The second message stated General Cornwallis remained in Philadelphia while General Howe had moved the balance of his force to Germantown; thus the number of British soldiers at Germantown was substantially fewer than those under Washington's command, and with the concurrence of his officers, Washington decided to attack them. See Freeman, *Washington,* pp. 356–60; Leckie, *George Washington's War,* pp. 359–65; Higginbotham, *The War of American Independence,* pp. 186–87.

For a perspective of the area around Germantown and the locations of the commands of the opposing armies as the battle approached and proceeded, see the map in Leckie, *George Washington's War,* p. 360.

Washington did in fact order that all British pickets be silenced, following which the Americans would make a bayonet charge. See Freeman, *Washington,* p. 357.

Both Caleb Dunson and Caleb Pryor are fictional characters.

The battle of Germantown, from beginning to end, is described. Included is the fact that the British had detected the advancing Americans as early as three o'clock the morning of October third and that General Howe had placed his entire command under arms to meet them. Notwithstanding, the American attack was so powerful that the British bugles were blowing "retreat," and the Americans had all but beaten them. Then the fiasco at the Chew House, Greene's force becoming lost, and the rising of the thick fog that resulted in Americans firing on Americans and a general chaotic confusion all over the battlefield, resulted in a reversal, and a final loss of the battle by the Americans. Following the battle General Washington was despondent, knowing that with the prior misfortunes of the summer of 1777, as previously described, he would certainly bear further humiliation. See Leckie, *George Washington's War*, pp. 359–65; Freeman, *Washington*, pp. 356–60; Mackesy, *The War for America, 1775–1783*, p. 129; Higginbotham, *The War of American Independence*, pp. 186–87.

PART TWO

CHAPTER XV

★ ★ ★

*A*t noon a chill breeze came gusting from the north, stirring the dead leaves that still clung to the trees, sending them fluttering to the forest floor. A little before one o'clock the breeze rose to a bitter wind, driving slate-gray clouds to blot out the bright midday sun and cast the southeastern Pennsylvania hills and valleys into a shadowless twilight. By two o'clock the wind was moaning in the pines and firs and rattling the stark, bare branches of the oak, poplar, and maple trees, sending the thick cover of brown, brittle leaves skittering along the forest floor southward. At half past four, wet sleet came slanting on the freezing wind.

Billy Weems drew up the collar of his summer coat, hunched his shoulders, and bowed his head as he walked on with the wind at his back. He carried his musket in his right hand and with his left, reached to hitch up the rope that went over his shoulder to his bedroll. He broke from the trees into a small field of wheat stubble jerking in the wind, now plastered white with the sticky sleet. His eyes narrowed as he peered about in the gathering gloom of early evening for the lights of the farm building that must be nearby. From a quarter mile to the west came a faint gleam, and he turned to his right, slogging through the stubble in soaked shoes that were separating at the seams and had holes in both soles.

He climbed the split-rail fence behind the low, slab-sided barn and paused at the south end, shielded from the wind and sleet to open the pan on his musket enough to be certain the powder was dry. He snapped the pan shut and drew the big hammer back to full cock, carrying the weapon loosely in both hands as he rounded the corner. Yellow lantern light glowed from two small square windows along the west wall of the barn, and he walked past a low enclosure where a sow lay on her belly inside a three-sided hutch connected to the barn, continued past an empty pen for milk cows, and turned again to pause near the front door. Carefully he pulled the latch rope, pushed the door open, and quickly stepped inside, blinking in the light, musket muzzle raised, ready, as the wind and sleet came whistling in.

To his right a startled man sitting on a one-legged milk stool jerked his head from the flank of a Jersey cow and started to rise until he saw the musket muzzle swing to bear on his chest. Straight ahead a boy with a pitchfork load of dried grass straightened to stare, frightened, indecisive, looking white-faced at his father for directions.

Billy's eyes swept the barn. There was no other movement, and he saw no weapon other than the pitchfork clutched by the boy. He lowered the musket, closed the door, and cleared his throat.

"Sir, I mean you no harm. I am passing through and would like to ask if I might take shelter in your barn for the night."

The man stood—average height, husky, black felt hat over black hair and beard, heavy coat—and faced Billy. The Jersey cow craned her neck in the stanchion to stare back for a moment, large brown eyes questioning the interruption in the familiar procedure of giving her milk.

"Who might you be?" The voice was high, strained, and there was a German accent.

"My name is Billy Weems. I am a soldier in the Continental Army. I'm just returning from the north and looking for the army camp."

"Where are you from?"

"Boston."

For long seconds the man studied Billy. Taller, sandy-reddish hair and beard, plain features, bullnecked, thick-shouldered, emanating a feeling of disciplined strength.

"If you are with the Continental Army, why are you not with them? Why were you in the north?"

"I was sent north by General Washington to join the fight against General Burgoyne."

Recognition flashed in the man's eyes. "You were at Bemis Heights? Saratoga?"

"Yes."

"You were there when Burgoyne laid down his arms?"

"I was at the surrender."

"Tell me, did the Hessians fight well?"

Billy could not miss the pride in the German eyes. "Yes. They fought well. At the Breymann redoubt."

A smiled flashed for a moment in the black beard, and the man bobbed his head. "I am glad they fought well. I am also glad General Burgoyne surrendered before all his army was killed." He hesitated, then spoke bluntly. "Are you a Loyalist? Pretending to be a patriot?"

"No." Billy slipped his finger into the musket trigger guard. "Are you?"

The man squared his shoulders. "I believe the United States should be free from the British, but I will not bear arms. I have my family." He glanced at the boy, who laid down the pitchfork and walked to his father's side to stare up at Billy. He was wrapped in a great coat, with a knit cap pulled low.

Billy drew his finger from the trigger. "Are the British nearby?"

"They have patrols. We never know when they will come. If they find you here they will shoot you and burn my farm. They have done it to others. Many times."

"Would it be better if I did not stop?"

For a time the man did not move. "It will be all right if you stay in the barn. There is fresh straw." He pointed. "When it is dark I will send Hans with some food and some clothes." He glanced at the boy, who nodded his understanding.

Billy answered, "I have no money to pay. I will cut some firewood."

"No. You might be seen. Stay inside the barn. Be certain you are gone before daylight, and leave no trace."

"I will."

"Do you know where you are?"

"North of the Delaware. When I left last June, the army was in Morristown. I was told they marched to Middlebrook, but they are no longer there. They are somewhere to the south."

"That is correct. Across the Delaware, perhaps twenty miles, at a placed called Whitemarsh, the last I heard."

"How far to the river?"

"Four miles due south to Coryell's Ferry. You will need to take the ferry across. Whitemarsh is south and east. You'll have to ask."

"Coryell's Ferry? Above McKonkey's Ferry?"

"Yes."

"I was at Trenton."

"Whitemarsh is about thirty miles nearly due east of Trenton, on the Missahickon Creek."

"I'll find it. May I know your name?"

The man probed Billy's eyes, then decided. "Yes. Karl Steinman. We will finish now with the cow. Hans will come after dark. Bury the pail in straw in the corner when you are finished." He pointed. "And take your old clothes with you."

"Thank you."

Ten minutes later the man led the boy out the door, carrying the lantern and wooden milk bucket, and Billy was left to listen to the wind and sleet while his eyes adjusted to the darkness. For a time he stood beside the door with his musket still cocked, but there was no break in the sound of the storm. He uncocked the weapon and sat down on an empty keg to wait, shivering while he listened to the cow working on her cud as she dozed.

He judged it to be half an hour before there was a sound at the door, and instantly he was on his feet with the musket leveled when a shadow entered. With the sounds of the storm raging, the boy handed him a covered pail and a large bundle tied with cord, then turned without a word and was gone.

Billy set the pail on the hard-packed dirt floor and laid the bundle on the keg while he worked with the knot. He could not force his numb fingers to undo it, so he cut it with his belt knife, and in the near total darkness he unfolded the layers. There was a heavy, long-sleeved wool shirt, trousers, knee-length cotton stockings, a knitted cap, and a pair of heavy, stiff-soled work shoes. They were wrapped in a thick wool coat that closed in the front with six huge buttons and a belt.

Shaking in the freezing air, he stripped off his wet summer clothing, pulled on the woolen shirt, then the trousers and stockings, the cap over the matted ice in his hair, and finally the heavy coat. The shoes were too wide, but by pulling the laces tight he closed them enough that he could wear them.

For a moment he stood still, luxuriating in the warmth of the dry clothing. Then he picked the pail from the floor and sat down on the keg.

The potato was steaming, the ham hot, the cheese and thick slice of brown bread rich, made by the hands of a good German woman. She had also sent a pewter jar of fresh milk, heavy with cream and still warm from the Jersey cow, and a slab of apple strudel wrapped in a napkin. Billy set aside a portion of the bread and cheese and the ham, then ate slowly, unable to remember the last time food tasted so good. Finished, he folded the napkin into the pail and buried it in the straw, then wrapped the portions he had saved in his discarded shirt. He gathered the remainder of his wet clothing, rolled it inside his summer coat, tied it with the cord, and set it on the keg with his bedroll, stiff with ice.

Wrapped in the heavy coat, minutes later he was burrowed into the straw, with the warmth of the food in his midsection and the luxury of dry clothing bringing on drowsiness. Disconnected thoughts that had long been denied came with a will of their own.

Mother and Trudy—are they all right?—did they find buyers for their candles?— must write—Mother will worry—Matthew on the sea—has he survived?— Kathleen—they must get together—they'll get together—a just God would not deny them—Brigitte—loves her British captain—is she still waiting for him?—Eli—found his sister—seventeen years searching—never saw such joy in a man—so good—so good—he'll be coming down soon—down from the north—to find Mary—where's Mary?—he'll find her—must find her—never dreamed a war could scatter families, loved ones, so far—so far . . .

At four o'clock the sleet dwindled and stopped, and the clouds thinned and parted to show the stars and a quarter-moon waning. Minutes later the wind slowed and stopped, the temperature dropped, and the night became a silent, frozen world. Billy sat bolt upright, listening for what had wakened him, and realized it was the quiet. He rose from the straw and opened the door to peer outside, where the morning star was dropping toward the eastern skyline. Quickly he slung his bedroll over his back, tucked his bundled clothing under his left arm, and walked silently out the door with his musket in his right hand. There were no lights in the house as he hurried to the back of the barn, climbed over the rail fence, and walked across the frozen field, feet crunching in the frozen sleet, working his way south through the stubble field with his breath a cloud of vapor trailing behind his head.

He reached the Delaware with the sun half risen to turn the frozen sleet on the fields and trees into an endless blanket of diamonds. He turned left, southeast, onto a rutted, frozen dirt road that followed the river to Coryell's Ferry. He helped a man load two Guernsey bulls onto the ferry to pay his fare and crossed the black, ice-choked Delaware with the sun half an hour above the eastern tree line. The sun was climbing when he came to McKonkey's Ferry, and he paused at the memories and the scenes that came before his eyes, vivid and powerful, as though he were seeing them as they had happened eleven months before.

The starving men—no shoes—blood in the snow—sickness—no shelter—no food—the desperate realization that all enlistments would expire at midnight, December 31, 1776—the Continental Army would disband, the revolution lost—the wild plan to cross the Delaware at night on December 25—John Glover's Marblehead fishermen and the great Durham boats—loading at dusk as snow began to fall—Glover's men crossing the river at night in a driving blizzard with two-ton ice floes battering the boats—men, cannon, horses, all across safely—a miracle—a miracle—the march in the dark, nine and one-half miles downriver to Trenton—the attack in the blizzard at eight o'clock—three hours late—the chaotic battle in the streets—routing the entire Hessian garrison of one thousand four hundred of the best fighting men in the world—pushing them into the wheat field and orchard east of town—surrounding them—their commanding officer, Colonel Johnann Rall—Eli knocking him from his horse with two shots from his long Pennsylvania rifle—Washington visiting the dying Rall in the church in town—accepting his surrender—the casualty count—all fourteen hundred Hessians killed or captured—four Americans wounded, none dead—unbelievable, impossible— the march back to McKonkey's Ferry, recrossing from the New Jersey to the Pennsylvania side.

For a time Billy walked through the abandoned campsite at McKonkey's Ferry, scuffing in the snow where he remembered the firepits, searching for the lean-tos they had hastily built to shield them from the freezing storms of winter. There was almost nothing left to mark the place the Americans had suffered and fought and won a victory that rocked the world.

He hitched at his bedroll and walked on south, down the river. At noon he paused to peer five hundred yards across the waters of the Delaware at the south end of Trenton and at the bridge they had held at the foot of King and Queen Streets. He knocked the frozen sleet from a log, sat down, unwrapped the ham and bread and cheese he had saved, and while he ate he was seeing the scenes once again.

British General Cornwallis coming with his eight thousand troops under orders of General Howe to find and destroy the entire American army—including General Washington—Washington sitting his gray horse at the south end of the Trenton Bridge in the gathering dusk of January 2, 1777, while Colonel Edward Hand led his intrepid band of riflemen running across—the roar of British cannon and muskets kicking dirt and water fifty feet into the air as they tried to kill him and Washington—the American guns blasting out their defiant answer—holding the bridge until dark—moving the entire army around the British camp at the north end of Trenton overnight—marching twelve miles on Old Quaker Road—taking Princeton from British Colonel Mawhood the next morning—Cornwallis and his officers sitting their horses on the banks of the Delaware at sunrise, dumbfounded that the only sign the Americans had ever been there were the campfires they had left burning in the night to trick the British—the towering fury of

Cornwallis and Howe when they learned the American rabble had done the impossible—
taken both Trenton and Princeton.

Billy finished his scant meal, wiped the crumbs from his beard, repacked his old summer clothing, and left the Delaware behind as he struck out south and west in bright, frigid sunlight, cross-country, searching for Whitemarsh and the Continental Army. The sun had slipped below the western rim, and the cloudless heavens were taking on ever-deeper hues of purple when he walked past the outbuildings to rap on the back door of a log farm home. A stout woman with two small children clinging to her ankle-length dress opened the door, and the lantern glow cast a long, misshapen shaft of yellow light on the frozen ground around Billy as he spoke.

"I do not mean to frighten you, ma'am. I'm looking for Whitemarsh. The American army."

Her husband was away, but she could spare a little food.

He ate cold sliced pork and bread and drank water for his supper, slept on straw in the barn, cut half a cord of firewood to pay for his keep, and moved on. The sun was two hours past its zenith when he met a man with two sheltie dogs driving sheep on the winding wagon ruts that passed for a road, and Billy stopped to inquire.

The man turned to point due south. "Whitemarsh's that way, two miles and a little more. Army's there."

The sun was a frozen yellow ball touching the bare branches of the trees to the west when Billy crested one of the gentle, rolling hills of southeastern Pennsylvania and stopped at the rare sight spread before him. With the sun at his back, casting long shadows eastward, he drew the thick, gray, knitted cap from his head and for a time studied the random sprawl of the American army camp that lay in the cup of a broad valley, with a tiny settlement beyond, toward the southwest. Columns of cook-fire smoke rose straight as a die into the dead, frigid air, glowing golden with the rays of the setting sun. The tents and the lean-tos were not set in orderly rows, nor were the divisions and regiments organized according to any plan. Rather, they were scattered, each according to its own whim and fancy.

He tugged his cap back onto his head and walked on down the trace of a road through the woods, toward the sprawling muddle of the American camp, watching for the first sign of a Massachusetts regiment and a bandy-legged little sergeant with a scraggly beard and a high, raspy voice.

Notes

Following the battle of Germantown, General Washington camped his army at Whitemarsh, about eight miles north of Germantown, on the Missahickon Creek. See the map in Freeman, *Washington*, p. 321.

CHAPTER XVI

★ ★ ★

*I*n gathering dusk, Sergeant Alvin Turlock, Boston Company, Massachusetts Regiment, dumped an armload of firewood onto the growing heap next to a leg of the tall, iron tripod. Diminutive, thin, hawk-faced, he rammed two sticks into the fire beneath the great, black, pot-bellied cook kettle that hung from the chain. Vapor rose from his face as he stepped back from the heat of the fire, intently watching, studying his men as they moved about, making camp for the night. And once again the pain rose within.

Half his company had no shoes. A few had wrapped their feet in strips of canvas cut and stolen from tarps that covered the army's freight wagons. Others had taken the woolen coats from men who had been killed in battle or who had died from disease or freezing to fashion wraps for their feet. Too many were barefooted, feet blue and bleeding from the days of marching on frozen ridges of mud and snow and rocks. Turlock had cut the leg from the trousers of a dead soldier, wrapped it over the top of his head, and tied it beneath his chin to keep his ears from freezing, but most of his men were bareheaded, vapor trailing behind as they moved about.

He watched the ones assigned to cooking detail for the evening meal. Eight days ago as they passed by a farm some of them had stolen and slaughtered a pig. By eating everything—the meat, hocks, tongue, brain, lungs, heart, liver, kidneys—they had made it last six days, even cutting the skin into chunks and frying it in the lard to make pork cracklings. All that remained was the empty stomach and the intestines. Turlock grimly watched while they washed them as best they could in snow water, chopped them, and threw them into the smoking cook kettle.

One backwoodsman returned from a nearby stream, where he had dug fourteen toads from the frozen mud and bundled them in a dirty, ragged piece of cloth to carry them back to camp. He dumped them into a bucket of snow water to wash them, then tossed them into the pot, just as they were. Another brought the skinned head of a sheep, eyes and tongue still intact, and dropped it splashing into the steaming water. An old soldier, limping on a bare foot with two toes gone black, dropped the skinned carcass of a porcupine into the great, black kettle.

They had used the last of their turnips ten days ago. There were no potatoes nor cabbages. Some men were stripping the inner bark from maple and sycamore trees to add to the mix. A few came with jimson roots and a handful of nuts and seeds the squirrels had missed in their gather for the winter. Turlock set his jaw at the stench that rose from the pot to reach out in the still, frigid air.

With the sun below the horizon, the temperature dropped. White spots began to appear on the faces of his men, and their breath froze white in their beards. The sparse talk dwindled to nothing as they cut branches from pines and firs for bedding for the night, while their eyes continually diverted to the fires and the kettles in anticipation of something hot in their shriveled bellies. They had eaten nothing since dawn, when they were given one wooden spoonful of the last of the rice boiled in creek water.

Turlock wiped at the frozen moisture in his beard and called his orders. "All right, you lovelies, get your utensils. Time to eat this banquet."

He watched as they went to their bedrolls for wooden bowls and spoons and their canteens and formed the line. Cooks dipped the simmering gruel with their mouths clamped shut, breathing light against the reeking odor.

Turlock heard the murmured questions, "No salt? No bread? No turnips?"

His voice rose high, raspy, loud. "You want to ruin the taste of this stew?"

A few men grinned. Most did not.

Standing in the frigid air, watching his men silently file past the cook kettle, from the corner of his eye Turlock caught unexpected movement on the wagon ruts they called a road, and he turned his head to look. His eyes narrowed as he studied a man in a heavy, dark woolen coat, striding steadily eastward. He had a full, sandy-red beard, and his hair was tied back with a leather lace. He carried his musket in his right hand, with the thumb of his left hand hooked under the rope that held his bedroll on his back.

Recognition flashed, and Turlock started, then raised a hand to call, "Weems! Corporal Billy Weems! Is that you?"

Billy's head swung toward the familiar sound as he stopped in his tracks, searching. In the twilight he saw the small, wiry figure trotting toward him, and for a moment a feeling of deep gratitude rose to choke him. *He's alive!* Then a grin formed in his beard as he turned and quickened his pace toward the little man. They stopped with three feet separating them, and Turlock reached to grasp Billy by both arms and shake him roughly.

"You're back! I was beginnin' to worry the Mohawk got you."

Billy was grinning broadly. "Not likely. I'm fine. You?"

"Alive." An instant of fear flashed in his eyes. "Eli?"

"Alive. Good. A long story."

"Good or bad story?"

"The best."

Turlock's eyes widened and he blurted, "Found his sister?"

"Sister, husband, and two children."

Turlock's head rolled back, and his eyes closed as he uttered a long, "Ohhhhh. The Almighty smiled on him."

"He surely did. You camped nearby?"

Turlock hooked a thumb over his shoulder. "Over there. Come on.

Just in time for evening mess. Got a real good meal goin' in the pot. Pig paunch, sheep's head, porcupine, toads, tree bark, and some nuts the squirrels missed. Wish King George was here to help eat it. Might end the war right on the spot."

Billy shook his head with a cryptic smile. "Things don't change much, do they?"

With the meal finished and the kettle scrubbed with sand and snow and ice, Billy and Turlock rolled a six-foot section of pine log close to the fire and sat down in full darkness. Overhead, countless points of light dotted the frigid, black heavens. With hands extended and palms outward toward the warmth of the flames, Turlock spoke.

"Eli?"

"It was after the battle at Saratoga. The last battle. We went looking. We found a captain named Ben Fielding from the New Hampshire regiment. Tall, good man. Turned out his father was Cyrus Fielding, the man who took in Eli's sister eighteen years ago when the two of them were orphaned. The Iroquois got Eli."

"What's her name? Eli could only remember 'Iddi.'"

"Lydia."

Turlock smiled. "Lydia. A little brother would remember it as Iddi."

"Ben Fielding took us to his home. Lydia is a tall, strong, beautiful woman. Good woman. He married her. They built their own home. Cleared their own farm. Two children—a boy and a girl."

Turlock turned, with the firelight making crags and shadow ridges in his weathered face. "What names?"

"Samuel and Hannah. Hannah's four. Samuel's two. Hannah looks like her mother. Samuel looks a little like his father but maybe more like Eli."

Billy could see the deep pleasure in Turlock's eyes as he spoke. "Eli stayed there?"

"For a while. He'll be coming when they finish the harvest and have meat smoked for the winter."

"I'm glad. Glad for him."

The two men let a little time pass while Turlock created mental images of Eli with the profound joy and the peace of being with the sister he had lost and found; of working side by side with her and her husband to finish the work of harvest and preparing for winter; of sitting at the hearth at night with a small, tow-headed, blocky little boy on his knee while the family read from the Bible or listening while Ben and Eli told stories of the forest or while Lydia sang.

Billy turned his head to speak. "I promised Eli to ask about Mary Flint. Do you remember her?"

Turlock brightened. "I surely do. She was nursin' at the hospital in Morristown when we marched out. She came there lookin' for Eli. She has a strong feelin' for him."

"Seen her lately?"

"No. But as soon as we get to our winter campground and get a hospital, she'll likely show up. Life has sure dealt her some hardships. Husband gone, baby gone, family gone, lost everything she ever had." He bowed his head for a moment. "She's pure gold, that girl is. Does Eli have a feelin' for her?"

"He does. Made me promise to find her and tell her he's all right. He'll be coming down soon, and he intends finding her."

Turlock smiled. "That's the way it should be."

They sat quietly for a while before Turlock spoke again. "What happened up there with the Iroquois? Did you find Joseph Brant?"

"We found him."

"What's his Mohawk name?"

"Thayendanegea."

"Where'd you find him?"

"Up at Three Rivers, near Fort Stanwix. Eli went right into their camp at night, in a storm. Knocked the Indian picket unconscious and dumped him through the flap into Brant's lodge. Brant came out, and Eli faced him less than six feet away. Eli could have killed Brant, and Brant knew it. Eli did it so Brant would talk with him later. He left, and Brant didn't follow him."

A small sound came from Turlock as he rounded his lips and blew air that rose in vapor.

Billy continued. "Brant and his Mohawk ambushed Herkimer a few days later. That was probably the bloodiest fight I ever saw."

"Saw? You weren't in it?"

"Eli and I were in it. Herkimer died from it, along with over half his command." Billy paused, and Turlock saw his eyes narrow as the terrible memories came flooding.

"Afterward General Washington sent General Benedict Arnold to help. Eli saw a prisoner named Han Yost who is not right in the head. Slow. Eli told Arnold that the Mohawk regard such people as touched by Taronhiawagon."

"Taronhiawagon?"

"The Mohawk god. So Eli and Arnold arranged to have an Indian guide named Ponsee take Yost to Joseph Brant to tell him that it was useless to fight the Americans because they were coming in such numbers that they could not be stopped. Yost did it. Then later Eli walked right into Brant's camp in daylight carrying a wampum belt he had made. It gave us safe passage into camp but not back out again. He asked to talk to Brant, and Brant came, and Brant remembered Eli from the night he faced him in the storm. He remembered Eli could have killed him but didn't."

"Where were you?"

"With him."

"Scared?"

Billy shook his head. "You'll never know how bad. Right there, surrounded by more painted warriors than I've ever seen before or since, all wanting to kill us on the spot, Eli told Brant of an old Indian legend about General Washington. Washington was with Braddock when the Mohawk ambushed and killed Braddock years ago, and the Mohawk sent eight warriors to kill Washington. They got close and shot but couldn't hit him. They said they could feel a power protecting him. Their chief said he felt it, too. He made a prophecy. He said the Great Spirit had told him that Washington could not be killed by a musket or a cannon, that he would live to become the father of a great nation."

Turlock leaned back slightly, mouth fallen open as he listened.

"Brant knew of the prophecy. That was when he led his Mohawk away. They quit."

"They *what?*"

"Quit the British."

"You and Eli got Brant to do that?"

Slowly Billy shook his head and for a time stared into the flames before he spoke. "No, not Eli, not me, the Almighty."

For a long time Turlock stared, aware of a feeling that rose quietly in his breast to fill him. Finally he licked at his dry lips and spoke.

"Either one of you get hurt in all this?"

"No. Well, yes. I got hit by a tomahawk. On my back."

"When?"

"On the way up the Hudson. The Mohawk sent about ten warriors down to get us. There was a fight."

"How bad?"

"We killed about half of them. One got me with his tomahawk before I got him. Eighteen stitches or so."

"Eli sewed you up?"

Billy nodded. "He got gall from a deer to wash it clean, and stitched it closed. Bound it up with jimson weed to draw out the pus and start to heal. Taught me a lot about the woods. A whole new world for me. The Indians can teach us a lot if we'd only listen."

"I know. How'd you get away from those ten Mohawk assassins?"

"Eli got us to an Indian burial ground. Sacred. The Mohawk wouldn't come in to fight."

For a time Turlock stared into the fire, lost in thought at the story he had heard. "Anything else?"

"One thing. We built a sweat lodge. Stayed in it for two days."

Turlock stopped all movement. "You have a vision?"

Billy shook his head. "No vision. But we both knew we had to use the wampum belt to get into Brant's camp and that we had to talk to him. We didn't know if we'd get out alive, but while we were there, something happened. It didn't matter if we got out. It only mattered that we were there, doing what we had to do and that we were doing it for free-dom. Liberty. I can hardly explain it."

"You don't have to. I've felt it."

Billy shifted and rubbed his hands together for a moment. "How about you? I been tracking the army from Morristown, and I never heard of such wanderings. What happened?"

Turlock shook his head. "I can't hardly believe it myself. Gen'l Howe loaded his whole army onto Admiral Howe's boats and sailed 'em all over the east coast, with us marchin' up and down ready to fight 'em when they landed. North one day, south the next, east, west, up and down, until we wore out our shoes and our horses and most of the men for no good reason we ever knew. Then finally Howe landed clean down at Head of Elk on the Chesapeake Bay and started north towards Philadelphia. He was just as far from Philadelphia at Head of Elk as he was when he sailed out from Staten Island. Only him and the Almighty knows what was goin' through his head, and sometimes I think it might have confused the Almighty."

Billy nodded. "I heard about some of it."

"Then when it looked like he was goin' after Philadelphia, we engaged him on the Brandywine Creek. Things got pretty confused, and we lost it, but we scared 'em. Then Howe headed for Germantown and divided his army, so Washington decided to attack him at Germantown. We had the British bugles blowin' the retreat when a heavy fog rolled in and everybody lost track of everybody else. Wound up with Wayne shootin' at Stephen in the fog and Greene gettin' lost because his guide couldn't find his way, and we lost that one, too. But at Germantown, the British knew we had 'em beat until the fog saved 'em. Scared 'em bad."

"I didn't hear about the fog."

"Before that Howe made like he was headed for Reading to capture all our stores, and Washington went up there to stop him. Howe doubled back quick and sent Cornwallis in to take Philadelphia, and he did it without firing a shot."

Billy shook his head. "I was told."

"That gets us down to right now. Rumor is, Gen'l Conway's goin' behind Washington's back to tell Congress that Washington's not the man to lead the army. Seems Conway thinks he's the one ought to have command. Him or Gates. And there's some officers and a lot of Congressmen givin' that some thought."

"Gates?"

"Horatio Gates."

"The one at Saratoga?"

"The same."

Billy shook his head violently. "Not him. He stayed in his tent four miles from the lines the whole time. Benedict Arnold won that battle. Eli and I were with Arnold at the Breymann redoubt. Got his horse shot out from under him and his left leg broken by a musketball, but he led the charge that took the redoubt and got us in behind the British lines. Three days later Burgoyne surrendered. If Gates is getting the credit, someone's got it all backwards."

"Well, he is. Some are calling him our 'savior.'"

"He wasn't. It was Arnold."

"Nobody's talkin' about Arnold."

"Somebody better set them straight."

"How do you set 'em straight? We're findin' out that dealin' with politicians isn't like dealin' with regular humans. Their heads get lost goin' so many directions that there isn't no way to make 'em see the truth. Like that French general, du Coudray. Deane sent him over here from France with fourteen bodyguards and three officers to protect him, and a written agreement that we had to pay him more'n any other officer in this army, 'cept Gen'l Washington hisself, because he won't take pay. Only expenses. Congress was told to make this Coudray a major general before he'd served a day in the army, and Congress figured to do it. When the rest of our generals heard about it, we dang near had a mutiny. Greene and Knox and Sullivan said if Coudray was given rank above them, after what they been through for America, they was goin' to resign their commissions an' quit."

Billy was gaping, wide-eyed. "What's Washington saying?"

"As it turned out, Washington didn't have to say anything. Last

September, the nineteenth, I think, this Coudray showed up at the Schuylkill Ferry dressed like a peacock and insisted he wasn't goin' to dismount from that high-blooded nag he was ridin', just to get on the ferry. So he tried to ride the horse onto the boat, and it spooked. Went crazy. Reared up and busted through the railing and both Coudray and the horse went into the river. The horse came up, but we never saw Coudray again. That's a pretty sorry story, but there's a lot of people that smile when they tell it."

"Congress have anything to say about it?"

"Not about Coudray, but there's others. Lately it looks like that other French officer—the one I mentioned—Thomas Conway—is givin' Congress a lot of reasons why he ought to have Washington's position. And I hear Congress is startin' to listen. Like I said, those politicians got their heads someplace most of us out here can't understand. What they need is about six months out here, eatin' pig belly an' walkin' around with feet that's froze and bloody, and havin' musketballs and grapeshot buzzin' like hornets, and watchin' men on both sides of 'em droppin' dead."

Pain crossed Billy's face. "I watched your men before it got dark. Half of them bedded down with only pine boughs under and on top. No blankets. No shoes."

"Wait 'til mornin'. We got just enough horses and oxen to pull the wagons, but none to pull the cannon. They starved to death, and we ate most of 'em. These men have to buckle theirselves into the harnesses to bring the cannon. You can track this army by the blood in the snow, from their feet. Sometimes I see all this, and I get this strong feelin' we ought to go get those politicians at bayonet point and bring 'em here, and in the strongest bonds of love give 'em an education in what this war is all about. Can't think of anything that would do more for gettin' it over with."

The lonesome sound of a distant drum sounding tattoo brought both men's heads around to stare into the blackness. They listened while thoughts came flooding of how many times soldiers had gone to their beds with those sounds floating over battlefields or camps or hospitals.

The last echo died in the forest, and still they sat, suddenly seized by an unexpected melancholy that held them for a time.

Finally Turlock stirred. "I got to make my rounds. My blanket's over there. Bed down next to it. You're still a corporal. Ought to be enough pine boughs for both of us."

He stood. "Tomorrow mornin', first thing, you got to report to Gen'l Washington. It was him sent you and Eli up north. He'll be expecting you."

Notes

By November 1777, the American army was in desperate need of food, blankets, shoes, and clothing. The suffering that followed them to Valley Forge had begun. See Freeman, *Washington*, p. 363.

The finding of the lost sister of Eli Stroud, together with her husband and two children, is described in volume 4, *The Hand of Providence*, chapter XXXII.

The Iroquois name for Joseph Brant was *Thayendanegea*. The name of the chief god of the Iroquois was *Taronhiawagon*. See Graymont, *The Iroquois in the American Revolution*, pp. 52–53; Hale, *The Iroquois Book of Rites*, p. 74.

The meeting between Eli Stroud and Chief Joseph Brant, the stratagem of using Han Yost to influence the Mohawk to leave the British, and their leaving are set forth in volume 4, *The Hand of Providence*, chapter XXVIII.

General Horatio Gates was commander in chief of the American forces on the Hudson River to engage British General John Burgoyne. That Gates never left his tent but rather let General Benedict Arnold lead the American forces in battle, was described in volume 4, *The Hand of Providence*, chapter XXXI.

A much disliked French General named du Coudray refused to dismount his horse when boarding the Schuylkill River ferry. The horse reared overboard, and Coudray drowned, which tragedy saved much acrimony and anger among senior American officers. See Freeman, *Washington*, p. 364; Higginbotham, *The War of American Independence*, p. 215.

The blatant criticism by General Thomas Conway of General Washington was becoming notorious by November 1777. Conway wished to have Washington's position. See Higginbotham, *The War of American Independence*, p. 216.

Command tent of General Washington, Continental Army on the march,
moving toward the Schuylkill River, southeastern Pennsylvania

Late November 1777

CHAPTER XVII

★ ★ ★

*S*oldiers passing the command tent saw the misshapen shadow cast on the canvas wall by the yellow light of a single lantern on the worktable within. General Washington was sitting, leaning forward, elbows on the table, head in his hands, not moving. When the drum sounded tattoo, he slowly raised his head, listening while the drummer tapped out the rhythm and the echoes died in the dark forest.

He rose from his chair and walked out the flap of his tent, towering over the two pickets, who separated to allow him free passage. Vapor trailed behind his head as he walked a short distance and stopped, watching soldiers lay down on pine boughs and then pull more branches over themselves—their only protection from the bitter cold of the night.

How many thousands have no blankets?—no shoes?—leaving blood in the snow— what did they find to eat for supper?—when did they get their last pay?—how long can this go on before they mutiny?

The familiar, deep, galling frustration rose in Washington's breast, and he turned back to his tent to enter without a word to the pickets. There was no fire inside, and he sat down at his worktable, still wearing his heavy cape and boots against the cold. Wisps of vapor rose from his breathing as he interlaced stiff, cold fingers on the table before him and struggled to force a focus to the jumble of thoughts that filled his head.

A rustle at the tent entrance brought his head around, and he heard the picket at the tent flap challenge, and the voice of his aide Colonel John Laurens, answer. He rose and stepped rapidly to the tent flap to draw it back. His two aides, Colonel Alexander Hamilton and Colonel John Laurens, were standing in the snow.

"Gentlemen, do you need to see me?"

Hamilton spoke. "Yes, sir."

Washington held the flap open, they entered, and Washington gestured them into chairs facing his worktable.

"I'm sorry I do not have refreshment here to offer you."

Laurens shrugged. "No matter. We thought you would like to know that Congress has completed the Articles of Confederation. A copy was delivered for you a few minutes ago." He held out a sealed document.

For a moment Washington stared at the document. *The first such writing in the recorded history of man.* With a sense of reverence he accepted it and laid it carefully on his worktable.

Laurens continued. "Copies have been sent to all thirteen states for ratification. I don't recall such an event, ever. Remarkable."

Washington spoke quietly. "Yes, it is. I wonder how long it will survive. The world thought King Arthur's Round Table was the answer and then the Magna Carta. Both failed."

For several seconds Laurens studied the face of his commander in chief. In the subdued light of the single lantern, Washington's eyes were sunken shadows, and the deep lines in his forehead and around his mouth were softened. An aura of great weariness, bordering on melancholy, reached out from him. Both Laurens and Hamilton understood and accepted the fact that Washington must maintain a wall between himself and those he commanded—a sense of distance, of decorum, of protocol—as must all men whose duty it is to order other men to their deaths. They also knew that on Washington's side of that wall, where few men were allowed to venture, Washington was a deeply compassionate man who felt the pain of every soldier in the Continental Army. At times when Washington was unaware, both men had seen him with his head bowed, beseeching the Almighty to intercede for his men, and they had seen him with his shoulders shaking as he wept for them.

And both Hamilton and Laurens also knew that sometimes such a man needed to talk with others who understood and had the skill to reach over the wall for a few moments without abusing the privilege. Was this such a time for Washington? They broke off their gaze, and Laurens answered.

"I might disagree with that, sir. The germ of Arthur's idea has never died. The rights spelled out in the Magna Carta have never been out of the minds of men, no matter how bad things got. Maybe that's what those two events were all about."

Washington leaned back in his chair, startled by the unexpected contradiction from Laurens. He was aware that both men possessed unusual intelligence and a deep understanding of their proper place in the scheme of the military. If these two aides, whom he trusted implicitly, were pushing beyond the well-established barriers, there was a reason. Washington moved out to meet them. He flexed his cold fingers before he spoke.

"You think they were prologue?"

Laurens eyes narrowed. "I think they were sent by a Higher Hand. Each in its time. Each to prepare for what was to come. I don't think either one failed. I think both did exactly what the Almighty meant them to do."

"Which was what?"

"Prepare for what was coming."

Washington's mind made the leap, and he picked up the sealed Articles of Confederation. "These Articles?"

Hamilton interrupted, eyes glistening. "They're the next step."

"After the Magna Carta?"

"That, and the Declaration of Independence. Yes."

Washington stared into Hamilton's face for a long time before he spoke. "You think there's more to come?"

Hamilton drew and released a great breath. "Yes."

"What?"

"I don't know. I only hope it comes in my lifetime, and I hope I know it when I see it."

All three men knew they were now in an arena seldom entered, and each sensed he had nothing to fear from the others. Washington leaned forward, one arm on the table before him. Never had the two aides seen the expression that came onto his face. There was an intense hunger in his eyes, almost as though he were pleading for the answer to an all-consuming inner torment.

Washington spoke. "I've thought . . . felt . . . many times that the Almighty . . ." He paused, and both aides saw the momentary hesitancy to permit himself to be seen as other men, with doubts and fears, and questions and flaws. After a moment, Washington continued, "I've felt the hand of the Almighty many times in this revolution. Have you?"

Laurens's response was instant, emphatic. "Yes. This is His work, not ours."

Washington dropped his eyes to his hands on the table, and Laurens saw a look of profound relief come into his face. He watched him working to find words that would not harm the unexpected thing that had developed between them.

"Even when we . . . when we've made many mistakes?"

Hamilton heard Washington's spoken words, but he also heard the silent ones Washington could not speak. When things were darkest, when the sins and errors of men plunged the Revolution into the pit, when battles were lost that should have been won, when those all around were nearing open rebellion—officers resigning, conniving against each other, seeking to destroy their leaders to sate their own ambitions—when the common men in the rank and file were dying for want of food and shelter, was the Almighty aware? Was He angered? Had He turned his back? Was all lost?

Hamilton heard it all and answered softly.

"We bring most of our grief on ourselves. But when we do, and it seems that everything is lost, He's there. Maybe that's when He's most among us. This Revolution is in His hands. One step at a time, He's prepared the way, and He'll never fail us. Failure will come only if we abandon Him."

Washington lowered his face for a moment, and they saw the muscles of his jaw form small ridges along his jawline. An unexpected feeling rose within each man, and for a time no one moved or spoke. The cold and misery of a small tent in the Pennsylvania wilderness were forgotten as the impression spread throughout their beings, filling them with a sureness that dispelled all doubt, all fears. The two aides waited, trying to gauge if they had been too bold. Washington shifted in his chair.

"You know about General Nash? And the others?" Washington asked.

They both sensed the long-denied need in Washington to talk, and Laurens answered.

"You mean General Nash's death? From wounds at Brandywine? I know. I regret it very much. He was a good officer." Laurens eased back in his chair. "But I don't know what you meant about the others."

Washington replied, "General Sullivan. Stephen. Maxwell. Wayne. De Borre."

"I heard about General Stephen. Facing charges for drunkenness and dereliction at Germantown?" Laurens asked.

"Yes. Maxwell the same."

"Sullivan? Wayne?"

Washington's voice was flat. "Sullivan's charged with misconduct for failing to scout the terrain he had to defend at Germantown and for not maintaining patrols that would have prevented the British from coming in behind him as they did. A repeat of the battle of Long Island. General Wayne must explain to Congress how the British could surprise him so completely at Paoli." Washington's eyes dropped. "The Paoli Massacre. Terrible."

"De Borre?"

"Intoxication and dereliction in the face of the enemy. He resigned. Congress has appointed a committee to investigate and hear the other four matters."

Hamilton slowly shook his head. "Another committee? They can talk more and accomplish less than any governmental function I've ever heard of. I fear for the generals if some committee is after them. I've lately thought the best thing we could do for these committees is require them to come here with us and carry a musket for six months. March when these men march. Eat what they eat. Freeze with them. Be sick with them." He caught himself and paused for a moment to let his anger cool.

Washington observed, "I hardly recognize the Congress now in session. Almost none of the original Congressmen remain." The general looked down at his hands for a moment. "Only seven."

Laurens looked at him, waiting.

"John and Sam Adams, John Hancock, Eliphalet Dyer, James Duane, Samuel Chase, and Richard Lee. Sam Chase is leaving now, and the three senior Massachusetts members will be gone shortly. That will leave but two who were there at the beginning. Those who were there from the beginning—the ones who understand the foundations on which this revolution rests—are nearly all gone. But we do have one faithful supporter. Your father, Henry Laurens."

Laurens sighed. "Father believes in this army. But it's true we're losing the ones who know. And the ones who are replacing them . . . ? His voice trailed off for a moment. "It seems they don't know why they're there. They get lost in their own interests. Some are starting to listen to Conway and Gates."

Laurens raised his eyes to Washington's for a moment, testing to see if he had opened a subject too painful for Washington.

Washington quietly said, "I've heard."

Laurens pushed on. "I'd like to know if Wilkinson knew what he was stirring up when he told McWilliams about the statement Conway made. Did Wilkinson intend that McWilliams would take it to his commander?—Lord Stirling?—and that Stirling would pass it on to you?"

Washington's eyes never left Laurens. "I've wondered."

Hamilton cleared his throat. "There's talk both ways. A lot of officers and most in Congress don't know the truth about what happened, so they invent." Hamilton stopped and waited, hoping Washington understood what he was after. Washington did.

"Wilkinson is aide-de-camp to General Gates. At this moment Gates enjoys high favor with Congress because of the victory at Saratoga. It apparently is of no consequence to the new congressmen, that Arnold, and not Gates, was responsible for winning that battle. Gates has missed no opportunity to promote himself with anyone in Congress who will listen. He chose not to report the Saratoga campaign to me as his commander in chief, but rather, he sent it directly to Congress. Conway likewise wrote to Congress in terms highly critical of me and presumed to let that body know he is prepared to assume my position."

Washington stopped, and Hamilton waited for a moment before he responded.

"You wrote something to Conway? There's talk about it."

"Yes."

Both aides straightened when Washington drew two documents from a stack on his worktable, glanced at them, and offered them. Their duties included opening and reading the general's mail and answering it when directed by Washington. But at times Washington wrote his own answers, and these they had not seen. They had never expected the general would draw them into such a delicate, personal conversation.

Washington gestured. "There is the note I received from Stirling on November eighth and a copy of the note I sent to Conway the next day."

Laurens spread the note from Stirling to Washington on the table-top, and both he and Hamilton leaned forward to read it: "The enclosed was communicated by Col. Wilkinson to Major McWilliams, my aide. Such wicked duplicity of conduct I shall always think it my duty to detect."

The enclosure read: "In a letter from Genl. Conway to Genl. Gates he says—'Heaven has been determined to save your country; or a weak general and bad counsellors would have ruined it.'"

Both men had seen the correspondence when it was received, and they recalled the shock that a general officer would dare refer to General Washington, in writing, as a "weak general." They again felt the outrage that such subversive correspondence would pass between a major general and a brigadier general in the Continental Army.

Laurens raised the second document. "This is a copy of the note you sent to Conway in response?"

"Yes."

Washington had written the note and sent it by private courier. Neither Laurens or Hamilton had seen it. Laurens unfolded and they read:

November 9, 1777

Sir:

A letter which I received last night, contain'd the following paragraph. In a letter from Genl. Conway to Genl. Gates he says: "Heaven has been determined to save your country, or a weak general and bad counsellors would have ruined it."

I am, Sir, Yr. Hble Servt.
Genl. Thos. Conway.

For several seconds Laurens and Hamilton sat with their eyes locked onto the brief document, instantly aware of the devastating impact that such a blunt, brutal statement from the commander in chief would have on a brigadier general. Hamilton spoke. "This is what you wrote back to Conway?"

"Yes."

"I understand Conway responded to you in writing."

"He did." Washington drew another document from the paperwork and handed it to Hamilton. Again, this document had come by private courier, and neither aide had seen it.

"I am willing that my original letter to General Gates should be handed to you. This, I trust, will convince you of my way of thinking. I know, sir, that several unfavorable hints have been reported by some of your aides de camp as the author of some discourse which I never uttered. These advices never gave me the least uneasiness because I was conscious I never said anything but what I could mention to yourself."

Hamilton lowered the document, surprised at Conway's candor.

"Did you reply to him?"

"No. On November fourteenth Conway submitted his resignation to Congress."

Laurens started, then settled back. "Did they accept it?"

"Not yet. A committee is considering the entire matter."

Laurens shook his head. "Another committee. Like the one they sent here to determine where we should establish winter camp for the army. Have you heard the results of their visit?"

"Not yet. They inquired far beyond the question of selecting a site for winter quarters. They were interested in the reasons for our failures at Brandywine and Germantown. The statements and recommendations of most of our officers were generally the same. We made mistakes, but the real reason for our failures was the inability of Congress to provide the necessary things to sustain an army."

Washington paused, then went on. "As for winter quarters, I can wait no longer. Most of the scouting reports support the decision to winter in Valley Forge. That is where we are going."

Laurens laid the documents back on the desk, and Hamilton spoke. "I know Conway and maybe Gates are ambitious men. They want command. Rush and Pickering and some others are in league with them, pushing Congress for a change. Rumors are out that General Greene and Knox and a few others are going to resign if Conway is advanced in rank ahead of them."

"I've heard. Conway is junior to all the twenty-three brigadiers in this army. If Congress advances him ahead of them, it could create a serious problem. I wrote to Richard Lee in Congress about Conway's efforts to replace me." He handed Laurens another document, and Laurens read:

"The appointment of Conway would be as unfortunate a measure as ever was adopted, and I may add (and I think with truth) that it will give a fatal blow to the existence of the army. General Conway's merit as an officer, and his importance in this army, exists more in his imagination than in reality; for it is a maxim with him to leave no service of his untold, nor to want anything that is to be had by importunity."

Both aides recognized that they had been allowed to see one of the games that is played at the highest levels of governmental control, and Hamilton responded.

"Did Lee answer?"

"Yes. He assured me Conway would not be advanced in rank so long as it would produce 'evil consequences' to the army. But he also said that Congress was discussing the reorganization of the Board of War. They were considering placing Timothy Pickering on the board. You will recall that Pickering is presently the adjutant general. They're considering replacing him with Conway as adjutant general."

Laurens's mouth fell open. "What? Conway? They'll commission him a major general if he replaces Pickering!"

Washington nodded, and for five full seconds no one made a sound. Then Hamilton rounded his mouth and blew air lightly. Vapors rose from his face.

"That explains it. Greene, Knox, Schuyler, Lafayette, Stirling, Cadwalader, Varnum, Morgan, Hamilton, Tilghman—they've been talking. And they are all using the same words: *Conspiracy. Cabal.* They know Rush and Mifflin and Pickering and some others are listening to Conway and Gates, and they're incensed. Should matters come to it, they're prepared to descend on Congress en masse to set them straight."

Washington nodded. "I've heard. And apparently so has Gates. I received a letter from him in which he does everything possible to distance himself from Conway. It is apparent he does not want to risk damaging his own ambition to replace me, should these matters erupt in Congress. He not only wrote a letter to me denying any support of Conway, but to Congress as well."

"Did you answer Gates?"

"Yes. In uncomplimentary terms."

"Congress?"

"I do not know how they received Gates's letter to them. I suppose I will in due time."

"This whole thing is dividing the army," Laurens said.

"And Congress," Washington added.

"What can be done about it?" Hamilton asked.

Washington shook his head. "Tell them the truth and move on. Hope they see what's happening. Despite all the weaknesses of that body, despite all their misguided efforts, I will not do anything that will undermine their control of military affairs. The military of this country must

. . . *must* . . . remain subject to civilian authority. When the military is the foundation of any government, wars will never cease."

Washington watched their eyes, and he saw the profound glimmer that crept into them as they began to comprehend the depths of the great truth Washington had laid before them. Laurens closed his mouth, then wiped at it, unable to speak a word for a time as he recognized that he had been given the gift of a brief glimpse into the heart of one of the great souls of his time. A sense of near reverence came welling up in his chest as he stared at Washington.

While Laurens sought to bring himself back under control, Washington stood, and the two aides immediately got to their feet.

Hamilton spoke.

"Sir, there is one more thing."

"What is that?"

"You recall the two young men you sent north to do what they could against Burgoyne? Both from the Massachusetts Regiment? Their names are Billy Weems and Eli Stroud."

A light came into Washington's eyes at the recollection of the two young men—one from the city, one from the wilds of the northern wilderness. "I do."

"Corporal Weems returned to camp this evening. His company captain thought you might like to hear his report."

All three men recognized that the rare minutes of intimacy, of talking openly and frankly of personal things, painful things, were over, and the men accepted it. Each had given the others something needed, something precious. They had reached over the wall, and they had given and taken without injury. Each knew they would never speak of these things outside the tent, nor would he share them with others.

Washington nodded. "I'll take his report in the morning. Nine o'clock."

Hamilton nodded. "I'll arrange it, sir."

"Thank you, gentlemen."

"Thank you, sir. Good night."

Notes

Following the American defeat in the battle of Germantown, the five American generals named in this chapter were in serious jeopardy, as herein described. Further, only seven men remained in Congress from those who had supported the commission granted to General George Washington to serve as commander in chief of the Continental Army. See Freeman, *Washington*, pp. 364, 366.

Congress did send a committee to investigate the proper place for the Continental Army to establish winter quarters, but they were dilatory in their conclusions, and Washington had to push ahead. He selected Valley Forge. See Freeman, *Washington*, p. 371.

The exchange of letters between Conway, Gates, Stirling, Washington, and Congress, with the resulting rising alarm that a conspiracy, or a cabal, was developing with the objective of replacing Washington with either Gates or Conway is accurate. The whole affair became known in history as "The Conway Cabal." See Freeman, *Washington*, pp. 368–69; Higginbotham, *The War of American Independence*, p. 220.

The Conway Cabal caused a split in the officers of the army, with nine stalwarts supporting Washington and others taking a position adverse to him. The officers on both sides are named in this chapter. See Higginbotham, *The War of American Independence*, pp. 218–21.

CHAPTER XVIII

★ ★ ★

*I*n the spotless, austere parlor of her Quaker home, midwife Lydia Darragh, small, thin, frail, aging, sat facing her flax clock-reel, feeding the long, thin threads of spun flax thread onto the cross-arms as they revolved. On the fortieth revolution the clock ticked. She stopped the cross-arms to carefully remove the thread, loop the thread end around the coil, and tie it. She laid the coil on top of those already finished and said quietly, "Eighteen. Two more and the skein will be finished."

She touched the nearly finished skein gently, almost reverently, as did most women who paid the price of making their own flax thread for knitting and making clothing. It was early May when she had scattered last year's flax seed in a cleared field not far from her home, quietly reciting to herself the verse:

> Good flax and good hemp to have of her own,
> In May a good huswife will see it be sown,
> And afterwards trim it to serve in a need,
> The fimble to spin, the card for her need.

When the plants were four inches high, she and two of her grown children had moved through the crop to thin it, barefooted to avoid damaging the tender plants, facing the wind so that injured plants would be brought back to standing position. In early July they pulled the ripe flax plants and turned them in the sun for two days to dry. Then they rippled them by drawing them through a large iron comb that stripped the bobs onto a sheet to be saved for seed for next year's crop, and the remaining stalks were tied in beats. The beats were stacked crosswise in water vats, covered with boards, weighted with rocks, and left for five days to soak the leaves rotten and get rid of them. The cleaned flax was again tied in bundles, dried, and taken to the flax brake in the kitchen to be methodically smashed by the heavy arm. It was then scutched for further cleaning, scutched again, bundled into strikes, swingled, pounded soft with a pestle-shaped beetle, hackled, and finally laid out in long threads to be sorted, spread, drawn ready for the spinning wheel, and finally, spun into thread to be coiled on the clock-reel, forty rounds to the knot, and bundled into skeins, twenty knots to the skein.

Considering the unending labor to bring them into being, the finished skeins of flax thread were looked on by women with much the same pride and affection they felt for their own children.

Lydia was reaching for the next long threads to be mounted on the cross-arms of the clock-reel when movement in the narrow cobblestone street caught her eye, and she paused to peer out through the lace curtains. Her breath caught for a moment as she recognized the black tricorns with the gold braid, the heavy black capes, and the crimson tunics of four approaching British officers in the frigid, late afternoon sun of a wintry Philadelphia day. She moved the curtains aside for a moment to be certain, then turned and hurried into the kitchen to move a large copper teakettle from the top of the oven onto the round, black iron plate of the stove. She gathered her apron in her hand to lift the hot latch and swing open the small door to the firebox. She thrust in two more sticks of kindling, slammed the door shut, gave the handle to the grate two hard shakes, and turned toward the breadbox, with its hand-painted scene of springtime in Pennsylvania on the lid.

How vividly she remembered the confusion in late September when General Washington marched the Continental Army through the streets of the city, moving south to meet the British one day. And then almost immediately, on September twenty-sixth, thousands of British soldiers marched into Philadelphia from the west, led by General Charles Earl

Cornwallis, to claim the city without firing a shot. Without notice or inquiry, the British officers simply commandeered the homes they wanted for their own quarters, invited the owners and residents to go elsewhere, and moved in while the soldiers filled the city.

Terrified when the pounding came at her door, Lydia had stood trembling behind William, her stern schoolteacher husband while he faced two British officers to inform them that he and his wife were of such an age that they could not, and would not, be ousted from their home of thirty years. The British officer peered at both of them for a moment before he tossed a hand indifferently. "So be it," he declared. "You both may remain on the sole condition that you will be house servants for all needs of myself and my staff. You will take quarters in the attic or the cellar." He paused a moment before he finished. "And you will interfere with nothing, absolutely nothing, pertaining to the business of this army."

He was General Albert Dunphy, the adjutant general of the British under command of William Howe. With smoldering indignation her husband nodded, and the two of them became servants, living in the attic of their own home.

She lifted a loaf of fresh-baked cinnamon bread from the box, laid it on the cutting board, and with quick, deft strokes sliced it, then arranged the pieces on a china platter as the teakettle began its piercing shriek. She stood on tiptoes to reach her silver serving tray from the second shelf in the cupboard, then set the platter of cinnamon bread on it before she reached back into the cupboard for her large, silver teapot. Hastily she poured the boiling water into the teapot, set it on the tray, followed by the silver bowl of crushed tea leaves, the matching sugar bowl, four silver spoons, four snowy-white, ironed linen napkins, and four china cups and saucers.

She heard the front door open, then the muffled voices of four men as they unhooked their capes and hung them on the pegs by the door, together with their tricorn hats. They walked into the parlor to stand before the stone fireplace for a few minutes, hands extended, palms outward toward the flame. They rubbed their hands together, exclaimed about the cold, extended their hands again, then turned to peer at her as she entered the room, carrying the great silver tray. She set it carefully on the table in the center of the parlor, curtsied, and had turned back toward the kitchen when Dunphy's voice stopped her.

"Thank you. You may serve our evening meal at precisely half past six o'clock in the library. In the meantime we will require absolute privacy."

She silently bowed, then turned and hurried back through the kitchen, out the back door to the root cellar. She heaved the heavy plank door upward and descended the five steps into the chill darkness. Quickly she seized a jar of cream and hastened back to the kitchen to pour a small silver pitcher half full, then hesitantly approach the archway into the parlor. She could hear the voices of the men, sometimes low, intense, sometimes loud, occasionally a laugh. She gathered her courage and walked into the parlor with quick steps, where the men were all seated around the table, working with their steaming cups of tea. In the moment of her appearance the talk ceased and all heads turned to follow her as she placed the cream pitcher on the large, silver tray beside the sugar. She straightened and nearly trotted back to the archway into the kitchen. She could feel the stern stare from General Dunphy boring into her back as she disappeared from their sight.

She stood in the kitchen, shaking, and heard a chuckle from the parlor, followed by the voice of Dunphy saying, "Don't be concerned. She's a Quaker. Harmless," and once again the voices continued in their low conversation while the teacups clinked.

Don't be concerned! She's harmless! She stood wide-eyed as she pondered, and then her breath caught in her throat as realization opened in her mind. *What are they discussing that they should be concerned about me?*

She had set a pot of potatoes boiling on the stove and the ham in the oven to warm when she heard the four officers set their teacups clattering on the silver tray, followed by the sound of their boot heels clicking on the hardwood floor as they moved down the hallway to the small library in which her husband kept his books and papers for teaching school. How her husband despised them for dispossessing him of his small room, the one place in the world where he was lord and master, where he could be alone with his beloved books to wander in the magic of faraway places or engage in mental jousting with the great philosophers from antiquity.

The library door closed, and then she heard the chairs scrape on the polished floor as the men drew them close to the large, plain, square desk, facing Dunphy, who was seated behind. The faint sounds of voices, rising and falling in close, sometimes emphatic conversation, reached her in the kitchen.

Four of them!—behind closed doors—what could be so critical?

Quietly she crept down the hall to stand outside the library door, head bowed, eyes closed, straining to catch the words, but only a few were distinguishable. She understood the words *attack* and *Washington* and *troops.*

Attack by whom? The British, or Washington? Whose troops?

She felt a clutch of fear in her heart at the realization that her son, Ensign Daniel Darragh, was with Washington's Continentals, camped near Whitemarsh. If the attack were to be made by the British on the Americans, her Daniel would be in mortal danger.

She jerked erect at the sound of the front door opening and silently fled down the hall to the parlor to see her husband, William, strict, judgmental, but withal a good man, hanging his heavy coat and hat on the pegs next to the cloaks of the despised British officers.

Dared she tell him her fears? Did she have enough information to convince him their son might be in danger? And worst of all, would he countenance the fact that she had gained the information by eavesdropping? In his rigidly structured Puritan view, eavesdropping was an abomination—one of the sources of much of the mischief of life. She drew a deep breath and approached him.

"It is good to have you home."

He glanced at her, then nodded his greeting. "I see the British are here. In the library?"

"Yes."

She saw the flash of anger rise in his face, then fade. "It is a cold day. I presume a hot supper is being prepared."

"It is. Ham and potatoes."

He nodded once more, then turned to the fireplace to absorb the warmth.

At six o'clock Lydia lighted the lamps in the parlor and kitchen and set the table for William. He took his place and stiffly bowed his head to drone out his standard grace, then looked at her, still standing near her chair.

"You do intend taking your place?"

"I am under orders to serve the British in the library at half past six. I will take my supper afterwards."

He nodded and reached for a thick slice of her freshly baked bread.

At twenty-eight minutes past six, Lydia rapped on the library door, waited for the command from within, and entered. The men opened a way for her, and she set the great silver tray on the desktop, then quickly strode from the room to return with a second tray. She set china, silverware, and goblets for four and removed the lids from steaming bowls of creamed potatoes, carrots, and yams cooked in brown sugar. To the side was a large plate of her sliced bread and a bowl of home-churned butter. There were two bottles of marionberry wine, with a dozen sweet apple tarts.

The officers swallowed in anticipation of the feast, reached for their napkins, and Lydia was forgotten as they portioned out large helpings of the steaming foods. She backed deferentially toward the door, stepped out into the hallway, and drew the door to within half an inch of being closed, then walked down the hallway, being certain her heels clicked loudly all the way.

She took her place opposite William at the dining table next to the kitchen, portioned herself small amounts of ham and creamed potatoes and watched as he finished his second apple tart. He gave her a brusque nod, rose, and walked to his favorite chair facing the hearth, where he packed his pipe and settled back with a book.

Lydia quickly ate the small portions on her plate, cleared the table, and set water to heat to wash the dishes. Minutes later she silently stole into the parlor, to find William's head tipped forward, clay pipe clutched in one hand and his book in the other, breathing slowly and deeply as he slept.

She did not hesitate. Without a sound she crept down the hall and flattened herself against the wall next to the door, still slightly ajar. She listened intently to the sounds of voices within.

The voice was Dunphy's. "Pass the wine."

There was the sound of wine leaving a bottle, tumbling into a goblet, and then silence as he drank.

"Good. Wonder who made it."

She heard the bottle thump onto the tray, and for the first time she caught the aroma of pipe smoke in the air.

They've finished eating. They're having pipes and wine.

Another voice spoke. "Five thousand you said? Who'll be in command?"

Dunphy answered. "Probably Grey and Grant. If Howe decides to send some Germans, Knyphausen will be with them."

"How will they be armed?"

"Thirteen cannon. Baggage wagons. Eleven boats on wheels. They'll have to cross the Schuylkill."

"Have they been notified? Received orders?"

"Not yet. Howe intends putting all commands under orders to be ready to march tomorrow morning. Everybody will think it's one of his standard orders to be prepared. He won't give written orders to Grey and Grant until the next morning, one hour before they're to leave. That way no one will suspect what he has in mind, so it can't be leaked. No one will know Grey and Grant are going to attack, even when they march out. It has to be a total surprise if we're to get them all."

Lydia felt her breathing constrict.

"Do we know where Washington's camped? He has a habit of not being where he's reported."

She heard soft chuckles. "Were you at Trenton?"

"No. Were you?"

"We marched down to the south end of town with Cornwallis that morning—January second, I think it was—ready to annihilate the entire

Continental Army, including Washington. We found about one hundred campfires still burning and not one living soul."

Again there were muffled chuckles.

Dunphy spoke. "We know where he is. Camped at Whitemarsh. The route our forces will take runs in a fourteen-mile arc that will bring them in right on top of him. The battle should be over within two hours. Once we have Washington, the rebellion will be finished."

The blood left Lydia's face, and she stood rigid for a moment, mind whirling. Then she turned and silently returned to the parlor where William was stirring. His book fell to the floor, and his eyes opened, staring for a moment before he rose. He started to speak when the sounds of boot heels clicking in the hallway came loud, and he stopped. Terror leaped in Lydia's heart at the thought the British had noticed the library door ajar and were coming to take her prisoner. Her breathing stopped as she peered into their faces.

They paid scant attention to Lydia and William as they walked to the pegs by the front door, where three of them snapped their capes about their shoulders. With their tricorns in their hands, they turned to General Dunphy.

"Good evening, sir."

He nodded. "I shall see you in the morning."

There was nothing else said as they opened the door, and the freezing night air flooded into the room as they walked out into the frigid, starry darkness. Dunphy closed the door behind them, shivered involuntarily, and strode past Lydia.

"You may clear the library, the sooner the better," he said, and added as a lackluster afterthought, "The meal was acceptable."

She waited until she heard the door to the master bedroom that she and her husband had shared for thirty years close before she walked to the library and gathered the utensils and the bowls onto the trays. She carried the heavier tray to the kitchen first, then returned for the second one, all the while struggling to maintain control of her growing fear. *The British are going to attack the Continental Army—take General Washington—and my Daniel!*

She had finished the dishes, taken the supper leftovers to the cold of the root cellar, banked the fire for the night, extinguished all the lamps in the house except for the one on her nightstand, knelt beside their bed in the attic while Aaron chanted the evening prayer, blown out the lamp, and slipped between the sheets in her bed in her floor-length, flannel nightshirt and cap before the plan took shape in her brain. Her eyes opened wide in the darkness, and she put one hand over her mouth, then turned her head far enough to see if she had disturbed William. There was no break in his soft snoring.

Frankford! Of course! Frankford! The British will let women through their lines to leave Philadelphia if they're going to Frankford to get flour from the mill. Surely, surely, there will be someone—an American officer, a soldier, someone—I can give the message to take on to General Washington. Warn him, they're coming.

She lay in the darkness a long time, pondering. *Dare I tell William? He will ask how I know, and I will tell him I listened at the library door—eavesdropped— a sin—and he will be furious—might demand I remain in the house—I cannot tell him—I will not.* She lay awake until the early hours of the morning, tormented with the knowledge that she was deliberately planning to commit the sin of deceiving her husband. She finally drifted into troubled sleep, silently repeating to herself that saving her son and General Washington and the Continental Army rose far above her duty of complete, subservient honesty with her husband.

She arose with the morning star fading in the east to begin her day of preparing meals, housecleaning, baking, and today, ironing. In near total silence she served Aaron his breakfast of steaming oatmeal porridge in the kitchen, and General Dunphy his breakfast of eggs and griddlecakes in the master bedroom. Afterward, both men wrapped themselves in their heavy clothing and scarves and left the house—Dunphy to go to the command headquarters of General Howe, Aaron to the school. Each would remain away until evening.

The moment they were gone, Lydia quickly finished cleaning the breakfast dishes, made the beds, finished the ironing, and set out a shoulder of mutton and turnips for the evening meal of stew. Then she walked quickly to the library, drew a small piece of paper from the desk drawer, dipped Aaron's quill in the inkwell, and wrote. She read the message, then rolled it into a small cylinder and walked back to the parlor. From her sewing basket she selected a needlebook and inserted the rolled paper into one of the small pockets and thrust it into her purse. Two minutes later she paused at the door, pulled her scarf tightly about her neck, and walked out into the freezing, bright Philadelphia sunlight.

She nearly trotted through the cobblestone streets to the British soldiers who were guarding the road northeast out of the city and stopped before them as two faced her with muskets and the long bayonets. There was a fire by the roadside with two other soldiers standing over it, hands extended to the warmth as they watched.

The older of the two before her spoke. "Show your written permission to leave the city."

She shook her head. "I have none. I understood women were allowed to leave to go to the mill for flour. At Frankford. It's just down this road a few miles."

The man shook his head. "Written permission."

Lydia battled the panic rising within. "I was not told." She shook her head. "General Dunphy will be angry. I have no flour left for bread."

The soldier started. "General Dunphy? Did you say Dunphy?"

"Yes. He is quartered at my house. I prepare his meals. He'll be badly disappointed when I have no bread."

"General Dunphy? The adjutant general?"

Lydia's eyes widened. "I don't know the meaning of adjutant general. I only know he is a general, and on occasion other officers come to his quarters."

The soldier looked uneasily at his companion, suddenly caught in a bind not to his liking. "Uh . . . are you carrying anything?"

Lydia thrust her purse forward. "Only my purse."

The man took it, tugged it open, and quickly sorted through the contents. He drew out a small change purse, opened it, counted the coins, then drew out the needlebook, opened it, glanced, tossed it back in, and drew the strings to close it before he handed it back. He studied

Lydia. Aging, frail, round-shouldered, gray hair showing beneath her bonnet that was tied tightly beneath her chin.

"Your name?"

"Lydia Darragh. My husband is a schoolteacher in Philadelphia. You can ask."

His face was stern. "All right. You may pass. But when you return, you come past this picket post. And you had better have a sack of flour."

Lydia bobbed her head. "Thank you, sir."

Lydia picked her way northeast, hurrying, stumbling on the frozen ruts of the dirt road, moving steadily toward Frankford, some two miles distant. She went directly to the mill, counted out her six shillings, received back her change, and the miller helped her take the twenty-five-pound sack of flour on her back. He followed her to open the door and spoke as she made her way outside.

"You intend carrying that back to Philadelphia?"

"Yes."

He shook his head as he watched her walk away with measured strides.

She reached the woods and followed the road as it angled to the west, out of sight of the mill, before she stopped. Carefully she turned both directions to be certain no one was watching, then walked quickly ten yards into the thick woods, where she laid the sack of flour behind a large tree stump, then straightened, hands on her hips to relieve the ache. She returned to the road and walked half a mile further west, to the fork that led back north toward Whitemarsh, six miles distant. In her heart was a prayer. *Merciful and Almighty Creator, may I meet someone who can carry my message to General Washington.*

She had gone one-half mile when the sound of an oncoming horse stopped her, and she stepped from the roadbed to hide in the trees. She watched the horseman approaching from the direction of Whitemarsh, and at the last instant saw gold epaulets on the shoulders of his heavy woolen coat. Instantly she threw up a hand and called out to him. He reined his horse around facing her and jerked a large pistol from his saddle holster and brought it to bear on her midsection. Terrified, she stood without moving, hand still raised.

"Approach and identify yourself," he demanded.

"Don't hurt me! I am Lydia Darragh. I'm lost. May I ask, sir, who you are, and if you could help me find my way?"

His eyes narrowed in surprise. "Mrs. Darragh? Is that you?"

Lydia stared. "Captain Craig? John Craig? Of the Pulaski Cavalry?"

Captain John Craig dismounted and swept his hat from his head. "It's I, Mrs. Darragh. I cannot imagine what you are doing out here in the countryside."

Lydia's head fell back and her eyes closed for a moment as relief flooded through her being. "Oh, John! The Almighty has answered my prayer. Can you take a message to General Washington?"

"I can. What message might you have for the general?"

"General Howe is planning a surprise attack on your army at Whitemarsh tomorrow. Five thousand soldiers with thirteen cannon, and they plan to bring eleven boats on wheels."

Craig's eyes widened in surprise. "How do you know this?"

"I overheard the plan in my home. A British general has his quarters there."

"Which general?"

"General Dunphy. Albert Dunphy."

Craig started. "Dunphy? The adjutant general?"

"Yes. I heard him called that this morning. The adjutant general."

"Who was with him?"

"Three other officers. Generals, I think."

"What else did you hear?"

"I heard the names of an officer named Grey and one named Grant."

Craig rounded his lips to blow air for a moment. Vapors rose from his face. "That would be Generals "No-Flint" Grey and James Grant. You're certain?"

"As the Almighty is my witness, John. You know my son Daniel— you grew up with him. He's in the Philadelphia Militia. I have to do something to save him. Could you please be certain the militia knows?"

Craig was incredulous. "Yes, ma'am, I will be certain. Do you know their route? Did they talk about it?"

"Only that it will be a fourteen-mile march, and it is in a curve. And, John, I beg of you, do not use my name. If the British find out what I've done, my life will be worth nothing."

Craig mounted his horse. "I'll see to it, Mrs. Darragh. And if this all works out, you can live with the knowledge that you have likely saved the Continental Army."

He spun his horse, rammed his blunted spurs home, and the animal hit racing stride in three jumps.

Lydia watched him ride out of sight before she turned. She had retraced her steps for one hundred yards before she stopped. *What if he's captured—has an accident—can't deliver the message?* She stood still for a time, struggling with indecision. Then she turned and started rapidly up the road where Craig had disappeared. *The Rising Sun Tavern is half a mile ahead. Surely someone will be there who can help.*

The road wound through the Pennsylvania forest. The Rising Sun Tavern was hidden until the last turn brought her within fifty yards of the hitching post in front, with three horses standing hip-shot, one hind leg cocked forward, heads down as they dozed. Above the door was a large, carved wooden sign of a rising sun. She studied the horses for a moment before pushing through the rough plank door into the dimly lighted room.

Half a dozen travelers were seated at a table, finishing their meal, waiting for the next coach to Whitemarsh. Two men sat at a table with pewter ale tankards before them. One man sat alone near a corner with a tankard of rum before him. He appeared relaxed, except for his eyes, which missed nothing. On the table in front of him was his tricorn, and on the face of it was gold braid.

Lydia could not remember having been in a tavern in her entire life, certainly not in the past thirty years, during her marriage to William. Visiting taverns, like eavesdropping, was a sin that required severe punishment.

She walked to the table nearest the tricorn hat with the gold braid and sat down. Trying to remain unnoticed, she glanced at the hat, then the man, only to discover his eyes were boring into her.

"Ma'am, is something wrong?"

She started at the sound of his voice.

"No. Oh, no. I'm just traveling. Waiting for a coach."

"You arrived on foot?"

"I live nearby."

He looked at her bonnet, then at her shoes. "Philadelphia?"

"No." She dropped her eyes. Lying was nearly an impossibility for her. "Yes."

The man sipped at his rum. "Is there something I can help with?"

She stared at his hat. "I see you're an officer."

"Yes, ma'am."

"American?"

He set his rum tankard on the table, and his voice was low. "Elias Boudinot. I am chief of intelligence services for General Washington."

For one split second, Lydia gaped. Then she rose and moved to sit at his table, next to him, to speak softly. "Sir, can you carry a message to General Washington?"

For a time Boudinot studied the frail, aging woman. "That depends."

In two minutes Lydia quietly related what she knew, and Boudinot straightened in his chair, stunned.

"How did you learn this?"

"I overheard it discussed in my home between General Alfred Dunphy and three of his officers. They have taken residence in my house."

Boudinot's head dropped forward. "Adjutant General Dunphy?"

"Yes."

"When did you hear it?"

"During supper yesterday evening."

"Are you certain?"

"Yes. I told all this to Captain John Craig—I've known John most of his life—he's in the cavalry—less than an hour ago. He promised to tell General Washington. I tell you because I must be certain General Washington gets it."

Boudinot's mind was racing, searching for all other information he had received in the past twenty-four hours. *This morning Howe put all his troops under orders to be prepared to march. Grey? Grant? Who better to lead an attack on what's left of the rebels? Howe had eleven boats taken off the river last night and hauled ashore. Could this little woman be part of a scheme to draw us one way while Howe attacks from another?*

"Ma'am, what route does Howe intend taking?"

"I don't know. Only that it will be a fourteen-mile march, and that it will bring his soldiers in from behind. A surprise attack."

Boudinot raised a mental image of Whitemarsh in his mind, and for ten seconds labored, inventing routes from Philadelphia to Whitemarsh that would involve eleven large boats and cover fourteen miles. *He plans to cross the river moving toward New York, then recross at night above Bristol and come in on our rear!*

Lydia glanced about the dim room, aware of prying eyes. She fumbled with her purse for a moment, then quietly laid the old needlebook on the table before Boudinot. He picked it up, opened it, and quickly felt each of the pockets. There was nothing until he came to the last one, and he removed the small cylinder of rolled paper. He closed the needlebook and thrust it back across the table to Lydia, holding the paper out of sight. He reached for his tricorn and stood.

Lydia spoke quietly. "Sir, please do not use my name. If the British discovered this, they might burn my home or do worse to my husband and myself."

"I understand."

He set his hat squarely on his head and spoke loudly enough to be heard by those nearest. "It has been a delight to see you again. Be certain to give my regards to Uncle Benjamin and the grandchildren."

Lydia nodded deeply, stood, and watched Boudinot walk out the front door, into the sunshine. She sat silent while listening to the sound of his galloping horse fade, moving up the road, northeast. She glanced at the large clock on the mantel above the huge stone fireplace. It was now past two o'clock. Hurriedly she walked out the door and retraced her steps back to the woods where she had left her sack of flour. She lifted it onto a large stone nearby, then backed up to it and took it on her back, one hand over her shoulder clutching one of the ears of the stitched sack, the other curled behind her waist to support it from beneath.

She had to stop to rest three times before she reached the cobble-stone street in front of her house, and she was staggering when she opened the door and entered the parlor. She let the sack fall and col-lapsed into the nearest chair. It was a full five minutes before she raised her head to look at the clock. It was twenty minutes before five o'clock.

With what was left of her strength she dragged the flour across the kitchen into the pantry and hid it behind a keg of molasses and a small cask of salt. Ten minutes later she was standing in the kitchen dicing mutton and turnips for stew when the front door rattled and she heard William's voice.

"Another cold day. Will there be a warm supper?"

Eleven miles north and a little east, General Washington leaned for-ward in his chair. The sun was making stark silhouettes of the leafless trees to the west as he interlaced his fingers, forearms on the table in his command tent. For a time he sat still in deep concentration, then raised his head.

"Are you both convinced this woman told the truth?"

Boudinot glanced at Craig. "I am, sir. I'd stake my life on it."

Craig nodded agreement. "I've known her for as far as I can remem-ber. Went to school with her son, Daniel. She's a good and honest woman. I'd trust Lydia Darragh with my life."

"Eleven boats? Only eleven, for five thousand troops and thirteen cannon?" Washington shook his head, doubt clear in his eyes.

"I've thought about that, sir," Boudinot said. "At first I thought he meant to cross the Delaware like he was headed for New York, then recross at night and come in from behind us. Now I think the boats might be a decoy."

Washington nodded. "That is my conclusion. I think he intends making a feint to the east, then circle back and come at us directly from the south."

Boudinot and Craig nodded in agreement.

"Then we need to send out scouts to track their movements. We must not let them know we are watching."

"Yes, sir."

"We must send enough Continentals, with militia and cannon, down to Chestnut Hill to stop them, if we have guessed right about their true intention. And we must send all the tents and baggage to Trappe. With winter coming on, we can't risk losing them."

"Yes, sir."

"I'll hold a war council and issue written orders yet tonight. One last thing. No one is to know the name of that little Quaker woman. Under no circumstance is she or her husband or their home to be put in danger because of anything we say or do. She may well have saved the army and the revolution by herself."

At half past eight o'clock, beneath a black velvet dome speckled with countless diamonds, on horses with winter hair hanging from their jaws and bellies and vapor streaming from their nostrils, the officers of the war council came to the command tent. The pickets held the flap for them, and they entered in silence, wondering the purpose of being gathered on short notice.

At ten minutes before ten o'clock, they walked back through the flap into the frigid, starry night, silent, breathing shallow to protect their lungs from frostbite. In the hand of General James Irvine of the Pennsylvania militia were signed orders. Six hundred of his men were to proceed south immediately, to take up positions with cannon on Chestnut Hill as an advance guard. The New York division was to dig in behind him with more cannon—fifty-two in all—in the event of an all-out assault by the British.

At precisely three o'clock A.M., the Americans saw the lanterns swinging and swaying from their attachments on the thirteen cannon the British were maneuvering into position at the base of Chestnut Hill, and ten seconds later the silence and the darkness were shattered by the roar of the American artillery. Flame leaped fifteen feet from the gun muzzles, and for an instant everyone on the hill saw the crimson tunics and the crossed white belts on the red-coated regulars below.

Caught by surprise, the British were desperately trying to load their cannon to return fire when the second American volley of grapeshot came ripping into them. With the echo of the cannon still ringing in the wooded hills, General James Irvine drew his sword, stood, shouted, "Follow me, boys!" and led his militiamen down the hill at a run. He was the first to meet the British in the dark, swinging his sword with all his strength, driving the startled British backwards in a hand-to-hand fight in the dark. He felt a sting on his left hand and fought on, his howling men right behind him. It was only after they had cut deeply into the leading British ranks that Irvine realized he had led his men into the center of the five thousand redcoats.

He halted, turned, and shouted, "Fall back! Fall back!" and they began a controlled retreat. Within minutes Irvine, and those around him, were surrounded on all sides by the British, and only then did Irvine lower his sword. He raised his left hand, trying to see what had hit him, to discover the last three fingers missing, and he could not remember when or how it had happened. Slowly he dropped his sword and raised his hands, and twenty of his men laid down their weapons in surrender. The others—more than five hundred fifty—had safely withdrawn.

He listened as the British moved them off the slope of Chestnut Hill. The British were withdrawing their cannon, and he heard the British officers shouting.

"Fall back! Fall back! Too many big guns on the hill."

Dawn was breaking when a British surgeon finished binding Irvine's mutilated hand. It was eight o'clock when the British began a movement to the east, probing for a soft spot in the American lines.

There wasn't one.

Orders came. "Prepare to march. Prepare to march. South. Back to Philadelphia."

With his bloodied left hand clasped against his chest, Irvine and his twenty men exchanged smiles. They were captured, but their command—

six hundred Pennsylvania militiamen—had hit the center of the five thousand British regulars with such ferocity in the night that they had slowed them, stopped them, turned them, given the British better than they got. And more than five hundred fifty of their men had made it back to the American lines.

They had turned Howe's surprise night attack into a rout. Irvine and his men marched back to Philadelphia surrounded by their British captors, but their heads were high, their step firm.

By nine o'clock the reports reached Washington. The British were in full retreat, moving south toward Philadelphia. They were beaten.

Washington sat at his table and carefully unrolled the small cylinder of paper to read it once more. *Five thousand men. Thirteen cannon. Eleven boats.*

He raised the chimney on the desk lamp that still burned and touched the paper to the flame. He dropped the burning message to the dirt of the tent floor and watched it turn to a small, fragile ash, then ground it beneath his heel.

Whoever she is, may the Almighty attend her every need.

A rustle at the tent flap brought his head up. Alexander Hamilton stood before him.

"Sir, when did you have it in mind to continue our march to winter quarters?"

"Are the British still in full retreat to Philadelphia?"

Hamilton set his jaw for a moment before he answered. "Yes, sir, they are, but reports are coming in from dozens of scouts to the south. The British are burning farms and crops and slaughtering sheep and pigs wherever they find them. They burned part of Beggarstown. They burned the Rising Sun Tavern to the ground. They're driving seven hundred head of cattle back to Philadelphia for meat."

Washington's eyes narrowed in outrage, and for a moment his hand trembled before he brought himself under control. "A day will come when they will regret such things." He cleared his throat. "We'll march as soon as the men are prepared."

"Valley Forge?"

"Yes. Valley Forge. Get the men ready."

Notes

The Lydia Darragh story is accurately presented, including the names of the two American officers she met, who carried her message to General Washington. She met officer Boudinot at the Rising Sun Tavern. General James Irvine lost three fingers in his attack on the British. In their retreat, the furious British burned homes and farms near Beggarstown and burned the Rising Sun Tavern to the ground. See Cleghorn, *Women Patriots of the American Revolution*, pp. 60–61; Wildes, *Valley Forge*, pp. 142–44.

CHAPTER XIX

★ ★ ★

*T*hey came west, eleven thousand and a few more, strung out for more than six miles on the crooked, frozen wagon tracks that had been cut through the thick Pennsylvania woods to connect Whitemarsh with the farms and taverns and villages that depended on the Schuylkill River. They were the Continentals—the army that had been beaten at Brandywine and at Germantown. The army that Congress had sent to defend Philadelphia and had been made foolish by the British when they led them twenty miles toward Reading, then marched back to Philadelphia in the night to take the city without firing a shot. The army that was dressed in the rags that were left of their summer clothing and that had learned to eat toads and snakes and tree bark to stay alive. The army that could be tracked by the blood from their feet, left on the frozen mud and ice ridges of the back roads as they struggled on.

They harnessed their few starving horses and oxen to their cannon and wagons, and drove them until the beasts dropped in their tracks. Then they ate them, and emaciated men hooked themselves into the harnesses and drew on their last strength to move the cannon and the wagons onward through the snows and the bitter cold of winter.

The officers rode horses with ribs and hipbones showing through their splotchy winter hides, and they watched the eyes of their troops, judging, waiting for the first signs of mutiny. None of them believed that men would, or could, long stand such purgatory without breaking. They

357

sat their emaciated mounts and grimly watched the wretched mob creep slowly to the west, and they waited.

They came to Swede's Ford, where they had to cross to the south bank of the Schuylkill River, and in late dusk, with snow slanting in a freezing wind, they approached the narrow bridge. The men in the leading company bit down on their fear and began the crossing in the dark, walking single file on a bridge that was shifting, moving in the wind. Seven hours later the last of them crossed to no food, no blankets, no fires, no tents. Nine were found drowned the next morning and were hastily buried in the church cemetery of the small hamlet of Swedesford, nearby, and they moved on.

They arrived at the Gulph, where orders were given to distribute axes so the men could build fires and brush huts for one night. They would march farther west the next morning. In the night the snow turned to sleet, then freezing rain. For two days the rains held, and the Continental Army huddled about fires that sputtered and refused to burn—without blankets, without shelter, while the countryside became a morass of mud that mired their wagons and cannon past the axles and made it impossible to move.

Once again the soldiers tightened their belts, set their chins, and endured. Talk began in the ranks, quietly at first, then insistent. *Where are we going? Winter quarters where?*

The word was passed down, from John Laurens, then General Enoch Poor. *Valley Forge. Not far. We can make it. Take courage.*

On December eighteenth, but one day's march from journey's end, Washington dug a thumb and finger into weary eyes and rubbed them for a time before he heaved a great sigh. He read again the declaration he had received from Congress, under date of November 1, 1777.

". . . December 18th is to be observed by all as a day for public Thanksgiving and Praise . . ."

One more day. Just one more day, and the ordeal will be ended. Congress could not have done worse than stopping us today. If I refuse to follow their declaration? If I march my men this day and observe their day of thanksgiving tomorrow?

Slowly he shook his head. *I cannot. This army will remain subject to the will* of Congress, no matter the price. This revolution is based on the subjection of military authority to civilian authority.

He drew paper and quill before him on the table and wrote.

" . . . I extol the courage and perseverance of the troops in support of the measures necessary for our defence; we shall finally obtain the end of our Warfare, Independence, Liberty and Peace. . . . We shall observe the Eighteenth day of December, 1777, to show our grateful acknowledgments to God for the manifold blessings he has granted us. We shall remain in our present quarters and the Chaplains are instructed to conduct divine services before their respective regiments and brigades. A supper of thanksgiving shall be prepared and served to all for the evening meal on that day. All marching orders shall therefore be postponed until the following morning, December nineteenth, at which time the wagons shall proceed at 7 o'clock A.M., followed by the troops at 10 o'clock A.M."

Thanksgiving supper? The men stared at each other in disbelief. There was no beef, pork, or mutton, no potatoes, turnips, cabbages, flour—nothing. Thanksgiving supper of what?

With the setting sun casting long shadows in the early evening of December eighteenth, the men formed their lines with wooden bowls in hand to receive their Thanksgiving supper.

Each received one-half cup of rice and one tablespoon of vinegar.

Their Thanksgiving supper had been served.

The morning of December nineteenth broke gray in that strange, muffled quiet that comes with snow falling in dead air. At seven o'clock the wagons rolled out. At ten o'clock the leading division of the Continentals once again set their feet on the frozen mud and ice and followed, moving west on Gulph Road. Two miles to their right the Schuylkill River rolled east. To their left were the gently rolling hills of Pennsylvania with the oak and the poplar and the birch trees stark and bare, the conifers green and snow covered in their winter hibernation.

Valley Forge! Just over the next rise? Or the next one? Winter quarters! The freezing and the starving over! Winter quarters!

A little after one o'clock the snow dwindled and stopped, and a raw north wind came quartering in. They crested the last rise and slowed, then stopped, and the heart went out of them.

There was no valley. There was no town. Only the forested, rolling hills of Pennsylvania lay before them, broken with an occasional field of what had been wheat or rye or corn. A few log homes were scattered about. To the south, scarcely visible in the trees, were a few more. Ahead was the King of Prussia Inn but no village. In the distance they could see Valley Creek and the wreckage of the forge where Isaac Potts and William Dewees had pounded white hot pig iron into farm implements until the British burned the structure to the ground, on September nineteenth, as they passed through on their way to take Philadelphia. Across the creek from the forge was the dam and the water wheel that had turned the grinding stone inside the grist mill. The British had intended to burn the mill along with the forge, but for reasons unknown had failed to do so.

Scattered about the mill and the black wreckage of the forge were the homes of Abijah Stephens, Wilsey Bodles, John Brown and his son, David Stephens, and Zachary Davis and no others. Just past the forge were the homes of Potts and Dewees.

There was little else. No granaries. No cattle. No barns filled with winter fodder for horses or oxen. No orchards. No corn silos. No storage sheds. No shelter for an army. Nothing.

The Continentals hitched up their muskets and marched on, spiritless, freezing, bellies empty and gnawing, with a growing anger that Congress and their officers had brought them to this forsaken place. The sun traveled its eternal arc westward and touched the western rim, and still they came. Dusk had settled when the last of them arrived.

The wagons with the tents rolled in from Trappe, and while some of the ravaged, exhausted men struggled to erect tents against the frigid north wind, others slowly set about erecting the tripods for their cook kettles. It was only then they learned the nearest water was the Schuylkill River, over a mile to the north. In the dark they trudged barefooted over trackless ground with buckets, while others swung the axes to cut firewood. They boiled whatever they could find and drank it scalding.

Never had General Washington seen his army as they now were. Disillusioned, spiritless, angry, betrayed, starving, freezing, hopeless. Scarcely able to control the pain in his heart, he issued his orders for the night. There would be no pickets posted tonight. There would be no camp protocol, no tattoo, no discipline. The men were to seek their own comfort, and Washington would not sleep in better conditions than they had until their lot was improved. General Washington spent the night, as did some of his men, huddled in a tent with the sides billowing from the north wind. The thousands who were without blankets built crude windbreaks and sat huddled around fires to keep from freezing to death.

The troops could not know that Washington had desired to take the entire army to a location closer to their sources of supply. But the Pennsylvania Supreme Executive Council had insisted that the army be stationed as near Philadelphia as possible, to protect the eastern section of Pennsylvania from the British, and they were adamant that Valley Forge was the location of their choice. The members of the national Congress had long since fled across the Susquehanna River to York, eighty miles south and west, where they intended to remain until they could return to Philadelphia. And once again Washington chose to allow the military to be guided by the civilian government. At whatever cost, the army would winter in Valley Forge.

Sometime in the night the snow began again, driven by the north wind. Dawn came gray, and the wind died. To the north the Schuylkill River was frozen solid. To keep from freezing, the starving, emaciated men fed their fires and once more picked up their axes to build crude shelters.

With the snow falling on his shoulders and collecting in his brows, General Washington left his tent to walk slowly through the camp, scattered four miles east to west, parallel to the river. He saw the scarecrow men gritting their teeth to swing the axes, and he saw the blood from their blue feet in the snow. More than half had no coats, and their ragged shirts showed their bare shoulders and backs through the holes. Open sores on their faces wept pus and blood into their beards. He saw their diverted eyes, and he said nothing when he passed men who did not salute.

A smoldering rage began to take shape in his chest. He returned to his tent, dug a pencil and paper from his pack, drew up a wooden crate for a desk, and did the only thing he could. He drafted orders by which his men would begin, immediately, to build their camp.

"Divide the men into squads of twelve. Build huts in rows facing each other, with a street between, doors facing the street. The huts shall be fourteen feet by sixteen feet each, sides, ends, and roofs made of logs, the roof made tight with split slabs, the sides made tight with clay. Opposite the door will be a fireplace made of wood, secured with clay eighteen inches thick. Doors to be made of split oak slabs, unless boards are available. Side walls to be six and one half feet high. Bunks, six to the side, shall be arranged against the two long walls. All available straw from the citizens near camp shall be obtained to cover the roofs and for bedding for the soldiers. A proclamation shall be issued to all citizens within seventy miles of camp that they are to thresh all their grain within sixty days and make the straw available to the army, and should they fail, their grain shall be seized in the sheaves and paid for as straw."

Washington paused, and his forehead wrinkled in thought before he continued.

"I shall reward that party in each regiment, which finishes their hut in the quickest and most workmanlike manner with twelve dollars, drawn from my own pocket. Further, I shall reward any officer or soldier with one hundred dollars, who in the opinion of Generals Sullivan, Greene, and Stirling, shall discover or invent some other covering for the huts that may be cheaper and quicker made than boards, since finding boards will be nearly impossible, and there is no time to saw them."

With his written orders in hand, he stood and walked from his tent to find Alexander Hamilton.

"Gather the officers. We must be about the business of sheltering and feeding and clothing these men or this army will disintegrate."

"Yes, sir."

Notes

The horrible, destitute condition of the Continental Army as it marched toward Valley Forge is accurately described herein. The heartbreak felt by the men as they first saw Valley Forge is also accurate. Valley Forge is not a valley but hilly country. The forge itself had been burned by the British on September 19. The description of the homes and buildings and the owners is correct. The men had to go more than one mile to get fresh water. Sensing the desolate mood of his men and with snow commencing, Washington rescinded all orders for military protocol for the night of December 19, 1777. Washington desired to locate winter quarters nearer their source of supply but deferred to the will of Congress. The morning of December 20, Washington drafted and issued orders to his army to begin building their small huts, the dimensions and construction of which are quoted nearly verbatim from his written orders. See Martin, *Private Yankee Doodle*, pp. 100, 102, 103, 167; Higginbotham, *The War of American Independence*, pp. 303–4; Wildes, *Valley Forge*, pp. 144–51; Leckie, *George Washington's War*, p. 434; Reed, *Valley Forge: Crucible of Victory*, pp. 5, 9–10; Jackson, *Valley Forge: Pinnacle of Courage*, pp. 17–19.

CHAPTER XX

★ ★ ★

*T*hey moved slowly, the younger man with the hand-driven cross-cut saw cutting the trimmed tree trunks to measured eighteen-foot lengths, the older man with a broadax, notching the ends so they would form a wall sixteen feet in length when assembled. Two other men in their twelve-man squad were mixing clods of frozen clay with hot water in a hole three feet in diameter and one foot deep that they had hacked in the frozen ground. Four others were hoisting the finished logs into place on the wall, matching the notches with those beneath, while the last four men were carrying the thick clay mix from the hole in the ground to the wall, where they jammed it between the logs, careful to seal every cleft and gap.

They stopped often, weak, exhausted, their breath coming fast with vapors rising in the gray overcast. Seven of the twelve men were without shoes, working on numb, bloodied feet that were in the first stages of frostbite. They glanced often at the heavens, gauging time by the position of the sun, which was a dull ball behind the cloud cover. It was cold enough to snow again, but no flakes had yet fallen. They guessed it was shortly past ten o'clock, and they swallowed at the thought of something—anything—hot for their midday meal. They had had nothing to eat since noon, twenty-two hours earlier and had learned to work hunched over to relieve the cramps in their empty bellies.

Unexpected movement toward the Schuylkill caught the eye of the older man, and he turned his head, then stopped work, and straightened. He laid his broadax down and picked up his musket, his face drawn as he studied a man striding toward them. The younger man stared, searching for what had stopped his companion.

The man approaching them was dressed in a gray wolf-skin coat that reached nearly to his knees. His breeches were soft, tanned deerskin. A parka covered his face. His legs from the knees down were covered with gray wolf-skin moccasins. He wore a weapons belt drawn about his midsection, with a black tomahawk thrust through on the right side, a belt knife in a beaded sheath on his left, together with a leather bullet pouch and a powder horn that hung from his neck. He carried a long, beautifully tooled Pennsylvania rifle loosely in his right hand as he swung along. The footprints he left in the snow were nearly in line.

The older man cocked his musket. "Injun."

The incoming man raised his rifle high above his head and continued striding toward them, with the musket aimed at his chest. He stopped at twenty feet and drew back his parka. His eyes narrowed as he studied the emaciated, hollow-cheek, barefoot men before him, who were staring back at him from sunken eyes.

"I didn't see pickets." The voice was white, not Indian. The face was regular, dark from summer sun and winter storms, with a strong Roman nose. The hair was long, drawn back by a leather thong.

"Got no pickets out. Who are you?"

"Eli Stroud. Returning from a scout to the north. I'm looking for the Massachusetts Division."

"Don't recall seein' you hereabouts before."

"Haven't been hereabouts before, at least since you got here. I'm coming in from far to the north. Above Fort Ticonderoga."

"The fighting up there was over last fall."

"I was there. Have you seen the Massachusetts soldiers?"

The younger soldier pointed east. "I think they're back there, maybe two miles."

Eli nodded and continued on without further comment, rifle at his side. He did not look back at the twelve men who watched him out of sight, unable to tear their eyes from the wolf-skin coat and the moccasins. Warmth. Clearly this man was part of the wilderness, part of the woods, and there would be risk if they interfered.

Eli left his parka pulled back, watching everything as he strode east through the camp. Silent men in threadbare clothing, legs and feet bare, shivering, sores visible on their faces and bodies, doggedly working slowly in squads of twelve to erect huts that would turn the snow and the wind. He saw no iron tripods, no kettles, no one bringing wood to start the midday cooking fires. Men glanced at him with listless eyes, then watched him out of sight. A few officers mounted on thin, spiritless horses moved through the camp, eyeing him suspiciously, but none stopped him.

He had not gone half a mile when he understood he was witnessing a momentous calamity. The army he had left six months earlier, when he and Billy had walked out of Morristown on orders of General Washington, had nothing to do with the army he was now seeing. He had been with them one year earlier, when they were freezing and starving on the banks of the Delaware and had crossed the river to take Trenton from the Hessians. That was bad enough. But this? Never could he have guessed he would find eleven thousand of them in the death throes of extinction.

"Eli! Over here!"·

The shout came from his left, toward the river, and he recognized the voice at the instant of hearing. He swung around and stopped, eyes searching, and then he saw the thick-shouldered, thick-necked man running toward him, long sandy-red hair tied back, round face grinning through a thick rusty beard. He wore a thick woolen coat and heavy leather shoes. Eli trotted to meet him, and the two men stopped to grasp each other by the shoulders.

"Billy! You made it back!"

"Weeks ago. Are you all right?"

"Good."

"Are Ben and Lydia and the children all right?"

Billy saw the light in Eli's eyes as he answered. "Fine. Fine. Ready for winter."

"Did you get the room finished? Harvest finished? The meat salted?"

"All done. Lydia said you've got to come back."

A great smile spread on Billy's face. "As soon as I can. Come on. Sergeant—"

Billy got no further. The high, nasal, raspy voice came piercing. "Stroud! Is that you?"

Eli peered past Billy to see the feisty little sergeant trotting as fast as his bowed legs would allow.

"It's me."

"You two lovelies over here, and not inviting me?"

Billy replied, "We were just coming to find you."

Sergeant Alvin Turlock eyed Eli, top to bottom. "Don't look like that little skirmish up north did you any harm."

"I'm fine."

"Your sister—Lydia? She and her family all right?"

"Yes."

For a moment Turlock's eyes closed, and his head rolled back. "I'm glad for you. I truly am. You back to stay?"

"So far as I know. I notice things have changed since I've been gone."

Turlock glanced about. "You mean the look of this army?"

Eli nodded.

Turlock shook his head, searching for words. "We fought good this summer—twice—but we lost at Brandywine and Germantown, both. Brandywine because we was outgeneraled, and Germantown because of fog. Then Howe tricked us into goin' up to Reading to save our stores while he went back to Philadelphia and took it without a fight. Not one shot."

Eli's face drew down, and his eyes narrowed in disbelief. Turlock continued.

"Things went from bad to worse. Food stopped. No blankets. No clothes." He gestured toward the camp with his hand. "We're goin' to lose it all if something isn't done."

He paused, and Eli saw a flinty look come into the eyes of the gritty little man. "But we aren't goin' to solve that standin' here. Come on.

You're part of a squad. Twelve of us got to build us a hut or freeze to death. Makes choices real simple when you say it that way, don't it?"

Eli paused to thoughtfully stroke the three-inch scar on his jawbone. "No food?"

"You want somethin' to eat? Sorry to say, we got nothin'. Likely won't get rations for the next two, three days."

Eli drew a deep breath. "When did these men last eat?"

"Yesterday. Gruel. And then two days before that."

"No clothes?"

"Six thousand don't have blankets. More'n half don't have shoes. Most don't have coats. You see what they're wearin'. Rags."

Eli was incredulous. "Washington let all this happen?"

Turlock shook his head. "Not Washington. Congress. The High Supreme Council of Pennsylvania, if that's what they call theirselves. Washington's been with us all the way. His command tent's up at the other end of camp, and he's freezin' and starvin' just like the rest of us. From what I hear, he's about ready to march this whole army on Congress or on the Pennsylvania Supreme Council, or whatever it's called. Maybe a few bayonets in their faces will sober 'em up. Come on. We got work to do."

Eli spoke. "One more thing. Either of you know what became of Mary Flint?"

Both Turlock and Billy saw the fear, the need in Eli's eyes, and Turlock answered.

"She wintered with us at Morristown. Worked in the hospital. Came there to find you. We talked the day the army marched out. She told me to look out for you. Said she'll come when she can." Turlock rubbed the back of his hand across his bearded mouth. "She's a special lady, that one."

"Was she well? Healthy?"

Turlock's eyes dropped. "Mostly. Had a cough. A touch of pneumonia."

Eli's breath caught. "Was she in the hospital?"

"Oh, no. She was up and workin'. Workin' too hard. She'll come. Don't ever think she won't come."

For a moment the three stood there, two feeling the pain for the third.

Turlock broke it off. "Well, we'll have time for all the little stuff later. We better get back to buildin' this hut."

Eli followed Turlock and Billy back to the edge of the woods, where axes rang as their squad cut and trimmed pine trees, measured, sawed, and notched them. The men stopped at the approach of the three, and Billy made the necessary brief introductions. Each man nodded to Eli in silence as he eyed his wolf-skin coat and leggings and moccasins, and Eli read the all-too-familiar question in their eyes.

He waited until Billy stopped before he spoke.

"I'm white. I was orphaned and raised Iroquois. I went north with Billy. I'm back."

It was enough. They all settled into their assigned work. It was then that Eli realized he was the twelfth man. Turlock had saved a place for him.

Noon came and there was no meal. The men ate snow and sat down. Turlock gave them half an hour before he gave orders.

"Back on your feet. The sooner we finish, the sooner we're out of the cold."

Eli watched the eyes of the nine men as they struggled to their feet. *Not far from mutiny.*

The sun was two hours past its zenith when a tall, angular man working a handsaw coughed, then coughed again, and suddenly sat down. He began to tremble, then shake uncontrollably. Eli unbuckled his weapons belt and unbuttoned the three large bone buttons on his wolf-skin coat. He shrugged it off and wrapped it around the shoulders of the man. The man started to protest, but Eli raised the parka to cover his long hair. The others saw the look in the man's face as he stared up at Eli, and they turned away for a moment. Eli buckled his weapons belt back around his middle and pulled it tight over his long, deerskin hunting shirt with the quill and beadwork across the shoulders and breast, picked up his ax, and resumed the work of notching logs.

Long shadows were slanting eastward when Turlock suddenly straightened. "What have I been thinkin' about? Gen'l Washington'll want a report from you. You been to see him yet?"

Eli shook his head.

Billy interrupted. "I've made a report. He knows most of it."

Eli looked at Turlock. "Why does he need to hear it twice?"

"That isn't the point. Point is, he might have some questions. Or maybe somethin' else he wants you to do. He's the one sent you, he's the one you report back to. Follow the river clean up to the west end of camp, more'n two miles. Can't miss his command tent. You git movin'."

Eli left his coat wrapped about the sick man, and with his rifle in his right hand he left at the ground-eating trot he had learned from living seven years as an Iroquois warrior. He held the pace through camp, with half the men he passed lifting their heads to watch him. A few of them nervously reached for their muskets at the sight of his beaded leather shirt and breeches and the wolf-skin, knee-high moccasins. He passed the King of Prussia Tavern, crossed Valley Creek on the narrow bridge, and slowed as he recognized Washington's command tent to his right, not far from the frozen Schuylkill River.

The pickets both raised their muskets, and one challenged.

"Who comes there?"

"Eli Stroud. Returning from a scout up north. I ought to report to General Washington."

"One of his aides can take your report."

"My sergeant said General Washington. He's the one that sent me."

The picket sneered. "You saying Gen'l Washington himself gave you your orders? What's your rank?"

"I'm not an officer. I don't have a rank. I'm a scout. Maybe I'm a private."

The picket cocked his musket. "Gen'l Washington don't give orders to privates. I think we better put you under arrest."

In one fluid motion, the muzzle of Eli's rifle, held belt high in his right hand, was raised to bear on the center of the picket's chest, and the sound of the hammer coming back to full cock sounded loud in the freezing air. Eli's left hand had not moved. He spoke evenly, nearly casually.

"Might want to tell the general that Scout Eli Stroud is reporting back from the north. Three Rivers. Fort Ticonderoga. The Saratoga fight."

Both pickets started, wide-eyed, and the one with the cocked musket spoke. "You was up there? With Gates and Arnold? We heard things. Did Arnold lead that charge? At that redoubt?"

"He did. Tell the general. Eli Stroud."

The picket uncocked his musket.

Eli uncocked and lowered his rifle. "With a lot of other good men. Tell the general."

The picket disappeared into the tent and thirty seconds later held the flap aside and took Eli's rifle as he entered.

There was no fire. Alexander Hamilton sat on one side of a worktable, with General Washington seated at the head. Both men stood to face Eli, their breath rising as vapor in the frigid air. Hamilton carefully studied him as Washington spoke.

"Scout Eli Stroud?"

"Yes."

"I've heard remarkable things about your work up north. It is good to know you're back. Are you all right?"

"Yes."

"This is Colonel Alexander Hamilton, one of my aides."

Eli remembered Hamilton and his cannon at Trenton and Princeton. He nodded, and a quizzical expression flitted over Hamilton's face. *Hasn't anyone ever taught this man to salute?*

Washington continued. "Your companion reported several weeks ago. I take it you remained there?"

"With my sister. We were separated when the Iroquois took me. I hadn't seen her for seventeen years. I hope it wasn't a wrong thing—to stay for a while."

"It was right. Is she well?"

Washington saw the look that came into Eli's eyes, and the general felt the warmth it brought to his heart.

"She's fine. Married. Two children. Happy. Good husband. Captain Benjamin Fielding, New Hampshire Militia. He was with us at the Saratoga fight."

For a moment Washington paused to savor the story before he went on. "Your companion—Corporal Weems?—reported earlier. I know about your activities at Three Rivers, and with the Mohawk. Chief Joseph. General Benedict Arnold—your stratagem with that demented man—Han Yost?"

"Yes."

"Were you with Corporal Weems at Saratoga?"

"Yes."

"At the Breymann redoubt?"

"With Billy and Benedict Arnold."

"You saw it?"

"Billy and I were inside the redoubt with the Hessians."

"Remarkable."

"I got to ask one thing. Is Gates getting credit for taking down Burgoyne?"

Hamilton tensed, waiting for the answer.

"As it now stands, he is receiving much praise. Yes."

Eli's voice rose, and there was lightning in his eyes. "It's wrong. He never got within four miles of the fight. It was Arnold. He turned that whole campaign. I was there when his horse went down and pinned his broken leg. Still had his sword in his hand. Still shouting to us to go on, take the redoubt. And we did. It was him. Not Gates."

Hamilton grimaced. Washington's back stiffened. "I've heard. The truth is a stubborn thing. Somehow it will all come out. There is one thing I would like to hear from you."

Eli waited. Washington's eyes narrowed slightly. "Considering conditions as they saw them, did either General Schuyler or General St. Clair make major errors in the actions they took? Giving up Fort Ticonderoga and retreating?"

Eli's answer was instant. "No. Neither man. What they did saved most of the army they had, and that army is what stopped Burgoyne, finally. They did right."

For several seconds Washington remained silent. "Is there anything else?"

"About up north? I doubt it. If Billy reported, you likely heard it all. But I got a few other questions."

Washington's eyebrows arched. "Yes?"

Eli hooked a thumb over his shoulder. "Good men out there, freezing. Starving. Sick. No shoes. No clothes. What's happened?"

Washington drew a great breath and slowly let it out. "It seems Congress and the Pennsylvania Supreme Executive Council do not understand the conditions we are facing here. We receive encouragement and instruction from them, but little else. There is nothing more I can say."

"There's food out in the countryside. Cattle. I came through it on my way here. Can't they get it to us?"

"The administration is young. Just learning its business. We have to be patient."

"Two more months of this and half those men will be dead. Or gone."

Washington returned his steady gaze and said nothing.

"Have you asked some of those men in Congress to come here and see?"

"I have, and they did. They made their report, and little happened."

Eli shifted his weight and took control of a rising anger. "It's a hard thing to see these men the way they are, when there's grain and cattle and clothes out there."

"I agree. The problem is, how do we get it?"

"Isn't there some kind of law—I've heard about it—that you can just take it if you have to?"

"Yes, there is. And maybe we'll have to do it. But this whole revolution is being fought to determine what powers government should and should not have."

Eli slowly shook his head, baffled, struggling. "Congress gave you an army and orders to drive out the British, but they won't feed or clothe your army, and they won't let you do it yourself. Is that where we are?"

"It isn't that Congress won't take care of us. The hard truth is, they can't. The Articles of Confederation give them no such powers."

"Then someone better take a hard look at those articles."

Washington remained silent. Hamilton shifted his weight, eyes intently following both Washington and Eli.

Suddenly Eli wiped at his mouth. "I've said too much . . . I . . . it's just that seeing those men out there . . . I shouldn't have said so much."

"Is there anything else?"

"No. Yes. One thing. If there's anything I can do—if I can go scout out the British, where their supplies are—maybe capture some of them—try to find a way to get food and clothes and blankets—anything."

"I understand. Should that be needed you will hear from me."

"That's all I have to say."

"Your report will go into the orderly book. You are dismissed."

Eli turned and walked out without looking back. He took his rifle from the picket and walked east in the early shades of a purple dusk. There were fires with shoeless, coatless men huddled around in the bitter cold, without blankets, and there were no cook kettles in sight. It was full dark when he approached the fire where Billy and Turlock and their squad was gathered. Eli's wolf-skin coat lay on a log nearby. He picked it up and had it on when he stopped beside Billy, who was staring into the dancing flames.

"Where's the man who had this?"

Billy shook his head, and Turlock answered quietly.

"He died."

Back in his tent, Washington rose from his table, no longer able to remain seated with the smoldering anger that had ridden him raw for days. For a time he paced as he struggled to maintain a tenuous control of the outrage that surged each time he saw in his mind's eye his men, slowly dying for want of everything it took to maintain an army in winter. It was approaching midnight before he sat down on his cot, fully dressed, including his cloak, unbuckled the spurs from his boots, tossed them clattering on the table, and lay down.

Rose and yellow colors were high in the eastern sky when the voice of Alexander Hamilton wakened him.

"Sir, I have a report you should read."

Washington sat up, stiff from the cold, squinting as his mind came back to reality.

Hamilton handed him the paper, and Washington read the scrolled handwriting.

"Yesterday a column of British cavalry and infantry marched from Philadelphia towards Derby on what is certainly a foraging expedition."

He looked at Hamilton. "Have you read this?"

"Yes, sir."

"We must march against that column. Give my orders to our general officers to have their commands ready to march at once. Have Colonel Laurens help you."

"Yes, sir."

Washington broke ice from the top of the water in the porcelain pitcher on the washstand in the corner, poured a basin half full, shaved, washed himself, and was ready when Hamilton returned. John Laurens was with him.

Hamilton cleared his throat and came straight to it.

"Sir, we notified all general officers of your orders. To a man, their response was the same." He paused to lick at dry, chapped lips. "Each reported that his command is unable to move from this camp."

Washington stood in shock. Never in his life had he received such a report, not from this army, nor from any other in which he had served, as far back as the French and Indian War in 1755, when he had fought side by side with General Braddock! An army that cannot leave camp? Preposterous! Unthinkable!

"Tell them I rescind the order and then you return here. I will have a document that must be delivered at once."

Laurens looked at Hamilton, and Hamilton looked at Laurens, and both men pivoted and walked out.

Washington sat down at his worktable and in seconds had quill and paper at hand. He wrote with very little pause.

December 22, 1777

To the Hnble Henry Laurens, President, Congress of the United States:

Sir:

It is with infinite pain and concern that I must again dwell on the state of the Commissary's department. I do not know from what cause this alarming deficiency or rather total failure of supplies arises, but unless more vigorous exertions and better regulations take place, and immediately, this Army must dissolve. The presently vacant offices of Quartermaster General and Commissary General should be filled as soon as possible. Unless some great and capital change suddenly takes place in those departments, this army must inevitably be reduced to one or other of these three things: starve, dissolve, or disperse, in order to obtain subsistence in the best manner they can. This is not an exaggerated picture. Vinegar to combat scurvy, and other such articles we see none of. As of this date, no one in this camp has had food for two days. Our stores are depleted. There is no meat, no flour, no vegetables. Men are starving to death daily. Sickness is becoming epidemic. Soap is nearly non existent. Few men have more than one shirt, many only the moiety of, and some none at all. An exceeding number of the troops are confined to hospitals and to local farmhouses for no other reason than a want of shoes and other clothing. By a field return this day made, no less than 2,898 men are now in camp unfit for duty because they are barefoot and otherwise naked. Exclusive of the troops sent to Wilmington with General Smallwood some time ago, those remaining in this camp are reduced to the perilous number of no more than 8,200, though more than 17,000 men were carried on the paper returns of the army.

Regarding the Pennsylvania Supreme Executive Council and their declared wish that this army should attack the enemy, I can assure those Gentlemen that it is a much easier and less distressing thing to draw remonstrances in a comfortable room by a good fireside than to occupy a cold, bleak hill, and sleep under frost and snow without clothes or blankets. However, although the Council seems to have little feeling for the naked and distressed soldiers, I feel superabundantly for them, and from my soul pity those miseries they are now suffering, which it is neither in my power to relieve nor prevent.

He stopped, laid down his quill, and reread all he had written. He saw his anger leaping off the paper, and he did not care. If Congress, or the Pennsylvania Supreme Executive Council, took offense, then let them do as they wished. If they should find it necessary to relieve him as the commander in chief, then so be it. At that moment there was but one thought in Washington's mind: His men had suffered enough. He would defy both the national Congress and the Pennsylvania Council, if he must, to feed and clothe his army.

He signed and folded the paper, sealed it, and stood. "Colonel Hamilton, are you there?"

Hamilton pushed through the tent flap. "Yes, sir?"

"Find the horse and man most fit for travel and have this missive delivered to Henry Laurens at York. He is currently president of our national Congress."

"I know who he is, sir. May I suggest, sir, that the man most fit for travel is probably Scout Eli Stroud. He has eaten regularly until when he arrived yesterday, and he has clothing that will turn the cold."

"Find him a good horse."

"Yes, sir." Hamilton turned to leave, then paused. "Sir, hasn't anyone ever taught Stroud to salute?"

Washington's face clouded for a moment. "Unfortunately, no. But, notwithstanding, I wish I had a thousand more just like him."

Notes

The horrible condition of the Continental Army at Valley Forge in late December is again partially chronicled. Six thousand soldiers lacked blankets, half lacked shoes, few had coats and were wearing rags. See Martin, *Private Yankee Doodle*, pp. 100–4

On December 21, 1777, pursuant to information that a British column was marching toward the small town of Derby on an expedition to obtain food and supplies, Washington ordered his army to prepare to march to meet it. He was informed that the Continental Army was incapable of marching out of camp. Stunned, shocked, and angered, Washington sat at his table on December 22–23 and wrote his now famous letter to Congress, addressing it to the president, Henry Laurens, who was father of Washington's trusted aide, John Laurens. The text of his writing is presented herein, most of it verbatim, and clearly shows Washington's anger at both Congress and the Pennsylvania Supreme Executive Council for their failure to sustain the army. It is from this letter that the phrase "a cold, bleak hill" is taken, the title of this volume of the series. See Reed, *Valley Forge: Crucible of Victory*, pp. 9–10; Wildes, *Valley Forge*, p. 153; Freeman, *Washington*, p. 172.

Valley Forge
December 26, 1777

CHAPTER XXI

★ ★ ★

*T*he snow that began falling on December twenty-fifth held through the night. Dawn on December twenty-sixth was little more than a change from blackness to deep gray as a thick blanket of clouds shrouded the world, and the great flakes continued to fall in dead air, steadily piling in the forests and the fields and on the winding dirt roads.

Paunchy, balding, aging Dr. Leonard Folsom, major in the Continental Army, sat on the driver's seat of the lead wagon of his column of eight as it moved west, intently watching the snow-covered ground ahead for mounds, listening to the muffled sounds of horses' hooves and wagon wheels plowing through six inches of snow. Too many times in the past thirty days, the road-weary horses, pulling the heavy wagons, had stumbled on logs or tree stumps or stones hidden beneath the white blanket that covered the narrow, rutted, winding road. Twice wagons had slammed into rocks hard enough to shatter wheels, one in front, two in back. The first time it had cost them half a day to unload the sealed wooden crates of medicines and surgical equipment, cut and trim a sapling pine, roll a rock into place to serve as a fulcrum, and lever the wagon off the ground, one side at a time. Then they labored in the cold and wet to remove the master bolts, pull the three undamaged wheels, lash them to the side of Folsom's lead wagon, load the crated medical supplies on the remaining wagons, abandon the wrecked one, and push on. The second time they used the spare wheels from the abandoned wagon at the cost of another half a day. Folsom had no more half-days to spare, so he watched the road for potential hazards.

Since leaving Morristown with nine wagons and the remains of his medical staff and their equipment in late August, he had pursued the wandering Continental Army over half the eastern section of the state of Pennsylvania, frustration mounting daily at what appeared to be the army's insane wanderings to all points on the compass. Three times he had blundered to within one mile of the British army. That he and his precious medical supplies and his skeleton staff had not been captured by the redcoats was a matter of profound mystery to him. He had lately been told at Whitemarsh that once again he was six days behind General Washington and the army, that they had marched out westward, to a place called Valley Forge. He had rested the horses and his staff for one day, then doggedly pushed on through the winter rains and snows and the freezing nights.

The thirty-two horses pulling the eight remaining wagons were nearing the breaking point. The winter hair hanging from their jaws and bellies was ragged, and their bones were showing beneath their hides. Many of their iron shoes had worked loose, and the five men remaining with the Folsom column had jerked the nails and pulled the shoes to keep them from crippling the horses. The frogs on the hind feet of two horses had been critically bruised by rocks in crossing the Raritan River, and the horses had to be let out of harness for more than ten days while they healed. Eight times the men had used sharpened sticks to dig caked ice out of the hooves to keep from freezing the frogs of all the horses.

The fourteen women in the column had long since taken their share of the work—cooking, mending, standing night picket, taking their rotation of sleeping in the wagons and on the open, frozen ground, insisting they take the same dwindling rations as the men, taking their turn driving the horses. They bore it all in stoic silence, living on the hope that one day soon they would reach the Continental Army. Food. Warmth. Blankets. Shelter. Cheeks hollow and with sunken eyes, the twenty had pushed on through it all, living on hope.

Folsom turned for a moment to peer inside the lurching wagon, where Mary Flint sat with two other women, bundled in blankets, heads nodded forward, eyes closed. They were silent, unmoving, unfeeling of the endless pitching of the wagon. None had energy that could be used other than on the necessities of surviving one more day.

He turned back to watch the rhythmic rise and fall of the horses' heads as they plowed on, and a look of deep concern, of fear, came into his eyes. *She's getting worse. I can hear her lungs rattle sometimes. She needs six months in a hospital bed with good food—No other way I know to stop the pneumonia. She ought not be out in this cold—ought not be working—I'll have to declare her unfit—confine her to the wagon—maybe that will stop her—save her.*

The narrow road had been cut through the thick woods years before, meandering through the places of least resistance. It curved to the left a quarter mile ahead, out of sight behind the snow-covered pines. Folsom's thoughts ran on.

She's living to see that man—Stroud. If anything has happened to him—or it turns out he has no feelings for her—it might kill her.

He shifted his weight, then removed his flat-brimmed felt hat to throw the snow off and then settle it back on his head.

Time will tell.

They nooned beyond the stand of pines. The men built fires and set the kettles and filled them with snow. The women diced the last of the salt pork belly and shriveled potatoes, added what salt they had left, and portioned it out steaming into wooden bowls, with army hardtack. They all moved into the shelter of the trees to sip at the scalding gruel and work at the brittle hardtack while the snow covered their heads and shoulders. Then they cleaned their utensils and cook pots and moved on.

It was just past two o'clock when they broke into a clearing and heard the unmistakable sound of axes ringing in the far distance. Folsom half stood in the wagon box, peering into the veil of falling snow, holding his breath.

British axes or American?

Then he saw the downward slope of the land before them, and at the bottom the black, winding course of a river, and his heart leaped.

The Schuylkill? Let it be the Schuylkill.

He slapped the leather reins on the rumps of the wheel horses and gigged them, and they raised their pace. He was nearly to the river when he saw through the swirling snow men on the other side of the river— thousands of bearded men up and down the banks as far as he could see, in tattered clothing, with few tents, swinging axes and pushing saws to make logs to raise walls of small huts. He found the bridge that crossed the river to Pennypacker's Mill and led his diminutive column thumping across. Everyone on his staff was peering out, faces bright, hope shining in their eyes.

Two barefoot, bearded, scarecrow men laid down their axes and picked up their muskets. "Who are you?"

"Major Leonard Folsom. Doctor. From Morristown. These are members of my medical staff. Are you the Continental Army?"

"What's left of it. Do you have any food in those wagons? Beef? Pork? Any shoes? Clothes?"

For an instant Folsom and all his people stared, and then they looked at other men nearby who had stopped work at the sight of the wagons. It was all wrong! These men were not soldiers, fed, clothed, sheltered, robust. These men were emaciated, in tatters, without shoes, starving, freezing. The people in the wagons stared while their brains struggled to comprehend what they had come into.

Folsom shook his head. "No food or clothes. We have medical supplies in the wagons. Where can I find the surgeon in charge?"

The light in the man's eyes died. "No food?"

"None. Who's the surgeon?"

The man wiped a wet hand across a wet beard. "Albigence Waldo. At a house—brick—about a mile due east, on that trail." He pointed.

The teams picked their way through the sprawl of the camp, with Folsom and the others staring in disbelief at the destitute men and the filth. They counted thirteen dead horses within one hundred feet of the wagon, some carcasses half eaten, some frozen stiff, some still warm. There were no latrines; human waste was wherever men had stopped to relieve themselves. Folsom counted three hundred men seated on logs, shaking with fever. He stopped counting.

They came to the brick house, and the wagons stopped. Folsom clambered down and walked to the door to bang on it with a balled fist. A woman—short, heavy, hair awry, tired eyes—opened the door.

"Yes?"

Folsom removed his hat. "I'm Major Leonard Folsom. A doctor. I'm told Albigence Waldo is here."

"He is."

Folsom pointed over his shoulder. "I'm here with my staff and some medical supplies from Morristown. I'm under orders to deliver them to the Continental Army. I presume Dr. Waldo is the proper person to receive them."

"Won't you come in? I'll get him."

"My staff?"

"There is no room."

"I'll wait here."

The door closed, and one minute later it opened again. Dr. Albigence Waldo stood in the door frame, average height and build, goatee beard, piercing dark eyes that were sunken, hollow. His shirt was open at the throat, soiled, and his vest was worn, wrinkled.

"Dr. Folsom?"

"Yes. Reporting. I have some people and medical supplies."

Waldo's shoulders slumped. "You don't know how welcome you are. I'll get some men to help unload."

"The lady said you have no room inside."

Waldo's eyes hardened. "We have one hundred eighty men in here. There is scarcely room for one hundred. We'll put the supplies in the stables."

"Do you have any food? Any place my people can take shelter? We are without."

Waldo wiped at his mouth. "I'll find some. Somehow. For now, drive the wagons behind the house and take shelter in the horse barn. It's stone. Tear down the partitions for wood to start a fire. There's straw for bedding. I'll deliver what blankets I can."

Waldo started to turn and Folsom stopped him.

"I've never seen a . . . catastrophe . . . like this."

Waldo shook his head. There was a look of fear in his eyes. "Nor have I. We have a great deal of fever. And pneumonia. The filth—I can't believe the filth. Two men inside have smallpox, but I don't dare say it aloud. If an epidemic starts in this camp . . ." Folsom saw the near panic in Waldo's eyes as he finished. "Dr. Folsom, you don't know how badly we need your supplies and your people."

The barn was tight. The men used a pick and an ax to smash three partitions to kindling. Minutes later they had a fire burning in the center of the floor, and a window open in the hayloft to draw the smoke. They unloaded crates of medical supplies for the women to sit on and brought blankets to wrap about their shoulders.

Soldiers came to unload the wagons into the long, low stable building next to the barn, then unhitched the horses and led them inside to throw them what little dried grass remained from the fall harvest. The horses buried their noses and didn't move as the sounds of grinding began.

Men brought one peck of potatoes sprouting eyes, one strip of salt sowbelly, half a venison ham, a basket of shriveled apples, four loaves of three-day-old bread, and two buckets of buttermilk. The women erected the tripod and hung the cook kettle above the fire, the men brought snow to melt, and half an hour later they bowed their heads while Folsom returned a heartfelt thanks for the bounty. They portioned out a steaming, saltless stew with thick slices of butterless bread and drank thick buttermilk and chewed on soft, shriveled apples. No one spoke a word as the warmth spread from their pinched stomachs. No one could remember food ever tasting sweeter.

In late dusk Folsom gave his small command their orders to prepare sleeping quarters in the barn, pulled his hat low, and walked out into the freezing night. Nearly two hours later he returned. All but one of his staff had gone to their beds, the men at one end of the barn, the women at the other, with blankets strung on a line to separate them. The single person sitting on a wooden crate, wrapped in a blanket, watching the low flames of the dying fire rose to face him.

Folsom saw the mixed emotions in Mary's eyes—hope, fear, anticipation, hesitancy—and he heard it in her voice as she quietly spoke.

"Did you go to find Eli Stroud?"

Folsom nodded.

"Did you find him?"

"I found the Massachusetts Regiment. Talked with a corporal—Billy Weems—and a sergeant. A little man named Turlock."

Mary raised a hand to cover her mouth, and Folsom saw the leap of terror in her eyes.

"No, he's not harmed. He came in from the north a few days ago. General Washington sent him to carry a message to Congress. They're sitting in York, west of here, about seventy or eighty miles. He has at least two rivers to cross and a lot of ground to cover. In this weather it will take a few days. He has a horse. Should be back anytime."

Mary dropped her hand. "He's unharmed?"

"He's fit. That's why Washington picked him. That and the fact he apparently knows how to take care of himself in the woods."

Mary's dark eyes closed for a moment, and her shoulders sagged in relief. "Thank you. Thank you."

"Get to your bed. You need rest more than anything else right now."

With the fire coals banked for morning, Mary burrowed into the straw fully dressed, as were the others, and pulled her blanket under her chin. *He's alive—unharmed—carrying a message to Congress—return soon— soon—soon.*

She drifted into sleep seeing his face—the eyes—the chin—the scar along his jawline . . .

Twenty-eight miles to the west, in the hush of deep woods in snow, Eli sat cross-legged on pine boughs piled a foot deep beneath the lean-to he had built at nightfall—one for himself, another for the bay gelding that had carried him to York, where he had delivered two messages to Henry Laurens. One from General George Washington, the second from his son, Colonel John Laurens, personal aide-de-camp to the general. Laurens requested he remain for one day while he decided if there would be a return message. There were two, one for Washington, the other for his son. Laurens thanked Eli warmly, gave him a sack of oats for the horse, a second pouch of meat and potatoes for himself, and watched him out of sight as he raised the gelding to a gentle lope to disappear in the falling snow, traveling east with both sacks tied to the saddle.

★ ★ ★ ★ ★

Eli looked across the five-foot gap between himself and the lean-to sheltering the horse, where the firelight reflected ruby-red in the horse's eyes. For a time Eli listened to the grinding as the horse worked on the oats, and he let his thoughts go as they would.

Peaceful—always peaceful in heavy snow—Laurens is a good man—he'll help Washington if he can—if no help comes the army will fall to pieces—the revolution will be finished—must find help.

He stopped to listen for sounds in the forest, and there were none, save the crackle and hiss of his small fire and the grinding of his horse's teeth. In heavy snow the wild creatures knew to find their nests or their burrows or their caves.

I've seen no British—no patrols—must all be in Philadelphia in comfort. Not the Continentals—never seen an army in that condition.

He reached to bank the fire, then lay down on the pine boughs and pulled his blanket up.

I wonder if Mary is coming—is she all right?—when will I see her? He yearned to touch her, hold her close. The beautiful dark eyes and the generous mouth were the last thing he saw as sleep came.

Four o'clock found him mounting the bay gelding, with a breakfast of sizzling meat and baked potato in his belly and what remained of his food in the two sacks wrapped in his blanket and tied behind the saddle. At eight o'clock the snow stopped, and a bright winter sun came through the clouds to turn the Pennsylvania woods into a blinding, shining world of white. Nine o'clock found horse and rider fourteen miles farther east, pushing steadily on through the snow, two-feet deep in places where it had drifted. A little past ten o'clock the horse tossed its head and pricked its ears, and Eli eased back on the reins, instantly searching for what the horse had seen or heard that he had not. His rifle lay balanced across his thighs, behind the saddle bow, muzzle pointing left.

Movement brought his head around, eyes narrowed, as he watched five mounted horsemen break clear of the woods one hundred fifty yards away, each with a musket, bringing their horses in at a lope from the north, to his left. The heavily bearded men wore black, flat-brimmed felt hats, and on the shoulders of their leader were the epaulets of a captain. On the captain's signal, the four riders behind him spread slightly, opening a clear line between themselves and Eli. Eli had his reins in his left hand. His right hand was away from the approaching riders, and they could not see him move it far enough to cock his rifle and slip his finger inside the trigger guard.

They were fifty yards away when the leader pulled his horse down to a walk and raised his right hand, then called, his voice echoing in the silence.

"Identify yourself."

"Stroud."

"White or Injun? You look Injun."

"White."

"Loyalist or patriot?"

Eli had two seconds to make up his mind. "American. Who are you?" He moved the rifle far enough to bring the muzzle in line with the leader, and he waited.

"Pennsylvania Militia. Where are you going?"

"To the army camp. Valley Forge. You?"

"Same place. We'll ride along with you."

"You out on patrol?"

"Yes."

"From Valley Forge?"

"Yes."

Eli studied them as they walked their horses toward him. They all wore heavy woolen coats. Their horses were in good flesh. All wore boots. Their cheeks were full, ruddy. Each man carried his musket across his thighs, with his right hand on the hammer and trigger.

At ten feet their leader reined his horse to a stop, a broad smile showing through his beard. "We thought for sure you was an Injun, with that wolf-skin coat and them moccasins and all and that rifle."

"I spent some time with the Iroquois." The eyes of the four silent men were going over Eli and his rifle, his horse, his saddle.

Eli continued. "Been out on patrol long?"

"Yesterday. Got to report back today. Heard the British were out stealing from the farmers. We was sent to find out. What are you doing out here?"

"Sent to deliver a message."

"To who?"

"A man in York. West of here. Who sent you out on scout?"

There was a pause. The smile disappeared in the beard. "You with the Pennsylvania Division at camp?"

"No, but I know most of the officers. Which one sent you?"

All five men started to raise their muskets to swing the barrels to bear on Eli when Eli raised his rifle, the muzzle steady on the middle button of the thick woolen coat on the leader, and Eli's voice rang out.

"Stop where you are or this man dies."

Looking into the muzzle of the long Pennsylvania rifle, the five immediately eased their muskets back down across their thighs.

"Now open the pans and empty out all the powder and then drop your muskets in the snow."

The leader shook his head. "You can't get us all."

"After the first shot, you won't much care. Empty the powder and drop the muskets. Now!"

For three full seconds the five men battled indecision before their leader nodded. He hit the frizzen on his musket, opened the pan, dumped the powder, and tossed his musket away. It disappeared in the snow. The others dumped the powder and threw theirs down.

"Undo your weapons belts and throw them away."

All five weapons belts, with the belt knives, were thrown into the snow.

"You four get off those horses and tie the reins of your horse to the tail of the one next to you. You've got one minute. Make a break if you feel like it. It's all the same to me if your leader goes down."

The reins were quickly knotted in the long winter tails, and the four horses strung out in a line.

"Now hand the reins of the lead horse to your captain, and then the four of you run west. I'm going to watch you out of sight. Move!"

Five minutes later all four men had disappeared in the woods, and Eli turned to their leader, still sitting his horse, holding the reins of the lead horse in the string. His face was a study in venomous hatred.

Eli still held his cocked rifle trained on the man's midsection. "Head due east and lead those horses. I'm right here beside you. Make a try for freedom whenever it suits you."

The man stared at the muzzle of the rifle for a moment, then back at Eli's eyes, and made his decision. He licked his lips, dug his spurs into the flanks of his horse, and the bunch started east at a trot, their breath streaming behind their heads as they plowed through the smooth field of white before them.

Eli paced the horses—trot, walk, trot, walk—to keep from sweating them in the frigid air. He stopped twice to let them catch their wind, both times remaining mounted with his rifle covering the bearded man with the epaulets.

It was midafternoon when the distant sound of axes reached them, and ten minutes later when they passed a neck of snow-covered oak trees, the west end of the Continental Army camp was before them. Men stopped to stare as Eli pushed on with his cocked rifle still trained on the man leading the four horses, across the bridge that spanned Valley Creek, and reined in at the command tent of General Washington.

The pickets gaped as Eli ordered his prisoner to dismount, then stepped down and walked him to the tent.

The taller picket was just under eighteen years of age, rawboned, feet wrapped in canvas. "Uh . . . who . . . what is your business here?"

"Tell General Washington that Eli Stroud is returning with messages from York. And a prisoner."

"I . . . yes, sir."

The picket dodged inside the flap and burst back out in ten seconds to hold the flap high. General Washington ducked to clear the opening and stepped into the brilliant, late afternoon, cold sunlight, followed by Hamilton and Laurens. The three men stared for a few moments at the strange assembly standing before them in ten inches of new snow, vapors rising from the heads of six horses and two men.

Washington broke the quiet. "Come in."

The picket looked at Eli. "I . . . that rifle . . . I think I'm supposed to take the rifle."

Eli uncocked it and handed it to the boy, then drew his tomahawk from his weapons belt, slipped the leather thong over his wrist to let it dangle, and gave his prisoner a nod. They followed Washington, Hamilton, and Laurens into the tent and stood before the table, waiting for Washington to speak.

Washington took his seat, Hamilton and Laurens at either side. "Report."

Eli reached inside his coat and drew out an oilcloth packet. "I delivered the two messages to Henry Laurens. He sent back these two. One to you and one to his son."

Washington accepted the packet and laid it on the table. "Continue."

"On the way back this man with four others stopped me. Said they were on scout from the Pennsylvania Militia camped here. They wore good coats, boots, and rode horses that were in good flesh. None of the five looked like they'd missed a meal. They were taking an interest in my rifle and my horse and saddle." Eli looked at the prisoner, standing rigid, anger fairly dripping from him. "I asked him the name of his commanding officer. He didn't give it. I took this one and turned the other four loose because I couldn't bring in all five, but I brought their horses."

Washington looked at the man for a time. "Can you name your commanding officer?"

The man's face grew red as he stammered, then blurted. "Nash. General Nash."

Washington's voice was controlled. "Unfortunately General Nash died of wounds sustained at the battle of Germantown." He turned to Laurens. "Have the pickets place this man under arrest."

A wild look crossed the man's face as though he would bolt for the entrance, and in that instant Eli grasped the handle of his tomahawk and turned to face him, feet spread, balanced, ready. The man froze, then slowly raised his hands, eyes never leaving the dreaded black tomahawk. Laurens quickly brought the pickets while Hamilton ran to get half a dozen more soldiers, and the eight of them left the tent with their bayonets high, their muskets cocked, and their prisoner locked between them.

Washington sat back down and waited for a few moments before he spoke.

"We've had reports from the local citizens that there are roving bands of robbers and thieves masquerading as our soldiers. They steal from anyone—the citizens, the British, our soldiers. Some have committed murder. I think you've just brought one in. He will be tried, and if he is such a man, he'll be hanged."

Eli slipped the tomahawk back in his weapons belt, with Hamilton and Laurens staring at it.

"You also brought in their horses?"

"Outside."

Washington turned to Hamilton. "Do what you can to find out if any of those animals were stolen from local citizens. If anyone can support a claim, return the horse to him. If not, keep them for our officers."

"Yes, sir."

Washington turned back to Eli. "Is there anything else?"

Eli reflected for a moment. "Not that I can think of. You have the messages."

Washington picked up the packet and opened it, then handed a sealed envelope to John Laurens. "Sir, that is for you from your father."

"Thank you, sir."

Washington turned back to Eli. "You are dismissed."

Eli nodded, turned, and walked out of the tent, continuing steadily through the camp. With the sun setting, he slowed as he came to the Massachusetts regiment. He stopped at the hut his squad had been working on. The walls were raised and the rafters partly in place, ready for the roofing. He found Billy helping with the firewood for the evening fires and came in from behind him.

"You've been busy while I was gone."

Billy turned. "We're ready to roof." He paused for a moment. "Mary's here."

Eli's head jerked forward. "Where?"

Turlock came running as Billy continued.

"She's billeted in a barn behind the house where the head surgeon is staying. His name's Albigence Waldo. About a mile back to the west."

Turlock cut in. "You go."

"Is she all right?"

Billy answered, "She looks tired. Thin. But she can see you. Go on."

"What's the name of that surgeon?"

"Waldo. Albigence Waldo. Ask if you don't find him."

Without a word Eli handed his rifle to Billy, turned on his heel, and left at a run. He didn't slow until he saw the stone house with the wagons at the side and the large stone barn behind, with the stables. He stopped at the door and pounded. A thin, sad-faced nurse opened it.

"What's the commotion?"

"Ma'am, I'm looking for a woman named Mary Flint. A nurse. She's supposed to be billeted in a barn behind a stone house where a surgeon named Waldo is staying."

"Dr. Waldo is staying here. You must be talking about one of the nurses who arrived yesterday from Morristown."

"Where are they?"

"In the stone barn behind the house."

Without a word Eli sprinted around the house, angling toward the barn, when the door opened and a paunchy, balding man hurried out, walking rapidly toward the back door of the house. The man lifted his head at the sound of Eli running and raised a hand to stop him.

"This is a hospital. What's your business here?"

"I'm looking for a nurse. Mary Flint."

Folsom's eyes widened. "You're Stroud?"

"I am. Is Mary here?"

"Young man, you follow me back to the barn, and you wait outside."

Two minutes later Eli stopped, and Folsom walked into the dark interior of the barn. He left the door open.

Eli's breath came short, and his heart was singing. *She's here, she's here, she's here.*

As if by magic she was standing in the doorway. All she had planned, all she had dreamed of saying and doing when she saw him vanished. Everything he had thought, all he had expected to do was gone. For two full seconds they stood ten feet apart, staring in disbelief, and then Mary threw open her arms and ran to him, and he ran to her. He swept her into his arms, and they clung to each other in the golden glow of the sunset, knowing only that they were together, lost in the wonder of the touch and the feel of it. Mary tipped her head back to look into his face, and she reached to kiss him. In his life Eli had never kissed a woman, and for a moment he did not know what to do. Mary kissed him again, and he kissed her back, and they stood in the snow, wrapped in each other's arms. For them the world was forgotten.

Standing just inside the darkened barn, Leonard Folsom quietly watched, remembering, seeing a girl named Emily that he had once held close and who had borne his children and grown old with him. He reached to wipe at his eyes and then closed the door.

Notes

The reader is familiar with Major Leonard Folsom, a doctor who brought his staff, including Mary Flint, and medical supplies from Morristown to find the Continental Army. Both Dr. Folsom and Mary Flint are fictional characters.

Hospital conditions at Valley Forge were deplorable. See Reed, *Valley Forge: Crucible of Victory*, pp. 13–14, 25.

Eli Stroud's meeting with the five men on his return to Valley Forge is included to inform the reader that there were robbers and murderers roving the farms and roads in and around Pennsylvania. They called themselves "volunteers" and blamed their plundering on the Continental Army. Washington issued orders to arrest them when possible. The Doane Gang of Bucks County and the gang led by a man named Fitzpatrick—"Captain Fitz"—in Chester County were notorious. Captain Fitz was caught and hanged. See Reed, *Valley Forge: Crucible of Victory*, pp. 15–16.

CHAPTER XXII

★ ★ ★

*T*hick ice covered the Schuylkill River, bank to bank. Men swung axes three times a day to reopen holes for fresh water. Eight inches of snow was frozen to a crystallized powder that crunched and squeaked beneath the feet of the soldiers and the wagon wheels. When the wind blew, it moaned in the chimneys, and when it did not, deathly silence ruled the nights. The twelve-man squads that shared the huts kept the fires burning in the fireplaces around the clock, huddled close, wrapped in whatever they could find. The green firewood smoldered, filling the crude, unfinished huts with smoke that made the soldiers squint and wipe at their watering eyes, enduring the pain to absorb what little warmth they could.

The thousands who had no blankets used what they could find to cover themselves at night, including the few canvas summer tents that had survived. No squad had enough shoes or trousers or coats or shirts to stand guard duty, and they had learned to give the best they had to the man leaving to take his two-hour shift, hunched over from cramps in his empty belly, shivering in the deep, bitter cold. When that man returned, he stripped off all he had and handed it to the next man going out to stand picket, then wrapped himself in a blanket to crouch near the smoking fire, shivering, teeth chattering, coughing, eyes watering. If he had no shoes, a man endured his two-hour picket duty standing on a felt hat to keep his bare feet from freezing to the ground. Toes turned black, then putrid, and every day surgeons laid men on rough-sawed wooden tables in homes or barns or log cabins that were called hospitals. They gave them half a cup of whiskey to dull their senses, strapped them down, thrust a leather belt between their teeth, and used scalpel and saw to remove the dead member while the men writhed and groaned. When the surgeons ran out of scalpels, they turned to the razors used to shave.

At five minutes past midnight, Sergeant Randolph O'Malley pushed through the plank door of the hut he shared with his squad and closed it quickly. His red beard and sandy-red hair and eyebrows were white with frost. He leaned his musket against the wall and stepped around two of his men wrapped in blankets, sitting cross-legged close to the fireplace, and leaned forward to thrust out his hands until they were nearly in the flames. No one spoke.

After a time, O'Malley turned to peer toward Caleb Dunson, lying in a lower bunk against the south wall, completely hidden beneath a canvas tent he had folded twice to lay under for cover. Caleb's head appeared, and he raised on one elbow.

"Your duty," O'Malley said and untied the old gray scarf he had tied over his head to keep his ears from freezing. He shrugged out of the threadbare woolen coat each man wore as he went to stand his time. He shivered as he sat down to untie his shoes and toss them onto the hard-packed dirt floor beside Caleb's bunk. The shoes were old and battered and too large for O'Malley, and there was a hole in the sole of each. The men had cut and laid a piece of old harness leather inside to cover the holes.

The only light in the shelter was from the fireplace, where green wood smoldered and smoked and hissed, casting the room in a dim pall. O'Malley sat down and began rubbing his numb feet, peering intently to see if any of his toes were turning black.

Caleb shuddered as he pulled his stockings up, then reached for the shoes. His stockings had holes in both toes and both heels and gave no warmth inside the worn, hard-leather shoes. He slipped his feet in carefully to avoid moving the piece of harness leather that plugged the holes, then reached for the coat. He looped the scarf over his head and tied it beneath his chin, stepped around men to reach the door, and picked up his musket. Without a word he walked out into the frozen night, feeling the searing grab in his lungs. He clamped his mouth shut and breathed shallow as he headed for the river.

Overhead a brilliant quarter-moon and a million frozen diamonds turned the camp and the woods into a world of black and gray shadows. He had not gone ten paces when he felt the cold coming through his shoes and his face turning numb. Vapor streamed behind as he marched on toward the river, the snow creaking with each step.

His sentry post was a place less than fifty yards from the frozen Schuylkill, beneath a great pine tree where the men had cleared away most of the snow, down to the rock-hard dirt. He leaned his musket against the tree and backed up to the trunk, arms wrapped about himself for the little warmth it would bring, and began the torturous two-hour wait in the dead silence. His feet grew numb, and he moved them and slapped his arms about his chest to keep the blood flowing. He reached to rub his face until feeling came back and again stamped his feet until the numbness was gone and feeling returned.

Minutes that seemed an eternity crept by, and he found his mind wandering to places of more comfort and to happier scenes. His mother—the hearth and fire in their small Boston home—a table laden with roast mutton and steaming potatoes—the pungent aroma of mince pies baking—little Trudy with her plain face and shy smile—Matthew at the door—Brigitte at the church—old Silas thrusting a finger into the air as he preached from the raised pulpit—

Drowsiness came, and it frightened him. Since Christmas four men had grown drowsy on picket duty and sat down to let it pass. The warmth had come, and they had drifted into a peaceful sleep. They were found still sitting, frozen stiff.

He judged that one hour had passed before he allowed the thought and the question to take shape in his mind. *Will she come again tonight?* Three times in the last seven days she had appeared in the darkness, bundled in a coat and a hooded cape, to bring him something warm and to talk for a few moments. He let himself think her name—*Nancy*—*Nancy*—and he brought her face up as though she were there. The auburn hair, the green eyes, the smiling mouth, and he knew he had never seen a face as beautiful.

Will she come? Will she?

The creak of footfalls in the snow and the whisper came at the same moment. "Caleb?"

He peered into the darkness, searching. "I'm here."

She came to him, a shape wrapped in a hooded cape, dark against the snow, and she stopped, her face turned upward.

"I brought you something hot. Tea." She brought her hands from beneath the heavy cape. "Here." She handed him a pewter jar.

He took it between his hands and felt the warmth. "You shouldn't have come—it's so cold."

"Drink it while it's warm."

He pried off the lid and saw the steam rise, then raised it to sip. It was rich and sweet, and he sipped again. "So good. Thank you."

She stood silent for a time, watching him savoring the tea. "We have so many men coming to the hospital. Are you all right?"

"I'm fine."

"Frozen feet and ears. Pneumonia. Scabs. So much sickness. I think the doctor fears an epidemic. Smallpox. The fever."

Caleb looked down into her face. "I worry about you in that hospital. Are you well?"

"Tired. Not sick. Just tired."

"You should be back there. Not out here. You need your rest."

She lowered her gaze. "I can't stay there. I lie awake. It helps to get away. To come here."

Caleb felt his heart leap within. *To come here! To be near him!* She could not have said it more clearly. He fumbled for words, but none would come.

She raised her face once more, and the moonlight defined her eyes and her mouth. "Do you mind? Should I not come?"

He lowered the jar of tea. "You should come. I want you to."

She reached to lay her hand on his arm and then stepped close, face turned upward, looking him full in the face. She stood on tiptoes and brushed a kiss, then stepped back. "I . . . Caleb, I'm sorry. I didn't mean . . ."

He reached and drew her against him, and he kissed her, and then held her close for a time, her arms about his neck, his cheek on hers.

She released him and stepped back, and he saw the smile. "Your tea is getting cold."

He grinned. "I don't mind." He raised the jar and drank.

"Have you finished your cabin?"

"Close. The roof leaks."

"Have you been doing any writing?"

"For the orderly book?"

"That. Or anything."

"A few days ago. Some things about the regiment. Bad. Too many officers resigning. Fifty in one regiment. Too many men sick. Nearly three thousand. Six thousand without blankets. Half without shoes. Commissary empty—no food. If the British came tomorrow the generals believe we could lose the whole army."

"That bad?"

"That bad."

"Do you ever write letters to your mother?"

"I did. I lost it."

"Lost it?"

"At a battle."

"You should write another."

"I will."

"You should write to people you care for."

Looking down into her face, Caleb could not miss her meaning. "Yes, I should. If I wrote to you, would you read it?"

She raised a hand to her throat. "Yes. I would. Truly I would."

He finished the tea, pressed the lid back on the heavy jar, and handed it back to her. "Thank you. Out here in the cold, something warm means more than you know."

"I'm glad. I should go back. I'll sleep now."

"I hope so."

She turned, then stopped as he spoke.

"Nancy, I'm glad you came."

"So am I." She had gone five paces when she stopped and turned once more. "Write me that letter."

"I will."

He watched her disappear into the trees and stood for a full half minute, heart racing at the remembrance of her face—the feel of her as he held her—the transcendent magic of their kiss—her request that he write her a letter.

The creeping numbness and pain brought him back to the reality of standing on a riverbank in the dead of winter, and he stomped his feet, then threw his arms about himself, slapping his sides to keep the blood circulating. The slow arc of the moon settling toward the tree line was his clock, and when he gauged enough time had passed, he walked back to the hut and pushed inside, into the dim light and the smoke and the huddle of eleven men. With nearly frozen fingers, he fumbled to unlace and pull off the shoes, then peeled off the coat and the scarf for the man who was to take next picket duty, and watched him slowly put them on, stand, and step to the door. The man stood for a long time, hand on the latch, taking a last look at the sputtering fire. Then he opened the door and was gone.

Caleb was shivering when he got back into his bunk and pulled the folded tent completely over his head. He curled into a ball, and slowly the warmth came. The last clear thought before he slipped into sleep was of her—the sweetness of holding her for that brief time, the feel of her kiss.

The sun rose to turn the thick frost that coated every tree, every hut, into endless, shimmering, tiny prisms of blue, green, yellow, and rose. Smoke from two hundred chimneys rose straight into a blue sky. Men squinted against the brilliant sunlight reflecting off the frozen, crusted snow as they went about their duties of gathering firewood and drill. There was no food for breakfast—nothing—and they tightened their belts and promised themselves there would be food for supper. Savory meat. Meat and bread. Potatoes. Butter, home-churned butter, laid thick on the bread, and berry jam. Fresh milk in a tall, heavy, porcelain pitcher with trees and cows painted on the sides. And pie. Hot apple pie. They wiped at their mouths and hunched forward to relieve the pangs in their empty, clamoring bellies.

Four men scaled handmade ladders to take their positions on the roof while the other eight passed rough-cut planks up to be laid in place on the framed roof. Then they passed cut pine boughs up the ladders, to be laid thick on top of the planks. While they worked they watched for the officers walking or riding through camp. When one passed, they waited until he was five yards beyond their hut before they all chanted, "No meat, no soldier, no meat, no soldier."

Most officers slowed but did not turn. They had heard the chant a hundred times in the past few days, and they knew there was nothing they could do about it. Any officer who turned to reprimand the complainers would see only a squad of men working on their cabin as though nothing had been said.

At noon O'Malley climbed down from the ladder and put his hands on his hips. "Two more days and we'll be finished. Take one hour of rest. Get off your feet."

The men went to the shelter wall facing the sun and sat down on one of the logs to absorb what warmth they could. Two massaged their bare feet, trying to work the blue color from their toes. Caleb leaned back against the wall, eyes closed, head resting against the rough pine logs and the mud chinking, trying not to think of the ache in his belly and the weariness that had become a constant torment. He opened his eyes to scoop snow and thrust it into his mouth to ease his thirst. He scooped more and sucked and swallowed, then leaned back once more and closed his eyes. The noises and sounds of a massive army camp under construction blended into a oneness as drowsiness came, and then he was seeing her again, the moonlight on her upturned face, her dark eyes, and he was holding her and feeling the thrill of her kiss.

O'Malley's bark roused him. "All right. Back on your feet. We have a roof to finish."

The men silently rose to stretch set muscles and gather their strength for the afternoon. They squinted up at the sun, calculating time, then slowly moved back to their work positions. Caleb was walking toward the ladder, shoulder to shoulder with O'Malley, when a thought struck him for the first time.

Billy Weems! Is Billy in camp?

He wondered why he had not thought of it before and turned to O'Malley. "Is there a Boston regiment in camp? Or a Massachusetts regiment?"

O'Malley shrugged. "I don't know. Probably. Why?"

"No reason. Just wondered about a friend."

"From home? Boston?"

"Yes. Billy Weems. My older brother's best friend." A wistful look came into Caleb's eyes. "I can't remember not knowing Billy. I wonder why I never thought of him being here."

"You sure he joined the army?"

"Yes. He was nearly killed at Concord. Shot and bayoneted. Took him a year to mend, and then he left to join."

O'Malley started up the ladder. "There's bound to be a Massachusetts division somewhere in camp. Ask."

Caleb followed him up the rungs. "I will."

They crawled on their hands and knees to their positions on the sloped roof and waited for the men on the ground to pass up the clumped pine boughs. Without nails they could only jam the boughs into the cracks between the uneven planks and stack them deep, knowing that snow would sift through and wind would move them and they would leak when the spring thaws and rains came. They were counting the days until they would have shakes and nails.

Caleb took the first load of deep green boughs and began jamming the smaller branches into the cracks.

Billy. He'll want to know why I left Mother and Trudy, and I'll have to tell him— to punish the British. Make them pay for what they did to Father and Mother and the family. And to him. What will he say? Will he preach?—tell me that this revolution is in the hands of the Almighty? If it's in the hands of the Almighty, then why is the whole

Continental Army starving and freezing to death out here in the wilderness? Where's the Almighty when we need Him? What will Billy tell Mother?

Do I really want to find him?

Caleb paused, knowing he should find the oldest and dearest friend Matthew had ever known but unable to reconcile himself to what such a meeting might bring. A sense of peace would not come.

He accepted the next load of pine boughs and worked on.

Notes

In late December 1777 and early January 1778, the deplorable, wretched conditions at Valley Forge continued and worsened. The men lacked food, blankets, clothing, and shoes, and they were freezing. They used useless army tents to cover themselves against the cold. They shared clothing and stood barefoot on felt hats to keep from freezing their feet while on picket duty. Leckie, *George Washington's War*, pp. 435–436; Freeman, *Washington*, p. 363; Jackson, *Valley Forge: Pinnacle of Courage*, pp. 48–50, 64, 68, 70; Stokesbury, *A Short History of the American Revolution*, p. 176.

With medical equipment in critically short supply, when they had no scalpels for surgery, the doctors substituted razors used by the men to shave. Fisk, "The Organization and Operation of the Medical Services of the Continental Army, 1775–1783," p. 97.

CHAPTER XXIII

★ ★ ★

Vapors streamed behind their heads, and frozen snow crackled beneath their feet as Turlock and Billy made their way through the stark, frigid twilight toward the supply wagon that had rumbled into camp at sunset. Their eyebrows and beards were crusted with frost. Both men had ragged strips of cloth tied over their heads to protect their ears, and they walked hunched forward, trying to relieve the hunger pangs that gnawed in their empty bellies. They said nothing as they took their place in the line that was rapidly forming, two men from each company in the Massachusetts Regiment.

Seven men worked in the bed of the wagon, where eight flour barrels had their tops knocked out. Two men stood with muskets at the ready. Two held large flour scoops. Two reached over the sideboards of the wagon to take sacks or buckets or wooden boxes or whatever the soldier from each company handed up to them to get their ration. The last man in the wagon asked the number of the company and the name of the soldier, then with numb fingers penciled entries on a paper while the flour ration was scooped from the barrels into the container.

The line moved slowly, and the men stomped their feet to keep the blood flowing and shivered, teeth chattering, as they waited their turn. They looked at the four horses that stood in the harnesses, winter hair long and ragged, heads down, withers and hips pointed, ribs showing through their hides. There was little talk.

The man with the scoop reached over the side, and Turlock pulled the empty flour sack from within his coat and handed it up, then turned to the man with the pad.

"Turlock. Massachusetts—"

The man cut him off. "I know who you are, Sergeant." He made the entries as one man held the sack and the other scooped four loads into it, then lifted it over the side to Billy.

Turlock peered up. "Meat?"

The man with the pad shook his head but did not look at Turlock.

"When?"

Again the man shook his head as Billy peered into the half-filled sack. His eyes narrowed before he twisted the neck of the sack, then hoisted it onto his shoulder and walked away with Turlock beside him. They were halfway back to their hut before Turlock spoke.

"Been three days without meat. Nothing but flour. How much you got there?"

"Maybe forty pounds. A little less."

"What's it look like?"

"Mold. Weevil. Pretty bad."

"Forty pounds of bad flour for the company. Less than one pound per man. How long will it last? Two days? Three if we eat once a day? Keep this up, there won't be a Massachusetts Regiment." Billy glanced at Turlock. Breeches in tatters, feet wrapped in blood-stained sailcloth, a ragged, threadbare coat he had cut and sewn from the blanket of a dead man. The beginnings of deep fear for his men was in the eyes and the hawk-nosed face of the little man.

They stopped at their hut, and the men of the company came with a gourd or a wooden bowl or whatever they had to carry flour and stood in line while Billy held the sack and Turlock carefully portioned out a share to each man. "Don't know when you'll get more, so make it last."

The only question that was asked, over and over, was, "Meat?" And the only answer Turlock could give was, "Later."

Eli stood behind Turlock until the last man had received his share and silently walked away. With aching hearts the three of them watched the men gather snow and knew what their supper would be tonight—the same as it had been last night and would be tomorrow. They would melt snow at the fireplace inside their huts and, with smoke from green wood smarting their eyes, would pick what weevil they could from a halfcup of flour, ignore the mold, mix the flour with snow-water, shape it into a small, thin cake, and lay it on the coals at the edge of the fire to bake. They had no salt, no leavening, no lard—nothing but bad flour and snow-water. When the cakes were browned they would work them out of the coals with a stick and sit at the rough plank table in the center of the dirt floor and break off small pieces of the thin, hard cake and chew slowly, to get all the flavor, all the good they could from it. They drank melted snow-water and waited for the hunger pangs to leave for a time. They could not remember the last time they had anything to eat with their firecakes.

In full darkness Turlock turned the flour sack inside out, shook it, folded it, and stuffed it inside his coat. He picked up his wooden bowl of flour and without a word he, Billy, and Eli entered their smoke-filled hut. They paused for a moment to peer at the emaciated men, who were gathered about the fireplace, each watching his firecake with sunken eyes as it browned.

Eli spoke quietly. "This army won't last without meat. Vegetables. Straw. Something besides a dirt floor or boards to sleep on."

Turlock stared at his men but did not answer.

Billy answered. "How long before they break?"

There was no answer.

A banging at the door brought all heads around, and Eli's hand dropped to his tomahawk. Turlock lifted the latch and opened the door six inches and peered out. The dim light from the room reflected off the bearded face of a tall man in a tattered woolen coat.

"Lieutenant Nathan Wasserman. Sent by Colonel Hamilton for Gen'l. Washington. You from the Massachusetts Regiment?"

"Yes. What's your business?"

"Got someone in there named Stroud? Eli Stroud?"

Eli stepped to the door, behind Turlock, and Turlock answered. "Stroud's here."

"Gen'l Washington wants to see him at eight o'clock in the morning."

Eli's eyes widened. "What about?"

"Who are you?"

"Stroud."

Wasserman's eyes widened at the sight of a man clad in a wolf-skin coat, with an Iroquois weapons belt and tomahawk at his waist. "Didn't say. Just be there. Know where Washington's headquarters is?"

"Big stone house up by the creek? Valley Creek?"

"Eight o'clock." The man turned and vanished into the night.

Turlock closed the door and turned to Eli. "Any idea what Washington wants with you?"

Eli shrugged. "None."

"Anything in your report that could cause trouble?"

"Nothing I can think of. I told him the men were in hard times."

Turlock shook his head. "I imagine he had that figgered out by hisself. Well, you go see him in the morning."

Eli wiped at his beard. "I'm going to be gone a while. Up to see Mary."

Turlock nodded. "If anybody challenges, tell 'em I sent you for medical supplies."

Billy and Turlock watched Eli walk out the door into the frozen night before they set about mixing and shaping their own firecakes. When they were finished eating, Billy went to his bunk to draw out an oilcloth and laid it on the table. He unfolded it, then carefully lifted the writing pad from inside and laid it on the table. It was dog-eared and frayed, and he treated it with a reverence that Turlock could not miss.

"You writing to that girl again—Brigitte?" Turlock waited.

Billy nodded.

"How many letters you got there for her?"

Billy shrugged. "A few."

"You ever going to mail 'em?"

"Don't know yet."

"That the girl who's got her eye set on a British captain?"

"Yes."

"Might be wastin' your time."

"Maybe. Probably."

Turlock shook his head and remained silent. He knew only too well the futility of interfering in matters of the heart. There are some things in life that each person must learn for himself, in his own way, and in his own time. He turned away, toward his own bunk as Billy reached for his pencil and began to write.

> My Dear Brigitte:
>
> I am sitting at the table in the hut we have nearly finished here at Valley Forge. The fireplace is warming the room, and we have finished supper.

Billy stopped and for a time sat in the chill twilight of the tiny room, crowded with ten other men, uncertain in his heart what his duty was to Brigitte. *Do I tell her the truth about camp?—starving—freezing—dying—or do I use softer words—everything I write to Brigitte, or to Mother, will be shared between the families—do I spare them the pain of the truth?—do I?*

With cold fingers he continued.

> There are some things in camp that are unfavorable, but we will manage.

A voice from behind brought his head around. A middle-aged man sitting cross-legged before the fire was turned around, staring at him. His beard was full, clothing ragged, feet wrapped in burlap from a bean sack.

"Writing a letter home?"

Billy nodded. The man's eyes dropped, and Billy saw the embarrassment as he spoke.

"I . . . uh . . ." He stopped, rose, and came to the table to sit opposite Billy. He leaned forward to speak softly.

"I ought to . . . I got a wife and three kids at home. A house me and Maudie built. Logs." The pride and the longing shined in his face as he went on. "I ought to write to her."

Billy asked, "Need paper? I got a few sheets."

"I'd appreciate it. I asked for some from the captain. He said it's hard to get. They got to save it for the army. Reports and orders and such."

Billy carefully tore two sheets from the back of his pad and pushed them across the rough tabletop. "Need a pencil?"

The man nodded, and Billy laid his pencil on the paper.

Surprise showed in the man's face. "I oughtn't stop you from finishing your letter."

"It's all right. I can finish anytime. You go ahead."

For twenty minutes the man labored with the pencil, thinking, slowly forming words on the paper, pondering, and finally finishing. He raised his head and with downcast eyes haltingly said, "I didn't have no schoolin'. I . . . my Maudie learned me to write a little. I don't know if . . ." He stopped.

Billy spoke. "Want me to read it? Maybe look at the spelling?"

"I'd look kindly on it if you would."

Billy turned the paper, and in the flickering firelight read silently:

My Wife Maudie:

    I am riting in my hut that was bilt by me and elevn other soljers. It is small but it is shelter. The wether has been cold. We had no tents nor anithing to cook our provisions in, and that was prity poor, for beef was very lean and no salt, nor any way to cook it but to throw it on the coles and brile it; and the warter we had to drink and to mix our flower with was out of a brook that run along by the camps, and so many dippin and washin it which maid it very dirt and muddy. I am all rite. Tell the childrun to mind. I hope the new calf was a heffer. I will rite again when I can. Papir is scarse. I think of you offen. Eviry day.

                          Your husband.
                          Elijah Fisher.

Billy finished and raised his eyes to Fisher. "You did fine. I wouldn't change a thing. Maudie and the children will be proud."

The man's eyes shined. "I sure do thank you. Aren't you the company corporal?"

"I'm a corporal."

"Could you see that gets mailed out? I don't know exactly how to do it."

"I'll take care of it."

"I surely do thank you."

"Anytime."

Nearly two miles to the west, Eli stopped at the heavy oak door of a large, two-storied home with stone walls a foot thick, where Dr. Folsom and his staff had been given quarters. For a moment he peered about, looking for pickets, and there were none. He rapped loudly, and a moment later the door swung open. Warm air washed over him as he spoke to the slight, hunch-shouldered, elderly woman with tired eyes who stood before him with yellow lamplight on her gray hair and shoulders.

"I'm Eli Stroud. I've come to see Mary Flint."

The woman nodded recognition and stepped aside. "I recognize you. Come in from the cold. I'll get her."

Eli watched her hurry through the small parlor and listened to her rapid footsteps clicking down the long hallway. A door opened, then closed, and the sound of a longer stride on the polished hardwood hallway floor reached him. Face radiant, eyes glowing, Mary entered the parlor, and Eli felt his heart quicken at the sight of her. She came to him, and for a moment they held each other before she spoke.

"Give me your coat."

She hung it on a peg by the door, then led him to a couch against the wall in the small, sparsely furnished room, and they sat down. She held his hand between hers as she spoke.

"I'm so glad you came."

"I thought I better tell you, I'm supposed to see General Washington in the morning."

Mary stiffened. "About what?"

"I don't know. A lieutenant came about an hour ago and told me."

Mary felt the panic begin in her chest. "Is he going to send you away again? Like he sent you up north?"

"I don't know."

"Billy?"

"The lieutenant said only me."

Eli saw the fear and the pain in her eyes. Her shoulders sagged, and her head tipped forward. Eli reached to lift her chin and look her in the face. "You're not to worry. I'll be all right."

"You might be all right, but you'll be away. I don't know if I can stand that again."

"If I go, I'll come back. Don't dwell on me being gone. Dwell on knowing I'll be back."

She nodded, but he knew the saying of it would not take the fear from her heart. He waited a moment and changed directions. "There were no pickets at the door when I came. Something wrong?"

She drew a heavy breath and let it out slowly, the weariness apparent. "Sickness. Two of them with the fever."

"Is it getting worse at the hospital?"

She nodded her head. "You would hardly believe it. General Washington gave us permission to use homes and churches and government buildings for the sick. We've crowded our patients into barns and churches and Quaker meetinghouses all around Valley Forge. We've sent some to the Moravian Brethren's house at Bethlehem, some to Easton, Allentown, Lititz, Lancaster, and we have men out right now, looking at Trenton and Princeton in New Jersey. Smallpox is spreading, and Dr. Cochrane has ordered inoculations with cowpox for everyone who wasn't inoculated earlier. He's ordered a new hospital—a big one—to be opened at Yellow Springs for all with contagious diseases. Medicine? Nearly gone. Short of blankets. Short of food. Short of trained people. Short of everything we need to save these poor men."

She paused for a moment. "Our army captured a British ship with fifteen hundred pairs of shoes that were too small to fit any of our soldiers. So we passed them out to the troops with orders to boil them and eat them! Think of it! Eating leather shoes! An army so destitute it must boil and eat leather shoes for whatever strength they can give!"

Eli sat in stunned silence for several seconds. "No one set aside food for the sick?"

"None! We're desperate. And almost no medicine."

"Are you losing many men?"

"Dozens. Every day. Besides smallpox, we've got typhoid in camp. Malnutrition. Scurvy. Fever. Scabs. Open sores that won't stop running, and no way to stop them. Amputations of frozen toes and fingers and sometimes feet and hands that have gone black and dead—nothing to deaden pain—we simply strap them to a table and hold them down while they scream." She shook her head sadly. "I've never seen anything like it—never dreamed I would be in such a place."

Eli felt the grab in his heart and remained silent for a moment while it dwindled. "I'm sorry you have to be here. I don't know what I can do about it."

Mary leaned forward. "Oh, Eli, I didn't mean to cause you alarm. You're here because this is where you belong, doing what you're doing, and I'm here because I choose to be near you. I would have it no other way."

He looked steadily into her eyes. "Mary, make me a promise."

"Anything."

"I can still hear the sounds in your lungs. You're not well. Promise me you'll be careful with your health. Promise me. I don't know what I'd do . . ."

His voice trailed off and stopped, and Mary saw the fear in his eyes, and she reached with both hands to grasp his, and she spoke with an earnestness he had not heard before.

"I promise."

Eli sighed and rose. "I should get back. I don't know what tomorrow will bring, but if Washington sends me away, I'll get word to you. Probably through Billy or Turlock."

Mary rose to face him. "I'll be waiting. And I won't dwell on you being gone. I'll think only of the day you return."

He drew her close and kissed her, then walked to the door and reached for his wolf-skin coat.

Mary smiled. "Every man in this camp is jealous of that coat."

Eli grinned. "Want one?"

Mary's eyes widened. "A wolf-skin coat? I hadn't thought of it. Yes, I would like one."

Eli bobbed his head as he reached for the doorknob. "I'll see what I can do."

Mary stood in the doorway and watched him until he was out of sight, then closed the door and locked it before she turned back to walk down the long hallway to her small room.

In full darkness Eli made his way through camp on the trail that thousands of feet had tromped in the snow. He saw the pickets as he passed through, but none challenged him. He was halfway back to the Massachusetts Regiment when a sound to his left brought him to a stop, and he peered into the darkness to see a small, dark form moving through the trees. For a moment he waited, deciding whether he should follow. Then he heard a voice and a response. A picket had challenged. Eli moved on, glancing back but once. There was no further movement nor sound.

Behind Eli, at a sentry post in the trees, Caleb took Nancy in his arms and held her for a moment before he kissed her. He remained silent, heart racing at the touch and feel of her.

She looked up at him. "I brought you something warm."

He took the jar and removed the lid. Steam rose. "Soup?"

"It's not much—the best I could do with what we have."

He sipped. "Good. Thank you."

She waited while he sipped. "Did you write the letter?"

"Part of it. I'll finish it in the morning."

"I can hardly wait." She let a little time pass while he worked on the soup. "Are things any better in your company?"

He shook his head. "Worse."

"Are you doing any more writing in that book?"

"The orderly book? I wrote a little more today."

"Did they say anything about hope for food soon? Clothing? The sick men in our hospital need food so badly."

"No. Officers are resigning in every company. Desertions everywhere. Men haven't eaten for two days. They're living on moldy flour—making firecakes out of it. General Washington said if the British were to attack this camp right now, the revolution would be over. We aren't fit to fight."

Nancy slowly shook her head. "We can only pray the British don't learn of all this."

Caleb finished the soup and handed her the jar. "Thank you for coming. It's the best part of the day for me." He gazed earnestly into her face, shining in the dim light. He wanted to say more—much more—but he was yet too shy.

She drew close and whispered, "It's all that keeps me going, knowing I can see you."

He gathered her close and kissed her again. "Tomorrow night?"

"I promise. Finish the letter. Please."

"I will." He watched her turn and move away through the trees, the sounds of crunching snow dying until there was only the silence of the night, broken occasionally by the distant sound of wolves baying at the moon.

Morning broke clear and frigid, and at eight o'clock Eli faced the pickets at the entrance to Washington's headquarters, south and east of the junction of Valley Creek and the Schuylkill River. The two-storied stone building had previously been owned by Isaac Potts.

"Who comes there?"

"Eli Stroud. I was told to report to General Washington at eight o'clock."

The picket nodded. "He's expecting you. Hand me the rifle, and you may enter."

Three minutes later Eli was standing in the center of what had been the library, facing a plain oak table. General Washington remained seated on the other side. To Washington's right stood John Laurens, holding a paper in one hand.

Washington gestured. "Be seated."

Both Laurens and Eli settled onto hardwood, straight-backed chairs, and Washington came directly to the point.

"It will not be a surprise when I tell you this army is in need of almost everything needed to sustain itself."

Eli nodded but remained silent.

"I have great need for an accurate report on what is available in the countryside within seventy miles of this camp. Specifically, we must have clean straw for bedding the men. Meat of any kind, beef if at all possible. Grain of any kind. Flour. Blankets and bedding. Clothing. Shoes. Vegetables and fruits, fresh or dried. Horses and fodder. Medicines of any kind. Bandages."

He paused for several moments, and Eli shifted in his chair. Washington went on.

"To get that information I want you to leave camp and make a scout, seventy miles in all directions. Locate such things and mark where they are. On your return it is my intention to send out a command to gather them."

Eli's eyes widened. Washington continued. "I have been authorized to do so." He turned to Laurens. "Would you read the document under which such action is authorized?"

Laurens raised the paper and read.

December 27, 1776

In Congress assembled. Resolved:

That General Washington shall be, and is hereby, vested with full, ample and complete powers to raise and collect together, in the most speedy and effectual manner, from any or all of these United States, sixteen battalions of infantry . . . to appoint officers . . . equipt with three thousand light horse . . . to take, wherever he may be, whatever he may want for the use of the army, if the inhabitants will not sell it, allowing reasonable price for the same; to arrest and confine persons who refuse to take the continental currency, or are otherwise disaffected to the American cause; and to return to the states of

which they are citizens, their names, and the nature of
their offences, together with the witnesses to prove them:

That the foregoing powers be vested in General
Washington for and during the term of six months from
the date hereof, unless sooner determined by Congress.

Eli's eyes narrowed in near disbelief. That Congress would vest such
powers in one man was unbelievable, and it suddenly broke clear in his
mind that he had just heard the most profound tribute ever given to a man
by the highest body politic of the United States. The terrible, frighten-
ing trust and faith they had vested in George Washington left Eli silent,
mind groping.

Washington took a breath. "Those powers were granted thirteen
months ago and expired June twenty-ninth of this year. However, they
were again granted one month ago. I have no choice. This revolution lives
or dies on what we do in the next several days. Have I stated this strongly
enough that you understand the importance of what you are to do?"

Eli licked dry lips. "Yes."

"Do you want to take anyone with you? I recall you work well with
one other man."

Billy? Eli dropped his eyes for a moment of thought. "I don't see the
need. If you want the truth about what's out there, I won't be talking to
very many people. Ask them what they got, you'll get the answer they
want you to have, and that might not be the truth. I'll be looking in
barns and granaries and root cellars and storehouses. I'll likely do that at
night, or whenever they're not around. No, I think this is better done
alone."

Washington looked steadily into Eli's eyes. "I do not have one day,
or one half day to spare. Can you return within five days?"

Eli rounded his mouth and blew air and shook his head. "Five days.
Maybe. With a good horse."

"Do you want two horses? In the event that one breaks down?"

"No. One. Two will slow me down. Have you got a horse in good
flesh? I haven't seen one around here."

"You recall the five horses you brought in, along with the man suspected of being a robber?"

"Yes."

"His name is Percy Walters. He was a member of a mob in Bucks County called the Doane Gang. Thieves and murderers. The Bucks County authorities hanged him yesterday. The horse he was riding is a strong gelding in good strength and flesh. It has not been claimed by anyone yet, and I have no reservations about turning it over to you."

Eli reflected. "Yes, that was a good horse. When do you want me to leave?"

"How long before you can be ready?"

"I'm ready now."

Washington turned to Laurens. "Is the horse ready?"

"Saddled and waiting in the stable, sir."

Washington plucked a piece of paper from his desk and handed it to Eli. "Here are my written orders authorizing you to do whatever is needed."

Eli's eyebrows raised. *The horse saddled and waiting? Orders already in writing?* A wry smile crossed his face. "I'll stop at my hut long enough to get powder and shot and be on my way."

"Will you need food? I can give you rations from my personal store."

"No, I can live off the land."

Washington nodded. "Report back here, to me, immediately on your return. Day or night."

Eli nodded and turned to follow Laurens out the door. Fifteen minutes later he reined the big brown gelding to a halt in front of his hut and stepped down. Vapors streamed from the horse's nostrils, and the animal moved sideways, wanting to move, to run in the cold air. Eli tied the reins to a log and ducked through the doorway into the dark, smoky interior. Minutes later he stepped back into the bright sunlight, weapons belt strapped around his middle, shot pouch and powder horn hung around his neck and under his left arm. He mounted the horse and peered about, looking for Billy or Turlock. He found them cutting green firewood.

Eli remained mounted to speak. "General Washington is sending me on scout for five days. Alone. Will one of you tell Mary?"

Billy nodded. "Scouting for what? The British?"

"No. Anything I can find to help this army."

Turlock broke in. "He's going to just go out into the countryside and take it? Food? Clothes?"

Eli nodded. "Congress gave him authority, and he's going to use it."

"I knew he'd find a way. I knew it."

Notes

For a time "firecakes" became the only food available to the American soldiers at Valley Forge. They have been described. Straw was in critical shortage, as was food, clothing, medicines, soap, and every other item necessary to sustain an army. The incident of boiling 1,500 pairs of too-small shoes for food is factual. The list of diseases and maladies prevalent in the Valley Forge camp is also accurate. See Wildes, *Valley Forge*, p. 165; Leckie, *George Washington's War*, pp. 436–38; Freeman, *Washington*, p. 374.

Elijah Fisher was a soldier. The letter attributed to him was actually written; part of it is quoted herein, verbatim, from the original writing. Paper was in very short supply. Wildes, *Valley Forge*, p. 177; Reed, *Valley Forge: Crucible of Victory*, p. 14; Jackson, *Valley Forge: Pinnacle of Courage*, p. 46.

The overwhelming need for hospitals resulted in converting homes, meetinghouses, barns, and other buildings in towns as far away as Trenton and Princeton to hospitals, as described herein. Reed, *Valley Forge: Crucible of Victory*, p. 25; Busch, *Winter Quarters*, p. 68.

Washington sent scouts out on reconnaissance missions, limiting their scope to seventy miles from Valley Forge, according to the authority and the mileage limitation granted him by Congress. Some of his scouts were General Nathanael Greene and Colonel Tench Tilghman. Eli, a fictional character, is herein depicted as such a scout. Jackson, *Valley Forge: Pinnacle of Courage*, p. 85; Reed, *Valley Forge: Crucible of Victory*, p. 16.

On December 27, 1776, Congress granted astounding powers to George Washington, which it has not bestowed on any other man since, to essentially go into the countryside and take what he needed, paying a fair price in continental currency to farmers and other persons, who would rather have sold to the British for gold. The powers enumerated herein are abstracted from the larger document issued by Congress. Said powers expired in June 1777 but were reinstated in favor of Washington in December 1777, to enable him to survive at Valley Forge. Freeman, *Washington*, p. 323; Leckie; *George Washington's War*, p. 324; Higginbotham, *The War of American Independence*, p. 182; Reed, *Valley Forge: Crucible of Victory*, p. 16.

CHAPTER XXIV

★ ★ ★

olonel John Laurens's boots echoed as he strode briskly down the bare hardwood hall to stop before the library door and rap twice. From within came the familiar voice, and he tugged at his tunic, opened the door, and entered. Seated at a plain table, in a small, sparsely furnished room with hardwood bookshelves lining two walls, General Washington, proper in his uniform, nodded. Laurens advanced two steps and saluted. Washington returned it, and Laurens waited.

"You have the mail?"

"Yes, sir." He handed the general several messages, and Washington asked, "Anything of unusual import?"

"Two things, sir. First, a letter from General Lafayette. It might be of interest."

"Concerning what?"

"An apology. General Lafayette lately came to understand the entire matter of the cabal set in motion by Generals Conway and Gates. He had made it a point to be friendly to all his fellow officers and just realized that it was a mistake to attempt to ingratiate himself with either Gates or Conway. He wants you to know that he is in no way part of their . . . uh . . . conspiracy, if that's an accurate description, to be disruptive with Congress. He reaffirms his unswerving commitment to serve you and the American cause."

Washington gestured for Laurens to be seated while he drew the

Lafayette letter from the bundle and opened it. Carefully he read every word.

" . . . the friendliest of relations have not been impaired by my ignorance of the truth surrounding Generals Conway and Gates. Every assurance and proof of your affection fills my heart with joy. . . ."

Washington finished reading the letter and laid it on the tabletop. "General Lafayette sent a letter about a month ago, expressing the same sentiments. I wrote to him then, giving him my assurances of my continued confidence and trust in him. Since then, he has written to Henry Laurens in Congress, steadfastly supporting me and our efforts in behalf of the army. This letter confirms his loyalty. Young General Lafayette is coming of age. I believe he will mature into a great help to our cause."

"I agree, sir."

"Have you heard anything more about the so-called Conway Cabal since Congress made General Conway inspector general and he came here to perform his inspection of the army?"

"Not since he left here. I know he complained to Congress that his reception here was . . . cool."

Washington's reply was instant. "He understated. It was not cool, it was cold, but it was proper in every particular. He was extended every courtesy, every point of protocol due his station. I find it impossible to be warm toward one of the most dangerous men in the Continental Army. I wrote Congress to that effect, as you know."

Laurens nodded. "I recall. In any event, it is apparent that since General Conway left here, his cabal has died of its own weight. I believe it is of no further concern."

"Was General Lafayette successful in extracting himself from Congress' plan to put him in command of another attempt to invade Canada?"

"Yes, sir. He was willing to do what Congress required but informed the members rather forcefully that he thought placing Conway as his second in command would be a serious mistake. And he was not at all impressed with the proposition that Canada could be won with just twelve hundred men. It appears Congress is going to abandon the entire project. Lafayette was overjoyed at being ordered to return here."

"Good." Washington glanced at the remaining messages. "You said there were two matters of import. What is the second?"

"A message from General Howe, sir. I believe he wants to discuss an exchange of prisoners."

Washington leaned forward. "An exchange! Enlisted men or officers?"

"Both. Mainly officers."

Quickly Washington searched through the papers until he found the one with the British lion impressed on the parchment. He opened it, scanned the salutation, and studied the wording.

" . . . it now seems appropriate to both sides to accept your prior offer to exchange prisoners of war, officer for officer of equal rank, or, several officers of inferior rank for one of superior rank, and soldier for soldier held by either side to be freed on parole until exchanged . . ."

Washington turned to Laurens. "He's proposing to accept our terms. Would you draft a response advising that we will refine the terms as soon as possible. Specifically, I need to know whether he means that the officers shall be exchanged immediately, before any such final terms are agreed to, or whether he intends they should be retained where they are and considered to be on parole until the final terms are concluded. Further, I propose that I send two commissioners to meet with two commissioners he shall appoint to represent him, and they shall meet at the King of Prussia Tavern in Germantown on March tenth to make any changes that are just and fair, and any other matters that may arise. I would like to receive from him the names and ranks of the officers he intends to return to us. Specifically, does he intend delivering General Charles Lee to us under this arrangement?"

For a moment Laurens bowed his head to hide a smile, remembering that the highly touted Major General Charles Lee, British trained but serving in the American army, had been taken prisoner by young British Ensign Banastre Tarleton on Friday, December 13, 1776, when Tarleton caught him in his slippers, mid-morning, just after Lee finished his breakfast in the boarding house of Mrs. White near Basking Ridge, not far from Trenton. No one in the American army had ever learned just what Lee was doing in a boarding house, wearing slippers mid-morning, nine miles from his command, without sufficient soldiers to protect him.

"I'll draft a proposal for you earliest, sir."

Washington leaned back in his chair reflectively. "Colonel, there is a matter—a personal matter—that is of concern. Mrs. Washington is coming to Valley Forge for a time, and I have not had word of her travels. I would very much appreciate knowing if she is safe, and if possible, when she is expected to arrive here."

"I will do what I can to find out, sir. Is there anything else?"

"Yes. It appears that from time to time critically important information that is privy to some of our officers is reaching the British. I would like yourself and Colonel Hamilton to address a plan to find which officers are responsible, whether by carelessness or otherwise."

"Do I presume this should be done . . . discreetly?"

"As quietly as possible. I do not want to ruin the reputation of innocent officers, but I tell you now, should we find proof one of them is abetting the British, he will be hanged summarily for treason."

"Anyone in particular under suspicion?"

"At this time, no."

"I'll discuss it with Colonel Hamilton, and we will do—"

There was an insistent rap at the door, and both men turned their heads to look as Washington spoke.

"Who's there?"

"Colonel Hamilton, sir. Scout Eli Stroud has returned and states his orders are to report to you immediately."

Washington's back stiffened. "Enter."

Hamilton opened the door, stepped aside, and Eli walked into the room. He still wore his wolf-skin coat with the parka thrown back, and his weapons belt remained buckled about his midsection. His jaw was set, his beard a five-day growth. He waited for Washington's direction.

Washington turned to Laurens and Hamilton. "Both of you remain. All of you be seated." He turned to Eli. "Make your report."

Eli proceeded immediately.

"Do you have a map of the country around here?"

Quickly Washington unrolled a scrolled map. Eli stood, studied it for a moment, then dropped an index finger on the area just north and west of Trenton.

"There are about seven hundred barrels of salt fish here." He shifted his finger slightly to the west. "And here, not far, are over ten thousand barrels of pork."

Washington started but held his silence as Eli continued.

His finger slid on the map, from Allentown on the east to Coryell's Ferry on the west. "All through this country, farmers are salting their beef—thousands of barrels."

Hamilton came to his feet, followed by Laurens, who leaned forward to study the places Eli was indicating.

"From where we are, here at Valley Forge, moving north past Princeton, on to New Brunswick, here, east as far as English Town, and west to Bethlehem, then south to the Susquehanna River, there is enough flour in barrels to fill more than five hundred wagons."

Washington was incredulous. Hamilton straightened, wide-eyed.

"Within seventy miles in all directions are hundreds—thousands— of cattle, fat and ready for market. Thousands of tons of grain—oats, barley, wheat—stored in barns."

Laurens raised a hand as though to speak, thought better of it, and remained silent. Eli went on.

"Blankets, shoes, clothes—the merchants and the farmers have all of them."

Eli stopped, considered, and raised his eyes to Washington, waiting.

Washington cleared his throat. "Why have we not known this?"

"Farmers and merchants are selling their goods to the British. The reason is the British are paying good prices, and they're paying in gold. We pay less, and we pay in Continental paper money, and the farmers know our paper money is nearly worthless. It doesn't take much to figure out why the farmers would rather deal with the British than with us. So the farmers hide their goods and tell us they have nothing to sell and deal instead with the British."

"You talked with the farmers?"

"No. I watched them sell to British patrols when they came, and I watched them refuse to sell to our men, so I stopped at half a dozen taverns and listened. That's what I heard over and over again. I went to the farms—dozens of them—and counted their goods myself. The supplies are there, hidden."

"Could you show a large force of our troops where these things are stored if they were ordered to take those goods?"

"Yes, but that's not the trouble."

"What is?"

"Wagons and roads and horses." Eli waited until he saw understanding creep into the eyes of the three officers.

"I found over two thousand barrels of flour sitting in a warehouse less than forty miles from here. Six hundred barrels of fish sitting on a dock, rotten. Fifty wagon loads of clothing in a storage shed. But in the whole five days I was out there, I didn't see more than ten wagons. There are no wagons within eighty miles of here. Without wagons, nothing moves."

"And the roads?"

"Frozen hard as stone. If we did somehow find wagons, not one of them would make it ten miles on the roads the way they are right now. They're frozen hard enough and they're rutted enough to break the wheels and axles of a loaded wagon. It might be possible to load wagons light—maybe one third of a load—and move them on the roads, but that would be the only chance."

"Horses?"

"Very few to be found anywhere, including this camp. I've seen three hundred dead horses in this camp, and without horses, I've seen men harness themselves to sleds loaded with firewood to drag it from the forest to the campfires. They left blood from their feet in the snow. Eight days ago we got four barrels of salt fish delivered to our Massachusetts Regiment. It was spoiled so rotten you couldn't lift out the fish one at a time. We had to shovel it out like soup. And the men pounced on it and ate half of it raw. Vomited most of it up and ate some more. When supply wagons do make it into camp with barrels of salt beef, we find the wagoneers have poured off the salt brine to lighten the loads to get through the snow in the mountain passes, and the meat's gone to mush. Some wagons come in with the flour dumped from the barrels into the wagon box and left uncovered to the weather so the flour's gone. Useless. Everything we need is out there, but the way this thing is working right now, we'll all be dead or gone before we ever get any of it here."

Eli swallowed hard and straightened while he regained control. He did not realize how hard he had been talking to General George Washington.

For five full seconds Washington, Hamilton, and Laurens remained silent, letting the full impact of Eli's outburst sink in, take shape, form a picture in their minds. Then Washington shifted his feet.

"Is there anything else?"

"Yes. I saw a lot of British patrols. They're out getting whatever they want."

"Are you all right? Sick? Injured?"

"I'm all right."

"You found enough to eat?"

"Yes. Rabbit. Partridge. Nuts."

"Unless there is something else, you are dismissed."

Eli nodded, turned on his heel, walked out the door and closed it and treaded softly down the hallway to the parlor, where he collected his rifle from a sergeant and walked out into the frigid, bright sunlight.

In the library Washington sat down and gestured for Laurens and Hamilton to take their seats.

"I believe this man. Do you?"

"Absolutely."

"Last evening I received a copy of a hand-delivered message from an inspecting officer named Francis Dana, written to Congress." Washington opened his desk drawer and drew out a small sheet of paper. "Colonel Dana wrote, and I quote, 'Should the enemy, encouraged by the growing weakness of your troops, be led to make a successful impression upon your camp, your artillery would now undoubtedly fall into their hands for want of horses to remove it. Further, the loss of the artillery, catastrophic as it would be, is a much smaller and more tolerable evil than the imminence of famine.'"

Washington's eyes became blue-gray flecks of obsidian. "Colonel Hamilton, before your arrival today, I spoke to Colonel Laurens of the fact that information such as this is somehow reaching the British. Should they learn of the true conditions of this army, a heavy attack might end the revolution in half a day. We absolutely must stop the leaking of such things to the British. I asked Colonel Laurens to cooperate with you in studying the problem and reaching a proposal to stop it. I repeat that order to both of you now."

"Yes, sir."

"Now, as for the wretched state of affairs of our commissary, I have no compunctions in stating that in my opinion much of it is the result of the inaction of General Mifflin. He commands the commissary, but he remains sitting in Reading, spending his time trying to revive the now defunct Conway Cabal against me and ignoring this army altogether. Couple Mifflin's neglect with a Congress that is nearly paralyzed with infighting and politics that are meaningless, and that leaves our men exactly as Colonel Dana described them—facing the imminent and real threat of dying from famine, to say nothing of a British assault. Unless General Mifflin corrects himself immediately, I'm going to recommend to Congress a massive reorganization of this army and nominate General Nathanael Greene to replace General Mifflin."

Hamilton and Laurens watched the controlled anger rise to color Washington's face. "Famine! Our men starving to death here in a section of the country famous for an abundance of everything! I will not tolerate it!"

The two aides sat without moving, without a change of expression.

"The only way I can see to stop the practice of selling flour to the British rather than to us is to disable the flour mills engaged in it. So, Colonel Hamilton, draft a proposed order for my signature, directing that our troops are to disable such mills by sawing off the teeth of the wheel that drives the grindstone."

Washington paused to bring his raging anger under control.

"Have General Anthony Wayne in this office tomorrow morning at nine o'clock. As soon as possible, I'm sending him with five hundred troops to go into the countryside and get the supplies that Scout Stroud has located—at bayonet point if necessary. General Wayne will be authorized to pay a fair price in Continental money for it, but get it he will!"

Hamilton interrupted. "Sir, General Wayne is . . . uh . . . badly discouraged. More than one hundred officers have lately resigned from his command. There is rumor that he himself has intimated he will leave unless something changes very quickly."

"I know of that, but General Wayne will obey orders if they are given to him. Get him here."

"Yes, sir."

"And be certain that what we've discussed here today remains in this room until I give further orders. Do you understand?"

"Yes, sir."

***

Notes

Upon discovering that General Thomas Conway was undermining General Washington, General Lafayette wrote to General Washington assuring him of his distaste for Conway and of his ongoing support of General Washington. Washington and Lafayette exchanged letters, as stated herein. The quotation from a Lafayette letter is verbatim. Reed, *Valley Forge: Crucible of Victory*, pp. 16–17.

Following his appointment as inspector general, General Conway visited Valley Forge. General Washington extended him every required military courtesy; however, Washington was cold and formal. Conway complained to Congress. See Reed, *Valley Forge: Crucible of Victory*, p. 22; Freeman, *Washington*, p. 378.

Congress resolved to attempt to invade Canada with 1,200 men and intended to appoint General Lafayette to be in command, with General Conway second in command. Lafayette informed Congress it would be a serious mistake, both to invade Canada and to appoint Conway his second in command. The expedition never materialized. Much to his relief, Lafayette was ordered to return to Valley Forge. Higginbotham, *The War of American Independence*, p. 220.

General Washington wrote to British General Howe with an offer to exchange prisoners. General Howe responded. The quotations of their exchange are accurate. Reed, *Valley Forge: Crucible of Victory*, p. 34.

The list of items discovered by Eli Stroud on his scouting mission is accurate, including those found in abundance, as well as the fact that the lack of wagons and horses and of roads frozen so hard that they would destroy wagons made it impossible to bring the critically needed supplies to Valley Forge. The description of freighters dumping brine from salt beef and dumping barrels of flour into the wagon beds is accurate. Food prices were highly inflated. Jackson, *Valley Forge: Pinnacle of Courage*, pp. 85–86; Leckie, *George Washington's War*, p. 438; Wildes, *Valley Forge*, p. 172.

The letter attributed to Colonal Francis Dana is accurate and quoted verbatim in part. Wildes, *Valley Forge*, p. 167.

To stop the local farmers from selling their flour to the British for gold and not to the Americans for paper money, General Washington ordered the flour mills of the offenders disabled by sawing off the wooden teeth that drove the grinding stone. Reed, *Valley Forge: Crucible of Victory*, p. 31.

General Anthony Wayne was deeply discouraged by conditions at Valley Forge, and it was rumored he was considering leaving. Wildes, *Valley Forge*, p. 170.

CHAPTER XXV

★ ★ ★

*S*he came in her coach on the old Gulph Road, angling west through the frozen, rolling Pennsylvania hills of Valley Forge. With an armed, mounted guard riding on all four sides, the coach traveled slowly to keep from sweating the horses in the frigid air. Steam rose from their hides and trailed from their dilated nostrils as they picked their way through the rock-hard ruts, past the divisions commanded by General Poor on the left and General Glover on the right, on past the old schoolhouse at the junction of Gulph Road and Baptist Road.

Scarcely five feet tall, plump, face plain and round, blue eyes, quiet, industrious, always busy, tirelessly helping her husband and his soldiers, she was Martha Custis Washington, wife of General George Washington. Widowed with four children, two of whom died, she had married Washington and become completely devoted to him, and he to her. It was she who had put herself at risk to visit her husband wherever the fortunes of war took him, whenever she could. At Baltimore, Cambridge, Eltham, Fredericksburg, Hartford, New Windsor, Philadelphia, Williamsburg, and now at Valley Forge. No one knew how many sewing bees she had arranged to sew shirts and knit socks for the soldiers or how many projects she had sponsored to gather food. No one could tell how many times she had gone into the hospitals with meals she had prepared with her own hands and patiently fed to the crippled soldiers, then sat at their bedsides to read to them or kneel to pray for them. Over time and in her own calm way, she had earned the adoration, the love, and the respect of the soldiers in the Continental Army. No one knew who first turned the title or when it came to be, but she was known, not as Mrs. Washington or the general's wife; with a reverence reserved only for her, she was "Lady Washington" to her army.

The coach jolted on in the late February morning, between the divisions commanded by General Maxwell on the left and General Huntington on the right. By her orders the curtains in the coach had been thrown open so she could see the country and the soldiers as she passed. With a blanket drawn about her legs and feet, she sat wide-eyed, appalled at the sight of hollow-cheek, scarecrow-like soldiers with sunken eyes on all sides. Those who recognized the coach or her stopped working to come to attention, paying their silent respects as the coach lurched on. The frozen, half-decayed carcasses of dead horses were scattered about. A wagon rolled past, traveling in the opposite direction, and Lady Washington gasped when she recognized an arm thrust above the sideboard, fingers black and clutching, frozen solid. She turned to peer, and there were half a dozen legs, hard as stone, feet bare and black, thrust out the back of the wagon box. Inside were the remains of fourteen soldiers dressed in rags and tatters, who had frozen to death. She thought she had seen all the horrors war could inflict on men, but never had she seen anything like the world through which she was now moving.

She stared, her face a blank, her mouth compressed to a straight line as the coach moved on, across Inner Line Drive, past the junction with Port Kennedy Road, and on to the junction with Valley Road, where they turned right and suddenly were there, in front of the Potts home, just past the small spread of buildings in which General Washington had established his personal quarters and command offices.

Lady Washington was stunned. Gathered in rank and file, a company of Virginia soldiers raised a raucous welcome, with Colonel John Laurens at the head. The men's tumultuous shout rang in the woods as the door opened and General Washington strode out to the waiting coach. Without a word he opened the carriage door, extended his hand, and brought his lady out on his arm.

The soldiers quieted as the general, six feet and three inches tall, leaned forward to gather his beloved Martha, just under five feet, close to him. He held her for a moment, kissed her on the cheek, and turned, beaming, to escort her into the home. Behind him, some of the soldiers wiped at their eyes as Laurens turned to the Virginia Regiment. "You are dismissed. Return to your duties."

Two pickets took their positions beside the door. By order of Laurens, the general and his lady were going to have a little time to talk before the crushing duties of commanding a starving, freezing army once again made their demands.

At noon Washington walked back to his office in the headquarters building. At one o'clock Alexander Hamilton came to inform him, "Lady Washington requests your company for dinner, sir. She has prepared a meal."

Hamilton could not miss the glow in Washington's eyes and the lightness of his step as he strode back to the home and into the small, austere dining room where Martha waited, her plain, round face beaming. A fire burned in the stone fireplace, casting a little heat into the bare-walled room. The chairs were straight-backed hardwood. The single sofa was covered with aging, scarred leather. Washington held his wife's chair to seat her, then took his own. They bowed their heads for a silent grace, then Martha passed him a bowl of steaming potatoes.

"The rooms are quite small," she said.

He nodded as he cut the potatoes and added butter.

Martha continued, "But they're solid, and with a few little things they'll be cheerful. And I see you've built a small dining hall at the rear of the building. For entertaining?"

"Yes. Dining and entertaining, should we ever find time and substance to do so." Her face sobered. "I've seen the conditions in camp." She shook her head, and there was compassion in her eyes. "Terrible."

Washington met her with his direct gaze. "The worst I have ever seen."

"What's happened?"

"In concise terms, we lack everything on which an army depends to survive. Food, blankets, clothing, shoes, money, wagons—everything. We'll talk more of it when we have more time."

"Is there anything I can do?"

The tall, gaunt man paused. "Yes. Go out among the soldiers as you always do. I've never known greater need for it."

She stared into his eyes for a time, nodded her head faintly, and passed him the platter of hot sliced mutton.

"Would it be troublesome for me to visit the hospitals this afternoon? Would I need an escort?"

He shook his head. "I will arrange it. When do you wish to go?"

"Two o'clock?"

"Colonel Alexander Hamilton will escort you." He paused for a moment. "It has been some time since food tasted so good." His eyes met hers, and she blushed and bowed her head. "It's just mutton and potatoes."

At five minutes past two o'clock Hamilton took the hand and arm of Lady Washington and watched her put her foot on the iron cleat, then hoist herself inside the coach to take her seat. He quickly followed to take his place opposite her.

He pointed. "Madam, the foot warmer is filled with hot bricks. Your feet will remain warm."

Martha smiled. "Oh, thank you." She placed her feet on the iron lid, with the hundreds of small holes in rows, then spread the blanket over her legs and feet. "That's much better."

Hamilton leaned from the window to give hand signals, the coach driver slapped the reins on the rumps of the wheel horses and gigged at them, and the coach lurched into motion, the wheels crunching in the frozen snow and ice. Four mounted escort soldiers tapped spur, and their mounts swung in around the coach, one leading, one following, and one on each side. They rode with their muskets across their thighs, behind the saddle bow.

The driver swung the coach around to Gulph Road, then turned left onto the Port Kennedy Road. They proceeded past the grounds where General McIntosh had his division camped, past a rifle pit where green soldiers were trained in the proper use of musket and cannon, and past the junction with Baptist Road, where the driver reined the coach in at a small wooden structure on the south side of the road, less than four hundred yards from the tiny stone home that served as personal quarters for General Varnum. The horses blew and stamped their impatience as Hamilton reached to help Lady Washington from the coach.

"This building was a barn that we have been forced to use as a hospital. I am sorry it is so wanting, but the general's orders were that you should see this winter camp in its true light. I hope you understand." He opened the door and stepped aside to allow Lady Washington to enter the cold, dimly lit room first.

The stench of filthy bodies and decaying human flesh and the sounds of human beings in agony flooded over them. For several seconds neither of them could breathe, and both of them backed up one step and covered their noses and mouths with a hand. Lady Washington coughed, then moved through the doorway and waited for her eyes to adjust to the twilight, while she listened to the moaning and an occasional shriek.

The sole source of heat was a large, black stove that had been moved into the far end of the barn, where a hole had been cut in the barn ceiling for the pipe. The stalls and stanchions had been torn out, and makeshift cots of wood and canvas were placed everywhere one would fit on the bare dirt floor. Blankets had been laid beneath the cots, and emaciated, sunken-eyed men lay on the blankets, some with raging fever, others with fingers or toes or feet or hands missing. Most had open sores every place their skin could be seen. Sores were in their beards, clogging them with running pus and putrid matter.

Six women, hair awry, exhausted beyond words, gaped at Lady Washington as she slowly made her way between cots, staring in shock at soldiers who looked back with dead, flat, sunken eyes that had lost all hope. A tall, wiry woman came forward to meet them.

Hamilton cleared his throat. "I am Colonel Hamilton. On orders of General Washington, I am escorting Lady Martha Washington on a tour of the hospitals. I trust you will cooperate."

Martha placed a hand on his arm, and he fell silent. She turned to the nurse. "Who is in charge here?"

"Dr. Parkinson."

"Is he present?"

"He's asleep at the rear of the building. By the stove."

"How many men are you caring for here?"

"One hundred four. We lost six more this morning."

Martha nodded. "Taken away in a wagon?"

"Yes."

"I saw the wagon. Do you have any medicines?"

"Almost none. Only enough for the most severe cases."

"Some of these men have fever?"

"Yes. Typhus. Maybe smallpox. You should not be here."

Martha brushed it aside. "Do you have enough food?"

"Hardly any. Half these men would recover if we could feed them properly."

"Thank you. May I continue through the room?"

Twenty minutes later Hamilton again opened the door, and the two emerged from the tormented room into the clear, frigid fresh air, and each drew a deep breath, then coughed as the freezing air hit their lungs.

Hamilton spoke. "I apologize, madam, that you had to be witness to that . . . that deplorable scene inside."

"Let's continue on."

The coach lurched forward, jostling, wrenching over ruts and ridges frozen hard as rocks, with Lady Washington locked in silence as she stared out the window at the men and at the camp. She began to count the men with bare legs and bare feet and ten minutes later stopped. In spite of the snow, more than half had no shoes or long trousers. Most were dressed in ragged clothing that did little to turn the freezing cold. Few had coats. Almost none had hats.

The driver leaned over to call to Hamilton through the window. "We're coming to the big hospital, sir, but the wagon's parked in front."

Hamilton's eyebrows raised. "The wagon?"

"Yes, sir. The one . . . you might want to take a look, sir."

Hamilton leaned his head far out the window and quickly understood the driver's reluctance to speak. Standing in front of the two-
storied stone building that had once been a great stable for high-bred
horses, with a loft for one hundred tons of hay, was a wagon with high
sideboards, hitched to four horses blowing steam, anxious to be on with
the day's work. Two soldiers were walking from the front door of the
building to the wagon with a stretcher between them, and on the
stretcher, uncovered, was the shriveled, shrunken body of a dead soldier.
Without ceremony the two soldiers dumped the remains into the wagon
and started back into the building for the next corpse.

The soldiers had given the vehicle the infamous name "the Meat
Wagon."

Hamilton called up to the driver. "Stop the coach here and wait until
it's gone."

"Yes, sir."

Martha leaned forward. "What seems to be in the way?"

Hamilton cleared his throat. "Madam . . . uh . . . they are removing
the remains of those who have passed on."

"The wagon?"

"Yes."

Martha moved to the window and leaned out. For ten minutes she
silently watched while four more bodies were brought out and loaded
into the wagon. With the last one loaded, one soldier called up to the
driver, "That's all for now," and the wagon rolled out.

Martha settled back into her seat without a word, and she studied
her folded hands in her lap until her coach stopped at the front door.
Hamilton assisted her to the ground, and they walked side by side to the
front door of the massive building. He opened it into the dark interior
of the converted stable, and once again they were assaulted by the putrid
odor and the sounds of human suffering.

They had not gone three steps into the morass of cots and men
when they were stopped by a high, shrill shriek. "No! No! Don't!
Don't!" Instantly the voice rose to a heartbreaking crescendo that filled
the building and then trailed off, lost in the ongoing chorus of pitiful

moans from men lost in the nightmare world of fever deliriums and unrelenting pain.

Martha peered through the gloom to the far end of the massive room where two lanterns hanging from the ceiling cast their yellow light onto the body of a man lying on a rough-sawn pine table. A man was leaning over the table, working with his hands. After several seconds, he straightened, shook his head, and took a step backward. Opposite him, a woman drew a sheet forward, backed away from the table, and began to make her way through the jumble of men and cots toward the door behind Martha. She was less than ten feet from Martha before she raised her head and saw her.

Hamilton spoke. "Are we interfering?"

The woman shook her head. "No. It's over."

"I'm Colonel Alexander Hamilton. I am escorting Lady Martha Washington on a tour of our medical facilities under orders of General Washington."

The woman's eyes widened. "Oh, I didn't know. I'm sorry. My name is Mary Flint. I am surgical assistant to Dr. Folsom."

Martha exclaimed, "Child, you're shaking! Something's wrong."

Mary's dark eyes filled with tears. "That man—the one you heard scream—has died. Dr. Folsom had to remove most of his leg, and his body would not stand the shock. I . . . I've seen it before, many times, but this is the fourth man we've lost on the surgical table since yesterday afternoon. I just . . . I'm sorry . . . it doesn't usually affect me this way." She wiped at her dark eyes, squared her shoulders, and straightened her spine.

Martha stared into her face. The cheeks were hollow, the eyes sunken. "You're ill! When did you last rest? Eat?"

Mary shook her head. "It doesn't matter. There's just so much to do . . . endless."

"It *does* matter! How many sick do you have in this building?"

"Two hundred ninety seven left."

"Why, there's barely room for half that! How long has it been like this?"

"Since we got here. Over a month. It's getting worse." Suddenly Mary reached to grasp Martha's arm. "Oh! You shouldn't be in this room. We have smallpox and typhus! You must leave!"

Martha raised her eyes at the approach of Dr. Folsom, behind Mary, and Folsom spoke. "I'm Dr. Folsom. May I know who you are?"

Hamilton broke in. "I'm Colonel Hamilton. I am escorting Lady Martha Washington through our hospitals. Orders of General Washington."

Folsom bowed. "I am honored. I would happily shake hands, but as you can see, I am not prepared to do so." His shirtsleeves were splattered with blood, and there were traces still on his hands. He looked directly at Martha. "I regret that you will have to leave at once. There are three contagious diseases in this room, and I will not be responsible for allowing you to contract any of them."

Martha spoke. "Doctor, how many on your staff?"

"Six remaining. One died of typhus, five days ago."

"The others?"

"We take shifts. Besides Mary, there is one more on duty right now. He's back there, disposing of . . . the results of surgeries." He shifted his eyes to Hamilton. "Colonel, I'm certain you'll understand. Would you please escort Mrs. Washington out of this building?"

Martha remained silent, somber, while the coach worked its way back west. As they approached the grounds where General Varnum's division had built their huts, she looked right half a mile, to the place where the bare branches of poplar and oak trees lined the Schuylkill River, and then the coach turned right on Valley Road and the driver stopped in front of the plain, square stone house. Hamilton assisted her to the ground and bowed.

"It has been an honor. It would be my privilege to escort you whenever you wish."

Martha reached to grasp his arm and looked up into his eyes. "Thank you, Colonel Hamilton. Thank you for not sparing me. I shall look forward to seeing you again." He walked her to the door, opened it, and stepped aside as she entered. One minute later the driver gigged the horses into motion, and the coach moved away.

The old, carved clock on the fireplace mantel in the parlor had just struck nine o'clock when Martha stopped her gentle rocking and laid her knitting in her lap. General Washington knew the signs. He laid his quill down on the document he had been writing on the small desk in the corner, turned in his chair to look at her, and waited.

Martha spoke in a quiet, even voice. "Could you arrange to have food delivered here, to this kitchen, tomorrow morning as soon as possible? As much flour and meat as you can gather. And any vegetables you can get. I will spend some time delivering food among the sick."

"Anyone in particular?"

She shook her head. "I would appreciate it."

The general nodded, turned back to his desk, plucked up his quill, and continued writing.

★   ★   ★   ★   ★

The gray of approaching dawn found Martha in her kitchen, quietly kneading bread dough. Six smoking loaves sat cooling on towels on the kitchen cupboard. Six more were in the hot, black oven. The rich aroma of baking bread filled every corner of the kitchen and wafted out into the hallway.

At fifteen minutes before seven o'clock she used thick pads to remove the loaves from the oven, drop them from the pans onto the kitchen cupboard, set them in rows on towels to cool, and rub the tops with fresh butter. Quickly she greased and floured the pans, rolled out fresh dough, cut it to exact lengths, and plopped it into the waiting tins to rise.

At ten minutes past seven she served the general his breakfast of ham, eggs, steaming fresh bread and butter, and hot chocolate. At seven-thirty she stood before him and reached high to fasten his heavy woolen cape, then raised to tiptoes to kiss him on the cheek before he walked out into the crisp air. At eight o'clock she quickly wiped her hands on her flour-spotted apron to answer a rap at the front door.

A stocky sergeant with bare legs and his feet wrapped in filthy, ragged sailcloth stood on the doorstep. Behind him four men stood beside a great, two-wheeled cart they had dragged three miles over the rough road through camp. The sergeant's bushy red beard moved as he spoke.

"Ma'am, I'm sergeant Randolph O'Malley, New York Third Company. I got orders to deliver some supplies here to Lady Washington."

Martha nodded. "I'm Mrs. Washington."

O'Malley brightened. "There's flour here, ma'am, and a little meat and a few things we hunted down. Where would you like us to unload?"

"Around at the side of the house, please. There's a door into the kitchen and the pantry. I'll open it for you."

"That would be fine, ma'am."

O'Malley turned and called, "Bring it around to the side of the house," while Martha closed the door and hurried through the house, through the kitchen, and unlatched the door. She was standing on the flagstone entryway when O'Malley led his small command around the corner, two men between the shafts pulling, and two men behind the cart pushing. Of the five men, only one had shoes, and four had their feet wrapped in anything they could find. None had winter coats.

She pointed and stood aside while they carried the goods inside to set them on the pantry shelves or the kitchen table as Martha directed. The men worked silently, their eyes seldom leaving the golden brown tops of the smoking loaves of bread cooling on the kitchen cupboard. Martha studied the men as they moved. Their arms and legs were thin, knees and elbows and wrist joints too large. Their eyes were sunken, cheeks hollow, their skin a sallow, sickly color.

She gestured, and O'Malley spoke to a young soldier, thin, nearly smooth-cheeked, who held a small sack of potatoes with sprouts in every eye.

"She wants it there on the table, Dunson."

Caleb set the sack down and backed toward the door, waiting.

O'Malley faced Martha. "That's the last of it, ma'am. I surely do hope you and the general enjoy it."

"I thank you all for delivering it, but it isn't for myself or the general."

O'Malley's bushy red brows raised. "Not for you? Then who?"

O'Malley saw the pain come into her face. "I visited the hospitals yesterday. I hope to have some of this ready to deliver to those men by one o'clock."

O'Malley hooked a thumb toward the pantry and the table. "You're going to cook all this for the sick?"

"It's the least I can do."

O'Malley stood in dead, incredulous silence for a moment, then raised a hand to scratch his beard. "Ma'am, if ever you need more such, you say so. We'll get it here, one way or another."

"You're very kind. Thank you."

O'Malley turned to his men. "We're finished. We've got a ways to go to get back to camp."

They had the door open when Martha suddenly said, "Wait a moment."

O'Malley turned, puzzled.

Martha pointed. "Load these loaves of bread in one of those clean sacks on the cupboard and take it back to your company. Don't tell a soul where you got it."

Caleb's mouth dropped open in shock. In his life he had seen a thousand loaves of fresh-baked bread in his mother's Boston kitchen, but he could not remember bread that looked and smelled so good.

O'Malley stammered, "You . . . this bread is for us?"

"Take it. Share it with your company. You've earned it."

"Ma'am, I can't hardly believe you'd offer, but that doesn't seem fair to the rest of the army."

"It's a start. Now you take it." She grasped a clean flour sack from those on the cupboard and handed it to Caleb. "Would you help him?"

With a sense of reverence they loaded the twelve heavy loaves of golden brown bread, six loaves warm, six still smoking hot, into the clean sack, then all five men stopped to stare at Martha. In their eyes and their faces was a look akin to worship.

O'Malley cleared his throat. "Ma'am, there just isn't a word I can think of that will let you know how grateful we are. I'll see these loaves get back to Third Company, and we'll divide 'em out fair. We'll tell the men an angel give 'em to us, and I don't think that's far from the truth. You don't know what you've done for my men."

"It was nothing. Now go on, while they're still hot."

The men filed out, and Martha stood in the doorway until they disappeared around the corner: four men pushing and pulling the cart, and Sergeant O'Malley carrying the sacked bread over his shoulder.

The winter sun had passed its zenith and was beginning its arc toward the western rim when Martha once again climbed into her coach. Seated opposite her was Alexander Hamilton. On the floor of the coach, beside the foot warmer, were three large, heavy kettles of meat and potato stew, lids fastened down. On the seats beside herself and Hamilton were twenty-four loaves of bread in clean flour sacks, packed in wooden crates.

At twenty minutes past one o'clock the coach rocked to a stop before the huge, two-storied stone building that had been converted from a stable into a hospital. Twenty-five minutes later the food was inside the makeshift hospital, and Mary Flint and Martha were portioning out the steaming stew as rapidly as they could spoon it into wooden bowls, while Dr. Folsom and his two assistants cut bread as fast as they could.

Men ate their stew with spoons if they had them. If they did not, they raised the wooden bowls to their lips and sipped at it, and dipped their bread into it, and then wiped their bowls clean with the last crust. For half an hour the only sounds were those of famished, starving men filling shrunken stomachs with a meal they would never forget. They finished, and as Martha passed among them, touching one on the forehead, another on the hand, they reached to touch her. Some tried to speak but could not.

By half past three the wooden bowls had been gathered and water was boiling on the stove to wash them. Dr. Folsom beckoned Martha and Mary back to his cot.

"I don't know what to say. That's the first food these men have had in weeks, that had any strength to it. But more than that, I saw hope come back into their eyes. It's a terrible thing when men lose hope. I'll never forget this. I thank you."

Martha shrugged it off. "I need to get back. The general will be coming home soon for supper, and I have a kitchen to clean up. I'll be back when I can. May the Almighty bless you and your staff for what you're doing."

She had turned and started away when Mary reached to take her arm. "Mrs. Washington, I've held back a little—"

Martha cut her off. "Please, call me Martha."

Mary started again. "I've held back a little stew and bread. Nearby there's a sergeant with a young wife. He's dying. We sent him home yesterday because there's nothing we can do for him, and he wanted to be with her. Would you come with me to their little hut? It won't take much time."

Martha looked up into Mary's dark eyes. "Of course." She turned to Colonel Hamilton, standing behind her, waiting.

"Colonel, I hope you won't mind waiting for just a short time."

Hamilton shook his head. "Of course not."

Bundled in their heavy cloaks, parkas over their heads, the two women walked out the front door, Mary carrying a jar of stew, Martha a loaf of bread. They marched west through the snow, with the sun in their eyes and the shadows of trees lengthening eastward. Mary pointed, and they approached a small hut with smoke rising straight into the blue sky. Mary knocked on the door, and it was opened by a girl not yet seventeen. Her face was pretty, eyes red and tired, her hair awry, her ankle-length, gray dress wrinkled.

"Yes?" In the moment she spoke she recognized Mary. "Oh! Do come in."

She opened the door and stepped back while Mary led Martha inside the cabin. There was a fireplace at one end, a table in the center of the room on a cold dirt floor. Straw was piled two-feet deep against one wall, and a young man lay on it, beneath blankets. He was sweating and shaking, and his teeth were chattering as he opened his eyes and tried to focus in the dim light of the single lantern that burned on the table.

"Polly? Did someone come?"

"Yes. It's Mary Flint. From the hospital. She has a friend."

"Mary? Bless Mary."

Mary pulled a stool beside his bed and sat down. "Enoch, I have someone who wants to meet you. Someone special. Do you know General Washington?"

"Yes. He's my commander."

"His wife has come to visit you. Martha Washington."

The man's eyes widened. "His wife? Lady Washington?"

"Yes. Lady Washington."

Martha drew a chair up beside him and placed a cool hand on his forehead. She felt the sweat running.

"Sergeant, Mary said you're special. I wanted to meet you."

By force of will the man stopped his shaking and brought his eyes to meet hers. "I am honored. I am deeply honored."

"Have you been with the general long?"

"From the beginning, ma'am. The battle of Long Island. I've marched through it all with him."

Martha took his hand and felt the weakness as he clutched at hers. "I'll tell him. He'll be proud. Is this your wife?"

A light sprang into his eyes. "It is. Polly. Polly Linderman. Been married a little over a year. So proud of her."

"You should be." Martha brought the wrapped loaf of bread from the folds of her cloak. "I brought you something, and so did Mary." She laid the bread on the table, and Mary set the jar of stew beside it. "Some fresh bread and beef stew. I thought it might be fitting."

"For us? Bread and stew? Can't remember the last time we had food like that. I want to thank you. For me and for Polly."

Martha turned to Polly, who stood in disbelief at the sight and smell of the bread and stew. "Do you have a bowl? Could he eat a little of it now?"

For fifteen minutes Martha patiently dipped small amounts of stew from a wooden bowl and held it to the man's lips while he chewed and swallowed. She broke bread into small chunks to go with it, and he ate ravenously.

Martha set the bowl on the table. "That's enough for now. We'll leave the rest for later. Polly can help you. I have to go, but I'll return when I can. I'll tell the general about you, Sergeant."

He reached to seize her arm. "If I . . . if things go . . . wrong, take care of Polly for me. Will you do that?"

"I promise."

He relaxed, and a look of peace stole across his face. "Thank you."

For a moment Martha stood beside him, and then suddenly she knelt beside him, and she bowed her head and clasped her hands before her chest. Instinctively Polly and Mary bowed their heads and waited as Martha spoke.

"Almighty Father, Creator of all, humbly we thank Thee for Thy blessings. Forgive us our trespasses. We beseech Thee to look down upon this, Thy son, Enoch Linderman, with compassion. He has offered all he possesses in Thy holy cause of freedom. May Thy blessed Spirit be with him, and with Polly, now and always, to give them peace in the sure knowledge their offering has been accepted of Thee. In the name of Thy Beloved Son, Jesus, Amen."

Martha raised her head, and Enoch reached to tenderly touch her cheek.

"I thank you, Lady Washington."

"God bless you, Enoch."

From behind, Martha heard a quiet sob catch in Polly's throat, and she rose and turned. She reached for the girl and drew her close and held her while Polly buried her face on her shoulder and sobbed. When the shaking stopped, Martha turned to Mary, who wiped at her eyes.

"We must go."

Mary nodded. "I know."

Martha turned back to Enoch. "I'll remember my promise. Polly will be all right."

Polly held the door while the two women walked out into the snow and turned their backs to the westering sun. They walked together back toward the hospital, each aware of a quiet sense of peace that came stealing over them in the bitter cold.

Martha spoke without turning her head. "Tell me when he leaves us. I must take care of Polly."

Mary answered, "I will."

They walked on in silence.

Notes

The entire American camp at Valley Forge was about ten miles in length, on the south side of the Schuylkill River. The route traveled by Martha Washington as described here is accurate, including the location of some of the divisions of soldiers. For an excellent diagram, see the fold-out map preceding the preface page in Wilde, *Valley Forge*.

Martha Washington is accurately described, both physically and by character and personality. Because of their love and respect for her, the American soldiers called her "Lady Washington." On her arrival at Valley Forge the soldiers gave her a loud welcome. Once in the residence with General Washington, she commented on the smallness of the rooms and the fact that a log building had been erected behind the home for dining and entertaining. Leckie, *George Washington's War*, p. 142; Busch, *Winter Quarters*, pp. 94–95; Reed, *Valley Forge: Crucible of Victory*, p. 34; Freeman, *Washington*, p. 375; Jackson, *Valley Forge: Pinnacle of Courage*, p. 171.

Martha Washington's observations of the terrible condition of the soldiers as her coach passed through the Valley Forge camp is accurate. Many carcasses of dead horses littered the campsite. Leckie, *George Washington's War*, p. 436; Busch, *Winter Quarters*, p. 71.

The horrendous odor and sounds and general condition of the hospitals are accurate as described. Wagons, called "meat wagons" by the soldiers, were sent through camp daily to pick up the bodies of dead soldiers. Jackson, *Valley Forge: Pinnacle of Courage*, p. 154; Leckie, *George Washington's War*, p. 436–38.

For an excellent view of a "surgical suite" in a Valley Forge hospital as described here, see the photo in Wilde, *Valley Forge*, p. 179.

For an authoritative presentation of the true, deplorable conditions in the American medical staff and the hospitals, see Fisk, "The Organization and Operation of the Medical Services of the Continental Army, 1775–1783," pp. 94–142.

The incident of Martha Washington visiting a dying sergeant and his wife in their small hut is accurately described here, including the fact that she knelt by his bedside and prayed for him; however, the names Polly and Enoch Linderman are fictional names. A young girl accompanied Martha and told of the experience many years later. For purposes of our story, we have substituted Mary Flint in place of the young girl. Busch, *Winter Quarters*, pp. 94–95.

CHAPTER XXVI

★ ★ ★

ergeant Randolph O'Malley breathed shallow under the moonless, black-vaulted heavens and hunched his shoulders against the bitter cold as he covered the last ten yards to the small hut he shared with eleven others from Third Company. His beard and eyebrows were white with frost from his two hours of picket duty in a night thirty-one degrees below freezing. His feet and fingers and nose were numb as he leaned his shoulder against the rough plank door and forced it inward into the single room. Sixteen feet opposite the door, the coals of the fire glowed dully where they had been banked earlier. The thick stench of unwashed bodies that had worn the same clothing night and day for five weeks and the thin hint of smoke from green wood made him squint.

He walked past the crude table and the two-tiered bunks on both sides of the room to stand his musket against the wall and drop to his haunches close to the glowing coals. He stirred them with a piece of kindling, then added three more sticks and waited for the first hesitant flames to come licking. There was a small, muffled sound as the sap in the green wood began to run, boiling and popping. He stood, stepped to the nearest upper bunk on the west wall, and reached up to shake the form lying covered by an old army tent. His whisper was hoarse, too loud.

"Dunson, your duty."

The form stirred, and a head appeared from beneath the dirty folds of the battered canvas tent. Caleb shivered as he lifted his legs over the side to drop to the chill dirt floor. He was wearing the same summer clothing he had on the day he joined the Continental Army eight months earlier. Then it had been whole and had fit him; now it was in tatters and hung loose on his wasted, shrunken frame.

In silence O'Malley shrugged out of the only winter coat in the hut and handed it to Caleb, who pulled it on, then waited while O'Malley sat on a pine bench to unlace the shoes all twelve men shared for picket duty. They were too small, but Caleb had learned to leave the laces loose and endure the pinch for the two hours he had to wear them. He stood, tied a strip of cloth taken from the trousers of a dead man over his head to protect his ears, turned the coat collar up, picked up his musket from his bunk, and walked out the door into the blackness. The snow crunched as he walked to his picket post beneath the unnumbered frozen stars overhead, feeling the bite of the air in his lungs. He felt his face begin to numb, and knew white spots were already forming. He raised a hand to rub his cheeks and forehead, then quickly thrust it back into the coat pocket.

At his picket post he leaned his musket against the trunk of a pine tree and wrapped his arms around himself for what warmth they would give. To remain still was to freeze to death, so he kept moving, shuffling his feet, head pulled low inside the coat collar. Brutal experience had taught him that time became unbearable torture if he allowed himself to dwell on the pain of the deadly cold, and he forced his thoughts away from the silence and the misery and the black loneliness.

The bread—Lady Washington—no meat, no butter, just bread—golden brown— like Moses and the manna from heaven—one slice per man in the company—holding it in my mouth—don't chew and swallow because it would be gone—so good—so good— like Mother's—how is Mother?—Brigitte?—Prissy?—Adam?—home in bed—a warm bed—a warm breakfast—what will it be this morning?—oatmeal porridge?— Mother will cook oatmeal porridge this morning—steaming—thick—with dried apple slices soft and sweet mixed in—cinnamon on top—thick cream poured on—hot cider— a big pitcher of hot, sweet apple cider—

He raised a hand to rub again at his numb face, and his thoughts changed direction.

Where's Matthew?—alive?—wounded?—crippled?—captured?—at sea?— Matthew—and Billy—so unalike and so alike—odd—where's Billy?—alive?—in this camp somewhere?—haven't gone to find him—why?—why haven't I gone?—would he know I'm here?—no, he doesn't know—if he did he would have found me—because Billy is Billy, and that's the kind of thing he'd do—so why haven't I gone to find him?— something wrong with me?—

The sound of feet crunching snow brought him up short, and he reached with numb fingers for his musket. He fumbled it, and it fell onto the hard, frozen snow. He scooped it up and turned toward the incoming sound.

"Who comes there?" He had spoken it softly, but it seemed loud— too loud—in the great, frozen silence.

"Nancy."

Nancy—Nancy! The realization flooded through him like a great, warm, comforting wave. He watched as she appeared, a dark form moving through the trees. He dropped his musket and gathered her in his arms, and he held her while she wrapped her arms about him and laid her head against his chest. They stood without moving for a long time before he spoke.

"It's so cold. You shouldn't have come."

"I had to. I brought you something." She brought a jar from the folds of her heavy cape and put it in his hands. "Broth. Beef broth."

He loosened the clasp and removed the lid and raised it steaming to sip at the rich, brown mix.

"Where did you get beef?"

"Lady Washington brought a small piece of brisket to the hospital. We boiled it. I saved this much of the broth for you."

He worked on it for several seconds and could not remember anything that had ever tasted better. "You shouldn't have. You should have eaten it. You need your strength."

She shook her head. "You need it. You've lost twenty pounds! Have you looked at yourself?"

He shook his head.

"And I brought you this." She thrust a folded paper into his hands. "A letter I wrote. In answer to yours."

He raised startled eyes and peered into her face, a pale whiteness inside her parka. "You wrote this? For me?"

"Yes."

"I'll read it when it's light enough. I . . . I don't know what to say."

"You needn't say anything."

He finished the broth, locked the lid back on the heavy pewter jar, and handed it to her. "Nothing ever tasted better. I'm grateful. And for the letter." He pushed it inside his coat.

"Some of the soldiers in the hospital are talking. Is it true the army may be leaving here?" He could hear the earnestness in her voice.

"Not that I've heard. A lot of officers are resigning. Hundreds of soldiers are leaving—just walking away. Some regiments can't muster one full company. It's been two days since most of us have seen food of any kind—meat, flour—anything. No wagons, no horses, nothing. I've heard that General Washington is going to send General Wayne—Anthony Wayne—out to get whatever he can find. Take it at bayonet point if he has to. Congress gave Washington authority to do it. Some officers are talking against General Washington, but so far it's only been talk."

"What! Talk against General Washington? Impossible! Who?"

"Gates. Conway. Dr. Rush. Mifflin. A few others. But so far no one has said General Washington will be replaced, and no one has said we're going to leave."

"You're sure? I . . . can't stand the thought of you leaving."

"I wrote up the standing orders in the orderly book yesterday. This army could not withstand a heavy attack right now but not a word about leaving."

"Thank heaven."

He drew her to him once again, and she reached to kiss him.

He spoke reluctantly. "You go on back. You'll freeze out here."

"Answer my letter when you can."

"I will. I promise. Now go."

He watched her slender, dark form disappear into the trees, and he stood for a time, until the sound of her feet breaking through the hard-crusted snow had faded and died. He reached once more inside his coat to feel the letter, remembering the thrill of holding her, of the brief touch as she kissed him, the sound of concern in her voice. He was still filled with the wonder of her when the black of the eastern skyline imperceptibly became deep purple and the morning star faded. His hand was inside his coat holding the letter when the purple yielded to the first glow of a sun not yet risen, and for a few moments the heavens were caught in the magic between night and day as the light skiff of clouds burst into a vast play of reds and golds and yellows. Then the first arc of the sun rose above the barren trees, the colors faded, and were gone, and another day of starvation and sickness and hopelessness was upon Valley Forge.

Before he picked up his musket to leave his picket post, Caleb unfolded the letter with a tender reverence and read the meticulously scrolled lines.

> My Dear Caleb:
>
> Dare I refer to you as 'my Caleb'? Something inside will not let me say less. I only know that my day is not complete without the thought, and that being able to see you at night as you stand your picket duty is what gives me the will and the strength to work through the trials of the day. I look forward to the time when this wretched war will have ended and the joy and happiness of normal and peaceful life come once again. Until then, I am so proud of you for all you do in the cause of liberty. I beg of you, take care of your health, and know that I am thinking of you always.
>
> > With deep affection,
> > Nancy Fremont.

My Caleb. My dear Caleb. I am thinking of you always. With affection—deep affection. That's what she wrote. To me. Me.

For a time the cold and the hunger and the hopelessness were forgotten as the words ran over and over again, through his brain and his heart. He took one last look at the letter and read the signature one more time—the beautifully scripted *N* and *F* and the carefully formed letters of her name. Then he gently folded the paper and worked it inside the coat, picked up his musket, and walked southwest, back to the hut, and pushed through the door.

He breathed shallow at the stench inside and squinted at the smoke from the green wood in the fireplace. A small smoke-blackened kettle was settled among the coals, steaming. O'Malley glanced at him and gestured at the pot.

"We got the bones of a dead partridge we found in there, and part of the innards of a froze horse, and what flour we could scrape from the empty sack, and one big chunk of hardtack Ellison found in the bottom of his knapsack, mold and all. Tossed it all in with the snow water. Get out your bowl. We're about to have breakfast."

Caleb took the coat and shoes off and laid them on his bunk and got his worn wooden bowl. The men sat at the table or hunkered down near the fire and held the warmth of their bowls in both hands and nursed the steaming gruel, waiting for it to cool enough to sip at it. The mold on the hardtack and the horse parts came strong, tainting the greasy mix with a stink and a taste that turned their stomachs. Two men gagged and waited for a time before they tried again. Caleb got his portion down and sat for ten seconds battling the need to wretch it all up onto the cold dirt floor. He swallowed hard and held it.

O'Malley took a deep breath. "This is the third day without rations. I don't know when we'll see more food. If this goes on, I'll go see Gen'l Washington."

All heads turned to him in surprise, and he saw the sores on their faces and in their beards, and he felt the stab of pain at the fading of hope in their eyes. Caleb stared into his own empty bowl while the next man struggled into the coat and sat down to tie the shoes onto his bare feet.

O'Malley set his bowl clattering on the table. "We got to set this hut in order, and then we'll go out to get firewood and water from the creek. We got a new officer comin' in today. German. Likely to have some sort of armed guard. If he comes this way we're supposed to come to attention and salute."

"German? On our side?"

"Yes. Supposed to have fought with Frederick. Frederick the Great. Whoever that was. Anyway, remember to come to attention if he passes."

The wood crew loaded three axes onto the pine sled. Two of the men slipped looped ropes over their shoulders and leaned into them. The sled runners cracked loose from the ice, and the crew trudged south, away from the river, toward the green-black of the woods, with the empty sled, six feet by ten feet, cutting a path through the frozen snow. They had gone only twenty yards when the sounds of a running horse brought them to a stop. They watched a rider with lieutenant's epaulets on his shoulders rein a laboring sorrel mare in from the east and continue past them toward the west at a run.

O'Malley shook his head in disgust. "He's goin' to break that horse down in this weather if he keeps that up."

The crew had covered another fifteen yards when Caleb stopped and turned his head to listen. O'Malley slowed.

"What's wrong?"

Caleb pointed east. "Bells. Hear 'em? Sleigh bells."

The whole crew stopped to peer east, and O'Malley's forehead wrinkled in puzzlement as the jangle of distant sleigh bells grew louder in the crisp, thin air. Then, half a mile away, they saw two armed, uniformed riders emerge from the trees side by side, and behind them a great, open sleigh drawn by two heavy, black Percheron draft horses. Arched over the broad withers of the horses was a heavy metal frame, anchored in the horse collars and harnesses, from which dangled twenty-four bells, ringing incessantly to announce their approach. The huge sleigh was shiny black, with wrought-iron decoration on the driver's seat and down both sides. Behind the sleigh, four more draft horses drew a large, ornately decorated black coach. An armed rider rode on either side of the sleigh, and two more rode behind.

Not one man in the wood crew uttered a word as the strange entourage approached. No one thought to give the order to stand at attention as the horses trotted past, pulling the two vehicles. Every man gaped in utter astonishment at the sight of the passengers riding in the open sleigh.

A round-faced man, the obvious leader, sat in the forward-facing seat, dressed in a new buff and blue American officer's uniform, a spotless tricorn set squarely on his sizable head. His silk-lined cape was thrown back, and on his left breast they could see row upon row of medals and decorations clustered about a huge one that sparkled golden in the morning sunlight. On the seat next to him was a tall, lean, long-snouted, perfectly groomed Italian greyhound. O'Malley's mouth dropped open, and Caleb's head jerked forward in disbelief. Seated next to the greyhound was a uniformed officer with his hawkish face set straight forward, looking neither right nor left. Facing them in the opposite seat were three more officers, all sitting like statues.

The wood crew, dressed in tatters, feet wrapped in rags, watched the sleigh pass, then turned to watch the enclosed coach rumble past, with the trotting horses blowing steam and vapor that trailed four feet behind their heads. They could see at least six dark figures inside, all officers, but nothing more. The two mounted, armed guards bringing up the rear followed ten yards behind, and then the entire column turned to follow the trail through camp and disappeared behind a neck of trees.

For five seconds the wood crew neither moved nor spoke. Then O'Malley shifted his feet in the crackling snow and wiped the frost from his beard.

"Was that the German officer we're waiting for? If it is, either he's in for a big surprise or we are. I wonder what Gen'l Washington's going to think."

Nearly three miles to the west the rider pulled the sweating sorrel mare to a sliding stop before the austere stone headquarters building, answered the pickets' challenge, and was immediately admitted to General Washington's office.

"Sir, that German general you spoke of is about fifteen minutes behind me. He has a sleigh and a coach, both full of officers, with about six mounted, armed guards. General Picket sent me to tell you. He thought you should know."

Washington's eyes narrowed in question. *Sleigh? Coach? Armed escort?* He spoke to the young lieutenant. "I take it he is coming here."

"He is. Sir, I left my horse in front, sweating bad. I should tend to her in this cold."

"You are dismissed. Would you tell the orderly in the·foyer to have Colonels Hamilton and Laurens in my office at once?"

"Yes, sir."

Quickly Washington selected four sheets of paper from those stacked on the corner of his desk, glanced at the signatures, selected one, and read steadily.

" . . . *Lieutenant General Friedrich Ludolf Gerhard Wilhelm Augustin von Steuben . . . aide-de-camp to King Frederick the Great of Prussia, the greatest soldier of his age . . . born in Magdeburg, Prussia, 1730 . . . son of an army engineer . . . educated in Breslau by Jesuits . . . an officer in the Prussian army at age seventeen. . . . Discharged in 1762 . . . served as chamberlain to the court of Hohnenzollermn-Hechingen . . . fell into debt . . . traveled to Paris . . . met Benjamin Franklin . . . Franklin obtained a loan from Beaumarchais . . . sent him to America . . . extraordinary abilities as an officer . . . capable of organizing and training the Continental Army . . . concur altogether with Ambassador Franklin's assessment of the contribution he can make to our cause . . . recommend he be given instant commission as an officer and assigned to the duties related to training our soldiery.*"

Washington glanced once more at the signature of Silas Deane.

A brisk rap at the door brought Washington's head up. "Who comes?"

"Colonel Hamilton, sir, and Colonel Laurens."

"Enter."

The door opened, and the two aides entered to stand at attention, awaiting orders.

"Be seated. I have just received word that General von Steuben is arriving shortly. You both speak French and have some grasp of German. Would you remain here in the event interpreters are needed?"

"Of course, sir."

"Have either of you read the information I received regarding General von Steuben?"

"From Ambassador Franklin and Silas Deane? Part of it, sir."

Washington slid the Deane letter across the table. "Read this while I review Ambassador Franklin's letter."

Silence held as the men pored over the documents, while Washington carefully read every word from Ben Franklin, one of the shrewdest judges of men of his time.

"*. . . has no grandiose perceptions of his own abilities . . . self-effacing . . . protege of Frederick the Great of Prussia . . . well grounded in all things pertaining to military matters . . . has the unmistakable bearing of an officer . . . awarded the prestigious Order of Baden knighthood . . . wishes to be judged on merit and not on birth or reputation . . . in my judgment capable of contributing mightily to the advancement of the Continental Army. . . . Signed, yr obdn't serv't Benjamin Franklin.*"

Washington pushed Franklin's letter across the table and picked up the two-page letter signed by von Steuben himself.

"*. . . much honored by the reception extended me by Ambassador Benjamin Franklin and his associate Silas Deane . . . it was they who urged and arranged for my passage to America . . . am aware of the letters they have written in my behalf . . . they have some-what overstated my credentials. . . .*"

Washington paused for a moment, then read the next statement slowly, carefully, putting every word in proper context.

"*If the distinguished ranks in which I have served in Europe should be an obstacle, I had rather serve under your Excellency as a volunteer than to be a subject of discontent to such deserving officers as have already distinguished themselves amongst you. Signed, your obedient servant, Baron von Steuben.*"

Slowly Washington straightened and slid the letter across the desk to Hamilton and Laurens. "The last paragraph is most revealing. This man is willing to commence service without rank and without pay. Remarkable. Does that bring back remembrance of the last European officer Franklin personally recommended?"

The answer was instant. "General Lafayette."

Washington nodded. "This man—Baron von Steuben—appears to have possibilities."

The sound of rapid footsteps in the hallway was followed by a brisk rap at the door.

"Who comes?"

"Your orderly, sir."

"Enter."

The door swung open and Washington started at the look of profound astonishment on the face of his orderly. "What has happened?" Washington demanded. "Is something wrong?"

"Sir, a German officer has arrived with a . . . uh . . . rather large delegation of . . . uh . . . people, sir, and a . . . a great big dog."

Washington's eyes widened. Hamilton grinned. Laurens laughed out loud.

"Bring in the officer and one interpreter if he wishes."

"Yes, sir."

The young orderly walked out without closing the door, and they heard his hesitant footsteps march down the plain, hardwood hallway, stop, then proceed back, accompanied by the cadence of clicking boot heels. The orderly entered the room, stepped to one side at attention, and Baron von Steuben entered the room.

He walked ramrod straight, chest out, chin tucked in, the living epitome of military bearing, all of which gave the impression he was taller than his five feet nine and one-half inches. He had regular features, a large nose, ruddy cheeks, and gray eyes, which Washington would learn were capable of all ranges of human emotions, from humor to pinpoints that froze men in their tracks. Behind him came Pierre Etioenne Du Ponceau, in the uniform of a brigadier general, to act as von Steuben's interpreter.

The Baron halted, clacked his boot heels together, and snapped his arm up in a perfect salute. "Baron von Steuben at your service, sir."

Washington returned the salute. "It is my honor to receive you."

Von Steuben's arm dropped. "May I present my interpreter, Brigadier General Du Ponceau."

Du Ponceau bowed.

Washington said, "I am honored. May I present my two aides, Colonels Laurens and Hamilton."

Both von Steuben and Du Ponceau bowed stiffly, and the two Americans returned it.

"Please be seated."

Von Steuben gathered his coattails into his lap and sat down, followed by Du Ponceau, while Hamilton and Laurens took their chairs beside the general's desk. Washington dispensed with the formalities rapidly. "I trust your voyage and your trip here were acceptable."

"Excellent."

Du Ponceau was interpreting for von Steuben. Laurens was listening and quietly nodding his approval as Du Ponceau spoke.

"I am certain you understand that I am unable to extend you an appointment without the approval of our Congress."

"I understand. I do not wish to cause conflict. I will be happy to serve as a volunteer in any capacity pleasing to yourself, Excellency."

Washington leaned forward in his chair. "Your offer is most gratifying."

Von Steuben's expression did not change. "I do not desire rank until I have learned the language and the genius and the manners of the people."

Hamilton leaned forward, unsure he had heard correctly. Laurens turned to look at Washington. General Washington's eyes narrowed, and for five seconds no one made a sound as the three Americans accepted the profound implications of von Steuben's statement.

This man intended taking on the rigors of learning American ways and of qualifying himself before he would accept rank or pay. If his notions of training an army in the craft of military discipline were built on the same principle by demanding that the soldiers begin by learning the rock-bottom foundations . . .

Washington drew a deep breath. "General, I cannot—"

Von Steuben interrupted, "Captain, not general."

Washington reached for the letters. "I believe the letters indicate . . ."

"They are incorrect. I was a captain in the Prussian army when I served on the staff of General Frederick. When his staff was dissolved, someone listed my rank as general. I gave no such permission, nor was it correct."

Again the three Americans fell silent, stunned by the candor of this man, who sat like a statue and would not allow himself to be thought more than he was.

Washington continued. "Until such time as Congress grants rank and pay, may I request that you move about this military camp, making such observations as you deem proper in any particulars you see fit. Make a written summary and submit it to me. Would that be agreeable?"

Von Steuben bobbed his head once. "It would be my great honor."

Washington turned to Laurens. "I will dictate proposed orders to that effect for my signature. When they're signed, deliver them personally to Baron von Steuben."

"Yes, sir."

Washington turned to Hamilton. "Would you find suitable quarters for Baron von Steuben and his staff?"

"Yes, sir."

Washington turned back to von Steuben. "Is there anything else I can do for you at this time, sir?"

"Accept my thanks. I am deeply honored."

Washington stood, and the others stood with him. "Then, sir, would you follow Colonel Hamilton? He will show you to your quarters."

Washington was caught in deep thought as he listened to the footsteps fading down the hallway. Laurens remained and said, "I wonder what Baron von Steuben will think of the terrible condition of our army. This camp."

For several seconds Washington stared out the window. "I hope Dr. Franklin was right about him. We shall see."

In front of the headquarters building, von Steuben stepped into the sleigh with the tall, gaunt Italian greyhound at his side on a leash. Hamilton, and the balance of his entourage, stood waiting for him to take his seat before they followed. Von Steuben gathered his heavy cloak and started to sit when movement to the south caught his eye, and he straightened, eyes narrowed as he peered. A knot of soldiers had gathered less than thirty yards away, vapors rising from their faces. The men were dressed in the tatters that remained from their summer clothing, feet wrapped in bloody rags, hair long, beards full, running sores on their faces. They stood hunched forward to relieve the hunger pains that had not left their bellies in days.

In the strange silence that held for a few moments, von Steuben stared at the ghoulish-looking clump of men, then listened as they began a hollow chant. He turned to look at Du Ponceau for the translation into German. Du Ponceau raised his face and spoke in German, then turned to Hamilton and repeated it in English to be certain.

"They said, 'No meat, no bread, no soldier.'"

Hamilton's eyes dropped for a moment, then raised back to Du Ponceau. "That is correct."

Du Ponceau nodded his affirmation to von Steuben, and for a long time the stout German officer stared at the scarecrow men with shock and disbelief plain in his slitted gray eyes.

Notes

General Washington sent Brigadier General Anthony Wayne, General Nathanael Greene, and five hundred fifty hand-picked men out into the countryside to forage for food and supplies under written orders to take what was needed, at bayonet point if necessary, under authority granted by Congress to General Washngton. Reed, *Valley Forge: Crucible of Victory*, p. 35; Wildes, *Valley Forge*, pp. 170–74; Jackson, *Valley Forge: Pinnacle of Courage*, p. 89.

Some generals openly opposed General Washington. Freeman, *Washington*, p. 381; Higginbotham, *The War of American Independence*, p. 218; Jackson, *Valley Forge: Pinnacle of Courage*, pp. 196–98.

The army was in peril of disbanding; it could not withstand a heavy British attack. Wildes, *Valley Forge*, p. 170; Jackson, *Valley Forge: Pinnacle of Courage*, p. 88.

The description of Baron von Steuben's entourage, including the Italian greyhound dog, his aides, translators, and the belled sleigh and coach, are set forth in Leckie, *George Washington's War*, p. 439.

Colonel John Laurens spoke German and acted as an interpreter for General Washington in the exchanges with Baron von Steuben. Jackson, *Valley Forge: Pinnacle of Courage*, p. 124.

General Washington had received letters of recommendation for von Steuben from both Silas Deane and Benjamin Franklin, as well as from von Steuben himself. Von Steuben magnanimously offered to serve as a volunteer at no rank or pay until he had learned American ways, which statement heavily impressed General Washington. Portions of said letters are quoted verbatim herein. The history of von Steuben is accurate. He was not a general in the Prussian army but a captain, and he did not represent himself otherwise. Leckie, *George Washington's War*, pp. 438–40; Jackson, *Valley Forge: Pinnacle of Courage*, 125–26; Reed, *Valley Forge: Crucible of Victory*, pp. 38–39.

CHAPTER XXVII

★ ★ ★

*T*he cracking report of the distant musket came strangely loud in the silence of the frozen night, and Caleb Dunson jerked awake, staring wide-eyed into the dark of the hut, lighted only by the remains of the coals banked in the fireplace. He waited until the sleep-fog cleared from his brain and he could make out the dark form of the table on the floor before he raised on one elbow to listen intently, aware something had awakened him but unsure what it was. From miles away came the sound of wolves talking to each other as they ran their prey to ground. Seconds passed in silence, broken only by the sounds of men sleeping. Half a minute later Caleb lay back down and was pulling the folded tent over his head when O'Malley's voice came quietly in the dim shadows.

"Dunson, you awake?"

"Yes."

"Did you hear it?"

"Something woke me. Might have been wolves."

"No, it was a musket shot."

Caleb reared up on his elbow. "Musket? Close?"

"No. Maybe three hundred yards. North. Towards the river."

Caleb made mental calculations. "Our picket line?"

"That direction."

"Who's out there on duty now?"

"Ellison, I think."

Men began stirring as Caleb continued, "Maybe someone ought to go take a look."

"He's due back in about ten minutes. If he doesn't come, I'll send someone. When do you stand duty tonight?"

"Two o'clock."

An irritated voice came loud from the bunk below Caleb. "Quiet."

O'Malley said, "I'll give Ellison ten more minutes."

Seconds stretched to minutes, and Caleb lost track of time as he listened in the silence. The baying of wolves sounded again, farther off, nearly indiscernible. The faint creaking of feet on frozen snow reached the hut, and Caleb held his breath to listen. The sounds came stronger, then they were outside the door, and suddenly the door burst open.

Caleb and O'Malley jerked upright in their bunks as other men grunted and wakened, and Caleb saw a figure lurch into the darkness of the room to slam into the table, fall to one knee, then rise, hunched forward, one hand flat on the tabletop, the other clamped on his left hip. Behind him a second vague figure entered, and Caleb saw the musket and the bayonet, level, pointing, ready, as Ellison's voice boomed, "Sergeant, you awake?"

Caleb dropped from his upper bunk as O'Malley's stockinged feet hit the cold, dirt floor.

"Here. What's happening?"

"This man was skulking through the trees out there, and I challenged. When he ran, I shot him."

"How bad?"

"Don't know. He's still walkin'."

"British or ours?"

"Says he was sent here by the New Jersey Militia. Got lost and was tryin' to find some place to keep from freezin' until mornin'. Gave a name, but I forget what it was."

Caleb stirred the coals and added kindling to the fire, then fumbled to light the single lantern on the table. Four of the other men were now on their feet, staring at the man who remained beside the table, leaning on his right arm, left hand clutching his left hip. O'Malley raised the lantern to look him full in the face. The prisoner was wiry, bearded, eyes narrowed beneath heavy brows, wearing a heavy woolen coat.

"What's your name?"

"Ferguson. Nathan Ferguson."

"What were you doing out there in the middle of the night?" O'Malley's face was a study in doubt and anger.

"Tryin' to find someplace to keep from freezin' to death."

O'Malley snorted. "By sneakin' around in the trees and runnin' when Ellison challenged?"

"I didn't know who he was. And I wasn't runnin'. I was standin', facin' him, waitin' for him to come."

O'Malley snorted, and half the men in the room laughed out loud.

"Where'd the ball hit you?"

"Left hip."

"Pull off that coat and show me."

The man winced as he raised his right hand from the table and his legs took his full weight. Seconds later his coat was on the table, and O'Malley was holding the lantern waist high, looking at the large, black splotch of blood on the man's trousers and shirt.

He touched the man's hip on the back side. "Went in here?"

The man cringed. "Yes."

"I don't see where it come out. Still in there?"

"Yes. It burns."

O'Malley raised his face. "How'd that ball hit you back there if you was facin' Ellison?"

The man stammered. "I . . . was just turnin' when he fired."

Groans of disbelief came from every man in the room as O'Malley continued. "You from New Jersey? Where in New Jersey?"

"Amboy."

"Militia?"

"Yes."

"If you was sent here to join the Continentals, where's the rest of your company? No militia ever sent just one man."

"They deserted. Went back. I come on alone."

"Where's your musket?"

"Lost it."

O'Malley set the lantern on the table. A thin haze of smoke hung in the room from the green wood smoldering in the fireplace. He turned to Ellison.

"I think you brought in a spy. We was told to be watchin'. I'm goin' for the captain and a doctor."

He turned to Caleb. "While I'm gone, strip him and search him. Everything. Coat, pants, shoes—everything."

He spoke to the rest of the men. "Bolt the door and watch careful. See he don't eat no hidden poison or got a knife hid somewhere. I got a hunch the captain'll want a long talk with this man, and it won't do to have him dead."

Five minutes later O'Malley walked out the door, musket in hand, clad in the coat and shoes used for picket duty, and Caleb watched his back disappear in the frigid night. Caleb closed the door, dropped the heavy bar into its brackets, and turned to face the man.

"Strip off all your clothes."

The man was wild-eyed, trembling like a caged animal, and instead of removing his clothes, he reached quickly inside his coat with his right hand. When he withdrew it, a knife blade flashed in the yellow lantern light. He lunged at Caleb, slashing wildly at his vitals. Caleb avoided the thrust and in the same motion slammed his left fist into the man's face. The blow caught him flush on the jaw, knocking him backward into the table and sending him sprawling onto the dirt floor. In an instant four men were on top of him, clawing for the knife hand, choking him, pinning his arms and legs to the dirt floor.

Ellison turned frightened eyes to Caleb. "You hurt? He get that knife in you?"

Caleb shook his head. "Strip him. Everything."

Ellison mumbled, "Why don't we just stick that knife in him and tell O'Malley he fell on it?"

Caleb watched as half a dozen men wrestled every garment off the struggling, cursing man and laid them in a heap on the dirt floor. They tied him, hand and foot, and strapped him with belts to one of the crude benches at the table, then draped a blanket over his shoulders against the cold. They turned back to Caleb, waiting.

"Search everything." He reached for the coat.

Minutes passed while the men silently, systematically, went through everything. Suddenly one straightened, holding up a small, folded square of paper. "In the toe of his shoe!"

He handed it to Caleb, who held it to the lantern light for a moment, then began to carefully unfold it. Screaming and cursing, the man lunged against the belts that held him on the bench and the cords on his wrists and ankles. Four men pounced on him, and two minutes later he was gagged and tied spread-eagle in a lower bunk, covered with a ragged, filthy blanket.

Caleb sat at the table with every man gathered around, waiting, and finished unfolding the small paper. He laid it on the table and smoothed it the best he could with his hand, then raised it and read aloud.

"The wheat has been winnowed. It is ready for grinding. Nathan Ferguson." The words were printed; the signature written in scrolled English.

Caleb's forehead furrowed, and his eyes narrowed in puzzlement. The men around him turned to each other, exclaiming, asking questions no one could answer.

Caleb read it once more, then laid it on the table, unable to force a conclusion to the questions the brief message raised.

"That don't say one word about us or the British."

"Sounds like some sort of orders for a mill to grind someone's wheat."

One man picked up the paper and studied it closely, then glanced at Ferguson, tied, struggling, making muffled sounds in the bunk. "He don't print so good, but he signs his name real pretty."

Caleb took the slip and turned it to the light and carefully studied the signature. The letters were perfectly formed—the *N* and the *F* in a distinctive English scroll.

The recognition began quietly in the back of his brain and in an instant exploded to seize him. With trembling hands he laid the paper flat on the tabletop and dropped his face to within six inches of the signature to study every detail of every line.

The writing—the N *and the* F—*I've seen them before.*

He raised his head, his brain paralyzed. For ten seconds he stared, dumb, speechless. Then he cleared his throat and said softly, "Untie the man. Get him over here to the table."

While they struggled with the man, Caleb went to his bunk and unwrapped the few sheets of paper he had with his things and found his pencil. With the bleeding man sitting at the table, held in place by two men, Caleb moved the lantern directly in front of him. He laid the paper and pencil before the man, then reached for the nearest musket. He popped open the frizzen, checked the powder, snapped it shut, cocked the weapon, and pressed the muzzle against the man's jaw, just below his left ear.

"Sign your name, exactly the way you signed that message."

Animal sounds came from the man, indiscernible through the gag that filled his mouth. He struggled to rise, but eight hands jammed him back down on the bench.

"You have to the count of ten before I blow half your head off."

The room went dead silent, and the man looked into Caleb's eyes. What he saw brought his struggling to a stop. He picked up the pencil, squared the paper, and slowly formed "Nathan Furgusson."

Caleb lowered the musket, turned the paper, and studied the signature. It was crude, partly printed, partly written, and the last name was misspelled. He turned the paper back and said, "Sign it again, exactly as it is on that message we found." He raised the musket muzzle and pressed the cold metal just behind the man's ear.

Again the man formed the words on the page, and again Caleb examined them. They were again, crude, scrawled, as before. He took the paper, picked up the note they had found, and went to his bunk. While he dug into his belongings he said, "Tie him back in the bunk and watch him."

From within the folds of his belongings he drew out the letter he had received from Nancy. Hoping with all his soul that he was mistaken, he brought the lantern from the table and held the letter and the note in the yellow light. Behind him the men looked at each other in puzzlement while Caleb scrutinized every mark.

There was no doubt.

Carefully he folded his letter, then the sheet that the prisoner had signed on threat of being shot, and sat down at the table with them and the secret message in his hand.

"We wait for O'Malley."

The men knew only that something catastrophic had seized Caleb, and they did not interfere with him as they waited. Caleb sat as though in a trance, staring at the badly wrinkled note, mindless of the chill and the smoke in the hut. Time was without meaning, and he started at the sound of O'Malley banging at the door. A man lifted the bar and swung it open, and O'Malley entered, followed by two officers and a man bundled in an oversized coat, carrying a black case. It took O'Malley a few seconds to locate the man, gagged and tied in a bunk.

He spoke to the nearest man. "Untie him."

Caleb had not moved, and O'Malley looked at him in question. "You all right? What's happened?"

Caleb handed him the small note. "We found this in one of his shoes."

The two officers instantly crowded beside O'Malley to look at the tiny document, and for fifteen seconds silence held as they read and reread it. O'Malley spoke while Caleb and the others waited.

"This is Captain Wiebe and Lieutenant Thorson. Dr. Bristol come along to take a look at the wound."

Captain Wiebe suddenly exclaimed, "It's in code! It sounds like they're saying this camp is ready for the harvest—it can be taken by the British at any time!"

Lieutenant Thorson, shorter, huskier, spoke to O'Malley. "How was this man dressed?"

O'Malley looked at Ellison, who answered. "Clothes are right there, on the floor."

Quickly both officers went through them, then the shorter one turned to the prisoner, still tied to the cot. He untied the gag and cleared the struggling man's mouth. "You were dressed as a civilian. If you're a spy, you'll be hanged. It's possible you can save your life by telling us who gave this to you and where you were taking it."

The man's face drew into an ugly snarl. "I'm tellin' you nothin'."

Captain Wiebe shook his head. "It's your life." He tied the gag back in the man's mouth.

Dr. Bristol interrupted. "I thought this man was shot—needed medical attention."

O'Malley nodded. "In the hip."

"Let's take a look."

They untied one arm and one ankle and rolled the man on his side. Caleb held the lantern while the doctor looked at the smeared blood and the purple hole on the back side of the left hip. He pressed, and the prisoner groaned.

"Ball's still in there. From the angle I'd say it hit the pelvis. The hip bone. Ought to come out, if it's not stuck in the bone." He straightened. "Better get him dressed. We'll have to take him to the hospital. I'll operate as soon as he's ready."

Caleb spoke. "Which hospital?"

"The one near General Varnum's quarters, on Port Kennedy Road. Why?"

"The one where Nancy Fremont works?"

"Miss Fremont's there, yes."

"Will she be there tonight?"

The doctor shrugged. "She's not a surgical assistant, but we'll need two general nurses. She might be on call. I don't know."

"I'll help move the prisoner to the hospital."

O'Malley protested. "You got picket duty."

Caleb shook his head. "Someone'll have to trade with me. I'm going."

O'Malley sensed the need and let it pass. "Let's get him dressed. If that hip stiffens up we might have to carry him."

Forty minutes later the doctor answered the challenge of the picket at the front door of the hospital, opened the door, and the small column of men entered. The stench of putrid flesh and carbolics swamped them as they walked between the cots and the men on blankets spread on the floor, through the building to the place where a table with leather belts attached stood in an open area.

"This is it," the doctor said. "I'll get a surgical assistant and some nurses. I'll have to probe and maybe cut. This could take a while. While I'm gone, get his hip exposed and strap him down. And get some water heating on that stove over there. Light those overhead lamps."

Fifteen minutes later the doctor returned with a man and two women. Nancy Fremont was not one of them. The doctor inspected the hip of the wounded prisoner, jerked the leather belts to be certain they were tight, and nodded to his surgical assistant. The man quickly brought steaming water from the stove and washed the pucker around the black hole where the big lead ball had punched in, then assembled the few necessary surgical tools on a pewter tray.

The doctor picked up a long steel probe and spoke to the prisoner. "This is going to hurt. Want something in your teeth?"

The man nodded, and the doctor offered a six-inch piece of leather belt. The man bit down, nodded, and the doctor heaved a weary sigh and began the uncertain task of shoving the probe into the bullet channel, hoping to strike the ball on the first try. The two officers, O'Malley, and the others who had brought the prisoner stood in the yellow light, caught in the strange fascination of the time and the place and the sight of one man pushing a steel probe into the body of another.

Caleb turned to the closest general assistant and spoke quietly. "Do you know Nancy Fremont?"

The woman looked at him. "Yes."

"Where is she?"

"Asleep."

"Where? In what building?"

The woman looked at the doctor, who stood with his eyes closed, intensely feeling for the first contact with the bullet. Sweat had formed on his forehead. The prisoner was groaning through clenched teeth. She dared not interrupt.

"Across the way, in the servants' quarters," she whispered and pointed west. "Why do you want to know?"

Caleb did not answer. He turned and silently walked away from the surgical table to the door at the rear of the building and out into the night.

O'Malley glanced at Caleb as he left. *Can't stand watching the doctor probe? This whole thing too much for him?*

Outside Caleb paused while his eyes adjusted enough to make out a low, stone building thirty yards away—square, weathered, with a thin column of smoke rising straight into the black-domed heavens. The shades in the windows glowed dully. He walked to the front door and rapped. From within came a woman's voice.

"Who's there?"

"A soldier. The doctor sent me. He's operating on a wounded man."

The door opened a crack. "What does he want?"

"A nurse named Nancy Fremont. Is she here?"

"She's in her bed."

"He needs her."

The door opened hesitantly, and an aging woman wrapped in a heavy woolen housecoat, with her gray hair in a long braid stepped aside. "Come inside. I'll fetch her."

The room was small, lighted by a single lamp on the wall. The only break in the plain walls was a row of pegs for hanging coats behind the door. Caleb stepped inside and closed the door while the woman disappeared through a small archway into the larger room inside.

Caleb drew the three pieces of paper from inside his light summer coat and waited. His brain and his heart were numb. He felt no anger, no outrage. It was as though all feeling, all emotion, were disconnected from his being.

He heard the approaching footsteps, and then she was there, standing in the archway, dressed, heavy coat pulled tight by the belt at her waist, a scarf tied over her head to protect her hair and her ears from the freezing cold outside. She saw him and stood without speaking, eyes wide, mouth partly open. For three seconds neither spoke, and then she broke the silence.

"Caleb! What are you doing here?"

He said nothing. He handed her the crumpled little note taken from the prisoner and then the letter she had written to him. In the dim yellow light she quickly scanned one, then the other, and raised her eyes back to his. He saw the sudden rush of fear and watched the blood leave her face.

"I don't understand," she said.

He looked steadily into her eyes and said nothing.

For a time—neither knew or cared how long—she stood silent, unable to tear her eyes from his. Quietly a sureness came into both their hearts, and each knew.

"What are you going to do?" It was nearly a whisper.

He reached and took the two papers from her hand, opened the door, and held it, waiting. For five long seconds she stared at him, then she walked steadily out the door. He closed it behind them, and they walked, shoulder to shoulder, the thirty yards back to the hospital. Caleb held the rear door for her, she entered behind the surgical suite, and he led her to the edge of the light, where the doctor was bandaging the hip of the wounded prisoner.

Startled, O'Malley broke from the circle of men and walked to him. "I was worried. Might I know who this young lady is?"

Caleb spoke steadily. "Her name is Nancy Fremont, so far as I know. The message we found on that man was written by her. She got the information on it from me. I believe she is a British spy."

O'Malley gaped, speechless for a moment. "How . . . on what proof?"

"These three pieces of paper. One is a letter she wrote me. One is the message we took from that man's shoe. The third is the signature he made back in the hut. The signature on the secret message was made by this woman, not him."

"You can prove that man didn't sign the message we got from him?"

"Yes. I made him sign his name twice. Look at it. He can hardly write—couldn't even spell his own last name, or the name he claimed to be his. Then look at her signature on the letter and the one on the message. They were made by the same person. Her."

O'Malley turned to face Nancy. He could not recall a more beautiful young face. His eyes met hers, and in hers O'Malley saw her confession. "Ma'am, until this is all straightened out, you're under arrest. Don't try to leave."

He turned to the men surrounding the surgical table, where Dr. Bristol had stepped back and was washing his hands. "That's all I can do for now." He looked at his assistants. "Get him to a cot and then clean up, will you?"

The cluster of men backed away, and for the first time talk broke out among them. O'Malley motioned to the two officers, who came to him, clearly puzzled.

O'Malley pointed. "This young lady is accused of being a British spy. That man we just operated on is likely her courier."

Wiebe's mouth dropped open in astonishment. "What?"

"I've put her under arrest. You ought to take her to a cell while proper charges are written out."

Dr. Bristol broke in. "Preposterous! I've worked with this young lady long enough to know this business of her being a spy is utterly ridiculous. I demand you release her at once."

O'Malley raised a hand. "You'll have your chance at her hearing, Doctor. Until then she stays under arrest." He turned back to the two officers. "She's in your charge now."

Lieutenant Thorson found his voice. "On what evidence are these charges brought?"

O'Malley handed him the three pieces of paper. "These. Compare 'em. She signed two of them. He signed the third."

For twenty seconds the officers held the papers in the light and pored over them. "How did you get these?"

"From him." He gestured to Caleb.

"He brought her in?"

"Yes. Alone."

"He'll testify to all of this?"

"Yes."

"Is he implicated? Is he a spy, too?"

O'Malley shook his head. "No. We're lucky. It just all happened in one place tonight, where he could see it. He put it all together and got her."

The officers shook their heads in bewilderment, clearly disliking the business of bringing in a beautiful young woman to be tried as a spy. One folded the papers and carefully slipped them inside his tunic. "I'll be responsible for these."

One reached for Nancy, and Caleb stepped forward. "Could I see her alone for just a minute. You can watch if you like."

The officers looked at each other. "Over there."

Caleb led her ten feet to the edge of the lantern light and for a moment looked into her face. He memorized every line, every feature before he spoke.

"Why?"

"For England. My native country. You would do the same for America."

"Can you tell me your real name?"

"I cannot."

"How old are you?"

"Eighteen."

"Was it all an illusion?"

She looked him steadily in the eyes. "No. I loved you. I didn't expect that to happen, but it did."

He saw the slightest quiver in her chin, and she reached to wipe at a single tear that started in the corner of her eye.

Caleb took her arm, turned, and led her back to the waiting men. He said nothing as he watched the two officers take her between them and walk her through the hospital, out into the black, cold world.

He turned to O'Malley. "What'll happen to her?"

O'Malley drew a heavy breath. "First, what does she mean to you?"

"I met her months ago. We became friends. Good friends."

"Do you love her?"

Caleb was startled that such a question could come from a grizzled, hard soldier. The thought that O'Malley had ever felt such feelings for a woman had never entered Caleb's mind.

"I think I did. Yes."

O'Malley shook his head, and a softness that Caleb had never heard before came into his voice. "I'm sorry. So sorry. Worse that you had to bring her in. You did a brave thing."

Caleb spoke, and O'Malley saw the deep need in his face. "What will happen to her, O'Malley?"

"She'll be tried as a spy. If she's found guilty, she might hang. I don't know the last time we hanged a woman spy, but that's what the rules call for."

"Isn't there something besides hanging?"

"It's possible they could send her to England on orders that if she ever returns she'll be hanged."

"Can that happen? Can someone recommend it?"

For a time O'Malley studied the pain in Caleb's face. "Yes. Maybe me."

"Will you?"

O'Malley's answer came slowly. "I'll try."

Note

The events depicted in this chapter are fictional.

CHAPTER XXVIII

★ ★ ★

*E*li ducked to enter the low door of the hut and softly closed it against the cold, then reached to wipe at the thick, white frost that had collected in his beard from his two hours on picket duty. He leaned his long Pennsylvania rifle against the wall and silently stepped to Billy's bunk to lay a hand his shoulder. Billy's eyes opened in the darkness of the small hut, and Eli said softly, "Your duty."

Billy lay still for a moment, then swung his legs out of his bunk. He still wore his trousers and shirt and socks, and he shivered as he reached for the shoes that had been given to him five months earlier by the German family who had allowed him a night's sleep in their barn. The banked coals in the fireplace cast everything in the small, square room as dim shapes, and Eli loomed large in his wolf-skin coat and moccasins, with his parka still over his head. He added two sticks of green kindling, then spoke softly.

"I'll be back not long after sunup. Tell Turlock."

"Where you going?"

"I heard wolves less than a half mile from camp on my way back from picket duty. I promised Mary a wolf-skin coat."

Billy shrugged. "I'll tell him." He watched Eli pick up the rifle and a coil of rawhide cord, and he felt the cold rush of air as Eli walked out the door and closed it.

The sap in the green kindling made a small hissing sound as it boiled

477

out and dripped into the flames, and Billy added one more stick before he picked up his musket and walked out into the night. A sliver of moon lay low on the eastern horizon, and Billy felt his breath freezing in his beard as he walked steadily to his picket post. He leaned his musket against a tree and began the nightly ritual of all who stood picket duty in the fierce cold. He wrapped his arms around himself and moved his feet. He pounded his open hands against his sides and on his thick legs. He rubbed his face until feeling returned, then began the ritual again.

He judged that an hour had passed when he heard the unmistakable crack of a rifle far to the south, away from the river. *Eli. I wonder if he hit in the dark.* He thought for a moment. *If he shot, he hit.*

At the end of his second hour he was shaking from the cold as he picked up his musket and walked back to the hut. He was at the door when the report of a second rifle shot reached him from the southwest, and he instinctively turned to look. *Did he get two?*

He entered the hut and touched one of the other men on the shoulder. "Your duty."

Dawn came clear and colorless to cast the camp in stark sunlight. Dark smoke from green wood rose up the chimneys of nine hundred huts, into the still air of a cloudless sky. Silent men, gaunt scarecrows dressed in rags, with feet wrapped in bloody, shredded strips of anything they could find, walked out to cut more wood—always more wood—to keep from freezing to death in their huts. The light of hope was gone from their eyes. Their only thought was finding a way to survive one more day. One more day.

Billy's clothes hung slack on his frame as he pulled on his coat and buttoned the front. The coat hung from his shoulders like a tent, and he wrapped a piece of cord around his middle and tied it tight to his body. With Turlock and two others from his hut, he walked out into the morning and loaded the four axes leaned against the front wall onto a crude sled. Two men looped the rope over their shoulders, and they started south, dragging the sled toward the trees. They had gone twenty yards when Turlock pointed.

"Eli's coming."

They all looked at Eli, walking out of the woods toward them, hunched forward, dragging two dead wolves in the snow behind. At his approach the wood crew stopped.

Billy pointed to the two wolves—one white, one gray. "Enough for the coat?"

Eli nodded. "Got to skin them." He waited a moment before he continued. "Wolf meat's a little tough and stringy and bitter, but a man can stay alive on it."

All four men on the wood crew raised a hand to wipe at their beards while they stared at the dead carcasses with but one thought.

Turlock said, "Let's get 'em loaded." Without a word they dragged the two dead wolves onto the sled and turned it around. Minutes later they stopped at the door of the hut and Turlock spoke.

"You men fill the pots with snow and get them heated inside. Eli, you need help skinnin' 'em?"

Eli shook his head. "They're frozen. I'll clean out the cavity out here, but I'll have to bring them inside to skin them."

Fifteen minutes later the men dumped diced heart and liver into three steaming pots. For the next forty minutes they waited while Eli peeled the skin back, careful not to score the pelts, and cut off the hams, then the loins, and finally the shoulders from the first carcass. The other men in the hut stripped the meat off the bones, diced it, and dropped it splashing into the pots. They wrinkled their noses at the piercing stench of boiling wolf meat, and they stirred it with sticks while Eli skinned the second carcass. He spread the gray pelt on the floor behind the door, laid the meat on it, and covered it with the white pelt. He walked outside to wash his hands in snow while Turlock got his wooden bowl and dipped some of the steaming broth into it. He raised it, held his breath, and sipped.

He shuddered and for a moment could not speak. "It's greasy and bitter, and it needs salt, but there's strength in it. Get your bowls."

They dipped the broth and chunks of the diced meat and sipped at it. Five of them gagged and turned their heads, but they held it down and continued dipping it up with their wooden spoons. The warmth spread from their bellies outward, and they slowed for a time, then dipped some more.

Finally Turlock set his empty bowl on the table. "Better slow down. Your bellies been empty too long. They won't take too much at first."

The men finished what was in their bowls and sat on the benches or on their bunks while their stomachs struggled to hold the wolf stew.

"We'll wait twenty minutes, then we got to go get the firewood. We'll keep the pots warm for dinner and supper."

They sat in silence, savoring the feel of meat in their bellies, struggling to choke down the urge to vomit up the bitter, greasy gruel. Turlock gave them twenty-five minutes before he stood.

"All right, you lovelies, the wood won't cut itself. Let's get at it."

The wood crew filed out the door as the sound of trotting horses brought their heads around, peering east. They watched a team of matched Percheron geldings, necks arched against the pull of the bit, trotting west, pulling a large, black sleigh. As it passed, the men saw a stout officer sitting stiffly straight, dressed in a buff and blue uniform, tricorn squarely on his head. There was an officer facing him in the opposing seat.

Turlock shook his head. "That German again. Been out riding around camp like that for three, four days. Looks like he's headed for headquarters. I wonder what he has to say to Gen'l Washington."

They watched the sleigh go out of sight before they once again loaded the axes on the sled and trudged south toward the trees.

Three miles west, seated in his small office, Washington concluded reading a document, nodded his approval, dipped his quill in the inkwell, and affixed his signature. He leaned back to let it dry and spoke to Hamilton, seated opposite him.

"There's the order for the trial. I understand one of the accused is a woman. Quite young, in fact."

"Eighteen. Beautiful girl."

Washington shook his head. "Will you arrange to have the men who caught her in this office by two o'clock today? They've done a remarkable thing. I want to commend them personally."

"Yes, sir."

Washington glanced at the clock on the fireplace mantel. "Are we expecting Baron von Steuben this morning?"

"In five minutes, sir."

"When he arrives, show him in. I understand he has requested audience for most of the morning."

Hamilton nodded. "Yes, he has. I think the general will be . . . uh . . . surprised at Baron von Steuben's views on our camp."

Washington's eyebrows raised. "Oh?" He reflected for a moment. "Is Colonel Laurens going to be here?"

"He is, sir."

The sound and ground vibrations of heavy horses approaching came, and instinctively both men looked out through the light lace of the window curtains.

Hamilton stood. "That should be him now, sir."

"Bring him in."

Hamilton left, and Washington leaned back in his plain, wooden chair, pondering while he waited. The clicking of boot heels in cadence came down the hallway, and Washington straightened in his chair. He answered the rap at the door, John Laurens opened it, entered, and stepped aside. Baron von Steuben strode in, his face a mask of military discipline, followed by General Du Ponceau. Von Steuben stopped a measured six feet from Washington's desk, and his arm snapped up in a salute. He spoke, and Du Ponceau translated.

"Baron von Steuben reporting as ordered, sir."

Washington stood, returned the salute, and gestured to them all to take their places, Laurens at the side of the desk, the two Germans facing him. All sat down on plain, straight-backed chairs. The only break in the austere walls was the stone fireplace built in one wall, where a fire burned. Above the fireplace was a simple mantel, with a clock that ticked steadily.

Washington leaned forward on his forearms, hands clasped. All too well he knew the destitute condition of the American army, but he refused to make excuses. "I trust your accommodations are adequate?"

Von Steuben nodded. "Yes. Fine."

"Have you had sufficient time to reach some conclusions concerning this camp?"

"I have made a writing." Du Ponceau handed von Steuben a sheaf of papers nearly half an inch thick. Washington masked his surprise.

"I would be happy to hear your recommendations."

Von Steuben bobbed his head once. "The general will forgive me if I speak too plainly, but it is my experience that plainness is sometimes required." Von Steuben stopped, and his eyes bored into Washington's.

Washington said, "I prefer plainness. Proceed."

Von Steuben worked with the papers for a moment, took a deep breath, and ripped into it, voice steady, words clipped with strict Prussian discipline.

"I will speak first of the regiments. I have not found one that is organized. The officers are elected by the vote of the men. This means the officers must maintain the good will of the men they lead or be replaced whenever the men wish. It strips the officers of any possibility of disciplining their soldiers. The practice is utterly ridiculous. It must stop at once. Officers must be selected on merit."

His eyes dropped to his paperwork. "I believe no regiment has more than one-third of its men fit for duty at this time. One company has but one man remaining—a corporal. Another company cannot mount a corporals' guard today. Not one regiment can muster a full company. I discovered a Massachusetts regiment under the command of a lieutenant! To call such a thing an army is unthinkable."

He cleared his throat, and his voice heightened almost imperceptibly. "I will now talk of the soldiers. Never have I seen men in this condition. They are dressed in rags. I have seen some soldiers absolutely naked. They are barefoot. They leave blood in the snow where they walk. As of this morning they have had no rations—not one thing—for eight days. Their bodies are racked with open sores. They suffer from fever, typhoid, smallpox. Every available building within ten miles is filled with the sick and dying. We call them hospitals, but in truth they are little more than breeding places for death. Every night men die from freezing. Every day wagons pass through camp to collect the dead bodies, and they are buried without ceremony, twenty or more to a grave, with no memorial of who they were or where they were from. I counted twenty-one dead bodies cast into a wagon like trash yesterday. There were great rats in the wagon, gnawing on the corpses. I watched as they were thrown in a shallow trench, like so many dead cattle. The men throwing them in fought over what little clothing they could strip from the corpses, like grave robbers. Ghouls! The practice is appalling!"

Washington's face was a mask of disciplined shock at the brutality of von Steuben's assault. Laurens sat like a stone statue. Von Steuben continued.

"The camp is filthy beyond anything I have ever seen. Three hundred twenty-nine dead horse carcasses scattered everywhere, putrid, decaying. The vaults used by the men to relieve their bowels are full and overflowing and unusable, so the men now evacuate their bowels and relieve themselves wherever they wish, like animals. Human excrement is everywhere! The stink is worse than any cattle or horse corral I have ever seen. The insides of the huts are little better. I do not believe a single soldier has cleaned his body in two months. They urinate against the walls. Their bedding is filthy. The floors of the huts are dirt. The roofs leak. There is no question the deplorable conditions in this camp have filled the hospitals with sick and dying men."

Von Steuben stopped to place a finger on his papers. In that moment the room was locked in a silence so tense that Hamilton dared not move.

The German went on. "Officers are dressed in uniforms made from bed quilts or from cast-off blankets. Every company has a different color, a different design for uniforms. No two companies appear to be from the same army. It is impossible to achieve unity in an army when no two companies appear the same."

Du Ponceau was watching von Steuben intently, not missing a word, translating everything exactly as it was spoken. Laurens had not moved nor spoken as he followed both von Steuben's Germanic presentation and Du Ponceau's translation.

"Every company drills its men according to its own notions—often by the whim of the officers in charge. There are at least fifty different systems of drill in this camp, no two alike. It is a travesty to call such an assembly of regiments an army! They are not an army! They are fifty small, separate groups of badly prepared officers and undisciplined soldiers, who are worse than no army at all."

Hamilton glanced at Washington, whose mouth was a slit above a chin set like granite.

"The equipment is very close to unusable. There is no uniformity. Most companies have muskets, fowling pieces, carbines, and rifles, all mixed together. Close to half the weapons are rusted so badly they will not fire a single shot. Parts must be exchanged or replaced—hammers, frizzens, triggers—and you cannot replace the hammer of a musket with that taken from a rifle, nor the frizzen on a rifle with one taken from a fowling piece. As for the bayonets, the men have never been trained to use them. Many have been thrown away. Most are used to skewer bits of food to cook over a fire, when they can find the food. Cartridge pouches are nearly nonexistent. Men are still carrying powder in cattle horns. The cannon are rusting. Should this camp be required to fight today, more than half the weapons would not fire. I am unable to understand how the muskets and cannon have been allowed to come into such a condition."

Von Steuben stopped again, and silence held while he reviewed his notes, then went on:

"It is my opinion this army is badly organized. The office of inspector general is very close to nonfunctional. I am told there are no financial records available, nor are there any records of the supplies that have been purchased, where they have gone, or how much remains available. Quartermasters are paid according to the amount of goods they purchase, and with no records to control the flow of goods, the result is that theft abounds at every turn. Goods bought for this army are being sold at inflated prices in Philadelphia and other places, while the quartermasters and their conspirators grow rich. The organization of this army was patterned after that of the British army. To state it in the simplest possible terms, this army is a very poor copy of a very poor original."

He paused to allow his words to settle in, then forged on. "The system of soldiers enlisting for three months or six months or nine months, and then leaving, will cripple this army until it is corrected. No sooner do we train a soldier than he is gone, and we must begin with a new one. We will never have a fully trained, effective army until we have the soldiers long enough to train them and then get the benefit of their training."

Von Steuben drew and released a great sigh, peered at his notes, and raised his eyes to Washington's. For a few moments there was a silent exchange between the two men, and then von Steuben continued.

"Many soldiers waste much time with cards and gambling. All forms of gambling must cease. The inevitable result of gambling is arguments and fights, sometimes killing. It makes soldiers lazy, undisciplined. It must stop at once."

Von Steuben rearranged his sheaf of papers to bring a new section to the top, cast his eyes at the floor while he determined he had finished the first half of his presentation, and raised his eyes back to Washington.

"I recognize I have said many critical things. May I repeat, there is a time for plain speaking. It is my opinion this is one of them. May I now continue with some thoughts and proposals that may be of a more positive nature?"

Hamilton's eyes widened. *In the name of heaven, I hope so! This man has demolished every part of this army. Is there something he missed?*

Washington nodded, and von Steuben glanced down at the new section of his paperwork.

"I begin with the soldiers. I state bluntly that no European army I have ever seen or read about would survive the conditions I find here. I am overpowered with admiration when I see your men as they are, freezing, starving, but standing to their duties. Refusing to mutiny. Refusing to desert. There is something in their spirit that is indomitable. Grand. If I . . . we . . . can find a way to harness that spirit, I thrill at the possibilities of the army we can produce. Think of it!"

A light broke in Washington's eyes. Von Steuben's voice rose, and there was a beginning of excitement about him as he continued.

"I believe I have discovered something that is very important to understanding how to reach your men." He stopped, searching for the right words. "In Europe you tell the soldier, 'Do this,' and he doeth it because that is what he was ordered to do." A shine came into his eyes. "But in this army, you tell the soldier, 'This is the *reason* you *ought* to do this, and he doeth it.'"

Washington started. Laurens gaped. Hamilton drew breath. Instantly each of them grasped that this rigid, stout Prussian officer had plumbed the depth of the American soldier and reached the foundations on which the army—the entire nation—rested. None of the three Americans in the room had ever heard it pronounced so clearly, so concisely. Order an American, and you have no guarantee. Give an American the reasons, and if the reasons are good enough, you will have a convert. Choice. Rob an American of choice, and he will fight.

Von Steuben went on. "I am writing a drill manual for the Continental Army. I have named it *Regulations for the Order and Discipline of the Troops of the United States.* It addresses all matters concerning the soldier and will train the entire army as one." He paused and looked at Laurens, then Hamilton, then back at Washington. "I am aware you have selected two extraordinary men to be your personal aides. I would be grateful if you would allow me to seek their advice on the manual before it is finished. I am certain their contribution will be invaluable."

Neither Laurens nor Hamilton could hide the startled expression that crossed his face.

Washington nodded. "They are available to you at any time."

"Without exceeding my position, may I suggest it has become necessary to obtain food and clothing for this army, at any cost. Foraging in the countryside if necessary?"

"I agree. I have sent Generals Greene and Wayne out on such assignments now. Food and clothing are beginning to arrive in small quantities." Washington stopped, then added, "I have done so under authority granted me in writing by the United States Congress."

Von Steuben leaned back, struck by the fact that the commander in chief openly recognized that his authority was subordinate to a civilian congress elected by the people. He knew of no other country with a government so structured.

He leaned forward, and his voice became animated. "This is the month of March. This army must be prepared to move by May. The answer to most of the problems is drill. Discipline. I have but seventy-five days to prepare them. I propose that I be given two men from each company, to be picked because they are intelligent and capable. I will drill them twice a day for thirty days, and then I will send them back to their companies, and they will train their own men. In this manner I will have your army prepared for battle for the summer campaign."

Washington's mind leaped at the simple genius of the plan. He glanced at Laurens. "Can you prepare such an order for my signature, today?"

"Absolutely, sir."

Washington turned back to von Steuben, who continued:

"Issue orders immediately, today, that this camp will be cleaned up. Dead horses will be buried. Hospitals cleaned. Deceased soldiers given military burials, with their names, homes, and families recorded, so letters can be sent to their next of kin. Old vaults will be buried and new ones dug for the soldiers to relieve themselves. Men will bathe regularly. Gambling in any form stops today. Officers will be selected on merit. Records will be required of the quartermaster's office showing all goods received, held, and delivered, and complete financial accounts of all monies handled. The inspector general's office should be notified that it has five days to correct its inaction or face the probability of being replaced by someone who will. We must obtain new weapons—from France if necessary—and make one musket standard throughout the army. The soldiers must be trained to use the bayonet and be required to keep their weapons in good repair."

Von Steuben paused, and Washington raised a hand. "Baron von Steuben, could you reduce these proposals to writing?"

Von Steuben turned to Du Ponceau, who handed him a second sheaf of papers. "I have already done so. This copy is for you." He pushed it across the desk to Washington.

Washington picked up the packet, read the cover sheet, and laid it back on his desk. "I presume this includes the notes you used in our discussion."

"Yes, everything."

"I and my two aides will study it and send word to you for another conference when we're prepared."

"That is good."

"Is there anything else you wish to discuss at this time?"

"No."

Washington stood, and they all stood with him. "You will hear from one of my aides. You are dismissed."

Von Steuben's heels clicked, and he bowed stiffly from the waist. "It is my great honor to be in your service."

Hamilton opened the door, von Steuben turned on his heel, and Du Ponceau followed him out of the room. Hamilton escorted them out of the building and quickly returned to Washington's office, where the general was holding the half-inch thick paperwork in his hand. Laurens was seated at the side of the desk.

Hamilton sat down. "Sir, I'm not quite sure what we just experienced."

Washington answered, "It was a great many things, but, finally, I think it might have been the message that will save this army." He dropped the papers on his desk. "Do either of you have any thoughts?"

Laurens raised his voice. "I'm concerned. Will our soldiers . . . accept . . . his Prussian sense of discipline?"

For several moments Washington stared down at the paperwork. "Perhaps not from an American officer, but there's something about this man. They might accept it from him."

Suddenly Washington looked at the clock on the mantel, startled at the time. It was as though his mind had returned from a far place to the crushing business of running an army well on its way to disintegrating. "It's half past twelve o'clock. I had no idea we had taken so much time. Don't we have men coming at two o'clock?"

Hamilton nodded. "Yes, sir. The ones who discovered the two spies.

And I must mention, the sergeant in question has requested a few minutes to speak to you."

"About what?"

"He didn't say."

"Very well. We shall be here. Right now I'm overdue for dinner with Mrs. Washington. I will return in time for the two o'clock meeting."

Both Laurens and Hamilton stood while Washington snapped on his cape and collected his tricorn. They followed him to the front door, well aware there was a lightness and a quickness to his step as he hurried down the front walkway and turned to his quarters and his Martha and a meal she had prepared with her own hands.

At ten minutes before two o'clock, Washington was back in his office chair. At two o'clock Hamilton rapped on the door.

"The two o'clock appointment is here, sir."

At five minutes past two, Sergeant Randolph O'Malley was seated across the desk from the general, with Caleb seated to his right and five other men from Third Company on his left and behind him. They wore the best clothing they had and still looked like exactly what they were— men who had starved too long, wearing the tattered rags that remained from their summer clothing, without shoes, feet wrapped in scraps and rags that showed blood splotches.

Washington's eyes swept the group, and he spoke to O'Malley. "I understand you are the sergeant of this company?"

"Yes, sir. Sergeant Randolph O'Malley, Third Company, Ninth New York Regiment."

"My information is that you and these men are the ones who discovered the two spies who have been sending information to the British."

"Yes, sir."

"I deemed it appropriate to extend my thanks to you. We have known that someone is conveying secret information to the British, but we had assumed that it was an officer. The message you intercepted urges the British to attack this camp with a major force. Whoever wrote it seems intimately acquainted with our weakened condition. It may well be that you have prevented a catastrophic defeat—that you have saved not only this army but the United States. I shall take steps to ensure that your action receives due recognition from Congress."

"Thank you, sir."

"Do I understand correctly, that it was a young soldier who discovered the plot?"

"Yes, sir. Private Caleb Dunson, seated here beside me."

Washington nodded to Caleb. "Private Dunson, would you please explain how you discovered the spy?"

"Yes, sir." Caleb took a deep breath. *Tell it straight. If you get hung, tell it straight.* "I believe I was the one giving out the information. From time to time I was assigned to make entries in the regimental orderly book. In conversations with a young lady, I mentioned some of what was there. The night Private Ellison shot the courier and brought him to the hut, we found a message in the toe of his shoe. I recognized the handwriting on the message. It had been written by the lady. I confronted her, and she confessed. I brought her in. I believe that's all, sir."

For five long seconds Washington studied Caleb through narrowed eyes. "Do I sense this was a matter of the heart between you and this young lady?"

"Yes, sir, it was. She was a nurse in the hospital. I had strong feelings for her. I did not know she was a British loyalist. The fault was mine."

"You're the one who arrested her?"

"I was, sir."

"Despite your . . . feelings . . . for her?"

"Yes, sir."

Washington said, "If I am seeing this matter correctly, the part she played as a British spy would have likely gone undetected if you had not grown close to her."

Caleb thought for a moment. "That is probable, sir."

"And when you knew the truth, you brought her in?"

"Yes, sir."

Washington leaned forward and spoke directly to Caleb. "Remarkable. Private Dunson, you must never punish yourself for what happened. To the contrary, your . . . feelings for this young lady seem to have been the key to discovering the plot. That you would bring her in, despite such feelings, is to your great credit. Do you understand?"

For one moment Caleb's chin trembled. "Yes, sir. Thank you, sir."

Washington turned back to O'Malley. "Sergeant, I am informed you have some matters you wish to discuss?"

"Yes, sir."

Washington waited. O'Malley gathered himself, took a deep breath, and spoke.

"Gen'l, sir, I'm no officer. I don't have no right, no . . . standing to talk to you this way, but I got to do it. I'm responsible for these men and some more besides. Look at us, sir. Every man in the company—in this army—has lost so much weight we look like sticks of wood. Today is eight days since we had anything—*anything*—give to us to eat. The last solid thing we had was some British shoes that wouldn't fit nobody. We boiled 'em for two days and drank the broth and chewed the leather 'til we could swallow it. We're wearin' our best clothes right now, and look at us, sir. Four of these men had their toes froze and had them cut off. Haven't seen soap for two months."

O'Malley stopped for a moment to gather his thoughts.

"Sir, we aren't complainin'. We'll stay here until we're dead, if that's what you ask. All I'm tryin' to say is, it's hard for me to be responsible for these men and watch 'em slowly dyin' and not be able to do nothin' about it. If there's anything can be done for 'em, I'll do whatever is asked. I hope you understand, sir."

O'Malley stopped. Hamilton's jaw was working, and he dared not look up from the floor. Laurens reached to cover his mouth. Washington waited until he could trust his voice.

"Sergeant, I have sent Generals Nathanael Greene and Anthony Wayne out into the countryside, with written orders to take whatever they can find, wherever they find it. They're to pay a fair price in continental money for it, and no more. They're to seize it at bayonet point if necessary. I am reliably informed that General Wayne has more than one hundred eighty cattle being driven to this camp, due to arrive soon. There is no feeling you have for your men that I do not share with you. I promise you, I give you my word of honor, I will find a way to feed and clothe these men."

The room fell silent. For five seconds no one moved or spoke while a feeling rose in the breast of every man that for a few moments lifted them above the discouragement, the pain, the suffering, and filled them with a hope that somehow they would survive the horrors of their trials and move on.

Washington broke the mood. "Sergeant, before you leave, would you give the names of the soldiers you have with you to Colonel Hamilton. I want their names to appear in the regimental orderly book."

"Yes, sir."

"Is there anything else?"

"Only this, sir. I didn't have no idea you'd listen to a sergeant. But you did. That is something . . . special. I don't know . . . I have nothing else I can think to say, sir."

"I am glad you came. If there is nothing else, you are dismissed."

★　★　★　★　★

Alone in the dark of night, in the light of a single lamp on his desk, Washington stood. He rubbed weary, bloodshot eyes, then stretched muscles that had cramped from nine hours at his desk, studying the detail in the papers von Steuben had delivered. In his memory he could not recall a commander who had faced so many heart-wrenching problems for which there was no solution. Congress, food, medicine, clothing, sickness, death, cold, officers seeking his ouster—the burden was crushing his soul.

He looked once more at von Steuben's papers. *Maybe. Maybe. If he can find a way to instill discipline. . . . It might be a start.*

Then he was seeing O'Malley. Stocky, bushy red beard, clothing in tatters, feet wrapped in bloody strips of a bean sack, hollow cheeks, sunken eyes, pleading, begging for his men. Washington felt the grab in his own heart and sat back down at his table. Minutes later he reached for his quill and wrote:

"Without arrogance or the smallest deviation from truth it may be said that no history, now extant, can furnish an instance of any army's suffering such uncommon hardships as ours has done and bearing them with the same patience and fortitude. To see men without clothes to cover their nakedness, without blankets to lie on, without shoes by which their marches might be traced by the blood from their feet and almost as often without provisions as with; marching through frost and snow, and at Christmas taking up their winter quarters within a day's march of the enemy, without a house or a hut to cover them till they could be built, and submitting to it without a murmur, is a mark of patience and obedience which in my opinion can scarce be paralleled."

He read it, then buried his face in his hands for a time. Finally he leaned back in his chair, then stood.

Congress will receive that message when the time is right. It must go into its records. Someone has to preserve the truth for future generations about what these men did here. The price they have paid.

He snapped on his cape, lifted his tricorn from the peg by the door, walked back to blow out the lamp, and walked out into the freezing night.

Notes

The thorough, blunt presentation by Baron von Steuben of the condition of the Continental Army at Valley Forge is stated correctly. There was no part of the army, including lack of supplies of every kind, officer incompetency, near total lack of discipline among the soldiers, terrible organization, failure of the quartermaster's office, critical neglect of the weapons, deplorable hospital conditions, and other matters, that escaped his scathing report, as set forth herein. Parts of his written appraisal are quoted verbatim. Von Steuben recognized the genius of explaining the purpose of military matters to the American soldiers. He wrote the "Blue Book" for American drill, called "Regulations for the Order and Discipline of the Troops of the United States." Reed, *Valley Forge: Crucible of Victory*, pp. 39–40; Jackson, *Valley Forge: Pinnacle of Victory*, p. 126; Leckie, *George Washington's War*, p. 440.

During the last seven days of February 1778, the soldiers received no meat and almost no other supplies. The officers were expecting a mutiny. Instead, the soldiers came to headquarters to present their case and plead for help in humble terms. Thus the appearance of the fictional character Sergeant Randolph O'Malley to plead for his men is consistent with the true history of Valley Forge. Wildes, *Valley Forge*, p. 170.

The writing attributed to George Washington in the closing pages of this chapter, wherein he prepared a written statement to be sent to Congress, in which he marveled at the patient suffering of his army, is a verbatim quote. The writing was sent to Congress and was preserved for history. Freeman, *Washington*, p. 385.

CHAPTER XXIX

★ ★ ★

*E*li stood near the door of the hut to buckle his weapons belt around his middle, then reached to pull his parka over his head. Billy dropped the last stick of kindling into the fireplace, rose from his haunches, and looked at Eli, inquiring.

"Going to the river for water."

"Creek's closer."

Eli shook his head. "Froze solid clear to the bottom. I won't be long."

"Water for what? We ate the last of the wolf meat two days ago."

"We got the bones. Crack them with an ax while I'm gone. The marrow has strength."

He opened the door, stooped to step through, closed it, and stood still for a moment to take the shock of the frigid air on his face and in his lungs. The large, heavy wooden water bucket was frozen to the ground beside the door, and Eli kicked it to break it loose, then grasped the rope handle, frozen stiff, and started for the river. The tip of the rising sun washed the camp in a blush of rose color for several moments and turned nine hundred wispy columns of rising smoke to golden pillars reaching into the blue heavens. The colors held until the sun was one-quarter risen, and then they faded, and the camp was once again a canvas of white snow and green-black forest.

Eli marched steadily towards the Schuylkill River, the north boundary of the camp. As far as he could see in all directions, disorderly rows of huts imposed themselves in the woods and on the hills and in the valleys, crude intrusions that defiled the great scheme of nature. His breath froze in his beard, and frost whitened his eyebrows as he moved through the silent camp. He could see fewer than half a dozen men moving outside their huts, loading their arms with firewood from the stack against the front wall of the huts, then quickly disappearing inside.

One more week without food, and this army will be gone—where's the cattle Wayne was bringing in?—the flour Greene said was up in New Jersey?

He shook his head. *The British can't beat us, but the Americans can—just keep selling their food to the British.*

Soldiers had hacked a path through the barren oak and poplar trees and the frozen, leafless willows that lined the riverbank to the water's edge, where they had cleared a place to dip water. The handle of a rusty ax, left there to chop through the ice that sealed the hole each night, leaned against a rock. In the bitter cold Eli set the bucket down, picked up the ax, and dropped to one knee beside the newly frozen ice. Minutes later he had cut a large enough hole through five inches of ice and laid the ax aside. He was reaching for the bucket when movement in the black water stopped him. He stared, then dropped his head lower to be certain, and instantly his voice rang out.

"Shad!"

He seized the ax and swung hard. Ice chips flew as he widened the hole to six feet, then once again stooped, gaping. The water was roiling with the swimming bodies of the huge fish as they responded to the mysterious compulsion to migrate to the headwaters of their origins, there to spawn and die. He thrust the ax away, seized the bucket, dunked it in the water, waited for two seconds, then jerked it out. Water sloshed as he turned to set it on the ice, then plunged both hands in and seized one of the four-pound, writhing, slippery, gray-and-white fish. He threw it flopping onto the bank, then grasped the second fish and stood, clutching it in both hands as it writhed, fighting.

The ice was thick close to the bank but thinned fifteen yards out, leaving an open, running channel in the center of the river. Eli stood motionless to study the black water as it flowed east. It was unsettled, riffled, choppy. There was no doubt.

"They're running," he exclaimed.

He dumped the water from the bucket, threw both fish in, pivoted, and started south at a run. He burst through the door of the hut, and every man in the room jumped, startled. He slammed the bucket down on the table, seized one fish in each hand, and held them high in the dim light while the men stared in wide-eyed disbelief.

"The shad are running in the river. Thousands. Fat—full of eggs. Get the axes and anything that will catch a fish and get down there." He threw the two fish back into the bucket and turned to Billy. "I'll go east, you go west. Tell every officer you see. They only run once a year, and we got to get them while we can. There's enough to feed this army until spring if we get them in time."

From behind came the sounds of men chewing, and Eli turned to look. Two men had cut strips of the white meat from the flopping fish, heavy with rich fish oil, and were stuffing the raw flesh into their mouths. Oil and blood ran from the corners of their mouths into their beards, and they did not care. They only knew that after eight days of famine, they had food in their mouths that would stay in their bellies and give nourishment to their gaunt bodies.

Eli could not find it in his heart to stop them. "When you've had your fill, get on up to the river. Billy, let's go."

By seven o'clock men were running in all directions, shouting, "The river—get to the river—the shad are running!" By eight o'clock mounted riders had reached both ends of the camp, shouting the news as they went. By nine o'clock most of the soldiers of the Continental Army were at the river, smashing holes in the ice with whatever they could find, then plunging into the frigid water up to their knees, grabbing the squirming fish with their hands and throwing them up on the banks as fast as they could. By ten o'clock riders were circulating through the adjacent farms, seizing the fishnets used by the citizens to catch the spring run. By noon the nets were strung across the river above the junction with Valley Creek, and every serviceable horse in camp was in the river seven miles below the nets, side by side, their riders spurring them west, breaking through the ice into water up to their bellies, driving the fish before them. Oxen were hooked to the nets, filled to overflowing with great piles of the writhing fish, to drag them ashore. On the banks teams of men slit them, vent to gills, stripped the eggs into buckets, dumped the entrails on the ground, quickly rinsed the fish in river water, and threw them into barrels or crates or onto blankets—anything that would hold them while the frantic work went on and on. Starving men everywhere were slicing chunks from the silver and gray shad and stuffing them into their mouths, to chew while they worked.

By two o'clock the horsemen were against the nets, and they reined their mounts out of the river, back to the east to start the second drive. The sun had dropped below the western horizon when the riders reached the nets the second time. They spurred their weary, ice-caked horses out of the water and quickly stripped the saddles and used the saddle blankets to rub them down.

With hands and feet that were numb from the cold and clothing stiff with ice, the exhausted soldiers left the catch in the barrels and crates and on the riverbank and trotted back to their huts to keep from freezing, knowing the shad would be there, frozen stiff, the next morning. Each man carried fish back to his hut and drew close to blazing fires, to roast the fish, watching the flesh split and the rich oil ooze out, dripping into the flames as his own frozen clothes thawed and steamed. They plucked the fish from the fire into their wooden bowls and picked at the flaky, white meat until it stopped sizzling, then crammed it into their mouths with their hands. They filled their battered, blackened skillets with fish eggs and stirred them until they were steaming, then portioned them out. They could not remember a time when food meant so much as it did that night.

Eli set his empty bowl on the table and looked at Billy. "How much did we take from the river today?"

Billy shook his head. "All together?" He shook his head. "No idea. Tons. Maybe fifty tons."

"They'll be running again tomorrow."

"I expect the army will be right there to take them."

"Don't need to salt it down in barrels. The cold will hold it for a month, maybe six weeks. Might get enough to see the whole army through to warm weather."

"It will probably save us."

An insistent knock at the door brought all eyes around. Turlock raised the bar and opened it six inches. A young lieutenant stood outside, shaking in the cold.

"Come in."

The young man entered, and Turlock pointed to the table. "Have some fish."

"No time. I'm looking for Sergeant Turlock. Alvin Turlock."

"That's me."

"Here are written orders from Captain Stemple."

"What about?"

"Drill."

"Drill? What about drill?"

"There are going to be some changes. That new German officer. You're to pick one man from this company. It's in the orders."

Turlock took the writing.

"That's all." The lieutenant looked longingly at the table, turned on his heel, and walked back out into the night.

Turlock opened the paper and held it to the light to read aloud.

"Each regiment will select two alert men who adapt quickly, to be trained in the science of military drill, discipline, and maneuvers for a period of thirty days, after which they will be returned to their regiment to train their men accordingly. The training of the men selected shall commence at eight o'clock in the morning, two days from date hereof, at the Star Redoubt on Port Kennedy Road."

Turlock puzzled at the implications. "Sounds like that new German officer has a plan." He scratched at his beard. "One man." He looked at Billy. "Weems, you're the one."

At three o'clock A.M., von Steuben arose from his bed and lighted the lamp in his second-floor bedroom of the plain stone home of Abijah Stephens, where he had been quartered. By disciplined habit he drank one cup of steaming coffee, smoked one pipe of tobacco, and sat down at the desk in the corner of the library. For ten minutes he reviewed and corrected the writing he had completed at ten o'clock the previous night, then picked up his quill, dipped it in the inkwell, and continued writing.

At ten o'clock he delivered the written documents to Du Ponceau for translation from German to English. At one o'clock, while von Steuben ate his simple midday meal, Du Ponceau delivered the translated documents to Colonel Alexander Hamilton for review by himself and John Laurens. He also picked up the sheets he had left the previous day with Hamilton's comments in the margins, and returned to his own quarters where he translated Hamilton's notes to German and delivered them back to von Steuben, who was hunched at his desk, poring over his writing. At seven o'clock, von Steuben delivered the day's work to Du Ponceau for translation, ate his light supper, then worked until ten o'clock before going to his bed.

At three o'clock in the dark of early morning he arose again, drank his coffee, smoked his pipe, and began the new day of work on the drill manual, which had to be completed as fast as he could write it and have it translated.

At five minutes before eight o'clock on the appointed day, von Steuben dismounted his brown gelding on the west side of the Star Redoubt and handed the reins to his aide. Ninety-two Americans stood in silent curiosity, staring at the two large, brass-studded pistols that protruded from holsters built into the German military saddle. They studied von Steuben, struck by his crisp, new uniform and the gaudy collection of silver and gold medals that graced the left breast of his tunic. They were dominated by the one in the center—a big one that resembled a great, gold sunburst. It meant nothing to the Americans, who did not know it was the Order of Baden, a symbol of knighthood in von Steuben's native Prussia.

At eight o'clock von Steuben strode to face the men, Du Ponceau at his side to translate. He stood ramrod straight, chin up, and spoke with the voice and precision of a Prussian officer.

"I am Baron Frederich von Steuben. I received my military training under Frederick the Great. I do not yet speak your language, but I shall learn. I am acting under written orders of his Excellency, General George Washington. He has authorized the training of this command to the basic drill and manual of arms, which shall become standard in the Continental Army."

He stopped, and his narrowed gray eyes scanned the gathering of men, standing loose and easy in a disorganized cluster.

"I have counted ninety-two of you. There should be one hundred twenty. Today we will not discipline those who arrive after eight o'clock. Tomorrow you will be here at precisely eight o'clock, in rank and file, or punishment shall be meted."

The startled Americans looked at each other, then back at von Steuben, and he saw the doubt in their eyes.

"The reason is, armies succeed or fail because of discipline or the lack of it. This army will succeed. You will succeed. For that reason you will be here on time."

The Americans shifted their feet and waited.

"This morning we shall begin with the basics. You will now form in rank and file, twenty men to the rank, six ranks to the file. A rank is a line of men, shoulder to shoulder, facing me. A file is many ranks, one behind the other. You should do this because order is necessary in an army. Form now!"

Slowly, uncertainly, the Americans shuffled into six lines—crooked, badly spaced.

"You will straighten the lines and you will space yourselves by one arm's length, each man in each rank and each rank in the file. You ought to do this because each man will require the length of one arm to do the maneuvers required of him. Straighten your lines and space yourselves now."

The Americans looked at each other, skepticism and reluctance plain in their faces, and began haphazardly straightening their ranks and spacing themselves. It became immediately apparent that one arm's length varied, tall man to short man.

"One arm's length is twenty-four inches." Von Steuben explained and waited while they adjusted.

"Now we will discuss marching. You should begin to march by moving your left foot. The marching stride is twenty-eight inches. This you ought to do because tall soldiers and short soldiers can both make a stride of twenty-eight inches, and it is necessary to maintain ranks in straight lines when you are marching and for the ranks to maintain their correct interval. I will show you the proper stride."

The Americans gaped, wide-eyed. None of them had ever seen an officer lower himself to the task of drilling men. Officers were far above such matters. Drill had always been the exclusive domain of drill sergeants. The soldiers looked at each other in stunned surprise, then back at von Steuben as he clicked his boot heels together, then marched forward ten paces. His stride was consistent, measured.

"That is how you should march."

It had begun. The demolition of the old Continental Army and the creation of a new one was under way.

Reluctantly, with doubts and deep reservations, the Americans listened to the instruction and watched the demonstrations and slowly began to form their judgment of this man who patiently, firmly, explained every move, every maneuver, and the reasons for each, in terms that could not be misunderstood. When they marched, he marched with them, at the end of one rank, then the next, watching, bawling out orders, "Straighten the rank, straighten it . . . you there, third man, you are too far back—straighten the rank."

At noon he called a halt. "You are dismissed. You will return to this place at half past two o'clock for afternoon drill. We will do this because you must be trained by thirty days, and then you will have thirty days to train your own regiments. We must have this army battle-ready in sixty days. You can do this. You are dismissed."

The closely grouped men broke from ranks, jostling as each made his way in his own direction. Billy worked his way toward Port Kennedy Road, anxious to reach his hut just over one mile to the east, where hot shad would be waiting. He slowed to give way to a man coming from his left. He glanced up as the soldier passed, and he saw the tattered summer clothing, the long hair, the light beard, and the sunken eyes above hollow cheeks, and a tingle began in his brain. The man was two paces past him when recognition struck.

Billy stopped dead in his tracks. "Caleb? Caleb Dunson? Is that you?"

Caleb turned, looking, and stared at Billy for five seconds before he recognized him, his once-heavy shoulders and bull neck shrunken, his sandy beard full.

"Billy!"

Caleb's doubts of what he would do if he met Billy were gone in an instant. He strode to him and threw his arms around him, and Billy clasped him to his breast like a brother. For a time the two stood in their embrace, saying nothing, lost in the joy of discovering someone from home—someone they had known as far back as memory could take them—someone they loved, who was part of the fabric of their lives.

Billy grasped Caleb by the shoulders and pushed him back. "Are you all right? I didn't know . . . how long have you been in the army?"

Caleb was grinning. "I'm all right. I joined about a year ago. I lost track of you up on the Hudson. When did you come back?"

"October. Have you heard from your mother? Any letters? Matthew? Brigitte? The children?"

"No letters. They were fine when I left."

"Come to my hut. We've got fish."

"I can't. I've got to finish some things for the regimental orderly book. I'll be finished by tonight. I can come then. Where's your company?"

"Just over a mile east. I'll draw a map and give it to you this afternoon. Have you been in battle?"

"Brandywine. Germantown. Paoli."

"You were at Paoli?"

"Yes. Bad. I better go."

"See you at two-thirty."

It was half past nine o'clock that night when Caleb closed the door of Billy's hut and began the two-mile walk back to his own company. The quarter-moon and countless stars shed a dim, silvery light on the snow as he walked through the woods and past the huts, head down, his thoughts running. The rattle of the tattoo drum came drifting as he opened the door to his own hut and entered. He quietly climbed to his own bunk and pulled the folded tent over his head to wait for warmth.

So good to see Billy and talk—so good—so many things—he worries about Matthew—Mother—Brigitte—his own mother—sister—carries so much in his heart—for how long?—when will he be gone—dead like Father—British almost killed him at Concord—shot, bayoneted—like those men at Paoli—dead and gone.

Caleb twisted in his bunk as the dark thoughts came once again.

What's it all for?—all the pain and suffering and death—it doesn't matter who wins or loses this war—we all die in the end anyway—suffer all our lives and die—like Nancy—she struggled and she suffered and now she will die—die or live in regret the rest of her life.

He closed his eyes at the remembrance of her, and his heart swelled with grief at knowing he had been the one who had brought her down. He remembered the magic of the feel of her when he held her close and the touch of her when he had kissed her.

Nothing good lasts—somehow it all becomes bitter and goes away—what's the use?—why struggle?—who says we should struggle to do good when nothing good lasts?— the Almighty?—where's He while we're struggling?—in His heaven?—safe and warm while we're down here freezing and starving and killing each other?—hopeless—it's all hopeless—nothing good lasts—finally it is all gone.

He drifted into a twisting, fitful, tormented sleep, seeing a mix of jumbled images: his father, mother, home, Billy and Matthew, dead men on a battlefield, and the beautiful face and the staring, accusing, green eyes of Nancy Fremont.

Notes

In March 1778 hundreds of thousands of shad fish migrated up the Schuylkill River, on the northern boundary of the Continental Army camp. The soldiers used cavalry horses and tree branches to force the spawning fish upriver into nets they had obtained from local residents. The soldiers salted tons of the fish for food supply, as described herein. Wildes, *Valley Forge*, pp. 174–75.

General von Steuben organized a team of 120 picked soldiers to train in one month, after which they went back to their own units to train them. Von Steuben's habit of arising at three o'clock A.M., drinking one cup of coffee, smoking one pipe of tobacco, and then entering his day's work is factual. He worked continually on creating his new manual of arms and drill, with input from John Laurens and Alexander Hamilton. He did in fact carry two large pistols in holsters on his saddle. Reed, *Valley Forge: Crucible of Victory*, pp. 39–40; Wildes, *Valley Forge*, p. 205.

CHAPTER XXX

★ ★ ★

The weather had warmed. The steady drip of snowmelt from the roofs of the huts and from the trees was a quiet drumming from one end of camp to the other. The snow had softened, then turned to slush. Muddy splotches appeared in the roadways and the paths that countless feet had made from one place to another. In the hope of spring, soldiers moved about with a slight lift in their step. A snatch of song was heard here and there.

Colonel Alexander Hamilton stopped on the threshold of the command headquarters, scraped the mud from his boots on the iron cleat, wiped them on the heavy-bristled mat, and walked in. He hung his cape and tricorn behind the door, adjusted his portfolio of papers, and walked rapidly down the narrow hallway to rap on the door of Washington's office.

"Who comes?"

"Colonel Hamilton, sir."

"Enter."

Hamilton pushed through the door to face General Washington, seated behind his desk, waiting expectantly in a freshly pressed uniform. "Be seated."

Hamilton drew his chair to the front of the desk, sat, and laid his papers before him. Washington could not miss the restrained excitement in his face.

"Something came in the mail?"

"Yes, sir." Hamilton took the top document from his stack. "This is a copy of a document brought by Silas Deane. He arrived on the French warship *Le Sensible* at Falmouth, Maine, on April twelfth." He handed it to Washington. "It is from our men in France—at the Court of Versailles." Washington instantly stiffened, and Hamilton hurried on. "The French have signed our treaty. They have recognized us as free and independent states."

Washington leaned back in his chair, his mind working to grasp the profound reach of what had happened. For a time he sat still, not moving, while his entire view of the Revolutionary War shifted from what was to what was to be.

"Has Congress ratified the treaty?"

"Not yet, sir. But it will in due time."

"Is there anything about French participation? Navy? Army?"

"Both, sir. And there's more." He handed Washington a second document. "The British are making plans to evacuate Philadelphia."

Washington's eyes widened. "Do we know why?"

"At least in part. The French have sent Admiral d'Estaing and part of his fleet with French infantry on board to the Mediterranean port of Toulon. His orders are to refit his ships and sail for American waters. The British fear he will blockade the Delaware and seal off Philadelphia. They are unwilling to take the risk of having their army trapped there."

"When do they plan to evacuate?"

"That isn't yet known. It is known that the British Parliament is in the process of accepting the resignation of General Howe. As soon as that's finished and the government appoints a new commander in chief in his place, it seems certain they'll abandon Philadelphia."

Washington drew a great breath. "Dr. Franklin?"

Hamilton grinned. "Dr. Franklin. Silas Deane was there, but it was Dr. Franklin's doing."

Washington shook his head. "The only minister plenipotentiary in the service of the United States. That old fox has done it again."

"Yes, sir, he has."

Washington leaned forward, hands clasped on the table, and for several moments stared at the documents, while his mind struggled with the unbelievable shift that had been thrust upon him within five minutes. The French were coming—ships and men. The British were retreating, abandoning Philadelphia. How many French ships? How many infantry, cavalry? What supplies could they deliver? When?

He straightened, and Hamilton watched his iron will take control. Washington asked, "Anything else?"

"Yes, sir, several items. General Wayne delivered one hundred eighty fat cattle late yesterday evening. With your permission I'll see that they are divided equally among the various regiments."

"Good."

Hamilton referred to a list. "We now have more than three hundred tons of shad fish salted down. General Greene sent six tons of salt in a wagon that arrived four days ago. It should see us through to the month of June."

Relief flooded through Washington. "Go on."

"The dead horses are all buried. The camp vaults where the soldiers relieve themselves are all covered and fresh ones dug. The huts are cleaned. All visible refuse has been picked up and buried. Records are being kept on the burials of soldiers, and each is given a separate grave with a marker. The hospitals are being cleaned, top to bottom."

"Excellent."

"However, sir, we are hearing some murmuring from the officers. They are of the opinion that Baron von Steuben's ban on gambling and an occasional mug of rum or spirits is excessive. Soldiers need some form of diversion. A few brigadiers have suggested they will resign unless some of von Steuben's rules are softened."

Washington dropped his eyes to reflect. "The ban stands. If you need it, prepare an order for me to sign. Should any brigadiers decide to resign, so be it."

Hamilton cleared his throat. "Sir, if I recall correctly, the general enjoys a game of whist from time to time."

A smile momentarily played at the corners of Washington's mouth. "The general will destroy his deck of whist cards today."

Hamilton's shoulders shook in a silent laugh. "Yes, sir. May I mention that to officers should the need arise?"

"Yes. What else?"

"The matter of the spy. The young lady. Nancy Fremont. There will be no trial. She readily confessed. She refused to identify any of her conspirators. The court sentenced her to be deported to England, to be hanged if she ever returns. Her courier refused to say a word. We never knew his correct name. He is to be hanged tomorrow at noon."

A look of compassion crossed Washington's face. "Would you get that information to that young soldier who brought her in? There was something between them. He needs to know."

"That was private Caleb Dunson, New York Third Company. I shall send him a private note, sir."

"I will sign it personally. Continue."

"Baron von Steuben has asked permission to have an American officer named Captain Benjamin Walker of the New York Second Regiment act as his interpreter for field drill. General Du Ponceau has been translating for him, but he lacks some American words. Captain Walker volunteered and has proven invaluable to von Steuben on the field. The Baron was heard to say of Captain Walker that had he seen an angel from heaven, he could not have been more rejoiced." Hamilton hesitated, and Washington leaned slightly forward while he continued. "I should mention, sir, that some of the words General Du Ponceau lacks in the English language are . . . uh . . . profanity. First-rate swearing, sir. The Baron is quite . . . colorful."

Washington started. "And Captain Walker knows those words in German or French?"

"Yes, sir."

Washington drummed his fingers on the table for a few seconds. "Permission granted. See to it that Captain Walker is relieved of any duties that would conflict with his service to Baron von Steuben."

"Yes, sir."

Hamilton shuffled through his papers, then continued. "The physical condition of the men is improving every day, sir. General Greene sent several hundred barrels of flour from his forage to the north, and the men have gorged on fish. We still lack fresh vegetables, but the flour and fish have put weight and color back into the men. They're standing straight now, sir, and their faces and bodies are beginning to fill out. There is also a trickle of clothing and blankets starting to come into camp. Their spirits are rising."

"You could not give me better news."

Hamilton pushed a paper to Washington. "That is a note delivered personally to me by Dr. Albigence Waldo. It is from his surgical assistant, a nurse named Mary Flint. It is for your wife, Lady Washington. A sergeant named Enoch Linderman has passed on. He leaves a young widow, Polly Linderman. Lady Washington wished to know when the sergeant passed on. She promised to look after the widow."

Washington took the paper and for a moment held it in his hands, pondering how many thousand such letters had already been written. "I shall deliver it to Mrs. Washington today."

"The next thing, sir. General von Steuben claims that the select command of men he has been training is prepared to demonstrate its skills before the entire army. He asks permission to let the men perform on the Grand Parade with the entire army watching, next week."

"After fewer than four weeks?"

"Yes, sir. This man is not to be underestimated. I have it reliably that he arises at three o'clock every morning, drinks one mug of coffee, smokes one pipe of tobacco, and works the rest of the day drilling that select group or drafting his manual. His sense of duty and discipline are set in granite, sir."

"He shall have his day. Arrange it."

"You will recall we have made arrangements for the exchange of prisoners, including Major General Charles Lee. General Howe and appropriate British escort will deliver General Lee to the British picket post near the Schuylkill Bridge two days from now. As you instructed, we shall have appropriate officers there to meet him, and he shall be received in camp with honors. Lady Washington will welcome him personally with a grand banquet, and he will be quartered temporarily in the second floor of this building. As soon as possible he will be given permanent quarters at the home of David Harvard."

"Very good."

Hamilton laid one more paper before Washington. "That is a resolution passed by Congress, which heard of the British plans to vacate Philadelphia and thought it appropriate to commemorate the event."

Washington unfolded the document and read: "Resolved that Congress set apart Wednesday, April 22nd to be universally observed as a day of Fasting, Humiliation, and Prayer, that at one time and with one voice the righteous dispensations of Providence may be acknowledged, and His Goodness and Mercy towards us and our Arms supplicated and implored."

Washington laid the paper down, thought for a moment, then said, "Colonel, would you take this down as I speak it?"

"Yes, sir." Washington pushed paper and quill across the desk, and Hamilton wrote while Washington spoke.

"The commander in chief orders that the day of April 22nd instant shall be most religiously observed in the Army as a day of Fasting, Humiliation, and Prayer for the righteous dispensations of Providence and His Goodness and Mercy towards us and against our enemies, and that no work be done thereon, and that the Chaplains prepare discourses suitable to the Occasion."

Hamilton finished writing, then waited. Washington went on. "Reduce that to proper form for my signature."

"Yes, sir."

"Is there anything else?"

"No, sir."

"Then you are dismissed to attend to those matters we have handled."

Hamilton stood and assembled the papers he was to retain. He tucked them under his arm and spoke.

"Sir, it might be . . . enlightening to observe Baron von Steuben on the drill field. I understand he is . . . entertaining at times."

"We shall see."

Three miles east of the headquarters building, near the walls of the large Star Redoubt, von Steuben stood in the slush and mud, face drawn down to a scowl. Beside him Captain Benjamin Walker maintained a discreet silence as the Baron began to pace before the men, who stood in rigid rank and file.

"Ven I say halt, you do not halt at that time. You take one more step and den you bring the other foot beside, and you halt. Do you understand? It is halt-one-two. Observe."

The Baron called a cadence in English with a thick German accent as he marched out in front of his men. "Vun-doo-dree-four—vun-doo-dree-four—Halt-vun-doo. The reason is that all soldiers must halt at the same time to maintain intervals in the rank and file. Now, you shall do it mit me."

He turned to face his men, and in his thick concoction of English corrupted by German, called the commands.

"Forward, MARCH! Vun-doo-dree-four—vun-doo-dree-four—Halt-vun-doo."

One hundred fourteen men stopped together. Six did not, plowing into the men ahead of them.

Von Steuben's neck veins expanded, and his face reddened. He turned to Captain Walker, and for fifteen seconds he ripped off a mix of French, German, and badly mangled English while the men stood silent, fascinated. He stopped. He was breathing heavily, body shaking. He threw up both hands and growled. "I gan gurse dem no more! Tell dem!"

Captain Walker swallowed hard, wiped at his mouth for a moment, and said, "Sir, do you want me to repeat every word you said to these men?"

Von Steuben's chin was set like granite. "Every vord. Exactly as I set it."

Walker sucked air. "Yes, sir." He turned to the one hundred twenty men and launched into it. Never had the men heard such a sustained torrent of profanity. The words did harm to every man, his ancestry, his stupidity, the human race, America, and Deity, and repeated most of it twice.

Walker finished the tirade, stood for a moment to be certain he had repeated it as von Steuben had said it, and in that moment a voice from the last rank murmured, "That was the best I ever heard. Sounded like it oughta be in the Bible!"

Von Steuben jerked toward the sound, eyes flashing, face dark, voice like the crack of Judgment Day. "Vat vas set? Who set someting?"

Walker started to translate, and the Baron raised a hand to stop him. "Who set someting?" he demanded.

The offender in the rear rank raised his hand. "Here, sir. Me."

In five seconds von Steuben was standing nose to nose with the man, and he barked at Walker, "Vat vas said?"

Walker cleared his throat, and his voice cracked. He started again. "Sir, he said that was the best swearing he had ever heard. He said it sounded like it came from the Bible."

Von Steuben's eyes popped wide. He stared at the man, speechless. From behind him someone chuckled, and then someone joined him, and then someone laughed out loud. Von Steuben swung around, and as he did, a dozen more men laughed.

Suddenly von Steuben grinned, and then he threw back his head, and laughed from his belly. In two seconds the entire command was wheezing with a laughing spasm that rang in the woods and stopped soldiers a half mile away.

Slowly von Steuben brought himself under control and wiped the tears from his cheeks. "You vill try vun more time. I vill call the command." Again he launched off in his pidgin English. "Forward, march! Vun-doo-dree-four—vun-doo-dree-four—Halt-vun-doo!"

The command came to a perfect halt, every man in his measured twenty-four-inch interval. Von Steuben's eyes sparkled. "Vunce more. Forward, march! Vun-doo-dree-four—vun-doo-dree-four—Halt-vun-doo!"

Again the command maintained perfect formation. Every man could see the light in von Steuben's face. "Again. Forward, march!" This time, as he began counting the cadence, half a dozen men called it out loud with him, and in an instant the entire command had joined in the chant, pronouncing each word exactly as von Steuben did. "Vun-doo-dree-four—vun-doo-dree-four—Halt!-vun-doo!"

They stopped in perfect formation, and every man held a straight face. For one moment von Steuben was uncertain whether he had been mocked or complimented, and then he realized. These men had accepted him as one of their own. He had bridged the gap. He owned his men, and they owned him.

"Goot, goot," he exclaimed. "Vunce again. Forward, march!" One hundred twenty-one lusty voices shouted the cadence. "Vun-doo-dree-four—vun-doo-dree-four—Halt-vun-doo!"

Every man in the formation felt it. Something had happened. Somehow they had come together as never before, in one mind, one purpose, one spirit. The afternoon wore on with the men calling the cadence along with von Steuben in each maneuver, each marching pattern. The right turns, left turns, obliques, mark time—all of it. Von Steuben was afire with what his men were doing, where they had arrived.

With the sun on the western rim, he brought them to a halt, and he stood before them, straight, proud, beaming. "Tomorrow ve continue as usual. Today . . . today you became as soldiers. Goot soldiers. In a few days you vill show the entire Continental Army what you have become. They vill watch you on the Grand Parade grounds as you march, and they vill be proud. *I* vill be proud. Then you will return to your own regiments, und you vill train your soldiers as you have been taught. You have done in four weeks what can only be done in eight weeks in my homeland. You do honor to your country." For a moment he stood in silence, steadily meeting the eyes of his men. "*Our* country."

Strong men looked at the ground for a moment. Von Steuben went on.

"And then ve vill have a banquet. Sauerkraut and water."

Laughter rippled through the ranks.

He looked at his army. The trousers of every man were in shreds, showing their bare legs.

Von Steuben grinned. "We will call it our 'sans culottes' banquet."

The men looked at Walker for a translation.

Walker looked at von Steuben, and von Steuben nodded, and Walker turned back to the ranks.

"*Sans culottes* means 'without pants.'"

The explosion of laughter could be heard a half mile away.

Von Steuben waited until he could be heard. "You are dismissed."

Notes

Silas Deane, one of the United States' emissaries to France, arrived in Falmouth, Maine, aboard the French ship *Le Sensible* on April 12, 1778, carrying the signed peace treaty between the United States and France, to General Washington and Congress. Congress had not yet approved the critically important treaty. Freeman, *Washington*, p. 389.

Having allied themselves with the Americans, the French sent Vice Admiral d'Estaing and a sizable command of French warships to Toulon in the Mediterranean, then on to America. The British feared they would blockade Philadelphia. Reed, *Valley Forge: Crucible of Victory*, p. 53.

Some American officers criticized Baron von Steuben's strict discipline and threatened to resign if he did not relent. He refused to listen. Whist was a card game of which General Washington was fond. Reed, *Valley Forge: Crucible of Victory*, p. 41; Pool, *What Jane Austen Ate and Charles Dickens Knew*, p. 65.

Baron von Steuben used Captain Benjamin Walker of the New York Second Regiment as a volunteer interpreter on the drill field since Du Ponceau did not know some of the American words. Von Steuben did refer to Walker as "an angel from heaven" for his services. Von Steuben obtained permission to march his select group of 120 on the Grand Parade before the entire Continental Army. Reed, *Valley Forge: Crucible of Victory*, p. 41.

Arrangements were made to receive Major General Charles Lee back from the British in a prisoner exchange; a banquet was to follow in his honor, hosted by Lady Washington. Lee was given quarters in the home of David Harvard. Reed, *Valley Forge: Crucible of Victory*, p. 48.

Congress passed a resolution, setting aside April 22, 1778, as a day of thanksgiving for the blessings from the Almighty. The quoted portion of the resolution is verbatim. Reed, *Valley Forge: Crucible of Victory*, p. 53.

The incident in which Baron von Steuben took over the drilling of his men, cursing them soundly, calling cadence in pidgin English "vun-doo-dree-four," provoking laughter, in which he joined, with the result of unifying his command, is correctly reported.

He trained his American troops in four weeks, a feat that would have required six weeks in Prussia, and took great pride in them, calling them his "apostles." When his troops were trained to a high degree of skill, he did hold a banquet, which he called his "Sans Culottes" banquet, the translation of *sans culottes* being "without pants." He transformed the boredom of the drill field into a means of promoting camaraderie and laughter, to the delight of his men. Jackson, *Valley Forge: Pinnacle of Courage*, p. 181; Leckie, *George Washington's War*, pp. 438–42; Reed, *Valley Forge: Crucible of Victory*, p. 41.

Valley Forge

May–June 1778

CHAPTER XXXI

★ ★ ★

Spring had come to New England, and the world was born anew—fresh, clean, pristine. All things in the rolling hills had once again answered the eternal call to awaken from the slumbers of winter and bring new life. The woods and the fields were clad in greens and golds and yellows and blues, and the sounds of living things filled the air and echoed in the forests.

The souls and the bodies of the soldiers of the Continental Army, camped along the banks of the Schuylkill River, had nearly mended from the horrors of the winter's starvation and cold. The warmth of mother earth and the deep, lush grasses gave comfort to those still without shoes and wearing rags. The men moved about their duties with a spring and a jaunty swing in their step, calling loudly to each other, humming, bellowing forth in a snatch of misbegotten song, reveling in the renewal that expanded their inner beings each day.

In the red blush of dawn, Billy sat quietly in the grass with his back against the east wall of his squad's small hut, paper and pencil in hand, knees drawn up as he labored in his mind for the words he needed. He paused to peer upward into the trees, where the quiet hum of insects mixed with the cacophony of the jays and ravens and robins arguing their territorial claims. The warmth of the morning sun was on his face as he carefully began to write.

My Dear Mother:

Much has happened. Spring has come, and the hard things of winter are past. I am well. I have gained back most of my lost weight, as have nearly all the soldiers. We still have salt fish, and General Anthony Wayne brought in several hundred cattle. The soldiers have begun to call him "Wayne the Drover," which he seems to like. We now have enough flour and even a small ration of vegetables. We will be all right.

I am sorry to say over three thousand of our soldiers died in the harsh winter. Fifteen hundred of our horses perished. Many of the officers and soldiers left and have not returned. However, I can say that those who remained and lived are of a nature that has made them an army that can scarce be beaten. I know in my heart that in this way the Almighty has turned our suffering into a blessing.

A short time ago I was mightily surprised to find Caleb Dunson. He is in a New York company. He looked poorly at the time but today looks like himself, except that he is a little older. We have talked many times, and I am aware he labors with his own inner troubles, which he will not share with me. I do not mean he has become a bad man. I only mean he must settle some things inside himself to come to peace with the world.

Caleb and I were part of a group of one hundred twenty men selected to be trained by a German officer, General von Steuben. He is an excellent officer, who taught us military drill in four weeks and then sent us back to train our own regiments. A short time ago those of us in the one hundred twenty had the privilege of marching before the entire Continental Army. It brought praise from every quarter. General Washington was heard to say that he believes General von Steuben has blessed this army more than any other single man. I believe he may be right. We are now training our regiments under the watchful eye of General von Steuben, and they are eagerly learning. For the first time we feel like we are an army. A good army.

We have information that General William Howe has resigned as commander of the British and will be returning to England soon. When that occurs we believe the British will abandon Philadelphia and march to New York. Should that happen it is thought that General Washington will follow and perhaps engage them in battle. I do not want you to worry. Our army is now well prepared. I will be all right.

I must mention, I previously wrote about camp fever and the sores and scabs and the itch that disabled so many of our men. I too suffered with such things. We could not get medicine, so our sergeant, Alvin Turlock, taught us to use an old remedy. We mixed gunpowder with tallow and smeared it on our sores. In fact, most of our bodies. The sulphur in the gunpowder mixed with the tallow healed us. My good friend Eli Stroud also taught us to use many herbs and plants from the forest as medicine.

Would you share this letter with Margaret Dunson and her family? I do not think a letter from you would reach me. I think of you every day. I know Trudy must be a young lady by now. I miss you both. I will write again when I can, and I will take a furlough when I receive permission and come home. I place you both in the hands of the Almighty.

Your loving son,
Billy Weems.

From the corner of the hut came a high, raspy voice. "Writing a letter?"

Billy glanced at Turlock. "To Mother."

"I thought it might be to that girl."

"I'll write her tomorrow."

"Weems, don't waste your time. You got at least six of those letters. Some so old you can hardly read 'em. Writing letters you won't send is a waste of paper and time."

Billy shrugged and rose to his feet and reached to brush the seat of his trousers. "You're probably right. We better get started. Regimental drill starts at eight o'clock, and we better be on time. Von Steuben's rules. One second past eight o'clock, you stand at attention for an hour."

He had reached the door of the hut when the sound of trotting horses stopped him short. In the distance, half a dozen officers were moving west on Gulph Road, epaulets glittering in the bright sunlight. Billy shaded his eyes for a moment to study them.

"Muhlenberg, Weedon, Patterson, Lafayette—a few others. Moving towards headquarters. I wonder what's happening."

Turlock scratched his stomach. "I got a hunch. Howe's leaving, and we're going after Philadelphia and then the British army." He pushed past Billy. "Well, if we expect to eat, we better get about fixing breakfast. We got a choice. Firecakes and beef, or firecakes and fish."

At eight o'clock, Washington glanced at the officers who surrounded the conference table in the library on the main floor of the headquarters building. Satisfied, he remained standing to speak.

"First, this is the first war council in which we have the honor of the presence of General Charles Lee since his return on April sixth." He bowed to Lee. "I wish to welcome you back, sir."

Tall, thin, hawkish, Lee stiffly nodded but remained silent. Guarded glances passed around the table, but no one looked directly at Lee. None had forgotten the humiliating circumstances that resulted in Lee's capture just days before the Trenton attack—caught in a dressing robe, finishing breakfast in a boarding house miles from his troops! No one had ever heard an explanation of his dereliction. That Washington had extended him a warm welcome when the Americans and the British exchanged prisoners and now had given him recognition at the war council were magnanimous gestures indeed!

Washington immediately launched into the business of the day.

"Gentlemen, I am sure you will understand the . . . pivotal . . . importance of what I am about to say." He waited until every eye at the table was on him, every face tense, waiting. "Congress has approved the treaty with France. The French are now officially our allies. We are to be the beneficiaries of the full strength of that nation's capabilities, military and otherwise."

Applause broke out. Loud exclamations filled the room. Washington waited until it quieted, then continued.

"I have drafted a statement, which I feel is appropriate to the event." He turned to Hamilton. "Colonel, would you read the statement."

"It having pleased the Almighty ruler of the universe propitiously to defend the cause of the United American States and finally by raising us up a powerful friend among the princes of the earth to establish our liberty and independence upon lasting foundations, it becomes us to set apart a day for gratefully acknowledging the divine goodness and celebrating the important event which we owe to His benign interposition."

Hamilton stopped and looked up to see each man in deep thought.

Washington went on. "Each of you will receive a copy as you leave this council. Tomorrow morning at nine o'clock, assemble your commands and read this statement to them. Assign your chaplains to deliver an appropriate address. One hour later we will form the entire army for inspection, followed by salutes from both cannon and muskets."

He paused, then turned to Lafayette. "I thought it appropriate that General Lafayette take command of those ceremonies. General, I presume you will accept my invitation to do so."

For a moment Lafayette could not speak. "It will be my great honor, your Excellency."

Washington picked up a paper, read his notes, and continued.

"We must move on. I am recommending to Congress that Captain von Steuben be appointed inspector general of the army and that he be given the rank of major general."

Instant comments of approval filled the room, and Washington let them go until they dwindled.

"Observance of the Sabbath is slipping. I am entering an order effective immediately that divine services be performed each Sunday at eleven o'clock. Officers of all ranks are expected to attend to be an example to their men. We must be ever mindful of our overriding duty of worship to that Supreme being whose providence and blessings we enjoy."

There was a moment of silence as each man dropped his eyes, caught by the suddenness of the reminder.

Washington cleared his throat, glanced at his prepared agenda, and continued. "The British Parliament has accepted General Howe's resignation. His farewell banquet—probably a grand meschianza—is being planned for the last part of this month, and he will sail for England soon after. General Clinton will likely be appointed to succeed him. It is expected that General Clinton will abandon Philadelphia and march the entire British force to New York. He knows Admiral d'Estaing has sailed from Toulon in the Mediterranean with a large part of the French navy, and Clinton fears being blockaded in New York Harbor. From a military point of view, New York Harbor is vastly more critical to the British than the city of Philadelphia."

He glanced at a paper. "I should mention, I lately received a letter from General Clinton."

Instantly the room fell silent. The only sound was of flies buzzing at the windows.

"He invited me to negotiate a settlement of our differences with the British."

Loud talk erupted.

Washington waited for quiet. "I advised him that Congress, and only Congress, has the power to declare war or make peace. He would have to negotiate with it, not me. He has not pursued it."

There was a moment of silence; then talk broke out and subsided.

Washington continued. "Assuming General Howe leaves and Clinton takes command and marches for New York, I propose the following."

He unrolled and anchored a map. "The day he marches out of

Philadelphia, General Arnold will occupy it with sufficient strength to hold it."

He raised his eyes to General Benedict Arnold, who peered at the map for a moment, then nodded.

"If the British march out, I believe the most likely route they will take will be here." He dropped his long index finger to the map. "Cross the Delaware at Philadelphia, then proceed northeast through Burlington, Bordentown, then angle more easterly to Monmouth, then north to Raritan Bay, across to Amboy, then east to Staten Island and on to either Long Island or Manhattan Island. There is good forage all the way for his animals, and the countryside will support an army that size. I expect his column to be well above ten miles in length."

Every combat-wise officer at the table instantly realized what was coming.

"As you know, an army is never so vulnerable as when it is strung out in retreat. Should my presumptions be correct, there will be half a dozen places that a well-planned attack could cripple or badly hurt General Clinton's army. I therefore propose that we prepare our forces to follow him and make such an attack at an appropriate place."

General Lee twisted in his chair, then raised his voice. "Sir, it is my opinion that our best course would be to attack and occupy Pittsburgh. It is in a position to afford a strong defense. Let the British come to retake it and engage in an ongoing battle of attrition. Eventually they will diminish in number sufficient to realize the entire campaign in America is futile and leave. I have written this plan and provided a copy to Congress."

Buzzing broke out around the table for a moment as the war council struggled with Lee's reasoning. Startled, caught totally by surprise, Washington raised a hand, waited for silence, and addressed Lee.

"I knew nothing of this until now. I shall of course consider your proposal, but for now, it is my intention to give command of the right wing of the army to yourself, General Lee, for purposes of the attack I am proposing on the British, should they march to New York."

Lee shifted in his chair, agitation and disagreement plain in his thin, sharp face. Washington waited, but Lee held his silence. Washington turned to Lafayette. "General, at the time of the farewell meschianza for General Howe, I am entering a written order for you to lead a command of two thousand men to Barren Hill, here." His finger dropped to the map. "The object of your foray is twofold. First, be cognizant of all maneuvers of the British, and second, harass them where in your judgment it is prudent to do so."

Lafayette nodded his understanding but said nothing.

"That having been said, let us now get down to the detail involved."

The animated, often loud, give and take of a war council commenced. Pittsburgh? What is there at Pittsburgh the British want? What if Clinton splits his force, part in Philadelphia, part to New York? Have we got enough wagons and munitions to pursue him? Food? He'll know we're following—will he attack us first?

By eleven o'clock the details had been twisted and turned and settled. Washington dismissed the war council, and the officers walked out of the building into the warm sunshine, where they chatted for a moment before mounting their horses and turning each in his own direction.

Four miles to the east the soldiers of the New York Regiment stood at rigid attention in rank and file, their faces shiny with sweat from three hours of rigorous close-order drill. At noon they were dismissed for their midday meal. At two o'clock they were reassembled at attention in perfect rank and file, muskets over their right shoulders. Caleb stood beside his captain, facing his company, ready to demonstrate further the intricacies of everything von Steuben had hammered into him. At five o'clock the New York Regiment was again at attention, waiting for the most blessed word in the military handbook von Steuben had created, and the captain bawled it out.

"Company, *dismissed!*"

Cheers erupted as the men broke ranks. Caleb grinned. It was spring. The men felt strong, good. The day's work was done. They had become an army—a good one—and they knew it. Loud, raucous talk was everywhere as they jostled their way toward the roads leading to their huts.

O'Malley stopped at Caleb's side, shirt sticking from sweat. "Better get back to the place. Got to prepare evening mess."

"Wait a minute for Dorman. He was coming over later."

Caleb stood tall, searching for the gray hair of the aging soldier, and seconds later he was there. He greeted O'Malley, then turned to Caleb as Caleb spoke.

"Coming over after mess? Maybe spar a little again?"

Dorman grinned. "Three times last week. Twice this week. You want to go again?"

"I do. See you after mess."

Dorman bobbed his head and was turning to go when a voice from behind stopped all three men, and they turned. Six feet away stood Conlin Murphy, thick-shouldered, bull-necked, bearded, square face dark. Three men flanked him, their silent, bearded faces a blank as they stared at Caleb.

Murphy's voice purred. "I thought you deserted, but there you are, right up front, like you was an officer."

O'Malley eyed the men next to Murphy. Dorman shifted his feet and flexed his hands. Caleb remained still, silent.

"That German taught you good—up in front showin' us, all your inferiors, how to drill."

Caleb spoke quietly. "I don't want trouble."

Murphy's face became ugly. "Trouble? No trouble. Just a lesson to teach you that you got no cause to be lookin' down on us."

Men walking past slowed and stopped. A crowd began to gather.

"I'm leaving, Murphy. I'm walking away."

"Not for a minute. Won't take long."

Those nearest heard the words and drew back to form a loose circle. The three men with Murphy spread out, facing Caleb.

The time for the inevitable clash between Caleb and Murphy had arrived, and no one knew it more clearly than Dorman. He shifted his weight and raised a hand to signal two of the men with Murphy to stand away. They looked at Murphy, who nodded, and then stepped back. O'Malley jammed a thick finger into the chest of the third man, and he also backed away. Officers passing by pushed through the circled crowd to the opening in the center. They instantly recognized what was about to happen and opened their mouths to bark orders. Fifty soldiers turned to stare them down, and one by one the officers closed their mouths. They sensed that somehow this conflict was more than two men settling their differences. It was more than that—a part of the eternal battle between right and wrong; evil, ugly power crushing all who opposed. This was every man's fight. The officers remained silent. Not one remembered or cared that it was their duty to stop all fighting among enlisted men. They became part of the silent, mesmerized crowd that was irresistibly drawn to the unequal combat.

Murphy flexed his hands, then raised them. Barrel-chested, heavy and muscled above the waist, he had thirty pounds' advantage over Caleb.

The Irishman did not hesitate. He moved directly at Caleb, who raised his hands and made his fists and took his stance. His thumbs were wrapped tightly about his fingertips, chin tucked into the cavity of his shoulder, left foot slightly ahead of his right. He began the shuffling circle to his left, staring at Murphy's chest, eyes taking in every move, every expression in Murphy's eyes and face. Murphy followed, eyes narrow slits as he tried to bring Caleb to a stand. His right hand flicked out, and Caleb slipped it and continued circling.

Murphy recovered and moved after him. Setting himself, he swung hard with his left hand. Caleb dropped his head to his left, and the punch grazed his right ear harmlessly. Caleb straightened and continued circling, seeing in Murphy's eyes the first hint of doubt. Once again Murphy recovered and suddenly rushed. He swung his left hand first, then his right. Caleb again slipped the left hand, then raised his own left forearm upward to deflect Murphy's right arm outward. In the same instant he set his feet and delivered a powerful right-hand punch to Murphy's chest. The blow landed over Murphy's heart, jolting him, causing him to stagger backward a full step.

Caleb instantly recovered his stance and continued circling, eyes on Murphy's chest, face expressionless. He glanced upwards once and saw the panic mounting in Murphy's eyes. He continued his patient circling, waiting. *He's going to rush—means to use his strength—wait—wait—he'll get foolish.*

Near total silence gripped the crowd. The men stood hypnotized by what they were seeing. Dorman was watching every move with a critical eye. O'Malley had his fists clenched, jaw set.

Once more Murphy rushed, and again Caleb slipped his punches, struck back, and quickly recovered. In that instant he saw it plain in Murphy's eyes. It was coming.

Murphy charged like a raging bull. A thick, animal sound erupting from his throat as he threw caution to the wind and came clawing, trying to seize Caleb, fold him inside massive arms, crush him, break his back.

The flurry came too fast to follow. Caleb was a blur as he stepped inside the huge arms and swung, left, right, left, hammering with all his strength into Murphy's middle. It stopped Murphy in his tracks, eyes bulging, wind gone out of him, arms still extended. Caleb danced back, dodged under Murphy's extended right arm, set his feet, and hooked with his left hand over Murphy's arm. His fist slammed against Murphy's right temple, snapping his head sideways while Caleb again shifted his feet and then swung his right hand with every pound he had. His fist crunched flush on Murphy's mouth and blood flew as his upper lip split wide open. Murphy's eyes started to glaze as Caleb jabbed with his left hand, then cocked his right hand again and delivered another vicious blow. The fist traveled less than twenty inches, this time to catch Murphy on his forehead. The Irishman's entire frame shook as Caleb swung again with his left hand, opening a two-inch gash above Murphy's right eye. With blood and gore covering Murphy's face, Caleb reset his feet and delivered his right hand once more. His fist caught Murphy flush on the point of his chin, and those nearest heard the crack as Murphy's jawbone broke.

Murphy's arms dropped and his eyes went glassy. Caleb set his feet once more and cocked his right hand to deliver another blow when he saw it. Murphy was unconscious on his feet. Caleb held his blow and stepped back. The big man's knees buckled, and he pitched forward, landing face first in the dirt. He did not move.

For seconds that seemed an eternity, no one moved or spoke. Then as the men realized what had happened, a murmur began in the crowd and reached a crescendo. The big man was down, beaten, lying in his own blood. The smaller man was standing, unhurt, unmarked. Evil, brute strength had failed. Officers turned and worked their way out of the crowd, aware that they should not interfere with what had happened and what was going to happen.

Caleb stood over Murphy, and suddenly Dorman was at his right side, O'Malley on his left. No one tried to touch Caleb or Murphy. They stood at a distance, awed by what they had witnessed.

Then O'Malley handed Caleb his old, scarred, wooden canteen, and Caleb pulled the stopper. He knelt beside Murphy, rolled him onto his back, and began to wash the dirt and blood and gore from his face. He saw the cut above the eye and the split lip and the jaw that would not close straight, and Caleb felt a sense of sadness, of pain.

He glanced at O'Malley. "Get a doctor."

Murphy stirred, then groaned, and a bloody froth came from his nose and mouth. Caleb rinsed it away, and Murphy tried to raise on one elbow.

Caleb pushed him down. "Lie still. The doctor's coming."

Murphy peered up, eyes still unable to focus.

The doctor came and knelt beside Murphy. He inspected his face, then raised unbelieving eyes to Caleb. "You did this?"

Caleb nodded but said nothing.

"With what? An ax handle?"

They rigged a stretcher, and the men who were with Murphy carried him off, following the doctor toward the nearest hospital. The crowd still remained, milling about, not yet able to approach or talk with Caleb. O'Malley gestured, Caleb followed, and Dorman called after them as they walked away.

"I'll be over after mess. Some things need to be said."

Later, in the warmth of the spring evening, Dorman sat down on a log outside Caleb's hut, and Caleb came to sit beside him. The younger man pulled a shred of bark from the log and began to work it with his fingers. For a time they sat in reflective silence, and then Dorman spoke.

"How do you feel?"

"All right."

"I mean inside?"

Caleb stopped peeling at the piece of bark in his hands. He did not raise his eyes. "Bad. I thought it would be different."

Relief flooded through Dorman, but his expression did not change. "Would you do it again?"

Caleb worked at the bark with his thumbnail for a time. "I don't know."

"There's a lot to think about. He's a bully. Someone had to stop him. I doubt he'll be as quick to pick a fight next time."

"I know that. Still, it was . . . a bad thing."

"No, not bad. It would have been bad if you had picked a fight with a lesser man just to beat him. This was the other way around. He picked the fight because he thought he could beat you. It was evil of him. Not you. Someone has to stand up to his kind. You did it. It wasn't bad. Sad, but not bad. Do you see?"

"I see. It was still ugly."

"You better think about one more thing."

Caleb raised questioning eyes.

"You're a marked man. By tomorrow night most of this army will know what you did today. There are men here who are going to pick fights with you just to find out if they can beat you. Better be ready."

"That happened to you?"

"Many times."

"What did you do?"

"Learned to walk away. Pride isn't worth it. I'm glad I learned that."

Dorman dropped his hands to his knees and stood. "Well, I better get back." He looked at Caleb. "You handled yourself well. In the fight, I mean. He never touched you."

"That wasn't me. I learned it from you."

"No, it was you. See you tomorrow."

Caleb watched the aging man walk away into the last rays of sunlight casting long shadows to the east, then picked at the bark with his thumbnail once more. *Billy's going to hear—what will he think?—what will he write to his mother?—How long before it reaches my mother?—What will she think?— Does it matter?—It seems like the bad in life goes on and the good dies or goes away— what does it matter?*

Two miles east, among the tiny log buildings of the Massachusetts Regiment, Billy finished scrubbing the large, black company cook kettle with sand and water and leaned it against the west wall of his hut. He wiped his hands on his tattered breeches and was walking toward the front door when color caught his eye, and he glanced west, into the glow of sunset. Fifteen yards away, Eli was seated on the trunk of an ancient, wind-felled pine. He was leaning forward, elbows on his knees, slowly working his hands together, head bowed in deep thought. Rarely had Billy seen him so. He turned away from the hut toward his friend and was five yards away when Eli raised his head to watch him come the last few paces and sit down.

Seconds passed in silence before Billy spoke. "Trouble?"

For a time Eli continued to study his hands. "Can't get my mind to come clear."

"About what?"

"Mary."

"What about her?" Billy saw the reluctance in Eli, and he left the question hanging for a time before Eli raised his head and looked him squarely in the eyes.

"I want to marry her, and I know it's wrong."

Billy slowly straightened, startled, shocked. "Wrong? How?"

"I'm more Iroquois than white. I know the woods. It's where I belong. I doubt I can live in a city. I own a rifle and a knife and a tomahawk and nothing more. I don't much like a lot of what people in towns do and think. Mary comes from New York. Wealth. Position. Power. She doesn't belong in the woods. She belongs in a city. I can't get my head to make it work."

"You talk to her about it?"

"No. Nothing to be gained by troubling her."

From the corner of the hut came the high, raspy voice of Turlock. "What are you two doing?"

Billy answered. "Nothing."

"Sounds dangerous." Without invitation Turlock walked over. Before he reached them he was aware something heavy had happened. He dropped to his haunches in the thick spring grass, facing them, and looked up at Eli and waited. Billy remained silent, giving Eli the choice of either opening up to Turlock or not.

For a time Eli remained silent, then spoke quietly. "It's Mary."

"The one you made that coat for? I hear every woman in camp is jealous of that wolf-skin coat."

"I want to marry her, but it's wrong."

Turlock's eyes widened. "Wrong?"

"I'm more Indian than white. She's a lady from the city. I doubt I can live in her world or that she can live in mine."

Turlock rounded his lips and blew air. "That does sound thorny. You talk to her about it?"

"No. No sense in it."

"You already made up her mind?"

It took Eli two seconds to catch it. "Me? Make up *her* mind?"

"I thought that's what you said. You won't talk to her because there's no sense to it. You already made up her mind."

"You think I should trouble her with this? She belongs in a city, with wealth and the things she knows. I can never give her that."

"You already decided she belongs in a city?"

Eli straightened, and a slight cutting edge crept into his voice. "She does! That's where she came from. That's the life she knows."

"You looked at her lately? It's been a long time since she saw a city. Money? Clothes? She's over there in that hospital, workin' herself to death in poverty and disease, and she's doin' it because that's where she wants to be. And she wants to be there because that's as close as she can get to you."

Billy saw the slow realization come into Eli's face.

Eli asked, "You think I should tell her?"

Turlock answered. "I think you should follow your heart. You got a head like few men I ever met, but you got a lot to learn about your heart. And more to learn about a woman's heart. You go talk to her."

Eli turned to Billy with imploring eyes, and Billy spoke.

"Go see her. Tell her just what you told us."

Eli slowly rose to his feet, and both men stood with him. He picked up his rifle, handed it to Billy, and without a word he left at a trot.

The first shades of purple evening were filtering into the woods when Eli rapped on the door of the long stone building behind the hospital. A plump woman opened the door.

"Oh. It's you. Wait here."

Three minutes later Mary appeared. She wore a plain, long-sleeved gray dress to her ankles. Her dark hair was held back by a white scarf. Her eyes were glowing as she came to him.

"Eli, it's so good to see you. Do come in."

"Is it all right if we walk?"

Mary sensed his need. "Of course."

He took her hand and led her into the trees twenty yards east of the building. Full twilight had set in. He stopped and faced her, and he knew no other way than to speak plainly.

"I'm more Indian than white. I was raised in the woods. It's the only life I know. I own a Pennsylvania rifle and this knife and tomahawk. I've never lived in a city, and I doubt I could."

He stopped for a moment to gather his thoughts. Mary started to speak, and he cut her off. "You were raised in New York City. Wealth. A grand home. Society. I could never give you those things."

Mary reached to cover his mouth with her hand. "Eli, you're trying to say something. Say it."

He looked down into her dark eyes, and his heart rose to choke him. "I want you to marry me, but I can't—"

Again she stopped him. "You can't what?"

"I can't ask you to live the only way I know, and I can't give you what you should have."

"What I should have? You haven't given me the only thing I need. How do you feel about me, Eli? Tell me how you feel about me."

His brow knitted down in bewilderment. "How I feel about you? I thought you knew. Understood. You hold my heart. I love you."

She threw her arms around his neck and raised her face and kissed him. After a moment she drew back. "That's all I need. You want me to marry you? Yes. Yes, Eli. You want me to come live in the forest with you? If that's where you are, that's where I belong. Yes, I will marry you. I love you with all my heart."

He started to speak, and she kissed him again, all the passion in her heart rising to reach him. He held her and never in his life had he known the fulfillment that surged through his being. Neither knew, nor cared, how long they stood in the twilight of the forest, lost in each other.

He released her, and she whispered, "When?"

"As soon as we finish our battle with Clinton. I can't leave before then."

"Leave?"

"When we're married, would you come with me north? To my sister? We can stay with her for a time—her and her husband and two children. They have a small home in the north woods. You'll love her, and she'll love you."

"How will we get there?"

"Walk. Canoe."

"Just the two of us?"

"Yes."

"It sounds like heaven. Of course we'll go."

Full darkness had set in when Eli returned to the hut. Billy sat on a pile of firewood near the door. Turlock walked out into the moonlight, waiting. Billy stood and spoke.

"Did you talk to her?"

"Yes."

"And?"

"We're going to marry as soon as we finish our fight with Clinton."

Turlock looked up into his face. Eli saw the strange tenderness in his eyes as the little man spoke. "I'm glad for you, son. Glad."

Turlock turned and disappeared into the hut, his mind reaching far back into memories of a girl who had passed on before he could speak to her of his love.

Notes

The letter written by Billy to his mother is fictional; however, the facts set forth therein are correct. General Anthony Wayne did bring in cattle and was given the nickname "Wayne the Drover." In the five months at Valley Forge, over 3,000 American soldiers died. Over 1,500 horses died. The 120 select soldiers did march in demonstration before the Continental Army. General Washington was lavish in his praise of the contribution made by Baron von Steuben. Lacking medicines, the men resorted to homemade cures, including a mixture of gunpowder (in which there was the necessary sulphur) and tallow, to smear on scabs, sores, and itches. Herbs and plants were used for cures. Leckie, *George Washington's War*, pp. 442–43; Reed, *Valley Forge: Crucible of Victory*, pp. 22, 35–36; Busch, *Winter Quarters*, pp. 71, 171.

General Washington extended every courtesy to General Charles Lee after his return as an exchanged prisoner of war. Reed, *Valley Forge: Crucible of Victory*, p. 50.

On May 4, 1778, Congress ratified and approved the treaty with France. To commemorate the critically important event, a great celebration was conducted on May 6 at Valley Forge in which Lafayette was given command of "the right of the first line." For full details as set forth herein, see Freeman, *Washington*, p. 390; Reed, *Valley Forge: Crucible of Victory*, pp. 55–56.

On Washington's recommendation, Baron von Steuben was in fact appointed inspector general and given the rank of major general. *Valley Forge Orderly Book*, p. 273; Reed, *Valley Forge: Crucible of Victory*, pp. 38–40.

General Washington entered an order that all officers and soldiers would attend church services on the Sabbath. *Valley Forge Orderly Book*, p. 303.

The British Parliament accepted Howe's resignation. A great farewell party called a *meschianza* was held in Philadelphia in his honor on May 18, 1778. The French sent Vice Admiral d'Estaing to Toulon in the Mediterranean, then on to America, which caused the British to fear he would blockade Philadelphia. Reed, *Valley Forge: Crucible of Victory*, pp. 59–63

General Henry Clinton contacted Washington to discuss matters between England and the United States. Washington replied that he did not have such powers; they were vested in Congress only. Freeman, *Washington*, p. 391.

General Benedict Arnold was ordered to occupy Philadelphia when the British abandoned it. General Lee was given command of the right wing of the Continental Army for purposes of attacking the retreat of General Clinton. General Lafayette was ordered to proceed with 2,200 men to Barren Hill for the purposes of observing the British and harassing them. Reed, *Valley Forge: Crucible of Freedom*, pp. 50, 57, 61, 68.

CHAPTER XXXII

★ ★ ★

*T*he evening star hung low and dim in the east, where the approaching day had defined earth from sky. The waning half-moon was fading in the south. The awful heat of June twenty-seventh had not cooled in the night; a hot, sultry, humid west wind had risen to sweat the Continental Army as the men lay on their blankets, fighting night insects, twisting, turning, unable to sleep.

Inside his command tent, General Washington looked at the clock on his small desk in the corner, then turned back to the table to count. There were fourteen general officers seated, tricorns on the table before them, sweat-stains showing on the necks of their shirts. Two were yet lacking. Seated beside Washington's chair at the head of the table, Hamilton and Laurens looked at their papers, impatient, anxious to move on. Behind them, toward the desk in the corner, Eli stood alone in his beaded buckskin hunting shirt and leggings and moccasins, with his weapons belt still buckled around his middle.

There was a commotion at the tent flap, and Generals Duportail and Huntington stepped in. They blinked in the lantern light while their eyes adjusted from the darkness. They realized they were late and quickly dropped into the two chairs that were left.

Washington drew a breath and started.

"A review is in order. General Lafayette returned from his mission to Barren Hill and brought much-needed information. The British have about sixteen thousand men and scores of heavy guns. We now have about eleven thousand men who are capable of combat and fewer than thirty cannon. We have divided our forces into five divisions under Generals Lee, Mifflin, Lafayette, DeKalb, and Stirling. We have been pursuing the British from the day they marched out of Philadelphia—the night of June eighteenth—until now, June twenty-eighth."

He referred to a map he had on the table before him. "We are here, at Cranbury." He pointed, then moved his finger. "The British are here, at Monmouth, camped around the courthouse, less than one day's march ahead of us. All too soon they will reach Amboy and go on to Sandy Hook, where ships are waiting to ferry them to Staten Island."

He straightened. "In short, we have no more time. Either we strike them now, or not at all."

A brief murmur went around the table and stopped.

"It is five o'clock. Scout Stroud reported minutes ago that the British were up and marching at half past four. General Clinton knows we're here, and he knows why. The only thing he does not know is when we will strike and where."

Some officers shifted in their chairs, then settled.

"This is the plan." Again he placed his index finger on the map. "General Lee and his command are here at Englishtown under my strictest written orders to contact the British and attack the rear of their column the moment he catches them and hold them until we can arrive in support."

His finger moved as he traced lines on the map. "General Morgan is here with six hundred riflemen, on the east flank of the British column, waiting to attack when General Lee engages. General Stirling has command of my left wing, General Greene my right. I will lead the main division of the army with seven thousand eight hundred men to here, Penelopen, where we will be in a position to move instantly to support General Lee when he has engaged and stopped the British column."

He straightened to face his war council. "I repeat, it is critical to understand that General Lee is under my written orders to attack as soon as he comes upon the British. When he does engage them, he will be totally dependent on us being there to support him. We cannot fail."

Washington stopped to look at his documents, then raised his head once again. "Does anyone have any questions of the overall plan or his part in it?"

No one spoke.

"The heat has been devastating, and it appears it will continue. Be certain your men fill their canteens. Nearly four hundred have already dropped from heat exhaustion. I have ordered the drummer to sound reveille in five minutes. Do whatever you must to have your men marching by half past five. They can eat hard rations while they're marching. We must catch the British today."

For a moment Washington peered into their faces. The tension in the sweltering tent was like a great, physical hand pushing down.

"Dismissed."

At nine o'clock the Continental Army was marching northeast, every man dripping sweat. By ten o'clock half the canteens were empty. Half an hour later one hundred fifty men had dropped in their tracks, delirious from heat exhaustion. Their companions quickly dragged them to the nearest tree for shade, poured what water they could spare over their heads, and left them. At eleven o'clock Washington called Eli, Alexander Hamilton, and General Knox to his side.

"I must know where General Lee is and when to expect the engagement to begin. Scout ahead and report back when you know."

At noon the first rumble of a single distant cannon shot reached the Americans, and Washington drew rein on a strong, white mare given him that morning by New Jersey Governor William Livingston. He turned his head and listened. Two—three—four—five cannon shots followed, and Washington breathed light, listening intently for the inevitable rattle of musketfire to follow.

There was no such sound.

Mystified, Washington felt the first chill of concern come into his mind. *Cannon, but no musketfire? How can that be?*

He tapped spur to the big white mare and moved ahead, holding her in check so he did not distance his command. Twenty minutes later Hamilton came in at a gallop and reined his sweated horse to a stop. Hamilton was panting, excited.

"Lee's about to engage. Is it time to turn Greene's troops south to cover the right flank if Lee is overrun?"

Washington's eyes narrowed as he considered, and then he turned to the sound of a second rider coming in at a dead run. Henry Knox pulled his mount to a sliding stop, dirt flying, and his face was filled with thunder and lightning.

Washington held his breath.

"Lee's men are in a state of mass confusion! They're breaking! They're going to retreat!"

Washington started. "Impossible."

At that moment a farmer from nearby rode up on a heavy-footed plow horse. "Gen'l Washington, sir, the countryside ahead is full of our troops in full retreat! They're comin', sir."

Washington shook his head in bewildered disbelief. "That cannot be! There is no musketfire, no sign of a battle! There has to be a—" He stopped at the sight of Eli bringing his horse in at stampede gait, the horse sweating, throwing its head at the pressure of the bit.

"Lee's command is in full retreat!" Eli exclaimed. "Maybe ten, fifteen minutes behind me, and ten minutes behind him half the British troops are coming as hard as they can run."

It flashed in Washington's mind—*This is Long Island all over again—in minutes this army will be in chaos—defeated—defeated—defeated.*

He rammed his spurs into the flanks of the white mare, and she was at a full-out gallop in three jumps, neck stretched low, forelock and mane flying as she skimmed the ground. Behind, coming as hard as his sweating mount could follow, came Eli, and behind him most of Washington's staff, and a few of his aides.

Washington put the horse down a slope, thundered across the wooden bridge that spanned the creek at the bottom of West Ravine, crested the hill beyond, pulled the horse to a stiff-legged, skidding halt, and gaped.

Spread before him the Continental Army came streaming through the trees and on the road, pell-mell, in a full, panic-driven retreat. Leading them was Colonel Israel Shreve of the Second New Jersey Regiment. Washington reined over into his path and forced him to a stop.

"What's the meaning of this?" Washington bellowed.

"I don't know, sir. All I know is that General Lee gave the order to retreat, and the men retreated. The officers didn't control it, and it became a rout!"

"*What?* Retreat from what? There is no sign of a battle."

"I don't know what, sir. I only know General Lee came riding back, shouting his order to retreat." Shreve twisted in his saddle. "He's right back there, sir, not more than three hundred yards."

Washington covered the distance in twenty seconds and reined his horse up in front of Lee's mount, nose to nose.

"What is the meaning of this, sir? What's this disorder and confusion all about,?" he roared. His face was flushed, his neck veins protruding.

Lee recoiled as though struck in the face.

"Sir?"

"I said, what's this retreat all about?"

Lee stammered for a moment, then blurted, "My scouts gave me misinformation that caused mass confusion that caused General Charles Scott to fall back from his favorable position, and I could not sustain an attack." His story took on its own bravado, and he snapped, "Besides, you will recall that I opposed this attack in the war council! We should be taking Pittsburgh, not engaging Clinton!"

At that moment Eli pulled his horse to a prancing stop, with half a dozen members of Washington's staff still following, including Tench Tilghman, one of the general's aides. The lot of them sat dumbfounded at what they heard next.

Washington leaned forward in his saddle, his voice crackling like Doomsday. For thirty seconds he cursed Lee, invoking profanity that no one had ever heard come from his mouth before. He ended by accusing

Lee of being an accursed paltroon, which was the gentlest description he had used.

Lee was white as a sheet, trembling, beyond any hope of framing an answer.

At that moment one thing was clear to Washington. In minutes, without warning, what had begun as an attack to hurt the British had become a trap in which he could lose nearly the entire Continental Army—the one thing he had sworn he would never let happen. He turned in his saddle and shouted orders to the officers around him. "We've got to save those men! We can't form a defense here on this low rise! Does anyone know this country?"

Tilghman pointed. "There, sir. David Rhea of the Fourth New Jersey. He knows this country."

Ten seconds later Rhea was sitting his horse in front of Washington, wide-eyed.

"We've got to make a stand. Is there cover around here? Anywhere?"

Instantly Rhea's hand shot up, pointing. "Yes, sir. Just over that rise. A hedgerow. It will cover a lot of men." He shifted his point. "This little rise where we are is part of a long elevation, sir, and right down there is a bad swamp, right in front of it. Over there, to the left, is a thick woods on a ridge. Get your army into those woods, and they'll have the swamp in front to slow down the British. There's no way the British are going to gain the high ground to rout them out of those trees."

Never had Washington felt the relief that rushed through his being. He spun his horse, shouting orders. Instantly the men leaped to his commands, some sprinting for the hedgerow, others for the woods.

Thirty feet behind Washington, General von Steuben sat on his bay horse, listening, watching, masking his fears of what his army would do. A full-blown retreat, men in blind chaos, the British coming, officers totally out of control—he could not recall a worse scene. It was one thing to teach men to drill smartly on a field in their own camp. It was quite another for them to obey orders instantly in the disaster he was watching unfold. He held his breath and watched and waited.

"Cannon!" shouted Washington.

Instantly Colonel Eleazer Oswald bawled out his orders, and his men grabbed four of the heavy guns and sprinted, rolling them forward to the crest of a small rise. They swung them around and went through the drill von Steuben had so laboriously taught them of how to quickly load and elevate a cannon.

General Stirling drew his sword and shouted orders at his men. Fifty of them grabbed the trails of ten cannon, and within minutes had them in the trees, hidden, waiting. Among them was John Hays, and with him was his wife, Mary, who had defied the American officers by refusing to leave her husband's side.

From the right Greene's men came marching across an open field in rank and file, following the cadence as their officers chanted.

"Right, *oblique!*" The entire command, rank and file, hit the ground with their left foot at the same instant and pivoted on a forty-five degree angle to the right, striding straight for the hedgerow. Thirty seconds later they closed on it, and the order came ringing, "Company, *halt!*"

Every soldier stopped on the count of two.

"Company, *fall out and take up defensive positions behind this hedgerow!*"

Shouting, the entire company broke ranks, and in thirty seconds had filled out the defensive line behind the hedgerow, muskets laid over the top, bayonets gleaming.

From the left General Anthony Wayne's brigade came marching, every man chanting the cadence, one-two-three-four, company, *halt.* The rank and file held its interval.

"Fall out and form a defensive line in those trees!"

In three minutes a line of Americans was kneeling at the edge of the trees, muskets at the ready, and behind them a second line of Americans stood, muskets and bayonets extended over the heads of those in front. Wayne was pacing behind his men, calling to them, "Steady—steady—wait—wait."

They heard them before they saw them. The rattle and clatter of British drums pounding out the beat coming first and then the horde of red-coated regulars pouring over the hills and through the fields.

Washington sucked air. *An all-out assault. We've never withstood an all-out assault.* Half a mile away, still mounted, von Steuben stiffened in his saddle. The brass trim on his huge pistols, mounted in the saddle holsters, sparkled in the sunlight as he licked at his lips and waited, his gray eyes mere slits in the bright June sunshine.

From behind the leading ranks of infantry, the vaunted British cavalry came at the gallop, screaming, swords high.

At the hedgerow General Wayne stood straight, sword in his hand, calming his men. "Hold your fire. Steady . . ."

The thunder of three hundred galloping horses rolled over them, and Wayne mentally measured the distance as they closed. At forty paces, he dropped his sword and shouted, "FIRE!"

The men in the front line cut loose, and the leading ranks of the charging cavalry took the first volley head-on. Riders and crippled horses went down all up and down the line. The first American line stepped back two paces and quickly reached for fresh cartridges to reload while the second row stepped forward two paces, muskets at the ready, and again the order came.

"FIRE!"

The second rank of the charging cavalry stumbled and went down.

The two rows of Americans again changed places, and the front line reloaded, waited.

"FIRE!"

Deadly orange flame spurted from their muskets, and the third rank of redcoated British cavalry faltered. The fourth rank stopped in its tracks. Before them, the ground was littered with men in crimson tunics, dead, dying, wounded, writhing, moaning, while crippled horses called out their pain. The fourth rank turned and ran.

Wayne was grinning ear to ear as he shouted, "Reload!"

Two hundred yards down the slight incline, British commander Henry Monckton bellowed commands, and his infantry rose up to charge. Determined to succeed where the cavalry had failed, or die in the attempt, carrying the pole with the British Union Jack fluttering in the wind, Monckton led them forward at a run.

Wayne paced behind his men. "Wait, wait, wait . . ." Again he judged distance. Ninety yards—eighty—seventy. "Here they come, men. Steady. Wait for my word; then pick out the king-birds."

At forty yards he shouted, "FIRE!" and once again white smoke and orange flame blasted from the American muskets, and the heavy musketballs ripped into the leading ranks of the charging redcoats. All up and down the line, officers and regulars buckled and staggered and went down. An American ball punched into Monckton's chest, halting his headlong dash and dropping him to his knees. He pitched forward onto his face, the proud flag lying limply in the grass and dirt before him. Instantly, two Americans leaped the hedgerow, pried the fallen colors from his dead grasp, and carried them back to the American lines.

Washington spurred his horse toward Wayne's command, and stumbled into a befuddled, indecisive Lee. Washington shouted to him, "You stay here and do what you can for these men. I'm going back to form the center of our line of defense."

Lee blustered, "Yes, sir. I will be the last to leave the field."

Alexander Hamilton, less than twenty yards distant, swung his sword and shouted at Lee, "That's right, my dear General, and I will stay and we will all die here on the spot!" Furious, Lee jerked around, and Hamilton stared him down.

Washington swung his horse around to gallop off to prepare the heart of his lines for the assault that was sure to come. He shouted orders to those in command of cannon as he went and reined his horse to a winded stop to watch. Soldiers leaped to swing the cannon muzzles northeast, then rammed powder and shot down the barrels, grasped the smoking linstocks, and waited.

From nine hundred yards, the heavy British guns blasted. Their thunder rolled across the open ground as white smoke blossomed from their muzzles.

Instantly the American guns answered. Cannister shot exploded above the British guns. One-inch diameter lead balls ripped downward, kicking up dirt, ricocheting off cannon barrels, knocking British gunners rolling on the ground. Grapeshot tore into them, full in the face. Solid shot shattered the huge, seven-foot, spoked wheels on the British cannon carriages, and the big guns dropped, muzzles pointing harmlessly into the blue heavens at crazy angles.

Again the British guns spoke in the unbearable heat, and again the American guns answered.

"Reload!" came the order, and John Hays raised the rammer to seat the powder load in the barrel of his cannon when suddenly he sagged to his knees and collapsed from heat exhaustion. Instantly Mary sprinted for the nearest water barrel, scooped a pitcher full, and ran back to her husband to bathe his face. The call came from others, "Water, water," and Mary ran dodging for another pitcher full and yet another for the men who were near collapse.

"FIRE!" Startled, Mary flinched then leaped to the position of her fallen husband, wrenched the rammer from his hands, drove it down the barrel to seat the powder, and a soldier in the gun crew dropped the cannonball down the muzzle. A gunner smacked the smoking linstock to the touch hole, and the cannon blasted. Mary wiped perspiration from her forehead, went for one more load of water, then stepped over her unconscious husband to take his position in the gun crew. The men glanced at her, nodded, and the gun crew continued loading and firing on command.

Slowly the musketfire from the British dwindled and then stopped as the regulars fell back under the withering fire from the heavy American guns. The men in the British cannon crews faltered, then threw down their rammers and powder ladles and wilted away to disappear into the trees and over the crest of the low rise. As by magic, the only crimson tunics remaining on the field of battle were those of the dead and wounded.

Washington's heart leaped. *We've beaten them! The best they had. We can get most of them if we attack!*

He rose in his stirrups to shout his orders, then settled back into his saddle. He looked at the men nearest him. In the unbearable heat, sweat was running in streams. Their clothing was soaked, their hair plastered to their heads. Some could not stand without support. They looked back at him, and he saw it in their eyes. *We'll attack if you order it, but not many of us can make it across to their lines.*

His heart went out to them. *I cannot ask more than I have. They've met the flower of the British army on an open field and taken the best the British had to give, and turned them—driven them from the field. They're dying of thirst and heat exhaustion. It is enough.*

He rose in his stirrups to shout, "Hold the lines! Hold where you are!"

It was shortly past five o'clock in the afternoon of June 28, 1778. The battle of Monmouth was over.

The Americans dug in, watching the abandoned British cannon like hawks. Evening shadows lengthened, and nothing stirred. Men brought water and cooked meat, and the Americans stood to their positions and their cannon until darkness fell. A cooling night breeze arose to drive away the unbearable heat. Pickets were posted and changed on the regular intervals.

At two o'clock, beneath a half-moon, Eli turned to Billy, seated at the west end of the hedgerow, peering intently into the dimly moonlit landscape for any light or movement at the British lines.

"I'll be back in a while."

"Where you going?"

"To have a look."

Billy nodded, and in five seconds Eli was gone, silent as a shadow.

At half past four Eli settled beside Billy. "They're gone."

"Gone?"

"Not a redcoat within four miles."

"Better go tell General Washington."

Twenty minutes later, in the gray of dawn, an apologetic picket thrust his head inside Washington's tent.

"Sir, beg pardon, there's a corporal and an Indian out here who say they should talk to you."

"An Indian?"

"Dressed like one. Talks like he's white."

"Send them in."

Billy entered, came to attention, and saluted. Eli stood easy at his side.

Washington peered at them in the yellow lantern light. "You have something I should hear?"

"I thought so, sir. Scout Stroud has been to the British camp tonight. He has a report."

Washington turned to Eli.

"The British are gone. All of them. Baggage, wagons, cannon— everything. They left in the night. There isn't a regular within four miles."

They abandoned the field! We're in command! We beat them! Beat them!

"You're certain?"

"Followed them for three miles. They're gone, and they're not coming back."

"I can have this army stand down?"

"There's no reason to hold them in the lines."

"Anything else?"

Eli shook his head.

"Thank you. You are dismissed."

At six o'clock Washington gave orders. "The men will finish their morning mess and then seek shade and water and rest until noon. In the meantime I'll consider mounting a command to pursue and attack the British."

At eight o'clock, the hot, sweltering wind was fluttering the flags and driving the men into the trees to seek shade. By ten o'clock it was evident; the heat, not the redcoats, was their real enemy. Reluctantly Washington gave the order.

"The men will continue their camp here. The commissary will hand out rations sufficient for two days or until further notice."

On the morning of June thirtieth, Hamilton entered the command tent. "I have been requested to deliver this to you, sir."

"What is it?"

"A message from General Lee."

Startled, Washington opened and read the document aloud.

"From the knowledge I have of your Excellency's character, I must conclude that nothing but misinformation of some very stupid, or mis-representation of some very wicked person, could have occasioned your making use of such very singular expressions as you did on my coming up to the ground where you had taken post; they implied that I was guilty either of disobedience of orders, of want of conduct, or want of courage. I wish to know on which of these three articles you ground your charge, that I may prepare for my justification . . ."

Washington turned to Hamilton. "He knows he will be called before a court-martial to defend his shameful retreat, and he's laying the groundwork for a defense." For a moment he set his teeth, and his eyes narrowed. "There is no defense for it. Be certain you save this document. I'll dictate an answer later this morning."

"Yes, sir."

Washington softened. "Have you seen von Steuben lately?"

"Yes, sir."

"How is he?"

"Proud, sir, of his men."

"He should be. Did you see our troops under fire? Cannon and musket?"

"I did, sir."

"I'll have to draft a letter to von Steuben. I believe his service at Valley Forge saved this army. Maybe the revolution. Remind me to write a letter."

"Yes, sir."

"One more thing. A report reached me that a woman—Mary Hays, I believe—took her husband's position in a gun crew after he collapsed. It was a Pennsylvania regiment. Men called her 'Molly Pitcher' because she carried water to them in a pitcher. Try to get the facts. If it's true, it's proper that she be recognized."

"I'll find out, sir."

Notes

The detail of all the names, times, places, sequences of action, and results, describing the battle of Monmouth, are far too numerous and complex to be effectively endnoted.

Thus, the names of the participants, the locations, the sequences of action, and the results, are all as herein described, save and except the name of Eli Stroud, who is a fictional character. The acts attributed to Eli were in fact performed by other persons, with the result that the only inaccuracy is the use of his name and not the events described. In particular, however, the profanity vented by General Washington on General Lee when he confronted him during Lee's retreat was as described, and the letter written by Lee to Washington after the battle was concluded is quoted verbatim. Many of the conversations are nearly verbatim. There is no other known incident of General Washington resorting to profanity in chastising an officer or soldier. It is in this battle that Mary Hays, known in history as "Molly Pitcher," performed her missions of mercy with her water pitcher and took the place of her fallen husband in his cannon crew. General Washington did reward her.

For details in support, see Leckie, *George Washington's War*, pp. 467–86, and in particular see the battle map on page 478; Freeman, *George Washington*, pp. 397–401; Higginbotham, *The War of American Independence*, pp. 246–47.

July 6, 1778

CHAPTER XXXIII

★ ★ ★

They came to the small, square stone courthouse in the cool of the morning, Billy and Sergeant Alvin Turlock wearing the best clothing they could find. A dozen men from the Massachusetts Regiment, barefooted, wearing the only clothing they had, nervous, ill at ease. Ten nurses in their uniforms. Caleb Dunson and Sergeant Randolph O'Malley, from the New York Third Company. Half a dozen officers with their epaulets gleaming and the gold trim prominent on their tricorns.

At nine o'clock they entered the high ceilinged, austere courtroom and sat on the first rows of the hard, worn benches, facing the raised platform where the judge sat to preside at court. There was already the promise of another hot, muggy day, and the windows were open to let what little breeze there was move the air.

At five minutes past nine o'clock the door into the small jury room at the rear of the hall creaked as it swung open, and Dr. Albigence Waldo, portly, aging, a major in the United States army, walked into the courtroom wearing an ill-fitting officer's uniform, carrying a large Bible under his right arm. The click of his heels on the old hardwood floor echoed slightly. Behind him came Eli, tall, clad in a white-ruffled shirt, royal blue tunic and breeches, white socks, and square-toed shoes borrowed from a Monmouth township alderman. On his arm was Mary Flint, glowing in a simple white cotton wedding dress that ten nurses had spent seven days making. She was smiling as they followed Dr. Waldo, who led them to a place just in front of the judge's bench. He took his position facing those assembled, and Mary and Eli stood facing him.

Dr. Waldo cleared his throat, settled his nerves, and began.

"As an officer in the Continental Army, I am authorized to perform marriage ceremonies under these circumstances, but I confess this is the first time I have been called on to do so." He stopped and for a moment puckered his mouth. "Mary has asked me . . . Mary Flint has asked me to join herself to Eli Stroud in holy matrimony. I've worked with Mary for a time, and I've come to love her, and I'm honored, but I wish I knew more about what to say and do." He paused to pull his thoughts together.

"It seems proper to mention that marriage is ordained of God. It is a high and holy thing between a man and a woman. With it comes the possibility of the greatest happiness this life can give. Love. Security. Companionship. Children. Every good thing."

He stopped for a moment and removed his spectacles to wipe at them with his handkerchief. "It is my sincerest hope that such can come to these two young people. I could talk longer, but I doubt I could add much, and besides, you haven't come to hear me. You've come to see this man and this woman join their lives together."

Quiet sniffles came from the ten nurses, and Dr. Waldo looked at them, surprise in his face. He turned back to Mary and Eli and opened his Bible. Inside he had placed a sheet of paper on which he had printed in bold letters the words necessary to make such a marriage legal. He adjusted his spectacles to read.

"Who gives this woman in marriage?"

Billy stepped one pace forward. "I do."

"By what authority?"

"She has no living kin. She has authorized me to give her in marriage."

Waldo looked at Mary. "Have you so authorized?"

"Yes."

He tipped his head forward to peer over his glasses. "Does anybody here have a reason this marriage cannot take place?"

The room fell silent.

"Very well." He looked at Eli, then read, "Do you, Eli Stroud, take this woman, Mary Flint, to be your legal and lawfully wedded wife, and do you promise to cleave unto her and her only for the rest of your life?"

"Yes. I do."

Waldo nodded and turned to Mary. "Do you, Mary Flint, take this man, Eli Stroud, to be your legal and lawfully wedded husband, and do you promise to obey and cleave unto him and him only for the rest of your life?"

"I do."

He reread what he had said and, satisfied, made his declaration.

"Then, by the power vested in me as a duly commissioned officer in the Continental Army, I pronounce you husband and wife, lawfully wedded before God and the laws of this commonwealth."

He stopped and fumbled for a moment. "Do you have a ring you wish to place on her finger, a symbol to the world of your covenants entered into freely this day?"

Billy stepped forward again and placed a simple gold band in Eli's hand.

Waldo nodded. "You may place the ring on her finger."

Gently Eli worked the ring onto the third finger of her left hand.

"Well," Waldo said, "I believe that concludes the legalities. You may kiss your wife if you so desire."

Eli bent to tenderly kiss Mary, and stifled sobs came from every woman in the room. The men shifted their feet and diverted their eyes for a moment, then quickly looked again.

Waldo concluded. "The ceremony is finished. You may congratulate the bride and groom."

The women surged forward to embrace Mary, wiping at their tears. The men walked to Eli to clap him on the shoulder and shake his hand. For a time the talk and the embracing continued. Billy stood back, a thousand memories racing through his mind of the things, great and small, that had bound him and Eli together. He looked at Mary, radiant, beautiful beyond words, clinging to Eli's arm, and he silently, fervently, wished them joy in their union. Turlock looked at them, then at the floor, then back at the two of them, then reached to wipe at his eyes.

In due time Eli turned to Mary, and a silent communication passed between them. He led her out through the large, heavy oak doors into the sunlight, where a Quaker woman took Mary by the arm and escorted her and Eli to her small home, next to the courthouse. Billy and Caleb and the others also made their way to the house and waited in the yard for the couple to change their clothing.

In the rising heat of the day, Turlock spoke quietly to Billy.

"Heard about Conway?

Billy shook his head. "The one who started that cabal against Washington?"

"The same."

"What happened?"

"Two days ago. Gen'l Cadwalader got tired of him degrading Washington and challenged him to a duel. Shot him through the mouth."

"Is he dead?"

"Close to it. This isn't exactly the time to bring it up, but I thought you'd like to know."

A minute passed before Turlock gestured toward the house. "They're going north? To his sister's place?"

"Yes."

"I hope he isn't gone too long."

Billy turned. "Why? Something happening?"

Turlock nodded. "Probably. Rumor is the British have found out beating us here in the northern states is a lot harder than they thought. Someone over there in England named Knox is trying to convince Parliament to forget the north and attack us in the south. The southern states. Then come on up north once they've got a base down there."

Billy's face drew down in surprise. "The south? They're going to attack the south?"

"Savannah. Charleston. Somewhere down there. They figure the slaves will help—rise up against their masters."

Billy stood silent, his mind racing.

"Anyway, I hope Eli gets back before all that breaks loose."

At that moment the door of the home opened, and Eli emerged into the sunlight. He was dressed once again in his leather hunting shirt and breeches and his moccasins. His weapons belt was at his middle, his rifle in his hand. On his back was a bedroll, and a pouch with a small amount of food was slung under his arm.

Mary came to stand beside him. She was dressed in an ankle-length, sturdy, gray cotton dress. She wore leather shoes, and her hair was pulled back by a gray bandanna. Never had Billy seen such happiness in two faces.

The nurses could not restrain themselves. Once again they crowded around Mary to hug her, wish her well, sniffle, and hug her one last time. Billy moved close to hold her for a moment, then embrace Eli. Turlock stepped up, embarrassed, gave Mary a peck on the cheek, clutched Eli's hand to shake it, then stepped back, relieved.

It was finished. The simple wedding of Eli and Mary was concluded. Without further words, Eli caught Mary by the hand, turned north, and led her into their journey through life. Those who loved them waved and then stood in silence, each lost in his or her own thoughts. They saw the sun on the two, and they watched as the couple followed the trail through the reds and yellows of the wildflowers, into the deep emerald green of the forest and were gone.

Notes

Dr. Albigence Waldo was a surgeon who went through the Valley Forge experience. Reed, *Valley Forge: Crucible of Victory,* pp. 12, 16, 22.

General John Cadwalader was a strong supporter of General Washington and detested General Thomas Conway for his attacks on Washington. He challenged Conway to a duel and shot him through the mouth on July 4, 1778; however, the wound was not fatal. Freeman, *Washington,* p. 403.

Following their defeat at Monmouth, the British accepted the proposition long argued by William Knox, under-secretary of the American Department in the cabinet of King George III, that the most effective approach to defeating the United States would be to conquer the southern states first, then proceed north. Mackesy, *The War for America, 1775–1783,* pp. 43–44, 158, 267.

BIBLIOGRAPHY

★ ★ ★

Busch, Noel F. *Winter Quarters.* New York: Liveright, 1974.

Claghorn, Charles E. *Women Patriots of the American Revolution.* Metuchen, N.J.: Scarecrow Press, 1991.

Earle, Alice Morse. *Home Life in Colonial Days.* New York: Grosset and Dunlap, 1898. Reprint, Stockbridge, Mass.: Berkshire House Publishers, 1993.

Eyewitness Accounts of the American Revolution: Valley Forge Orderly Book of General George Weedon. New York: New York Times and Arno, 1971.

Fisk, Anita Marie. "The Organization and Operation of the Medical Services of the Continental Army, 1775–1783." Master's thesis, University of Utah, 1979.

Flexner, James Thomas. *Washington: The Indispensable Man.* New York: Little, Brown, and Company, 1998.

Flint, Edward F., Jr., and Gwendolyn S. Flint. *Flint Family History of the Adventuresome Seven.* Baltimore: Gateway Press, 1984.

Graymont, Barbara. *The Iroquois.* New York: Chelsea House, 1988.

———. *The Iroquois in the American Revolution.* Syracuse: Syracuse University Press, 1972.

Hale, Horatio. *The Iroquois Book of Rites.* 1883. Reprint, New York: AMS Press, 1969.

Harwell, Richard Barksdale. *Washington.* New York: Simon & Schuster, 1995. A one-volume abridgment of Douglas Southall Freeman. *George Washington, a Biography,* 7 vols. (New York: Scribner, 1948–57).

Higginbotham, Don. *The War of American Independence.* Boston: Northeastern University Press, 1983.

Jackson, John W. *Valley Forge: Pinnacle of Courage.* Gettysburg, Pa.: Thomas Publications, 1992.

Joslin, J., B. Frisbie, and F. Rugles. *A History of the Town of Poultney, Vermont, from Its Settlement to the Year 1875.* New Hampshire: Poultney Journal Printing Office, 1979.

Ketchum, Richard M. *Saratoga.* New York: Henry Holt and Company, 1997.

Leckie, Robert. *George Washington's War.* New York: HarperCollins, Harper Perennial, 1992.

Mackesy, Piers. *The War for America, 1775–1783.* Lincoln, Nebr.: University of Nebraska Press, 1964.

Martin, Joseph Plumb. *Private Yankee Doodle*. Edited by George F. Scheer. New Stratford, N. H.: Ayer Company Publishers, 1998.

Morgan, Lewis H. *League of the Ho-de-no-sau-nee or Iroquois*. Vol. I. New York: Dodd, Mead & Co., 1901. Reprint, New Haven, Conn.: Human Relations Area Files, 1954.

Parry, Jay A., and Andrew M. Allison. *The Real George Washington*. Washington, D.C.: National Center for Constitutional Studies, 1990.

Pool, Daniel. *What Jane Austen Ate and Charles Dickens Knew*. New York: Simon & Schuster, 1993.

Reed, John F. *Valley Forge, Crucible of Victory*. Monmouth Beach, N.J.: Philip Freneau Press, 1969.

Stokesbury, James L. *A Short History of the American Revolution*. New York: William Morrow, 1991.

Trigger, Bruce G. *Children of the Aataentsic*. Montreal: McGill-Queens University Press, 1987.

Ulrich, Laurel Thatcher. *Good Wives*. New York: Vintage Books, 1991.

Von Riedesel, Frederika. *Baroness von Riedesel and the American Revolution*. Translated by Marvin L. Brown Jr. Chapel Hill: University of North Carolina Press, 1965.

Wilbur, C. Keith. *The Revolutionary Soldier, 1775–1783*. Old Saybrook, Conn.: Globe Pequot Press, 1993.

Wildes, Henry Emerson. *Valley Forge*. New York: Macmillan, 1938.

ACKNOWLEDGMENTS

★ ★ ★

Dr. Richard B. Bernstein, internationally recognized authority on the Revolutionary War, continues to make his tremendous contribution to the series, for which the author is most grateful. Jana Erickson has again spent much time and effort on the cover and the artwork. Richard Peterson has exercised his usual great patience and careful work of editing. Harriette Abels, consultant and editor, has guided the author with her wisdom and insight.

However, again, the men and women of the Revolution, whose spirit reaches across more than two centuries, are truly responsible for all that is good in this series.

The work proceeds only because of the contributions many.